AURORA'S ANGEL

Emily Noon

Aurora's Angel

Published by Bluefire Books Ltd.
New Zealand

ISBN 978-0-473-48832-1 (Ebook Edition)
ISBN 978-0-473-48831-4 (Paperback Edition)
ISBN 978-0-473-50513-4 (Softcover - Slimline Edition)

A catalogue record for this book is available from The National Library of New Zealand.

Book cover design by Bespokebookcovers.com

First Edition

DEDICATION/THANKS

To my amazing spouse – J, I couldn't have done this without your love and support. You are my rock and shelter in the storm. Thank you for always being on my side.

Elena – My dear friend and proofreader/editor. Thanks for herding my wayward tenses in the right direction, tempering my love for commas with something more appropriate and pointing out when my world building was getting out of hand (your comments in the margins made me laugh so hard I cried). The finished product is better because of your input. Oh, and I'm delighted to know your Google search history is now as dodgy as mine!

Mamma – After all these years of believing in your daughter you finally get to see my book. Thanks for helping out so I'd have more time to write and passing on your love of books and reading. By the way, I'm reasonably sure it's because you read me the riveting and very gory tales from the World Book of Mythology when I was little that I developed a love for dark fantasy. Just saying.

AURORA'S ANGEL

CHAPTER 1

A SONG IN THE DARK

Aurora was halfway up a mine shaft when she heard faint singing. She paused in her climb and frowned as she craned her neck to listen. The mine was locked up tight until morning and all the main lights were off; there shouldn't be anyone moving about in the murky depths. Maybe a drunk guard who'd taken a wrong turn and instead of going to the barracks to sleep it off, ended up wandering around lost and confused in the labyrinth of tunnels? Straining to hear, she realized it couldn't be a guard because the singer was female and this mine only hired male guards.

Aurora continued climbing, rotating her head to hone in on the song. Her unease grew the more she heard. The melody was hauntingly familiar and infused with the singer's desperation. When Aurora realized she was listening to an avian dawn song she cursed. She often heard their early morning praise drift from their tall towers and watched them raise their wings with the rising of the sun as they welcomed its return. They sang beautifully and even though she wasn't fond of the winged shapeshifters she would always pause to listen. This particular song happened to be her favorite. It was old, from the time when powerful monsters stalked the night and surviving until dawn was a victory. It was supposed to be sung while bathed in the first light of day as a joyous celebration of survival, *not* underground in the middle of the night!

This sharpened her interest. There was no way the owners had an avian working in the mine. The tall beings with their massive wings would find it almost impossible to maneuver in these narrow passages and there was no mistaking the fearful tremble in the singer's voice. Something was very wrong. Was the girl a prisoner? If so, was she the only one or were there others? If there was more than one shapeshifter in captivity it would mean there was a cutter's den operating in the hidden depths. She'd come across a few of those over the years and had hoped never to find another. Aurora fought to shut down the memories rising like bile in her throat. A cutter's den was a place of unimaginable horror, where shapeshifters were imprisoned while their bodies were systematically harvested for the high price their parts fetched on the black market.

Aurora pressed her forehead against the cold stone and wished the singing would stop. If it stopped, she could let herself imagine she'd heard something harmless and unimportant that she could ignore. After two days and nights of watching from the dark as miners carefully tended the living veins that fed the precious ethian crystals, and trying not to get bitten by the venomous spiders that inhabited the mine, she had finally found the prize she'd been after. Now all she had to do was get out of this dark pit and no one would know she'd been here. An hour at most and she would breathe crisp mountain air on route to her appointment. On the other hand, if she followed that song and found what she feared, things would get loud and ugly. But the avian's desperate song continued and Aurora could no more ignore it than she could the frightened cry of a child lost in the dark. She had to find that girl.

Her mind made up, Aurora climbed rapidly. She had excellent hearing but the mine was so large it was a miracle she'd heard the girl at all. If the avian stopped singing it would be a nightmare to find her in the labyrinth of tunnels that zigzagged underground. Aurora angled in the direction the song was coming from, climbed into a tunnel leading in that direction and ran. The mine was pitch dark aside from the custom-made lamps that kept the light-sensitive spiders from overrunning the main tunnels in the miners' absence. Placed intermittently the lamps poured pools of blue light onto the floors and walls so it felt like she was sprinting underwater. Occasionally she had to pause to listen and twice she had to retrace her steps after ending up at a dead end. When the girl's voice wavered, becoming almost inaudible, Aurora stood waiting, unsure which way to go. She heaved a sigh of relief when the girl continued singing with renewed vigor and raced to follow the tenuous link. This led her to a disused section of the mine where danger signs warned of a collapse and old mining equipment barred the way. Aurora made a gap, took one of the emergency lamps from the wall and pushed on into the rabbit warren of dark passages.

It was as the singing died away that Aurora found the locked door behind a sheet of rusty metal. She made short work of the lock but to her frustration the door wouldn't budge – something barred it from the other side. She pressed her ear against the door but heard nothing through the thick metal. Spotting a vent high on the wall she climbed up to listen and heard the faint sounds of a woman crying. Aurora briefly considered breaking down the door to get to her but there was no telling what was on the other side. Besides, she didn't want to alert every guard in the vicinity. There had to be another entrance.

Aurora sat down cross-legged on the stone floor and consulted the map in her head. She'd had a rudimentary idea of the layout of the mine before she entered and in the two days she'd spent crawling around inside had added a lot more detail. She knew she had to be close to the top of the mountain where she'd seen the lookout towers and the heavily guarded buildings. That area and the preceding three floors were restricted; none of the miners and only select guards had access. She had assumed it was because that was where the harvested ethian crystals were kept but now it seemed that wasn't the only reason. If her suspicion was correct an access tunnel ran from one of the buildings up top to this barred room. There was only one way to find out. Aurora got up, put her hand against the metal door and whispered, "Hold on, whoever you are. Help is on the way."

***

It took Aurora almost an hour to work her way through the barred floors with their numerous locked doors and to check the buildings up top to find the entrance to the hidden area. She was frustrated with her slow progress but it couldn't be helped. Lights burned brightly despite the late hour and there were guards everywhere. There was a heated card game underway in the kitchen and she caught a change of guard in progress. Slow minutes ticked past as she watched from hiding while men grumbled to each other about the miserable weather and traded insults as they ambled out to go relieve their buddies in the watchtowers. She had to hug the shadows on the windy roof where huge spotlights burned into the stormy night illuminating the sky, the sides of the mountain and the miners' huts far below.

By the time she made her way down the stairs to the hidden area Aurora had begun to second guess herself. What if she'd read too much into the girl's sad song and crying? She had overheard many conversations while sneaking around in the mine and not once did she hear anything that gave her the impression the miners knew of a cutter's den. She could be wasting her precious time because she'd jumped to the worst conclusion. Perhaps instead of being a prisoner, the avian girl was the lover of the mine manager or owner and the two had had a fight resulting in her bursting out into tearful, melodramatic song. That seemed unlikely but if she went through all this trouble to rescue the girl, only to find her in the throes of make-up sex Aurora would be tempted to bite her.

Midway down the staircase she paused to consider her options. There was a door on either side; which one to check first? She cautiously opened the door on the right and found a small apartment containing a tiny sitting room with a vent that drew in fresh air from outside, a bathroom made up of a chemical shower and toilet unit and a bedroom set into a small alcove. Entering the bedroom quietly she found a scrawny middle-aged blond man asleep on his back, no naked avian lover beside him. His breathing was deep and even, his arms and legs thrown wide as he sprawled on his comfy bed surrounded by plump pillows under a thick bedspread while a small lamp in the corner bathed the room in a bluish glow. On the desk next to his bed she found a ledger with the single word 'HARVEST' written in bold letters on the cover. Aurora felt herself go cold as she scanned the pages. The author had noted with business-like precision which body parts had been removed from over a dozen shapeshifters, down to the weight and size of each item harvested. It was a grisly read and damning evidence. Aurora wanted to beat the cutter to death with his ledger but instead slid it into her backpack and left his room as quietly as she'd entered.

In the hallway Aurora stared at the opposite door wishing she didn't have to go inside but after what she'd just read, she had no choice. She braced herself and pushed open the door. This room was also bathed in cool blue light and had a vent circulating air but that was where the similarity ended. Metallic shelves containing a multitude of jars and small boxes lined one wall. There was a long table with a draining hole under which rested a metal bucket and a big meat hook hung from the ceiling attached to a pulley system. Laid out neatly on a table with lots of drawers, Aurora saw an array of scalpels, saws and other equipment made to cut flesh and bone. She tried to remain detached as she scanned the contents of the jars, noting the labels and how the piles of bones and skulls were sorted according to the type of shifter. She forced herself to open the refrigeration unit to have a look and shuddered at what she saw. The anger she'd held in check since she entered the room flared into rage and it took all Aurora's self-control to resist the reddening haze that threatened to sweep her away. She could not afford to go on a rampage because she had at least one prisoner, maybe more, to rescue. She had to think and act rationally but there would be a reckoning for what was done here…just not right now.

Feeling more in control and with a rough plan in place she searched for something specific. She had hoped not to find the long-handled pole syringe but wasn't surprised when she found it next to a container of paralyzing agent. Unlike the scoped dart-gun on the shelf above that was designed to shoot knock-out darts from a distance the jab stick was used up close to inject the toxin that caused prolonged paralysis while keeping the victim awake. Some cutters used this instead of anesthesia because their buyers would pay more for parts that were harvested while the shifter was awake and actively trying to heal – such items were imbued with more potent magic. It meant the captive had to endure helplessly, aware of everything that was happening but unable to move or even scream. It was the most horrific torture to inflict on another living being for the sake of profit. A shifter's body would regenerate limbs and organs given enough time but a mind subjected to such horror may never heal.

With grim determination Aurora drew a little of the yellow liquid into a syringe as the one in the jab stick was preloaded to paralyze a large shapeshifter. If she used that much on the human his heart would stop and he didn't deserve to die that easily. She returned to the room next door and the sleeping man. She woke him with a hand clamped over his mouth so he couldn't scream, yanked down the covers to bare his stomach and stuck him with the needle. It took only seconds for his pupils to dilate and his body to become limp. His pulse beat rapidly but didn't become irregular, a good sign. She threw the man, clad only in his green boxers, over her shoulder and carried him back to the lab where she dumped him on the cold metal slab. She tilted the cutter's head so that he had to stare into her eyes. She let him see her rage then she shifted just enough to give him a glimpse of her beast. Terror bloomed in his eyes and he tried to speak, possibly to plead for his life, but no words came out.

Aurora bared her teeth in a feral smile and said, "Not a nice feeling being on the other side, is it? I'm going to unlock the cages but when I get back, you and I will have a reckoning." Aurora picked up a pair of gleaming secateurs, studied them thoughtfully for a moment before laying them back down with the rest of the tools. "So many sharp toys to choose from. Where to start? I'll ask your prisoner if you have a personal favorite." With those parting words Aurora removed the ring of keys from the wall and without sparing the cutter a backward glance left the room.

***

At the bottom of the staircase Aurora found two more rooms. From one emanated the scent of dirty fur and pungent male wolf in human form while from the other came the delicate scent of feathers. The space that held the wolves was well lit and held four large cages, two of which were occupied. The winged girl was alone in the other room, a weak lamp above her cage the only illumination in an otherwise pitch-black room. Aurora discovered she was right about the door to the mine being blocked from the inside and once she removed the heavy bar, she pushed it open. Having another exit immediately made her feel less trapped and she breathed a little easier.

Aurora decided to start by freeing the two wolf-shifters. Best to get them out and on the move before approaching the avian. There was a lot of bad history between wolves and avians and the current situation was difficult enough without adding more tension. At first glance the cage on the left contained only a pile of filthy straw but Aurora wasn't fooled; there was someone under there desperately trying to hide. The cage beside it held a man who was chained and muzzled like a dog. Aurora unlocked the cage on the left but couldn't bring herself to go in. The reek emanating from under the soiled straw was stomach-turning. It was the stench of sickness mixed liberally with blood, piss and fear so thick it was cloying. Her sensitive nose told her the person hiding under the straw was in bad shape, possibly beyond help. Best she saw to the man first. After freeing him she would see what, if anything, could be done for the other poor creature.

A low growl from the adjoining cage drew her attention. The wolf-shifter watched her intently, his eyes darting between her and the figure hidden under the straw. Trying to get closer he strained against the chains that restricted his movements and kept him away from the bars.

"Yours?" Aurora pointed into the cage. "Is she a member of your pack?"

The growling stopped and Aurora had the impression that if he had wolf ears they would have pricked up in interest.

"Pack. Yes. *Mine.*" The words came out muffled from around the muzzle with a rough edge as if from a throat that hadn't attempted human speech in some time.

Aurora nodded her understanding and moved away from the female's cage to show him she wasn't a threat to his vulnerable pack-mate. "I'm here to set you both free. Do you need my help to get out of the mine or will you be able to find your own way out?"

There was a pause as if he had to take a moment to decipher her words. "I can find the way out. Don't need your help."

"Good."

She unlocked his cage then motioned for him to stand back. He stood motionless for a moment before shuffling back a half step, his chains making a clanking sound as he did. Aurora didn't like the way he lowered his head to stare at her through hooded eyes or the way his lips curled back in a snarl and his body hunched as if ready to charge or fend off blows. He reminded her of an abused pit-bull she'd seen tied at the back of a shop years ago. Covered in scars and maddened with fear and rage the dog would growl and snap at anyone who came near, unable to tell friend from foe. This man had been a captive for so long he couldn't help but respond to certain triggers and that made him dangerous. His association with people coming into his cage would be the stuff of nightmares and in his current state he might not be able to tell the difference between her and the people who'd tortured him.

"Listen carefully, wolf. I am not your enemy. Friend. Don't attack me. If you try to kill me I will break your bones. Understood?"

"You could try..." the man scoffed and the feral sheen in his eyes intensified as reason fled, replaced by battle lust.

Aurora sighed. Yup, he *definitely* wasn't thinking clearly. Exasperated she said, "We don't have time for a pissing contest. If you don't want me to help you then free yourself."

She unhooked a key that looked like it would fit his shackles and threw it at his chest. He tried clumsily to catch it but it bounced off and rolled between his feet. Instantly he went down on his knees scrambling to find it. Aurora backed away from the entrance and watched him struggle to slot the key in the right way and turn the hinges with only the thumb and index finger of his right hand. Those were the only functional fingers he had as the rest were stumpy things in the process of regrowth. There were healing scars all over his body and the big uneven stitches used to close him up after harvest had puckered his skin in hard ridges. The cutter had really done a number on him. She felt a surge of admiration for the wolf; she'd seen beast-shifters who'd endured a lot less die from shock. It was a testament to the man's resilience and fighting spirit that he was still alive.

Gradually his animalistic snarls became curses as he was forced to push back his rage to focus on the task of undoing the multiple locks. By the time he undid the last one, a tricky lock on the tight band around his neck, the intermittent glances he gave Aurora had turned from manic as if expecting her to pounce when he wasn't looking, to merely wary. Aurora deliberately kept her posture non-threatening but refused to lower her eyes when he glared at her. As soon as the chains fell off the man surged out of the cage to rock to a halt a mere arm's length from her. Aurora knew she was taller than most; she'd stopped measuring herself in her early teens and by then she had stood well over six feet. That meant she rarely had to look up at anyone and she found it mildly alarming that the man in front of her topped her by at least a foot. When he was well fed and at full strength he'd be an imposing giant of a man. Even with his body reduced to ropey muscle and bony edges he radiated power. He was also furious and spoiling for a fight. He wanted to kill someone and she was right in front of him.

"Don't do it," she warned. "You think you can crush me with a single blow but it won't be that easy. Test my scent, wolf. Let your beast tell you what I am."

The man's nostrils flared as he inhaled, drawing in Aurora's scent. His eyes flew wide and he stared at her for a long moment before he averted his gaze. "Your smell and size…you must be Aurora? Clan Blood Moon has heard stories of a female by that name." When Aurora inclined her head in acknowledgment the tension that had been pulling the man's shoulders taut visibly released and he said, "I am Duzan."

"Duzan, if you've heard of me then you should know I'm not your enemy. Go see to your pack-mate. We need to be away from this place as soon as possible."

He warily skirted around Aurora but didn't hesitate to enter the other cage. He fell to his knees in front of the straw and dug, revealing the emaciated body of a female wolf. Her fur was so matted with blood and filth it was hard to determine the color aside from it being some dark shade. He made a choking sound as he carefully lifted and cradled the limp body against his chest. The she-wolf remained motionless in his arms and made no sound as he carried her out.

"How is she?"

"She's barely alive. It is almost over for Asha." His voice trembled and he looked away but not before Aurora saw his eyes luminous with unshed tears.

"Let me see. I may be able to help."

He nodded and she approached slowly not wanting to spook him into alarm when he'd just calmed down enough to be reasoned with. That he was allowing her, a stranger, this close to an injured pack-mate spoke to the level of his desperation and affection for the she-wolf. It made her wonder what Asha was to him and if she was perhaps the reason he had fought so hard to stay alive. A quick examination proved Duzan was right: the she-wolf was barely alive. Her breathing was shallow, her heartbeat irregular and the stench of infection and rot oozed from her. Still, as long as there was life... Aurora removed the pack from her back and carefully extracted a dark glass vial. She tilted it from side to side so Duzan could see there was liquid inside.

"This might help," she told him.

His eyes lit up. "Is it a healing potion?" he asked hopefully.

"Yes. It's powerful and has saved my life more than once but I don't want to give you false hope. The state Asha's in...it may be too late already."

"*Please* give it to her. Any hope is better than none."

Aurora gently pried open the wolf's jaw, tilting the head to pour the contents down her throat. The unconscious creature shuddered, made a small whining noise and one paw feebly stirred.

"You will know soon if it's worked."

Duzan rubbed his cheek against the she-wolf's head. "I owe you an apology. Before with the keys, I could tell you wanted to free me but I couldn't help myself. So *angry*. Wanted to bite someone."

"It's understandable. But now that you can think again you have to keep a clear head. Don't allow the scent of your enemies to drive you into such a rage you lose control of your beast and shift. No matter how much you want to tear them to shreds remember you need to take care of Asha first. She needs you to carry her away from this awful place. The potion will help her body but only she can decide if she wants to live. She needs a reason. She needs to hear the forest and smell fresh air to know she is free. If that's not enough and she dies let it be where her spirit can run free under open skies, not trapped underground in this place of torment."

Duzan made a noise half-way between a whine and a growl. "I will take her outside. But there is a human...he's near." He used his chin to point towards the steps. "He did the cutting. *He must die*. And the guards who did those unspeakable things to my little sister must pay. I've promised her I'll make them *suffer*." He bared his teeth in a furious snarl then his eyes drifted to the limp she-wolf in his arms and he howled softly.

"Duzan, calm yourself," Aurora said gently. "If you shift you won't be able to carry her."

He nodded and took deep calming breaths. When he spoke his voice was low and guttural. "Die. *They must all die*. Blood is owed for what they've done."

"I agree but vengeance can wait. We *must* be gone before this place becomes as busy as an anthill. If it will make it easier for you to go, know that I have found the cutter."

"He's dead?"

"Not yet but soon. You have my word."

"Make him pay." Duzan's voice was a growl thick with anger and remembered pain. "He is an enemy of our kind. He called us animals but no animal would do this to another."

"He *will* pay. Go now, quickly and quietly. I've already unlocked the door into the passages. Outside there are guards huddled in their towers but they're only human and you should have no difficulty sneaking past in the shadows."

Duzan nodded and the gleam in his eyes told Aurora he wouldn't hesitate to kill anyone who tried to stop him from leaving. He was halfway to the exit when he paused to ask, "Which way are you going?"

"I have unfinished business. The cutter and the girl whose song drew me here."

"Will you free the winged girl?"

"Yes. Are you going to tell me I should leave her because she's an avian?"

Duzan grimaced. "No. No one deserves to be in a place like this but be careful. I saw an avian with the cutter and smelled others. Not her but she may be with them."

"That seems unlikely. Why would they stuff one of their own into a cage?"

Duzan shrugged. "Avians are treacherous. Who can understand them?" With those parting words the big man disappeared into the mine carrying his precious cargo.

With a frown Aurora watched him go. She didn't trust avians and Duzan's words made her even more apprehensive about helping the girl. But…she couldn't leave her here. Bad things happened in this place and she couldn't live with herself if she abandoned the girl to her fate. She would free the singer as she'd set out to do which shouldn't take too long. Then she would kill the cutter and be on her way.

CHAPTER 2

ESCAPE

From the shadows Aurora stared at the girl in the cage. She looked like a golden angel wreathed in shadows as she stood under the only light in the room. Her head was bowed as if in prayer and her beautiful wings were so large they strained against the top and sides of the cage despite being tightly bound. Aurora silently swore when it dawned on her that those wings would make it harder to rescue the avian than she'd expected. She had planned to lead her to safety through the mine, despite the tunnels being a tight fit for someone with wings, but that was *before* she saw that impressive wingspan. Even if the girl didn't get stuck it would be just a matter of time before she brushed a spider lurking in one of the dark corners and provoked an attack. Aurora grimaced, imagining the avian's screams of agony as spider venom burned through her veins. No, going through the mine was no longer an option. There was only one way out with her and that was up via the broad stairway that led to the flattened mountain roof. A well-lit area that happened to have two lookout towers manned with watchful armed guards. It would be almost impossible to get the avian to a spot where she would have enough room to launch without the guards noticing them. Even if they could pull that off, once the girl spread those massive golden wings to take flight it would be as good as hoisting a sail. Anyone on the roof of the mountain would see that and once the avian was in the air even the guards in the camp would notice her with all those spotlights pointing at the sky. All hell would break loose and Aurora would be the one left behind fighting to get away. To prevent that she'd have to neutralize the guards on the roof beforehand and then leave with the avian. The question was: would the girl agree to carry Aurora to safety as payment for setting her free and if she did, could she be trusted to keep her word? She could fly off while Aurora's back was turned or drop her. The wolf was right that avians had a reputation for acting treacherously, even with each other, and they were infamous for selling out other shifters to the humans. If this girl was an associate of the avians who ran this place she would be risking her life to save a viper.

Aurora studied the girl in the cage, uncertain what to do. She didn't look like a viper. She was young and very pretty and when she sang that song she'd sounded desperately afraid. She would let her out of the cage, that much was a given. Aurora wished she could leave the avian to escape on her own like she did with the wolves but she looked so fragile it seemed unlikely that someone like that could overpower multiple armed guards to make her way to freedom. She really wanted to see that beautiful creature soar away from this place while she was still relatively unharmed. Aurora's heightened sense of smell confirmed there wasn't blood or foreign body fluids on the girl so if she freed the avian tonight she would save her from the fate that had befallen the she-wolf. That was worth some risk. She would talk to the girl, see what she could learn about her and then decide whether to offer a deal.

Staying in the shadows Aurora tapped on the floor to get the girl's attention. The avian immediately stood up straighter and squinted as she tried to see into the dark.

"Is someone there?"

"Yes. I'm here to help but before I do – tell me how you ended up in that cage."

"You must be a miner? I was hoping someone would hear me. Please let me out."

"You haven't answered my question…" Aurora put a warning into her voice. She wanted to hurry the conversation along because they didn't have time to waste.

"Please don't leave! I got blown off course in a storm and needed to rest and get out of the bad weather. I saw this place had an avian landing platform so I thought it would be a safe place to find shelter but as you can see, I was wrong. I'd barely landed when someone shot me with a tranquilizer dart. I tried to fly away but I collapsed and there were people running at me with a net. It got blurry after that but I remember being carried down here and thrown in this cage. That was hours ago and no one has been to see me or talk to me. Until you." The girl finished in a rush and her words lay heavily in the silence. "Hello? Are you still there? Who are you?"

"Who I am is not important. What matters is that I'm willing to help you. I have a proposition for you so listen carefully. I can get you out of this cage and to the roof but in return, I expect you to take me with you.

You don't have to take me far, just a safe distance from this place. Will you swear an oath to do this if I help you?"

"If I don't agree, what then? You'll leave me here?" the avian asked anxiously.

"You'd be stupid to turn me down. I'll let you out of this cage anyway but if you're not willing to take me with you when you fly away then you're on your own after that. If you make it to the roof the guards will instantly be on you and you'll be back in that cage so fast you'll have whiplash."

The girl cringed at her words. "You're offering to help me but you sound as desperate as I am to get away from here. Why is that? I could be wrong but you don't sound like a miner which begs the question: what *are* you doing here?"

"Why does that matter?"

"It matters *because* you're still hiding in the dark but you expect me to swear an oath and put my life in your hands. That's asking a lot and after the day I've had my trust levels are at an all-time low."

Aurora emerged from the shadows. She gripped the bars above the girl's hands and pressed her face so close she felt the avian's startled inhale. "Is this better?"

"Yes, *much* better."

"I snuck into the mine to harvest ethian crystals. Call me a thief if you want. Personally, I don't believe that crystals made by nature can be claimed as a person's property while still growing inside a mountain. I was leaving when I heard your song. Avians don't belong underground nor do they sing dawn songs in the middle of the night as far as I'm aware and it made me think you were here against your will so I came to have a look and found this cutter's den. I've already let the wolf-shifters go. I don't know if you saw what was done to them; it'll be a miracle if the she-wolf lives to see the dawn. I want to help you because you're still whole and unscarred and I'd like you to remain that way but to get you to safety will cost me. It's not enough to just open your cage and point you in the right direction. I'll have to take additional risks, the kind that could get me killed and you're a total stranger. Is it so unreasonable that I ask for help in return so we can both get away from this place?"

The girl studied Aurora closely while she spoke, hanging on to her every word. "No, not unreasonable. A partnership. You help me and I'll help you." She put her hands over Aurora's on the bars. "I, Evie, swear to you on the blood of my lineage that I will take you with me when we leave this place and put you to ground safely. Now please, *get me out of here!*"

Aurora stared at Evie's hands. They looked so delicate against her own. The skin soft and creamy and yet her grip was surprisingly firm. She met searching blue eyes only inches away. Such expressive kind eyes. Aurora saw hope warring with fear and something else that flitted past so quickly she couldn't catch it. She had the oddest sensation that she was being drawn into those deep blue depths and she had an urge to reassure the girl that everything would be all right. Mentally Aurora shook herself and withdrew her hands. The avian was waiting to be freed and a guard could at any moment discover one of the broken locks she'd left in her wake. The clock was ticking and she couldn't afford to be distracted by soft hands and pretty eyes, no matter how attractive she found them. Aurora unlocked the cage, took her knife from its sheath behind her back and sliced through the girl's bindings with the dark blade, taking care to keep the razor-sharp edge away from vulnerable skin and feathers.

"Evie, until we're in the air you need to do what I say immediately, no questions asked. I have a plan but there's no time to explain it to you. Understood?" At Evie's nod, Aurora continued. "How difficult will it be for you to get into the air with my added weight? Can you launch us straight up or do I need to get us to the edge?"

"Going over the side will be better because I don't want to stand there flapping my wings, making an easy target of myself. As for carrying you…if we had more time I'd make a harness but I'll just have to wrap my arms around your chest. It might get rough if we hit turbulence but don't worry, I won't let you fall. Once we have enough altitude I can glide and we'll literally be floating on air. Let your body drift in tandem with mine and try to relax. I'll take care of everything."

"I've flown before so I understand what I have to do. You just need to let me know when you want to land because I don't want to break my legs if you decide to make a quick landing."

"It's great that you've been flown before. I worried you might panic because most people do the first time up."

"Unless you drop me you don't have to worry about me panicking but there is something you need to know."

"What?"

"There's a storm brewing out there and we might get lightning."

Evie grimaced. "Lightning is the last thing we need."

"Yeah, we both have our jobs cut out for us tonight. It's going to be a bumpy ride."

"No kidding. Let's do this. I'll be right behind you."

The girl rustled her powerful wings and arched them aggressively. That, the determined set of her jaw and the way her eyes sparked made her look formidable, dangerous even. The transformation from a scared girl in a cage to pissed off fallen angel, ready to do battle, was so sudden it made Aurora do a double take. Maybe the avian wasn't as fragile and helpless as she thought after all. Good. That would make things a lot easier.

***

Evie followed her rescuer out of the room and up a flight of stairs. As they passed a set of doors the tall woman gave the door on the right such a furious scowl it made Evie pause. Her curiosity aroused she asked, "What's behind that door?"

"You don't want to go in there."

"Why not?"

"Behind that door is a torture chamber and slaughter pen. That's where the cutters harvested whatever was in demand on the black market from their captives. They'd wait for the shapeshifters to regenerate and do it over and over until the shifter died. There's a lifetime worth of nightmares in that room. Don't open that door unless you're prepared for that."

Evie hesitated as she considered the woman's words and her grim expression. "I don't want to look but I have to. I've only ever heard of places like this and I need to see if what I imagined might happen to me is as bad as I thought."

"Why?"

"When I tell my flock what happened to me and about this place they'll seek retribution so I need to have my facts straight. I can't have any doubts. All I saw in passing was a chained man with missing fingers and a scarred chest. I think I know what that means but I need to see for myself."

"I understand. Do what you have to but brace yourself before you go in. That's a chamber of evil and some things once seen will remain with you for the rest of your life."

The warning sent a chill down Evie's spine but she squared her shoulders and opened the door anyway. She immediately wished she hadn't. The smell of disinfectant, blood and harsh chemicals burned her nose but it was nothing compared to the horror that assailed her sight. She skimmed over the contents of the shelves and her stomach heaved as she realized the things in the jars and the pelts stretched out on the drying racks were the remains of shapeshifters. Her eye snagged on a contraption in the corner with lots of hooks and chains set up in a square cubicle. The walls and floor were stained in muted reds and blacks as if it had been washed down but the stone had absorbed so much blood no amount of bleach could completely wash it away. That must be where they butchered the captives when they were dead. Or was that done while they were still alive? Evie put a hand over her mouth to stifle the sound of a sob she couldn't keep inside. Her mind was making connections between what she was seeing and what must have happened in that room and the horror was overwhelming. She desperately wanted to look away to make it stop but she couldn't move.

The door closed in front of her and the woman turned Evie to face her. Strong hands squeezed her shoulders and a reassuring voice said, "That will not happen to you. I won't let it. Do you hear me? You will be in the air shortly and on your way home. Concentrate on that."

Evie took a shuddering breath as if she was coming up for air. She realized she was crying and angrily wiped at the tears streaming down her face. "How could anyone do such things to another living being? I don't understand...it's monstrous." Her voice sounded shaky to her. Weak. That was unacceptable. She had to pull herself together. Evie shook her head to dislodge the images and forced herself to stop huddling under her wings like a scared child. She stood a little taller and said, "Thank you for closing the door. Seeing that...it was…horrifying."

"Are you all right?"

"No, but I won't break down on you either. Please get us out of here as quickly as possible."

"That's the plan so let's keep going."

"Oh wait…I saw a man on the table. I think his eyes were open so maybe he's still alive? Can you please have a look and see if we can save him?"

"That's the cutter responsible for all the blood spilled in that room. I put him there and no, he's not dead...yet."

Evie heard the implication loud and clear. To spill the blood of another without just cause created blood-debt and that cutter was due to pay a price he couldn't survive. Evie stared at the closed door and her mind flashed to the horrible things she'd just seen. What a living nightmare it must have been for the people who suffered in that room. If she had remained a captive here would that cutter have strung her up by those hooks to cut into her as he'd done with the others?

Evie resisted the urge to heave and said in a formal tone, "Blood is owed. The cutter can't be allowed to harm anyone ever again but I've never killed a person and I don't think I have it in me to kill a helpless man no matter how guilty he is. Is it something you are able to do? I'll stand by and bear witness if you need me to."

"I will take care of him before we leave but you don't need to be a part of that. Come on. I'm taking you upstairs."

Grateful that the other woman would do what she could not Evie nodded and followed. When they got into a large office that appeared to double as an area to entertain guests Evie was told to wait behind a cupboard.

"From here you can see anyone who enters the room but they can't see you. I'm going to take care of the guards on the roof. Don't move until I get back." With those words, her new partner disappeared into the night.

Evie waited in the quiet room as the minutes ticked past, acutely aware of her loud breathing and thumping heart. She breathed a sigh of relief when the woman returned.

"It's done. I need to go back downstairs but I won't be long. Wait here until I give you the signal to come out then join me outside."

"What kind of signal?"

"There'll be a loud noise. You'll know when you hear it."

***

In the laboratory Aurora pulled the shelving out of the freezer and dumped the grisly contents back in. She hurriedly emptied all the drawers and shelves of the potions, the packets of dried powder and jars of organs suspended in fluids and threw everything into the freezer. The glint of the surgical tools caught her eye so she added those as well. Then she went over to the cutter, who lay where she'd left him. His eyes wide and wild, he followed her every move. When he saw the purposeful way she walked towards him he tried to speak but could only manage a muffled moan like a man in a nightmare trying to wake himself.

She leaned over him so they were eye to eye and said, "What comes next is better than you deserve. It will be over quickly and that is more mercy than you gave the poor souls you tortured."

She picked him up and threw him into the freezer on top of his handiwork. She hadn't planned it but it seemed fitting that the scalpels were directly under him slicing into his bare flesh. The freezer was too full to accommodate a full-grown man but she made him fit and she wasn't gentle about it. Once he was in she secured the lid with tape and set about maneuvering the freezer out the door and onto the stairs. She rammed a large hook into the side and used it as a handle to drag the thing upstairs. The weight didn't bother her but the noise she made did even though she was reasonably sure there was no one left to raise the alarm. Fortunately, all the doors were wide enough so the freezer slid through easily and soon she was on the flattened roof of the mountain dragging it behind her to the spot she'd chosen earlier. Aurora peered over the side of the cliff and saw she was directly over the loading dock. Far below trucks were parked in a tight square illuminated by a single spotlight. Aurora shoved the freezer over the side. It tumbled in slow motion and hit the cab of a truck with a loud boom. The lid flew open and the grizzly contents flew out in a wide arc, raining down on the other vehicles with a succession of thumps along with the sound of breaking glass as windows broke and jars shattered, splattering fluids and body parts everywhere. Even from where she stood the loading dock looked like the site of a massacre.

"What did you push over the side? It made enough noise to wake the dead so I assume this was the signal for me to come?"

Turning, Aurora found the girl jogging towards her while trying to do some kind of crouching maneuver. If Evie was trying to be stealthy it was an utter failure as the spotlights illuminated her wings like giant golden flags. She tried to go around Aurora to have a peek over the side but Aurora blocked her and took her gently but firmly by the arm and led her away. It was a long way down and the light below wasn't as bright as on the roof but it was still possible that the avian might see more than was good for her. Aurora wanted to shield her from the sight below and if she was honest with herself, she didn't want to risk Evie seeing what she'd done to the cutter. She didn't feel she'd been excessive under the circumstances but since the girl didn't know her, she might justifiably conclude she was in the company of a psychopath and make a run for it without Aurora. Or in this case, leap off the edge and fly away as fast as she could.

When Aurora didn't answer her immediately Evie rustled her wings impatiently. "Well…what *was* that?"

"I gathered the contents of the cutter's lab and dumped it over the side, along with the cutter."

"Eeew…that's seems a little extreme. Was that really necessary?"

"Yes, I had to make an example of him and send a message to the miners. I don't think they knew what's been going on here but now they will. If they remain after seeing the evidence then they can't claim to be ignorant when the wolves come for vengeance. That big scarred man *will* return and he won't come alone. He's out for blood and I don't think he will take the time to ask who knew what before the killing starts."

Looking grim Evie said, "A pack of angry wolves would rip the camp apart. There are many people here and it'd be a massacre."

"Yes, that's why I wanted to warn the miners."

"That's a gruesome warning but if that doesn't get their attention nothing will. So, we can go now? I *really* want to leave."

"Will this spot work? You can launch us over the side from here. Time for you to deliver on your part of the deal and get us away from here."

Evie pointed at the pack on Aurora's back. "We can't have that between us. You'll either have to move it to your chest or leave it behind."

"There is *no way* I'm leaving it here. It took me two days and nights of searching and finally crawling into a giant spider's nest to find those crystals, none of which was fun. I'll move it."

As soon as she refastened her pack the avian stepped up behind her and wrapped her arms around Aurora's chest under her armpits, locking at the wrists. She was shorter than Aurora and her face brushed Aurora's shoulder standing so close. Aurora overlapped her own arms and took a firm hold of the girl's arms.

Evie winced. "Wow, you have a powerful grip. I'm going to have bruises tomorrow."

Standing on the side of the mountain staring down at the jagged rocks far below, Aurora wanted to step away from the edge and let the avian take off without her. What had possessed her to put her life in the hands of a stranger? This was madness. She turned her head to lock eyes with Evie. "You won't let me fall, will you? You gave your word."

There was a flash of mischief in Evie's eyes and as she nudged Aurora closer to the edge she said, "It's too late for you to worry about that, don't you think?" Then she launched them into open space.

Aurora's stomach lurched as they dropped into the dark abyss and slow seconds ticked past as she waited for the avian to let her fall. Instead, Evie's arms around her chest tightened almost painfully, she spread her huge golden wings and they soared. She angled them upwards and Aurora heard the whoosh of those wings as they worked to take them higher.

"Get us further away before you try to climb," Aurora shouted over her shoulder. "They have all kinds of weapons down there!"

"What did you say?"

BOOM! BOOM!

As if on cue there was a thunderous noise and something whistled past Aurora's face. She saw the next projectile coming on course to hit her in the chest. The avian banked, trying to get out of the way but it was too late. Aurora felt the impact as something hit the wing to her right and Evie screamed in agony, her wing crumpled and they spun wildly. Aurora held on for dear life while the girl fought to regain control and extend her injured wing. She managed to get it open all the way but in the process Aurora was ripped out of her arms. Turning in the air she saw the look of shock and horror on Evie's face as she fell away from her. Then in a move that stunned Aurora, Evie folded her wings and dove with arms extended, reaching for her. Aurora opened her own arms and suddenly they were in an embrace, falling together.

The avian had her wings open again but only a third of the way. From the painful grimace on her face, Aurora guessed she was finding it difficult to keep her right wing open even that much and Evie struggled to guide them down in something between a glide and a controlled fall. Peering over her shoulder Aurora saw the ground approaching fast. She saw dark crevices and jagged rocks everywhere. It was a terrible place to land. Twisting in Evie's arms so she could see better she shoved herself free from the girl's hold about ten feet from the ground to land in a small clearing. The avian landed on her feet but tumbled over, one wing tucked properly but the other partly extended at an awkward angle, with the girl landing on top of it. There was a wail of pain and the sound of something snapping. Aurora rushed to the girl, lifting her under her shoulders to get her up and off the injured wing.

Evie's eyes were glazed with pain and she was shaking. "My wing…my wing. I think I broke it."

A quick glance told Aurora she was right. The wing dragged on the ground at an odd angle and there was a bone sticking out. To make matters worse, there was a fist-sized hole near the joint where the girl had been hit and blood flowed from the wound.

"Yes, you broke it."

"No, no, no! This is terrible. What am I going to do? I'm stuck on the ground and we're only a little way from the mine. They'll come for us!"

Taking stock of their surroundings Aurora realized she was right. They were close to the mine on a bare slope strewn with the jagged stumps of harvested trees. To make matters worse their pursuers had a projectile weapon powerful enough to take an avian out of the air and someone skilled enough to use it with precision. This was bad. She had to get them moving and fast. There was only one way to do that and Evie wouldn't like it.

"Listen to me. You have to shift your wings away. Quickly."

***

Evie stared at the woman holding her up, struggling to believe what she just heard. "Shift my wings away? Are you insane? I have a broken wing!"

"Exactly why you need to get rid of it. It's useless to you right now and it will slow us down. Dragging on the ground like that you'll only damage it more and you'll leave such wide tracks that even the rain won't wash it all away."

"I can't. Not quickly! Even when my wings are fine it takes me at least half an hour or longer to shift."

"I know avians keep their wings on almost permanently but you've got to be kidding! Don't your people practice quick shifts for an emergency?"

"This is not the time to lecture me! I *can't* quick-shift! I need lots of time and peaceful surroundings. We have neither and I can hear dogs. Oh no…they have dogs. They're coming for us!"

Her companion tilted her head sideways. In the poor light it was hard to read her expression but Evie thought she looked perplexed.

"The dogs are going in the wrong direction. They've found a scent but it's not ours."

"How can you tell?"

"I can hear them," she said this slowly as if she was trying to explain something to a child. "That doesn't mean we should waste time. We have an advantage with the rain and poor visibility so we need to push it. At the very least we need to be away from here before sunrise."

"But what will we do if the dogs catch our scent?"

"I'll take care of the dogs if they get too close. It's the men that follow them and whoever is using that weapon that could be a problem especially with you like this." She went quiet and stared over her shoulder thoughtfully. "If the guards found the wolves' trail they could be in serious trouble. He can look after himself but if the female is still alive he will have his hands full carrying her and evading the hunters. This is my fault…it's because I made so much noise dropping that fridge on the trucks that the mine is on high alert. I have to make sure the wolves are all right. Wait under this overhang. The guards wouldn't have seen where we landed, only that we went down on this side of the mountain, so you should be safe until I get back. While I'm away shift your wings. Push through the pain, *do whatever you have to.* Once they're gone you will feel much better. Your injured wing will start to heal and in a few days you'll be able to fly again." She abruptly turned away from Evie and started back towards the mine.

"Wait!" Evie grabbed her arm, desperation giving her strength. "You won't leave me here like this? Promise me you're coming back?"

The tall stranger stared at the hand on her arm for a moment before prying Evie's fingers loose. "Don't worry, I'll come back." She pressed her backpack into Evie's arms. "At the very least I'll come back for my things." Then between one blink and the next she disappeared, swallowed by the night as a dark cluster of clouds once again obscured the moon.

Alone in the dark Evie pressed as close to the outcropping as her wings would allow. The motion had her doubled over in agony and she was grateful she couldn't see the extent of the damage to her wing because what her bloody fingers told her was bad enough. Taking deep breaths she forced down the fear. She could not afford to go into shock or curl up into a whimpering ball. If she wanted to survive her ordeal and get home in one piece she had to focus and deal with one problem at a time. As much as she hated to admit it the woman was right, she had to get rid of her wings. Evie shuddered at the thought. Her wings were as much a part of her as any of her other limbs and they defined who she was: an avian, a creature of the skies. But right now one of her wings was a useless liability that made her an easy target. If she didn't shift she was as good as recaptured and after what she saw in the cutter's lab she'd rather be dead.

Evie gritted her teeth and prepared to shift. For her, it was akin to hauling something heavy out of a powerful current with a slippery rope. It was a painful, difficult process and she knew other avians avoided shifting for the same reason. That and the stigma associated with going wingless. Among her kind, being seen without one's wings was the equivalent of going naked in public. None of that mattered right now. If she wanted to see dawn as a free woman she'd have to do it. Evie pushed harder. With the added layer of pain from the injury it felt like the rope she visualized had thorns. Soon despite the cold she could feel sweat pouring from her body, her heart pounded in her ears and her vision narrowed as she fought not to pass out from the excruciating pain.

Finally, there was a popping sensation like something just gave way under great pressure and her wings disappeared. The sudden absence of pain was such a relief that Evie sobbed. She slumped against the rock and rode out the waves of fatigue that rolled over her. She didn't know how long it had taken. Longer than normal for sure but at least she'd got it done before the woman returned. There was a small triumph in that. Hopefully she had a few moments to gather herself because she didn't want to be seen looking as weak as a newborn kitten. It had been the worst shift she'd ever endured and it felt like she had just been spat out of a hurricane-sized twister. If she'd been at home she would have taken a large dose of mira essence to speed up her healing, had a hearty meal and then collapsed onto her soft warm bed for at least ten hours.

A gust of freezing air buffeted Evie, chilling her sweat-drenched body as if in cruel reminder that there would be no such luxuries for her tonight. She was a long way from home and her ordeal far from over. When her rescuer returned she would have to draw on every scrap of reserve she had to keep up with her on foot. That's assuming she came back. Evie clutched the bag left in her care tighter to her chest. If there really were precious ethian crystals in it she would surely be back for them? Unless she couldn't because she'd been captured or killed. This was a very real possibility and it would mean that Evie would have to get off the mountain and to safety on her own. It was a daunting prospect. Even by day, this place with its ragged stumps, hidden crevices, and sheer cliffs would be a minefield for her. Walking it by night would be one of the most dangerous things she'd ever attempted. It may even kill her. But hiding here until morning wasn't an option. The area around the mine was like a festering sore; where once tall trees grew it was now mostly barren rock. She'd be seen for sure. Not only that but in her experience places like this drew lightning and if she lingered here during what sounded like the rumblings of a thunderstorm overhead she could be struck by it. Evie felt drops hit her face and knew it was a prelude to the deluge that would soon follow. She had to get moving. She couldn't afford to wait for someone who may not be coming back.

"Good, you took care of the wings."

The words spoken from only about a foot away made Evie jump. "Where did you come from so suddenly?" she hissed. "I could have sworn you weren't here a moment ago."

"I just got back. Here, I found you a pair of walking boots." From around her neck the woman removed a pair of shoes tied together by the laces and held them out to Evie. "What you have on is fine for flying but an hour travelling over rocks will rip those shoes and your feet to shreds. The boots I got you may be a little big but rather too big than too small."

"You got me shoes? Whose are these?"

"Does it matter? I didn't kill anyone for them…if that's what you're asking. I caused havoc in the camp to draw the hunters back, saw the shoes while I did that and thought they could be a fit. It was amazing good fortune to find such small boots in a mostly male camp."

When Evie made no move to take the boots she put them on the ground in front of her and snapped, "Hurry. Give me your flight boots so they can go in the bag." She took her backpack from Evie's limp hands, her eyes restlessly scanning in the mine's direction. She snatched the flight boots as soon as Evie had them off, wrapped them in a cloth and slid them into her bag. As soon as Evie put on the stolen boots she asked, "Do they fit?"

"They're a half size bigger than I prefer but with the laces pulled tight they're a reasonable fit. I've never worn another person's shoes before. It feels...odd."

"You'll feel a lot worse than odd with bleeding feet. We need to move. Stay close and step where I do because the path is treacherous."

Feeling clumsy in boots so much heavier than her own and struggling to see where she was going, it wasn't long before Evie stumbled. She corrected herself but only got a little further before again losing her footing on the uneven slippery slope and this time she couldn't stop the fall. She slammed down on her hands and knees so hard the impact jarred her teeth and she tasted blood on her tongue. The woman didn't comment and didn't help her up, she just watched and waited. However, when Evie slipped again, twisting her ankle in the process, a hand jerked her back from a chasm Evie hadn't even realized was there until she was about to fall into it.

"This really won't do. You're stumbling around like a wounded deer."

Evie wrenched her arm free, shame and fear making her angry and indignant. "I'm not *that bad*. I'm just not used to this kind of terrain. I'll get better, you'll see. I won't hold you back. Keep going and I'll follow." When the woman didn't move Evie tried to step around her and had to stifle a cry at the stab of pain that shot up from the newly twisted ankle. Instantly hands were on her shoulders holding her firmly, preventing her from moving. Evie tried to shake loose but it was like being held in a vise.

"You're off balance without your wings and not used to walking at night. We are on a rocky mountainside in the rain, you've already stumbled twice so it's just a matter of time before you fall and hurt yourself badly. I thought the hiking boots would help you but it's not enough." She rolled her shoulders in a motion that reminded Evie of a boxer loosening up before getting into the ring and said, "There's only one reasonable solution to this problem. Put my backpack on your back."

"You want me to carry your things?" Evie asked incredulously. "How is *that* going to help? I can hardly stay upright as it is."

"You carry my pack and I'll carry you. I'm used to running in the dark with weight on my back."

"It's my wing that's broken, not my legs and my ankle is just a little sore. There is no way I'm letting you piggyback me down a mountain like a child. It's bad enough I have to walk down it instead of fly!"

"If you don't get on my back I *will* leave you here. I don't have time to soothe your ego or whatever is going on with you. When we flew I followed your lead and I put myself into your hands because air is your domain. You are in my world now. I've been the hunter and the hunted; I know how to evade our pursuers. If you listen and do what I say I'll get us to safety. Fight me and you become too big a liability. Do you understand?"

Evie bit her lip, clamping down on the furious things she wanted to say. As much as she hated to admit it, she needed help. Reluctantly she nodded.

"Good. We have a lot of ground to cover before daybreak. If they find us here we'll be sitting ducks. They will try to pin us down for capture or attempt to kill us outright. The people responsible for that cutter's den in the mine will do whatever they can to destroy the evidence and prevent word from getting out. It's already too late for that but they'll try. They have to because that's what desperate people do. Just so you know…I'll fight to the death rather than have cutters capture me."

Evie didn't like the images flashing before her. She saw jeering men dragging her back to the cages to resume whatever they had planned for her and the woman beside her dead on the ground in a pool of blood. It made her feel sick to her core.

"But how can you carry me?" Evie asked almost meekly. "Without my wings I'm lighter than a human my size but it's not like I'm light as a feather and you may be bigger and stronger than me but it's not like you're a behemoth."

A face pressed close to hers in the dark and Evie had a moment of déjà vu. "I *can* and *will* carry you. I do not offer what I can't deliver. I got you out of that cage and onto the roof, didn't I?"

"Yes, you did."

"Don't be afraid that I'll drop you because I won't. Tighten my pack so it doesn't bump around then get on my back. Hurry! It's high time we got off this rock."

Her companion sounded impatient and Evie didn't blame her. It was a miracle she hadn't already abandoned her broken-winged, limping companion. Her pride was thoroughly bruised and Evie wished she didn't have to take the offer but she was out of options. The moon had disappeared behind the cloud cover, taking with it the meager light it had provided and the intermittent drops had turned into a drizzle so Evie struggled to make out anything beyond the shape of the woman directly in front of her. She could see for miles by day but unlike her companion she didn't have night vision and under these conditions she was as good as blind. The only way she was getting off this slippery death trap of a mountainside quickly was if she fell off it or accepted help but she wished it didn't involve being carried like a human-shaped backpack. If anyone from her flock or any of the other avian Houses ever heard about this the snickering would be endless.

"Promise you won't tell anyone about this?" Evie begged.

"About what? Me carrying you?"

"Yes."

"Sure. Who would I tell anyway?"

Evie was still mulling over the answer when she got hoisted unceremoniously onto a broad back. Instinctively she wrapped her arms and legs around the tall muscular frame. Blinking rain out of her eyes, Evie felt rather than saw the length of cloth that got wrapped over and under her legs, bottom and back securing her tightly against her companion's back.

"This should keep you in place. If you feel the material loosen or tear you need to let me know immediately."

"I get the impression you've done this before?"

"I have. Now for both our sakes be as still as you can. Don't panic if I make sudden directional changes, try not to strangle me and don't whack me in the back of the head with your forehead. If I lose my balance we'll have an awful tumble. Don't know about you but I prefer all my teeth in my mouth."

Before Evie could say anything they were off. The woman set a pace between a fast walk and a jog. The first time she jumped over a crevice Evie's heart lurched in her mouth. Terrified of falling off Evie tightened her arms until she felt the urgent tap on her forearm. Embarrassed, she lessened her grip and adjusted for a better hold on her companion's shoulders rather than strangling her.

This was ridiculous. She was being piggybacked like an infant, dependent on someone whose name she didn't even know. When she heard the stranger had stolen crystals worth a fortune from the mine, she had assumed that was why she didn't want to tell Evie her name when they first met. She had apparently also planned to cause major damage to a very lucrative black-market operation by freeing the prisoners and destroying a freezer full of grizzly contents. Those were good reasons to want to stay anonymous. But why didn't she just lie and make up a name? That's what most people would have done. Thinking it over Evie decided it was probably because her companion expected to spend so little time in Evie's company that she didn't think it was worth the effort. Well, so much for that plan. Now they were stuck with each other. At the first opportunity she would demand to know her name.

Soon the cold drizzle turned into a persistent downpour and it wasn't long before Evie was soaked. Normally her flight gear would keep her dry but she had lost the hood when she'd been taken and the rest of her outfit was designed around her wings. Without them rain poured into the slits on her back to pool around her hips, from where it seeped into her pants. Fatigued and battered by the day's events, the constant jostling made her feel even worse. She was wet and miserable. If she had to endure being cold as well it would have been unbearable but courtesy of the intense heat generated by the fast moving woman to whose back she was fused, she remained surprisingly warm.

With her arms and legs wrapped around her companion Evie was intensely aware of the other woman's body. Despite her undignified position Evie was fascinated with the feel of muscles rippling, tensing and releasing. Their pace never faltered and the woman steadfastly made her way over perilous terrain as if she was jogging in a well-lit park. She had to be a shapeshifter, that much was obvious. Humans couldn't see in the dark and she was super-agile and very strong. But what kind? It was rude to ask another shifter something so personal and if her companion was a beast-shifter as she suspected, she had to be careful because they were extra prickly about it. Taking on the form of a beast brought with it many strengths but also some undesirable traits associated with the creature they could become. Prejudices and old rivalries were rife in the shapeshifter community because of this. The only thing all shapeshifters had in common was their distrust of the new arrivals from the human world eager to carve out a life for themselves in Nordarra…by whatever means possible. Technically, she was a shifter as well but avians only grew wings, enabling them to fly. They couldn't turn into birds. They had light strong bones, enhanced eyesight by day and the ability to endure high altitude but other than that gained little from their shifter heritage. The flip side of that coin was that they didn't have major problems either. Most other shifters were not that fortunate. Wolves who ran in their beast form too long could become ferals who saw everyone else as little more than meat. Mers while in mermaid or merman form had the nasty tendency to drown and even take a bite out of anyone foolish enough to follow them into the water. Those were the shifters who were sociable and capable of working and playing reasonably well with others. Most of the time. There were shifters in the wild isolated places who rarely mingled with those not of their kind; they shunned the cities and only visited the trade stations and small towns when they had to. Then there were the shapeshifters who were so monstrous they were almost indiscernible from the terrifying wildlife that still roamed the ancient forests and the forbidden places. Presumably, their ancestors were also fully human ages ago before the magic of the land drifted into their blood changing them and their children, altering them more with every passing generation, at least according to one of the prevailing theories on how shifters came into existence. Another theory was that the ancient beings who inhabited this land long before humans first set foot here, the builders of all the great structures that now lay in ruin, changed humans, enabling them to shapeshift so they could survive the harsh environment and the potent magic of Nordarra as it was then.

The long-lived dragons with their love for hoarding knowledge and precious things probably knew the truth but they shared nothing. Besides, even if someone was desperate enough for an answer to ask a dragon they'd be hard-pressed to find one. Where once they were a common sight they were now so rarely seen people speculated the dragon-shifters were on the verge of dying out or had migrated to one of the other continents. Either way, their absence wasn't a bad thing in Evie's opinion as they were the most powerful and dangerous of all the shifters in this part of the world. Volatile and arrogant, their magical lineage put them in the ranks of the fabled Old Bloods, the firstborn of all shapeshifters. The dragons considered most other shifters as lesser beings and anyone with half a brain avoided them. Even before she could fly she'd been taught to hide at the first sighting of a dragon. To avians, dragons were the sharks of the sky and their fear of the magnificent monsters ran deep.

Evie's stomach dropped as her companion jumped over something she couldn't see, to land with cat-like grace. She must have made an anxious noise because she got a reassuring squeeze on her leg. Evie's thoughts circled back to the woman forging a way to safety for them in the dark. She was probably a nocturnal hunter. A wolf perhaps? Whatever she was at least she didn't consider Evie prey. A nuisance certainly but not something she was dragging along as a snack for when her beast came out to play. She'd gone out of her way to rescue Evie and she was carrying her down a mountain in the rain; even fresh meat wasn't worth that much trouble!

CHAPTER 3

SHELTER

It was mid-morning and by Evie's estimate they'd been moving through the forest for about two hours. The sun made a weak effort to brighten the grey skies but very little light and no warmth made it past the thick canopy to the forest floor. Thankfully, the rain had stopped for the moment but she was still getting plenty of cold drops from the overhanging branches. Not that it mattered, she couldn't be wetter if she'd taken a swim in a river fully clothed. She had asked her companion how far they had to go and her reply had been: 'Not far'. That was before dawn. She didn't want to pester or sound like a whiny child but her bladder was sending her urgent messages she couldn't ignore.

"Can I get down soon? We've been traveling for hours."

"We're almost there. I know a place we can rest and anyone looking will have a hard time finding us."

Good to her word a short time later she lowered a very stiff Evie off her back. Evie pulled the pack off her own back, almost groaning at the relief of pressure on her shoulder blades. She put the small backpack down gently on a stump that looked semi-dry. The last thing she wanted to do was damage her companion's property by being careless when she'd been so careful with her. Then Evie stretched and twisted trying to get the blood flowing in her tight muscles. Her injured ankle throbbed and her thighs ached from being wrapped around someone's hips for hours. She once had a friend describe to her what it had been like to go bareback horse riding. This, she decided, must be similar. Although thankfully she didn't get chafed raw around her nether regions and at no point had she worried that her mount was trying to dump her head first into a stream as her friend's had. Her 'mount' stood with hands on hips studying a huge tree, her eyes occasionally flickering to Evie.

"Are you all right?"

"I am, thanks to you. I'm just a little stiff. How about you?"

The woman nodded and went back to studying the tree. Evie realized this was the first time she'd gotten to see her entire face unobscured by hair or poor light. Evie had noticed her rescuer was attractive when she'd let her out of the cage but that had registered as background noise with everything else going on. Now she really looked, drinking her in. The woman was stunning. Very tall and built like an athlete with broad shoulders that tapered to narrow hips. With her dark hair pulled away into a low ponytail, Evie could see high cheekbones and a strong jaw. Sharp lines softened by almond-shaped eyes gave her an exotic slant and she had full lips that made Evie wonder if they would be as amazing to taste as they looked. Not that she had any illusion of finding out. Her companion wasn't unfriendly exactly but so far not particularly talkative and very guarded. There was a wary watchfulness in the way she studied everything, even Evie, which gave the impression she was ready to react swiftly to any perceived danger. Evie had seen that look on the battle-scarred veterans who protected her father from assassination attempts after he had taken over the leadership of House Aquilar from his own father and made some changes that were unpopular. There hadn't been an attempt on his life for a long time but the veterans still had that vigilant look about them as if they were always watching for an attack. It made her sad to see such a look on someone so young and beautiful.

The object of her scrutiny grabbed her backpack and said, "I'm going up. I'll be back soon." Not waiting for a response she leapt into the tree and disappeared.

Evie tried to find her in the thick foliage but it was hopeless. It was like the forest giant swallowed her. That was an unsettling thought. She'd heard many scary tales about forest dwelling predators. If one of those creatures hurt or killed her only guide what would happen to her? She couldn't fly and had no woodcraft to speak of. Evie caught the fear before it could bloom into full-blown panic and stomped on it. She couldn't allow the strangeness of the forest to mess with her head. She reminded herself that her companion was a strong, capable woman who didn't look like she'd tolerate being messed with. If anything attacked her she would probably slap it out of the tree.

Feeling less fearful but still on edge, Evie looked for something to distract her while she waited. She had a closer look at the tree and it occurred to her there was something unusual about it. She tilted her head and took a few steps to the side trying to figure it out. She couldn't decide if she was looking at one massive tree or several smaller ones clustered together. Roots wove around each other so it was impossible to tell where one ended and another began. It was probably one tree she decided after studying it more. Just an old one of a variety unknown to her which was hardly surprising as she didn't spend time in forests unless she absolutely had to. It wasn't that the tree was a tall giant. Instead of pushing upwards it had expanded sideways investing in its roots which was probably wise considering the fierce weather and heavy rains that hammered this area at the base of the mountains. During their trek into the forest she'd seen many trees lean precariously against their neighbors and numerous ones on the ground in various stages of being overgrown or cannibalized by colorful mushrooms. Squinting at the tree to keep random raindrops out of her eyes Evie got the peculiar impression she was looking at a stout matriarch weighed down by several layers of heavy skirts that ballooned out from her hips, obscuring her feet. This thought made Evie blink several times. She had to be very tired to see an old woman in a tree; her mind had a way of offering her odd perspectives when she was overtired or stressed.

Growing weary of craning her neck she found a spot that looked reasonably safe to relieve her overfull bladder. Feeling a lot lighter Evie settled down to wait on a log, hoping as she did so that nothing would crawl out to bite her in the behind. A troubling thought had occurred to her and she really hoped she was wrong. What if the woman expected her to climb that tree? Normally reaching a high place would be easy, but unable to fly it felt like she was facing an insurmountable obstacle. If she found the prospect of climbing a tree this daunting how was she going to cope with all the other challenges the forest would throw at her?

Evie took stock of her wingless body and didn't find the results encouraging. She had considered herself fit because she spent a lot of time flying and kept physically active. She wasn't muscular but her shifter side meant she was stronger than the average human, even a male in the prime of his life. However, her strengths were relative. In comparison to a wolf-shifter she was fragile and she had done nothing to prepare herself for the physical demands of the wild terrain she now found herself in. Why would she? Avians were vulnerable on the ground and going for a walk into an overgrown forest with large wings that could get snagged made no sense.

Her companion, on the other hand, radiated a level of physicality that took Evie's breath away. She was designed for this kind of environment and had clearly honed her body and skills to thrive in it. She moved with such agile grace she appeared almost slender despite her height and powerful build. It wasn't until one touched, as Evie had, the corded muscles sheathed in silken skin and felt the immense coiled strength unleashed in a contained burst of vicious energy, that one got a sense of what lay hidden. Once again Evie wondered what kind of beast the woman turned into. No doubt a predator. Evie could imagine her stalking the shadows while stealthily closing in on oblivious prey. As if called by her thoughts the stealthy predator in question dropped in front of Evie, barely making a sound. Startled Evie instinctively jumped, trying to launch herself into flight only to come down hard on her sore ankle. She winced as a stab of pain shot up her leg.

"I wish you would stop doing that! Are you trying to give me a heart attack?"

"Did I give you a fright? Sorry. It wasn't deliberate."

"Never mind. *Please* tell me you don't expect me to climb that tree? The bark looks as slippery as soap."

"I'll help you get to the shelter."

Evie stared at the other woman with a mixture of disbelief and trepidation. "Do I have a choice?"

"You *could* stay here but if you want to get dry you'll have to climb the tree."

"Dry?" This made Evie perk up a little.

"Yes, I have a change of clothing for you and I'll make us a hot drink before we sleep."

"Really? You're not just saying that to get me to climb the tree?"

The woman frowned. "Why would I lie? If I did that you would start to doubt me. Since we're going to be together for a while it's important that we trust each other. Out here with only each other to rely on that can mean the difference between life and death."

Evie studied the earnest green eyes that held her gaze. She had a feeling this conversation was no longer just about whether there really was a change of clothing waiting for her. She slowly let out a breath, sliding her eyes up the tree and away from the intense woman watching her. Very well…two could play this game.

"Talking about trust…there's something I want from you before I start climbing."

The woman's eyebrows shot up. "What?"

"I want to know your name. It's only fair since I told you mine. I understand why you didn't want to tell me earlier but do you *really* expect me to follow a nameless woman up a tree?"

"Oh…I forgot I didn't tell you my name. I'm Aurora." The amused smile transformed Aurora's guarded expression and her eyes danced with mirth. "There…now do you trust me enough to climb a tree with me?"

Evie stared at Aurora stunned at the metamorphosis she witnessed and her own response to that devastating smile. Wow! The woman was breathtaking when she smiled. Struggling to rally her thoughts into coherent speech Evie said the first thing that came to mind. "That's a lovely name. It beats Wolfie. That's what I've been calling you in my head."

Aurora wrinkled her nose and said with a hint of indignation, "I'm *not* a wolf."

"Good to know. That's one possibility off my list."

"You've been trying to figure it out?"

"It is obvious you're a beast-shifter. You can't blame a girl for trying to work out what kind."

"What gave away that I'm a shifter?"

"Oh, come on! The running in the dark and carrying me for hours without tiring?"

"There are humans who could do the same. I've met some remarkable people."

"Perhaps but I doubt even the most extraordinary human can see in the dark like you can or jump as high as you did to get in and out of that tree."

Aurora nodded thoughtfully. "Good point. I must remember that."

"Why hide that you're a shifter?"

"To pass as human."

"But why would you want to do that? Usually, humans want to be more like us."

Aurora shrugged and her expression once again became guarded. "No reason. Ready to climb?"

She wasn't but there was no point in delaying the inevitable so Evie took a fortifying breath and nodded. "Let's get this over with."

***

Resting with her head on her knees Evie tried to get her uneven breathing and the slight tremors in her limbs under control. She tried not to think about what it took for her to get to this shelter. There had been a lot of pushing and pulling, with Aurora doing most of the actual work and her feeling about as useful as a sack of potatoes. Yet again. She chalked it up as another experience in the last few days she would actively avoid reliving. Normally a confident person, her ego and her perception of her own competence had been dealt serious blows. At least she'd discovered her ankle was usable once she pushed through the pain. With a little rest, it would be fine. That was something positive at least. What wasn't good was the cold. Now that she'd stopped moving for more than a few minutes and no longer had the warmth of Aurora's body to shield her she could tell she was chilled to the bone. The wet clothing and the cold stone under her butt had just made things worse. To her surprise, their ascent into the tree hadn't ended in some leafy nest but in a cave which they entered by crawling through a narrow opening inside the tree. The tree must be ancient as it had had enough time to swallow, among other things, an entire rock formation, wrapping tendril-like branches around it. Getting to the cave inside that rock formation had been a surreal experience. The first part of the climb up the tree had gone as expected. But then Aurora led them inward, around intertwining limbs to get into the hollow trunk of the tree that turned out to be the cannibalized remnant of another tree. The tree that grew here before must have been gigantic as the trunk was wide enough for them to descend the husk side by side to get to the cave opening. In the distant past a parasitic plant must have latched onto the old tree. It had wrapped around the forest giant in a thickening weave, sinking tendrils into its woody flesh while it grew and spread its tentacle-like limbs. Now all that remained of the giant it fed on was the emptied wooden heart. If she wasn't so exhausted she'd ask Aurora how she had discovered there was a cave inside the tree. That Aurora had been here before and recently was apparent from the burnt candle stubs in various lengths and the thickness of the wax drippings keeping them wedged to the ledges onto which they were placed. On her previous climb Aurora had taken the time to light them all, something for which Evie was very grateful. Dark places made her anxious. The candles illuminated a space roughly thirty feet in diameter with a ceiling just high enough that the taller woman could move about without bending. The cave was swept clean and in one corner she saw what she assumed to be supplies covered by an oiled canvas. There was even a small sooty fire pit ringed with rocks.

"Evie, I have something for you."

Evie looked up to see Aurora squatting in front of her, offering a glass vial cradled in her cupped hand.

"What is it?"

"Drink it. It will speed up your healing."

"Where did you get that?"

"I had it stowed in the supplies as a backup. I gave the one I had on me to the dying wolf. Hopefully, it helped her pull through."

"What's in it?"

"It's my mother's secret formula and trust me, it is amazing. It's not a miracle cure but it is darn close."

"You won't tell me what's in it?"

"No."

Evie gave the dark liquid inside the vial a dubious look and slowly shook her head. "I'm not in the habit of drinking potions when I don't know what's in them."

Aurora froze and her green eyes gained an unsettling amber glow. Her voice stiff she said, "As your host, I feel insulted you think I'd poison you after everything we went through together. I will not offer this gift again." Aurora closed her hand and started to withdraw.

Quickly Evie grabbed onto her wrist, sensing as she did the tension in the tight muscles under her fingertips. Despite her fatigue she registered the words and the message that went with it. Alarm bells now rang loud and clear. How could she have missed this? When they crawled through the entrance of the cave Aurora had turned to face her and said, "Be welcome as my guest. My sanctuary is your sanctuary. My food, your food." At the time she'd nodded even though she found such formality odd considering their ragged appearance and the setting, essentially a hole in the rock, but thought no more of it. Now she recognized it for what it was. Aurora had offered her hospitality and all the solemn tradition that went with it and she, by entering, had accepted. It seemed fitting that someone as serious as Aurora would uphold such an ancient custom. In this cave, she considered herself Evie's host and protector. To turn down a host's food or any other sustenance was rude; to outright reject a healing gift the way she just did was a grave insult that could have dire repercussions.

"Aurora, thank you for this generous gift. I apologize for my poor manners, I didn't mean to imply you'd deliberately harm me. It's been a harrowing couple of days and I'm exhausted. I'm not at my best."

There was a slight hesitation then Aurora rolled her wrist, offering her the potion again. Evie carefully took it and poured the contents onto her tongue, grateful her big mouth hadn't alienated someone who had gone out of her way to help a stranger. The liquid tasted faintly salty with a metallic aftertaste and she felt a tingling sensation as it went down her throat all the way to her stomach as if she had just swallowed a small electrical current. Despite her misgivings about taking something unknown, she felt Aurora was sincere in her belief the potion would aid her healing. Whether it would make her better remained to be seen. Hopefully, she'd suffer no more than an upset stomach if the concoction didn't agree with her.

"Understandable. A lot has happened to you in a short time and some of it was traumatic. You look cold sitting in a puddle like that. I thought flight gear was supposed to be insulated and waterproof?"

"No wings." Evie pointed a thumb at her back. "The water just ran into the slits."

"Ah, of course. I'll bring you some dry clothes and get a fire going to warm the place a little. Enjoy the fire while you can. There's a small draft that constantly draws in fresh air but it's still not safe to keep the fire going too long. I'll go get water so we can have hot drinks."

"Where are you going to get water? Not all the way back outside the way we came?"

"I don't have to do that because I made a rainwater collector; by now the little reservoir will be overflowing with fresh water. It's near."

Aurora went to the covered supplies and turned her body in such a way that Evie couldn't see what was under the canvas. Shortly she came back with several items of clothing which she put beside Evie.

"Pants, shirt, jersey, socks. The cloth is for drying. You really need to get out of those wet things quickly – you're shivering and your lips are turning blue. Do you…need help?"

"No! Ah no, I'm fine thanks. I can undress myself."

Aurora nodded and hurried back to the other side.

Trying to break the silence after her small outburst Evie asked, "Do you live here?" As soon as she said it Evie wanted to kick herself. Why did she ask such a stupid question? It was obvious from the rudimentary setup the cave wasn't used as a home.

Aurora gave her an amused smile. "No, my home is a little nicer than this. It's just a place I use sometimes. I leave a few things here for when I'm in the area. This location is close, but not too close, to several roads and other places of interest and there is plenty of food in the forest."

Turning her back on Evie all the way Aurora produced kindling and dry wood from under the canvas and built a fire. Evie took this as her cue to change. Peeling the wet clothing from her body with clumsy cold fingers proved a challenge. She cast a furtive look to see if Aurora had caught her awkward undressing but she remained in the same position, her head slightly bowed and her hands busy. She never looked, not even when Evie muttered a few choice words as she struggled to get the tight fitting pants past her swollen ankle.

As soon as she could, Evie hobbled over on socked feet to join Aurora by the small fire. Sticking her hands over the licking flames she angled her chilled body as close to the meager warmth as she could. Aurora gave her a speculative look but didn't comment. Instead, she picked up a small blackened pot with a makeshift handle fashioned from wire along with a bundle of clothing. She went outside, scooping up Evie's wet things on the way. She came back a little while later dressed in faded green canvas pants and a loose fitting grey long-sleeved top. The pot, now two-thirds full of clear water, she put on a small metal tripod in the fire pit. She tipped half the contents of a jar into the pot, stirred once then put the lid on.

"What did you do with our wet clothing?"

"It's drying."

When Aurora didn't elaborate Evie decided not to ask how she planned to get their clothing dry when everything outside was so wet.

"Here." Aurora held out a dented tin decorated with faded pictures of a family sitting around a table opening presents. "We can share. Half each."

"What is it?"

"Fruitcake."

"You're kidding..."

"I'm not. I carry fruitcake with me whenever I can. It lasts for ages as long as I keep it away from direct heat and the ants don't get to it."

"Did you make it?"

"Yes. It's a sweet treat for the road. It's not as nice as chocolate but it doesn't melt and turn into a gooey mess."

Evie tried to pry the lid open but it wouldn't budge. Frustrated she pushed the tin back at Aurora. "The lid is on too tight and I can't get it open."

"I forgot it can be a little hard to open. It needs to fit tight to keep the bugs out."

Aurora took the tin from Evie and popped the lid in one smooth motion to reveal half a container of dark brown fruitcake cut into thick squares. The rich fruity sweet smell hit Evie hard and she could feel herself salivating. She took a bite from the piece Aurora offered her and the explosion of taste made her moan. Aurora savored her own slice, taking her time. She watched in amusement as Evie devoured two more slices in rapid succession and licked her fingers to get all the sugary goodness.

"You must really like fruitcake, Evie. Either that or you're very hungry."

"I love fruit and this is the cake version of the things I love to eat. It's been an awful couple of days and to have this now, so unexpectedly, I can't tell you how much this means."

Aurora paused mid-chew, took one more slice from the tin and offered Evie the remaining piece of fruitcake.

"Oh no, I can't," Evie protested. "I've already eaten my share."

"That's all right, you have the rest. That is probably the most I will ever see anyone enjoy anything I've made. I rarely get to share my cooking. You deserve extra just for that."

"I shouldn't," Evie said as she longingly eyed the last slice.

"But you must accept. You are my guest remember." Grinning Aurora twirled a finger indicating the cave. "I know it's just a crappy damp cave but the rules of hospitality still apply."

"Well, I'd hate to be a rude guest and risk insulting my host."

Quickly Evie snatched up the last piece. She forced herself to eat slower this time and ignored Aurora's low chuckle. The broth when it was finally ready to drink was less pleasant.

"Not to be rude but what is in that? The smell is…intense. What were those granules you added?"

"Mostly dehydrated protein in concentrated form and dried seaweed. It doesn't taste great either but it makes a nutritious broth."

"What kind of protein?"

"Mostly animal."

"Oh. I see."

The drink tasted only marginally better than it smelled and Evie tried not to think of what may be in it. She wasn't entirely vegetarian but she hadn't eaten red meat since she was a child. Evie forced herself to empty her cup knowing she needed the nourishment and warmth. The small fire had already burned down to a pile that was more grey ash than red coal, the receding warmth not nearly enough to banish the chill in her bones. That combined with fatigue and possibly delayed shock was making her feel shaky and dizzy. However, when Aurora offered her more of the broth she felt her stomach heave in protest and she adamantly shook her head.

"You have that. I had extra fruit cake so it's only fair you have more broth."

"Thanks. After we've had a sleep I'll make us a heartier meal. It's raining again, much harder than before, so we might as well hunker down and rest while we can. I'll roll out my sleeping bag for you near the fire."

"What will you use if I take your sleeping bag?"

"I have a cloak and I'll wrap up in that. It's a good travel cloak and I'm used to sleeping on the ground so I'll be fine." Aurora wet her fingertips and snuffed out a candle. "Once you're in bed I'll put out all but one candle. I don't normally burn so many at once."

"Do you have to? Can you leave more than one candle? Please? The dark…I find it unsettling."

"I can leave two burning. I hope that's enough. I'd leave them all on for you but I'm trying to conserve the candles and we have to be mindful of our air supply."

"Thank you. I appreciate it."

"It's not a big deal, Evie."

Evie briefly put her hand on the other woman's arm. "It is in my eyes."

Aurora self-consciously tucked a lock of hair behind her ear. "Um…all right. Let me get that bed ready for you."

Aurora laid out a thin mat and unrolled a brown sleeping bag on top. She held open the sleeping bag and motioned for Evie to get in. Evie crawled in and curled up in a tight ball, desperate to get warm. At first, she thought she was getting better but then the shivering turned into shudders that caused her body to spasm painfully. Her teeth chattered and her mind felt foggy. Evie longed for her wings. She so rarely went without them that she felt traumatized by their absence. Not only that, she really needed them right now. If she had her wings, she would have wrapped them around herself and fallen asleep cocooned in the luxurious warmth of her feathers. Instead, she had to endure cold misery in a borrowed sleeping bag.

"You're still cold," Aurora said from somewhere above her.

With her head inside the sleeping bag Evie didn't answer, though she could hardly deny it.

"Hey." A tentative hand touched her shoulder and then drew the cover away from Evie's face. "Please look at me."

"W-what do y-you w-want?"

Feeling wretched and hating to be seen in such a state she glared at Aurora, or she tried to. It was hard to look fierce while shivering. Aurora stared down at her with concern, her green eyes compassionate. Evie felt a wave of relief because she had steeled herself for contempt at yet another display of her weakness.

"Evie, you're freezing." Aurora bit her lip and a look of uncertainty crossed her face. "Um…will you allow me to warm you?"

"H-how?" Evie stuttered. The words getting stuck between her teeth.

"Body heat."

"I'm n-not getting n-naked with you. I hardly kn-know you."

Aurora's eyebrows shot up. "That's extreme and not what I had in mind."

"Oh?"

"We can share the sleeping bag. I'm warm. Feel." Aurora cupped Evie's face and the heat radiating from her palms made Evie groan.

"Yes, p-please. More. So *warm*."

Aurora removed her cloak and long-sleeved shirt so she only wore her pants and a black singlet then maneuvered Evie's jersey off her shivering body so she was down to the t-shirt and the soft charcoal drawstring pants. She slid in next to Evie, arranged their clothing on top of the sleeping bag like a blanket then gently gathered Evie's shivering body into her arms.

As soon as she felt the heat that radiated from Aurora, Evie burrowed into her, all thoughts of pride forgotten at the delicious warmth thawing her chilled limbs. Evie heard Aurora gasp but that was hardly surprising; it must have felt like she was cuddling an ice block. Greedy for more body heat she uncrossed her arms from around her own chest and crept them up Aurora's sides until her frozen hands lodged in Aurora's armpits. Her cheek pillowed against luxurious softness, her hip and right leg found a comfortable position wedged between warm thighs. When she felt Aurora stiffen and push her leg away it dawned on Evie what she had done. Mortified at her body's instinctive response and the way she took liberties with a near stranger's body she tried to roll away but strong arms wrapped around and kept her close.

"It's all right, Evie. Relax and try to sleep."

The voice was so reassuring, so soothing and she was so very tired and cold. Evie stopped struggling and relaxed into the warm embrace. Her shivers became less frequent and while she listened to the steady heartbeat under her ear oblivion claimed her.

***

Aurora lay rigid while her mind raced to come to grips with the surreal situation she found herself in. She'd expected to free the avian and never see her again once she flew away. Never could she have anticipated the turn of events that would lead to that same girl lying in her arms. Not a young girl, she corrected but a full-grown woman. Shapeshifters aged slower than humans and she'd forgotten that avians had lighter bones, giving some of them a delicate almost fragile look. Evie looked so young especially when she was afraid that it initially threw her. After spending time with her she realized Evie was probably in her late twenties, if not older, which put her around Aurora's age. She found this disconcerting. It was one thing to shelter and care for a young girl barely out of her teens but what she had nestled against her was a soft, curvaceous, golden-haired woman with eyes the deep blue of the sea after a storm who smelled faintly of jasmine. Aurora suppressed a sigh. At least she had successfully dislodged the leg Evie pressed dangerously close to her core. When she offered to share body heat she thought Evie would lie on her side with her back to her but she'd made herself comfortable as if they shared a bed all the time. The woman liked to snuggle, that much was obvious. She didn't. Or at least she didn't think so. It was hard to know for sure because she never felt relaxed enough with anyone to linger after sex, never mind cuddle.

Once Evie fell asleep, which didn't take long once she stopped shivering, Aurora relaxed. Since she had the opportunity she might as well explore what it felt like to have someone snuggle up to her, even if it was only to stave off hypothermia. Aurora decided she liked the way the soft feminine body curled up against her and it was strangely soothing to feel someone stir and make little noises in the abandon of sleep. If it was this good with a stranger it must be amazing to cuddle with someone special, especially after sex. Unfortunately, it had been a long time since she'd had someone like that in her life and she didn't see that changing in the foreseeable future. Aurora wished she did have a mate to share her life with or even just a trusted lover because that would make going into heat a pleasurable rather than agonizing experience. It wouldn't be so bad if she had fewer hang-ups about who she let that close to her or if she could convince herself that the drive to have sex, like hunger or thirst, was just a physical need to be met like any other. But for her having sex without the intimacy and connection she craved left her feeling sad and sullied. Going into heat like a lust-crazed animal who was driven to couple with anyone who seemed even vaguely suitable was downright humiliating. There were many advantages to being the kind of shifter she was but this she hated. Every time she fought it, vowing to wait out the discomfort that grew into a searing agony but it was a dangerous game. When she became distressed it unsettled her beasts and brought them too close to the surface. At the best of times she walked a tightrope containing them and it was a balancing act that required her to be calm and in control. The agitation of resisting a shift on top of fighting the need to have sex pushed her to the edge. With such a potent cocktail of hormones and who knows what else flooding her system she had three options: fuck, fight or go out of her bloody mind. Since her overriding instinct in a fight was to kill, sex remained the only viable outlet…unless she actually wanted to go on a slaughtering rampage.

Evie muttered something in her sleep and gave Aurora a jolt when she slid a hand under the hem of her shirt onto bare stomach. Aurora carefully removed the hand and firmly kept it in her own. This was not a good time to be thinking about sex or lamenting her non-existent love life, inevitable as it was with a beautiful woman draped over her. It was keeping her awake when she needed to rest while she could. Aurora closed her eyes and waited for sleep to claim her.

CHAPTER 4

AGREEMENT

The first thing Evie saw when she opened her eyes was Aurora leaning over her. She smiled and lifted her hand in greeting. "Sorry for waking you. I'm heading out but I'll be back in a little while. I didn't want you to wake alone thinking I abandoned you." She stood up and slung a satchel over her chest.

"You're leaving right now?" Evie sat up quickly. "But I have to talk to you, there are things we need to discuss."

"Can it wait till I get back? The rain stopped so I need to make sure nothing followed us here and I want to scout ahead in the direction we are going."

"Where *are* we heading? That's what I want to talk to you about. I want to go to Porta Belua. My home is there."

"I'm not going to Porta Belua. I'm going in a different direction but if you come with me, I'll make sure you get home."

"How long will that take?"

"Depending on what happens and the condition of the routes I'm planning on taking… about a week. If there's been a landslide in the mountains it could take two or three weeks as you probably can't manage the harder routes."

"That's too long. Will you take me to the nearest trading post? I should be able to arrange transportation from there."

"Same thing. I'm not heading towards a trading post."

"If it's about money, Aurora, I can pay. I have little on me but when you get me home I will make sure you're rewarded generously. I'm an important member of a prosperous House and I can afford to make it worth your while."

Aurora studied Evie for a few seconds then said, "I don't expect to get paid for helping you. If I didn't have other plans I'd take you to Porta Belua straight away."

"Then don't think of it as getting paid but as thanks. My House will be very grateful to have me back."

"I don't need your money. Have you forgotten I have ethian crystals? The ones I harvested are worth a fortune."

"True, but you still have to sell the crystals. If you want to get the best price you will have to negotiate with buyers and that takes time. I can compensate you for your troubles immediately. All you have to do is take me to Porta Belua straight away."

Aurora shook her head. "No. I'm on a tight schedule. I have an appointment to keep and nothing short of death or catastrophe will keep me from getting there on time." She held up her hand when she saw Evie about to speak. "Before you say anything else or offer me more money, which will just annoy me, you need to come up top with me. There is something I want to show you."

"All the way up through the tree? Just for a look?"

"This is important and no, not all the way to the top. It's a short climb."

"I need to get dressed first. Can I have my clothes back? The pants you lent me are comfortable for sleeping in but way too big for me to walk or climb in."

Aurora left the cave and returned with Evie's clothing. She put it down beside her and said, "I washed and dried your clothing along with my own so everything is clean. Keep the things I gave you. You'll need them." Aurora rummaged under the canvas and pulled out a brown jacket with a hood and held it out to Evie. "Take this as well and wear it instead of your flight jacket. It's waterproof and sturdy and will keep you dry and protect your skin from branches and other sharp things."

Evie took the jacket from Aurora. It was made with soft brown leather and surprisingly light. Holding it to her chest it came to mid-thigh on her; on Aurora it would probably only reach to her hips. "Aurora, I can't thank you enough for everything you've done for me."

Aurora merely nodded. "When we get back I'll give you a bag to carry your things. I'll go get more water while you change."

As soon as she left Evie jumped up, extracted her underwear from the neatly folded pile of clothing and shrugged out of Aurora's clothing to slip on her own. She quickly put on her bra. Feeling dubious about the panty she'd worn for several days she gave it a quick sniff and felt a mixture of relief and embarrassment that Aurora had washed it as well. Relief because she got to put on clean underwear, embarrassment because the other woman had cleaned something so intimate of hers.

She'd stripped off her underwear last night because it was wet. In her delirious half-frozen state she'd thought nothing of discarding everything in a pile as she was in a hurry to slip into the dry clothing Aurora had offered her. She didn't think Aurora would take it upon herself to hand wash her clothing. Who just washes a stranger's clothing for them, panties and all? She didn't know how to deal with that. Come to think of it, she didn't know how to deal with Aurora either. The woman was an enigma.

Hurriedly Evie pulled the grey t-shirt Aurora had given her back on and it was as she was balancing on one leg to get into her own pants that she realized the ankle she injured the previous day was healed. Taking stock of the rest of herself she noticed how good she felt. No aches and pains, no bruises as far as she could see and she should have plenty from the previous day. Not even residual stiffness from sleeping on a stone floor. Granted, she'd slept more on her companion than on the floor but the point was she felt way better than she had any right to feel. There was only one explanation for that – Aurora's potion worked. Evie's House cultivated mira flowers for the creation of healing potions and she oversaw much of that personally so she knew a lot about potion making. Nothing her House produced came close to being this effective. To think she initially refused Aurora's gift and came close to insulting her hostess. What a disaster that almost turned into.

As soon as Aurora came back carrying the pot of water she blurted out, "That potion you gave me last night worked wonders. It healed my ankle and I feel great."

That made Aurora smile. "I told you it was amazing. Give it time to work and it will do wonders for your wing as well."

"Any chance you'll tell me how to make it?"

That made Aurora grin. "Nope. It's a family secret. You ready to go, Evie?"

Evie gave the laces on her boots an extra tug to make sure they were securely tied. She didn't want to lose her shoe or re-twist her ankle because she'd done a shoddy job on such a simple task. "I am now. Lead the way."

***

Twenty minutes later they were on a thick branch high above the forest. Dawn was struggling to make a showing, the world still overlaid in heavy shades of grey with just the barest hint of color as light crept into the horizon. Aurora squatted next to Evie and pointed at the forest that in the predawn light was a dense, dark mass as far as the eye could see.

"The trade station is about two days travel that way once you get on the little dirt road that cuts through the forest, that's if the road is still there after all that rain. To get to that road from here you'll have to cross the river. Even if I didn't have other plans I wouldn't take you to that trading post because Black Paw runs it. You might have heard of them? They're a mix of beast-shifters and humans. They call themselves a clan but what they really are is a bunch of lowlife rejects and mercenary thugs for hire. To say they are a rough crowd is putting it mildly. However, if you feel confident you can negotiate with people like that to take you to Porta Belua I won't stand in your way."

"That's wild country," Evie said taking in the rain-soaked forest. Nearby she could hear a waterfall, or was that the river Aurora had mentioned? If so, that river was a raging torrent. If she tried to cross something like that on her own she'd be courting disaster.

"Yes, it's a dense forest with lots of wildlife and I know from experience there are many predators down there. If you don't know how to survive in that kind of terrain it's a dangerous place."

"Aurora, are you sure I can't convince you to escort me to Porta Belua straight away? I can make it worth your while, just name your price. If not money my House has a lot of influence in the city and beyond. Everyone wants something. What do *you* want?"

"What I want lies that way," Aurora pointed towards a mountain range to their left. If you come with me to my appointment then as soon as I'm done I will take you to friends of mine on the coast who I trust to get you safely to Porta Belua."

"But not for at least a week or more."

Aurora shrugged, "That's the best I can offer you."

"Is there nothing I can do to convince you to take me home immediately? If I could fly I'd be back in a day. I've never been earthbound like this before and it's awful. Please take me to Porta Belua...*I need to go home*."

"I already told you no. Don't ask me again because my answer won't change."

"But I'm really worried about what's happening in my absence. My father isn't well and—"

"That's enough!" Aurora stood up abruptly and took a deep breath as if calming herself. "I'm sorry your father is sick but I don't have the time to play escort for you. I have a very important appointment and as it is offering to take you along means I'll be cutting it close to get there on time."

Evie didn't have to see Aurora's stormy expression to realize she'd pushed too hard. She'd been so focused on talking Aurora into taking her home she'd not listened when the other woman told her she had her own important business to take care of. Gentling her voice, she asked, "Then why offer to take me with you? Why risk missing your meeting because of me?"

"Because…" Aurora sighed and squatted beside Evie again. "Because you dove to catch me when I fell. My body is strong and resilient but if I'd hit the rocks from that height I would have been a broken mess. If you'd let me fall you could have glided on the air currents for hours, even with that damaged wing. You may even have reached the outskirts of Porta Belua. Diving for me meant you couldn't reopen your wing and because of my added weight you were off balance during landing and broke your injured wing. Until your wing heals you're earthbound and I won't abandon you out here unable to fly. Don't take this the wrong way but I don't like your odds trudging around the forest by yourself."

"I see." Evie was quiet for a moment. "But you would have let me go off by myself if I insisted?"

"Yes, if that was your choice. I'm not your keeper, Evie. If you come with me you must do so willingly because where I'm going it's not safe either. I will, however, do everything in my power to protect you. So my offer stands – come with me and I *will* get you home. Just not as quickly as you would like."

Evie took another long look at the forest and imagined trying to forge a way through it solo. She had many skills but woodcraft wasn't on the list. She'd get lost and likely kill herself by eating a poisonous plant or become something's dinner. She'd rather take the long way home with Aurora than risk not making it back at all. She turned to face Aurora more directly and said, "I'm coming with you. Thank you for the offer and for what you did for me yesterday. I'm still embarrassed you had to carry me."

"Why?" Aurora looked genuinely curious.

"Because, as you so eloquently put it, I stumbled like a wounded deer. I felt awful being such a burden to you."

"I didn't see you as a burden. I carried you because we made a deal.

We agreed to work together to get away from that place. A partnership, remember? I wasn't confident you would keep your word. I thought you would try to leave me behind as soon as we got outside or drop me the first chance you got. That's why I held on to you so tightly. Instead of betraying me, you did the unexpected and risked your life to save mine. That made a powerful impression. So, when I saw you needed help to get down the mountain I carried you. You carried me in the air and I carried you on the ground. Do you see? We took turns helping each other. There's no reason for you to feel embarrassed."

"Aurora, you only offered to get me out of that cage onto the roof. You fulfilled your part of our agreement. I'm not surprised you thought I'd betray you. Unfortunately, I've come up against the perception that avians are untrustworthy my whole life and I know how much other shifters dislike us. Most would not have felt the need to help me beyond what was strictly agreed upon."

"Hmm." There was an amused smile on Aurora's lips. "You'll find I'm not like most people."

"That's a good thing."

Aurora shrugged and her expression became guarded. "Maybe – it depends on who you talk to. You know very little about me."

Evie put her hand on Aurora's arm and squeezed gently. "I know enough already to realize how lucky I am that someone like you came around when you did."

"Even though I'm not willing to take you straight home?" Aurora was smiling again; it was a small thing that just tugged at the corners of her mouth but reached all the way to her eyes and it warmed Evie to see it.

"Despite that. Let me know if you change your mind. I didn't exaggerate when I said my House would compensate you handsomely."

Aurora snorted a laugh. "You are *very* persistent."

"You can't blame a girl for trying."

"No, I suppose not. I'll get you home as soon as I can. Right now, I have work to do before we head out. Do you think you can make your way back to the cave on your own?"

"I can manage that. Anything I can do while I wait for you?"

"Get a fire going and boil the water? I'll catch something to add to the pot while I'm out; we both need a hearty meal."

"You're going to hunt?"

"Yes."

"I ah…well I suppose this is a good a time to tell you I prefer not to eat meat. I don't mind fish and shellfish. If I must I'll eat poultry but I won't touch red meat."

"Why not?"

"Does there have to be a reason?"

"I'd like one. Since I'm the one who will be foraging for your meals in a waterlogged forest. I know most avians eat meat. I've seen the field of carcasses left behind by hunting flocks. I watched a group of young avians cut the beating heart out of a fawn and take turns eating it raw."

"That's revolting."

"I thought so too. They should have given it a quick, clean death first. The animal was terrified and in pain. There was no reason to make it suffer like that."

"That's awful and I would never do something like that. We are not savages! There's no excuse for that kind of behavior and avians who act like that are no better than feral wolves!"

Aurora held her palms up in a placating gesture. "Okay, I can see that struck a nerve. You still haven't explained why you won't eat red meat but you clearly feel strongly about it. I respect that. Since we're on the topic of food you should know I'm a meat eater. In fact, I will eat just about anything. It's a matter of survival. I burn a lot of energy and I need to replenish it constantly or it becomes difficult to control my beast. As the saying goes, 'A hungry beast is an angry beast…' and I try to keep mine nice and calm. I'll do my best not to offend you with what I eat but it may be inevitable."

"As long as you don't eat something while it's alive or rip bloody chunks out of your food in front of me, I'll be fine."

Aurora's mouth quirked into a wry smile. "I think I can contain myself enough not to do that."

***

When Aurora returned to the cave her satchel was bulging. She gave Evie an approving nod when she saw the well-tended fire and the pot of boiling water. Aurora opened the satchel to reveal an assortment of mushrooms, different colored eggs, white roots that looked like they had been freshly washed and a selection of greens that Evie thought looked vaguely familiar from their trek through the forest the previous day.

"Eggs?" Aurora asked as she scooted Evie out of the way in front of the fire and cut the roots into thin slivers onto a plate in quick precise motions.

"I eat eggs."

"Good. We are having mushroom and egg omelet and whatever this will be when it's done." Aurora pointed at the boiling pot into which she added the sliced roots followed by the chopped greens before removing it from the small fire and placing the lid on tightly. She produced a small pan and true to her word made a thick omelet with lots of mushrooms. The delicious aroma of fried mushrooms had Evie salivating and she eagerly accepted the omelet Aurora slid onto her plate. Next Aurora made one for herself which she ate directly from the pan with a spoon. The veggie and herb broth she let sit for a little while before dividing it equally, pouring Evie's portion into a large ceramic mug and hers into a bowl of the same make.

"I'm short on cutlery and such since it's usually just me. Everything for one. I know it's not polite to eat directly out of the pan in company."

Evie waved her off with her fork. "I don't care about that. You're feeding me and this is marvelous. My tongue is doing a happy dance. These mushrooms are so nutty and I don't know how you cooked the omelet without burning it. Every time I try to cook on an open fire my food is charred to a crisp." Evie took a sip of the veggie soup and her eyebrows shot up. "Wow. This is fantastic. Spicy and herby but in a good way and that root reminds me of carrot but it's tangier."

"You're hungry. Everything tastes better when you're hungry."

"True, but that doesn't mean I'm exaggerating."

Between bites of her omelet Evie asked, "Did you see any sign of the wolves? Do you think they made it?"

"I saw a brief glimpse of them in the forest. He was carrying the female but her head was up so she is still alive. My guess is he'll find shelter and hunker down so he can hunt and tend to her until she's well enough to walk again."

"That's great news, Aurora!"

"Yes, it is," Aurora said with a smile and kept eating.

Evie waited for her to say more when she didn't she prompted, "Did they see you?"

"No, I was under cover and on the opposite side of the river. They would not have seen me."

"You didn't call to them?"

Aurora paused with the spoon halfway to her mouth. "Why would I do that?"

"To say hello? To tell them you're happy they got away?"

Aurora's brow furrowed. "If I shouted to get their attention it would have given away their position and mine. Sound travels and there is no way of knowing who or what is out there listening."

Evie felt her face heat. "Yes, of course. I didn't think about that."

They ate in silence after that. Aurora finished long before Evie even though she started after her and bustled about tiding the fireplace, extracting things from under the canvas and packing into a rucksack. The smaller backpack she'd used the previous day she emptied of its contents and put it down next to Evie.

"You can use this to carry your things." She stuck a water bottle next to the backpack. "This is yours as well."

Evie hurried through the rest of her meal. Miraculously she did it without burning her tongue on the hot soup. She finished by scraping at the bottom of her cup with the fork to gather the stray greens and bits of root that got stuck there for one last delicious crunchy bite. With a good meal in her tummy and feeding off the energetic way Aurora moved she felt a buzz of excitement. She was a firm believer in planning for the future but living in the moment. She refused to dwell on things she couldn't control and tried to find enjoyment in whatever she did. It was a philosophy that served her well. She would have preferred to be heading straight home but having resigned herself to the inevitable delay she was looking forward to experiencing something she never thought she would do. She was traveling through the wilderness with a beast-shifter, on foot. It was a far cry from how she usually spent her days. At home she would have been in a meeting by now, the first of many, feeling the burden of her responsibilities firmly pressing down on her. Seen in that context it almost felt like she was on holiday. It didn't hurt that her guide was a very interesting and attractive woman who apparently could whip up amazing meals out of almost nothing. She could think of less pleasant ways to spend the next week.

CHAPTER 5

NEW FRIENDS, OLD SCARS

It was mid-morning and Aurora led the way along a faint animal trail on a ridge to keep them out of the worst of the wet forest. The rainfall during the night had been heavy and water was flowing down from the surrounding mountains so that small streams that usually trickled along lazily were bursting with noisy energy. The forest had evolved to deal with these downpours and in a few days most of it would be siphoned away or have found its way into the larger rivers but for the moment the soil was saturated and water pooled in every available dip and fern-covered hollow so it would be easy to misjudge and end up ankle deep in water. That wasn't really a big deal when she was in beast form but she didn't relish walking around in wet socks and shoes for hours on end and as much as possible she wanted to keep Evie dry. She looked fully recovered from the previous day but Aurora didn't want to take chances with Evie getting sick. Shifters were robust and rarely became ill but she was mindful that the previous day had been a massive shock to Evie's system in more ways than one. Some part of her even at this moment would be busy repairing her injured wing and it would be a steady drain on her despite the lingering healing effect of the potion in her system. She needed to make sure Evie ate well and she would continue to add things to their meals that she knew to be good for healing.

It amused Aurora that she was so concerned with the other woman's wellbeing and she tried to write it off as being practical. If her companion got sick or injured again she would slow them down. This was true and a good reason to look out for her but Aurora knew there was more to it. Normally it took her a while to warm to strangers but she'd felt drawn to Evie from the moment she saw her and it had taken very little time for her to decide she liked her. Evie exuded a warmth that was hard to resist and she impressed Aurora with how well she adjusted to her situation. She was an earthbound avian forced to follow a stranger in a direction she didn't want to go and yet once she realized she couldn't persuade Aurora to take her home immediately she didn't sulk or drag her feet. Quite the opposite. Evie was doing her best to keep up even though the uneven terrain had her watching her footing the whole time and she had to pause occasionally to catch her breath. What had pleasantly surprised her was how interested Evie seemed in their surroundings. She looked around her with wide-eyed curiosity and occasionally she'd point at an unfamiliar plant or creature and ask Aurora to tell her more about it. Aurora loved forests, especially the ancient ones, and while some people found such places intimidating or scary to her it felt like a second home so she found it pleasing that Evie looked at it with so much wonder. All of this contributed to her growing fondness for the avian.

There was however something she was having difficulty with. Evie had a habit of casually wandering into her personal space and touching her. It was just a brief touch, usually on the arm, but she did it with alarming frequency. She did it to get Aurora's attention when a word or gesture would have done the same or when she was talking and trying to make a point. This was baffling behavior and it put her on edge. Beast-shifters never stood that close or touched someone who wasn't family or a trusted member of the pack and of the adult humans she knew well enough to allow close few touched her and none so casually. She'd never had an avian friend or spent enough time with one to get to know their mannerisms so she had no idea how to interpret Evie's behavior. Her own behavior equally baffled her. Normally she wouldn't tolerate someone she barely knew touching her and yet she couldn't bring herself to tell Evie to keep her distance. Maybe it was because she held the sleeping woman in her arms for hours. It seemed silly after that to make a fuss about her standing too close but Aurora still felt a jolt every time she was touched and watched Evie warily.

By the early afternoon Aurora concluded that Evie was oblivious that she was taking dangerous liberties. She was just a very tactile person, that's why she was constantly reaching for Aurora. Her hands were always busy touching something and when she got excited they became animated. As for how close she stood to Aurora, Evie was too physically fragile a creature for it to be a challenge for dominance and since she didn't smell arousal Aurora knew it wasn't a signal the other woman wanted to have sex. She just had a much smaller personal space, which made sense as she lived in a tower surrounded by other avians. Once she got that sorted in her head Aurora was able to relax more around Evie. She still wasn't comfortable having Evie in her personal space but she was slowly getting used to her.

***

Aurora halted and squinted up at the sky measuring how much daylight they had left. They had made better time than she expected. "Ready for a hot meal and a rest? We can stop over there next to the stream. We've covered over half the distance we need to travel today."

"Phew, that's a relief. I was beginning to think we were going to walk non-stop all day. I could kill for a hot meal and I'd be thankful to sit a little while."

"Why didn't you say something earlier? I would have stopped if you told me you needed a rest."

"We'd already had to stop several times for me to pee and you probably think I have the bladder of a small child by now. I didn't want to slow us down even more. Just so you know, I'm not usually like this."

This made Aurora laugh. "It's probably the sound of all the running water that is getting to you."

"Let's go with that. I'm more than happy to let the rain take the blame for my overactive bladder."

Despite how wet everything was Aurora quickly had a small smokeless fire going using dried moss and kindling she'd gathered along the way. Without being asked Evie filled their little pot with water from the stream and put it down next to where Aurora was getting things from her rucksack for their meal.

"Anything I can do to help?"

"Get off your feet, Evie. Rest. I will let you know when the food is ready. We can't stop for long."

Too tired to protest Evie sat down on the other side of the small fire with her back against a rock. Looking up she saw wisps of cloud streaking overhead through gaps in the canopy. She stared at this absentmindedly while she listened to the birds singing all around them in the forest. The sound of the crackling fire drew her eyes back down and she watched the confident precise way Aurora moved while she washed, chopped and added things to the pot.

"What are you making?"

"We'll just have to see what it becomes when I'm done."

This made Evie smile. Aurora had said something similar at

breakfast. If what she was making was half as tasty as that soup and omelet their lunch would be yummy. Already the food smelled so good it made her mouth water.

"Aurora, I think I've worked out what kind of shifter you are. Do you mind if I take a guess?"

Aurora looked up from what she was doing. "Go ahead. What do you think I am?"

"Do you have a feline beast form?"

Aurora's eyebrows shot up. "Yes. How did you figure it out? Few people get that right."

"It's subtle. If I wasn't able to study you so carefully I might not have guessed. It's not like I have any sense of smell to speak of so I don't know if other shifters could pick it up from that."

"How then?"

"It's the graceful way you move, the way you watch things and how still you can be one moment to become a blur of motion the next. I'm a cat lover and I'm not the only one; there are always cats underfoot in our tower so I've had plenty of time to study them. Some of your mannerisms are similar. Altogether it was an educated guess based on what I can remember my wolf-shifter godfather told me about how to identify different beast-shifters."

Aurora paused in stirring the food to give Evie an incredulous stare, "You, an avian, had a wolf as a godfather? Really?"

"Yes really. He used to be my father's best friend when I was little so I got to spend a lot of time with him. He felt it was important I be knowledgeable about such things. I was a tempestuous, curious kid and my mouth got me into all kinds of trouble. I think he worried I would accidentally lock eyes with the wrong beast-shifter and get myself hurt or killed in a mistaken challenge for dominance."

"I'm still struggling to get my head around an avian having a wolf-shifter as a godfather. How extraordinary! How did this happen? I mean I know it rarely happens now but when I was a child avians were infamous among other shifters, the wolves in particular, for being the paid scouts and sky hunters of slavers, cutters and other unsavory types wanting to kill them or capture their young. Avians were hated because of that. Even now resentment still lingers over it. How did the things avians were responsible for sit with your godfather? He must have known about it. It wasn't that long ago after all. Most shifters I know still keep a wary eye on the skies for that very reason."

"It wasn't my people who did those horrible things!" Evie could feel her cheeks flush with heat as it always did when this topic came up. "Well, not *my* flock and not since before I was born. My father abolished those practices. It was due to his friend. They grew up together and became the best of friends so when my father took over from my grandfather he decreed none of his people would participate in those kinds of aerial hunts. To do so would mean expulsion. He uncollared the few bound servants we had, his friend included. He gave them resources to start new lives or the option to stay with us but as paid retainers. He didn't want anyone in our tower who wasn't there freely."

Aurora didn't comment, instead she busied herself with pouring the steaming broth into a mug. She filled it almost to the brim then handed the mug to Evie who took it gingerly, careful not to spill any of the liquid and burn herself. Aurora waited for Evie to take a sip and nodded in satisfaction when Evie made a sound of pleasure at the tastiness of the food before pouring the rest into a bowl for herself. She ate so quickly Evie paused between sips to stare and wonder how Aurora could down the hot food so easily. Only when she finished did Aurora speak.

"I heard about the flock that broke away from the rest – House Aquilar. It caused quite a stir. If your father is the head of your House that must make you Evangeline Aquilar, the oldest child of Lord Augustus Aquilar?"

"Yes, that's right. You're well informed. My friends and family call me Evie. I'm only Evangeline on official documents and at formal gatherings."

"Ah, that explains why I didn't make the connection earlier. If I remember correctly other avians gave your House a rough time because of your father's decision?"

"Some of them were very upset. Our business suffered, we weren't invited to the yearly gathering and there were several assassination attempts on my father's life. But that was many years ago and things have changed a lot since then. My father took a gamble on cultivating the mira flowers. They are very difficult to grow and capturing their essence at the peak of potency is an art he mastered. I'm building on his legacy. It's exciting work. We make the best and strongest regeneration potions on the market, best for healing and restoring spent magic. My father built an empire around Aquimar, our brand name for the mira products we produce. That and the impeccable reputation of our House. It's well known that we will not do business with slavers, cutters or sky hunters.

It has been a painstaking process but we now sell to many shapeshifter clans across Nordarra. Our products are renowned for being the most potent, pure and long-lasting and we deal fairly with our clients and allies. Others are trying to compete with us but we are far ahead in our field. Where once we were a lesser House with almost no influence or power, other flocks now vie for our favor. Those who partner with us find the prosperity and prestige of their flock grow exponentially and it doesn't involve making money off the suffering of others or being reviled and always having to be on guard for a revenge kill. It's a new era. In his quiet way my father was a revolutionary. He couldn't use force to make the other flocks see things his way so he persuaded them with the lure of profit and respectability."

"That is quite a story, Evie. Your father sounds like a good man and smart. I think I would like him."

"Yes, he's a good man and a great father."

"Is your father's wolf friend still with your House or did he leave?"

Evie shook her head a sad expression on her face. "He died when I was little. He saved my father's life during an assassination attempt but it cost him his own. I miss him. Before I could fly he used to carry me on his back in wolf form while my parents flew above. He could run so fast it felt like we flew."

"My father used to do that with me!" Aurora exclaimed. "He could run like the wind."

"Your father must have been so proud when you first shifted. I know my parents were so happy when my wings sprouted and I finally learned to fly."

"I can imagine. It must have been an amazing moment."

"It was," Evie said her smile wide and happy at the memory. "It's a shame my mother wasn't there to see my sister Oriana take her first flight. She died in childbirth."

"I'm sorry to hear that, Evie."

"Thank you. It's horrible that something as joyous as the birth of my sister is forever marred by my mother's death. It makes celebrating her birthday weird, especially for my dad. I know he adores Oriana but he must miss his wife."

"He didn't remarry?"

"No, and there hasn't been a serious contender as far as I'm aware. Not that he's left himself time for romance. He spends all his time either with House business, tinkering with Aquimar or talking to Oriana and me. Before he got sick his light would be on way past midnight all the time and I'd find him still hard at work."

"A very dedicated man."

"Yes. I have the greatest respect and admiration for my father even though we clash occasionally. He says I inherited my mother's temper and stubbornness. I was young when she died so I don't remember that part of her and it's strangely comforting to think a part of her remains within me even though I know he doesn't mean it as a compliment."

Aurora was smiling at Evie. "I can attest to the stubbornness. Not seen much of that temper yet but I'll take your word for it."

Evie returned her smile and took another cautious sip of her hot meal. "Did your father teach you to be so stealthy? You move so quietly most of the time I don't hear you and you do this thing where you are there one moment then suddenly…you're gone!"

"Yes," Aurora said with a fond smile. "That was the first thing he taught me. He was such a great teacher and every moment was an opportunity to learn something, a game in every lesson so it was fun even when it was hard. He took me everywhere with him. He taught me to hunt, to swim, how to survive just about anywhere. We were inseparable."

"Where is he now?"

"He's dead."

"Oh. I'm sorry. When did he die?"

"When I was a child."

"How did he die?"

Aurora was no longer smiling, in fact, her expression had become decidedly unfriendly. "Why do you want to know something like that?"

Evie hesitated with the cup halfway to her mouth sensing she had somehow wandered into dangerous waters. There was something too still in the way Aurora held herself. Her voice held a strain that hinted at a strong dark current beneath. Carefully Evie put down her cup.

"It's something people ask when they hear a friend's parent passed away. I didn't mean to pry. I just told you how my mother died, remember?"

Aurora studied her for what felt like a small eternity. Her green eyes pinned Evie, the intensity of her gaze almost unbearable and Evie struggled not to squirm. Unable to tolerate it any longer she said, "Aurora, why are you angry with me? I'd apologize but I don't know what I've done wrong."

Aurora sighed and looked away. "You did nothing wrong." She spoke so quietly Evie had to strain to hear her. "I believe you meant it as a casual question, nothing more. If you hadn't been so open with me I would have let you think his death was an accident. I wish that was true. He was murdered because he could shift to a tiger, something highly sought after by the lowlifes your father will not do business with. I was there when it happened and as you can imagine it's a sensitive topic for me."

"Aurora, I'm so sorry I brought that up. You don't have to tell me any more if you don't want to. I didn't mean to upset you. You were there?" Evie grimaced. "I can't even imagine how awful that must have been."

Aurora meant to stay silent as she always did when friends tried to pry things about that terrible time from her but she found to her surprise she wanted to talk, needed to actually. Maybe it was the events of the preceding days stirring up old memories that were to blame.

"It was an ambush. They wanted my father's body. Talismans and potions made from any tiger are worth a fortune on the black market. Any part of a tiger-shifter is worth a hundred times more because of the additional magical properties attributed to us and my father was exceptionally large. His pelt would have been a trophy fit for an emperor. It was the most beautiful thing I'd ever seen and stroking his thick silky fur felt amazing. For me, they had a cage and other plans. It was my fault: I fell into the trap they set for us. My father would never have been so stupid. Once they had me, he came. He died because he tried to save me."

"You can't blame yourself for your father's death, Aurora. Any parent would try to save their child."

"You don't understand. My father was like a shadow in the night, he could have picked them off one by one even by day with enough time. If I hadn't screamed, he wouldn't have rushed in the way he did. He was so strong, my father, so ferocious but he was a hunter not a warrior and there were so many of them and they had come prepared to capture him."

"That's horrible! I'm so sorry. I'm just happy you got away. What a nightmare that must have been!"

Aurora nodded and a deep furrow creased her brow. Hard lines appeared around her mouth and her eyes looked hollowed by old grief. "My father did not die a quick painless death. They took trophies from him while he was still alive because it's believed to be more magically potent that way and therefore more valuable. He felt them hacking into him but he didn't scream. Instead he used his last breaths to tell me what I had to do to escape. It was the hardest thing he ever asked of me but I obeyed and because of that I got away while the person who meant everything to me died like an animal on a butcher's block."

Evie hissed in a sharp breath. "How old were you when this happened?"

"I had just turned eleven."

"Aurora…I'm so sorry. I wish that had never happened to you."

Aurora gave a bitter smile and said, "Yeah. You and me both."

After a moment's silence Evie asked, "Do you know what became of the people who killed your father?"

"I do. My mother killed a few and even though it took me a while to find them all I killed the rest. So now they are all dead. All but one. He escaped through the portal to the human world and I couldn't follow. None of the people I paid to track him on the other side found any trace of him after he reached a place called America so unless there is a miracle, he's gotten away and I have to live with that."

Evie picked up her cup, craving the remembered warmth because the way Aurora spoke about killing people so casually sent a chill into her body. She wanted to ask how many people there had been, how many Aurora had killed but found she couldn't. She didn't really want to know but she couldn't let it go either.

"How long did it take you to find all the killers?"

"Years. I was also trying to retrieve my father's body at the same time and once they realized I was hunting them they did their best to disappear. I was twenty-two when I found the last killer, aside from the human that got away that is."

"I don't understand…retrieve how? Did they take off with his body?"

"They were cutters – they cut him up and sold his body. They would have harvested every part of him from tail to nose if they hadn't been interrupted. They had already skinned him and removed the most valuable parts before they were made to stop. I found his organs in a large jar with one of the first men I killed. I was lucky with that. The rest that was taken I found piece by piece. I made a vow that I would keep hunting until I found all of him. It has taken me much longer than I ever imagined but now I only need to find his top right fang and hopefully, I have a good lead on that last piece. The person I'm going to meet is an old friend of my father's and someone who has helped me over the years. He sent me a message that he'd heard of someone who may know where the fang is and that he is investigating. He told me to meet him two days from now. He sounded excited so I'm cautiously hopeful he has located it. He's my friend as well and doesn't expect me to pay him for his help but I know from experience information is expensive so that's why I went to the mine for crystals. The ones I harvested are of exceptional quality and even one would cover any expenses he may have had and be a very handsome finder's fee on top. If he's retrieved it for me as well I will give him all the ethian crystals, a fortune many times over, as a show of gratitude."

"Ah..." Evie's face lit up with understanding. "No wonder you snapped at me when I kept trying to persuade you to take me home first instead of going to meet your friend. If this works out it would mean you can fulfill your oath and lay your father to rest."

"Yes, and I'll finally be free. I'll always carry my father in my heart but I want to forget what happened. I want to move on. That's what I desire most."

"It sounds like you've dedicated your life to this?" Evie asked.

"Yes. But I got to travel far and I saw amazing sights while searching. I learned a lot and found things I enjoy doing. I saw I could be more than a hunter. I would have gladly taken up any of a dozen professions but I couldn't, not until my search was over. I had to keep going even when the trail went stone cold and I had nothing to go on."

"Because of the vow you made?"

Aurora nodded. "It was a true blood oath. The kind made with old magic and sealed with my blood. I was a child; I didn't know I was placing a powerful binding on myself and I didn't realize the implication it would have for my life. I wanted to stop hunting years ago but the vow wouldn't let me. It has been like a hungry wolf that harries me with sharp nips. It won't let me rest until I've finished what I started."

Evie's mind reeled as she tried to process everything Aurora had told her. "It must be a terrible burden carrying all of that around. I feel honored that you shared so much with me."

"Thank you for listening. I very rarely talk about this because it's not exactly uplifting conversation."

"Um," Evie shifted uncomfortably as the question and the sick dread that accompanied it rose in her mind. "There's something I have to ask you."

"Ok..." Aurora said cautiously as she watched Evie squirm. "Why do

I get the feeling I'm not going to like this?"

"Probably because I'm worried what your answer will be. Aurora, were there avians involved in your father's murder?" When Aurora silently nodded Evie bit her lip and stared at the ground for a moment before asking, "You killed them?"

Aurora grimaced. "You already know the answer. Do you really want me to say it out loud?"

Guilt at what other avians had done warred with her natural protective instinct towards her people. Evie felt she should apologize but instead what came out of her mouth was, "How many avians have you killed?" She knew that was a mistake the moment she saw the way Aurora's expression darkened.

"How about I ask you a question now. Would you like to tell me how your family first amassed enough riches and followers to rise above being merely a flock to become a House? Or why your ancestors chose the title of 'House Aquilar' which means, if my translation is correct, the house of eagles. An eagle is a predatory bird that swoops down from above and takes its prey by stealth and brute force. We both know why your family would have chosen such a name. Would you like me to drag all the beast-shifter skeletons out of your family's closet to sit between us?"

Evie felt her cheeks burn and she struggled to look Aurora in the eye. "No. I don't want that."

"Neither do I. I'm tired of old grudges and vengeance for blood long spilled and dried. I'd like us to judge each other fairly and not on what our kind might have done to each other in the past. If it helps, I never went after anyone from House Aquilar. Thanks to your father's stance against working with cutters and slavers I had no reason to."

"It's a huge relief to hear you say that. For the record I'm glad you killed those evil people who murdered your father, even if some of them were avians."

"Oh..." Aurora sounded so surprised and relieved that Evie suspected the other woman had braced herself for a very different response.

"After everything you've told me I now understand your determination to get me out and why you were so furious with the cutter. For you going into a place like that must be horrific and seeing all those harvested parts a reminder of—" Evie registered the look on Aurora's face and clamped a hand over her own mouth. "I'm sorry. That was so insensitive of me."

Aurora gave her a rueful smile. "It's all right, Evie but let's not talk about this anymore. For both our sakes. Please finish your meal so we can go."

Evie nodded and made herself finish her meal even though it had cooled and it was hard to swallow past the lump in her throat.

CHAPTER 6

DANGER AND TRUST

After lunch, Aurora led them into a part of the forest that was so old and dense the light dimmed to twilight and the air smelled of damp earth and rotting vegetation. It was cold in the perpetual shade and she was grateful for the jacket Aurora had loaned her. It was eerily quiet aside from the birds chirping so high above that she never got to see them and the occasional sound of something scurrying just out of view. It wasn't long before Evie longed for the sun and the sight of open skies and when they eventually broke into a clearing she sighed with relief. Aurora paused and took a slow turn studying their surroundings. Following her example Evie saw they were on a ridge that granted a birds-eye view of the surrounding forest and the mountains in the distance. Aurora silently sat down on a rock, took out her water bottle and had a drink. Evie took this as a sign they were taking a short break and sat down on a stump a short distance from her.

Evie found this Aurora unsettling. After their conversation by the fire she had become withdrawn, not cold exactly but closed off and she had barely spoken a word. Evie tried to give her space but she missed the comradery they had developed during the morning and the patient way Aurora would answer her questions about different plants and animals. There had been times she'd told Evie to be silent but that was because they had to be stealthy. It quickly became a game for her to watch Aurora's body language to figure out when it was okay to speak and when not. She rarely saw the reason for Aurora's caution but knew that she was aware of things happening in the forest that Evie was oblivious to. Like the time she made her lie down next to her in the tall ferns and whispered in her ear to watch the clearing between two trees about twenty feet away. After a short wait, a doe and her fawn appeared in that exact spot. While the doe paused to graze the fawn had suckled enthusiastically. The sight had filled her with wonder and she'd realized when she saw the way Aurora watched her that she had made them wait there so Evie could see that. It was such a sweet thing to do. Barely an hour later she'd repaid that kindness by poking a stick into what for Aurora was an old but unhealed wound. She'd been trying to think of a way to make up for it ever since but came up blank. Evie got jarred out of her thoughts when Aurora grabbed her arm and dragged her under cover.

"What is it?"

"Wings in the sky," Aurora said pointing towards the mountain where the mine was located.

Evie saw the avian in the sky and she gave a small cry of joy. Finally, one of her people had come for her. "I'm here! Here!" she shouted. She took a step towards the clearing waving wildly. Instantly Aurora caught her around the waist and clamped a hand over her mouth. The sudden and unexpected way Aurora grabbed her and the strength of her hold made Evie go cold. Scared and confused she turned her head to stare at Aurora.

"Evie, wait. Listen to me for a moment. If you still want to run out there and get the attention of whoever is up there when I'm done talking I'll let you. Agreed?"

Evie gave a small nod.

Aurora took her hand away from Evie's mouth and said, "You told me you ended up at the mine because you got blown off course by a storm. How far off course? Would it be reasonable for a search party to be so far away from Porta Belua and on this side of the mountains looking for you? Shouldn't that person be wearing the official colors of your House so you can identify him or her as a member of your flock? Look at the outfit, Evie. That avian is wearing the camouflage gear of a sky-hunter. Why would one of your people dress like that?"

This gave Evie pause. Peering at the avian soaring on high she realized Aurora was right. The stranger wore a full face cover and clothing designed to help the hunter blend into the sky for added stealth. She tried to make an identification based solely on wingspan and feather color but came up blank.

"You're right. That isn't someone from House Aquilar but it is another avian and I'll ask whoever it is to notify my father where I am. He'll send the sentinels to come get me. I could be home by tomorrow."

"Or it could be one of the avians from the mine looking for us. Don't you think it's suspicious that whoever is up there is circling outward from the mine in a search pattern?"

"What do you mean 'avians from the mine'? Wasn't I the only avian there?"

"You were the only one in captivity and there were no avians at the mine when I set you free. But others of your kind are definitely in on that filthy business."

That made Evie frown. "If you didn't see other avians you can't make such an assumption. That is dangerous talk."

"It is not an assumption. I know."

"How?"

"The wolf told me when I freed him and my nose confirmed his story. The fresh scent of an avian male was all over the place. He'd been in the room they kept you in. Your cage was lit while the rest of the room was in darkness and that was on purpose. He stood in the dark and watched you."

Evie felt a chill run up her spine at Aurora's words. "Why didn't you tell me this before?"

"When was I supposed to tell you? When we were falling down the mountain? Or maybe when we were running for our lives with hunters on our trail? Besides, I assumed you knew."

"How would I know this? How? I can't see in the dark and I don't have the nose of a wolf! I am an avian, all I can do is fly and without my wings, not even that!"

"But you have a brain – use it. Think. Why does the mine have a platform designed for avians to land and launch more easily? It was kept clear even though the rest of the roof space was covered in gear. Why bother to do that if it was not being used? You said yourself seeing that made you think the mine must be friendly to avians and yet as soon as you landed you were tranquilized and thrown into a cage. Why? Maybe because another avian was there and he worried you'd seen too much? Didn't you say your father refuses to do business with cutters and their associates? What if that person is someone you know? Or perhaps it was an avian from a rival House who'd be happy to have Evangeline Aquilar as a captive to use as a bargaining piece in negotiations with House Aquilar?"

Evie exhaled loudly and sagged down on a stump. Her eyes still tracked the other avian but she made no move to draw the flyer's attention. Aurora squatted next to her and together they watched the avian search along the foothills of the mountain closest to the mine and make broad circular sweeps over the nearby forest before heading toward the Black Paw trade station.

"I hate that I'm now afraid that another avian will see me. I hate that the sight of wings in the sky that I always found such a friendly sight now fills me with dread. Those are my people and it shouldn't be like this."

Aurora kept her expression carefully blank and said nothing.

Evie stared at the disappearing avian for a while then turned troubled blue eyes on Aurora. "Why did you help me if you knew before you let me out of that cage that avians were involved with that dreadful business at the mine?"

"I figured they must have a grudge to imprison you alongside wolves."

"I see your point but I'm still an avian and from what you've told me during our conversation earlier you have plenty of reasons to hate us. As much as I don't like to admit it we do have a long and bloody history of working with cutters and slavers."

"Evie, you were a girl in a cage. It didn't matter who you were, I could not leave you there. I realized it was possible you knew the other avians but I still didn't want the scared girl I saw to get hurt like I knew she would if I left her there. Also, it gave me immense satisfaction to steal their catch from right under their noses before they got to get their teeth into you."

"I see."

"Are you ready to keep going now?"

"Yeah."

Aurora led the way along a narrow trail, taking care to keep under cover and Evie followed.

"Aurora?"

"Yes?"

"We haven't known each other long so I can hardly expect you to believe me but I promise you I'm not like those other avians."

"I know."

"*How* do you know? I could be an amazing actress and a terrible, deceitful person."

"No, you're not."

"You say that with such conviction but how can you know for sure? I'd hate for you to think I'm like that."

Aurora stopped so suddenly Evie almost walked into her.

"I don't like how worked up you are getting – it makes you smell weird. You're upset about what you imagine I'm thinking and you've got it all wrong so let's clear this up right now. Evie, I've encountered a lot of bad people so I think of myself as a reasonable judge of character. I've observed you closely since we met and you don't strike me as the kind of person who could torture and murder others for profit. Remember I was with you when you opened the door of the cutter's lab and I saw you go into shock. It looked like someone punched you so hard in the gut you couldn't breathe, your eyes were wild and I smelled the distinct odor of intense fear. No one can fake that kind of physical response. That was the moment I *knew* you had nothing to do with that place."

"I heard stories but that didn't prepare me for what I saw. That was the first time I've come face-to-face with something like that."

"I know, I could tell. You don't have to convince me. I don't blame you for what other avians have done and in my eyes you are as much a victim as the wolves I set free. Does that settle this now?"

"Yes, and now I also know how you knew I wasn't lying." Evie said with a frown.

"So…do you feel better now?"

"Why do you ask? Can't you tell from my smell?"

"Now you're upset about something else." Aurora sighed and rubbed at her temple. "What did I say?"

"I'm not upset, I'm amused."

Aurora snorted. "Yeah right. If that's what you look like when you're amused then I don't want to see your angry face."

Evie slowly let out her breath while she thought how to put what she wanted to say. "I'm still in shock and furious to discover avians were involved in my capture and the horrible things done at that place. I honestly thought, or at least hoped, avian involvement with such despicable things were a thing of the past despite how the shame of it still clings to us. Hearing you can tell from my smell how I feel when I was still reeling from what you told me freaked me out. I knew beast-shifters have a great sense of smell but I didn't realize it went that far. It means you know things about me that I can't know about you in the same way. I love my wings but sometimes I resent that other shifters have all these enhanced senses. Don't even get me started on how unfair it is that you are so much stronger than me!"

Aurora opened her hands in a helpless motion. "I can't help what I am and trust me, some days being me is no fun at all. I'm sorry I freaked you out. I'll try to be more careful about what I say. Keep in mind I've had little contact with avians and I'm still trying to figure out how to deal with you. I'm doing the best I can."

"Oh no...I've upset you again. I'm such an idiot. You tried to reassure me and make me feel better and I made a big fuss about nothing." Evie took one of Aurora's hands in hers and cradled it between her palms. "I was feeling insecure and acted like an ass. I'm sorry. There was nothing wrong with what you said. I want you to feel that you can speak to me freely and hopefully if I shoot off my mouth and say something stupid you'll forgive me."

While Evie spoke Aurora remained motionless her head slightly cocked as she listened. Her expression gave very little away but Evie had already learned to watch Aurora's eyes to gauge her emotions and to watch for any sign of amber the way she would watch the sky for the telltale signs a storm was imminent. Aurora was a predatory shapeshifter and Evie knew any significant change in eye color was a sign that strong emotions, like anger or distress, were drawing her beast closer to the surface. To her relief she saw that the amber sparks that moments before had flared up like fireworks in Aurora's eyes, warning Evie she was a lot more upset than she was letting on, were dimming. She wasn't sure what would happen if Aurora's eyes turned amber entirely and she didn't want to find out.

"Aurora, please say something."

"You confuse me. Just as I think I'm beginning to understand you something like this happens and I don't know what to make of it."

"We are still in the early stages of getting to know each other and I don't really know how to read you either. It's normal that we'll have a few misunderstandings but as long as we are honest and talk to each other we can work things out, don't you think? Personally, I find this process of discovery exciting. I already like you and I think we can become good friends, despite how different we are."

That made Aurora smile. "I'd like that...to be friends and you make a good point. I should've realized you'd find me baffling as well and I too am enjoying getting to know you."

Evie beamed at Aurora. "I'm so glad to hear that. As your friend can I just ask one thing? Please don't give me the silent treatment like you did earlier. I'm a talker, freezing me out is the worst thing you can do. I knew you were thinking about things that happened in the past but I worried I'd alienated you by dredging it up in the first place and this when we were just becoming comfortable with each other. I'd much rather you shout at me if I've upset you because then at least I can shout back and we can get to the bottom of what's wrong."

"But I wasn't giving you the silent treatment. I just go quiet when I have a lot to think about."

"Oh, ok. I'll keep that in mind. See I've already learned another new thing about you! So, are we all right?"

"Yes, Evie, we're fine." Aurora squeezed her fingers gently and withdrew her hand.

"You have very expressive eyes," Evie blurted out.

"Uh…I do?" Clearly confused by the random statement Aurora gave her a curious look.

"You do. That's how I know when you're upset. Your eyes really are the windows to your emotions."

"They are?"

"Yes. Has no one told you that? They are such a beautiful green and when those amber sparks flare up in your eyes, they're mesmerizing. I think of those as your warning flares: pretty but dangerous."

Aurora slowly shook her head. "You're definitely the first to say that. Humans have told me I have scary eyes or that it looks weird when they change color. Other beast-shifters don't look me in the eye for long because that could be considered a challenge. They never said what they thought of my eyes, not to my face anyway. Probably because they are more concerned with my claws and what I might do with my teeth if they anger me."

"Yes, I can see how that would be a bigger concern," Evie said trying to keep a straight face. It wasn't easy as she could feel her lips wanting to twitch into a grin but she so didn't want Aurora to think she was laughing at her. Their conversation had become a bit surreal and yet the other woman was so earnest Evie knew Aurora had no idea how strange it was to talk about teeth and claws and possibly biting someone. Or perhaps it was only odd to Evie because she wasn't a beast-shifter. Among creatures who grew fur and paws this was probably a normal topic but since she rarely spent time with non-avians how would she know? At that moment it struck Evie that although she had always assumed she knew a lot about other shifters she probably had a lot to learn, especially about beast-shifters. She should take this opportunity to improve her understanding by carefully observing her new friend. *Friends with a tigress.* Evie decided she really liked the sound of that.

"Evie, can we get going now? We still have a way to go before we reach the spot by the river I have in mind for our camp tonight and I'd like to catch as many fish as possible for dinner. I'm already hungry enough to eat a shark. Nothing that big in there, unfortunately, well nothing I consider edible anyway."

Evie smiled at the absurd visual of Aurora jumping in to wrestle an angry shark out of the water for their dinner. "Yes, I'm ready. Lead the way and I'll be right behind you. Before I forget to say it…thank you for believing me and saving me from myself when that avian flew past."

Aurora lifted a tree that had fallen across the path blocking their way and motioned for Evie to go underneath while she held it up. "That's all right. You don't have to thank me."

Evie patted her leg as she squeezed under. "Yes, I really do."

***

"Aurora?"

"Yes?" She turned slightly expecting Evie to be pointing at something of interest wanting to know more about it as she had several times since their last stop but she was standing still her head tilted like she was listening.

"Do you hear bees? I'm sure I hear bees."

"Yes, I hear them too. There must be a hive nearby, a big one by the sound of things."

"That's great news. Help me find it?"

"Why?"

"What kind of question is that? Where there is a beehive there is honey. Don't you like honey?"

"What kind of question is that?" Aurora countered. "Who doesn't like honey? Honey is nature's candy. But finding a hive doesn't mean we can necessarily get to the honey and we're almost at our campsite. It's next to a river and if we hurry you can take a swim before it gets dark. Wouldn't you like that?"

"I would love that but we are talking honey, Aurora. Honey! After chocolate that's my favorite thing. Let's go have a look. Please? Come on, you said yourself the nest is near and it won't take long to get to our campsite from here. Surely we can spare a few minutes?"

She could hardly argue the point so she nodded and followed the sound of the bees. It wasn't long before she found the hive sandwiched between two layers of rock overlooking a small ravine.

"There!" Evie grinned and pointed at the hive bouncing on the spot in her excitement. "It's not too high, I can still get to it even without wings."

Aurora studied the huge hive, dark with thousands of bees swarming all over it and gave Evie a dubious look. "You might be able to get to it but they will most certainly get to you as well."

"No, I'll be fine. Just help me up to the first ledge then I can climb the rest of the way."

"Evie, I don't have time to get the things ready that I need to calm the bees before we approach their hive and this variety is very aggressive. Why else do you think none of the animals has tried to get near that hive? That thing is huge. We are already attracting attention and we're not even near. See?" She pointed at several bees hovering inches from her face buzzing angrily.

"I'll be fine. I have a knack with bees."

"Really? What are you going to do? Sing them a lullaby so they won't sting you?"

Evie's smile broadened. "Something like that. Do you have a container for me and a knife? I lost mine when I got taken."

Aurora pulled the tin that previously held the fruitcake from her bag. "Will this do? I assume you mean to cut a comb? We can decant the honey later." She reached behind her back and produced a black knife in a sheath. She pulled it out to show Evie the long thin blade. "Be careful because this is very sharp. Just a touch against the skin will cut."

"Is this the same knife you used to cut me loose?"

"Yes."

"I'll be careful. I remember it slicing through those bindings like it was nothing."

"Go work your magic. This I want to see. I will stay here because bees get really agitated around me."

"Because you steal their honey?" Evie asked with a smirk.

"That and they don't like my smell. Watch." She held her hand near a hovering bee, the buzzing instantly intensified and it dove at her hand stinging furiously. "See? Take note how they can sting repeatedly; these bees do not lose their barb after the first sting."

"Are you going to let it keep stinging you like that?"

"It doesn't really hurt as I'm not affected by their venom." Aurora caught the bee, popped it into her mouth and chomped down. "Hmm, not bad."

Evie pulled a face and pointed a finger at Aurora. "I thought we agreed you wouldn't eat live things in front of me."

Aurora's jaw paused and she looked like a kid caught with her hand in a cookie jar. "But it stung me."

"And you said it didn't hurt. Miss '*I'm so tough I'll just let the bee sting me.*'"

A faint color rose on Aurora's cheeks. "How about you get on with trying to steal honey Miss *Bee Charmer*. I want to see how kindly you feel towards the bees after a few dozen stings. I bet you'll want to bite them too by the time they're done with you."

"Want to bet I don't get stung at all?"

Aurora cocked her head in interest. "What do you want to bet?"

"If I win you have to make me a soft bed. I want to sleep like a queen tonight."

Aurora's eyes narrowed. "You drive a hard bargain. What do I get if you lose?"

"You get to use the sleeping bag tonight."

"Evie, you'll be cold. I'm used to sleeping in my cloak, you're not. Pick something else."

"Oooo, Bad Kitty, are you scared you'll be beaten by little old me?"

Aurora's eyebrows flew up. "That's fighting talk. I'll take your bet and you'd better be prepared to sleep on stones and shiver like a plucked chicken tonight."

Evie gasped. "Who's living dangerously now? I can't believe you just compared me to a chicken and took a jab at me being without my wings."

"Don't ruffle Kitty's fur if you don't want to play, Evie. Go, you have a bet to lose."

"I'm so going to make you pay for that. I will *not* lose."

"You do have an advantage; all covered in my jacket like that. By the time you put up the hood the bees will only be able to target your face and hands. Which will be swollen shortly by the way."

Locking eyes with Aurora, Evie shimmied out of the jacket so she was down to her t-shirt. She held the jacket dramatically in the air for a moment then dropped it at Aurora's feet. "Watch me and weep, Aurora. You are *so* going down."

"Nope. It's you who will be weeping soon. Don't worry I can make you an ointment out of fresh boar dung that will ease the pain. I'll even smear it on for you, nice and thick."

"You wouldn't dare."

That made Aurora grin. "You'll beg me to do it."

Evie gave Aurora a disgusted look that just made her grin harder. "Not on your life."

She bent to pick up the tin and knife she'd put down to get out of the jacket. She motioned for Aurora to lift her up to the ledge. Aurora paused with her hands on Evie's hips frowning at the dark mass of bees around the hive.

"You don't have to do this. You could get hurt badly."

"I know I don't have to do this. I want to. You've provided every meal so far and I want to contribute too. Trust me, I can do this. Lift me. I'm going to get us honey."

Wordlessly, Aurora complied, lifting Evie straight up above her head enabling her to climb onto the ledge. As soon as Evie took a step towards the hive the bees reacted and a squadron of black buzzing bodies launched her way.

"Evie…" Aurora's voice was laced with concern.

"Hush, let me work. Quiet now."

Evie took a deep breath and started to hum. She stood still, allowing the bees to approach her. They hovered inches from her but didn't land on her or attack. Aurora watched in astonishment as Evie slowly made her way along the narrow ledge towards the nest humming continuously. It was a low melodious sound not dissimilar to what the bees were making but there was something more to it. Using her other senses Aurora listened more intently and heard the intricate weaving of magic entwined with the bee-song like a second melody. Using her magic to inspect what Evie was doing roused her beasts. Her tiger stirred from its slumber, lifted its head to listen and found the song soothing like the sound of a gentle stream winding its way through a forest. Her other beast stirred as well, drawn in curiosity, not to Evie's voice, but the magic she used to enthrall the bees. It wanted to taste that magic and the girl who wielded it as innocently as a child playing with a sharp knife. Aurora sensed its interest in Evie so she blocked its view. It would not be good for anyone if it became fixated on Evie. It huffed at her in annoyance but lay its head back down on the tiger's flank.

"She is becoming my friend," she whispered to her beasts. "Mine to protect. I like her."

"Ours," they echoed back at her in agreement. They too liked the girl but for different reasons. This amused Aurora. What would Evie's reaction be if she knew she had more than one beast and that they were

not only aware enough to communicate with her, they'd been studying Evie and formed a favorable opinion? Unfortunately, this was something she could never share with her. Too much depended on her keeping that secret. The only other person who knew was her mother and she was the one who'd taught Aurora how to hide what she was. As far as the world knew she was only a tiger-shifter and even that caused her trouble.

Aurora waited for her beasts to settle, their presence dimming, before she looked back up to follow Evie's progress. She was almost within reach of the hive. Evie was lucky she only grew wings. She might admire Aurora's greater strength and other enhanced abilities but she didn't have to keep a leash on her emotions to keep her beasts calm and contained. They were a part of her, Aurora understood this. They lent her their shapes and perceptions so she could draw on their strengths and magic. In exchange, she had to deal with their more primal natures bleeding into how she saw the world and sometimes it was a battle to impose reason and restraint over instinct. For instance, at that moment her instinct was to charge in and haul Evie bodily away from that beehive to keep her safe even though it was clear the woman had a handle on the situation.

Aurora watched in growing admiration as Evie carefully slid a thick chunk of honeycomb into the tin and started back. She was still humming when she handed the tin and knife down to Aurora before jumping down herself. Evie landed with an 'oomph' sound and for a moment Aurora worried she might have hurt her ankle again but she straightened and held her arms out to the side for Aurora to see before making a full turn on the spot.

"Witness, no bee stings."

"Amazing. I am in awe of your bee-wooing abilities."

Evie gave a regal nod. "I won the bet. I told you I would. What do you have to say to that?"

Aurora trailed a finger through the honey that dribbled over the outside of the tin and licked it off. A wide grin broke out on her face, she tore off a small piece of honeycomb and popped it into her mouth.

"Hmm, I love honey. It's a shame the bees won't give it up that easily for me. They at least expect me to blow smoke in their eyes first. As for losing the bet? Defeat has never tasted so sweet."

Evie tried to maintain her haughty composure but the corners of her mouth were twitching and her eyes danced with laughter. "I'm not sure you're still talking about the honey bees give…but enjoy. Just remember

I expect a bed soft enough for a queen tonight."

"You will have it. Nifty trick with the bees. How did you learn that?"

"My House cultivates mira flowers and we need bees to pollinate them so we keep hives. Tending the hives was one of my responsibilities when I was little so I know a thing or two about how to work with bees. The honey from those hives is worth almost as much as the mira extract we use in our products and the taste is exquisite. When I get home I'll send you a jar as a gift."

"Yum, I haven't had mira honey in a while so that will be a lovely treat. I'm still curious about who taught you to sing to the bees like that. Is it a family secret you aren't allowed to share?"

"Pfft, what family secret?" Evie scoffed. "No one taught me to sing to the bees. I discovered by accident that the bees find it soothing when I hum to them. I didn't like how upset they got when I had to clean the hives so, being a kid, I thought I'd try to tell the bees in their singsong language I meant them no harm. To my amazement it made them go all docile so from that day I've always hummed to the bees."

"So, you're a natural."

"A natural at what? Humming?" Evie laughed. "It's not a skill, Aurora. Admittedly, I'm the only one in the flock who can hum the bees into a daze but I'm only mediocre when it comes to singing fit for human ears." Noticing Aurora's amused grin she asked, "What's so funny? Why are you looking at me like that?"

"I'm smiling because you are more extraordinary than you realize, Evie."

"You're just saying that because I brought back so much honey. Don't think I haven't noticed you nibbling."

"But it's so tasty."

"Tastier than a bee?"

"Definitely and there is no furry aftertaste on my tongue."

Evie grimaced. "That right there is another great reason *not* to eat bees. Let them make honey and eat that instead."

"Funny…just for that I'm going to tell you when I said we are almost at our camp spot I exaggerated to make you feel better. We have at least another hour to go."

"Aargh, you will kill me with all this walking Aurora. I swear I've walked more today than in the last few years combined. It'll be a miracle if I can put my shoes on tomorrow, never mind walk."

"You'll be fine. You still have the potion I gave you working through your system and after a good night's sleep in your soft bed you will be as good as new tomorrow. Ready to do the same as today. Over the mountains. Your legs will *love* the climb."

Evie struck a dramatic pose and put a hand over her heart like she was the starlet in a play and said, "Such cruel words to torment me and this after I risked my life to give her the sweet gift of nature's candy. How will I recover?"

Aurora laughed and held the tin out to Evie. "Have a piece of honeycomb to chew on while we walk. That will make you feel better."

CHAPTER 7

WHAT WE FEAR

Evie lay on the soft nest of moss and ferns Aurora made for her with a stomach so full she was pleased she'd crawled into the sleeping bag in just her freshly washed and mostly dry panties, socks, t-shirt and the thick oversized jersey Aurora told her to keep while they were traveling. She was even clean. Well, as clean as one could be after a soapy wash and swim in a deep forest pool. Even her mouth felt fresh. She'd almost kissed Aurora when she produced a small tube of toothpaste, asking her to use it sparingly.

"Aurora, have I told you how impressed I am with your fishing skill and cooking? Dinner was *amazing*. I haven't eaten so much in one sitting in ages." She wasn't exaggerating. The fish and rice dish with the tree mushrooms had been delectable and the sweet and spicy drink Aurora had made had left Evie feeling warm all over and very relaxed.

Aurora's smile was wide and pleased. "You did, several times. I'm glad you liked dinner."

"I wish you hadn't put out the fire though. It will be dark soon and without light it'll be pitch black."

"A fire at night draws attention. It won't be pitch black. The sky is clear tonight and the moon and stars will be out later and we'll see them through the trees."

"Yes, but aren't you afraid of wild animals and things like that? There must be lots of dangerous predators out there and we'll be easy pickings. At least a fire would keep them away."

"You don't need a fire to do that. *I* will keep them away. I told you I would protect you. I won't let anything drag you off in the night. Most animal predators once they get a whiff of my scent avoid me. Relax, Evie, I'm more than capable and willing to make a meal of anything stupid enough to attack our camp."

This gave Evie pause. "I keep forgetting you're a beast-shifter. Mostly I just think of you as another woman. A very competent woman but not as someone who goes all furry."

"That's good, to be thought of as just a person I mean. I just think of you as Evie, not someone who grows wings and becomes all feathery."

"I don't become all feathery, it's just the wings. I've heard the rumor that avians sprout downy feathers over our private bits when we're winged. That's nonsense. I only have skin on my chest and the normal things covering down below."

There was a moment of silence then an amused sounding Aurora said, "I'm not sure I needed to know that but since you brought up rumors I'd better address the one about hairy beasts. I can't speak for other beast-shifters but in my case, unless I'm in my tiger form, I don't have fur on my private areas or anywhere else on my body. The hair on my head grows quickly but I don't have excessive body hair. Actually, I'm smooth all over, in case you were wondering."

This made Evie giggle. "How did we get into this kind of conversation? My face is on fire."

"I have no idea. I was following your lead. If you start talking about 'that time of the month' or ask me what it's like to go into heat I'll find an excuse to scout around the camp sooner rather than later. My girl to girl small talk skills are pretty much non-existent. I'm flying blind here."

"What do you mean 'scout around the camp'?" Evie asked, her voice sharp with alarm. "You're not planning to leave me here alone and go wandering in the forest, are you?"

"I will be moving around within earshot, just checking on things."

"But why do you have to go out there when you have such great hearing and sense of smell?"

"You'll be fine on your own, there's nothing to be afraid of," Aurora said soothingly.

"Easy for you to say! You can see in the dark and hear everything whereas I'm as good as blind and I hear just enough to know there's something out there but I don't know what. Do you have any idea how helpless that makes me feel? At least when you're near I know I'm not alone and it doesn't feel so bad."

"Evie, are you afraid of the dark? I'm asking because this is the second time you've mentioned something about not wanting to be in the dark. Last night with the candles and now this."

Evie fidgeted with the zipper on the sleeping bag. "It's embarrassing. I'm a grown woman, I shouldn't still be afraid of the dark but…I am. It's not like I'm paralyzed with fear but it's a very unpleasant sensation being alone in the dark. It feels like there's something in the shadows watching and if I let my guard down for even a moment it will get me. It's nerve-wracking."

"Put like that it explains a lot." Aurora got the sleeping mat from her rucksack and rolled it out beside Evie's forest bed. Next, she draped the cloak around herself and lay down on the mat facing Evie. "I'll be right here the whole night. If you can't see me put out your hand and you will feel I'm still here."

"You must think I'm stupid. This is so embarrassing."

"No need to be embarrassed. Everyone is afraid of something."

"Even you? I find it hard to believe anything could scare you."

"Of course."

"What are you afraid of, Aurora?"

The question took Aurora off guard and she didn't know what to say. How could she tell someone she barely knew that she was terrified she would die like her father? How could she tell Evie she was afraid if she disappeared that no one would come looking for her? That it made her feel sad and incredibly lonely to know if she died no lover would mourn her passing? No, she could not share such private thoughts and Evie was probably not thinking of that type of fear anyway.

"Aurora? Are you still there? It's gone so dark all of a sudden and all I can see are the vague outline of the trees. Aurora?" Evie's voice was higher the second time she said Aurora's name and a little panicky.

"I'm still here."

There was the sound of the sleeping bag being unzipped and a hand reached for her. Aurora moved a little allowing Evie to find her arm.

"I'm here."

"You didn't answer my question and you're so quiet I can't even hear you breathe. I thought for a moment you had gone."

"You are not alone. Try to sleep, I'll be right next to you all night. I promise."

Evie's hand slid down to clasp her wrist and held on as though she was afraid Aurora would leave if she let go. Once again Aurora marveled at the strength in those delicate hands and despite how cool Evie's fingers were against her skin her touch made her feel warm in a way she could not explain. She waited until Evie's breathing became deep and even before she carefully removed Evie's hand and tucked her arm into the warmth of the sleeping bag.

***

When Evie woke in the night she didn't know where she was and it took her sleep-befuddled mind a moment to process that she was really seeing stars and moonlight through an opening in the treetops and not just dreaming it. Before panic could set in she saw Aurora sitting beside her. She sat with her arms draped around her legs and her chin resting on her knees as she stared up at the night sky. She sat so still she looked like a statue, the only movement on her caused by the slight breeze stirring her long dark hair and cloak.

Evie felt a wave of gratitude towards Aurora. She'd kept her word and remained by Evie's side. Lifting herself up on her elbows Evie immediately felt the chilly bite of the night air on her sleep-warmed face. Aurora turned her head to look at her and for a moment the way the light from the moon reflected in her eyes they shone with a greenish yellow glow before her face was cast into shadows.

Keeping her voice at a whisper Evie asked, "Why aren't you sleeping? Are you cold?"

"No, I'm not cold." Aurora pointed at the moon. "That is my sunrise and the moon calls to me. It is to me as the sun is to you, my light and guide. The stars my signposts so I'm never lost."

Evie gave Aurora a thoughtful look. "You're traveling by day because of me, aren't you? You're nocturnal."

"Yes, I am. It's also safer to travel by night. For me anyway."

Evie looked up at the sky. The stars looked like silver blotches against the dark canvas and the moon drifting above was a luminous orb. She'd seen the moon countless times but being beside Aurora and seeing the reverence with which she watched it made her see it in a different light. It really was beautiful. No match for sunrise but she was a creature of the day and she could see how for a creature of the night the moon would hold a similar appeal.

"You should try to get more sleep, Evie," Aurora said quietly. "I'm going to get us moving very early and tomorrow will be a long grueling day."

"What about you?"

"I'll sleep soon. I want to watch the moon and listen to the night a while longer."

"You sure you aren't cold? The bed you made me is so cozy and snug I probably don't even need the sleeping bag. Do you want it?"

Aurora leaned over and cupped Evie's cheek in her palm. Heat radiated from it and despite being cocooned within the sleeping bag Evie leaned into that warmth wanting more.

"Wow, you really do run hot. I thought it was just because I was so cold last night that you felt so warm."

"I'm like this most of the time. Cold weather rarely bothers me, it's the hot summer days I find uncomfortable." Aurora removed her hand and went back to staring at the moon.

Evie lay back down and pulled the sleeping bag up around her head to block out the cold. She could still feel the warm outline where Aurora's fingers had been just moments ago and she wished she could think of a reasonable excuse to entice Aurora to join her in the comfy nest. Just that small touch was enough to make her crave more and she could imagine how amazing it would be to snuggle up to Aurora's warm back. Or even better, in her warm arms again. Evie suppressed a groan and made herself lie still despite the sudden restless feeling in her limbs at the memory of how she'd slept draped over Aurora the previous night. She was being silly – she couldn't start thinking of Aurora as her personal bed warmer or a potential lover. Evie watched Aurora sitting quietly next to her until her eyelids drooped shut and she drifted off to sleep, reassured by Aurora's watchful presence.

CHAPTER 8

MOUNTAIN

Evie was having a lovely dream when she felt someone shake her shoulder. She cracked open an eye, saw it was still dark and swatted the hand away. When the hand came back she grumbled, "Leave me alone, Oriana, it's too early to get up."

There was a low chuckle and someone said, "I hate to break it to you, Evie but I'm not your sister and staying in bed is not an option."

Blearily Evie opened her eyes to find Aurora's face inches away.

"Wake up, sleepyhead. Time to go."

Sitting up Evie stared around her in disbelief. "But it's the middle of the night. The stars are gone and it's pitch black. I can't see a thing!"

"It's around four in the morning. Full dawn won't be for a while but there is already enough light for you to follow me. Here…" Aurora pressed a cup into Evie's hands making sure she had a hold on the handle before she let go. "Drink this while your eyes adjust."

Feeling stunned and barely awake Evie sipped the drink. It was mint tea with so much honey it was like drinking a slightly diluted version of the stuff and by the time she finished her cup she could feel the sugary buzz energizing her. She dressed mostly by feel and racked her memory for any useful tips on how to trek safely through a dark forest. Not surprisingly she came up blank.

"Ready, Evie?"

"Almost, just let me double check my shoelaces. Yup, good to go…except I really can't see much. It isn't as dark as I thought at first but I still can't see more than a few feet in front of me."

"But I thought avians have enhanced eyesight?"

"We do but it only really works by day. I can see for miles and hone in on small details but I need light to do that. My night vision is pathetic. If we were in the open I could probably manage but here in the forest it's too bloody dark. If you insist on leaving now it will be just a matter of time before I trip or impale myself on a branch."

There was a moment of thoughtful silence then Aurora's said, "That just means I'll have to help you until there is enough light for you to see properly."

Evie vehemently shook her head. "You are *not* piggybacking me again. Seriously Aurora, we are not doing that."

"I wasn't going to suggest that."

"No? What do you have in mind?"

"How about taking my hand for a little while? I can guide you."

"Oh, okay. I can live with that."

A short while later Evie found herself holding Aurora's hand as they walked through the forest. She focused all her attention on reading Aurora's signals by the way she moved and did her best to follow in Aurora's footsteps. When they'd set off she had worried that Aurora would drag her along at breakneck speed but she set a slow steady pace, the grip of her hand firm but gentle. Twice Evie tripped and had to grab hold of Aurora to prevent a fall. The other woman stood still and waited patiently for Evie to let go before continuing. Evie was concentrating so hard that it caught her by surprise when they suddenly stepped into the open. Looking around she realized they were at the foot of a mountain and that she could see enough to no longer need a guide. She let go of Aurora's hand.

"I can see now. Thank you."

"Let me know if I'm going too fast or when you need a rest. We have to get over the mountain today and I'm aiming to get us to the top of the ridge before noon."

Evie craned her neck trying to measure the distance to the top of the mountain. Struggling to keep the dismay from her voice she said, "That's a long way up."

"Yes, that's why it's important that we get most of the climb out of the way while it's still cool and we're fresh. Here…I made these for our breakfast. We can eat while we walk."

Evie took the leafy bundle Aurora held out to her in both hands. It was slightly charred and still warm.

"What is it?"

"Just a little something I made. We need to keep our strength up. The outer leaves are edible but very bitter so unless you are starving I'd suggest you make a hole and eat out the contents."

"I have to give it to you, Aurora, you might kill me with the walking but you keep me well fed. Whatever you put in this little parcel feels substantial. I'll not go home slimmer even with all this exercise at the rate you're feeding me."

"It's still early. Trust me, by mid-morning you will have burned so many calories you'll wonder if you should have eaten the leaves too."

***

They were walking up yet another steep incline when Evie said, "Aurora, tell me how you learned to cook so well. You amazed me with that breakfast parcel – it was delicious. You turn ingredients I'd consider inedible into tasty meals."

Aurora gave Evie an incredulous look. "You want to talk about my cooking? Now? Maybe you should save your breath for walking because you sound a little winded."

"I'm not winded, I'm just breathing with enthusiasm. We've been walking for what feels like forever and mostly in silence. Not that the mountainside isn't pretty but at this point I couldn't care less about the view. I'm bored and I need to focus on something other than how much my legs are punishing me right now. Talk to me, tell me how you learned to cook…or anything else, I don't care. Just make it interesting."

"Wow, talk about pressure. I doubt you'll find this interesting but my father taught me how to cook. He loved trying new dishes and he liked to bake. He said just because his tiger liked raw meat it didn't mean he couldn't have a cultivated palate. Then there was the old shepherd who taught me. I got to know him when I signed on to guard a flock of sheep in the high mountains."

"You're kidding. You, a shepherd? I'm trying to imagine it and I just can't."

"True story. I was between things and I sort of stumbled into the job. It was just me and the old human. They hired me to protect the flock and he was supposed to take care of the animals. He was good with the animals but he had arthritis and the cold weather just about crippled him so once he showed me what to do I took over all the outside work while he did the inside stuff and cooked our meals. Turned out he was a great cook and he used to hire himself out as a cook when he was younger. Wherever he went he took his cookbooks. They were his pride and joy and full of handwritten notes and his own recipes. It was amazing what he could make with just a few ingredients and he was bush savvy too so he could make a meal out of just about anything. It's a shame he never got his dream of opening a restaurant in town, people would have loved his food."

"Why didn't he?"

"Drink and gambling. He couldn't stay away from either and once he started he couldn't stop. He spent his money quicker than he made it and would end up in jail or wake up in a ditch, all beat up with no memory of what happened. In a sober moment he realized if he wanted to stay alive past thirty he had to keep away from towns and large camps. That was his story anyway."

"Sounds like you liked him."

"Yes, we got on well. We respected each other's space. I didn't have much to say but I enjoyed listening to him talk about his life and since I rarely drink and he couldn't, that worked too. I asked him to teach me his favorite dishes and in exchange I offered to let him read the books I'd brought with me. He didn't want to at first but boredom got the better of him. He turned out to be an excellent teacher. He never said so but I think he enjoyed passing on his skills and showing off."

"That's a sweet story but I'm still stuck on you looking after sheep. Could they sense your beast? How did they react to you?"

Aurora gave a toothy grin. "Let's just say they quickly learned to come when I called. Even the cantankerous ram behaved. I spent a lot of time walking with or near them and once they got used to my scent I slept in their midst. Those mountain sheep were a wily lot, much smarter than the ones in the low-lands in my opinion. It didn't take them long to figure out I was keeping the other predators away. After a while, they followed me and stayed close to me while they grazed. It was oddly soothing watching over them and listening to their noises in the night. To my surprise, I became fond of them especially the lambs. They were so inquisitive and playful; I didn't know sheep could be like that."

"Do you still keep in contact with the shepherd?"

"No. There was an incident. I didn't think he'd want to see me or hear from me again after that."

"What happened?"

Aurora frowned. "That's not a good story. Not one of my proudest moments."

"Now I'm curious. You can't tell me that and not continue because it will drive me crazy. Don't make me try to work out what happened because I have a very fertile imagination. Oh no…don't tell me you developed a craving for the feel of well-aged wrinkly man and tried to put the moves on him? *Please* tell me that's not what happened?"

"Evie…that's gross. I was barely twenty and he was in his seventies."

"Then tell me, I mean how bad can it be?"

"That depends on how you feel about me almost disemboweling someone."

"Was it an accident?"

"An accident?" Aurora sounded incredulous. "You must have a *very* creative imagination. How would something like that happen accidentally?"

"Come on…just tell me already." Evie narrowed her eyes at Aurora in mock threat. "Unless you *want* me to keep guessing what happened? I can keep doing this all day…"

Aurora grinned and put her hands up as if to ward Evie off. "All right you win…just remember you made me tell you. So, I'd been there for several months when human men came to visit the shepherd. At that time in my life, I found it difficult to be around groups of strangers, especially males. So I stayed away from the buildings but close enough in case of trouble. They stayed all day and overnight in the hut with the old man. I had a peek and they were playing dice and drinking. In the morning he came to me and told me to let the men take several sheep. Since the animals did not belong to them I said no. He told me that the winters in those mountains were brutal on humans and that the men needed meat for their families to survive. He said at least a dozen sheep were taken by predators every season but since we'd lost none yet the owner would not become suspicious if we let the men have a few."

"That doesn't sound right," Evie murmured.

Aurora shook her head. "I didn't think so either. I gave my word to protect the flock and I had kept them safe. I was proud of that." Aurora's expression became pensive and troubled. "I told him there was an abundance of food in those mountains; plenty of deer, goats and other things. There was no need for those people to go hungry. There were tracks everywhere and even a half decent tracker could find the wild herds. If they couldn't manage that much then those men had no business dragging their families into such wild country."

"What did the shepherd say?"

"He got upset. Said he'd already told them they could have the sheep. I told him it wasn't up to him, that the flock was under my care and I didn't agree to anything with those men. He told me it was a done deal. I disagreed. I spoke with the men and told them about the deer and the lake with lots of fish. I even offered to hunt for them so their children wouldn't starve but they wouldn't listen. They tried to take the sheep even though I made it very clear they were not to go near them. The ewes and lambs were confused and afraid of the men and their barking dogs and they didn't want to go with them. Their bleating sounded like the screams of terrified children. It felt like they were begging me for help."

"What happened?"

"Mentally I wasn't in a good place, Evie. The angry men shouting at me, crowding me and the sound of the animals all upset like that set me off. I lost control. I shifted and attacked. Fortunately, I came to my senses before I killed the men but I hurt them badly. Their dogs didn't survive. I still feel bad about that because they were just trying to protect their masters. I didn't touch the shepherd but he fled with the men and he never came back, not even to collect his cookbooks. After that, I tended the flock for the rest of the season and didn't see another soul until the owner came to check on things. I told him what happened, collected my pay and left."

Evie came to a stop and rested with her hands on her hips breathing hard. "I have to give you credit, Aurora, that story wasn't boring. Strange and violent but definitely not boring."

"That was a long time ago. I had issues. I don't want you to worry that I'll shift uncontrollably or act like a feral beast. I have superb control and hardly ever lose my temper. I promise you are safe with me in case you're planning on running away as soon as I turn my back."

"I wouldn't dream of running."

"That's good."

"I've seen how fast you move so running would be stupid. I'd fly away if I could."

Seeing Aurora's worried look Evie gave her a wide smile and a pat on the shoulder. "I'm just joking with you."

"Evie, if that's what you consider a passable joke you seriously need to work on your repertoire."

"But it was funny…you should have seen your face. All jokes aside I feel very safe with you and that story just made me realize why."

"Really? This I've got to hear."

"Theme, I see a theme. You fiercely protect what is under your care." Evie paused and bent down to retie a shoelace.

"So?" It was Aurora's turn to sound impatient.

"You said I'm under your protection. Several times and I feel good about that. For the record, if a group of people tries to drag me away kicking and screaming please don't hold back, use those claws and teeth all you want." Evie had meant it as a semi-joke to set her new friend at ease but realized she'd wound Aurora up instead when she saw the fierce expression on her face and the way her eyes swam in amber.

"I will not allow *anyone* to forcibly take you away or hurt you while you're with me. Any fool who tries will regret it."

Moving slowly Evie rested a hand on Aurora's arm. She felt a spike of energy under her fingertips but ignored the warning that Aurora's beast was close to the surface and squeezed gently. "Coming from you that is a sweet thing to say." Evie felt the tension ease off and saw the amber in Aurora's eyes fade until they were once again a deep forest green. She stroked Aurora's arm in a soothing gesture and it occurred to her calming a tigress was the same as soothing an angry house cat. It had to be done gently and carefully.

Aurora gave her a small smile, covered Evie's hand on her arm with her own for a moment then she stepped away, continuing up the path. Over her shoulder she said, "Now you have to tell me a story, it's only fair. Your turn to try and be entertaining and see how you like it."

"You set the bar kind of high. I don't have stories like that. No blood and guts and people running away screaming. My life seems boring in comparison."

"Nonsense. Your world is so different from mine that things that seem ordinary to you will be fascinating to me. For instance, what's it like living with so many people in your home all the time? Doesn't that drive you crazy?"

"Aurora, remember I grew up with lots of people around me all the time and I'm used to it so no, it doesn't drive me crazy. I like the hustle and bustle and there is always something happening or some kind of drama or intrigue. Granted, sometimes it gets too much and I feel like I could strangle the next person who wants something from me but I have ways of escaping. I can fly higher than anyone in my flock so when I need silence and open space I go for a long solo flight. There are also areas only my father and I have access to because of our work and the family wing is restricted so there is that and there's a lock on my suite. Not that it seems to keep my sister out. I'm sure she's made herself a copy of my key because she always seems to get into my wardrobe. She doesn't have boobs to speak of so I don't understand why she keeps borrowing my tops when they look weird on her. But does she listen?

Nope. Don't even get me started on her getting into my makeup and perfumes and eating on my bed when she knows I hate that. Oh, I got carried away. I think it's because I miss Oriana so much. You might regret asking me about life in my tower because now you got me talking, I might not stop."

"I'm astounded you could say all that so quickly almost without taking a breath but I'm not regretting it yet. Still waiting for the story though."

"Yes, I've thought of a good one to tell you. This should give you an idea of how difficult it is to do anything sneakily in a tower full of nosy avians. It's about my sister and the first time she went on a date. It was such a disaster but in a funny way. Well, it was funny to me and everyone else in the flock but she's still embarrassed about it and she'll make me pay if she finds out I told you this story but I'm going to tell you anyway. What's the point of being an older sister if I can't occasionally dish on Oriana after all the trouble that little fireball has caused me over the years?"

"I'm already fascinated and you've not even started. Do tell, my lips are sealed. Your sister will never know you told me."

"So, what happened was…"

***

As Aurora reached the top of yet another ridge she gave the sun an angry glare. She wished, not for the first time, that it was something she could pounce on and shred to pieces for the agony it was inflicting on her. She usually traveled by night and if she had to be out by day she sought shelter and rested during the hottest part of the day. Unfortunately, since Evie didn't have night vision and got nervous and jumpy after sundown they had to travel all day if she wanted to reach her appointment on time. When they started up the mountain this meant they had been walking with the sun in front of them most of the time. In the morning the sun had been weak and their twisting path only occasionally had them facing the glare directly and there had been plenty of shady spots along the way. Since then they had climbed so high that vegetation had become sparse and what little there was grew no taller than her ankle, leaving her exposed to the merciless mid-day sun without even the cool breeze she had expected at this height. To make things worse, for the last two hours the sun had hovered right in her line of sight like a giant burning orb sent to torment her. Despite her cap and keeping her eyes down to only occasionally sweep the landscape the glare coming off the rocks was searing her eyeballs and the headache it had given her was rapidly becoming worse. On top of that, she was hot. Boiling hot. She had stripped off as much clothing as she could without being indecent. She was down to just her singlet and a pair of boxer briefs which were almost like shorts. The singlet was sweat soaked and clung to her breasts in a way she'd find embarrassing if she wasn't so irritated and the damp boxer briefs chafed. She wished she could strip entirely but didn't want to walk around naked in front of Evie.

Adding to her ill temper Evie seemed to be enjoying herself, relishing the heat and the light if not the actual walking. Earlier in the day she had enjoyed their conversation. True to her word once Evie got going she had lots to say telling one story after another and more than once she'd had Aurora laughing out loud. The woman had a way with words. She was witty, charming and being around her was a pleasure. That made her feel awful that she'd not been able to muster more than a dismissive grunt the last few times Evie had tried to break the silence. She was not a great conversationalist to start with and casual friendly banter was way beyond her at this point. She was doing her best not to snap at Evie or let on how much the light and heat was bothering her.

Another hour of the sun beating down on her and Aurora couldn't take it anymore. She *really* had to find shelter. As much as she didn't want to reveal her weakness her headache had become epic and her eyes burned and wept. She was so irritable she barely resisted the urge to snarl when Evie asked her if she was all right which meant her control was fraying along with her temper. She had to do something fast. Spotting a small outcropping of trees in the distance she took off for it at a run. As soon as she got there she realized the trees with their small trunks twisted by fierce high-altitude winds and tiny leaves did not provide nearly as much cover as she needed in her current state. Frustrated and desperate she peeled off the hot singlet but kept on the briefs so as not to be entirely naked and shifted her arms and hands to accommodate powerful claws. She dug under the gnarled roots that anchored the trees, to get to the moist soil beneath, raking chunks of rock out of the way along with the dirt. Soon she created a hole wide and deep enough to fit her body and lowered herself into the blessed cool shelter.

She'd barely changed her hands and arms back when she saw a worried looking Evie peering into her little hidey-hole. She hated being seen in such a state because it made her feel vulnerable, cornered and as defensive as a wounded bear. Before she could stop it a growl sprung from her lips, she locked eyes with Evie and she felt her muscles bunch in readiness to meet assault head-on. What the woman saw was enough to make her go deathly pale and she backed away carefully. Aurora felt an instant rush of shame. Another beast-shifter would have known not to approach her while she was like this but Evie didn't know better and she was just acting out of concern. Evie must think she was acting like a feral and this after she boasted to her she had superb control. She expected Evie to turn tail and run away as quickly as she could but she sat down a few feet away under the shade with her back against the tree. After a little while she retrieved Aurora's pack from where she dropped it, put her cap on top and gingerly picked up her sodden singlet spreading it over a branch to dry.

"Evie, I'm sorry I growled at you."

Without looking at her Evie said, "Have a rest, I bet you didn't sleep much last night. I'll keep watch as you did for me during the night. We can travel when the sun is not so fierce."

"The sun hurts my eyes," Aurora grumbled. "It's too much. Too hot."

"I imagine so with those sensitive eyes of yours and how warm you seem to be even when it is freezing. We should find a time of day to travel when we both function reasonably. No more four in the morning stumbling around a dark forest for me so I have to be led like a child and no walking for hours under the brutal sun for you. We can discuss it and work out a travel plan together."

"Good idea."

Evie got Aurora's water bottle from her pack and shook it. When she heard the slosh of liquid she handed it to Aurora without looking directly at her. Aurora took the bottle gratefully and sipped the tepid liquid until it was all gone.

"I need to stay here a while. You'll wake me if you see something?"

"I will. I'll stay right here beside you. The view is excellent and I can see for miles so nothing will get close without me spotting it."

"Good."

Aurora lay her pounding head down and curled up for a sleep. It was comforting that Evie wanted to guard her while she slept; it was the sort of thing a pack-mate would do. She didn't really need that as her beasts would wake her the moment they sensed danger but she still felt more relaxed knowing Evie with her eagle-eyed vision was keeping watch.

***

When Aurora woke in her earth shelter she was instantly on high alert. Something was wrong. Trying to pinpoint the danger she found there was none. Her tiger was curious and amused but not alarmed, it was her other beast's agitation that woke her. Highly attuned to all things magical it was beside itself at the way Evie was attempting to shift her wings. Or at least she assumed that was what Evie was trying to do. Her face was rigid with concentration, beads of sweat rolled down her temples and the way she drew on her magic grated against Aurora's senses like a high-pitched screech.

"Evie, who taught you to shift like that? Your technique is awful."

Her voice startled Evie and she lost concentration. She scowled at Aurora. "My grandmother taught me to shift. She was the best and quickest shifter of all the avians in our House."

"If she was the best you had you have my condolences because your grandmother knew fuck all about shifting. Either that or you were a terrible student."

Aurora rubbed at her temples where the throb was down to a dull ache. She crawled out of her shelter and after dislodging a twig from her briefs and dusting herself down as best she could she quickly put her clothes back on.

Evie's eyes sparked with anger and she looked like she was about to give Aurora a verbal blast but paused with her mouth hanging open to watch her dress. The way her eyes traveled up and down Aurora's body and lingered on her bare chest made her skin heat again, but for a very different reason. Aurora told herself not to read too much into it. She'd noticed women often looked at each other's bodies to compare, like the way men instinctively noted each other's size and strength. It was nothing to get excited about.

She sat down next to Evie in the shade, retied her hair and tried to get the soil from between her toes before she put her shoes back on. She was so going to need a good wash after her crawling into the earth episode but at least she felt better and the sun was bearable.

"It was rude to insult my grandmother like that. Are you going to apologize?"

"No. In fact, your grandmother is the one who should apologize to you for teaching such a horrendous technique. An infant beast-shifter could do better."

"My grandmother is dead…"

"That doesn't excuse what she did. Why didn't your father ask your wolf-shifter godfather to teach you?"

"Only similar shifters can teach each other, avians teach avians, wolves teach wolves and so on. Different shifters can't teach each other. Everyone knows that."

Aurora just stared. "Who passed on that dung-ball of a gem as truth? That is utter drivel."

"You're grumpy when you wake up from an afternoon snooze. Or was it sleeping in a hole among tree roots that's made you so catty?"

Aurora shrugged. "I'm just calling it as I see it."

She retrieved her knife and began to rid her nails of the dirt left over from digging into the soil. She hated feeling dirty. She saw Evie wrinkle her nose at what she was doing. Her cheeks flushed and she hurried to finish. She should have known better than to clean her nails in company; now Evie probably thought she was crude on top of semi-feral. It shouldn't matter what Evie thought of her but it did and she knew why. She was drawn to Evie and she wanted to impress the beautiful woman despite knowing it was most likely a one-sided attraction. To think she'd crawled in the dirt like a mole creature and ate a bee. That was no way to make a good impression. Next, she'd probably go all furry and kill a baby deer in front of Evie.

"Hey, are you still half asleep? Did you hear what I said to you?"

Aurora wrenched her thoughts out of her dark musings to find Evie staring at her in a mixture of annoyance and concern. "I'm sorry, my mind wandered off for a moment. What were you saying?"

Evie raised a questioning eyebrow at her. "Are you all right? You're very flushed. Do you have heatstroke?"

"No, I'm fine. Just a momentary lapse of concentration. Please continue, you have my undivided attention."

"We are talking about shifting, in case you forgot. You said my wolf-shifter godfather should have taught me instead of my grandmother but I don't see how that would have made any difference. All avians are terrible at shifting so that's why we rarely do it. It's better to arrange our lives around our wings than to go through the agony of shifting unless we absolutely have to."

"Nonsense. I can guarantee it doesn't have to be like that. Granted avians don't seem to have a natural affinity for shifting but with the right technique and regular practice it should be a lot quicker and easier. I can't guarantee it will become painless, Evie, but when you shift it shouldn't look like you're sweating blood."

"You really believe that?"

"Absolutely."

"So…can you teach me to do it better?"

This gave Aurora pause, "I can…but you might find it too invasive."

"Invasive how? Explain."

"You have formed the equivalent of magical pathways that have been deeply ingrained since you were a child. I couldn't just tell you how to do it differently, I'd have to use my magic to override those pathways and forge new ones for you. That is very intimate and requires a certain level of trust. If you were a beast-shifter I would not even attempt such a thing as your beast and mine would rise to guard the gates so to speak. Unless we had such a deep bond that your beast would allow me past unopposed, we'd end up with a battle of wills and I would have to make your beast yield to gain entry. I'd never do such a thing to you as that's too close to mental rape for my liking. Ah…that's probably why it only gets taught in families and within clans. Similar beasts, similar magic, familiarity and all that. Never really thought about that. Now it makes more sense where the idea comes from that different shifters can't teach each other. It's not true, just easier and probably safer."

Aurora faltered when she noticed the way Evie was glaring at her. "What is it? What did I say? You look like you want to hit me."

"Aurora, you just told me my way of shifting is so shitty an infant could do it better. Then you tell me you can help me improve greatly but wait…oh no, it's probably too invasive and risky to try. That's really not helpful. *At all.* Now I feel even worse about the way I struggle to shift and it'll eat at me knowing I can be better at it but only if I'm brave enough to let you mess around with my magical pathways."

Aurora held her hands up defensively. "Maybe I shouldn't have said anything but I couldn't stand to see you strain like that because it put my teeth on edge. Plus, I'd just woken up. It takes a few minutes for all my faculties to kick in and I tend to say whatever pops into my head. Let's forget I said anything."

"No. I will not forget – this is too important. Shifting quicker would be life altering for me. I just need to think about this a little. Please don't be offended that I'm hesitant. It doesn't mean I don't trust you it's just…this is a big thing all of a sudden. I assume you were serious about teaching me? You won't let me agonize about this and then say you changed your mind or some rubbish like that?"

"No offense taken. I'd worry if you accepted my offer without carefully considering the risks. You hardly know me after all. Take your time thinking this through...my offer to teach you will remain on the table as long as we are traveling together. Hopefully, by now you know me well enough to realize I don't offer my help unless I intend to follow through. My word is my bond. You need to know I've never taught anyone how to shift but I'm confident I can guide you through it and make it much easier for you. I'm very good at shifting. I know all beast-shifters say this and you haven't seen me do it at all but trust me when I say that I have a knack for it."

"Thank you for being honest about that. I'll let you know as soon as I've decided."

"We'll be together for a few more days at least so you don't have to rush into a decision." Aurora stood up, gave the sun a speculative look and rammed her cap down low on her head. "We'd better get going. I want to get to the lake before dark."

Evie gave a tired sigh and said, "I've worked out where we are and it will take us hours to get to the lake on foot. Do we really have to go that far today? We've been walking since before daybreak."

"Unfortunately, we do. My appointment is tomorrow and if I want to get there on time we have to reach the lake tonight."

"Yikes, then we really need to keep going."

"Think of it this way, Evie, when we get there we can have a wash. You can even have a swim if you want to brave that water."

"What's wrong with the water?"

"A glacier feeds into it at the spot by the lake I want to camp tonight. It means the water is fresh and good for drinking but very cold."

Evie groaned and got up slowly. Aurora thought of offering to pull her up but she didn't want to touch Evie with her filthy hands.

"I'm sorry I growled at you and got all menacing before. That's not how one behaves towards a friend. I wasn't at my best. My beast comes close to the surface when I'm under duress or not functioning properly."

Evie smiled and put her hand on Aurora's arm. "It's all right. I could tell something was wrong."

"Still, I feel bad."

"You've apologized, that's enough. Let it go now, okay? We're fine. Trust me I'll let you know loud and clear if we have a problem. I don't suffer in silence and I don't believe in letting things slide."

"That's true...I've noticed that about you. You're...not

confrontational exactly but very direct. I like that. It means I know where I stand with you."

Evie's smile widened and she gave Aurora's arm a squeeze. "I'll remind you of that when you start finding it annoying."

CHAPTER 9

LAKE

Evie found Aurora had not exaggerated when she said the water in the lake was very cold. Dipping her fingers in the water felt like putting them into liquid fire and she instantly decided to make do with washing herself with a soapy cloth rather than submerge her body in the freezing water. Aurora, on the other hand, stripped out of her clothing and dove in but it must have been too cold even for her because she came up gasping and only had a quick swim before getting out of the water. Aurora had chosen a spot a short distance from her to undress and all Evie saw between the bushes was Aurora's back and glimpses of a very shapely bare butt. That was enough to make her a little breathless and confirmed she didn't also suffer from heatstroke in the afternoon and hallucinate that amazing body. The tall woman was very muscular but instead of being bulky like a man she was all long sleek muscles and feminine curves. Evie thought Aurora was stunning clothed but seeing that gorgeous body clad only in briefs as she came crawling out of that hole had made her temporarily speechless and unable to do anything but stare.

She almost wished she didn't find Aurora so attractive. She was the sort of woman that, had Evie seen her enter a nightclub, she immediately would have stood up to go talk to her before every single man and not-so-straight woman honed in on her. It wasn't just the other woman's appearance that drew her, there was also the way she moved that made it hard to look away. That husky voice was dreamy and those incredible eyes gave her the shivers but in a good way. Unfortunately, Aurora wasn't an attractive stranger in a club. She was the person who'd saved Evie from a horrible fate and who even now held her life in her hands. So, no matter how appealing she found her, flirting with her companion just to see what would happen was a terrible idea. It wasn't like she could just shrug and walk away if it turned out Aurora was the kind of person who took offense if another woman found her attractive and expressed an interest in sharing more than a drink. Besides, she was a new friend that Evie really liked and admired and she hoped their friendship would continue to grow. As a rule she didn't make a move on her friends, not the ones she wanted to keep anyway. In her experience sex complicated relationships and there was nothing like a messy breakup to ruin a beautiful friendship. However, there was no harm in looking and if Aurora wanted to walk around in her underwear or swim naked Evie would enjoy the view.

***

After her swim Aurora felt refreshed. It felt good to wash away the sweat and remnants of the dirt from earlier in the day. Mindful there wasn't a lot of time before sundown and that she needed to get back before dark for Evie's sake she hurriedly washed her dirty clothing before laying them out on sun-warmed rocks. She let Evie know she was going to get them dinner and headed into the wooded area beside the lake. She planned to collect eggs from the birds nesting in the area for Evie's dinner and catch something meaty for her own meal but at the last moment she had a flash of inspiration and headed to the river instead.

By the time she got back to their camp the sun was a red smudge in the sky. She was pleased and pleasantly surprised to find Evie had already got a cozy fire going. Evie also had a pot of water almost at a boil, gathered plenty of dried wood and she had their washing strung up on a makeshift clothing line. The washing made Aurora do a double take. Seeing their underwear side by side, her boxer briefs touching Evie's cute pink panties, gave her a fuzzy feeling inside.

"You've been busy."

"So have you, that satchel of yours is bulging. What do you have for us? I'm starving."

This made Aurora grin. "How do you feel about freshwater crayfish?"

"Seriously?"

Aurora carefully extracted a creature the size of a dinner plate that looked like a cross between a scorpion and a crab for Evie to see. "These live inside the crevices carved into the rocks by the river. They must prefer cold water because this is the only area I've ever found them. Catching them is a challenge but they're so tasty it's worth the effort. You said you eat shellfish, right? If you tell me I spent all that time up to my boobs in freezing water getting my fingers nipped for nothing I'm eating these all by myself."

"Were you naked?"

The random question and the intensity of Evie's gaze momentarily threw Aurora. "Um…was I naked when?"

"In the water – were you naked?"

"Yeah? Why would I be clothed? If I had any sand left in my nether regions after the swim it's definitely gone now."

Evie opened her mouth to say something, bit her lip and instead reached out to touch Aurora's arm. "You're so cold. How long were you in that freezing water? Come sit next to me by the fire."

Aurora sat beside Evie on the rock and held her hands over the fire to warm them. "About an hour, possibly longer. I had to find the critters by feel and it's not easy getting them out of those holes. I'm still waiting for you to answer my question. Will you eat what I caught for our dinner? I got enough for two people."

"Yes, even though that creature is probably one of the ugliest things I've ever seen. It was sweet of you to catch something we can both eat but you didn't have to go to so much effort." Evie went and got Aurora's cloak and draped it around her back and shoulders. "You need to look after yourself better. You almost fried yourself today and now you're icy cold and I don't care how strong you are, such extremes are bad for your body."

Aurora smiled and patted Evie's leg. "I'm fine. Let's get dinner started. Once you've tasted one of those things you'll understand why I said it was worth the effort."

***

An hour later Evie groaned and pushed her plate away. "I'm stuffed. I can't have another even though I really want to. You were right, they are delicious but you have the rest."

"But you only had three. You sure?"

"I am sure. I already had to loosen my pants – there's a lot of meat on those things."

"I won't say no. I could eat a dozen more."

"You could not. You'd burst. There's no way you could fit that much food in that flat tummy of yours."

Aurora gave Evie a toothy grin. "I'd make space."

Shaking her head in disbelief Evie got up to inspect her makeshift clothesline. "I think our clothing is dry enough. If we leave it out it will just get dew-soaked overnight."

Her mouth full of food Aurora merely nodded and watched as Evie folded their clothing, laying her neat pile on her rucksack with the underwear on top. She couldn't be sure but she thought there was something very deliberate in the way Evie smoothed her briefs and fingered her bra and she felt her cheeks heat at having another woman handle her underwear that way. Although to be fair she'd once washed Evie's clothing, under things and all, so she was probably just returning the favor.

"I'll go get bedding to put under your sleeping bag as insulation as soon as I'm done eating. It will get cold tonight."

"You don't have to do that. I've already made our beds," Evie said and pointed at the place Aurora had mentioned as a good spot for them to sleep.

Craning her neck to look, Aurora saw their bedding laid out together on a thick nest of greenery. She turned to stare at Evie.

"Don't look so surprised. My hands aren't made of porcelain. I live in a tower, not a castle. I know my wilderness skills are rusty but it's coming back to me and I've been watching how you do things. Besides, you spoiled me with that soft bed last night and I couldn't stand to sleep on the hard rocky ground after that."

"I'm impressed. Everything you've done is very helpful."

Evie's face broke into a pleased smile. "Partners remember? I can't let you do all the work. I want to feel like I'm contributing my share. If I have to keep us fed we'll starve unless there happens to be another beehive in the area but this..." Evie spread her arms to indicate the fire and their beds, "I can do."

***

Aurora eased herself onto the sleeping mat next to Evie and marveled at how springy their little nest felt. Evie had really put in some effort.

"Aurora?"

"Yes?"

"Why don't we share the sleeping bag again? There's no reason for me to have it all to myself while you huddle under just a cloak right next to me. Look, there's more than enough room." Evie held open one side to show Aurora the space beside her. "You said yourself it's going to get cold tonight so it will be so much warmer for both of us if we sleep together."

Unsure how to respond, Aurora fiddled with her cloak. She'd love to have Evie's warm body pressed against hers and the thought of Evie lying draped across her again like she did the first night made her body respond in unsettling ways. That was why she could not get into that sleeping bag with her. If it was a wide bed she could manage by scooting to the edge of the bed to allow space between them. In the confines of the sleeping bag she'd be struggling with herself all night long to keep her hands to herself and not 'accidentally' brush against parts of Evie she had no business thinking about, never mind touching. That would mean she'd get little or no sleep and she was tired. The previous night she'd gotten less than an hour's sleep before the nightmare started and she had barely managed to wake herself before it got to where she no longer knew she was dreaming and had to endure the horrors it brought. Afterwards, she couldn't go back to sleep and had spent the rest of the night looking at the moon, thinking dark thoughts and feeling frustrated that the dreams had started again. She'd hoped it had finally stopped but she wasn't surprised the nightmare was back as it returned like clockwork for days on end every time she dealt with something that reminded her of the things that happened to her when she was a child. She had ached to shift and go for a run in the cool dark forest hoping it would bring her relief but she had promised Evie she would stay by her side. At first she'd felt resentment, stark and bitter, at having to watch over the sleeping woman when the forest called to her as it did. Gradually, hearing Evie's deep even breathing and knowing it was her presence that kept Evie's fears at bay so she could sleep so peacefully, soothed her more than any run would have. She wasn't able to keep her own terrors at bay but at least she could do it for someone else.

"Aurora?"

She noticed Evie was still holding open the sleeping bag, an expectant look on her face. She lay down close to Evie and zipped her bag back up most of the way. "You made us a lovely warm nest and I'll be comfortable right here next to you." Seeing Evie about to protest she quickly added, "I'm a light sleeper, more so when I'm out in the open like this. I'll be awake and prowling about at the slightest suspicious sound and I don't want to wake you every time I get up."

"You aren't staying with me?"

"It will be a bright clear night once the full moon rises. I don't plan to leave you but if I need to investigate something I promise I will stay close enough to hear if you whisper my name."

"Oh. Okay." The disappointment in Evie's voice was palpable.

Aurora felt a little bad about the half-truth but it was way better than blurting out, "You'd make me too horny to sleep."

They lay side by side watching the colors change and fade to shades of grey as night descended over the lake. It was as the last flickers of light disappeared that Aurora heard Evie pull the zipper down a little and she automatically put her hand where Evie could find it. This time instead of merely grabbing hold of her wrist Evie drew Aurora's hand inside the warmth of the sleeping bag and kept it there cradled between her palms. Despite how used to Evie's casual physical affection she'd already become, it was still startling to feel Evie's thumb stroke the side of her hand. Unlike when they first met she no longer felt the desire to pull away, actually quite the opposite. She'd come to enjoy Evie's touch, in fact, she secretly looked forward to it. This caress sent warm tingles all the way up her arm and she'd never been so aware of the nerve endings in her own hand in her entire life. It felt so good, it was embarrassing how much she wanted Evie to keep touching her. It had been so long since anyone reached for her or held any part of her with such gentle affection. She didn't want to count how many years it had been since she'd had a girlfriend, it was too depressing. It was no wonder she was drawn to Evie's warmth. She was so lovely Aurora occasionally caught herself staring, mesmerized by the beautiful woman in her company. It was a stupid thing to do but she couldn't help it – she allowed herself to fantasize what it would be like to have Evie caress her all over. The thought brought such a flush of heat to her face and other parts of her body that for once she was grateful Evie couldn't see in the dark.

***

It was around midnight when Aurora clawed her way to wakefulness just ahead of the nightmare chasing her. She woke with the taste of blood on her tongue and she barely managed to put a hand over her mouth to smother the sound of her scream. It was close, too close. She almost didn't make it out in time, just a few seconds more and she wouldn't have been able to stop the dream sequence. Her heart hammered in her chest and her stomach filled with the acid dread of the horror she'd barely escaped. She quietly crawled out from under the cloak and away from Evie. She felt awful but at least Evie didn't wake up to see the state she was in.

A stone's throw away from their camp she sagged down against a tall rock, pulled her knees up to her chest and stared up at the moonlit sky trying her best not to think of the nightmare despite the after-effects lingering like a bad taste. After all this time and the countless repeats of the nightmare it shouldn't still affect her so badly but wishing it wasn't so changed nothing.

She allowed her eyes to drift across the stars tracing the patterns that formed familiar constellations. It was an old ritual and she found it soothing to recall the names of individual stars and the myths of how the constellations came to be. There were so many tales of great battles and epic quests, of lovers lost and reborn as other things and even more tales of the people who lived their lives bound to those stars or the moon in some way. She still fondly remembered the stories her father told her while they walked under the starry skies. After he died and she traveled the night alone she would retell herself those stories over and over trying to recall the exact inflection of his voice. She used to comfort herself with the memory of his huge hands resting gently on her shoulders while he waited patiently for her to point out which stars they ought to follow to get where they were going. It became a hobby of sorts to gather more stories wherever she went. She scoured books and happily sat down to listen to old men and women recall the things taught them by their own elders. In this way, she'd gathered a strange treasure trove of stories that were a mix of myth, legend, and religion. When she came across an interesting or funny story she always wished her dad was still around so she could share it with him. Despite her best efforts his voice had become a dull echo years ago but at least she could still remember his laughter. It was a deep, rumbly, joyful sound that had made her smile no matter how grumpy she felt. What she wouldn't give to hear her dad laugh like that one more time.

Aurora sighed and tucked a strand of hair behind her ear. What would her dad have thought of Evie? Would he have liked her? Probably, because Evie was easy to like. He wouldn't have cared that she was an avian. Her father judged people on how they conducted themselves, not based on species or magical lineage. It was this open-mindedness that allowed him to fall in love with her mother despite the hatred between their people. Would Evie have liked her father? Would she have enjoyed his stories as much as Aurora did? Would she find it fascinating to hear myths and legends or would she find it silly and uninteresting, something only fit to entertain children? If Evie pestered her for another story as she did on the mountain, she'd test Evie's reaction by telling her one of her favorites. It was a story from the human world about a moon goddess who fell in love with a fisherman and pretended to be an ordinary girl to win his heart. It was funny and sweet as well as a little sad and definitely too adult to be a children's story.

Aurora caught a flicker of movement out of the corner of her eye. Turning her head she saw a cluster of stars momentarily obscured by shadows drifting past. She knew what they were before she saw the massive wings. She quickly moved under cover keeping a wary eye on the dragons. She expected them to fly past but they headed to the lake and she soon realized they would be there a while. She quietly made her way back to Evie to wake her so she could see what the dragons were doing. This was too good to miss. It would beat the best story she could tell Evie hands down. If this didn't impress Evie, nothing would.

***

"Evie, wake up."

"Is it time to get up already?" Groggily Evie rose on one elbow and wiped at her face to clear the fog from her mind.

"Hush…keep your voice down," Aurora whispered.

"What's wrong?" she whispered back.

"Do you want to see dragons?"

"Dragons? Here?" Her voice came out as a squeak.

"Yes. They are over the lake."

"Is it safe?"

"Nothing is safe around dragons but if we're careful they won't notice us. They're preoccupied."

"Feeding?"

"Breeding."

That made Evie wrinkle her nose. "Um…I'm not sure I'm up to watching that. But out of curiosity are they doing it as people or winged and scaly?"

"They aren't having sex, not yet anyway. I meant they are doing a mating dance. It's done in flight and quite impressive to see. I thought since you can also fly you'd appreciate seeing something so rare."

"Yes, that I definitely want to see."

Evie didn't know there was such a thing as a dragon mating dance but then she knew very little about living breathing dragons. The stories she'd heard focused heavily on their might and were vague on dragon romance and how they produced offspring. Presumably because no one has been brave enough to ask an actual dragon something so intimate and lived to talk about it. Excitedly Evie extracted herself from the sleeping bag. She was as eager as a child who'd just been told she was about to see something as mythical but infinitely scarier than Santa Clause do something a lot more interesting than climb down a chimney.

Aurora grabbed the sleeping bag and made them crawl to a small outcropping covered by soft grass and dwarfish trees. She got Evie to lay down next to her then unzipped the dark sleeping bag quietly and drew it over them like a blanket making a point of covering their heads. Evie tried to push her head out but Aurora stopped her.

"It's camouflage. Your blond hair is bright in the moonlight and dragons have incredible eyesight. We need to get you a hat."

"Oh."

Evie settled with her head on her arms and looked out at the world from under the material shelter. The moon hung full and bright in the clear sky, not a single cloud across the canopy of stars. Under it the lake looked like a silver pool. It was such a perfect reflection of the world above that it was hard to tell where the one ended and the other began. The air was so still it felt like the world was holding its breath and it was so quiet that even the slightest sound seemed as loud as the ringing of a bell. It was a storybook sight. She herself would have loved to fly on a night as clear and bright as this when everything below was cast in eerie shadow giving familiar landscapes an otherworldly feel, like she had awoken to find the place she thought she knew altered to adjust to the secret life it led at night. It was magical.

Evie leaned in to speak quietly in Aurora's ear, "It's beautiful."

"Yes, it is." Aurora's reply was a warm whisper of breath against her cheek and the way it made Evie's heart skip a beat was a different sort of magic.

"Where are they?"

Aurora gently tilted Evie's face to the right and she saw two dark shadows over the surface of the lake. The dragons flew so close together their wings almost touched. As they came past Evie heard the whoosh of their giant wings, saw the gleam of the moonlight on their scales and the way they took turns to skim the tip of a wing or clawed toe into the silvery water casting a fine spray that glittered with the light of a thousand stars. The dragons flew the length of the lake until it curved out of sight between the mountains then they rose straight up into the sky while circling each other in a complicated ballet. Once they were high enough they dipped back towards the lake until they once again flew side by side, so close to the surface of the lake they almost skimmed the water. Their movements were so well coordinated that Evie could see why Aurora called it a mating dance. It was like the dragons flew in tune to a song that only they could hear and their dance was a graceful display of precision and power.

"Wow…that is…just wow. They are magnificent. What a privilege to see this, thank you, Aurora. That's an impressive flight pattern. I'm surprised something that huge can maneuver so well, especially so close to the water."

"Probably better to do that over the lake than close to the ground. At least here if they make a mistake it will only mean a swim."

Evie imagined one of the great dragons tumbling head over wing into the lake in an undignified splash and it made her grin. She bumped Aurora's shoulder and whispered, "I'd pay to see that."

The dragons performed a move that made it look like they were embracing mid-flight mimicking each other's moves so closely they became a singular giant shadow. Evie heard Aurora sigh, it was a deep heavy sound in the enclosed space they shared. Curious she tilted her head so she could watch Aurora watch the dragons on their next pass. To her surprise, she saw longing in Aurora's unguarded expression. Evie had seen a similar look on the faces of people staring up at her as she flew past. It was a yearning for something they could never experience.

"When my wing is healed we should go for another flight. I'll take you up so you can feel what it is like to glide on the wind."

Aurora gave her a small smile. "That's kind of you." She inclined her chin towards the dragons in the distance circling upwards again. "Does that make you want to fly?"

"Yes, but definitely not with them."

Aurora showed white teeth in the moonlight. "That wouldn't be wise. It would be like going for a swim with sharks." After a moment she added, "Especially right now. Who knows what kind of appetizer those lusty dragons would make out of you, young pretty thing that you are."

Evie clamped a hand over her mouth to silence her giggles. "Dragon sandwich…eeew. Don't make me laugh," she whispered urgently. Beside her she felt Aurora shake in her own fit of quiet laughter.

"That male is so large he dwarfs the poor female. Not that she's small but there is definitely a size discrepancy there. Hopefully, their bodies are more evenly matched when they take their human form or she's going to be squashed."

Aurora playfully elbowed Evie and said, "That's an image I could have lived without. For the record, the larger one is the female. Female dragons are always larger than males of the same age."

"They are?"

"Yes, I know this for a fact."

They were silent for a while watching the incredible display as two of the most powerful creatures in Nordarra playfully courted.

"Aurora, this has turned into a truly memorable evening. I'll never forget this. I thought dragons were almost extinct and now here are two of them right in front of us. I wish my sister could see this. I've only seen one before tonight and only from far away."

"There are still plenty of dragons. They are not as numerous as they used to be but they're far from extinct. They just prefer isolated places and those who live among those not of their kind try to blend and hide what they are."

"Why?"

"Same reason any great predator with intelligence tries to blend in when it's outnumbered. People hunt what they fear, Evie and even ancient powerful dragons can be killed. It is better to pretend to be a sheep and graze peacefully among the flock than to proclaim to be a lion and have every trophy hunter in existence on your trail night and day."

"How do you know this?"

"It's logical when you think about it. Besides..." Aurora tapped her nose, "I can spot a dragon even in human form. There are more around than you think."

Evie sighed and said wistfully, "They are magnificent. What an honor it would be to fly with them. It's a shame they are such arrogant assholes."

"I couldn't have said it better myself."

"You know so much more about dragons than I do. Have you spoken with one?"

Aurora was quiet so long Evie thought she might not have heard her.

"I have."

"What was that like?"

Aurora turned her head to look at the dragons and then back at Evie. The moonlight reflected in her eyes and for a moment they shone with an eerie amber luminescence. "Memorable."

They stared at each other their breath mingling in the closeness. Evie waited for Aurora to say more. When enough time passed that it became clear she didn't intend to elaborate Evie briefly touched Aurora's cheek.

"I bet there's quite a story behind that one word. Maybe you will tell me one day?"

"Perhaps."

The dragons continued their breath-taking aerial ballet, a thing of beauty only rivaled by the magnificence of the giants themselves. It was such a rare spectacle that Evie told herself she would watch as long as the dragons were there but it had been a long tiring day and it was so cozy under the sleeping bag with Aurora's warm body against her side. Eventually, she gave up the fight and allowed herself to drift off.

***

When Evie woke in the early morning hours to the sound of birds singing their own version of the dawn song she found Aurora asleep beside her. She lay very still not wanting to wake her. She'd seen for herself how the smallest sound could wake the woman from her light sleep and she relished the rare opportunity to look at Aurora openly. She studied Aurora's profile, saw the flickering under her eyelids indicating she was dreaming. She watched the slow steady rise of her chest and thought that as amazing as it had been to witness the dragon's mating dance it was even better to wake up next to this amazing woman. It was a shame they weren't waking in each other's arms and with a lot less clothing but she would take what she could get.

In her sleep Aurora's hair had escaped the hair tie to fan out around her head and shoulders. Her hair looked wild, thick and silky. It reminded Evie of the luxurious fur on the long-haired cat her mother owned when she was a child. She'd been fascinated with the aloof creature and would play with it whenever it would let her. When it climbed into her lap and lay there purring while she stroked its fur she had felt inexplicably happy. Looking at Aurora's hair she had the same childlike urge to touch and rub her face against it to see what that would feel like. Evie smiled thinking how awkward it would be if Aurora woke to find her doing that. However, nothing prevented her from breathing in Aurora's scent while she lay so close. She didn't have Aurora's sense of smell but she'd been near her often enough to recognize Aurora's tantalizing scent. It reminded her of a fine wine in that it was layered and seemed to change subtly depending on Aurora's mood. She smelled of spice, heated caramel and sometimes Evie thought she caught traces of something that reminded her of incense. She knew for a fact Aurora didn't wear perfume and from borrowing her soap she knew it didn't smell of anything so all of that must be her. She must have made a noise or perhaps her prolonged study was enough to rouse her bed mate because Aurora's eyes flew open. Instantly alert she scanned for danger.

"It's all right, it's just me." Evie put a soothing hand on Aurora's cheek and when she turned to stare at her Evie added, "We both dozed off."

Evie yawned, stretched and noted with interest the way Aurora watched her and how her eyes lingered on the swell of Evie's breasts as she stretched before she averted her gaze.

"We slept together again." Aurora sounded like she was talking to herself rather than to Evie. She looked bewildered, like she had just seen a flying deer and wasn't sure she could believe her eyes.

"So? We are traveling together and sleeping like this is a great way to keep each other warm."

"You're right but I'm not used to falling asleep like this next to someone and I slept so soundly."

"It doesn't bother me at all. I'm used to sharing. My cousins have sleepovers and my sister used to sneak into my bed for years when she was little. She was such a sweet cuddly little thing I didn't mind that she wanted to sleep with me but as soon as she got her wings I told her it had to stop."

"Why?" Aurora rolled onto her side and propped her head on her palm, a curious expression on her face. A lock of dark hair tumbled across her cheek and Evie tucked it behind Aurora's ear, marveling at the silky feel.

"My sister is a restless sleeper. She would stretch her wings in her sleep and whack me in the face so I looked like someone beat me up. I had to crawl out of my own bed because she made it a health risk to stay. Besides, by that time I wanted different company in bed. I didn't want my little sister sneaking into my bedroom and catching me in the act."

"Your family sounds so close it must be nice."

"Most of the time. They are also very opinionated and it's infuriating when they can't keep their noses out of my business."

"Even with that drawback I can't help but envy you, Evie."

"Don't you have family?"

"I do but I'm an outcast. My parent's bonding was very unpopular with both sides as there was bad blood between their people. To make matters worse my parents were supposed to pick mates from among their own kind to continue honored bloodlines. Instead, they chose to be together and had me. Things were so bad they had to make a home in the middle of nowhere to be together. As you can imagine I'm not exactly welcome at family gatherings."

"Aurora, I'm so sorry to hear that."

"Don't be. I've known nothing different and at this point in my life I don't give a fuck about the disapproval of people I don't know. I think family only counts as family if they treat you as such. Otherwise, they are just blood-related strangers."

"I suppose…but that can't be pleasant."

"Let's talk about something more pleasant than my relatives. Food. How do you feel about hot porridge sweetened with honey and tea for breakfast?"

"That sounds lovely."

CHAPTER 10

FACING WOLVES

They'd been making their way around the edge of the lake for over an hour when Aurora said, "I need to talk to you about something."

"What is it?"

"We will reach our first destination this morning. In fact, we're close now."

"Are you finally going to tell me who you're meeting?"

"Do you see how the lake bends just ahead?"

"Yeah?"

"Around that corner is a bay and on the other side of the lake a large wolf-shifter village. That's where I'm heading as my meeting is with Yutu, their retired chief."

Evie stopped walking. "That could be a problem. Wolves are not fond of avians last time I checked."

"No, and this clan has a huge grudge. So here's the thing…do you want to wait here while I go to my appointment or come with me?"

"What will happen if I come with you? Will I get chewed on?"

"No. You most certainly will not," Aurora said with such heat that Evie gave her a second look.

"You can protect me?"

"Yes. They will not touch you once I make it clear you're with me."

"In that case lead the way. Waiting around twiddling my thumbs for who knows how long seems a waste of time, especially if you have to backtrack to come get me."

"Evie, if you're coming with me we need to go over some basic ground rules. I know you had a wolf for a godfather and you said he taught you how to interact with beast-shifters but you seem to have gaps in your education. It doesn't matter when it's just you and me but there are things you really need to know before we head into the village. First rule: whatever happens, don't run and don't make sudden movements.

The ones who carry their beast too close to the surface won't be able to resist chasing something that acts like prey."

"*Everyone* knows that. That's common sense when dealing with predatory shifters."

Aurora ignored Evie's eye roll and kept going. "Next rule: don't look any of the dominants directly in the eye but don't look down either. You are not a submissive and you're not in their clan. As for your ranking, because you are with me you are under the mantle of my status. I have high status with clan Swift Foot and I do not submit to anyone, not even their chief. If anyone tries to scare you act like you've been hanging out with a bigger, meaner predator and that you're unimpressed with the posturing because that's all it will be. The wolves won't dare hurt you and risk antagonizing me. It will help that you've been wearing my clothing and we've been living so close together. At the moment my scent is on you and that in itself will make a statement and give you extra protection. Even if we get separated one sniff will make it clear to the wolves you're with me."

"Aurora…*have* I been hanging out with a bigger, meaner predator?"

"In comparison to a wolf? Definitely. I don't like to rub it in their faces that my beast is more powerful but I can't allow a direct challenge either, not from them or any other beast-shifter as it would be seen as a sign of weakness. The wolves know what will happen if they try to play dominance games with me so we shouldn't have to deal with that nonsense. If they need a reminder, I'll have to put on the sort of show they understand and respect. Act like you've seen it before, play along. It's important that whatever happens you don't show fear."

Evie was quiet for a while, a thoughtful expression on her face. "You told me the men who killed your father were interrupted before they could finish harvesting. Who stopped them? Was it you?"

Aurora's expression became grim. "Yes, I went back and took care of those who remained. The ones tasked with finishing up and clearing the evidence."

"How? You were just a kid so how did you…I mean…" Evie faltered. "I'm so sorry I shouldn't have brought that awful business up. Me and my big mouth *again*."

"It's all right. I understand it may be hard to believe. I hunted them in beast form, not as a child. It was a dark night and I took my time."

Evie grappled with the thought of a traumatized eleven-year-old girl returning to the horrendous scene she'd just escaped, to kill the hunting party of grown men who'd murdered her father, a mature tiger-shifter. What tremendous strength of will Aurora must have possessed at that age to force herself to go back when she must have wanted to hide or keep running. And just how powerful was Aurora's beast that she was able to do something like that and apparently had the respect of a wolf-clan? Curious, Evie studied the tall woman beside her.

"Aurora, will you please allow me to see your beast? Not right now obviously but when you're in the mood to show me?"

Aurora stopped to stare at her. She looked taken aback by the bold request. "No. I don't want you to see me like that."

"Why not?" Evie stubbornly persisted.

Aurora frowned and started walking again and for the first time since they met Evie had to jog to keep up with her. She'd clearly rattled her. She was about to apologize for being so pushy when Aurora slowed down and said, "Because…I'd like you to keep thinking of me as just another woman who, like you, happens to be a shifter. I like the way you treat me. Once you've seen my beast form you may not be so relaxed with me anymore. I've found people don't look at me the same once they've seen me like that and I'd hate for you to be afraid of me because of what I can become."

"I can handle it," Evie assured her. "I've seen beast-shifters in their altered form countless times. I can guarantee I won't act like a scared rabbit just because you go furry in front of me."

"Perhaps. However, you are not the first to say that to me and I'm not keen on history repeating itself. We still have a long road ahead of us and it would be miserable for both of us if it turns out the sight of my beast is too much for you."

Evie huffed and said, "You worry needlessly. You turn into a tiger, not a dragon or some kind of mythical monster. I have seen tigers before. It was from above and I don't think they were shifters but how different can it be? I don't know who these wimpy people were who scared so easily but don't insult me by assuming I'll act the same without even giving me a chance."

Aurora cocked her head and studied Evie thoughtfully. "You are fierce when you're annoyed. Fine, you made your point."

"Does that mean you will show me your beast?"

Aurora snorted a laugh, "*Very* persistent too."

"Well?"

"Maybe. I won't make a show of myself just to find out how much you can handle."

"Fair enough but if a situation comes up that requires you to shift you will let me see? *Please*?" Evie begged.

"You are like a burr in the fur once you get your mind set on something; you're really hard to shake." Aurora tried to sound exasperated but there was a hint of amusement in her tone. "All right...*if* I have to shift then I'll let you see."

"Excellent!" Evie grinned like she'd just won a prize. "Now I *almost* hope the wolves act like assholes so you have to shift to put them in their place."

Aurora shook her head and laughed.

***

Aurora called a halt once they were in sight of the wolf-shifter village on the other side of the lake. Huts and wooden building sprawled amidst trees stretching along a good portion of the shore and by the look of things into the tree-clad mountainside behind it. Aurora took a deep breath and gave a piercingly loud whistle. A moment later there was a whistle from the other side followed by multiple howls.

"What happens now?" Evie asked.

"Now we wait. They won't be long."

Aurora was right. It wasn't long before a single rowboat made its way across the lake towards them.

"They're collecting us by boat?"

"Yup. There's no other way across and I don't feel like swimming."

"The feeling is mutual."

Evie sat down next to Aurora on the rock she was using as a seat. Close enough that their legs and arms touched. She was probably too close but she liked being near Aurora as her presence was reassuring and she needed a little bolstering ahead of going into the wolf village. Seeing Aurora's questioning look she said, "I want to make sure your scent remains fresh. You said smelling like you will help keep the wolves off me. I'm all for that."

Aurora's smile was amused. "I did say that."

Together they watched as the boat drew nearer, the woman at the oars propelling the little vessel through the water with strong strokes. On the other side of the lake Evie could see a steadily growing crowd on the pier. For some reason the gathering crowd stirred an old memory. It reminded Evie of how people gathered around the body of an avian who'd been mauled to death by a wolf-shifter gone feral. From a block away she'd seen the tip of a blood-soaked wing poking up into the air like a flag on a battlefield. Her friends had begged her to stay back with them and wait for the adults to investigate but she'd been drawn to that wing and had rushed over terrified it might belong to a family member or friend. Thankfully, it hadn't been but she recognized the victim. It was the handsome avian boy who'd flirted with her and her friends while they were having cold drinks at a rooftop restaurant less than an hour before. It had been a massive shock to see that same boy sprawled on his back with his neck torn open, huge chunks of flesh missing from his chest and his beautiful wings that she'd openly admired a mangled, broken mess of bone and feather.

Evie felt her mouth go dry and she struggled to swallow. She reached into her pack for her water bottle but all the while she kept an eye on the approaching boat and the wolf-shifter coming to transport them to the other side. Evie realized Aurora was watching her carefully, her expression concerned.

"Evie, do you know the woman in the boat? Has she harmed you?"

Evie didn't think she had shown any outward signs of distress but Aurora, ever observant, noticed something was wrong. "It's nothing. Just a bad memory."

"Of wolves?"

"Yes. But not something that happened to me. Something I saw."

"It scared you?"

"It gave me nightmares for a long time."

Aurora grimaced. "I hate nightmares." She leaned back on the rock, one arm behind Evie so her shoulder braced the other woman's back. Not one to waste an opportunity Evie relaxed against Aurora, allowing the warmth of her nearness to chase away the chill brought on by the bad memory.

"Evie?"

"Yes?"

"Don't be afraid. If someone dares to bare a fang at you I will rip it out and give it to you as a souvenir."

Evie quietly pondered this, as the comment was somewhat disturbing and yet reassuring. She didn't know if Aurora could or would do such a thing but she understood it was her way of telling Evie she would keep her safe and she did feel safe with her. So safe that on Aurora's word alone she was about to do the inconceivable – she was going wingless into a den of wolves.

***

The woman who came to pick them up was pretty with skin the color of polished bronze. She had long black hair that flowed loosely around her shoulders and brown eyes that shone with a lust for life. She let her eyes roam over Aurora's body in open appreciation and gave her a sly smile that said in her mind they'd just fucked each other's brains out and she was ready for round two. Evie stole a glance at Aurora to gauge her reaction at being appraised like she was a piece of prime steak that the woman was eager to get her teeth into. Aurora didn't return the smile, her face an unreadable mask. Evie couldn't tell if she was oblivious to the other woman's interest or ignoring it. Either way, there was no encouragement in that look.

"Aurora, it's good to see you again. We've been expecting you."

"Aisha. Thank you for the transfer."

"My pleasure and it means we finally get to talk. I seem to miss you every time you are here. You're not avoiding me, are you? Who's the girl with you? Everyone is dying to know."

"This is Evie, my friend and traveling companion."

Her smile lukewarm Aisha turned her attention on Evie. She let her eyes wander over Evie's body and her smile brightened. Then her nostrils flared and anger replaced the spark of interest.

"She's an avian!" Aisha hissed. "How can you travel with *that*?" Aisha pulled a face like she smelled something rotten.

"I am aware she's an avian. Like I said Evie is my friend and you would do well to remember that and consider carefully what you say next."

Aurora got into the boat and held out a hand to Evie. She seated her in the back then placed herself between Aisha and Evie blocking their view of each other.

"Aurora, please," the woman protested in a low whine, "I can't take an avian across. Nesa will have my pelt!"

"You are not taking an avian across, you're taking me. Evie happens to be with me. Don't overthink this, Aisha."

"But—"

"Are you tired? Is a delicate avian woman too much extra weight for you? Would you prefer I row? Or better yet would you like to get out and wait for someone to collect you?"

"No, of course not!"

"Then please, get going." Aurora had spoken politely but there was no mistaking the steely command in her voice.

Wordlessly Aisha lowered the oars to the water and they were underway. Not another word was said. Even though Evie couldn't see Aisha's face she could feel her seething. She didn't blame her. Aisha just had her fangs pulled with such ruthless efficiency she was probably still trying to figure out what just happened.

They docked between fishing vessels offloading the night's catch. They had to scoot around a long table where people were quickly cleaning the fish while others carried it off to a large smokehouse. That explained all the people she saw streaming towards the pier, Evie thought. The gathering crowd wasn't there for them but had come for the fish. Her relief was short lived however because as they passed nostrils flared, knifes paused and heads turned to track their progress. She found it utterly unnerving. Aurora, on the other hand, seemed unfazed. She said hello to people in passing and her stride remained confident and purposeful. All the while she made sure Evie was right beside her.

At the end of the pier a woman with hair cropped Mohawk style, skin the color of light chocolate and the lean, wiry build of someone who did a lot of running prowled up and down. Her eyes were glued to them and she was very agitated. She was right in the path of the people going back and forth between the long table and the smokehouse but she didn't veer from her route. It was the workers who carefully stepped around her, taking care not to get in her way. Aurora came to a halt about six feet from her and watched her pace. The woman rocked to a standstill and snapped out, "You're late."

"No, I am not." Aurora's voice was calm but firm. "This is the date Yutu told me to be here."

The woman looked at Aurora's eyes and what she saw there must have belied Aurora's calm outward appearance because she quickly averted her own. "No, you're not late but I really wish you had come sooner."

"What is wrong, Nesa? Has something happened to your grandfather?"

The woman sagged a little, concern and fatigue tempering the fierce spark. "While he slept he had a stroke. It was bad. He's healed some but he still can't walk. Since it happened he won't go to sleep and he keeps saying over and over he's waiting for you."

"How long?"

"Four days since it happened."

"He's remained awake that long?"

Nesa nodded. "He's been taking things to keep him awake that young wolves in their prime only use sparingly. It has not been kind on him."

"He's afraid he won't wake," Aurora said with understanding. "What a terrible strain to deny himself the thing he needs most to heal."

"We tried to find you, left word where we could. I even sent one of our fastest runners to your mountains but he hasn't come back yet. Have you seen him?"

"We wouldn't have crossed paths as I came from a different direction. I would have been here earlier but I had unexpected delays."

"Was the avian one of your delays?" Nesa just about spat the words. "Aurora, how could you bring one of their kind into our village? How could you break our trust like this?"

"I have not broken trust by bringing her here. You don't know why the avian is with me and yet you rush to judge. Considering how long we've known each other that is disappointing. That aside let me be clear – I will spend time with whoever I please. This woman is my friend and under my protection. You would do well to remember that and make sure this is understood. If Evie is harmed in any way I will take it very badly."

Nesa's head whipped back like she'd been slapped, her eyes narrowed in fury and she bared her teeth in a snarl. "You would threaten us over an avian? A sky killer, a pup stealer, an accursed body dealer?"

Aurora took a step towards Nesa and as she did she seemed to grow larger. A curious crowd had gathered during her conversation with Nesa and Aurora was already taller than most of the people but now she seemed to tower over them. The air around her hummed and there was a faint shimmering on the edges that was disorientating to look at. Evie fought not to take a step back and feigned being relaxed for all she was worth. Any show of fear right now would be like blood in the water to the people watching them, escalating an already dangerous situation. Aurora had warned her she might have to remind the wolves of her dominance. She wasn't sure exactly what Aurora was doing but it definitely made a powerful statement. She could feel the disturbance in the space around Aurora like there was something else there, something eager to expand into it. She knew without Aurora having shifted as much as a hair on her head to reveal her beast that she was in the presence of a very powerful and dangerous shapeshifter. Judging by the submissive body language and wary looks of the onlookers they were acutely aware of this and didn't want to see whatever it was emerge.

What *had* she been traveling with? She'd been in the presence of many different shapeshifters and never had she experienced anything like this. Granted, Aurora was the first tiger-shifter she'd ever met but this casual display of power was way beyond what she would have expected. Evie heard a voice in the back of her mind screaming, a primitive reaction to something understood at a subconscious level yelling at her to run, fly, anything just as long as she got away from this thing. She locked her limbs and reminded herself she knew this person. This was the woman who'd carried her down a mountain without complaining, who gave up her sleeping bag so Evie would be warm and kept watch over her while she slept.

"Evie is none of those things."

Aurora hadn't raised her voice but it carried in the sudden quiet and held an edge that made Evie think she was fighting to control her temper.

"Do you really think I would keep by my side such a creature? That I would bring such a deplorable thing into a village with vulnerable little ones? Do you think so little of my judgement? You know my history. You know what I have done to such creatures irrespective of whether they were shifters or just human. Do not paint her with the blood of those she did not slay. She is no more responsible for those things than you are accountable for the killing frenzy of a pack of feral wolves just because you are a wolf-shifter."

Nesa whimpered softly and there was an uncomfortable stirring in the crowd. Aurora took a deep breath like she was calming herself, reeling herself back in. She laid a hand on Nesa's shoulder who, to her credit, only flinched a little.

"I know a great wrong was done to your people as once it was done to me. But this girl is innocent. Her hands are clean. This is Evangeline Aquilar, the daughter of Lord Augustus Aquilar, the first avian leader to publicly oppose the aerial hunts. To this day Evie's flock won't do business with anyone who associates with slavers or cutters and it is not common knowledge but her godfather was a wolf. Evie shares her father's views and since she will be the next ruler of House Aquilar it has made her a target. Her own kind betrayed her and she found herself in a cutter's cage. That was where I found her imprisoned alongside wolves."

Nesa's head tilted up, shock and surprise making her eyes wide. "Truly?"

"Yes. Send word to clan Blood Moon and ask them if Duzan and Asha made it back home. Those were the wolves I set free. After I rescued Evie she repaid me by deflecting with her wing a shot that would have taken me in the chest. Because of that she's earthbound and traveling with me."

Evie bit her lip and wondered if any of the shock she felt registered on her face. She'd been too slow to dodge the projectile and it was unlikely she would have deliberately taken a hit to her wing for a stranger and Aurora probably knew this. As for how and why she ended up a captive she wasn't sure about anything so how could Aurora talk about it with such certainty unless she knew more than she was sharing? But this was not the time to argue. Aurora knew these wolves and she knew how best to spin their story. Already the change in Nesa was remarkable. Gone was the outright hostility and righteous anger. She seemed flustered and shot Evie a curious look.

"I hear your words, Aurora," Nesa said and bowed her head." I apologize for my rude greeting. I let anger get the best of me. Please do not let my lapse of judgement reflect badly on clan Swift Foot. Know you are always welcome among us. Evangeline Aquilar will not be harmed and I grant her hospitality befitting your companion. I offer this as a ruling member of clan Swift Foot."

"Thank you, Nesa. I accept the hospitality of clan Swift Foot. As always, I will conduct myself with restraint while in your territory. Now take me to your grandfather. He's waited long enough."

"He won't be ready to see you. He was explicit about how he wanted to receive you. The preparations won't take long, less than an hour."

"In that case, I'm sure you wouldn't mind providing me and my traveling companion an opportunity to refresh ourselves while we wait. We traveled hard to be here on time."

"Yes, of course. Please follow me."

Nesa led them to a long wooden building on stilts. It had four doors that opened onto a porch and faced the lake.

"These rooms have their own bathrooms and they are for honored guests. You can use the two rooms at the end."

"Thank you. Go see to your grandfather."

Nesa nodded and took off in a loping gait. Taking her cue from Aurora, Evie waited and watched her watching the disappearing woman and scanning the surrounding area. She saw the narrowing of her eyes as four shifters in wolf form appeared around the side of the building. The instant they saw Aurora glare at them they ducked out of view.

Her voice when she spoke was low and quiet, "I think it would be a good idea to stay together for now. Would you mind if I showered in your room?"

"Of course not. Let's go inside."

The room was small but clean and tidy featuring a wooden bed already made up with white sheets and a pretty patchwork blanket. A plump pillow lay precisely in the middle at the top of the bed. On seeing the plush blue chair beside the small table Evie groaned and just about threw herself onto it.

"That bed looks divine. If I wasn't so filthy I'd lie down on it straight away."

Aurora shut the door, gave the bed a passing glance, checked inside the tiny closet then disappeared into the bathroom. She poked her head out a moment later. "I'll shower quickly. Please don't leave the room."

Already busy wrestling off her boots Evie gave her a dismissive wave. "Enjoy your shower; I'm not going anywhere."

Aurora shot her an amused smile and retreated into the bathroom leaving the door open a crack. Evie heard pipes groan a moment before the shower sputtered to life. She thought she heard the other woman moan.

"Is the water hot?"

"It's gloriously warm," Aurora said sounding muffled. "There's shampoo in here too and the soap smells nice."

Evie opened her small pack. She already knew what was in it but she still hoped there would be something else to wear. The only change of clothing she had was her flight jacket, the pants Aurora lent her that were only good for sleeping in and an extra pair of socks. The jacket and socks were clean enough that she wouldn't shudder to wear them but she didn't look forward to it. She was accustomed to changing her clothing several times a day especially when she'd been working in the gardens or laboratory, loving the feel of crisp freshly laundered linens against her skin. At least she would feel more like herself in a jacket tailored to her build rather than Aurora's oversized clothing. She was tall although not as tall as Aurora and where the other woman looked strong her fine avian bone structure made her look almost fragile. The only thing that saved her from looking like a willowy teenager was her feminine curves which some distant ancestor had passed on to her in abundance. Since she was going to have a shower she would wear Aurora's jacket over her own flight jacket. It would hide the open slits designed for her wings and, most importantly, it still carried traces of the other woman's scent. If she could pick up the smell she'd come to associate with Aurora so would the wolves with their highly developed noses. It would give her a little extra insurance. It amused her that she was planning to use Aurora's scent like wolf repellent. Should she tell her? Would she think it was funny? She was the one who'd pointed out her scent would give Evie some protection but maybe she wouldn't find it flattering to be used like the shifter equivalent of bug repellent or worse, she might interpret it as Evie saying she was smelly. She was over thinking. Aurora didn't seem to mind that she sat close to her on that rock to refresh her scent so she would surely understand that after a shower she needed more of the same. Perhaps if she put it like that Aurora would do that scent marking thing where beast-shifters rubbed cheeks. Hmm…what would it be like to rub cheeks with Aurora? She wouldn't mind finding out.

Behind her, the floorboards creaked and Evie felt herself go cold. Turning she made a startled noise on finding right beside her an imposing woman with broad shoulders and a fresh cut that ran across the bridge of her nose. The woman gave her a sharp-toothed sneer, clearly delighted she caught Evie off guard.

"What do you want?"

As soon as Evie spoke the shower turned off. An instant later Aurora strode into the room, the white towel hastily wrapped around under her arms barely reaching to mid-thigh on her tall frame. Her hair was a heavy soaked mass against her back and rivulets of steamy water ran down her arms and legs. Her eyes honed in on the intruder and Evie saw the flash of anger that transformed her green eyes into a swirling mass of amber flame.

The smug smile slid off the woman's face replaced by something between awe and alarm at the sight of the half-naked Aurora bearing down on her. Sleek powerful muscles rippled as she moved and Aurora radiated enough simmering aggression to singe the air.

"Wow…you...I…" The woman cleared her throat and tried again.

"The old man is ready to see you now."

Aurora just kept coming. The woman took an involuntary step backward, her gaze sliding downwards in a show of submission. Realizing what she was doing the wolf's hands curled into fists, she planted her legs and met Aurora's gaze.

"You should—"

Whatever the woman had meant to say she didn't get to finish. Aurora clamped a hand on her shoulder and walked her backward through the open door onto the deck, ignoring the wolf-shifter's protests and attempts to dislodge her hand.

"Always knock and *never* enter without permission. Even a pup knows this."

Aurora gave her a shove and she tumbled gracelessly off the deck, scattering a group of teen girls and a lanky young man walking past. Quietly but firmly Aurora shut the door dimming the sound of the woman's outraged howl and the laughter of the girls. Aurora stayed by the door waiting motionless for long minutes while water pooled around her bare feet, her head slightly tilted as she listened.

Finally, Evie couldn't take it anymore. "What was that about? And why doesn't that door have a key or a latch?"

Not taking her eyes off the door Aurora said, "It's a wooden structure. Not much point having a latch or a lock when you're dealing with creatures who can rip the door off the hinges. A closed door is meant to be just that, closed. As for what just happened? Stupid power games. Wolves are the worst. They're supposed to run as a pack but with all the jostling for position they are constantly nipping at each other to see what will happen. Always testing their strength, always pushing to see how much they can get away with before they are put in their place. Wolves need strong leaders to keep them in check. No wonder their young are always getting into trouble when they go to town."

Staring down at her feet Aurora noted the puddle and swore. "I need another towel." Hurriedly she turned towards the bathroom, two hands clasping the soaked towel as if aware for the first time that the clinging material barely covered her nakedness. As she slipped past Evie her long strides caused the material to bunch up giving Evie an up-close view of a bared hip and a flash of damp thighs. The awareness of Aurora so close, all freshly washed and wet, caused a powerful stirring in her body. Evie licked her lips and imagined her hands stroking up on the inside of those thighs while her tongue lapped up the stray drops from heated skin. She felt heat flush her cheeks. Embarrassed, Evie turned away from staring at the bathroom door, relieved to have a moment to gather herself. The last thing she needed was her new traveling buddy seeing her lustful response to a flash of bare skin. This was ridiculous; she was acting like a horny teenager. Although in her defense Aurora was an exceptional woman with an extraordinary body and she'd have to be made of stone not to wonder what it would be like to bed her.

By the time Aurora came out, already dressed and toweling her wet hair, Evie had her libido more or less under control. All erotic images firmly banished she sincerely hoped Aurora wouldn't smell the residue of her arousal.

"The shower is all yours. Enjoy." Aurora sat down on the seat Evie had just vacated, one leg stretched out and the other bent slightly underneath it.

"Will you be here when I get out or are you going to your meeting now?"

"I'm not going anywhere until you've had your shower. I won't leave you alone in this wooden box that only has one exit if you don't count the tiny windows. I don't like it."

"Does that mean you don't trust the wolves to keep their word? You think someone might attack me?"

Aurora hesitated. "I trust Nesa to keep her word and the pack is honor bound to uphold her offer of hospitality however, something feels wrong. There's tension in the air. I felt it when we came into the village. I thought the wolves were just unsettled because I brought an avian into their midst but now, I'm not so sure. It is possible there's more going on. I did not expect that wolf-bitch to come into a guest's room uninvited, it's simply not done. Outside the room a test or minor challenge directed at me sure, that's normal. The way that wolf sneaked up on you was stalking behavior. She treated you like prey, Evie. Since you were granted protection by a clan leader what she did comes dangerously close to breach of hospitality. So, to answer your question: I trust most of the wolves but not the entire clan and I'm not willing to take risks with your life. It would only take one rogue wolf to hurt you and blood will flow."

"When you told Nesa there would be repercussions if something happened to me, you meant that?"

Aurora frowned at her. "Of course."

"If they injure or…kill me, what would you do?"

"I'd find those responsible and kill them."

"What, just like that?" Evie couldn't keep the disbelief out of her voice. "You'd take the wolves on all by yourself, here, with so many of them?"

Aurora rested her chin on her palm and regarded Evie impassively. "Clan Swift Foot's leaders would be honor bound to give me the guilty ones but if they refused, I'd take them by force. I'd have to – for the sake of my reputation as someone not to be messed with and the safety of everyone who's under my protection. The wolves understand this and they also know they'd have to kill me to stop me from punishing the offenders. It's possible they would try and they may manage it but not without suffering great losses. I'm a beast-shifter too and what I am...let's just say they're no match for me."

"Your tiger form is *that* powerful?"

Aurora sighed wearily. "Evie, I'm not in the mood for a discussion on what I'm capable of. Let's focus on making our brief stay here as uneventful as possible. When we leave this room it's likely we will be separated, at least while I talk to Yutu. You are smart and good with words, much better than me. Use that charm of yours and you're very pretty too so use it all. Remember the things I told you on the way here. Just…stay safe. I've managed to stay on peaceful terms with these shifter neighbors of mine for years even though some of them can be a massive pain in the ass. I'd appreciate it if you didn't put me in a position where I have to kill people I actually like."

"Meaning what? You'd have to kill people you like for someone you don't, just to make a point?"

"That's not what I said. At all. I like you a lot but that's beside the point. Go have your shower. Please go. I need a few minutes of quiet. This place, this conversation, none of it is calming. My beasts are agitated and too close to the surface. I need to be calm when I walk out that door and in control. For everyone's sake."

It wasn't until Evie was under the gloriously hot water, generously lathering herself with soap that it hit her, Aurora had said beasts, not beast. But that wasn't possible? No surely not…she'd never heard of anyone with more than one beast. She must have heard wrong.

***

When Evie came out of the bathroom feeling refreshed after her shower Aurora had her eyes closed, her head lolled back against the chair. She looked so relaxed that if it wasn't for the restless flickering under her eyelids Evie would have thought she had fallen asleep. Quietly she sat down on the bed and fished out her little fold-away brush from her jacket pocket. She'd already dried her long hair until the towel couldn't absorb more moisture so now she set about smoothing the damp tresses with the brush.

Evie became aware of the subtle weight of Aurora's gaze but didn't acknowledge it as she had a feeling Aurora would look away if she caught her staring. She didn't mind Aurora's lingering gaze, in fact, she had to keep herself from arching her back to better display her assets. Feeling a sense of urgency Evie started to braid her gold-blond hair. Soon she had the separate sections in the tight weave that had taken her ages to perfect. It secured her hair with only a few strategically placed clips and she liked how it complimented her facial structure.

There was the sound of wood creaking as Aurora shifted in her chair. "Your hair looks lovely. That pattern is so complicated I don't know how you kept track of all the sections."

Evie smiled. "Did you have a nice little cat-nap?"

"Something of the sort."

"Feeling better?" She looked directly at Aurora this time. Her eyes were their usual dark green with no speck of amber to be seen. She was looking at Evie with a soft wistful expression.

"Yes, thank you. You helped actually. It was soothing watching you brush your hair and braid those patterns."

Evie's smile broadened. "I'm glad." A knock at the door startled her. With regret she saw the mask slip back on Aurora's face and there was coiled predatory energy in the way she rose.

"You ready, Evie?"

She slid off the bed to stand next to Aurora. She felt the absence of her wings like an ache and without them she felt so incomplete and vulnerable, especially now. With her wings she could bowl over several adversaries with a well-aimed strike and launch herself out of reach before they got to their feet. She once saw a warrior with razor-thin blades bound to his wings rip a group of men to bloody shreds with a few quick lashes of his powerful wings. Granted, she didn't have blades on hers but she knew how to use them to deadly effect if she had to. Her father had seen to that. Evie lifted her chin and squared her shoulders, no point dwelling on that now. She may not have her wings but she would not show weakness. She would not appear like prey to a pack of carnivorous predators with an axe to grind. She gave Aurora an affirmative nod and said, "I'm as ready as I'm going to be. Let's do this."

Evie didn't realize her hands were shaking until Aurora took one and squeezed gently. The instant they touched it was like she'd tapped into a live connection and she felt the other woman's steady confidence and the fierce protectiveness directed at her. Instinctively Evie turned her hand over to intertwine their fingers. It felt so right, so good. The trembling in her fingers stilled and she found herself smiling up at the woman beside her. The instant their eyes locked something surged between them. Aurora's eyes flew wide and for several seconds she just stared. Then she angled her body closer so that their sides touched and her free hand pressed into the small of Evie's back. For a breathless moment the way Aurora focused on her lips Evie thought she was about to be kissed but another knock on the door broke the spell and Aurora pulled away.

Aurora shot Evie a toothy grin. "The wolves are at our door. I'll go play another round of 'Who's the top predator?' while you dazzle them with that lethal smile of yours."

Evie popped a hand on her hip and gave Aurora a conspiratorial smile. "I'm right with you, Bad-Kitty. Between your fiendish power and my irresistible charm they won't know what hit them."

Aurora threw her head back and laughed. Still smiling she stalked off to open the door.

On the porch waited Nesa. Towering beside her was a burly man with arms like small tree trunks and eyes the color of a frozen lake, and sandwiched between them the heavy-set female who sneaked into their room. She stood with legs braced wide and a disgruntled scowl on her broad face. Nesa gave Aurora a small bow which she acknowledged with a nod. Nesa's eyes flicked to Evie where she stood slightly behind Aurora and after a moment's hesitation gave her a stiff nod in greeting.

"Aurora, I've brought Tania to apologize. I sent her to deliver a message but I didn't expect her to barge into your room like an untrained pup. She has not been here long and she's still finding her place and learning our ways."

Tania sneered and spat at Evie's feet. "I'm sorry I scared your little avian whore. How's that for an apology?"

Beside Tania the big man moved several feet away, distancing himself.

Nesa sighed and shook her head. "You stupid bitch. Seriously, don't you ever listen? I warned you not to mess with her and like an inbred mutt you lift your leg to piss on Aurora. What happens now is on your own head."

"I'm not scared. I can take her. She just surprised me before." The woman bared her teeth. "This will be fun. Nothing like a good tussle to get the blood flowing."

"Evie?"

"Yes?"

"I have things to say to this ill-mannered wolf. It may get a little ugly and you probably don't want to be around for that. Can you please wait in the room and close the door? I will get you when it's over."

"No. I'll stay. I want to see this. I don't appreciate being called a whore."

"You sure? You just had a shower and washed your hair so I don't want to get blood and fleshy bits all over you."

Evie grimaced. "This is my last clean change of clothing; I had to throw away the last set you got blood on. I'll wait inside but I'm leaving the door open."

As soon as Evie stepped into the room Aurora allowed more of her beast to come to the surface and in a blur of motion she was behind Tania. The look in her amber eyes was terrible but nowhere near as terrifying as the massive paw-like hand that clamped at the back of Tania's head and wrapped all the way around her face and neck. Razor-sharp claws drew blood the instant Tania struggled. She tried to kick Aurora and tore at the fingers encasing her face. In response, Aurora tightened her vice-like grip and lifted her so she balanced precariously on the tips of her toes. This made the woman go still.

"Little wolf..." Aurora's voice was conversation-like and almost pleasant. "When I threw you out of the room I thought that would be enough for you to understand I'm stronger than you and that I don't appreciate your rude behavior. I thought the matter was settled and that we could move on like civilized beings. It seems I wasn't clear enough or perhaps you are too stupid to understand a gentle warning. Listen carefully while I lay things out for you. Evangeline Aquilar is not afraid of you but you should be afraid of me. I understand you are new here. You may have heard about me but you don't seem to know what I am capable of so let me explain things to you. I am not a wolf and I don't tussle for fun or status. If you provoke me into a fight, I *will* kill you. My friend is not fond of bloodshed so that and the bonds of hospitality are the only things that prevent me from crushing your head like a ripe melon for threatening and insulting someone under my protection. However, if you stalk her like prey ever again, even in jest, I will let you find out what your intestines taste like when I feed them to you."

The other paw wrapped around the wolf-shifter's stomach and a claw tapped for emphasis against the hollow of Tania's breastbone.

"Do you understand?"

Tania made a muffled sound, her eyes wide and frantic.

"Oh, I covered your mouth and you couldn't speak? How rude of me. Is that better? What were you trying to say?"

"Yes! Yes, I understand!"

"Are you sure? I would hate to repeat myself. I might lose my temper."

"I'm sorry, it was just a joke!"

Aurora's growl was that of a pissed off tiger. It was a vicious menacing sound that rumbled like thunder, promising pain and death. "No, it's not a joke to call my friend a whore and you spat on her, you mangy mutt!" Aurora lifted the wolf by her head and neck so she dangled in the air and shook her like she weighed no more than a dirty rag. Tania's eyes rolled back in her head and froth oozed past the soundless scream contorting her mouth.

"Apology not accepted. Try again. This time *think* before you speak."

"Aurora? Can I talk to you for a moment?" Evie stood in the doorway. She leaned her hip against the doorframe in a seemingly relaxed pose but her eyes were troubled.

"I'm a little busy right now. What is it, Evie?"

"It is about what you're doing that I want to talk to you about. Please stop, you're killing her."

"I'm not killing her. I'm just making a point."

"It's hard to tell the difference at the moment and we are guests here, remember? It wouldn't be neighborly to accidentally kill someone."

Aurora frowned as she considered Evie's words and she looked at the dangling wolf more carefully. The woman looked terrible. In her anger she must have squeezed harder than she intended. Aurora let go of Tania and she crumpled to the ground in a heap. She clutched her head, coughed and heaved big uneven breaths struggling to get enough air.

Speaking to Nesa Aurora said, "Your wolf is unharmed aside from a bruised ego. The cuts are minor and her larynx will heal in a few days."

Nesa shrugged. "She is alive. If she can't talk for a while she might stay out of trouble long enough to develop some sense. She's a strong fighter who we thought would be a good addition to the pack but I'm having doubts. We need brains as well as brawn. This one challenges *everyone* and she has as little sense as a stag in rut set on fucking anything that looks like it will stand still long enough. It is a miracle she's survived this long." Nesa poked the bleeding woman with a boot. "If my sick grandfather has a setback and isn't able to talk to Aurora today because you wasted precious time by challenging her, I won't be the only one seriously pissed off."

While Nesa spoke, Aurora licked the drops of blood off her claws in a gesture that reminded Evie so much of a cat cleaning its paws it was uncanny. It was fascinating and horrifying all at the same time. She wondered if Aurora was trying to intimidate the wolves or if she wasn't aware she was licking someone else's blood off monstrous claws. Nesa and the male wolf were careful not to make direct eye contact with Aurora but they didn't look disturbed by what she was doing. They either didn't care or they were acting tough. Aurora saw Evie staring and stopped licking. A faint blush colored her cheeks and she instantly shifted her hands back to human shape. Her shoulders hunched a little and she wouldn't meet Evie's eyes.

"Nesa, you didn't tell me that Yutu is so ill you fear he'll have another stroke. If that's the case we need to hurry." Aurora slung her rucksack over her shoulder and motioned for Evie to follow.

"Aurora, your friend can't come. My grandfather wants to see you, no one else. He said it was private business."

"That it is." Frowning Aurora watched the wolf-bitch stagger away. She had a hand on her throat and a furious scowl on her face. "Oswald, if Nesa doesn't need you elsewhere will you please keep Evie company? Maybe show her around while I'm gone?"

"I'm sure the big oaf would love to keep a pretty girl company instead of doing actual work and you don't have to worry he'll misbehave because Oswald is a gentleman. Aren't you Oswald?"

Grinning the big man said, "I'm no gentleman but I know not to act like a jackass and these," he flexed his massive arms so muscles bulged under the skin, "are useful for swatting unruly wolves who need to be reminded we treat our guests and pretty girls in particular with respect."

Nesa snorted and turned her attention back to Aurora. "Your timing is good. A trading caravan arrived early this morning and they should be done setting up by now and ready for business. Your avian could go have a look."

"Evie, does that sound good to you? Want to go see what the traders have? You must need a few things. Just put aside what you want and as soon as I'm done I'll meet you there and I'll settle with them. You and I can work things out later."

"I do need a few essentials but you don't have to pay for me. I have trader coins for an emergency and if that's not enough I can see if they'll accept a token from House Aquilar. My House has a good reputation among traders so I'd be surprised if they turn me down."

Aurora nodded but didn't move to follow Nesa who was impatiently shifting from foot to foot. Seeing how conflicted she looked, Evie left her position at the door to stand beside Aurora and took her hands. She could have touched her arm or shoulder instead but she deliberately went for the hands that just moments before had bloody claws. She was concerned by the look that had crossed Aurora's face when she'd seen Evie watching her lick the blood. It was the same expression she got after she growled at Evie the previous day. Shame and a look that said she feared Evie would run from her. Evie didn't like the pattern she was seeing. It was like Aurora feared Evie would reject her if she saw her beast side. She wanted to show her this wouldn't happen.

"I know how important this is to you, Aurora. Go, I'll be fine."

Aurora stared at their entwined fingers. When she looked up her eyes were dark and her voice low. "Just shout if you need me and I'll come. No matter what I'm doing I will come for you."

Another flicker of current passed between them and again Evie found herself lost in the depths of Aurora's eyes.

"I know you would but that won't be necessary. I'm wingless, not toothless. Besides, I now have a burly handsome wolf as an escort. Go, you're keeping me from shopping. There's a toothbrush with my name on it waiting for me to come and get it."

This made Aurora smile. "See if they have toothpaste too because we need more. You don't seem to understand what it means to use sparingly."

Evie laughed and gave her a little shove. "Off with you. You marched us like a slave driver to get here on time and it would be awful if you missed out on speaking to Yutu because I held you up. Seriously, I don't want that on my conscience."

"I'm very anxious to see him. I'll be back as soon as I can." Aurora gave Oswald a nod and took off at a fast jog leaving Nesa flat-footed and sprinting to catch up.

Evie watched her until she disappeared from sight then turned to Oswald who was openly staring at her.

"What is it?"

"You and Aurora… I've never seen her act like that with anyone. She doesn't normally let people touch her. If one of us tried to do what you just did she would probably bite something off."

"I wouldn't take it personally, Oswald. I'm an avian and no challenge to her whatsoever when it comes to the strength of our bodies, so she doesn't mind me close. Besides, we've been through a lot since we've met. Those kinds of experiences bring closeness."

"She really found you in a cage?"

Evie felt her body stiffen. "Yes. The wolves and me."

"Where?"

"Inside the ethian mine on the other side of the mountain. The cutter's den was hidden so carefully the workers didn't know we were there. I'm still amazed she found us. I don't want to talk about it. It was a bad place and I know how incredibly lucky I am she turned up when she did."

Oswald nodded thoughtfully. "Aurora's hatred for cutters is legendary. No matter where she goes if she catches their scent she'll find their nest and root them out. She has been more effective at stopping that foul business than all those proclamations making it illegal. You're not the only person to owe her your life or thanks for saving a loved one. I too am grateful to her. My cousin went to the city to meet up with a human girl he thought was keen for a walk on the wild side. It was a trap. We thought the horny bastard was just taking his sweet time coming home. It was days before we started looking and by then his trail had gone cold. If it wasn't for Aurora, we wouldn't have found him and the people responsible. She looked in places we never would have thought of and she was relentless. I wish we'd asked for her help sooner."

"Was your cousin still alive?"

"Barely. We brought him home. His body eventually recovered but his mind was never right after that. One day he left to run with the wild wolves and didn't come back. I loved him like a younger brother and I still miss him but even I think that was for the best."

"Wow…that's…I'm so sorry, Oswald."

"That happened several years ago and I didn't tell you this to make you pity me. I said it so you would know I owe Aurora. She was worried about you and she put you in my care so even though you're an avian, I'll tear out fur and break bones to keep you safe."

"That's…a little overwhelming. Um…thank you?"

Oswald grunted and pointed to a cluster of buildings a little way off. "The traders set up behind there. Ready to go see what they have?"

"Yes, please lead the way. I could really do with a pleasant distraction right now."

CHAPTER 11

TAINTED OFFERS

Jogging towards Yutu's cabin Aurora wished she could have taken Evie with her or somehow physically manifested her tiger separate from herself so she could leave it behind to guard Evie. At least she'd done the next best thing and left Evie with someone she trusted. She felt a little bad she'd put Oswald in the position of having to guard an avian against his own people but she couldn't leave Evie unprotected after what happened with the wolf-bitch. Despite how he might feel about avians she knew Oswald would keep Evie safe. He was solid as a rock and if he said he would do something he would. Having him near should deter any of the wolves from nipping at Evie literally or figuratively as he was a respected high-ranking clan member. He wasn't one to look for trouble but he was no submissive. Once provoked he was a vicious fighter who went for the throat, definitely not someone to challenge lightly. She had to think of an appropriate way to thank Oswald for agreeing to protect Evie. He'd let slip the last time they talked that he had a new lover in Porta Belua. Apparently, she had expensive tastes and complained he never took her anywhere nice when he came to visit. She'd heard the new five-star hotel had a couple's package that came with a luxury suite and an all-you-can-eat buffet. She would buy him a voucher for that. Oswald was a man of earthly pleasures who'd appreciate that.

Aurora heard Nesa running hard behind her so she slowed to allow her to catch up. She noticed a large tent being erected in the central clearing to their right and the bustle of activity around it. Pointing toward it she asked, "Is someone getting married in the big tent again?"

Nesa glanced at the tent and quickly away. "No. It's for clan business."

They continued on in silence for a little while. Nesa must have realized how short her answer sounded because she added almost apologetically, "It is being set up for a gathering of the clan followed by a shared feast tonight. There are things that must be discussed. The traders will be confined because we don't want outsiders eavesdropping."

"That sounds serious. As soon as I'm done talking to your grandfather I'll take Evie and go. Fewer outsiders for you to worry about."

"No! Please stay. The clan leaders want to talk to you before the gathering starts."

Aurora schooled her face not to show her dismay at this development. She now had confirmation that the undercurrent she felt since they arrived wasn't her imagination. She'd considered staying the night so Evie could sleep in a proper bed but now she would complete her business quickly so they could leave. She had no desire to get caught up in clan politics. Her dealings with clan Swift Foot had been mostly low key. She would stop to trade at their general store, say hello to a few people she knew, catch up on clan gossip with Oswald if he was around and go see Yutu. Even though Yutu and his life-mate were so much older than her she had found it easier to be around them then the younger wolves with their constant yipping and posturing. She found their company undemanding and filled with thoughtful conversation. The shrewd old wolf would never have tried to make her the center of a surprise gathering as he understood she hated being put on display or feeling cornered. Trying to haul her in front of a meeting of clan leaders like she was a wayward pup was not only insulting, it reeked of ambush. In her experience when a group of people ganged up to ask her for something, they were too invested in the outcome to take it well when she said no.

Aurora sighed inwardly. When she woke this morning the only thing she wanted from the day was to get a solid lead on her father's fang from Yutu. At the rate things were going he would probably have nothing concrete to offer her and she would spend the rest of the day trying to leave without offending the wolves.

"You need to tell me what is going on, Nesa. I don't like surprises. It gets my hackles up."

Nesa hesitated for a moment then said, "We want you to join our clan."

"That's...a surprise. Whose idea was that?"

"Mine but the others agreed with me."

"Why? I'm not a wolf-shifter and you're all wolves. Your clan has always been adamant about keeping it that way."

"It's time for change. It's all well and good for the puritans to say we should stick to our own kind but we are losing curious young wolves who find the old ways too stifling. Some come back once they've sated their curiosity but many don't. My best friend fell in love with one of the tree-folk and wanted to bring her home but couldn't so they settled in a mixed community on the coast. They have three children now with a fourth on the way and I've missed out on being a godmother. It didn't have to be like that." Nesa sighed regretfully. "Clan Swift Foot would have been so much stronger if we'd allowed mixed couples and invited powerful shifters like you to join us over the years. If we had we would not be scraping the bottom of the barrel now trying to add to our fighting strength by bringing in troublemakers like Tania."

Aurora gave Nesa a curious look. "What's happened that you're in such a hurry to add fighters?"

"Black Paw has been encroaching onto our hunting grounds, poaching stock and attacking our people."

"Black Paw? But their base is on the other side of the mountains, closer to Porta Belua. What are they doing all the way out here? I'm sure they have a few good hunters among them but they don't hold to the old ways and they mainly make their living selling out as mercenaries and muscle for hire to the highest bidder. Are you sure it is them?"

"We're sure."

"How bad is it?"

"At first they took only a few deer. We had a talk to them about that and thought it was settled. I think they were just testing to see what we would do and scouting our territory. Then a month ago we got hit with full raiding parties, hard and fast. They broke into the hunting cabins and carried away the meat we'd been gathering for winter. We use the whole animal so nothing is wasted and we sell what we don't need to buy the things we can't make or grow ourselves. They are threatening our livelihood, Aurora. Now we have to hunt and fish more to replace what they have stolen before winter comes which will put stress on our stock. Fishing here is good but only because we have been careful over the years not to take more than we had to. The same with our hunting grounds. It has been carefully tended and we cull out the older animals and weaker males so the females and their young can flourish. Those Black Paw fuckers slaughtered indiscriminately and left good meat to rot. What they did is as good as a declaration of war."

"I get why you want to recruit more fighters but why me?"

"Oh, come on, Aurora…you don't know why we want you? You need me to spell it out? You are a descendant of the Old Bloods. They are the only ones who can shift parts of the body at will, the rest of us have to be either in human skin or animal fur. I know you can do the mixed human-beast warrior form too, just like the Old Bloods could. That is very rare now. Then there is your reputation... Everyone knows when you unleash your beast there will be carnage on a grand scale. Whenever Oswald gets drunk he still goes on about how you tore through those reinforced walls and fucked up that den of cutters that grabbed Eddie. The way he tells it when you were done the walls that were still standing ran red with the blood of your prey."

Aurora grimaced and said, "When I saw what they did to Eddie and the others I lost my temper. Those were evil people and I don't regret killing them but your wolves shouldn't have displayed their bodies like that. Their families didn't deserve to see that."

Nesa shrugged. "Displaying those bodies so all of Porta Belua could see what was done to those cutters and their helpers sent a powerful warning to the others still in that bloody business. You helped us rescue Eddie and shut down one of those butcher shops but what about the rest? The bodies sent a message in a language those people understand. '*Take our kin and we will butcher you in turn.*' They got it. Since then none of our pups has been snatched."

"I'm happy that what I did helped protect your pups, truly I am, but I'm the one who had to deal with the fallout. Your people were so eager to tell anyone who would listen what had happened that the story spread everywhere. Along the way the number of dead quadrupled and I became a bloodthirsty monster. Some may enjoy that kind of notoriety but I don't."

"I can see how that might put a damper on your social life Aurora but you have to admit having a reputation that casts such a long and bloody shadow is useful. It precedes you; it makes your enemies tremble and keeps your allies safe. Why do you think other shifters avoid your village of pet humans?"

Aurora gave Nesa a warning look. "Those humans are my friends, *not* my pets."

"Perhaps but you *have* claimed them. Your scent and warning signs are all around Ingvild village and look at you...I haven't even threatened them and you are ready to rip out my throat. This is how you get when those under your protection are threatened. You did the same thing when you thought the avian was in danger. This is who you are and this is exactly the reason why we desperately need you on our side. With you here Black Paw would think twice about attacking clan Swift Foot because they would know, just like I do, you would rend them to a bloody pulp."

"Ah…I see clearly what you expect my role in the clan to be but what do I get out of it?"

"I'd think that would be obvious, Aurora. You don't have a clan and you don't have a mate. We would give you a home and a place to belong. We would become your family."

Aurora shook her head, "I already have a home and territory of my own."

"Yes, but you are always alone and that must be awful. I don't know how you stand it. There is strength in pack. Even the greatest beast that walks alone can be taken down by those in greater numbers and you have dangerous enemies. We would be your pack. We would watch your back and fight beside you. To show how serious we are we've set one of the best cabins aside for you and it already has all the basics in there ready for you to move in."

Aurora considered being diplomatic by pretending she needed time to consider the offer but that would just drag things out and give Nesa false hope.

"No."

Nesa stared at her in shock. "What, just like that? But you didn't even take time to think it over. Fuck…I was too blunt. I knew I should have let one of the others try to talk you into this."

"It wouldn't have made a difference. I'm not interested."

"Why not? We have always treated you with respect and made you welcome."

"You have," Aurora agreed.

"Then why not join us?"

"If your clan was at peace, asking me to join would have been a genuine offer to make a home among your people. You only asked because you need my teeth and claws. Once I've subdued Black Paw I would have outlived my usefulness. Will I still be welcome when the threat is gone or will your people be eager for me to leave?"

"But…it's not like that!" Nesa protested.

"Isn't it? I'm not a stray kitten in need of a feed and a place at someone's fire so don't offer me scraps and expect me to be thankful for it. Do you think your clan is the first to make me such an offer? Not by far. In fact, your rivals offered me something similar about a year ago."

The shock and dismay on Nesa's face was almost comical. "What did Black Paw offer you? You turned them down so I assume you didn't like what they brought to the table either."

"Black Paw was arrogant and ignorant. They approached me like I'm a killer for hire who gets off on fucking virgins while covered in the blood of my enemies. They wanted to pay me to join their clan and become their enforcer. I use the word clan lightly because what they are is a gang of thugs that take in the half-feral shifters other clans won't have. When I told them I wasn't interested they tried to get me drunk and added I could have the pick of their young or anyone else I wanted to warm my bed as long as I worked for them."

Nesa scowled. "That's messed up. What did you say?"

"Aside from no? I was reasonably restrained in my response considering how insulting the offer was. Things got out of hand when the chief got belligerent about my refusal and went into great detail on how he would find me and service me himself the next time I went into heat. Keep in mind he said this at the top of his voice in front of a full meeting hall."

Nesa swore and shook her head in disbelief. "Was he drunk when he said that? Obviously, the mutt wasn't right in the head. What did you do?"

"I broke a table on his thick skull. His people took exception to that and tried to keep me from leaving so I broke a few of them as well and collapsed their meeting hall. That was too much I know but by that time I was furious."

"I heard a small earthquake collapsed their meeting hall and badly injured the people inside. You're telling me that was all you? I saw that ugly monstrosity they built. How did you collapse that thing?"

Aurora grinned. "It was easy. They built it like a house of cards but with logs. All I had to do was rip out the weight bearing poles and gravity did the rest."

Nesa gave a strangled laugh and said, "If you were anyone else, I'd not believe that story but I know what you're capable of when you get angry and your beast is freaking *huge*. I almost pissed my pants the first time I saw you like that." Nesa's expression became thoughtful. "Um…I don't have to worry about you going on a rampage and smashing things before you leave, right? I didn't offend you?"

"What? No! Of course, I won't go on a rampage for something like that. Don't you know me well enough by now to realize that? However, if someone tried to prevent me from leaving…" she gave Nesa a mock threatening look.

Nesa gave her a sheepish smile and held her hands up in surrender, "We're desperate, not suicidal. As always, you can come and go as you please. I'm disappointed but there are no hard feelings."

"Good. I'd like to maintain good relations with your people. I've always liked clan Swift Foot. Well, not everyone in it obviously but as a whole you are good people and I have the greatest respect for your grandfather. As I said, if you offered me a place in your clan when you were not on the brink of war I might have considered it but I won't be anyone's monster on a leash. The thought makes me feel sick."

"But that's not what we want."

"Stop. Just stop, Nesa! You know I'm right because you told me as much. You might have used prettier words but when it comes down to it you want me for the same reasons Black Paw did. I'm supposed to intimidate your enemies and kill them if they don't behave. Tell me honestly, if you were in my position, would you accept an offer like that?"

Nesa frowned and reluctantly said, "When you put it like that? No. But you can't blame me for trying. We really need someone like you and I still think you would be much better off as a member of our clan than on your own. I will talk the others into sweetening the deal any way you like."

"You're not going to offer me bed mates and virgins too, are you?" Aurora asked dryly.

Grinning Nesa said, "You're hilarious. You know as well as I do the clan would tear out my throat if I did something like that. Besides, young wolves are so horny I'd be amazed if there is a single virgin over fifteen in the entire clan. However, if you're interested in lusty experienced wolves I could put the word out for volunteers who'd like some girl on girl time. You'd have an eager queue banging on your cabin door within the hour. Aisha will be right at the front; she's been trying to get into your pants for *ages*. Unless you've broadened your interest to include men? If that's the case it would be more like a stampede!"

Aurora shook her head vehemently but she was laughing and it made Nesa grin harder. They ran the rest of the way to Yutu's cabin together in amicable silence.

***

Aurora noticed the sickly stench overlaid with pungent herbs and disinfectant before she even put a foot on the first step leading up to the wide porch of the log cabin. She did her best to pretend she didn't notice but she wasn't the only one struggling; she could see Nesa's nose wrinkle.

She paused on the porch and asked, "Yutu is inside?"

Nesa nodded took off her shoes and went in. This more than the smell let Aurora know how bad things were. In all the years she's known Yutu, which was most of her life, she'd seen him inside his home only a handful of times. He embraced his wolf and loved the woods and mountains so much that they always talked outdoors and ate on his porch, never inside. As she understood it the only reason he'd built a cabin was to have a shelter for his family and because he felt that a chief ought to have a home as a thing of status to show he was a man and not just a wolf. It was his mate when she was alive who had made their cabin into a home and enticed him inside as only a lover could. However, since Noree died she had it on good authority Yutu slept on the thickly padded bench on the porch unless the weather was too abysmal even for him to endure.

Aurora slipped off her own shoes and padded after Nesa. She tried to focus on the cool feel and texture of the wood under her bare feet in an effort not to gag at how much stronger the stink was inside despite all the windows being wide open. She tried breathing through her mouth instead but that wasn't much better. Her only consolation was that Nesa's sense of smell was probably better than her own so she would find this even worse.

"He can't control his bowels," Nesa whispered, "and he's struggling to keep food down. That's why it smells like this. I had to make sure he was able to receive a guest before I brought you to see him. His speech is hard to understand and he drools so be prepared for that."

"Wouldn't it be better for him to be outside? He must hate being cooped up inside," Aurora whispered back.

"He hates it but he doesn't want to be seen in the state he is in. My mum and her sisters are the only ones allowed in the house. Me too but I am not allowed in the room when they wash or feed him. He hates everything and everyone right now and I don't blame him. You know how proud he's always been and it must be humiliating for him to be so helpless and dependent. If he could shift he would have tried to bite us for putting hands on him or dragged himself off to go die in the forest. I think the only thing that has kept him going is waiting for you. He asks if you've arrived several times an hour. That alone has just about driven my mother crazy. With the way he's been asking after you and how he always made time to see you whenever you visited, my mum started to concoct this notion you might be Yutu's love child."

This stopped Aurora in her tracks. "No. I'm not. I'm confident I know who my parents are so please reassure your mother."

"I did tell my mum she was barking up the wrong tree but I'll tell her what you said. Sending a message to you was the last thing Yutu did before he had a stroke. He was so excited I figured it must have something to do with him locating your father's fang. What happened to you and your father…my grandfather sometimes talked to me about that when we were alone. He'd get this troubled look when he mentioned how his friend Valen was one of those murdered by cutters. To him, there is no worse fate than dying with parts of the body missing because maimed hunters can't enter the eternal hunting grounds. He admired what you were doing. He was convinced if you succeeded your father's spirit would be made whole and be able to pass on."

"Your grandfather told me that too. He also said he would help me however he could. Yutu was the one who tracked down my father's pelt. I took it off the wall of the trophy hunter's lodge and brought it here first so he could see it before I carried it home. That was the closest I'd ever seen your grandfather to tears. Yutu and my father used to hunt together in beast form, did you know that? A tiger and wolf hunting together – what a formidable pair they must have been."

"I didn't know that."

"Your grandfather has been a steadfast ally and friend over the years. We'd discuss where I'd been, which trails I'd followed and what I was thinking of doing next. I think he was as disappointed as me every time it turned out to be a false trail but he still wanted to hear all about it. It was good to have someone to share this with. I promised him if he helped me find my father's fang I'd get for him something I knew he wanted for the clan. When I got the message to say he might have found it I went and got what I promised him." Aurora patted the pack on her back. "I did my part so I hope he was able to do the same."

"What if it turns out to be another false trail?"

"Then I keep looking. I've been at this for so many years and have had so many false leads and disappointments I'd be shocked if Yutu actually tracked it down."

"After Grandma Noree died and he stepped down from his position as Chief my grandfather became restless and grumpy. I saw a change in him after one of your visits and it was like he found a new purpose. He became obsessed with finding your father's fang. He must have written hundreds of letters and bugged every traveler that came through here about it. My mum wasn't pleased he spent so much time on something she thought was futile but I reckon it was good for him. He felt like he was doing something important. He couldn't run with the pack anymore but he was on a hunt, except instead of stalking a deer he was tracking down the last piece of your father's body. In his mind, if he succeeded it would mean he helped you fulfill your vow to retrieve all the trophies taken from your father and he'd get to see his friend Valen at the eternal hunting grounds."

"I'm speechless, Nesa. I had no idea Yutu spent so much time on this. He told me he was still looking but…I didn't know he was so dedicated."

"He probably didn't want to get your hopes up. He must have found a good lead otherwise he wouldn't have called for you to come."

"Let's hope so."

Their hushed conversation brought them to a door in a long hallway. Nesa knocked quietly. There was the sound of footsteps and a moment later an older woman who bore a striking resemblance to Nesa opened the door. She had dark circles under her eyes and fatigue and worry had carved stark lines into her face. When she saw them she slipped out of the room and quickly closed the door behind her. She leaned back against the door and let out a heavy sigh.

"About bloody time you turned up, Aurora. Go see that stubborn old wolf so I can tend to him properly once you are gone. He won't take anything for the pain in case it dulls his mind even more and he needs to sleep but he fights it, too afraid he won't wake again if he does. He is obstinate, unreasonable and as difficult as an overtired child." The woman bared her teeth in a half snarl. "If he wasn't my father and I didn't respect him so much I'd force the sleep potion down his throat and be done with it."

"Mum..." Nesa carefully took her mother by the arm and led her away from the door. "How about you shift and go for a run. You've been cooped up here for days."

Lesia yanked her arm out of her daughter's hands and came to a full stop. "I'm fine. You know I can't leave him alone."

"He won't be alone. I will be here and Aurora is here and you *really* need to get out of here for a while. Get some fresh air in your lungs and grass under your paws."

Lesia gave her daughter a steely look. "It sounds like you are trying to get rid of me."

"I'm trying to help. You're like Grandad – too long inside and your wolf gets snappy."

Lesia huffed but didn't disagree. "I could do with a break. I won't go far, just to the stream for a swim and maybe catch a rabbit or two. Yes, that'll do me good. You two better take good care of him while I'm gone."

While she was talking Lesia had removed her shirt so she stood only in a tank top. As Lesia reached for the zipper on her pants Nesa said, "Mum, please go change in the other room?"

"Why? We're all shifters here."

"Mum, please," Nesa hissed, "we talked about this. We don't get naked in front of our guests."

"Gods above and below…I don't know where you kids get these ridiculous notions from! There was a time we shifters hardly bothered with clothing. But all right, I won't offend Aurora with the sight of my saggy tits. Happy now?" Lesia stalked off down the hallway and Aurora heard a door open but not close.

Nesa folded her arms across her chest, muttered something indistinct under her breath and gave Aurora an apologetic look. Aurora bit her lip and tried not to laugh. A few minutes later a large grey wolf came down the hallway its claws clicking on the wooden floorboards. When it passed Nesa it gave her a haughty look and disappeared through the open door.

"I swear my family will drive me insane," Nesa said. "Stubborn, hard-headed, difficult wolves the lot of them. I can say it now you've already turned us down. You can see my grandfather now. I'm going to grab myself something to drink from the kitchen then I'll go sit on the porch. That way I can run interference if one of the aunties turn up. He was very specific about wanting no interruption and no one in the house eavesdropping on your conversation. I'll make sure my grandfather gets his wish."

"Thank you."

Nesa waved a hand over a shoulder in acknowledgment as she walked down the hall but did not look back. Aurora turned to face the door behind which Yutu lay, rolled her shoulders once then she went inside closing the door firmly behind her.

***

An hour later Aurora came out of the cabin and sat next to Nesa on the porch steps. Nesa took one look at Aurora's face and disappeared into the cabin. A few minutes later she came back with two tall glasses filled to the brim with a golden liquid. She held one out to Aurora who took it but didn't take a sip.

"There's no alcohol in that," Nesa said. "Well, not in your one anyway." She took a long drink from her glass and smacked her lips appreciatively. "I figured by how rough you look you could do with a strong drink but I know you don't drink so I'll have one for you."

Aurora took an experimental sip, waited a moment then thirstily downed the entire glass. "That was refreshing, thank you. I do drink alcohol by the way but only on the rare occasion and not much."

"Why is that? If you don't mind me asking."

"When I get drunk I do stupid things."

Nesa nodded knowingly. "Just about everyone does." After a moment she added almost hesitantly, "But sometimes doing stupid shit is a good way to let off a little steam. For shifters like us suppressing things can be dangerous. Better to vent than to let all that pressure build and build. As the saying goes: 'Unwind the man and you relax his beast. Cage his temper and you stoke the rage of his beast.' With a beast as fierce as yours that must be doubly true." When Aurora didn't comment Nesa took another sip of her drink cleared her throat and asked, "How was he when you left him?"

"Asleep."

"Oh? You convinced him to take the sleeping potion?"

"No. When we finished talking I gave him something else. He was so exhausted once he allowed himself to relax he fell asleep almost immediately."

Seeing Nesa's concerned look Aurora added, "No need to worry. I gave him a powerful healing potion, something I know works. I always carry some in case I get badly injured or I come across someone in dire need of it. It's fortunate I had one left; it has been an eventful trip."

"Will he be all right? Will my grandfather be himself again?"

"Yes, but don't expect him to be like he was before the stroke when he wakes up. He will be a lot better but full recovery will take time. He might be a beast-shifter but your grandfather is also an old man who suffered severe damage and his ability to regenerate is not what it used to be. But give him a day or two and he should be well enough to sleep outside again. Not feeling trapped between four walls will help him mentally while his body heals."

"But what about the problem with his down below area."

"You mean his legs?"

Nesa nodded and fidgeted with her glass.

"Yeah, I noticed you neglected to mention Yutu had tried to shift to wolf and his lower half got stuck in limbo. No wonder he was in such agony and the family didn't want anyone to see him like that. My potion gave him a boost and he was able to finish the shift."

"Aurora, I can't tell you how relieved I am to hear that. It was horrific seeing him with those twisted deformed limbs, part wolf and part man. It gives me the cold sweats just thinking about it. We tried everything we could to help him but nothing worked."

"It wasn't a pretty sight," Aurora agreed. "Neither was him flashing me his old man bits when he showed me why he couldn't walk."

Nesa who was in the process of taking another long drink snorted liquid through her nose and mouth and started coughing. Aurora gave her a few helpful slaps on the back.

Conversationally Aurora said, "I now know where your mother gets the whole 'unconcerned with nudity' thing from. I didn't realize it was a thing with your family until today."

When the coughing fit stopped Nesa used the hem of her shirt to wipe the worst of the drink from her neck and flushed face. She gave Aurora a sideways look. "It's only on my mother's side of the family. They see clothing as a matter of practicality to protect human skin and they don't see the difference between a wolf running around in its fur and a human without clothing. But they don't usually parade around naked in front of outsiders."

"In that case, they probably don't see me as an outsider."

"I suppose not," Nesa said with a grin. "So, did my grandfather manage to find what you were looking for?"

Aurora went very still, she swallowed hard and after a moment nodded. "Yes, he did. He came through for me. I'll forever be grateful to him."

"Where did he find it?"

Aurora held up a hand. "I'm not ready to talk about it and if you want to know the how and where of it you can ask him yourself." She reached into her backpack and extracted a tube designed for transporting fragile things. She carefully unscrewed the lid and tilted it so Nesa could see a single ethian crystal the size of a man's fist suspended in a gel-like substance.

Nesa inhaled sharply and carefully put down her glass. "Gods above and below...that is the biggest ethian crystal I've ever seen and what amazing clarity! It must be worth a fortune."

"It is. This was what I promised Yutu if he found my father's fang for me. When I offered it to him he told me to give it to you instead."

What Aurora kept to herself was that she'd presented Yutu with several crystals as a show of her gratitude but once the old man saw the size of the crystals he'd called her gift excessive and insisted that as a matter of honor he could only accept one. Not wanting to offend the proud man she had taken back all but one, the largest and most valuable of the crystals.

Nesa watched with greedy eyes as Aurora secured the lid on the tube and Aurora noted with mild amusement how Nesa's hands twitched as if she had to physically restrain herself not to reach for the crystal. Instead of giving it to her Aurora put the tube in her own lap and waited for Nesa to make eye contact with her before she spoke.

"Before I give this to you we need to come to an understanding. This crystal is not a gift to clan Swift Foot, it is payment for services rendered to your grandfather. He accepted it from my hand and then he requested I pass it on to you. That is all I'm doing here, giving something that belongs to him to you. He said you would know how to use it for the benefit of the pack. Yutu once confided in me that he believed out of all his children and grandchildren you were the wisest and would make a great chief someday. He didn't say it to me in so many words but I think that must be why he chose to give the crystal to you. Personally, I don't care what you do with it but I want to be very clear that I don't want to hear a rumor I gifted clan Swift Foot an ethian crystal. I mean it, Nesa. Your clan is not the only one I'm friendly with and if the other shapeshifters hear about this it will cause me no end of trouble. They will think I favor your clan if I don't start handing out ethian crystals like candy. I don't want to deal with that kind of petty jealousy or have to explain why I gave such a precious thing to your pack. Understood?"

Nesa made a solemn bow and said, "Yes I understand. I will give honor to my grandfather for this as is his due. His gift to clan Swift Foot from my hand. I will not mention you. I swear this to you on my clan, my lineage and the honor of my name."

"Good. I know he wanted a large crystal because with something like this your clan could generate a huge amount of energy. That means you can build things you were not able to before and once the infrastructure is in place the village will no longer be reliant on wood and coal. That would greatly enhance the prestige of clan Swift Foot and draw wolves from all over. Or, if you're ruthless and desperate enough, you can sell it and use the funds to hire mercenaries to wipe out Black Paw. Whatever you do with this crystal make sure not to credit me for it in any way. That is all I ask. Here take it. Use it wisely."

***

Evie found the trading caravan a revelation and delight. Operated by six humans and their two shapeshifter guards it consisted of four re-purposed Bedford military trucks parked in a semi-circle. Colorful canopies were strung up between the roofs of the trucks and the poles driven into the ground. In the shade of the canopies all manner of goods were displayed in a way that gave the area the feel of a cheerful mini-market. Evie was impressed with the variety and quality of things on display and the private area set aside for those with things to sell. As a whole, it attested to shrewd traders and it made sense they would have to be very successful to be able to afford and maintain four trucks. Vehicles were scarce and military trucks a remnant of the time when such things were allowed into Nordarra before the bloody upheaval that caused the portal to the human world to be shut. When it finally reopened weapons and many other things that came from the human world could no longer enter, parts for vehicles being one of the casualties. Instead of abandoning the precious vehicles to the rust pile, the mechanics adapted. They learned to make what they couldn't do without and replaced the broken engines with ethian generators powered by tiny crystals, removed the defunct wires and fed energy where it needed to go via a web of arcane runes.

It was like that with many things in Nordarra. People took whatever was available to create what they needed, not caring if it came from the human world or an invention left behind by the ancients. If it made their lives easier they would use it. The wolves of clan Swift Foot were no different Evie thought with amusement as she observed the milling crowd. They may live in an isolated area and probably believed themselves to be traditionalists who held to the old ways but she saw as many pairs of store brought jeans as buckskin pants and the wolves were as eager as children at the fair to inspect the goods on display. Not that she had any intention of pointing that out to anyone. She could feel the hostile stares directed at her but at least none of the upset wolves approached her. She figured it was because of Oswald looming near her and scowling at anyone who dared come too close.

Evie didn't know whether to be amused or embarrassed so she decided to pretend that having a wolf bodyguard while shopping was perfectly normal and tried to act as if this was just another visit to the market. She haggled with the traders and even managed a brief chat with a group of teenaged girls who were curious and bold enough to come up to her and say hello. Despite how strange it felt to have Oswald shadow her every step she had to admit she felt reassured by his presence because every time she looked around there seemed to be more wolves crowding into the area. She sincerely hoped they were there because of the traders but she had a suspicion she was probably as big a draw. She did her best to appear nonchalant but it was unnerving. Every time she touched an item she felt dozens of eyes follow her every movement. That much scrutiny made buying two new panties the most uncomfortable shopping experience she could remember. For the same reason, she bought a belt in case the trousers she bought were too large because there was no way she would strip to try them on in the small changing room set up between two of the trucks.

After a few more essential purchases Evie had had enough of being stared at. She had a good poker face but she could feel cracks forming in her composure. She had a quick look at the dried food items, taking stock of what was there but did not buy anything. She wanted to ask Aurora what she thought they really needed before adding more weight to their packs. She didn't want to lug around anything unnecessary when, by the sound of things, they still had a long way to travel.

Evie was getting ready to leave the market when a thought struck her. This was a trading caravan which meant they would stop here a few days at most before moving on. Moving on to where? If the traders were going to Porta Belua and not further inland she could negotiate a ride with them and be home in very little time and without having to walk most of the way. The traders were doing brisk business and it took her several minutes before she got the attention of one to ask her question.

"Where are you heading after this, good sir?"

"We have been on the road for twelve weeks, this is our last stop before we head back to Porta Belua."

Evie felt her heart skip with excitement. "Can I—" but before Evie could finish her sentence the man hastily excused himself when a woman heaved a pile of goods onto the table and waved her wallet at him in a beckoning motion. Evie sighed when they started haggling because the man would obviously be busy for a while. She berated herself for not pretending she wanted to buy something to keep his attention. The other traders were equally busy with buying and selling so she would just have to wait to speak to one of them.

"You're not a wolf are you, dearie?"

Swiveling around Evie saw an elderly human woman who vaguely resembled the man she'd just been talking to sitting on the step leading up to the truck's high cab. She looked disheveled and mismatched socks showed under the hem of her dress but her eyes were sharp and focused on Evie.

"No, I'm not."

"Ah…I thought you must be the one. Even without wings I could tell you were different. Yes, you must be the one."

"The one what?"

The woman pushed off the step and came to stand so close to Evie she got hit with a miasma of unwashed body odor underscored by a sharp pee-whiff. It took all Evie's self-control to not back away.

"The one who arrived this morning with *her*. I hear things you know. I listen to everything. Tell me, are you planning to continue traveling with *her*?"

Evie didn't like the woman's tone at all and it set her teeth on edge. "If you're asking me whether I intend to travel with Aurora then yes, that's the plan. We're going in the same direction and she offered to take me along."

"You'll be better off coming with us, child."

"Why is that?"

"Don't you know who she is?" The woman's voice became a low hiss. "That vicious monster has so much blood on her hands even the other beasts are afraid of her. Haven't you heard the stories they tell about her?" The woman gripped Evie's arm and leaned so close her fetid breath puffed against Evie's cheek when she whispered, "Come with us if you value your life. You can't trust something like that. She will murder you in your sleep and eat you."

Evie flinched and ripped her arm out of the woman's bony grip. She was so angry that for a moment she couldn't speak, convinced that if she did she would call the stupid woman every foul word under the sun and slap her. Was the old woman senile or didn't she know, despite being in a trade caravan, that wolves had superb hearing? Did she really think the wolves hovering close by couldn't hear her whispered words? Couldn't she tell from the stares and the way Oswald tensed how closely they were following this conversation? This was bad. If she bought a ride with the traders now after what this woman said it would be as good as her saying she agreed with the woman. If the old woman had just said Aurora was dangerous and had a bloody reputation she could have let it slide but this was a grave insult to her friend. Not only did the old woman call Aurora untrustworthy she'd also accused her friend of having such poor control of her beast she would murder and eat her own companion. The old crone as good as called Aurora a feral in front of a pack of wolves. These were the same wolves Aurora had faced down a short while ago by proclaiming herself Evie's protector. Aurora risked her reputation with these people by siding with an avian and declaring Evie wasn't like the avians the wolves learned to distrust and hate. No matter how urgently she wanted to get home, abandoning Aurora now to travel with these human traders was inconceivable. It would send a terrible message to the wolves and it would feel like she'd betrayed Aurora's trust. Without mutual trust and respect their tentative friendship and whatever else was blossoming between them would disappear in an instant. The thought of having her connection with the enigmatic woman severed made something in Evie's chest constrict. It was time to put the old woman in her place.

"I came here to trade not to have my companion insulted." Evie knew anger made her voice carry but she didn't care. "Aurora is my friend. I trust her with my life and I know she would never hurt me. You, on the other hand, don't have her protection and who knows what she'll do when she hears what you said about her. Although she wouldn't bother to eat an old hag like you – you're way too skinny and dried up. It would take her hours to pick all the bone and sinewy bits out of her teeth and that is just too much effort for so little meat."

Still fuming Evie stormed off. She heard Oswald chuckle as he trailed behind her.

***

When Aurora didn't find Evie with the traders she followed her scent. It would have been quicker to ask someone where Evie went but when among wolves that was not how these things were done. She found Evie sitting on a bench overlooking the lake in animated conversation with a cluster of young wolves of both sexes. Aurora recognized four of the girls as the teens who saw her throw the wolf-bitch out of their room. Evie said something in reply to a comment by one of the girls and everyone roared with laughter. When the wolves saw she was heading towards them everyone suddenly decided they had to be elsewhere but not before she caught a mix of curious glances and cheeky grins. Instead of going directly to Evie she angled towards Oswald where he stood watch with his arms folded and a hip rested against the trunk of a tree.

"What's going on there? Anything I need to know?"

In answer Oswald gave a long-suffering sigh and said, "Teenagers... Your pretty avian is a charmer. I tried to keep the whelps away but it was like trying to keep flies off honey. They're harmless though, just curious. Thought it might be a good experience for them to talk to an avian. Are you finished? I can go?"

"I am. Thanks for keeping an eye on her for me."

"No problem, it was entertaining and Evie seems like a decent person even though she is an avian. She's loyal, I respect that."

Curious, Aurora watched his retreating back because from Oswald that was quite the compliment. What had Evie been up to in her absence to make such a strong impression?

Her young admirers gone, Evie stood and smiled warmly at Aurora as she walked towards her. Aurora found herself smiling back and felt a rush of warmth and happiness spread through her body when Evie's hand lingered on her arm as a way of saying hello.

"How have you been, Evie? Did everyone treat you well?"

"Well enough. The young wolves remind me so much of my little sister, so inquisitive and mischievous. I enjoyed talking to them. It's a shame the older wolves aren't as much fun."

"Why were they all giggly and looking at me like that?" Aurora asked.

"Oh, they were just saying you look amazing in a wet towel. I suspect you may have several admirers after that lovely display on the porch when you threw that woman out. Just so you know, I got to hear their version of what happened from several angles and in every retelling your towel became shorter and clingier. By tomorrow you might have stridden out naked at the rate they are going."

Aurora's brows shot up. "Well…so much for my fearsome reputation."

"Don't worry, its intact," Evie said with a grin. "Now it's just a little *sexier*. That's what you get for showing off your legs like that."

Feeling a little flustered and unsure how to respond to Evie's teasing Aurora decided to ask the question that had been on her mind. "Talking about reputation…I went to the traders looking for you and I had the most peculiar conversation."

"Oh?"

"Did you tell the old woman who is the mother of one of the traders I would eat her? She was hysterical and the son kept trying to apologize and he begged me not to eat his mother."

Evie's smile was instantly replaced by a scowl. "That stupid woman. I distinctly said you *wouldn't* eat her."

Aurora frowned and looked from Evie towards where the traders were. "What brought that on? Why would she think I'm a feral?"

Evie interlinked their arms and urged Aurora into a walk in the opposite direction. "It's nothing to concern yourself with. That old hag is half senile."

"You don't want to tell me?"

"I'd rather not. It would upset you and I already got upset enough for both of us. As I said, she's a crazy old hag."

"Well, whatever you said the wolves thought it was hilarious. They kept snickering while he talked and she cried. It was so odd it was like I was in the middle of a play in which I had the main bits of dialogue but had no idea what was going on."

"What did you do?"

"I asked to buy a few things just to distract him and make it all stop." Aurora was quiet for a moment then she added, "It was the best trade session I've had in ages; he dropped his prices to almost nothing. I wish he had more things I actually wanted."

"That's good. Hope you got us some yummy food for the road."

"I did actually."

"Oooh, I like the sound of that! What did you get?"

"Nope. Not telling. Since you won't tell me what that woman said about me you will just have to wait and see."

"That's mean but I suppose I can wait. As long as you understand I now have high expectations."

Aurora groaned dramatically which earned her a playful smack.

"So your meeting, how did it go? All done?"

Aurora nodded all playfulness gone and her eyes became distant.

Evie winced. "It was that bad?"

"I had two meetings as things turned out and neither went badly, quite the opposite. It's just...Evie, I need to leave. I have so much to think about. For the sake of my immense respect for Yutu and my friendship with some of the people here I've tried to be as polite as possible but I've had about as much of clan Swift Foot's so-called hospitality as I can take. Any more and I might bite someone."

"Seriously?"

"Seriously."

When she turned to look at Evie Aurora's mask slipped and Evie saw old sorrow mingled with sparks of anger and resentment.

"Okay, we're *definitely* leaving. Do you need to tell someone we're going? I got the impression they were expecting you to be at the feast this evening. They have a special seat for you and there was going to be some kind of ceremony. One of the girls told me."

"They were going to invite me to join their clan."

"That's...nice? I didn't think wolves invited other shifters in easily so they must really like you. But you don't sound happy about it?"

"I'm not. They don't want me to stay because they like me. They want me to become their warlord or whatever one calls the person who does the dirty, ugly things that keep others safe. They seem to think giving me a cabin and allowing me to live among them even though I'm not a wolf is an amazing honor. It's such bullshit. I've been coming here for years and no one worried about me being on my own but now that they need my protection they're suddenly concerned with how lonely I must be without a clan." Aurora made a rumbling noise that sounded to Evie like a suppressed growl. "I have to get away from this place and these people. It feels like I can't breathe properly. My beast is so agitated my skin burns with the need to shift so like I said, any more of their so-called hospitality and I'm going to bite someone."

"Wow. No wonder you're not happy." Evie looked over her shoulder briefly. "Maybe we should walk a little faster – it looks like someone is trying to catch up."

"It would be most unfortunate for that person."

"Ah-ha." Evie turned and made a frantic shooing motion with her hands.

"Did it work?"

"Looks like it."

"Thanks."

"You're welcome. Now onto an important matter. Please tell me what goodies you bought for us. Chocolate? Please tell me you got chocolate."

Aurora snorted a laugh. "You are something else, the best distraction ever. For the record, I knew you wouldn't be able to wait and yes, I also bought chocolate. I remember you told me you like chocolate but I didn't know what kind so I got all three. The dark slab with salted caramel, the plain one and the one with nuts in it."

"You bought all three slabs?" Evie's voice was a delighted squeal. "You're my hero! I was joking about the chocolate and I didn't think you'd even look at it never mind buy some. I was tempted but it was way too expensive, over three times what I'd expect to pay for something like that in Porta Belua and the trader wouldn't budge on the price."

"I could afford to indulge after you scared the snot out of that man. Eat his mother…yuck. That dried out sour old thing would give even a carrion eater indigestion. She was smelly too. Imagine trying to get that taste out of your mouth." Seeing the expression on Evie's face Aurora held up her hands, "Joke, it was just a joke."

"Ah-ha, how about we agree you never make that joke again. It's really not as funny as you think."

CHAPTER 12

PROMISES KEPT

After a four hour walk Aurora called for a meal break and rest on the winding mountain path they'd been ascending. Evie had kept a close eye on Aurora, worried about her being out in the midday sun again but she seemed fine. She concluded it was probably because unlike the previous day there was a constant cool breeze and a decent cloud cover. The other difference Evie noticed was that unlike the previous days and even that morning Aurora set a slower pace so it no longer felt like they were on an endurance march. Coming up the mountain they had walked in comfortable silence interspersed with conversation, mostly Evie's doing, but she could tell Aurora listened attentively. In the silences between she could see Aurora was deep in thought and she wanted to ask her if Yutu found her father's fang but couldn't bring herself to do it. She still remembered the haunted look on Aurora's face the last time they talked about what happened to her dad and she didn't want to be the one to rake up those painful memories. She had a feeling Aurora would talk about it when she was ready, or so she hoped. She would simply have to wait and see.

Evie looked over the spot Aurora had led them to have their lunch and admired how well she had chosen. They could see for miles in every direction while they were sheltered from view. There was a tiny stream for them to refill their water bottles. Evie had already tried the water and it tasted fresh, sweet and icy like it was the thawed runoff from a glacier higher up. Splashing it on her heated face and neck had felt shockingly cold but very refreshing. It felt so good she took off her socks and shoes to give her tired feet a soak while she enjoyed the view. In the valley below, she could still make out clan Swift Foot's village although the figures moving about were now as indistinct as ants despite her enhanced vision.

She glanced at Aurora who was busy as usual. She had offered to help with getting a fire going or whatever needed doing but Aurora had been adamant that what she was planning for their late lunch did not need Evie's help. So she relaxed and admired the view. Curious she watched as Aurora laid out on a large flat rock a small square of yellow cloth and put a plate in the middle. Beside it she placed a large packet of crackers, a jar of pickles, a tin of smoked oysters, a jar of asparagus and a packet of mixed nuts. Next out of her bag came the tin that previously held the fruitcake. Aurora opened it carefully to reveal four ripe tomatoes, a small wedge of cheese and a large red onion. She washed her hands and knife higher up in the stream from Evie then sliced the cheese, tomatoes, and onion in a neat arrangement onto the plate. Evie looked on in amazement as the impromptu picnic unfolded in front of her.

"The trader had fresh tomatoes? That's amazing."

"No, I bartered for those from the general goods store. I asked about fresh fruit but they didn't have any. So I got this." She rummaged in her bag and extracted a large tin of peaches in syrup and held it up triumphantly.

This made Evie laugh. "You are amazing!"

Aurora grinned. "I figured I owed you something after denying you a proper bed to sleep in tonight and like I said, the trader just about threw things at me thanks to you." She held the tin of peaches out to Evie. "Put that in the water to chill and we can have it with our meal." Evie did as she was told. "For dessert I thought we could have chocolate. Or did you want to leave it for tonight?"

"No, definitely no waiting."

"Okay. Which block of chocolate would you like to try?"

"All of them."

"All of them?" This made Aurora pause in the motion of carefully shaking crackers onto the plate to stare at Evie. "Really?"

"Yes. You said yourself chocolate doesn't travel well so why wait until it's melted? We might as well enjoy it now."

"Melted chocolate still tastes good but we can taste test all the chocolate if that's what you want."

"It is."

Evie dried her feet and after putting her shoes back on she sat down with Aurora at the mini-feast she had prepared for them. Sitting side by side with the food in front of them and the magnificent view of the valley stretched out before them they made their cracker creations. Soon it turned into a competition to see who could make the highest edible tower without dropping anything. This caused lots of laughter and Evie found Aurora was not above cheating. Aurora 'accidentally' knocked her elbow at a critical moment causing cracker, pickles, cheese and a precariously balanced onion sliver atop a piece of tomato to fall inside her shirt. Watching her fish it all out of her bra had Aurora laughing so hard she ended up on her side breathless and helpless to prevent Evie from retaliating by stealing a portion of her allotment of nuts and eating them before Aurora could even gather enough breath to protest. Once she'd recovered Aurora retrieved the tin of chilled peaches from the stream and decanted the syrup so they had half a cup each with their meal. It was cold and super sweet, a refreshing drink to sip after a long walk on a warm day.

It was one of the strangest and most fun meals Evie could remember. She tried foods together she would never have considered, even wedging an oyster, a pickle, an almond and a slice of peach between two crackers in a bid to outdo Aurora's weird combinations. She inhaled the fresh mountain air deep into her lungs and thought how much she preferred this way of travel despite it being slower than rattling along in the back of a truck wedged between strangers. Maybe the crazy old lady had done her a favor because if she'd gone with the traders she would have missed out on this lovely afternoon with Aurora. She felt invigorated and didn't even mind that every muscle in her body had a complaint about all the walking and there was yet more to come. Aurora wanted them to camp at the top of the pass so they would have a good start the next day. She claimed it was an easy walk and that they had plenty of time to get there before nightfall. Evie didn't know if she believed her. Not because Aurora would deliberately lie to her but the other woman had a disconcerting habit of measuring distance and how hard things might be against her own considerable strength and stamina rather than against Evie's less impressive abilities. She decided not to worry about it because she would find out soon enough what lay ahead. She had something delicious that demanded her immediate attention. The promise of chocolate. Aurora finished tidying up the remnants of their meal and packed everything, even the empty tin, into her rucksack with care. She brought out the three blocks of chocolate and laid them out in front of Evie motioning for her to pick where they should start. She didn't have to be asked twice.

Fifteen glorious minutes later Evie moaned as she ate yet another piece of chocolate. "This is so good. I think you're right and the salted caramel is the best but the nutty chocolate was also very good and of course the plain one too."

Aurora's smile was amused. "You have an incredible sweet tooth. I'm still on my fourth piece and have had enough especially after those peaches. How can you eat so much chocolate?"

"How can you eat so much in general?" Evie countered. "You eat like a horse."

"Why like a horse?"

"They graze constantly and eat lots."

"Hmm, but unlike a horse I have never eaten grass. Well, not deliberately. I once face planted and ended up with a mouth full but I spat that out straight away along with the dirt so it doesn't count as eating it."

Aurora finished her piece of chocolate then wrapped up the rest of her share. "I can't have more. I'm on sugar overload."

"Aurora, can I ask you something?"

"Let me guess, you want my chocolate?"

"What? No. Although if you don't want your share…" Evie pretended to reach for Aurora's chocolate and had her hand playfully swatted away.

"I savor mine – no one told you to gobble it down so fast."

"Says the woman who normally just about inhales her food," Evie scoffed.

"I can't argue with that. Eating quickly is an old habit. Plus, like someone pointed out, I eat like a horse so I have a lot to get through."

"My question…it's personal."

"Oh? What is it you want to know?"

"What you did in the village, the way you changed just your hands, that was a partial shift. Only the Old Bloods, the direct descendants of the first shapeshifters can do that. So…that must mean that you *are* an Old Blood?"

"That depends…if I say yes are you going to pester me with questions?"

"Probably," Evie admitted. "There are so many things I'd like to know." At Aurora's groan she quickly added. "I'll settle for just a tiny bit of information. Please? I just want to know if you inherit the Old Blood bloodline from your father or your mother."

"What do I get if I tell you?" Aurora asked with a teasing smile.

"Ah, it's going to be like that is it? All right, the game is on. How about the rest of my chocolate?

"You hardly have any left. Trying to bribe me with a few pieces won't get you anything."

"How about cooking? I can help with that," Evie said hopefully.

"Are you a good cook?"

"I'm terrible," Evie admitted, "but I can throw things in a pot and boil everything until it is the same mushy consistency."

That made Aurora laugh. "I'll pass on that appetizing offer."

"Oh, I know! I'll do your hair."

"You want to do my hair? Why? What's wrong with my hair?" Aurora patted at her head where strands of hair had once again escaped her makeshift tie to float around her face.

"I can see it bothers you. You keep pushing it out of your face and you get this annoyed look. Which reminds me, I'm reasonably sure your hair has grown several inches since we met. Is that also part of your shifter thing?"

"My shifter thing…you make it sound like I have an exotic disease. You're a shifter too you know."

"Yes, but we're very different. Let me think what else I can offer you. How about a massage? I've been told I give a great massage. Come on, help me out Aurora – what *do* you want? There must be something I can do for you?"

"Evie…what kind of negotiating is that? Offering something so physical and ending on an open offer is reckless. What if I asked you to do something outrageous?"

"Will you?" Evie's eyebrows were raised and the way she locked eyes with Aurora was a playful challenge.

The corners of Aurora's mouth twitched and her eyes danced with amusement. "No, but that's beside the point. I really hope you're more careful with other beast-shifters. I know you said your godfather was a wolf and he taught you how to interact with us but from what I've seen so far he either didn't do a good job or you choose to ignore the advice you don't like. I've stopped counting the number of times you've done things that could be considered a challenge for dominance or an entirely different sort of invitation."

"And yet you haven't…so I can't be *that* bad."

Aurora snorted. "I let it slide because I like you. I don't know what other avians are like but you act more like a human than a shifter with how close you stand and not caring how you meet my eyes and you are by far the most tactile person I've ever known."

"You think I act like a human? I'm not sure how to take that."

"Some of my best friends are humans so it's not an insult. I'm trying to say you don't act like I'd expect another shifter to behave and I've made allowances for that. Not everyone will. To be honest I like that I don't constantly have to be on guard around you. I hate the constant challenges and pissing contests to see who is tougher."

"That's nice that you feel you can relax around me but stop being so evasive. Just tell me if you don't want to talk about your bloodline."

Aurora sighed. "My family ties are messy and complicated so it's not a comfortable topic for me. But I don't mind telling you that my father was an Old Blood. He was powerful enough to take on a warrior form that was a mix of tiger and human. He didn't like it and said it didn't feel right to him to be in-between like that but it's never bothered me and I've learned to shift individual parts of my body at will. I did tell you I have a knack for shifting."

"What about your mother? I assume she is also a shifter?"

"I don't want to talk about my mother. We are not close and there's no reason for you to know about her."

The way Aurora said it left no doubt in Evie's mind that her mother was a sore point and the faint amber glow in her eyes that wasn't there a moment ago warned Evie to back off.

"I see. What about your hair? It's grown quite a bit since this morning, hasn't it?"

"Yes. I told you it grows fast and it gets worse when I shift, or use the abilities tied to my beast magic, which is very annoying. I have to cut it constantly or I'd end up with hair down to my butt in no time."

"I'd *love* to see that!"

"I really don't. It's heavy, it gets caught on things and keeping it clean is a mission. I'm already uncomfortable and my hair is only halfway down my back." Aurora removed the hair tie and held up a handful of hair for Evie to see. "Look how tangled it is. This is what happens when the wind gets to it. I really need to cut it."

Aurora slipped a hand behind her back and a moment later held her knife. She tested the blade on a small lock of hair. When it slid through smoothly, she grabbed a large handful of hair, squinted sideways and made ready to cut again.

Alarmed, Evie asked, "What are you doing?"

"I told you my hair is too long. I need to trim it."

"So, you want to butcher it with a knife?"

"That *is* what I usually do when I can't tolerate it anymore."

Evie stared at Aurora incredulously. "You are *not* doing that this time."

"Oh? Why not?"

"Aurora, it'll look like a hack-job if you cut your hair like that. I already offered to do your hair so why not let me?"

"Does that mean you want to cut it instead?" Aurora held the knife out to her handle first.

Evie stared at the knife, dark as obsidian from hilt to blade, and pointedly pushed Aurora's wrist down.

"No, I do not want to hack off your beautiful hair with a knife. What I will do instead, until I can find scissors to style it properly, is braid your hair so it doesn't bother you and won't get snagged. I have long hair and I know from experience what will happen if I go flying without tying it up properly first."

Aurora absentmindedly tried to finger comb her loose hair away from her face while she considered Evie's offer. "My mother used to braid my hair when I was little. Nothing as complex as what you did for yourself but it looked good. I tried doing that myself when she wasn't around but I couldn't get it that tidy so my dad cut my hair and I trimmed his hair and beard. Later I learned to cut it myself with whatever was at hand."

"You mean butcher it."

"Hey, by then I was living alone and I had no one to ask. I'm not half bad considering I mostly have to do it without a mirror."

Evie groaned and held up her hands in protest. "Stop. Please stop. Come sit down in front of me so I can do your hair. The thought of you cutting your own hair like that makes me shudder."

"Can you do it without using clips? Having things in my hair when I shift can be a problem."

"I'll just use a small tie like the one you've been using. Will that be all right?"

"That's fine."

Bracing her back against a shady rock Evie made Aurora sit between her raised legs on the slope so she was a little lower than her. Aurora was right. Her windblown hair was full of tangles but as Evie patiently worked them out with a brush the thick tresses, the color of dark chocolate, became loose silk. It was so lush and shiny that touching it was a unique pleasure and every bit as amazing as she imagined it would be. She took her time brushing, wanting to prolong the experience for both of them. At first Aurora sat stiffly but gradually she relaxed and draped her arms around Evie's knees to anchor herself. As she brushed and worked the long strands she occasionally stroked Aurora's back and shoulders with her fingers. When she grazed the bare expanse of her neck she heard Aurora sigh. She was enjoying the task and she could tell Aurora enjoyed being tended to, something that probably did not happen often. It made her feel restful to do something so ordinary and familiar, something she had done for her younger sister many times. This wasn't the same though. Oriana could never be as quiet or still as Aurora. She'd be chattering away her hands fluttering in animated conversation and if Evie took too long, even with braiding a complex pattern, she'd fidget and complain she had things to do or other places to be. Evie smiled at the memory. No Oriana could never be still like this. Aurora, on the other hand, gave the impression she could be still for an eternity.

"Evie, do you want to know what happened with Yutu?"

Evie's hands paused for a moment before she continued braiding. "I've been wondering about that but I decided not to ask. You became upset the last time we talked about you trying to retrieve your father's body and I made things worse with my blabbering. So yeah, I've been curious but I wasn't going to bring it up."

"I appreciate that. I kind of need to talk about this though and you already know how much this means to me. Are you up to hearing a little more?"

"Absolutely. Share away."

"Yutu not only knew where to find my father's fang he gave it to me. It was the last piece, the one I've been searching for so long I'd almost given up hope of ever finding it. It has been fashioned into the handle of a ceremonial dagger. It's beautiful…which makes it all the more macabre because it means an artist labored to transform an object that was the result of a horrible death into a work of art." Aurora grimaced and rubbed her temple as if the very thought was giving her a headache.

"You're sure it's his?" Evie hesitantly asked.

"Yes. The moment I touched it I *knew* it was his. I told you I made a blood oath to find every part of him. It was an oath sealed with blood magic. I come from an ancient lineage and there are forces still at work within those of my bloodline that no longer have sway over other shifters in the same way. It's a blessing and a curse. That oath I made was a powerful thing that bound me in ways that are hard to explain.

Today when I touched my father's fang I heard a sound like a gong in my head; it went through my entire body and I felt the binding break and afterwards I was shaking like a leaf. I felt so light, like a huge weight had been lifted. That's when I knew it was over. I did it. I'm free. After all these years and more blood and pain than I care to recall I'm finally free."

"This is huge, a truly monumental day! What will this mean for you, Aurora?"

"It is. I'm still processing. It feels unreal that it's over. I've worked towards this since I was eleven years old. I often imagined what it would feel to finally fulfill my vow. I thought I'd be ecstatically happy and when I first touched the fang there was a moment of sheer joy knowing I'd finally done it but mostly I felt numb and shell-shocked. It was just so overwhelming. Unreal. I needed time to let things settle in my mind but with the wolves all around me and everything else going on I didn't have the room to think and come to grips with what happened. I've had a few hours to mull things over. I need more time but the initial shock has passed. Now I can think about my future differently. There are things I can do now I could not do before and it makes me excited and a little nervous."

"What kind of things?"

Aurora smiled over her shoulder and said, "That's a different conversation."

"You're not ready to talk about it?"

"No. Not right now. Are you done with my hair?"

"Almost, just one more twist. It looks great. I wish we had a mirror so I could show you."

Aurora ran an exploratory hand over her head and said, "Thank you, it feels much better this way."

"It was my pleasure. Any time you want me to braid your hair or help with anything else, all you have to do is ask."

"You've already helped just by being here and listening. I'm normally a very private person but for some reason I find it easy to share things with you."

Evie wrapped her arms around Aurora's shoulders from behind and hugged her. "I'm very pleased to hear that. I want you to be comfortable enough with me to talk about anything. I already feel comfortable with you and very safe."

Aurora awkwardly patted Evie's arm. "I'm glad you feel safe with me. That means a lot."

They sat like this for a while, Evie holding her loosely from behind and Aurora with her hand wrapped around Evie's arm. When Evie felt Aurora stir, no doubt ready to get back underway, she hurriedly said, "I'd like to ask you something else."

Aurora chuckled. "Sure, why not? You seem to be on a roll."

"Can you show me a better way to shift now? Or would it be better to wait until tonight? Is this a bad time to ask such a thing? You can tell me if you're not in the mood. I can wait but I just wanted you to know I'm ready when you are."

"You're taking me up on my offer?"

"To be taught by an Old Blood? Absolutely. It's a once in a lifetime opportunity."

"I doubt your wing has healed enough for you to fly but this is as good a time as any to have a look. I might as well show you how to improve your technique now. Maybe if you're lucky you'll be able to fly home from here and your ordeal traveling with me will be over."

"Spending time with you hasn't been an ordeal and some of the things we've done have been lots of fun."

"But not the walking?" Aurora asked with a grin.

"Admittedly, there has been a lot more of that than I expected. As much as I've enjoyed our time together I'd prefer to fly home rather than spend more time on my feet."

Aurora nodded in understanding. "Before we do this do you remember that I told you this will be invasive? How do you feel about that?"

"You offered to teach me how to quick-shift and as far as I'm aware that's something no avian has ever mastered. That, my friend, would be epic – my rivals will stress-molt in envy. I have no doubt after what I saw you do today and hearing you're an Old Blood that if anyone can teach me this you can. As for how invasive it will be, I could ask you to go into more detail but I'm afraid if you do I might be too scared to go ahead and I want this too badly. So I'd rather you talk me through it as we go. Besides, you've shared personal details about yourself. You entrusted me with that and with everything we have been through in the last couple of days I can honestly say at this point I trust you with my life."

Aurora gently squeezed Evie's arm. "I will be very careful with you."

"I know you will because you always are."

Aurora extracted herself from Evie's hold and got a long silk ribbon and pencil case from her pack. "Good thing I bought a few things in case you wanted to go ahead."

Curious, Evie watched as Aurora smoothed the material out on the flat rock and selected a stick of charcoal from the pencil case. She inhaled and exhaled slowly then began to draw.

"What are you doing?"

"Creating something that will make it easier to teach you. This will take a few minutes. There are things I need to know before we begin. What have you been taught about the nature of your magic?"

Evie made a helpless motion. "Nothing really. We wouldn't think of our wings as magical at all if we couldn't shift them in and out of existence. It's not like they just appear and we can suddenly fly. We are born with little nubs on our backs but they don't sprout until we are about five and our wings continue to grow as we mature. That's not a smooth process either because every growth spurt ranges from uncomfortable to downright painful. Mastering flight is like learning anything – it takes lots of practice. I suppose what I'm trying to say is for us it's just another part of growing up. Intellectually I know there is magic involved but as an experience I'd compare it to going through puberty. It's just something that happens. I started out with bee stings for boobs and then one day there was a lot more going on and I had to learn to manage all that. Same thing with my wings."

Aurora paused in her writing to flash Evie an amused grin. "Yes, but unlike your boobs, which are here to stay, you can materialize or dematerialize your wings at will. Well, not so much at will in your case but that is only because you don't understand enough. There's a massive gap in your education and it isn't your fault. Avians are one of the youngest races of shapeshifters. Your people were not around when magic was at its height and Nordarra a different place from what it is now. By the time avians came into being there were only a few of the Ancients still around and the rest had gone taking their knowledge with them. According to my father the Ancients were the ones who taught shapeshifters magic. Without their instruction your people had to teach themselves because the older shifter races were not interested in sharing what they knew. I know some things because I was fortunate enough to have parents who'd been instructed in the old ways. I'm going to show you how to tap the power that's at your disposal."

"What power? Aurora, we avians are not like the dragons who are still imbued with raw magic able to do all kinds of powerful and amazing things. We have our wings, our bodies are adapted for flight and we are stronger and more resilient than mere humans. That is basically it."

"That's not strictly true. Think of it like this: from a point of aerodynamics even though your wingspan is huge realistically you shouldn't be able to do more than soar but avians can fly even if there is no wind at all. Now think about the dragons we saw last night. They are so massive they shouldn't be able to get up into the air from the ground and yet they can perform the equivalent of aerial ballet. That's because when it comes to flying avians and dragons are not so different and you draw on the same sort of magic. What makes dragons so formidable is that they know what they are doing and this helps them utilize their magic much better. I want to show you how to do the same."

"Are you saying there's secret knowledge that could make me as powerful as a dragon?"

Aurora shook her head. "Sorry to disappoint you but that's a definite no. An avian could never match a dragon for raw power no matter how much you learn or practice. There are types of magic that can only be passed on along bloodlines and Old Bloods are carriers of the most powerful strains of magic."

"What do you mean…strains of magic?"

"Um…that's not relevant to you. Forget I mentioned it."

"Oh no, you can't throw that out there and then not want to tell me. That's a terrible thing to do!"

"Telling you about this won't help you shift quicker, Evie."

"But I feel I've been stumbling around in the dark all my life; oblivious to so many things. I don't like that feeling at all. What harm can it do for you to tell me? Think of me as an eager student. You're going to teach me how to quick-shift which means you've already taken on the role of my teacher so why not take that a little further?"

Aurora gave Evie a long thoughtful look then said, "Okay. Stop me if I tell you something you already know. Magic is like genetics but more fickle and a *lot* more complicated. It's usually passed on along bloodlines but doesn't always express in the same way. If the parents come from the same or similar magical bloodlines, it's likely they will pass that on to their child. The more branches of magic passed on to a descendent the higher the risk that one or more strain of magic will become diluted or disappear altogether or manifest undesirably. That's why the old bloodlines take such care to mate with their own kind at the risk of inbreeding and running into other problems. It's a two-edged sword: breed for power and magical consistency or healthy offspring that may not be able to shift or use magic at all? The mers have chosen the path of lots of offspring with anything humanoid enough to breed but since they rarely produce males they didn't have a choice. Mers used to drown the 'failed offspring' who didn't inherit their traits but now they are more likely to offer the child to the father's family or abandon the baby on land."

"I knew some of what you just said but I've only looked at it from the angle of shifters breeding with their own kind to assure the offspring will be of the same kind. Mixed pairing can result in the child taking after either parent or not being able to shift at all. I didn't realize there were potentially older types of magic passed on or lost as well."

"It is indeed a complicated and very serious business. The Old Bloods keep extensive records on their lineages and which pairings produced particular strains of magic and how it manifested. The pairing of mates is meticulously planned accordingly, often generations ahead."

"Wow, and your parents, instead of sticking to the plan, eloped and had you. That must have upset a few people."

Aurora grinned. "You have that right. No invitations to family gatherings or matchmaking events for me. I'm the mixed blood of two very different bloodlines. Even if I was interested in playing power games with my offspring no other Old Blood would touch me with a ten-foot pole because of the unpredictability of what I might produce. I inherited strains of magic from my parents that historically do not mix well and I'm now the carrier of something the Old Bloods have tried to eradicate. I'm the proverbial loaded gun. If I have a baby it's almost guaranteed I'll birth something monstrous like in the old tales of magic gone wrong."

"Seriously?"

"Apparently. Just as well I don't plan on having children."

"Aurora, that's so sad and very unfair. You can't help that your parents fell in love and had you. I still can't believe your relatives won't have anything to do with you. It's unbelievably cruel to reject a child just for being born."

"It's all right. Like I told you this morning I've never known anything different. Besides, until my father died I had a very happy childhood. He took me everywhere with him and he had lots of friends among other shapeshifters and even humans. That allowed me to get to know people I'd never have been allowed to associate with if his clan or my mother's people had claimed me as one of them."

Evie touched Aurora's cheek in a gentle caress and said, "It's their loss and our gain."

Aurora blushed and briefly held Evie's eyes before she looked away. Clearing her throat Aurora said, "I've gone way off topic. I'm supposed to teach you how to shift quicker not burden you with more of my problems." Aurora held up the silk strip she'd been writing on. "It's finished."

Evie had been so busy listening she hadn't paid attention to what Aurora was doing. Taking a careful look at the material fluttering between Aurora's fingers she saw it was covered in a complex web of interlocking runes that ran in circular patterns. She only recognized a few of the runes like the inscriptions for flow and connect. Some looked vaguely familiar but most of the runes she had never seen before. She had no idea what kind of spell Aurora had created.

"And the woman can draw advanced runes as well…are you trying to give me a complex, Aurora? What can't you do?"

"I only know a little rune magic, Evie. I probably know more than the average shifter but in comparison to my mother's understanding of such things I'm a toddler still learning to write. I could be a lot better but I've never been drawn to this kind of magic because it's incredibly tedious. To become a master would require several lifetimes of dedicated study, and as much as I enjoy learning new things, after a few hours of studying diagrams and trying to decipher the interconnecting patterns to predict how the flow of magic will affect the final working I want to pull out my hair."

"Was it your mother who taught you rune magic?"

Aurora shifted uncomfortably. "Yes. She insisted I learn at least the basics."

"Does your mother—"

"Evie..." Aurora's voice held a note of warning.

"I'm sorry. No more personal questions. The ribbon, what's it for?"

"It contains a spell that once activated will form a link between us. It will help me see more clearly what happens when you shift. You'll feel my presence and it will not be a comfortable experience especially when I start rearranging your magical pathways. Please don't fight me. I'll withdraw without fixing what's wrong rather than subject you to feeling forced or violated. I mean it."

Evie thoughtfully rubbed the corner of the material between her fingers. "Is this how the Old Bloods pass on knowledge?"

"Sometimes. It's a sledgehammer quick fix approach. I wish I could go about it more gently but we don't have the months or years it would take to slowly correct a lifetime's habit of shifting a certain way."

"This link…how much will it show you? Will you be able to see private things, like memories or my thoughts?"

"I've only ever been on the receiving end with this, Evie. I've never been the teacher. As I understand it all I will see is your magic. I'll try to be as quick as possible. While the link is active we will be exposed to a measure of each other's magic and since I'm a beast-shifter you might glimpse my beast. Please don't be afraid if that happens. Since I mean you no harm it won't hurt you. At most, it will be curious and try to get a better look at you."

Evie gave her a thoughtful look. "You were right. There is a lot more to this than I expected."

"Changed your mind? We don't have to do this."

"I want to. I've come this far and I'm not turning back now. Let's get on with it."

"As you wish."

Aurora held out the long length of silk material at arm's length and draped it on the ground to form a large circle. She pricked her finger for a drop of blood and smeared it on one of the runes while whispering something under her breath. Instantly the cloth circle transformed, snapping into place like it had been replaced by a metal hoop. It even had a metallic sheen and the black runes seemed to pulse on the blood-red surface. Aurora gave a satisfied grunt then rolled up the sleeves of her long-sleeved shirt, took off her shoes, stepped into the circle and sat down cross-legged. Palm up she indicated the open space in the circle. "Join me, Evie."

Evie pushed up the sleeves of her jacket and removed her own shoes and socks. She regarded the ribbon that was now so much more than just a length of material with the same trepidation she'd reserve for a ring of lava. She didn't want that thing touching her. It was only her trust in Aurora, who sat watching her with calm patient eyes, and her desire to learn what Aurora could teach her that allowed her to gingerly step inside the circle. She mirrored Aurora's pose and sat as close to her as she could. When Evie wiggled her toes it brushed the soles of Aurora's feet. The motion drew Aurora's attention and she stared at Evie's feet.

"You have such small feet. It's fascinating to me that a grown woman can have such tiny feet."

Evie giggled and wiggled her toes some more. "We could never borrow each other's shoes. When you lent me your socks the heel section came up past my ankle."

Aurora looked at Evie's hands fidgeting in her lap. She studied her own hands and put them between them palms up. Evie immediately laid her hands in Aurora's. They fit easily with room to spare. "And you have such dainty hands. Such dainty everything."

"I'm not a small woman," Evie protested. "I'm taller than most. It's my avian bone structure and being slender that makes me appear smaller than I am."

"I know, it's just that I feel so oversized next to you. I take after my father although thankfully I'm not as big. My mother is like you, delicately built and she only comes up to my shoulder. I try to blend but I always stand out in a crowd. I dwarf most women and even some men feel intimidated by my height. I don't like being noticed and having people give me sideways looks ruffles my fur. I try not to let it bother me but…it really does."

"You're not oversized. You just happen to be bigger than most people and so muscular and strong." Evie lay a finger on Aurora's bicep. At the contact the well-defined muscles jumped and Evie smiled as if she just proved a point. She lightly caressed Aurora's arm. "You're a gorgeous woman and you move with such grace and power that watching you is a treat. You look, for lack of a better description, sleek like a powerful predator stalking the shadows. It's incredibly sexy and also a little intimidating. It's probably the way you move that draws people's attention rather than your actual size. You make women half your size look like lumbering elephants."

"Truly?"

"Yes. Stop worrying about your height; it suits you. I don't know how much you value my opinion but personally, I love how tall you are and I think you have an amazing body. As for our difference in size, just wait until I have my wings on. You'll see we are more than evenly matched. In fact, I will dwarf you. Shopping at the bazaar is a challenge. People have to give me plenty of room or risk getting knocked on their ass when I make a quick turn and that's with my wings tightly tucked."

"You do have very large wings, some of the largest I've seen on an avian. I remember. They are magnificent." Aurora shook herself as if waking from a dream. "Which is what we should be retrieving for you right now. Sorry, I got distracted. Again."

"By my tiny hands and feet?" Evie asked teasingly.

"Something like that. You're very sweet and I do value your opinion so thanks for what you said. It makes me feel better about myself."

"I'm glad. That's my good deed done for the day."

Aurora smiled and asked, "Are you ready to continue? You looked tense before."

"I was nervous but I'm feeling better now. Comparing feet and hands was an amusing distraction and being able to touch you is reassuring. I can feel by how carefully you hold my hands you're going to take good care of me."

"Good. I'm going to start now so don't be alarmed by what you see or feel."

As Evie watched Aurora's green eyes lit up with amber sparks that shone like fire. Evie felt something large and furry brush up against her and a puff of warm breath tickled her ear. The otherworldly presence made her shiver and she gripped Aurora's hands tighter. There was a humming noise and Evie saw the circle was no longer on the ground but about a foot off the ground and spinning. The black runes were now overlaid with the same shades of amber and green as Aurora's eyes. The hair on the back of Evie's neck prickled and her breathing sped up.

Aurora's thumbs stroked Evie's palms in a soothing caress. "There's nothing to fear. I just activated the protective part of the spell. The sort of magic I'm about to use draws attention if not contained – power calls to power. I'm just making sure if there's anything old or sensitive to magic in the area that it won't come calling while my attention is elsewhere."

"What kind of—" Aurora shook her head and Evie bit down on the rest of her question.

"Evie, draw out your wings so I can see what is going on."

Evie nodded and started the process like she was taught. As always, it was excruciating and she soon felt sweat trickle down her back.

Aurora fought not to show her dismay. Being this close to Evie while she wrestled with her magic was like having to endure a high-pitched screech in her ears and she desperately wanted to make it stop. She tried to ignore her own discomfort, focusing instead on how Evie interacted with her magic. It didn't take her long to realize that it wasn't only poor technique at fault; Evie simply had a lot less magic. Aurora was so used to her own magic being easily accessible and available in abundance that it had never occurred to her Evie would have so little to work with. Whereas her own magic was like a deep, flowing river it was like Evie was pumping by hand from a small well deep underground. To make matters worse the well wasn't refilling quickly and magic trickled into it painstakingly slow. It saddened Aurora to see her friend struggle so hard with something that came to her as easily as breathing. She had been so arrogantly confident of her own abilities that she'd promised to teach Evie how to quick-shift without hesitation. It was shocking to realize there was nothing she could teach her that would make that possible. It would be like trying to teach a crippled person to leap over a ten-foot fence: it was impossible.

Aurora realized she was squeezing Evie's fingers when she felt the other woman try to pull her hands free. She immediately relaxed her grip and tried to soothe the hurt with her thumbs. Evie opened her eyes and gave Aurora a questioning look. Aurora was shocked at the pain she saw in Evie's eyes and her first thought was that she must have crushed her delicate fingers. Then she noticed the grim set of Evie's mouth and her rapid breathing and understanding dawned. "Shifting is very painful for you?"

Evie nodded wearily. "You want me to keep going? It will take me at least another half hour. Just so you know once I've drawn out my wings that's me done. I won't be able to shift again until tomorrow."

Aurora cringed. "Please stop. I've seen enough."

Evie let out a breath and sagged forward.

"Are you all right?"

Evie wiped the sweat from her forehead and sighed. "I'm used to it. I just wish you didn't have to see me like this. This is why we never let other shifters see us. It's embarrassing to be so much slower than everyone else and look like we are giving birth while we're at it. It is such a big deal to us we don't even shift in front of our own flock. Only family members or lovers are allowed to see each other like this. Did you know that?"

Aurora fidgeted uncomfortably remembering how openly critical she'd been of Evie's shifting. "I didn't know. You're my first avian friend and I'm sorry I was so hard on you. I thought it was just a lack of practice and poor technique. I didn't realize until now just how difficult this is for you."

"It's okay." Evie tried for a smile to lighten the mood but it was a half-hearted effort that just twisted the knife in Aurora's chest. "So, what's the verdict, doc? How do we fix this? I'm all ears. I'll do anything you say. If you can teach me how to do this even a little quicker I'll be eternally grateful."

Evie looked at her with such hope and trust Aurora knew there was no way she could tell her the truth. She had to think of a way to help her. She'd promised Evie she would and she always kept her word no matter the cost.

"Please say something. I don't like that look on your face. What's wrong? Can't you teach me? Is our magic too different?" Evie's voice had a desperate edge now.

"Hush…it's all right. The way you use your magic is different from what I expected so I can't teach you the way I planned." That wasn't a lie, strictly speaking.

"Can you still help me?"

"I will. Just give me a moment to think. No talking."

Evie made a motion with her hands as if she was zipping her lips.

Slow minutes ticked past as Aurora tried to think of a solution. When the idea came to her it was so simple she was astounded it could be that easy. All she had to do was take a thread of her own magic, weave it into the walls of Evie's little reservoir and imbue it with the command to draw magic. That was it. She couldn't give Evie more magic or a bigger reservoir but she could speed up her regeneration of magic so she didn't have to wait so long and work so hard to get to it. The spell would respond to how often Evie shifted, so the more she did it the quicker it would refill Evie's reservoir. That was as it should be, a measurable reward for perseverance and practice. There was the small matter of her leaving some of her magic inside Evie. Magically speaking it would amount to giving Evie only a drop of her blood but because of her bloodline the effect would be profound. She was about to give a member of one of the youngest races in Nordarra a massive boost in power. Her mother would be livid if she ever found out. The thought made Aurora smile and the last of her hesitation vanished.

"You thought of something?" Evie asked.

"Yes, I have. I just need to make a small change to how you access your magic then I will teach you how to shift properly. Do you give me permission to do this?"

"Please go ahead. Do whatever you think necessary."

Aurora's smile broadened. "Good. I promise you won't regret this."

***

A little while later Aurora slowly guided Evie through her shift, giving careful instruction and nudging her the right way when she tried to fall back on her old method. When her wings whooshed into existence Evie's laughter was filled with delight.

"This is *amazing*! That took less than fifteen minutes and it hardly hurt at all! I'm so happy I could kiss you! Thank you, my friend, I'll never forget this."

"I'm happy I could help. You'll find the more you practice the quicker and easier it will become."

"Nooo…really?" At Aurora's nod Evie did a happy dance on the spot.

Aurora laughed and picked up her pack. "You can practice those dance moves on the way. We still have to get to the top of the pass before dark. That's unless your wing is healed enough for flight?"

Evie experimentally stretched her injured wing and winced. "I wouldn't chance it, not yet. It's no longer broken and the hole is gone but it's definitely not safe to use yet."

"So, you know what that means?"

"More walking?"

"Yup, more walking."

CHAPTER 13

INVITATION TO THE TIGER'S LAIR

It had taken them two hours to get to their destination and despite Evie's concerns the climb to the summit hadn't been nearly as bad as she feared. What did have her worried was how withdrawn Aurora had become since they arrived. She had already become used to Aurora's occasional quiet spells and those didn't bother her but this did. Normally even when she was watching the trail or occupied with her own thoughts Aurora's eyes would light up in warm acknowledgment whenever their gazes met and that made Evie feel like they were constantly connecting without the need for words. Aurora had grown quieter as they neared the top of the pass and her eyes, when they flickered over Evie, were troubled and restless. As soon as they arrived at their camp spot Aurora had excused herself, sat down on a rock that granted her a panoramic view and stared off into the distance. She'd been sitting like that for a while, her arms wrapped around her legs and her chin rested on her knees. Evie wanted to give Aurora space to think about whatever was troubling her but she looked so unbearably lonely like that, a single figure silhouetted against the vast landscape and endless sky.

She resisted the urge to go to Aurora as long as she could and when she did approach her she sought Aurora's attention by gently touching her shoulder. When Aurora gave her a questioning look Evie said, "Do you mind if I sit next to you? This is the only spot with an unobscured view of the valleys below and I'd very much like to see the sunset in all its glory."

Aurora didn't say anything but scooted over making room for Evie on the slab of rock and patted the space beside her. Encouraged by the welcoming gesture Evie sat down allowing a hand span between them.

"I'd like to open my wings to sun them but this isn't a big space. Would it bother you if I do that? I know I have a habit of getting into your personal space and I don't want to bug you more than I already have."

Aurora gave her a gentle smile. "You really don't have much of a sense of personal space but I'm getting used to that. Sun your wings, Evie. You're no bother."

The sky had a golden glow infused with tints of red and the mellow heat from the sun was that of a dying ember. Evie arched her wings open as much as her injury would allow as she was eager to absorb as much warmth and light as possible before it was swallowed by the darkening sky. As she stretched her wings she allowed the inside of one to glide lightly over Aurora's back in an almost-caress. Aurora gave her a sideways glance and looked like she was about to say something but after a moment she continued her quiet contemplation staring out over the mountains and valleys below.

Evie's own thoughts drifted to what was happening at home. She hoped fervently that her father's health hadn't gotten worse. It was a constant worry to her, along with keeping an eye on his conniving half-brother. Evie's brow furrowed as she thought about Marcus. Hopefully she wouldn't be away long enough for her uncle to cause trouble or find a way to get his sticky fingers into the treasury. It frustrated her that her father treated Marcus like a troubled son rather than the arrogant, greedy, asshole he was. It was probably her father's misguided attempt to bring into the fold a younger brother he didn't know he had until a few years ago. Evie didn't share her father's affection for Marcus and she had no tolerance for his antics so she knew it was just a matter of time before she and Marcus had another serious altercation. But that was a problem for another day. Right now, she got to enjoy a magnificent sunset in the company of a beautiful woman.

Eventually, shadows crept all the way up to the outcropping while the pool of amber light they sat in receded with the sun sinking over the horizon. With no more sun to warm her wings Evie gradually folded them away. She learned that quick movements were not a good idea around Aurora, especially behind her back. She would instantly become alert and track Evie's movements with predatory wariness. It usually only lasted a few seconds but every time it happened Evie's neck prickled in alarm. Aurora looked more relaxed and she wanted her to stay that way so they could talk. She'd given Aurora enough time to say something so it was time to push.

"Aurora, when are you going to tell me what's going on?"

"What do you mean?"

"You've been extra quiet since our last stop and now you have this expression like you're making a serious decision and the way you've looked at me several times makes me concerned that your decision might affect me. If it does, I have the right to know."

Aurora shifted uncomfortably and said, "Most of it has nothing to do with you. I've been thinking about my plans for the future."

"But there is a part that involves me?"

"Yes. I need to go to a place not far from here to collect some things of mine. I'd prefer you to wait for me while I make a quick detour but even running I probably wouldn't get back until mid-day tomorrow at the earliest. I don't think it is safe to leave you here still unable to fly. I'd never forgive myself if something happens to you while I'm gone."

"Then take me with you. What's the big deal? You took me into wolf territory and we got through that just fine."

Aurora hesitated and Evie could just about see the wheels in her head turning as she weighed what to say next. "I've never taken anyone there. If you come with me you must promise you won't tell anyone about it or talk about the things you see on the way and you must give me your word you'll never try to go there without me. It's a place that used to belong to the Ancients. I use it as a sanctuary of sorts."

"Will I be in danger there?"

"Not from other people; it would be just you and I. As for the place itself…it still has active defenses but as long as you're there as my guest you will be safe. In fact, I think you'll like it there. We can rest without having to be on guard and have a hot soak."

"Will there be food as well and a proper table to sit at so I don't have to balance my meal on my lap?"

Aurora smiled. "Yes, that too. Even a big bed to sleep in."

"Sweetie, at this point for a hot bath and a soft bed with clean bedding I'd be willing to do all manner of things. But all jokes aside, yes, you have my word and I agree to all you've asked. You have my oath as a blood liege of House Aquilar."

"Good." Aurora nodded a pleased expression on her face. "Then it's settled."

"Was that so hard? Next time don't brood so much, just talk to me."

"I don't brood. I was thinking."

"You're a broody thinker."

"Is that supposed to make me feel bad?" Aurora asked, the corner of her mouth quirking in amusement.

Evie patted her leg. "It's merely an observation. It's probably a habit you picked up from spending so much time by yourself. In my home it's almost impossible to be alone long enough to get into a serious brood. If I want to be alone I have to hide in my rooms or try to sneak away for a solo flight which is very hard to do with so many people everywhere. I suppose that's why I was drawn to work in our mira gardens in the first place. Only a select few are allowed to enter and it is so gloriously tranquil there. It was a bonus it turned out I have a natural aptitude for working with the mira and don't mind the bees. Not to praise my own feathers but I'm very good at what I do. We have all kinds of investments but that's still our most lucrative source of income. My ability to get the best out of every crop and the fact I also seemed to have inherited my father's shrewd nose for business has been incredibly useful leverage in dealing with the more troublesome members of my flock. I'm easy going most of the time but they know if they try to push me into something I don't want, like another arranged marriage, heads will roll."

Aurora frowned. "Can your flock do that? The arranged marriage thing?"

"Yes and no. Avian Houses are like small kingdoms and ruled by the founders. House Aquilar is more progressive than most but we are by no means a democracy. So, if the head of my House, my father, insisted on a marriage I'd have to agree to the union or leave. I'm the oldest child and future ruler of House Aquilar and in the past arranged marriages were used to create alliances all the time. It's an archaic remnant of a bygone age and my father has encouraged way too much independence in his daughters to turn around and try to force us into something like that. It would go against everything he stands for."

"It's good to know you've got your father's support but why do I get the impression you've already had to fend off a marriage alliance? I don't like the sound of that at all."

"It was all my uncle Marcus's doing. I can't stand that man. He sponsored a petition by House Ravir to enter into an alliance with House Aquilar. Since my father has been training me to be his successor when this came up he stepped back to let me handle the whole thing solo. Personally, I didn't want any dealings with House Ravir but as the official representative of the head of House Aquilar I had to at least hear them out. Normally I don't talk about House business to anyone outside of the flock but I trust you."

Aurora smiled and said, "My lips are sealed. Do tell – I'm intrigued to find out what happened."

"During the meeting House Ravir offered to put their air power at our disposal to help protect and expand our trade routes in exchange for a mutual support alliance. This caught the interest of the flock as House Ravir still has a strong warrior culture whereas our focus is business orientated. Financially House Aquilar is far more prosperous than Ravir but they outnumber us with trained fighters. We have a sizable House guard to defend our tower but our air force is a fraction of what it used to be during my grandfather's reign. The shift was a deliberate act by my father as he was trying to distance House Aquilar from the sort of behavior that used to be the trademark of the hunting and scavenging flocks of old. Having a smaller air force hadn't been a problem until recently. Unfortunately, over the last ten months we've had ongoing losses due to attacks on our shipments. Nothing crippling but it is concerning. If we trained more sentinels or hired mercenaries we could patrol the routes better but that would divert resources from other important projects. I proposed we re-evaluate our existing trade routes and develop relationships with companies on the other side of the portal eager to market our mira honey to humans. Marcus openly opposed me, arguing it would be a sign of weakness to abandon old trade routes. Then he brought in the offer by House Ravir as his solution to the problem. He suggested my marriage to House Ravir would instantly gain us access to the use of their warriors with no additional expense to House Aquilar."

"That sounds like a move to get rid of you. Marry off the female heir to another House and take her position."

"My thoughts exactly! I entertained fantasies of ripping off his wings while I made a show of listening to him argue how beneficial such an arrangement between our Houses would be. According to my uncle I'd be joined in marriage to Titus of House Ravir for 'the good of the flock'. Utter rubbish. Firstly, if I wanted to form an alliance just for the sake of gaining warriors there are better options than House Ravir. Secondly, I'd like to see Marcus offer up his body and soul 'for the good of the flock'. That man only thinks of himself and he still carries a mountain-sized grudge that my grandfather didn't acknowledge him as his bastard son while he was alive. Marcus was the result of his brief affair with a woman from House Ravir whose husband was, by all accounts, a brute. It wasn't until after the death of her husband that the clause in my grandfather's will kicked in and Marcus was gifted the sizable inheritance set aside for him. Once Marcus got over the shock, he quickly decided he'd not been given a fraction of what he was due and he's been trying to claw his way to power ever since. So as far as I'm concerned, any proposal Marcus puts forth is suspect. As for marrying into House Ravir? They would have to bind and gag me to pull that off. I despise Titus Ravir. He was a spoiled vicious brat as a child and from what I've heard he's only gotten worse. His sister Raven is a psychotic bitch I want nowhere near me and don't even get me started on their father." Evie visibly shuddered. "A few minutes in the presence of Lord Nero makes me feel like I need to bathe in disinfectant."

"And your father? Where did he stand on all of this?"

"As I said, my father would never try to strong-arm me into marriage and he doesn't like or trust House Ravir. He said there were too many bad rumors about their flock for all of it to be false and he didn't want the name of our House sullied by association."

"So…what happened?"

"My father hasn't been well. I think I mentioned that to you. His declining health and the constant barrage from my uncle and members of the flock he riled up to push for the alliance was wearing on my father. I already made my position clear and that should have been the end of it but because of my uncle they kept going behind my back to harass my father like a bunch of crows. This was Marcus's way of publicly undermining my authority. I had to put a stop to it. He struts around like a royal peacock but he only gets to maintain the facade of wealth and power because my father discreetly gives him an allowance and houses him in a luxurious suite. Marcus squandered the fortune my grandfather left him and came crawling to my father for help because he had money lenders threatening to pluck his feathers as repayment for bad debts. My father took him in and quietly took care of all his debts. I called Marcus out on this in front of his cronies. Then I reminded him that one day I'll be the ruler of House Aquilar, not him. From that point on his position in the flock and the allowance he receives from my family's personal fortune will depend on my goodwill, which he's already worn thin. I also advised him to find ways to be useful to the flock, just like everyone else, because I will not tolerate a freeloader who spends his days gambling and partying like a sailor on a weekend pass. If looks could kill I would have dropped dead on the spot but that was the end of his little show of dissent. Marcus' supporters abandoned him quicker than flees on a dead dog. My father wasn't happy that I humiliated his brother like that but he understood that I had to put Marcus in his place."

Evie paused when she noticed Aurora was staring at her with wide eyes. "Why are you looking at me like that?"

Aurora shook her head. "You're quite extraordinary and a little scary. You're like a kitten that looks all sweet and cuddly but you have sharp claws. Remind me never to cross you. Or play cards with you. I bet you play a mean hand."

"Ooh, I love a good game of cards. I'm rather good at it."

"I bet," Aurora said dryly.

"For some reason, people don't want to play with me when we're playing for money. Only my sister and a few of the cousins but they're cunning; I have to watch them carefully to make sure they don't cheat. Do you play?"

"Now and then but I don't get enough practice to be good at it. The last time I played strip poker I ended up in my undies in only a few rounds. I would have been naked first for sure if it wasn't for the fire that broke out next door. Saved by a fire…it's not every day one gets to say that."

"How did that happen?"

"It was a grease fire in the kitchen. More smoke than fire. No one got hurt."

"I mean how did you end up playing strip poker? Where, how and most importantly, with whom?" Evie was fairly bouncing on the spot with curiosity.

"I was at a private party in a club. It was late, I had a few drinks and it sounded like it could be fun. It was…except that I played so badly. Then there was the fire of course."

"You at a party? Getting drunk and playing strip poker?" Evie struggled to get her head around the idea of Aurora partying but mostly her imagination snagged on Aurora in her bra and panties getting ready to take it all off.

Aurora tucked a wisp of hair behind her ear, a faint blush on her cheeks. "Don't sound so surprised. I don't live out in the wilderness all the time. I move around a lot and when I'm in town I like to unwind a little."

"Sounds like it. So how many people at this poker game? Anyone in particular you wanted to see naked? I want to know *everything*."

Aurora's cheeks flared to crimson. "It wasn't like that. Besides, if I want to see someone naked I can do better than a game of strip poker. It was just a fun evening that got a bit risqué."

With or without booze Evie could not imagine Aurora suddenly becoming an outrageous party animal but to be fair she hardly knew the woman. Even though at times they fell into such a comfortable familiarity that it felt like they'd been friends for years, in reality there was a lot they didn't know about each other. The way Aurora had become all defensive and evasive had Evie intrigued and she was dying to know more. She was tempted to tease Aurora until she relented but she could as easily get all guarded and refuse to say anything. She'd seen that happen a few times. Best to wait for an opportunity to get the saucy details of that poker game out of her. She just had to be patient or if she was lucky stumble across some good quality booze. Even better would be to find a deck of cards as well. Nothing wrong with offering to play a few rounds to help Aurora improve her game and if along the way things got risqué it would just be a bit of fun between friends.

Evie shook herself mentally. Wow...did she just plot how to get Aurora to peel off her clothing for her, layer by layer, until nothing covered that glorious body? Evie felt her own body's eager response to that idea and bit down on the groan that almost escaped her lips. She had to get a hold of herself. Besides, that plan wouldn't work after she just bragged that she was a great card player. On the other hand, if she could convince Aurora to play she could always lose the occasional hand to keep things moving in the right direction. A room with just the two of them, their clothing coming off in a slow tease. No touching allowed, just their eyes devouring until finally there were no barriers left between them and they simply had to touch or go out of their minds. She'd give several of her precious prime feathers for that fantasy to become a reality. Would Aurora be interested in that kind of game? If she was what would it be like to be with someone like her? Aurora was so focused and intense and yet at times she could be playful so what would she be like as a lover?

"So…do you agree?"

Evie realized Aurora was looking at her expectantly. "Do I agree with what?" Evie shifted uncomfortably. She wasn't used to lusty thoughts ambushing her with such enthusiasm that she lost track of the conversation. Especially when the source of the wicked thoughts sat right next to her.

"To leave now. If we do we'll be at the sanctuary in a few hours. That way we can rest all of tomorrow. That's if you don't mind traveling at night again. The moon will be out so that will make it easier for you to see. I've traveled these paths so many times I could lead us there in my sleep."

"Even at night?"

"Especially at night. That's when I usually travel. I'm a nocturnal beast-shifter, remember?"

"Why didn't you say something earlier? We probably could have been there already if we hadn't stayed here so long."

Aurora shrugged. "This would have made a reasonable place to camp for the night had we decided to stay. Besides, you needed the rest."

Evie narrowed her eyes at Aurora. "The fact that it will be dark and very difficult for me to find the way again has nothing to do with it I suppose?"

Aurora responded by holding her palms up in a gesture of supplication. "Of course not. If you prefer we can spend the night sleeping here on the cold hard rocks with rats and insects for company instead of in a warm soft bed. It's entirely up to you. It makes no difference to me because I'm used to sleeping rough. Not sure you'll get much rest though. Can you feel the wind picking up? The way it blows through this pass it will sound like the howling of a pack of wolves tonight."

Evie grimaced and said, "Fine. Let's go." She rustled her wings to show her displeasure at being so cleverly manipulated to travel in the mountains at night. Aurora had been positively devious dangling the comforts of a bed and bath in front of her. The woman must know there was no way Evie would choose to spend a night sleeping on stones in a windy pass after that. Perhaps Aurora wasn't nearly as bad at cards as she let on. Or was she more of a chess player, plotting how to back her opponent into a corner from the first move? Yeah, she fit the profile.

CHAPTER 14

DANGEROUS PATH

Aurora led them along paths that twisted and turned through the mountains. When it became harder to see she offered Evie her arm to lean on when there was enough space for them to walk side by side and her hand when there wasn't. The moon had just appeared when Aurora led them off the path to two tall rocks. She told Evie to wait and disappeared behind them. About a minute later Aurora reappeared and beckoned for Evie to follow. Squeezing through the gap Evie saw a smooth doorway cut into the sheer rock. Peering inside it was as dark as a grave and the sight of it filled her with dread.

"Aurora, you can't expect me to go in there. It's pitch dark and you know how I feel about the dark."

"I'll be able to create light once we're inside."

"Do we really have to go this way?"

"Yes, we do. Without this shortcut we won't get there tonight."

"What is this? A cave system?"

"It's one of the underground passages built by the Ancients. Think of it as a system of tunnels if that helps."

"Really? I thought those were only a myth? How did you know there's an entrance here?"

Aurora held out a hand. "Not the time for questions. Come on."

Evie put her hand in Aurora's and immediately felt comforted by the familiar warmth.

Aurora squeezed her hand and said, "You may see some curious things but please don't ask me questions while we are inside. We need to be very quiet and I need to focus so I don't lose track of where we are. You ready, Evie?"

"As ready as I can be since I've no idea what I'm supposed to be ready for."

Aurora grinned, showing white teeth in the moonlight and the next moment they were moving. They went from moonlight to utter darkness so suddenly Evie's impulse was to stop but Aurora kept them moving forward. Not being able to see, Evie feared she would stumble or walk into something despite Aurora leading the way but she quickly realized the surface underfoot was smooth as polished stone. Aurora paused and a few seconds later faint glyphs glowed to light in a circular design around her hand on the wall. Glancing around, Evie saw they were indeed in a tunnel and that the walls and ceiling appeared as smooth as the floor. Aurora drew on the wall with her finger and tiny lights reminiscent of a firefly's glow appeared on the floor revealing a small section of the tunnel ahead of them. Aurora gave a satisfied grunt and they were off following the dim lights. Glancing over her shoulder Evie saw the lights going out behind them. Her rational mind knew there was a logical explanation for what was happening but the part of her that feared the dark felt like there was a monster following on their heels devouring the light. She tightened her grip on Aurora's hand and decided to keep her eyes on the lights in front of them.

When they came to a crossroad of tunnels veering off into different directions Aurora paused to rest her palm on the wall of one of the tunnels and the little lights appeared again. This happened twice more and Evie realized their pathway must be part of a complex labyrinth of passages. It was a mystery to her how Aurora knew which direction to go and since Aurora had warned her to be quiet she didn't dare ask.

They came to what appeared to Evie to be a dead end but instead of turning them around to go back the way they came Aurora moved Evie's hand to her shoulder. Evie felt Aurora roll her shoulders as she tended to do when faced with a challenge. With alarm Evie watched the lights behind them fade to black. As darkness descended Evie wrapped her arms around Aurora's waist and shamelessly pressed herself flat against the other woman's back. She knew the moment Aurora drew on her magic because every part of her that touched Aurora felt like it was being pricked by tiny electric needles. The sensation verged on being painful but Evie gritted her teeth and held on. Aurora's arms moved in the dark and a complex set of runes encased in circular designs rose to the surface of the stone around her hands. Keeping one hand in place Aurora used the other to touch a rune and it rose above the rest, clinging to her fingers like a sticky orb of light. She moved the rune to a different location and as soon as she let it go the designs swirled and changed. She did this again and again. By the eerie lights of the runes Evie saw Aurora's face was rigid with concentration. After several minutes of this

Aurora's hands dropped to her side and a doorway appeared where moments before there had been solid rock. She tucked Evie's arm under hers and moved them at a jog through a pitch-black space towards a throbbing red orb that appeared to drift in space some distance away. When they got near enough Evie saw the orb was actually several rune-filled circles spinning independently of each other within a larger circular design above a gigantic doorway. The runes changed with every rotation of the inner circles, flashing just before the change and for some reason it made Evie think of a countdown. Aurora rushed them through the giant doorway into a passage that lit up with tiny lights as soon as she touched the wall. They were just in time it seems because when Evie looked back the doorway they had come through was gone. Thoroughly shaken, Evie tucked her wings around herself as tightly as she could and meekly followed her guide.

They had only gone a short distance when Aurora stopped. She tilted her head to the left and right as if listening then she put an arm around Evie and drew her close. She put a finger to her mouth motioning for silence as the lights around them dimmed and they were swallowed by the dark. Evie listened but aside from their breathing she heard absolutely nothing. It was like they were standing in a tomb of smoothed stone, so long vacant of life, light and sound that not even mice dared scurry about. Testing the air she noticed it smelled dry and stale like it had not been disturbed for some time. She had begun to wonder if Aurora imagined she'd heard something when she felt through the delicate membranes in her wings the change in air pressure as if a door had opened into an enclosed space. Straining to hear she caught fragments of indistinct sound bouncing around tunnel walls somewhere up ahead and to their left. As it drew nearer she could make out something that creaked and groaned with mechanical thumps as it moved. After their long quiet passage through the tunnels the sounds seemed so sharp and out of place that, combined with Aurora's warning, it felt to her whatever was up ahead fairly hummed with menace. The spike of alarm made her heart hammer so loudly in her chest that she worried it would be heard. They stood motionless, tracking the progress of the thing moving through the dark. Whatever it was it didn't need light because even when it went past what sounded like an adjoining passage Evie saw no lights. To her relief, the creature became quieter as it moved away until once again she only heard their breathing. The minutes ticked away but Aurora didn't move so neither did she, trusting in her companion's superior hearing. The whole time Aurora held her close, her solidity and the warmth of her body Evie's anchor in the dark. Tired of waiting and looking without being able to see Evie leaned her head against Aurora's shoulder and closed her eyes. Like this it didn't feel so different from the other times Aurora watched over her in the dark.

Aurora's lips brushed her ear and she whispered, "I've got you. Don't be afraid."

To her surprise, Evie realized that she wasn't really afraid. It was true her heart had felt like it would pound out of her chest when they went through that weird passage and even now in the dark she was far from comfortable. But at the same time, her nerve endings zinged with such an acute awareness of her own body and everything around her that it was exhilarating. This was the danger of the unknown and the discomfort of finding herself in a situation she could not control but she didn't fear for her life. The last time she'd felt truly afraid was just after she'd broken her wing on that mountainside. She'd been terrified that Aurora would abandon her to be recaptured and dragged back to that cage to face the cutter's scalpel. In retrospect that fear seemed silly. Not because the danger hadn't been real but because she now knew Aurora would never have left her behind. No, she wasn't afraid. She couldn't be when she had Aurora by her side.

***

With no way to measure the time it felt to Evie like a small eternity before they finally emerged above ground. The moon was high in the sky and the stars were so bright compared to the lights in the tunnels they burned her eyes.

"Are you all right, Evie?"

Evie nodded and rubbed her eyes. "Yes, although at some point we're going to have words about the whole going underground business. You conveniently left out any mention of pitch-black tunnels and scary monsters when you sold this night time excursion to me."

"That wasn't a monster – it was one of the guardians that maintain and protect the old passages. The noisy fellow that passed us mostly just goes about its business but I still do my best to avoid the guardians. I was being extra careful tonight because I had you with me."

"Would that thing have attacked us?"

"Only if I triggered the wards by using incorrect runes or we did something it perceived as threatening. You weren't in any real danger. I've used the passages since I was a child and I know how to get in and out without getting into trouble."

"We're done with those passages? Because just so you know, there is nothing you could offer me that would get me to go back in right now."

"Yes, and we are almost home. When we get there I'll run you the biggest bath you've ever seen. Having a relaxing soak in the pool is one of my favorite things about going home."

Home. Evie mulled over the word Aurora used. When Aurora had described where they were going earlier she'd made it sound like an impersonal sanctuary of sorts. Was it a slip of the tongue? Her friend was full of secrets. She'd been curious anyway to see where they would end up but now she was thoroughly intrigued. Aurora was taking her home. She'd never had an invitation to a tiger's lair before. This was going to be interesting.

CHAPTER 15

INTIMATE FRIENDS

The closer they got to her home the more nervous Aurora became. She'd never taken anyone home and now she was leading a beautiful woman by the hand to sleep in her bed. It hadn't occurred to her there would be an issue with sleeping arrangements until they were already on the way but walking had given her time to think things through more. There were currently only two bedrooms, her own and her mother's. Her mother's bedroom was behind impenetrable walls and even had she been in the mood to open the doorways leading there she wouldn't dream of sleeping in her mother's bed. She had a very nice couch in the library she could sleep on but she didn't want to be too far away from Evie in case she got it in her head to wander about looking for her. That would be bad. That left sleeping in the chair in the kitchen area. Aurora didn't relish the thought but she was more worried about what would happen if she shared a bed with Evie. Evie had been more physical than normal with her. Which said a lot considering how frequently Evie usually touched her. She could still feel the way Evie's front had molded to her back while she worked the spell to open the passage and all the other places Evie touched her while trying to stay close. Aurora knew it was only because Evie was afraid of the dark and needed the comfort of her presence but it was messing with her head and getting her libido all fired up. She already had a huge crush on the beautiful avian and she'd begun to get the feeling Evie was flirting with her but that could be just wishful thinking on her part. Either way, she had to tread lightly if she wanted to keep her heart intact. Falling in love right now did not fit into her plans for the future. If that wasn't enough reason for her to avoid sleeping in the same bed as Evie she also had to consider the possibility she would have a nightmare tonight. She'd already had nightmares two nights in a row and with her track record she was almost guaranteed to have another. Her lusty hands she could control but what she did in her sleep when she got caught in one of those nightmares she could not. She simply could not risk exposing Evie to that.

By the time Aurora opened the doorway to her home and set the protective spells to recognize Evie as a guest she had come up with a plan. Evie might be too tired to notice there was only one bedroom but if she did and insisted they share she would just stall going to bed until the other woman fell asleep. She would get Evie in the pool and usher her to bed with a soothing hot drink. Then she would take her time having a wash. Evie was so tired she would fall asleep quickly and not wake until the morning none the wiser that Aurora had slept in a chair. Yes, that's what she would do.

"Aurora, can you please hurry with whatever you're doing and show me the way to the toilet because I *really* need to pee."

"This way, it's right next to the bathing chamber. Give me your bag and I'll go put it in your room over there." Aurora pointed down the hallway. "I'll turn on the water and get something for you to sleep in."

"Wonderful…can't wait…now please for the love of all things sacred, get out of the way before I embarrass us both. I'm busting!"

Laughing, Aurora jumped out of the way as Evie hastily pushed past her to get to the toilet. She hurried to the bedroom to get a few things then to get the bathing chambers ready for Evie. By the time she heard the rustle of wings behind her she already had the pool half filled with steaming water.

Evie slowly turned to study the bathroom. "Wow…this room is massive. Aurora that's not a bath…that thing is the size of a swimming pool! It seems like a waste of water to use it for one person's bath."

"Think of this room as a small replica of a bathhouse. The pool is for relaxing and soaking, not for cleaning. I wash over there in that corner. Can you see the things along the wall for washing and rinsing? Feel free to use any of the soaps and lotions. There's also a shower unit if you prefer to wash that way. The water in the big pool will remain at a consistent temperature and be ready to use any time day or night. There are steps leading down into the pool so you can sit on those and rest your wings on the side of the pool if you don't want to get your feathers wet. I've laid out clean towels and things for you to sleep in on the bench. I won't come in until you're finished so you have all of this to yourself. Enjoy."

"I will! This is amazing, thanks Aurora."

***

As soon as Evie walked into the room and saw the massive high bed and the books on the table on the left side of the bed she suspected she was in Aurora's bedroom. Curious to see if she was right she opened a closet door and found clothing on coat hangers and size eleven shoes neatly arranged underneath. She removed a jacket, pressed her nose into the fabric and inhaled Aurora's familiar scent. Yes, this was her room. Evie found it curious that Aurora didn't mention they would be sharing but she didn't mind in the least. They'd been sleeping side by side since they met after all and it would be comforting to have Aurora near in this strange place. So far she'd not seen any windows or vents and yet the air did not smell stale. She suspected they were inside a mountain but other than that she had no clue where they were. At another time this would have bothered her a lot more but she was simply too tired to give it more than a passing thought. Besides, every part of her was gloriously clean and she was about to get into a proper bed for the first time in days. Evie was pleased with the comfort of the sleepwear Aurora had chosen for her and how considerate she'd been in her selection. The soft boxer shorts had a drawstring so she'd been able to adjust it to fit her smaller size and the sarong she'd been able to fasten around herself in such a way it covered all the important bits while leaving her wings free.

Evie slid between the crisp sheets and sighed contently. She ran her hand over the duvet admiring the intricate embroidery that depicted a mountain covered in flowers. It was so cheerful and added a much-needed splash of color and warmth to a room that was sparsely decorated. Evie wondered who had given Aurora the duvet. It was exquisite but she couldn't imagine Aurora buying bedding with pink and red ribbons stitched into the borders.

Evie settled her wings so she could sit up and have the steaming mug of tea Aurora had pushed into her hands as she ushered her towards the room. Taking an experimental sip she found it was a chamomile blend with a generous dollop of honey. A perfect bedtime drink. She drank it slowly enjoying the taste and soothing warmth.

By the time she put the mug down on her bedside table Evie was struggling to keep her eyes open. She was tempted to lie down but she knew if she did she would be asleep in moments and she wanted to be awake when Aurora came to bed. It had become her guilty pleasure to watch Aurora and she had a wicked fantasy of seeing her in her full naked glory. Not that she expected Aurora to come to bed wearing nothing but there would be bare legs and no bra and she didn't want to miss that.

As time dragged on Evie repeatedly caught herself nodding off and still no sign of Aurora. This was ridiculous; how long could it possibly take her to clean up? As she waited Evie became aware of silence that was so absolute it reminded her of being back in those tunnels and she could feel herself become agitated. What was taking Aurora so long? Had she perhaps gone to sleep somewhere else? Surely not. It wasn't like the Aurora she'd come to know to not at least say goodnight to her. What if she'd fallen asleep in the pool and was close to drowning? That seemed unlikely but the worry gnawed at her and Evie knew she wouldn't be able to relax until she found out what had happened to Aurora. Reluctantly she dragged her weary limbs out from under the soft covers and took up the hunt for her hostess.

She found her down the hallway they'd originally entered in a room that looked like it doubled as a kitchen/sitting room. Aurora slumped in a large chair, her long limbs awkwardly draped over the sides with a blanket covering her legs.

"Aurora…what are you doing here?"

Aurora cracked an eye open and said, "It's called trying to sleep."

"That's obvious, wise-ass, but why here? Are you guarding the door?"

"No. We should be safe here. It would take more than a battering ram to get in and we would hear that kind of ruckus."

"So why are you here instead of in bed?"

"I'm too tired to unlock more rooms. For now, what you've seen is all we've got. Right now there is only one bed and it's in my bedroom. I promised you a bed if you came with me so the room is yours. I'll be fine here. I'll set things up better for tomorrow night."

"So, let me get this straight. You plan to sleep in that chair while I sleep alone in that massive bed of yours?"

"I promised you a bed and I already explained there is only one right now."

Evie narrowed her eyes at Aurora. "Get out of that chair."

"Why? Evie, I'm tired. Go back to bed and let me sleep."

Evie's wings arched open and her feathers puffed up like someone had rubbed them the wrong way. She kicked the side of Aurora's chair and said, "Get out of that thing. You are crazy if you think I'll let you give up your bed for me while you sleep in that uncomfortable chair. I know cats squeeze themselves into ridiculously small spaces but you are not a feline right now and you need space to stretch out. Your bed is more than big enough for both of us. We've done just about everything together in the last couple of days, including sleep together, so I don't know why you are acting so silly. Get up and come to bed."

When Aurora just stared at her and didn't move Evie's wings deflated. "I can't take your bed. I'd feel awful knowing you're out here like this. If you insist on sleeping here I'll have to join you and I really don't want to sleep on the floor when there's a perfectly good bed nearby."

"Evie—"

"Let me finish. Aside from the passages we used tonight I've never been in a place that feels so odd. Maybe it's because there are no windows and the walls glow or maybe it's because in my home there's always noise with people moving about and talking whereas this place is as quiet as the tomb. Whatever it is I find it very unsettling and I'd really appreciate it if you don't leave me alone here on our first night."

***

Aurora's heart ached to see Evie look so embarrassed having to admit she didn't want to sleep alone. It never occurred to her that Evie would be afraid in her home, probably because she measured safety in how fortified or defendable a place was whereas Evie needed people to feel safe. Darn it if Evie hadn't just derailed her careful strategy and it was impossible to say no to her when she got that wide-eyed, vulnerable look. She would have to go to bed with her now, at least long enough for Evie to fall asleep. Aurora got out of the chair and led the way back to her room. She paused at the foot of the bed and asked, "Do you prefer a side?"

"Not really, I tend to drift to the middle."

"Then I'll take the left."

Aurora crawled under the covers and tried to relax. Her bed was large and more than spacious enough for the two of them to sleep without touching. Although if she was honest with herself, she really wanted there to be touching.

"Aurora?"

"Hmm?"

"Why didn't you want to sleep with me? Surely you can't be uncomfortable with me after all the time we've spent together? Or is it just that you needed some alone time?"

"I'm very comfortable with you, Evie and no I don't need to be alone. I've gotten so used to you being around it feels like something is missing when I don't see you."

Aurora arched her toes and stretched her arms out behind her until her fingertips touched the wall, an old ritual. It was rare that she got to sleep in a bed that could fully accommodate her size and it was a pleasure being back in her own comfortable bed. Even if it was just for a little while.

"So…what was the reason?"

Aurora suppressed a sigh. She should have known Evie would not be satisfied until she got an answer. The woman was relentless when she wanted something.

"Maybe I was afraid you'd stretch those massive wings in your sleep and give me a black eye or worse, suffocate me."

"You mean like this?"

Evie playfully unfurled a wing so it enclosed them in a canopy of golden feathers. Suddenly Aurora found herself drenched in Evie's scent, her senses in total overload. She couldn't help herself; she inhaled deeply, drawing the glorious aroma deep into her lungs and tasting it on her tongue. She almost moaned aloud at the intensity of her body's response. Why would Evie do something so provocative? Did she know so little about beast-shifters with sensitive noses that she didn't realize doing something like this, especially while they were in bed together, was the equivalent of rubbing herself all over Aurora? If she was on heat such an invitation would have had her all over Evie in an instant. As it was, she had a hard time keeping her hands to herself and acting civilized. Someone really needed to educate Evie on the finer points of beast-shifter etiquette because she was a danger to herself.

"You can touch it."

Dazed and confused Aurora turned to stare at Evie.

"My wing – I can tell you want to touch the feathers. Go ahead, I don't mind."

Aurora swallowed hard and reminded herself firmly that Evie was only offering her wing. She tentatively laid her hand on the inside of Evie's wing and glided her fingertips over the feathers ever so lightly. The sensation was exquisite, the heat from Evie's body making the feathers feel like warm silk. She needed to feel more. She flattened her palm against Evie's wing, stroking gently. One hand simply wasn't enough with so much to explore so she added another. She glanced at

Evie to make sure it was all right to continue. Evie didn't say anything, instead she opened her wing further which was all the permission Aurora needed. She touched and stroked exploring the fine texture of individual feathers between her fingertips and the intricate layering of feathers. Aurora lost track of time mesmerized by the sensation of feathers on palm and Evie's scent all around her. The contrast between the bare skin on Evie's back and the feathers of her wing caught her eye. Without thinking she slid her hand into the area where the two joined so she could touch both at the same time. Evie inhaled sharply and shuddered.

"Did I hurt you, Evie?"

"No. It is, however, a very *sensitive* area."

The way Evie put emphasis on the word 'sensitive' made Aurora think she had meant to use an entirely different word so she carefully removed her hand. As soon as she did Evie withdrew her wing. Aurora immediately felt a sense of loss and she had to tuck her hands under her to keep from reaching for her again. Evie was watching her with hooded eyes and the air between them felt so charged Aurora found it a little hard to breathe. Something had shifted between them while she touched Evie's wing. She wasn't exactly sure what but something was different. Aurora felt like she should say something but she had no idea what. She could hardly tell Evie she thought she was falling in love with her.

***

While Aurora touched her wing Evie had taken the opportunity to study her carefully. What she saw had fascinated her. What started out as a gentle touch had quickly turned into something close to a lover's caress. She'd watched Aurora's strong hands glide all over her wing and she imagined those hands exploring other parts of her body like that. She kept reminding herself Aurora was her friend, just her friend…but no 'just friend' had ever explored her wing with such reverence. She'd almost lost it when Aurora so innocently stroked the spot between her back and wing that no avian would touch without a lover's permission.

Now even though Evie had removed her wing so they were no longer enclosed, the intimacy of the moment lingered. The air between them was so heavy with expectation it seemed natural to Evie that they should kiss. She leaned in slowly giving Aurora plenty of time to pull away. Despite her own excitement Evie took care to keep the kiss light and chaste in case she'd misinterpreted the signs. Aurora's lips were velvety soft and Evie ached to part her lips and taste her more fully but made herself pull back after just a few seconds. She lay her head back on her own pillow and tried to look relaxed like it was no big deal she'd just kissed Aurora. In truth she was nervous and it didn't help that Aurora looked so serious.

"Why the kiss?" Aurora asked.

"That was for getting me away from that mine. I don't think I said thank you properly for saving my life."

"No thanks needed, we helped each other."

"No, it was all you. You didn't really need my help to get away from that place and you could have left me to fend for myself after I broke my wing. You didn't. You've been looking out for me this whole time and I want you to know I think you are amazing."

While Evie spoke Aurora's eyes had drifted to her mouth and her eyes had gone a green so dark they looked almost black. When she looked back up Evie felt her heart skip a beat. She might not have seen that expression on Aurora before but she recognized desire when she saw it. She licked her lips and instantly Aurora's eyes were back on her mouth. It was too much to resist and she kissed Aurora again. This time Aurora returned the kiss and Evie got a tantalizing hint of the sweetness of Aurora's mouth in the slight parting of lips just before she drew away. They were both breathing a little fast despite the relative innocence of the kiss.

"And that kiss was for?"

"That was for keeping your word and delivering that hot bath and a proper bed. Even if you dragged me through those awful tunnels to get here."

Aurora considered Evie's words for a moment then her eyes and mouth crinkled in amusement and she said, "If your kisses are anything to go by it would seem you're more appreciative about the hot water and bed than you are about me saving your life. If that's true your priorities are really skewed."

Evie giggled as much in relief that Aurora wasn't upset she'd kissed her twice as the realization that she spoke the truth. "I didn't think about it like that but I suppose you have a point. But this really is a very nice bed."

Aurora bounced her long body and it made the bed creak and move a little. "The bed is not *that* nice. I really need to rebuild the frame but the mattress is comfortable and the bedding is soft and clean so it definitely beats sleeping on rocks."

The bouncing looked like fun so Evie joined in and they laughed as their combined movement made the bed creak and sway like a ship in a storm. They stopped simultaneously when the bed made an ominous groan. Aurora looked so flushed and happy Evie simply had to kiss her again. This time she gave no warning and she absorbed the sound and feel of Aurora's laughter into her mouth. She just wanted to steal another quick taste but to her delight Aurora deepened the kiss. Evie lost herself in the moment savoring the flavor of Aurora's mouth and the delicate dance of their lips and tongues. Just as their bare legs tangled and it felt like things were about to heat up considerably Aurora drew away. Evie was tempted to pursue and press for more but the guarded expression on Aurora's face warned her to slow down.

"Evie..."

The deep husky tone of Aurora's voice when she said her name sent shivers of desire down Evie's spine.

"Before we go any further I need to know what this means to you. Surely it's not you still showing gratitude?"

"That kiss was *way* too passionate for that, don't you think? It felt so good to kiss you the first two times I wanted more. Is that all right?"

"It's more than all right, Evie, you're an amazing kisser. If I didn't like what you were doing I wouldn't have kissed you back or let you kiss me at all. I'm not sure what to make of what's happening between us right now though. What is it you want? Do you just need stress release after a difficult few days? If that's what this is I have to tell you I'm not built for a casual fling. Not that there's anything wrong with that kind of thing but it's just not for me."

Evie brought Aurora's hand up to her lips and pressed a kiss against the knuckles. "You think too much. I'm attracted to you and I wanted to kiss you so I did. I don't expect anything and if this goes further it doesn't have to be a big deal. If it helps, think of whatever happens between us as an affectionate sharing between friends."

Aurora frowned. "I don't understand what that means. I assume you're saying if we become intimate it's not meant to be taken seriously? For the record, I don't kiss my friends like that or kiss them while in bed together no matter how affectionate I feel towards them."

"That's good to know. Neither do I. Just to be clear on that."

"That's a relief. I was beginning to wonder what sorts of things go on in that tower of yours. Orgies breaking out like an unexpected rash came to mind."

"They do not!" Evie giggled and gave Aurora a playful smack. "One person at a time is quite enough for me. Besides, most of the people in my tower are related in one way or another so any orgy is likely to cross some icky boundaries. Also, did you have to bring up sex in the same sentence as rash? If the thought of incest wasn't enough to make me feel queasy that would do it. Yikes."

Grinning Aurora said, "Finally I get payback."

"For what?"

"For when you asked if the twenty-year-old version of me wanted to have sex with an elderly shepherd who was missing several teeth, chewed tobacco and only washed once every other week. The thought of that made *me* feel queasy."

"Eeew, I think we need to stop this conversation. I'm terrified of what you'll come up with next. If you were trying to kill the mood you've managed it quite nicely."

Aurora laughed and rolled onto her back leaving a small space between them but close enough for their hands to touch. It wasn't long before their fingers intertwined. It was like their hands, joined for so much of the day, sought to fill the emptiness left by the other's absence.

Evie found she was amused and more than a little perplexed after the heated kisses they'd shared to find herself oddly content to lie in bed with Aurora just holding hands. She was too tired to analyze what had just happened. At least she now knew Aurora didn't mind being kissed by a woman, which was good. On the other hand, it was also now apparent Aurora put sex and a serious relationship in the same basket. She wasn't sure how she felt about that so she filed it away for later.

***

Aurora lay as still as she could and waited for Evie to fall asleep. She was exhausted and conflicted on so many levels but one thing she knew for sure, staying in bed with Evie tonight was not an option. She didn't want to explain why she needed to leave so she waited for Evie to drift off so she could sneak away.

Aurora woke out of her semi-doze and realized with alarm she had been moments away from falling asleep herself. She got one leg out of bed and tried to let go of Evie's hand without alerting her but the other woman's eyes fluttered open. Perhaps she looked guilty because Evie raised a questioning brow.

"I almost fell asleep," Aurora tried to explain realizing as soon as she said it how odd that would sound.

"I thought that was the idea?" Evie sleepily pointed out.

"I'd love to stay but I really should get up and sleep elsewhere. I was going to do that after you fell asleep but I won't last much longer."

"Why would you do that?" Evie took a firmer hold of Aurora's hand and tucked it securely under her chest. "It is not still about my wings? I thought you were just joking about that but I can shift them away if they bother you and if it's about the kisses…I apologize. I promise never to do anything like that again if you don't want me to. I'll never forgive myself if I've just ruined our friendship."

"Nothing is ruined. You haven't done anything wrong and I was just joking about your wings." Aurora reached with her free hand and gently tucked a lock of Evie's hair that had come loose from the braid away from her face.

"Then why?"

"I'm not used to sleeping with someone like this. I'm so tired I'd like nothing better than to sleep next to you in my own bed but when I'm very tired I sleep deeply. That would normally be fine but it also means it's much harder for me to wake myself when I have a nightmare."

"You expect to have a nightmare? Is this a common thing?"

Aurora's expression became troubled. "I have a recurring nightmare. It comes and goes but when it returns I usually have it for several nights in a row. So far I've had it two nights in a row and as these things go I'll probably have it again tonight."

"Do you know what brings it on?"

"Yes. Every time I'm reminded of what happened to me and my dad it starts up again. Between going into the cutter's lab and retrieving my father's fang it's raked up old memories. In my dreams I'm a little girl again and I get to relive the worst days of my life. Needless to say, my nightmares are violent and when I'm not able to wake myself to make it stop…it's bad. I don't know how safe it would be for you if I had one while you're in bed with me."

"Why? What do you think could happen?"

"I really don't know. I don't have experience sleeping with someone else like this and I'm worried. I'm a beast-shifter, Evie. Sometimes when I'm stuck in the dream and can't tell it's not really happening I start to change. It's a defense mechanism, like the fight-or-flight response that pumps adrenaline into the body getting it all psyched up. In my case, because of what I am, subconsciously I want to be in a less vulnerable body so I start drawing on my beast. Most times the discomfort wakes me before the change is too far along but I don't want to scare you or accidentally hurt you."

"Hmm…" Evie considered for a moment. "Don't worry, if it looks like you're having a nightmare I'll kick you out of bed. Like so…" she made a shoving motion with her foot against Aurora's hip. "That will put some distance between us and this bed is so high the drop is bound to wake you. Would that work?"

"Yeah, it probably would," Aurora said thoughtfully then grinned. "I never thought I'd find myself in a scenario where I'm pleased a woman offered to kick me out of bed. That's new. You keep amazing and surprising me."

"Aurora, since I've met you I've had one hair-raising experience after another. This morning I went into a den of hostile wolves and earlier this evening I got dragged through what felt like the pit of the underworld complete with a skulking monster. Both those experiences were very disconcerting but because you were with me I knew whatever happened I would be fine. I knew you wouldn't let anything hurt me. So tonight, if you have a bad dream it'll be the other way around. You'll be okay because I'm right next to you. I *will* wake you, one way or another. Now let's get some rest. I have a feeling I'm going to need my strength for whatever tomorrow will bring. Being around you, I fully expect something extraordinary."

"Being around you, I have to say the same. Evie, could you do something for me?"

"What do you need? Anything just name it."

"Now that we've established I'm not going anywhere can you ease your grip on my hand a little? I can't feel my fingers anymore."

Evie gave a slow blink as she processed Aurora's words and then her cheeks flushed pink when she realized she held Aurora's hand pinned under her left breast. She quickly let go. "Oh wow, sorry."

Chuckling Aurora turned onto her stomach. "Sleep well, Evie."

"You too."

There was the rustle of wings settling, the sound of a pillow being vigorously thumped into shape and then everything went quiet.

***

The nightmare started as it always did. She stood in a river up to her knees in black water. The water was rising and she could feel the sickening dread that something awful was coming. She knew what was happening, knew she was falling into the dream again. Desperate she struggled to get to the bank, to safety, to wakefulness but she knew she would not make it. She felt phantom fists slam into her, hands tore off her clothing and meat hooks dug into her flesh, dragging her deeper into the icy river. Despite knowing it was futile she fought with all her might, tearing out the hooks so the water around her warmed with the heat of her own blood. The pain was excruciating and she wanted to scream but she knew if she did her father would come into the water to save her and then he would be caught as well. The water surged up to her neck and she saw the crimson wave bearing down on her. It was so large it blocked out the light so all she could see was the dismembered corpses and screaming mouths. She made one last feeble attempt to get away then the wave was on her. She tried to scream but blood filled her mouth and nose. She tried to spit it out so she could breathe but there was too much of it.

"Drink the blood or you will die," a voice said.

"No, please don't make me do this."

"Drink Aurora, swallow my gift and be healed."

The voice was familiar. It was someone she loved, someone she trusted. It was a voice she could not disobey. She did as she was told and swallowed the warm blood along with the acid of her tears. It burned, oh how it burned going down and she was seared by the agony of it.

Weights pressed down on her so that she struggled to breathe and she couldn't move. She was out of the river splayed face down in the dirt, naked in a pool of her own blood. There were weights on her arms and legs, men sitting on her holding her down. Something terrible was coming. She tried to lift her head to see and saw the man holding something that glowed. A pipe red hot like fire, like burning, the color of pain.

"Scream for us girl, scream so your daddy will come for you."

She didn't want to but she couldn't help it – the pain was beyond what she could endure. She screamed and screamed for her father to come and make it stop until the world tilted from red to black.

The darkness turned to murky light and she was in a pit in the ground. It was a cage. Her cage. She was in pain, so much pain. She hurt everywhere. There were things wrong with her body, too many things. Dying. She knew she was dying.

Drip. Drip. Drip.

There was something dripping on her from above. What was it? A creature was lying on top of her cage, an animal so large it blocked out the light. There was something dripping from it, something warm and salty. It smelled like death, like something too horrible to think about but it tasted like life. She was thirsty, so very thirsty and the drip had become a downpour splashing over her face and naked filth-encrusted body.

"Drink Aurora. Do it for me."

"Daddy, I'm so sorry. I love you. Please don't die."

"Drink."

She tilted her head, opened her broken jaw as wide as she could and drank. As she did she felt her body healing, felt the beginning of a shift to a form more suited to survival and ideal for shredding enemies. The agony in her body and mind became overwhelming and she felt something inside break. She felt part of her mind cave under the onslaught and retreat to a safer place while another more primal part rose ready to scream its rage into the reddening haze of bloodlust and madness.

There was the feeling of falling, of hitting something. Aurora's eyes flew open. She was breathing hard, her body trembled like she'd been running full speed for hours and her heart thundered in her chest. She tried to orientate herself. Floor…she was on a floor looking up at a dimly illuminated ceiling. She blinked when a head of golden hair and wings appeared into view. Wings? Why was she seeing wings? Aurora's mind clicked back into place. Nightmare. She'd had *that* nightmare while she was with Evie. Fuck. The back of her head hurt. She must have hit it when she fell out of bed. The face tilted sideways and a concerned crease furrowed the flawless brow. Aurora took a deep breath and held it for as long as she could before slowly exhaling. She tried to uncoil her tense muscles and willed her heartbeat to slow to a steadier pace.

"It's good to see you're awake. Aurora, how are you feeling?"

"You really did it…you threw me out of bed!"

"I told you I would."

"And I'm glad you did. It worked; the fall got me out of there. Although…" Aurora rubbed her hip, "did you have to kick so hard? A good shove would have worked too. I'm probably going to have a bruise tomorrow – you kick like a mule."

"Sorry. I saw those and panicked a little." Evie pointed at Aurora's hands.

Looking, Aurora saw her fingers were tipped with blade-like claws the color of obsidian. She quickly changed them back. Covering her face she felt the contours and ran her tongue along the inside of her mouth to check the shape and size of her teeth. Everything was still normal. She felt dizzy with relief. The change was minor, nothing too frightening for Evie to see. Her rough awakening had spared them both. Seeing how intently Evie watched her Aurora said, "That kick did the job, good call."

"Do you want to talk about the nightmare?"

She definitely didn't. "No."

"Will the dream continue if you go back to sleep? I'm asking because sometimes that happens to me."

"No, I won't have another nightmare tonight."

"Good." Evie disappeared from view and there was the sound of covers being drawn back. "Come back to bed."

"You still want me to sleep up there with you? I don't mind sleeping right here on the floor. Just hand me my pillow?"

Evie's head appeared again and her wings arched open slightly. That combined with her stormy expression told Aurora that Evie wasn't happy with her.

"We've already had this discussion. You are not sleeping in a chair and I won't let you sleep on the floor in front of your own bed. You're shivering so hurry up and get into bed before you catch a chill."

As soon as Aurora crawled back into bed Evie asked, "Have you spooned with someone before? Do you like it?"

"I sort of know what spooning is but I've never slept like that with someone."

"You are about to find out what it feels like. Turn on your side so you face the wall."

It wasn't really a request and Aurora was too battered from the lingering effects of the nightmare to argue about how she should sleep in her own bed. She turned on her side and Evie scooted up behind her. She wrapped an arm around Aurora's waist and unfurled a wing so it came to rest on her hip and shoulder blanketing her in an extra layer of warmth. She moved Aurora's hair out of the way and lay her head close so when she spoke her breath tickled the back of Aurora's neck and ear.

"This is spooning. Do you think you could sleep like this or is it too much? I like to be held after I've had a bad dream. I thought maybe you would as well."

Aurora considered the arm holding her close, the warm press of Evie's body against her back and legs, the silken weight of her wing. It was so comforting. It felt so good. In her entire adult life no one had ever held her like this. It made her feel strangely emotional, like she wanted to laugh and cry at the same time. She wrapped her fingers around Evie's arm. "It's not too much. Thank you." Her words were barely a whisper.

"Try to sleep. You're safe. I'm right here and I won't let you go. I promise."

As Aurora drifted off to sleep she thought she felt soft lips linger against the back of her neck but it could just have been the start of a dream. A good dream this time.

CHAPTER 16

SANCTUARY

When Aurora woke she found that during the night she had rolled onto her back. This in itself was not unusual. What was unusual was the presence of a half-naked woman sleeping almost on top of her. Evie lay sprawled beside her on her stomach. Her braid had come undone so her hair tumbled across her shoulders in golden waves. That wasn't all that had come undone during the night. The sarong was somewhere past her hips and Aurora could see the side of a creamy breast move with the rise and fall of Evie's chest as she breathed. Evie had tucked her wings and thrown her legs wide in the abandon of sleep. That resulted in her draping a leg over Aurora with the inside of her thigh coming to rest against the back of Aurora's hand.

Aurora swallowed and tried to ignore the way her heart rate picked up at the realization she could feel the heat of Evie's core inches away. The shorts she'd lent her were loose fitting and Evie was not wearing any underwear. All she had to do was move her hand slightly and she'd slide past the loose clothing and have Evie cupped in her palm. If she felt the pressure against her sex would Evie move against it in her sleep, pressing down and spreading herself wide so Aurora could feel the moist ready heat of her? Could she slip her fingers inside to explore and make Evie come?

Whoa, what was she thinking? This was not okay! She had to get out of bed before she did something phenomenally stupid. Evie might have kissed her the previous night but that didn't mean she wanted to wake up half naked with Aurora's hand between her legs. Slowly and carefully she extracted herself. Disturbed by the motion, Evie muttered in her sleep, stirring briefly so that Aurora saw the flash of a pink nipple, but didn't wake up.

Breathing a quiet sigh of relief Aurora sneaked out, hurrying to get the rest of her clothing and go outside before Evie woke and called her back. She felt flushed and flustered. If Evie saw her now she'd know something was wrong. Grabbing an empty backpack she slipped outside taking deep breaths of the cool cleansing air. She needed movement and lots of activity to distract her and she needed a swim in the ocean to wash the intoxicating scent of Evie from her skin. She wasn't convinced that would be enough to bring her body and lusty fantasies under control but she was determined to try.

***

Evie groaned as she walked into the kitchen.

"Sore?"

"You have no idea." Evie stretched her legs gingerly. "I thought I was fit but there is a big difference between being flying fit and walking fit. A different set of muscles entirely. All that walking did a real number on my legs, on my whole body really. I didn't feel like this yesterday and even last night I still felt reasonable but this morning everything is so stiff. I suppose that means that healing potion of yours has finally worn off." Evie rubbed her behind and winced. "My butt is so sore it is unbelievable!"

Aurora threw her head back and laughed.

Evie scowled at her. "You're probably not sore at all."

Aurora grinned. "No, I'm fine."

"You could at least *pretend* you're suffering to make me feel better."

"Nope, no such luck."

"Hmm, what's that smell? I can't tell what that is but it smells really yummy. You made breakfast?"

"Yes, I made congee. It's a kind of savory rice porridge. Although it is good for any time of the day really and very soothing. At least I find it soothing. I put it on low heat before I went out because it needs time to slow cook. It should be ready now. Want to try some?"

"Yes please, I'm starving."

Evie gingerly took a seat at the wooden table that was bare aside from a pretty bowl filled with red apples, knobby pears and figs arranged on top. Aurora was in front of the stove, her back half-turned to Evie. She was barefoot in faded blue jeans and a snug fitting dark blue short-sleeve shirt that looked soft and comfortable while showing off her toned arms and trim physique. Her hair looked damp like she had taken a shower or gone for a swim.

"You said you went out? Where did you go, Aurora?"

"To see if there was any fruit left in the orchard. It's late in the season but it's sheltered and sunny there. I was lucky and found some the birds didn't. On the way back the tide was out so I checked the tidal traps and found several good sized fish. I put those in the smoker for dinner."

"You have an orchard?"

"Not here but where I used to live."

"Is it nearby?"

"Near enough on a run and I know shortcuts."

"I bet you do," Evie said dryly. "So let me recap. While I slept you went for a run to get fruit, caught dinner and cooked breakfast. Did I miss anything?"

Aurora grinned at her. "I also had a swim after the run but I'm not sure that counts as it was just for fun."

"Shut up," Evie growled. "You make me feel like a slug."

"You don't look like a slug, you look really good. You didn't get that shapely ass by doing nothing all day."

"When did you check out my ass?"

In the process of dishing the rice porridge into bowls Aurora froze with the spoon suspended mid-air. "I noticed...I didn't specifically look."

Evie noticed the blush creep up Aurora's cheeks and it made her smile. "How very observant of you." Aurora fidgeted with the bowls and wouldn't make eye contact with her. Evie was tempted to tease her more but Aurora looked like she was ready to bolt so she pointed at the stove and asked, "What kind of tea did you make for us this morning?"

"I made red bush tea. If you prefer I can brew you a pot of coffee but you'll have to drink it black and with honey if you want it sweetened."

"Tea will be lovely."

Aurora brought the teapot to the table and then two cups in the same beautiful design as the bowls and a glass jar with honey the color of liquid gold. Next, she brought the steaming bowls of rice porridge to the table and placed one carefully in front of Evie.

Evie dipped a spoon into the creamy mixture and tasted it. "This is really good. Thank you."

Aurora shrugged. "It's nothing. I have to eat, so it was no trouble making enough for two."

Evie wondered if Aurora would have made herself a meaty breakfast instead if she wasn't here. She eyed the fresh fruit that Aurora especially went and got for her and suspected she knew the answer. Everything at this table was tailored to Evie's needs. Aurora was going out of her way to be considerate but acting like it was nothing. She was such an extraordinary woman. She contemplated asking Aurora how she'd slept after her nightmare and how she felt about them kissing in bed but it didn't feel like the right time or place for such serious questions.

Wanting to do something she poured them a cup of tea each, adding a teaspoon of honey to Aurora's cup and three to her own. Aurora smiled her thanks and took a sip before starting to eat. Pleased she'd been observant enough to note how Aurora like her tea Evie took a sip from her own cup. The tea was dark with a reddish tint and tasted faintly floral. She'd never heard of red bush tea but with the honey she found it pleasant. Aurora was already scraping her bowl and eyeing the pot for another helping so Evie set to her own tasty breakfast with enthusiasm. When Aurora finished her cup of tea Evie refilled it for her without asking. Her friend must have been starving because she was on her fifth bowl by the time Evie finished her first serving. Evie decided not to make another joke about how much Aurora ate. Instead, she made a mental note to make sure she ordered extra dishes if they were ever at a restaurant together so Aurora wouldn't go hungry for appearances' sake.

Evie pushed her bowl away and shook her head when Aurora offered to refill it. As much as she enjoyed the congee it was the fruit she was after. At home she would have fresh fruit every day and kept a bowl of whatever was in season in her rooms for the times she missed meals. It had been days since she'd had any and now she craved it. She picked up one of the pears, inhaled the sweet scent and took a bite. The explosion of sweet flavorful juice in her mouth made her moan with delight.

"This is so good I'm deliriously happy right now," she said, licking a trickle of juice from the corner of her mouth. "These are so juicy it's unbelievable."

Aurora picked up her cup and leaned back in her chair, a small pleased smile on her lips as she watched Evie eat. "I'm glad you're enjoying it. I had plenty of fruit while I was looking for good ones to bring home so have as many as you like."

"Thank you, I'll try not to eat everything so there's some left for tomorrow."

"When you're ready I'll show you around. I'm going to be busy today. There are things I have to take care of so you're going to be on your own part of the day. I want to show you where you can go."

"Don't worry, I'm sure I can find my way around. Just go do whatever you need to do. I've always liked exploring new places. I promise I won't snoop through your drawers or anything like that."

Aurora stared at the liquid in her cup for several moments then said, "That wouldn't be a good idea. There are places that wouldn't be safe for you to wander into on your own." The look she gave Evie was deadly serious. "I will show you where you can go. Please don't go anywhere else. Even if you see an interesting passage or an open door unless I've taken you there previously and told you it was safe, don't go in."

Evie exhaled through her mouth and said, "If this place is so dangerous why did you leave while I slept? What if I woke while you were gone and started looking for you? Are you saying something bad could have happened or is this your way of telling me not to pry into your business? If it's the latter all you had to do was say so. I'm not a nosy child. I won't go where I'm not wanted and I respect your privacy."

Aurora put her cup down and said, "I value my privacy but that's not why I don't want you wandering around. I'm trying to keep you safe. Remember I said this place used to belong to the Ancient Ones and I used it as a sort of sanctuary?"

"I remember you saying something like that."

"I left out some details. To be more precise, my mother's family have been caretakers of this place for many generations. After my father's murder she gifted it to me so as much as this place can belong to anyone it now belongs to me. From what she told me this sanctuary was already formidable before she added her own special touches. She feared for my life and wanted to know I had a safe place. Remember those passages last night? Do you recall how some walls moved out of my way and how doorways disappeared behind us? That can happen here. Some things are constant here but many things are not. This place was designed like a multi-layered vault; it hides and protects what belongs within and actively tries to trap and destroy anything it sees as a threat. I know this place well and it's attuned to me so I can go wherever I please but it's not that way for you. While you were asleep and I was away you weren't in danger because the rooms I left you in are stable and I set the wards for that area to recognize you as a guest. You couldn't have opened any of the restricted doorways even had you known they were there. Today many of those will open and stay open because I need to move about freely to get everything done before I leave. If you wander into one of those places without me it would be bad."

Evie was silent while she recalled things she'd seen the previous evening but only half remembered and not quite believed. "You know if it wasn't for those tunnels last night I would have called bullshit on your explanation but…wow, just wow! No wonder this place feels so odd. I'm going to need another cup of tea, maybe two to process what you just told me."

"How about we have it outside in the garden? There's a lovely sunny spot where you can relax and sun your wings. It will be good for you. Bring the bowl of fruit along."

"I assume the garden is one of the places I can go?"

"Yes. It's safe for you and it's one of my favorite places here. I find it difficult being inside too long as it starts to feel like the walls are closing in."

"Which is hardly surprising as here that might actually happen," Evie commented dryly.

"How true. It never occurred to me that maybe subconsciously that's the reason I can only stand it for so long."

***

Aurora led Evie outside into a mid-sized garden. The sides were enclosed by smooth stone and in places overgrown with climbing plants covered in little yellow flowers that released a pleasant fragrance. Originally the garden was strictly ornamental, a place to relax. Over the years she'd repurposed and replanted to suit her own needs. Now most of the plants were either edible, useful for flavoring food or medicinal. Her concession to pure aesthetics was the path that wound through the garden. Made from pretty colored stones it had been a labor of love to create the intricate swirling patterns.

"The walkway is beautiful and it looks new. Did you create this?"

"Yes, I was bored and it seemed like a good idea at the time. Halfway through I cursed myself but the end result was worth the bruised knees and aching back."

"It certainly was," Evie agreed.

Aurora led Evie to her favorite spot, a patch of thick soft grass under a cherry blossom tree next to the pond. The tree wasn't in bloom but it was still lovely and provided adequate shade. Aurora sat down on the grass and watched as Evie went to the water's edge to have a better look at the pond. After she'd made appreciative noises about the clarity of the water, the pretty lilies and colorful little fish she sat down beside Aurora.

"It's a lovely garden."

"I'm glad you like it, Evie."

"You said your mother gave you this place after your father died. Does that mean you didn't always live here?"

"I've always called these mountain ranges home but I used to live in a cabin my father built. I was born there. I loved everything about that place. I still remember those big rooms, the cozy kitchen, that stone fireplace and the way I could see for miles out of every window. The cabin is still standing but in bad shape and overgrown. The fruit trees are about the only sign we lived in that valley. It's my fault, I could not make myself go back there for years after he died. I had this weird idea if I stayed away I could make believe he was still there doing everyday things. Living there was unthinkable and it would have been just me in that empty place with the ghosts of everything that was lost. I couldn't do it."

"Why by yourself? Didn't your mother live with you and your dad?"

"My mother never lived there, she visited. She came and went as she pleased. Sometimes she would stay with us for months or visit frequently. Other times she would be gone for a season or only stay for a night or two between long absences. I remember them having fights over that. This place wasn't her home either but it belonged to her, an inheritance of sort. Originally they thought they would live here but he was such a huge man he couldn't stand how enclosed this felt so he built the cabin nearby."

"Your mother…it sounds like she had another life. I hate to say this but do you think she had another family?"

"I don't think so but she did lead an entire life away from us. My mother is someone of great standing among her people. She has abilities and knowledge that is invaluable to them and she had important responsibilities long before she met my father. Do you remember I told you their bonding was very unpopular with both sides, so much so they had to live apart from their people to be together?"

"Yes, I remember."

"My father could leave his clan's territories and go on living his life but it wasn't that easy for my mother. Her people would not allow her to just walk away. She could have fought them but she didn't want to go to war with her own relatives. To appease them she struck a deal where she would continue with her duties and they agreed to leave her new family in peace but it came at the price of her being away a lot. If she wanted to she could have had another family and we wouldn't have known because it's not like either of us had access to that part of her life. It was a matter of trust. My father believed her and I had no reason to doubt either of them. My childhood was happy and the way things were was all I knew. I believed my father when he said theirs was an incredible love story. He said that even though there was great animosity between his clan and my mother's people they fell in love almost as soon as they met and found a way to be together. I was their little miracle because they were not supposed to be able to have children together. He looked so happy and proud when he told me that last part it didn't occur to me to question the details. Not then anyway. Whatever the truth he loved my mother with utter devotion and I was the fruit of their love. When he looked at me I felt so safe and adored. No one could have asked for a better father."

"And your mother?"

"She cares about me. She definitely loved my father and I think she loved me when I was little and we were our own little strange family. She taught me how to work the old magic and other useful things. She would brush and braid my long hair in front of the fire while my dad cooked and she even played games with me. I remember falling asleep in her lap hearing her laugh at my father's stories about the things I'd gotten up to while she was away." Aurora sighed and her expression became pained. "All of that changed after my father died. I told her everything that happened. I told her how they used me as bait to catch him. Although she never said she blamed me for his death she didn't have to; how she acted spoke louder than words."

"That's horrible. Aurora, are you sure? You were only a child and those men were experienced trappers who planned it all very carefully by the sound of things. No parent could put the blame for something like that on their child. What did she do to make you think she blamed you for what happened?"

"After my father died her visits became even less frequent. When she did turn up it was to teach me or give me something she thought I needed but she hardly ever touched me and sometimes it was difficult for her to look at me directly. I could feel her discomfort. It was like I reminded her of something she wanted to forget. I was so lonely by myself I asked her several times to take me with her but she always refused saying it wouldn't be safe for me to go with her. That part I found out to be true; her people definitely don't want me around."

"You still won't tell me what or who your mother is? It's so weird when you talk like this."

"As you've probably guessed already she is also an Old Blood. Like my father she too is a direct descendant of the first shapeshifters. Her family was one of the first families that accidentally sailed into Nordarra millennia ago. In those days all of Nordarra was full of great and terrible beasts and old powerful magic. In comparison, humans were weak like little children in the land of giants. The beings who built the ancient structures took pity on them and taught them how to use the magic of the land to become shapeshifters. At least that's one version of the story. Another version states humans became the Ancients' servants in order to survive. There was interbreeding and the children born from those unions became the Old Bloods. Whatever the truth behind their origin my mother's people are very proud of being Old Bloods. They are powerful, ruthless, secretive and so convinced of their own superiority it's like a kind of madness. I can't tell you of which shapeshifter bloodline my mother descends because she made me promise never to tell anyone. If you think you've worked it out I'd really appreciate it if you don't mention it to anyone, for my sake and yours. They have always strived to keep their bloodline pure and they pretend I don't exist. My mixed blood is such an affront that if it wasn't for my mother I suspect they would have murdered me years ago. Linking me to them in any way will draw attention you won't like."

Evie made herself eat an entire apple while she thought this over. Aurora's answer put a chill down her spine and she wanted to be composed or at least appear so. This was heavy stuff. Her knowledge of the original shapeshifters was sketchy, not through lack of interest but because over the centuries what people thought they knew about them had become a muddled mix of fact and myth so it was hard to know what was true. The one thing that remained consistent in all the stories was that the Old Bloods were not friendly to those who came after. They looked down on them as lesser shifters and they would kill them with the same disregard as a lion would a common kitten that dared wandered into its den. Evie was a curious person with the tendency to poke at things till she got all the answers she sought and she was burning to ask Aurora more questions but she sensed her friend had already shared more than she was comfortable with. There was no question she could ask her that wouldn't push into territory that might be off limits for Aurora to discuss and she risked putting too much strain on their new friendship. It was time to change direction to safer waters.

"Your mother must love you though. She gave you this extraordinary place that has been in her family for generations. That must mean something? This place is like nothing I've ever seen. Most of what the Ancients built have been reduced to crumbling ruins but this place is intact, the wards and everything else fully functional. There are scholars who would kill for an opportunity to study a place like this."

"I have to agree this place is special. The builders were brilliant. This place slots into nature as if the two grew together in symbiosis. It's self-sustaining, well hidden, easily defendable and there is an abundance of resources in the area. It's a perfect sanctuary."

"Aurora, you took a huge risk bringing me here. I now understand why you took the precautions you did to try and confuse me so I wouldn't know where we are but we both know I could probably figure it out if I really wanted to. Why bring me here? I know you said you wanted to collect a few things but you could have made me wait in the pass instead of taking the risk I might talk about this place."

"I did think carefully about everything before bringing you here. Like I said I needed to come here and leaving you on the mountain to potentially get captured didn't sit right. My plans for after we leave, well, let's just say I'm not sure when I will come here again. It seemed a shame not to share my home with someone at least once. I've always wanted to. Then yesterday we were so close, I like you and I feel I can trust you so it occurred to me this might be my only opportunity."

"Then I suppose I was doubly lucky to have met you when I did."

"You might want to reserve judgement on that. Evie, aside from me wanting to keep this place a secret there is another reason I never brought someone here and why I made you promise not to look for it or tell anyone about it."

"What?"

"I've already told you to be careful not to wander because this place can be dangerous but even so you're relatively safe because I'm here. However, the moment I leave this place will go into a kind of lock-down. It does that every time and even if I wanted to I couldn't disable the defenses. Trust me when I say the wards in and around this place are lethal. I've found the remains of things that have tried to get in and what I saw turned my stomach. You must never come back here, Evie, not for any reason."

"I promised you I wouldn't! I swore an oath."

"You did but if you wanted to there are ways you could get around that. Ways to justify it to yourself." Evie tried to speak but Aurora held up a hand interrupting her. "I know right now you think you will never do such a thing but life has a way of putting us under pressure so the unthinkable seems to become the inevitable and like you said, people would kill for this place. If you ever find yourself in a situation where you're contemplating telling someone about this place or want to return here yourself please remember that breaking my trust will bring death to you and everyone involved."

Letting the words sink in Evie wondered if Aurora had intended the dual meaning. Was that a veiled threat? If she told someone about this place and Aurora found out would she turn a corner one dark night to find the tigress waiting for her? The thought was chilling. She didn't want to think that the woman she'd become so fond of was possibly threatening to kill her if she betrayed her. But it wasn't impossible either. In their short time together she'd learned that Aurora was deadly serious about some things and keeping her promises and expecting people to honor their word in return was at the top of that list. Evie found that her appetite was gone and even though moments ago she had planned to eat several more pieces of fruit she simply couldn't take another bite.

Aurora must have picked up on her distress because she gently touched her arm. Looking concerned she said, "Maybe I shouldn't have brought you here. Knowing things can be a burden. This has been a safe place for me and I wanted us to come here so we could rest and recover without having to watch the trail and the skies the whole time. I wanted you to feel safe and protected in my home but instead I scared you. I'm sorry. I'm going to leave you in peace to enjoy the sun and the rest of your fruit."

Evie instantly felt ashamed for what she'd been thinking. Aurora had taken such good care of her and been nothing but kind so how could she so quickly suspect her friend of having murderous intentions? "Please don't go. I know you have things to do but I'd like you to stay with me a little longer."

"You're sure?"

"Yes. I get the feeling if you leave now you are going to brood about what a mistake it was to bring me here. I don't want that. Besides, I need your help."

"With?"

"My injured wing. I can't open it all the way. I can't look behind me to see what's going on. It's no longer broken and the open wound has closed but something is wrong. Can you have a look for me, please?"

"Of course."

Evie opened her wings. The left one extended fully but the right would only go two-thirds of the way before she winced and had to stop. Standing behind her Aurora gently touched the injured wing, her fingers tracing connections. After several minutes of exploration she said, "I need to have a look from the other side. I think you have something lodged inside the joint of your wing."

Evie lifted her wing as high as she could and Aurora ducked to her front standing so close that their sides touched. The careful exploration of her wing resumed and Evie felt when Aurora pressed on an area that was particularly painful.

"Why are you frowning? You're making me worried."

"I wish you'd told me sooner. There's something on the inside and you've semi-healed over the top. I would have expected the shift to expel any foreign matter but this could be a bone splinter so it doesn't really count as foreign. I have to remove it or you won't be able to fly."

"Oh…" Evie's wings drooped. "But Aurora, what do you know about wings?"

"I know plenty about winged creatures and I've cared for and healed my share of battered beings. I can get this out and afterwards you'll heal as good as new. It's either that or you will have to wait until you get home to see one of your physicians but by that time at the rate you're healing they will have to cut deep to get to it."

"I can't afford to wait that long and I definitely don't want to arrive home like some maimed thing unable to fly." Evie took a fortifying breath and said, "If you think you can take care of it then do it."

"I can."

"Then go get whatever surgical instruments you'll need."

"I already have everything I need." Aurora held up a hand and wiggled her fingers for Evie to see. "I can do things with these you wouldn't believe."

Evie bit her lip to keep herself from giving that statement the sort of reply it was begging for. She cleared her throat and said, "Yes I'm sure you can but *what* exactly are you intending to do with your fingers?"

Aurora must have caught on because a faint blush colored her cheeks and she abruptly dropped her hand. "I'm going to do a small shift. Only the tips of my fingers so I retain the dexterity of my human hands."

"You can do that? That's a lot of control. You must be *very* good."

She really shouldn't have but Evie just couldn't help herself. She felt a little wicked and had to fight the laughter threatening to bubble to the surface because seeing Aurora off balance and blushing was just the most adorable thing ever. Aurora tilted her head and studied Evie carefully. Evie worked hard to maintain an innocent expression but she might have overplayed it because Aurora's eyes narrowed in suspicion.

"Yeah, what's the point of having certain abilities if I don't occasionally use them for the good of others?"

Evie arched a brow at Aurora and met her stare with a challenge of her own. The flames on Aurora's cheeks became more pronounced and she broke eye contact first, her gaze settling on Evie's injured wing.

"Offering to extract what is lodged in your wing with my fingers rather than using surgical instruments was probably weird and now I think of it that doesn't sound sterile. It *is* since what I'll be using wouldn't be just an extension of these nails, it's something different, but that's beside the point. I'll go get tools."

"You don't have to do that Aurora, I trust you. If you think you can do it better and quicker without tools then I believe you. Do it. Get this over with."

"I'll be very careful." Aurora put a gentle hand on Evie's chin and turned her head to look the other way. "You need to look away now."

"Why?"

"You may not like what you see."

"It's my wing so I want to see what you're doing."

"You may find the way I shift or what I'm doing upsetting to watch and I don't want you yanking your wing away at a crucial moment because you've had a fright. Maybe I should just go get the surgical tools and do it with them after all."

"Don't be silly. Besides now I'm curious and I definitely want to see. I don't understand why you're so worried I'll get a fright when I've seen you change your hands twice already. I didn't faint either of those times and I'm not going to now."

"Good. I will hold you to that."

Aurora took hold of Evie's wing with one hand, her grip so firm Evie doubted she could pull her wing away if she tried. The nails on the other hand darkened and grew. Using the nail on her thumb Aurora made a small cut over the wing joint then used the first two fingers of her hand, now shaped like sharp-tipped tweezers, to bore into the cut. Evie felt when Aurora latched onto something lodged in her flesh and started to pull. There was a sucking sound as Aurora extracted a bloody piece of bone about four inches long. Evie pulled a face when Aurora held out the bone shard for her to take so she flicked it away into the garden instead. She felt along the joint some more then nodded in satisfaction and let go of Evie's wing.

"There, all done. Quick and easy, hardly any blood at all. It will heal properly now. By tomorrow you should be able to fly again."

Evie flexed her wing experimentally and found she could extend it all the way. "That's amazing. You should have become a surgeon."

Aurora gave her a lopsided grin. "Somehow I don't think many patients would sit still for this kind of treatment."

"I don't know about that. You really are *very* good with your hands. I think you'd be surprised what a patient would be willing to do for such delicate healing." Evie put her hands on Aurora's shoulders and kissed the corner of her mouth. "Thank you."

Aurora's lips twitched in amusement and she touched the spot Evie kissed. "You're a dangerous woman."

"Nonsense, you're the one with claws. All I have are these adorable wings and I have it on good authority they make me look angelic, so how could I possibly be dangerous?" Evie asked batting her eyes, all wide-eyed innocence.

This made Aurora laugh. "Yeah right. I pity the fool who underestimates you and falls for that one." Still smiling, Aurora touched Evie's arm. "I'm so glad I got to know you. You've made me laugh more than I have in years and things that would upset other people just roll off you like it's water on your wings. I can't tell you how refreshing that is and how good for my soul. In case you weren't already aware you're really something special."

Evie gave a mock regal nod. "Yes, I am. Now we've settled that how about I repay you for fixing my wing by giving you that haircut I promised you. Then you can go slave away at whatever it is you need to do while I laze in the sun by this beautiful pond gorging on fruit like a decadent princess."

"Sounds like a plan. I'll be back in a flash."

True to her word Aurora was back a few minutes later carrying a large rectangular box. On opening it Evie found it only contained a pair of scissors, a comb and a small mirror made to stand by itself.

"Why such a large box?"

"I put my hair in there when I cut it."

"Oh...okay. I should have asked you to bring water so I can wet your hair and make it more manageable while I cut. Just wait a minute while I go get some from the kitchen."

"Not necessary."

Aurora knelt by the pond and unceremoniously dunked her entire head under by lowering herself on her forearms in the same way a large cat might while drinking. From where she stood right behind her it gave Evie quite an interesting view and she instantly had thoughts about what she could do with Aurora in such a position, minus the head under water. Evie felt her body heat in response. Not wanting Aurora to notice she made a display of ducking when Aurora stood up and vigorously shook her head so her long water-soaked hair sprayed drops everywhere.

"Aurora, you're such a barbarian! Look you got me all wet."

Grinning Aurora eyed the way the shirt clung to Evie's chest in patches. "It's so hot I just helped you cool down a little. Now let's see how good you are with those hands of yours. I've already proven myself so it's your turn. Wield those scissors well."

"How much do you want off?"

"Cut it short."

"Really? That much?"

"I prefer it shoulder length but since I have someone who claims she can cut my hair in a proper style I'd like to see that. Besides, it'll grow back quickly. The shorter it is the longer it will take before I have to cut it again."

"That makes sense."

Evie set to work but not without some regret. It felt wrong to cut off the beautiful locks but she kept that thought to herself. She would do what Aurora asked of her and do it well. When she was done she had to admit to herself she'd done a good job and the haircut looked great. It accentuated Aurora's high cheekbones and those stunning eyes and lips. Inside and out the woman was gorgeous. Evie slid her fingers through Aurora's short hair checking for uneven ends, loving the silken feel of it against her skin.

"Done. I think you'll like it."

"I look decent?"

"Stunning. See for yourself." Evie held up the mirror so Aurora could see her haircut. Studying her own reflection Aurora tilted her head from side to side.

"Well, do you like it?"

A brilliant smile broke out on Aurora's face. "You did a great job. I didn't know it could look like this."

"Hair tends to look better when someone else cut it for you and with *scissors* not a knife."

"I already knew that, smart-ass, but how you've cut it looks amazing. I absolutely love it. I can honestly say this is the best haircut I've ever had. Thank you."

Evie felt ridiculously pleased with Aurora's reaction. She'd given countless haircuts to family and friends over the years because it was something she enjoyed and seemed to have a knack for but none of their praise had ever come close to making her feel as good as seeing the surprised joy on Aurora's face.

Aurora closed the lid of the wooden box now stuffed with her hair and put the scissors, comb, and mirror on top.

"What are you going to do with your hair? Do you keep it somewhere?"

"No, if I kept all my hair I'd soon run out of space and have rooms full of hair. That would be creepy. I used to destroy it but now I have a better use for it."

"Oh?"

"Um…it's hard to explain but if you want to come with me I'll show you."

"When?"

"Now?"

"Sure. I can interrupt my lazing about for something interesting to do."

"Evie, I just realized something…I don't think your wings will fit through the gap. Are you up for a shift or is that too much to ask right now? I know how much you enjoy sunning your wings and this will be the first day since the injury you can have your wings out the whole time."

Evie didn't look forward to shifting her wings again so soon but the practice would be good for her and she really wanted to go with Aurora to…wherever really.

"I'll do it. I want to see what you want to show me. I prefer you don't watch me shift this time. I know I pull weird faces. My sister's description of what I look like when I shift was very unflattering."

"You did pull faces yesterday. It sort of looked like you were having a tooth pulled without anesthesia but considering how painful it used to be I'm not surprised. I found the facial thing entertaining but instead of watching you I'll go do a few things while you shift. You have ten minutes. If you don't want me to stand right in front of you and stare while you pull funny faces I suggest you hurry."

"You suck as a motivational teacher!" Evie shouted after Aurora as she jogged away. Aurora flashed her an unrepentant grin over her shoulder and tapped an imaginary watch on her wrist. Evie hurried to start the process. She didn't want to call Aurora's bluff because it was almost certain she'd lose.

Ten minutes later and Aurora was back. She squatted in front of a seated Evie. "How are you feeling? Looks like I missed the show."

Evie feebly swatted at her. She was feeling shaky and was perspiring like she'd done strenuous exercise.

"Hey listen to me...you did it faster than last time and without my help. That's impressive. You should feel proud of yourself. You are now probably the fastest avian shifter in all of Nordarra. Soon you'll be able to shift like a dragon and draw out your wings in a heartbeat."

"I am proud," Evie huffed. "I'm just too exhausted to gloat. Give me a few minutes to recover."

"You're fine. Come on, you can recover on the way."

Grumbling Evie accepted the hand Aurora offered and allowed herself to be pulled up. Aurora held open a large leather coat for her to put on.

"Why do you want me to wear that?"

"It's to protect your skin. I don't think you'll need it but I'm not taking any chances. I want this to be a nice experience for you, not have it turn into a medical emergency."

"Wow…you say such fun things. By the way never use that line on a first date – not unless you want your partner to take off in the opposite direction."

Aurora just smiled and shook the jacket motioning for Evie to hurry up.

"Fine. But I'm already warm and in that coat I'm going to get really hot and turn the color of an overripe plum."

"It's cool where we're going and you can leave the coat open until we get there."

"Ah-ha, and *where* are we going?"

"Telling you would spoil the surprise. It's not far from here."

That gave Evie pause. The last time Aurora told her their destination was 'not far' they walked for hours. Still, it seemed unlikely they were going a long way. At least she hoped so.

"Carry this for me?" Aurora held the box with her cut hair out to Evie.

She took it and watched as Aurora sprinted off reappearing moments later with one of the largest fish Evie had ever seen. It was at least six feet long and as broad as the length of her arm. The thing had a mouth like that of a shark with multiple rows of razor-sharp teeth and a ridged triangular forehead. Carrying it over her shoulder on a short pole attached to a hook Aurora made it look like the thing weighed nothing but Evie guessed it weighed more than her with wings on several times over.

"Where did you find that hideous monstrosity and what are you planning to do with it?"

"It's a type of eel and it was stuck in the fish traps this morning. Normally I would leave it alone and let the tide wash it out again but I have hungry mouths to feed. All right, we have everything. Let's go."

Thoroughly intrigued, Evie followed. Aurora led them to a section of the wall that was overgrown with vines. She pressed her hand to a spot underneath then stepped back and absently licked blood from her thumb. After a moment an archway appeared as if it had always been there revealing a winding stairway on the other side. Evie mutely followed Aurora, the box clutched tight to her chest. She told herself firmly she was not allowed to freak out. She stayed as close to Aurora as she could but far enough away that she wouldn't accidentally walk into the giant eel. It seemed to be glaring at her and those teeth were the stuff of nightmares and could probably bite a leg off in one go. She was having serious reservations about ever swimming in the ocean again. It was one thing knowing there were all kinds of nasties in the water but quite another to be confronted with the possibility that something like this was lurking nearby.

The enclosed stairway led upwards winding this way and that. Evie saw runes on the floor, ceiling, and sides. There was one design in particular that drew her attention. Roughly in the form of a lidless eye, it repeated before and after every landing and the circle that could have represented an iris lit up as they passed, providing an eerie violet glow to light their way. She tried not to think too much about what that meant, sticking as close to the other woman as the blasted eel would allow. Aurora took a left when the passage split and moments later they were outside. Relieved to be out in the open Evie inhaled deeply drawing the fresh sea breeze into her lungs. Aurora turned to check on her and Evie did her best to smile brightly.

"Are you okay Evie?"

"I'm fine," she lied. "How much further?"

"Almost there."

The rest of the walkway was covered by a domed roof held up by tall columns covered in vines blooming with tiny white and purple flowers that smelled like jasmine and passionfruit. Whenever they walked past one of the open sections Evie felt a blast of cold air rip at her clothing and heard the roar of the sea. Aurora squeezed through one of the openings. Evie followed and found they were in the open on a sheltered landing. Far below a forest stretched as far as the eye could see and where it met the sea on the left it was semi-shrouded in mist. It was a sight that took her breath away. The sea battered against sheer cliffs throwing foam high as it surged around tall spindly rocks that stuck up into the air like needles, interspersed with long stretches of rock curved and hollowed into impossible shapes by the endless pounding of the waves. Nothing could pass through that area without getting bashed to pieces by the unpredictable surge of the sea and the forest that adjoined it looked old and impenetrable. This was a wild untamed place.

"Wow."

"It's beautiful, isn't it? I love this view. I can sit here for hours." Aurora motioned Evie towards a bench carved from driftwood. "Have a seat over there and I'll be with you shortly."

Evie did as she was told. She put the box of hair under the seat and watched as Aurora lay the giant fish out on a slab of rock. While Aurora washed her hands in a small hollow in the rock filled with water she made high pitched trilling sounds. She dried her hands on her pants and stood with legs spread wide and her hands on her hips scanning the forest, obviously waiting for a response to her calls. After about a minute she repeated the trilling noise with greater urgency and waited again.

"Ah, here he comes."

"Who?"

"There," Aurora pointed at a winged creature coming towards them, its bat-like wings flapping rapidly.

"That's my pal Lucky, little flying furball extraordinaire. He's more active at night so he was probably having a nap."

"Aurora, is that a lynxhawk? You must be joking. Why would you call one of those things? Everyone knows lynxhawks are vicious."

"Nonsense. They're just misunderstood. They only swarm when their nest or family are under threat. Isn't he sweet? Listen to that commotion." Aurora smiled at Evie over her shoulder her face suffused with affection and joy as of a person who was about to be reunited with a beloved pet. "He's upset with me for being away so long. He's still a good distance away and he's already telling me off."

Evie listened but she couldn't hear anything over the raging sea bashing against the cliffs. "I don't hear it."

"His call is probably too high pitched for you to hear at this distance. You'll hear him when he lands. He's a vocal fellow when he gets going, quite a talker."

A creature that looked like a cross between a bat with its wings, large ears and narrow face and the sleek body and fur of a short-haired oriental cat with something extra thrown in on the side swooped towards Aurora. At the last moment the lynxhawk spread its wings, unsheathed claws like that of a large bird of prey on the hind legs and angled to land on the offered arm. Evie winced when she saw those vicious claws because they were going to rip Aurora's bare arm to shreds. Staring at Aurora's extended arm Evie experienced a disconcerting blur in her vision. One moment she was looking at smooth human skin and an instant later thick silvery grey fur streaked with black and russet oranges covered Aurora's arms from the wrists upwards causing the sleeves of her t-shirt to puff up with the added bulk. The sudden change was so startling Evie found herself blinking rapidly as her mind tried to process what she'd just seen.

"Hello Lucky, it's good to see you." Aurora smiled affectionately at the lynxhawk as it prowled on her forearm making agitated high-pitched noises, its huge round ears twitching this way and that independently of each other. "Did you miss me, handsome? Look at you…you're still getting bigger and your coat is so glossy you must be eating well. You are such a good hunter. No wonder you get so many girls. I bet all the other boys are jealous of you."

The lynxhawk went quiet. It stared intently at Aurora's face, both ears pitched forward, seemingly entranced by the low soothing tone of her voice.

"Time to put away those sharp claws. You can balance perfectly fine without them." Aurora stroked the hind feet and Lucky retracted his claws. "That's better." She brought the lynxhawk up against her chest and it immediately wrapped its forearms with the finger-like digits around her neck and crooned softly. Aurora stroked its sides, neck, and head with her free hand. "I missed you too, gorgeous boy. I'm glad to see you looking so healthy. I worry about you."

Evie watched in amazement as Aurora poured affection onto Lucky, talking to him like a small child and the lynxhawk responded with little noises of its own as if it understood. Several minutes passed that way then Lucky climbed onto Aurora's shoulder. He immediately spotted Evie on the bench and screeched loudly flashing a mouth full of pointy teeth.

"Hush Lucky, she's a friend. Darn…don't do that so close to my ear boy, you know better." Aurora stuck a finger in her ear and wiggled. Lucky made to screech again and she flicked him against the jaw. That got his attention. "No. Enough of that. Friend. Mine." Lucky ducked his head but looked no less suspicious and watched Evie with unnerving focus.

"I'd bring him over to say hello but he's not ready. Lynxhawks are naturally shy and very suspicious creatures and it takes time to win their trust."

Evie cleared her throat and said, "I've heard about the suspicious part and other things like that they are extremely aggressive. Did you know those creatures can down an avian? My friend barely survived an unprovoked attack by only two of those things. His wings were such a mess it took him weeks to recover and he suffered a seizure on the way home. I've been chased by those things as well. They're a menace."

"They are not a menace. It's about a lack of understanding and perspective. If you keep your distance from a bear it will usually leave you alone but if you approach when it has a cub it will attack. Ants will swarm and attack if you step on their nest and bees the same if you try to take their honey. Well, maybe bees wouldn't attack *you* but they would attack me if I didn't take precautions. What I'm trying to say is that how they react is an instinctive defense mechanism. Lynxhawks are social creatures and form lasting bonds with each other. Imagine being the size of this little guy guarding a nest with babies that can't fly yet and suddenly a huge winged predator hovers above. Wouldn't it seem prudent to call for reinforcements and drive the predator away?"

"Avians are *not* predators," Evie objected.

"Nonsense. Avians are vicious predators when they set their minds to it. Same as with humans. I know you don't see yourself as a predator,

Evie, and you're not as such things go but you are an avian and other creatures will instinctively react to the danger they associate with avians."

Evie narrowed her eyes at Aurora. She wanted to argue but she knew she was on shaky ground. Members of her flock still regularly went out on hunts to refresh the meat stocks and to keep their skills sharp. That at least was the official reasoning but she suspected that some of the hunters took greater joy in the act of killing than in providing for the flock.

"Fine. I don't like it but I can see where you are coming from. If you can tell me how to avoid being attacked by those things when I'm minding my own business and just going for a flight that happens to be over a forest with them in it, I'd like to hear it."

"The simple solution is to stay high. They don't like going more than a few meters above the forest canopy."

"We are more than a few meters above the forest here," Evie pointed out.

"True but Lucky came because I called him. Evie, please put your hand into the right-hand pocket and take out the chocolate."

Evie stuck her hand into the pocket and found loose bits of chocolate wrapped in a cloth.

"Take a piece for yourself, eat it then hand me one piece. He might hiss when you come close but he won't attack."

Curious Evie complied. Aurora took her piece of chocolate and ate it slowly making appreciative noises. Lucky sniffed her fingers and watched Aurora's mouth attentively. A little red tongue darted out and the lynxhawk licked its lips.

"Does your little friend by chance like chocolate?" Evie asked keeping an eye on the lynxhawk who seemed to have temporarily forgotten about her.

"He's crazy about it. Especially the kind with nuts."

"Do all lynxhawks eat chocolate?"

"No. Just him. As far as I know anyway. Give me another piece please and rub it between your fingers before you hand it to me. I want your scent on it."

"Do I get more as well? You know I love chocolate."

Aurora smiled fondly at Evie and said, "I know you do. Of course, you can have more. I didn't bring all that chocolate just for Lucky."

Evie handed Aurora another piece of chocolate and Lucky watched the exchange with intense focus. When Aurora held the chocolate against her lips and took a tiny bite Lucky made a high-pitched noise and put one of his front paws on Aurora's hand.

"You want some?"

Lucky stared intently at the chocolate she still held in front of her mouth. She offered it to him between thumb and forefinger allowing him to sniff it. He made a huffing noise presumably at the traces of Evie's scent on it then he took the chocolate between both paws. He made himself comfortable resting on his hind legs on Aurora's shoulder and ate his chocolate in precise bites.

"Wow, that's not something I thought I'd ever see," Evie mused aloud. "Why did you want me to handle the chocolate like that?"

"I wanted him to see I will accept food from you and I asked you to eat some first because that is how the adults test the food to make sure it is safe for the young ones to eat. In his world there is no greater demonstration of trust."

"So, what's with the monster fish? Surely that entire thing isn't for him?"

"No, he couldn't eat that much in one sitting even if he tried and try he would because he's a little guts. As soon as he's done with his chocolate I'm going to call the others so they can share the fish."

"You're calling more?"

"I was going to. I thought you would enjoy watching them eat but if you're afraid of them I can take you back first."

"I am not afraid of lynxhawks," Evie protested. "I just don't like them and I don't trust one near me. This feels like the whole dragon thing all over again…like this is a once in a lifetime opportunity. I want to watch because I doubt I'll get another opportunity like this. It's not like I know anyone else who can call lynxhawks at will."

"I can't call all lynxhawks, Evie. Just the ones who know me and it took years to gain their trust."

When Lucky finished his chocolate Aurora carried him over to the fish and put him down next to it. She cut a thin sliver from the raw fish, ate it and then cut Lucky a steak-sized hunk which he daintily accepted with his paws. He ripped into it with vigor. While he ate Aurora again made trilling noises similar to what she made before but followed it up with whooping roars.

Even though it was a friendly invitation and not the battle cry of a furious tiger, hearing Aurora roar like that sent chills down Evie's spine.

After she'd seen the deference and respect the wolves of clan Swift Foot showed Aurora it had dawned on her that Aurora had to be a powerful apex predator for them to treat her so cautiously. Since then she had seen glimpses of what her friend was capable of but mostly she had been very careful to keep that part of her hidden so it was easy to think of her as just another female shifter. Actually, most of the time Aurora acted more like a human than a beast-shifter and it was only the subtle things that gave her away, like her strength and the way she moved. There was nothing subtle about that roar. It was a declaration of who she was. It was primal and screamed:

I AM PREDATOR. HEAR ME AND TREMBLE.

All of that and she wasn't even in beast form.

Evie trembled but not in fear. She felt the same heart-thumping anticipation she got just before flying into a storm. Yes, there were risks but if she was brave and skillful enough she could ride the powerful wind currents to soar higher and further than any tame breeze could take her. It was like she was an adrenaline junkie and she'd just realized claiming Aurora for herself would be the biggest thrill ever. She couldn't remember the last time she was this aroused. She had an intense urge to crush herself against Aurora's body. She wanted to feel the power of that roar vibrate through her and then pull Aurora down on top of her and have wild sex. She'd already acknowledged her attraction to Aurora but seeing the other woman like this shot her interest to a different stratosphere. Standing there sending her calls into that wild untamed land that stretched before her, the tigress looked so powerful, so commanding, so *dangerous.* Yet this was the same woman who just a little while ago had playfully sprayed her with water and blushed like a young girl when Evie teased her. Every time she thought she had a handle on Aurora she revealed a little more of herself and her fascination with the woman deepened. She was hooked. She wanted more of everything Aurora. Just entertaining the possibility of them having sex for real and not just in her imagination made her brain melt a little.

Whoa, down girl. Take a deep breath. Slow down. Remember she is your friend first.

Evie shook her head trying to clear it of the lust haze. Aurora wasn't someone she could just have a bit of mutual fun with for the evening or a few days, she was way too intense and serious for that. Her stopping things last night after just a few kisses and saying she wasn't into casual sex instead of taking what was on offer confirmed that. Anything started with Aurora had to be carefully considered as there would be no going back. As much as she wanted to move things beyond the occasional touch and teasing banter she didn't want to fuck things up with her. They had a genuine connection, the kind that would grow deeper and stronger with time if nurtured properly. To lose her friendship and have that incredible woman cut her out of her life after everything they'd shared would be more devastating than never finding out if the rest of Aurora tasted as good as her amazing lips. On the other hand, if she didn't push to see if they could be more than friends she would wonder about it the rest of her life and it would drive her crazy.

Evie exhaled slowly and focused on the wild landscape while she grappled with her thoughts and the nervous flutter in her chest. If she was going to do this she had to move forward carefully. Going slowly and trying to be subtle when she knew what she wanted wasn't her style but for this incredible woman she would try. She had yet to see Aurora around many people but she didn't seem like the type of person who let people close easily and she had let Evie in deeper than most by the sound of things. She didn't want to scare Aurora and have her become distant and disappear behind those barriers of hers.

"Evie, come stand by me. I'd like you to see this."

"Over there?"

"Yes. Come. Please?"

Cautiously Evie moved to Aurora's side making sure to stay to the side furthest from the feeding Lucky. Aurora checked Evie's coat was closed properly and flipped the sides up to cover her throat.

"This is just a precaution. I don't think they will land on you but…just in case."

Noting Aurora's arms were still covered in fur Evie lifted one across her shoulders and draped it across her chest so Aurora's hand came to rest within inches of her breast. She secured her hold by entwining the fingers of one hand with Aurora's and resting her other hand just above Aurora's wrist in a loose hold. She had made no protest as Evie moved her arm into position but now her eyes questioned Evie. Wanting to put Aurora at ease Evie turned on her most reassuring smile.

"I want to make sure there is no doubt I'm with you. Just a precaution to make sure your fiendish little friends don't get it into their head to attack me. Those claws would rip right through the coat's material if they're determined and I don't have a layer of fur I can conjure to protect my fragile skin."

Aurora nodded and tightened her arm around Evie, drawing her closer so she stood with her back nestled against the taller woman's front. Evie almost groaned it felt so good. Together they watched in silence as all over the forest winged shapes rose and made their way towards them. Evie counted at first but soon gave up. There were just too many. Counting them was like trying to tally an infestation of quick moving fleas on the stomach of a giant dog. She was beginning to feel genuinely worried.

"Um…how many are you expecting?"

"It changes. We are getting a good turnout for this time of day."

"There are many more?"

"Yes. Some adults always remain with the nests and they come or stay away depending on what they're doing."

One after another the lynxhawks landed and crooned at Aurora in greeting. As soon as they saw Lucky gorging himself they rushed to join in the feast, tearing chunks of flesh from the fish then hopping away to devour it, allowing another lynxhawk access. Soon the clearing was covered in a mass of wings and furry bodies bumping against each other and jostling for position. With so many of them Evie expected there would be fights but aside from the occasional baring of teeth and the high pitch screeches they seemed to be feeding together quite amicably.

"It's like I'm not even here," Evie whispered. "They are totally ignoring me."

"It just looks like they are not aware of you. They're keeping an eye on you but they don't feel threatened by your presence because I'm here and there are so many of them. They are more concerned with getting a free meal before the eel is all gone. This is fresh fish, not a half-rotten carcass washed up on shore and I've fed them this kind before so they remember the flesh is tasty."

"Even raw?"

"Have you never had sashimi?"

"Ah...I see your point. Although I prefer it with condiments."

"Who doesn't? A good dipping sauce makes everything taste better, even raw fish."

They watched the lynxhawks chatter and eat and Evie had to admit they were kind of cute. That didn't mean she wanted to touch or cuddle one, she was too acutely aware of how efficiently those sharp teeth were rending flesh and she watched in fascinated horror as they cracked open the eel's armored scalp and scooped out the brain with their fingers.

"Aurora, can we please go sit down?"

"Is it too much for you?"

"No, it's fine. I'd just like to sit down and admire the whole view although not being so close that I can hear them crunch bone would be good too. You have to remember before today I did my best to avoid them. I keep imagining what those powerful teeth could do to my wings and it's very unsettling."

Aurora led them back to the seat. Heads turned to watch them go but only momentarily. "Your concern is understandable; for such small creatures they have surprisingly strong jaws. Did you know they have poison pouches around their claws? That's probably why your cousin had a seizure."

"No…really?"

"Yeah. The strength of the toxin and the side effects depend on what they've been eating. They eat all kinds of things other animals would leave well alone but they have a particular fondness for a little yellow frog that is highly toxic and excretes a slime that causes seizures and muscle weakness and yet the lynxhawks can eat them. Their bodies somehow redirect the toxin into the pouches around their claws and that comes in handy when they want to take down much larger prey. If they're desperate or cornered they smash the sacs open to release all the toxin at once and they usually go for the attacker's eyes to poison and blind at the same time. That's bloody effective and impressive. Nature did a great job with that design."

"It sounds like you admire them?"

"I do. It's a dangerous world out there and they've adapted magnificently, thriving despite the number of predators determined to make a meal out of them."

Evie noticed how happy and relaxed Aurora appeared while talking about her pets. She sat with her hands on her thighs and there was an indulgent fond smile on her lips as she watched the lynxhawks eat the food she'd provided for them. Evie, on the other hand didn't feel relaxed at all. She was too aware of the heat and feel of Aurora's leg against hers as they sat side by side on the bench and her fingers twitched with the need to find out if that luscious fur felt as soft as it looked.

"Aurora?"

"Hmm?"

"Can I touch your arm?"

"You didn't ask permission before."

"I know but that was different, that was me taking safety precautions. Now I want to feel your fur. May I? I've been dying to touch it but I wanted to ask first. I know how much I hate it when people touch my wings without permission."

"Um…sure. If you want to."

Evie lifted Aurora's arm over her own into her lap, wishing as she did so that there wasn't a jacket barrier between them. She made do with pushing up her sleeve so her bare forearm was pressed against Aurora's furry one, their hands right next to each other on her thigh. With her other hand she stroked Aurora's fur reveling in the sensations she was being bombarded with. It was like the nerve endings in her hand were doing a little happy dance.

"Oh wow, this feels *amazing*. Your fur is so thick and silky. So incredibly luxurious."

Aurora turned over her palm and entwined their fingers. "I enjoyed touching your feathers too. Your wings are so beautiful I'm not surprised people try to touch them."

They smiled at each other and Evie felt her heart might burst with how much affection she felt for Aurora at that moment. Evie suppressed a sigh. Now she was alternating between lust and tenderness. She really had it bad.

Evie put the rest of the chocolate in her lap and they shared it. She kept Aurora's hand in hers never letting go and resumed stroking her fur. After a while, gentle fingers stilled the motion of her hand. "Oh, I'm sorry. Too much?"

"A little. No one has ever done that. I'm happy you're comfortable enough with me to touch me when I'm like this but I'm getting a bit of sensory overload. Especially when you stroke in the wrong direction."

"So it's like a cat that will enjoy it if you stroke the fur one way and become agitated when you rub the other way?"

"I suppose. Never thought of it in those terms before. Some of the lynxhawks are getting ready to leave and I forgot to put the hair out for them. I'd better go do that now."

Aurora opened the box and tipped the hair out on the slab of rock away from the fish carcass. One of the lynxhawks, its wings already spread to leave, hurried over. It grabbed as much of the hair as its tiny paws could hold on to on top of the piece of fish it already carried and flew off. Soon the process was repeated and the pile rapidly dwindled.

When Aurora came to sit with Evie again her arms were back to normal and Evie didn't feel comfortable touching her the way she did before. Touching fur was one thing but stroking Aurora skin on skin without a good reason was crossing a boundary. Besides, maybe she'd had enough of Evie touching her and this was her polite way of saying so.

"We can go soon but I just want to see if Lucky wants to come with me for a while when he's done eating. I don't know when I'll see him again."

"Sure. I don't have any pressing plans. I'm flexible. So, what's with you giving them your hair?"

"They use it to line their nests. In long strands it's easy to weave, stronger than it looks and a great insulator. It also makes other predators think twice about attacking them in the nest because it smells like me. I've been here so long the other creatures that live here are familiar with my scent and they know what I am. I like that the little ones in the nest too young to fly learn to associate my smell with food, nest, and protection so when they finally meet me they are cautious at first but not afraid. I adore the lynxhawks, they're great company and extra eyes and ears out there. The other reason I let them have the hair is less altruistic. They nest all over the forest and that means they're spreading my scent liberally through the area. When other predatory shifters wander into the area they pick up my scent and know I've claimed this area but if they try to track me by scent alone it becomes confusing."

"I can imagine how upset the lynxhawks would become if a strange shapeshifter gets near their nests. They are bound to make a fuss?"

Aurora gave a predatory grin. "Ah yes, there is that. It is hard to sneak around or hunt with lynxhawks screeching to anything that will listen that there is danger down below."

"Do they make noise when you're in the forest?"

"Why would they? I don't hunt them. Besides, they know I always leave them something when I've made a kill. They've figured out it's to their advantage to be quiet and let me do my thing. They're cunning that way."

Evie looked at Aurora with new found respect. "I'd say you're the cunning one. Befriending the lynxhawks was a sound strategic move. You have your own little army out there."

"It's not like that," Aurora objected. "It's a mutually beneficial relationship; I help them and they help me."

"Fine, see it that way if you want. So how did this 'mutually beneficial relationship' start?"

"This little fellow." She pointed at Lucky who had sauntered over, his stomach almost dragging on the ground, hopped up onto Aurora's lap and made himself comfortable while pointedly ignoring Evie's presence.

"I found him when he was barely out of the nest. Something had taken a bite out of him and tore his wings so badly I thought he'd probably never fly again." Aurora slid her thumb along the outer edge of a wing and Lucky dutifully spread his wing for her to inspect the delicate inner membranes. "See the slight discoloration where I stitched the wing back together? That's all that remains and you'd never guess he almost died. It was touch and go there for a while and that's why I called him Lucky. He was such a feisty little thing he gave me some serious scratches and nips despite being half dead. Fortunately, he's smart and it didn't take him long to realize I was trying to help. I nursed him for almost a year carrying him everywhere with me before he was well enough to fly and take on the big bad world on his own again. By that time Lucky decided he was mine or more likely that I was his."

Hearing his name, Lucky tilted his head up to stare at Aurora and one large ear pointed at her while the other continued rotating. Aurora released his wing and scratched him under his chin. Lucky's eyes rolled half shut, he made a contented humming noise and arched his neck so she could have better access.

"He kept coming back for his treats and cuddle time and started bringing friends. When it came time to build his nest to impress prospective females he collected stray hairs from my clothing and even tried to gather ones still attached to my head. I got the picture and let him have the hair I cut rather than destroy it. He was so excited he crooned like I'd given him a great prize. I assume the addition to his nest was a hit with the ladies because he soon had several females and an expansive family of his own. This little fella has become quite the patriarch. Things developed from there."

***

It turned out Lucky did want to go with Aurora and on the way back Evie again kept a small distance between them. This time because Lucky was draped over Aurora's shoulders like a brown furry scarf with wings and he kept a watchful eye on Evie, silently baring his impressive set of teeth whenever she came too close. Evie couldn't decide if it was a territorial display or if Lucky was just being protective of Aurora. She was annoyed that she had to keep a few steps behind but at the same time she found it sweet that the little creature was guarding his mistress. She could have alerted Aurora to what Lucky was doing behind her back but that felt too much like getting an adult to settle a playground dispute. It was unlikely she would spend much time in the lynxhawk's company but if she had to she'd find a way to come to an understanding with Lucky on her own. She already knew Lucky was crazy about chocolate and she was more than willing to exploit that weakness ruthlessly to win him over.

As soon as they got to the garden Aurora excused herself and disappeared inside. Evie returned Aurora's jacket to their room, folded it neatly and left it on the foot of the bed. She stared at the side of the bed where Aurora had slept the previous night. What a sight Aurora had been. Her freshly washed hair had tumbled loose and untamed over her shoulders, her long muscular legs had been clad in just a pair of tiny shorts and the way that t-shirt had outlined Aurora's breasts had made Evie a little breathless. She'd been so turned on after their playful kisses and yet when she held Aurora tightly in the curve of her body after that nightmare her only thought was to comfort her friend and drive away whatever terrors had made her look so wild-eyed. Instinctively she'd snuggled up to Aurora and draped her wing over the trembling woman like she would have if her sister had woken from a bad dream. Aurora had looked battered and incredibly vulnerable curled up on her side, her arms and legs tucked tightly to her own chest as if to protect herself. It had been troubling to see such a defensive posture from the normally strong and confident woman and it had made her sad that Aurora was so scarred by her childhood trauma that she was still tormented by recurring nightmares.

Evie abruptly turned away from the bed and marched herself out of the bedroom before she got swept up in the powerful emotions of that memory. She was about at the limit of what she could deal with. She made a brief stop at the toilet then she got herself a drink from the kitchen and returned to the tree by the pond to have more fruit. She was actually pleased Aurora was busy elsewhere. She needed to be by herself for a while so she could process and let her emotions settle. She'd learned so many new things today, mostly about Aurora but also about herself. Her mind felt overfull with thoughts and emotions. Some she wasn't ready to examine too closely.

Evie decided not to shift her wings back. She was tired and she reasoned they would heal quicker if she left them alone. Besides, it allowed her a rare opportunity to lie on her back and look at the sunlight as it filtered through the leaves of the tree. A light breeze stirred the leaves and it made shadowy patterns dance on her skin. It was hypnotic and soothing to watch. It wasn't long before Evie drifted off to sleep and dreamt about soft fur and warm lips.

CHAPTER 17

NEW BEGINNINGS

When Evie woke, the light drifting through the leaves were tinted in shades of orange and red. The air on her face was cool but she felt warm and snug. Taking stock she found a soft blanket had been draped over her and another placed under her head as a pillow. This made her smile. Aurora must have been to check on her. Sitting up Evie stretch languidly. She felt refreshed after her long, deep sleep. Her tummy rumbled and this made her realize she'd not had anything substantial since breakfast. She was tempted to have another piece of fruit but aside from there not being a lot left she didn't want to risk spoiling her appetite as she was curious to see what Aurora had prepared for dinner. She'd mentioned smoked fish this morning and just the thought of it made Evie's mouth water so she quickly got up, shook out the blankets before folding them and headed to the room. She felt rumpled and there were probably leaves and other things in her hair from sleeping under the tree. If she hurried she could enjoy a soak in the bathing chambers and still be ready before dinner. Evie wished she had a pretty dress to put on and a little of her favorite perfume and make-up. At least after her wash she could slip into fresh clothing and put her hair into a soft looking braid. As preparations went that was the best she could do. She felt her heart thump a little faster; she was thinking like a woman going on a date. Which this wasn't…but there was definitely a spark between them. She had to make a move tonight or at least find out if Aurora was interested in being more than friends because tomorrow they were heading back to civilization and it was anyone's guess what would happen after that. Perhaps if she was lucky and played her cards right she would have ample reason to be grateful she'd had a rest in the afternoon.

***

Aurora heard Evie's terrified scream, dropped the book in her hand and ran. In the hallway outside the bathroom she was just in time to see

Evie fling a brown furry body from her chest. Lucky hit the wall, slid to the floor and turned on Evie, his ears tucked back and his teeth bared in a vicious snarl.

"Lucky, NOOOO!" She roared her fury and Lucky's head swiveled towards her. One look at her and his ears drooped. He made a pitiful mewing sound and propelled himself in a run along the wall until he got to the doorway then launched himself into the air and disappeared from view.

"Why did Lucky jump on me like that? He attacked me for no reason!"

"Did he scratch you?"

Not waiting for Evie's reply Aurora shoved the shirt off her shoulder. On seeing the welts welling with thin lines of blood she growled, wrapped her mouth over the wound and sucked.

Feeling Evie squirm she wrapped an arm around holding her firm. "Be still. I need to clean this quickly before the poison from his claws enters your bloodstream. Even a little will make you very sick."

Not waiting for a response she licked until the wound tasted clean and no longer bled. She nodded to herself in satisfaction and moved on to check the rest of Evie's shoulder. She spotted several smaller scratches near Evie's collarbone and between rounded peaks so she unbuttoned the shirt further to continue downwards with her tongue. She paused only long enough to swallow the poison and work her jaw to release more healing enzymes before continuing. She felt Evie moan and push at her shoulders but ignored her, determined to clean every single scratch before the toxin got into Evie's system. It didn't take long but she wanted to be thorough, going over the healing scratches several times. As the initial urgency lessened she drifted into the rhythm of her task, licking anything that remotely resembled a claw mark in long cat-like strokes. Mesmerized by the taste and feel of the creamy skin she became intent on finding and healing any mark that might mar the perfection and as she explored the scent rising from heated flesh was coming more intense and oh so tantalizing.

"Aurora, what are you doing?" Evie's voice sounded low and breathy and her fingers pressed into Aurora's shoulders with urgency.

This got her attention so she paused to say, "I told you lynxhawks have poison sacs under their claws. Lucky's scratches are dangerous. I'm neutralizing the toxins."

"With your tongue?"

"Yes, I can produce antigens for toxins in my saliva and I'm speeding up your healing. See the scratches are almost gone already."

"Oh, I see." There was a slight pause and then Evie continued, "Um, I'm grateful you're trying to heal me but I don't think he got me that far down."

Confused Aurora stopped licking to stare up at Evie. That's when it dawned on her that she was on her knees with her face pressed against Evie's navel. She did not recall getting down on her knees or peeling Evie shirt open so far that the only covering she had left was a lacy bra. Aurora felt stunned and for a moment her brain froze and she didn't know what to do.

"I ah…" She cleared her throat, let go of Evie's hips and jerked up and away. It felt like her face was on fire. "I thought I saw more scratches but I must have gotten them all. Did he scratch your arms? Anything on your back?" Concern replaced her embarrassment and Aurora nudged Evie trying to get her to turn around so she could take off her shirt to check for scratches.

Evie grabbed Aurora's arm with trembling fingers while the other hand fumbled to close her shirt. "My back is fine but if you keep working me over like this I definitely won't be. I generally prefer to be kissed on the lips first and to have a little foreplay over dinner or drinks before a woman ends up on her knees between mine. However, for you I'd make an exception. If that was your intention?" The last was said with a raised eyebrow and a seductive purr.

"I didn't mean to…your skin is so lovely and smells so nice I ah… I'm so sorry, Evie, I got carried away." Aurora didn't think it was possible for her cheeks to get any hotter but she was sure her body just managed it. She desperately wished the floor would open and swallow her but no such luck.

"Your lips have blisters forming. Are you all right?"

"It will heal in a minute; it just tingles a little."

Evie lightly traced her thumb along Aurora's lower lip. "I can feel it. It's more of a burning sensation than tingling."

"Careful, I just got that stuff off your skin." She grabbed Evie's hand and sucked her thumb into her mouth to lick off the toxin. She heard Evie moan and realized what she was doing. Mortified, Aurora let go and stumbled a step back. Glancing up she caught a peculiar expression on Evie's face and froze.

"Aurora, I didn't mean to make you so uncomfortable. I didn't realize…"

"Realize what?"

"I've seen you blush a few times but it didn't occur to me that you'd be this shy when it comes to sex. Or is it because I'm a woman? I thought from the way you are around me you must like women *that way*. Oh wow, how did I get that so wrong? But I was sure that—"

"You didn't get it wrong. I prefer women and I like you a lot. I think you are amazing and beautiful but I'm just not…" Unable to find the right words Aurora made a frustrated hand motion. "You may have noticed I'm a bit intense and when it comes to being with someone *that way*, I have serious trust issues. I don't do casual and my life hasn't been full of parties and opportunities to meet women in a relaxed, carefree environment to learn how not to be so…" again Aurora made the frustrated hand motion indicating herself. "Not that there hasn't been plenty of opportunities to you know…" She faltered and her eyes flickered in the direction Lucky had gone as if she considered making a run for it as well.

"Are you saying you've never had sex?" Evie sounded incredulous.

"Of course, I have." Aurora's voice was sharp. "My tiger goes into heat occasionally. When that happens it's very hard to not look for a partner but having sex when I'm like that is not a choice, it's a kind of madness and I have almost no self-control when the mating frenzy is at its worst. It's beyond humiliating. I don't normally allow strangers to touch me. It's a total mind fuck that things can get so out of hand I'd do it with someone I barely know or don't even like and who doesn't care about me in any way that matters. I hate that my beast can flood my body and mind with chemicals and override my will so I become more like an animal than a person. When I can feel it coming I see a discreet professional and pay for what I need. It's not intimacy, it's a business transaction. There is no real joy in it but the woman I see is good at what she does and at least that way I have some control over what happens."

Aurora was breathing hard and shaking. She flinched when Evie cupped her face but didn't pull away. Waiting until Aurora raised her eyes to meet hers, Evie leaned in slowly and pressed a feather-light kiss on her cheek. She leaned her forehead against Aurora's neck and rested her hands on her hips. They stood like that for a while, barely touching, a small space between their bodies. Neither said anything. Eventually, Aurora stopped shaking, sighed into Evie's hair and wrapped arms around to pull her closer.

Running her hands up and down Aurora's back in a soothing motion Evie said, "I believe you owe me dinner. I'm starving."

"You are? Of course, you are. You missed lunch and it's getting late. Time to have something to eat," Aurora said but made no move to leave.

Evie nestled a little closer and gently said, "Thank you for sharing that with me."

"It slipped out. I don't usually share such embarrassing things but you had me a little worked up."

"The feeling is mutual but there is no need to feel embarrassed or tense around me. I'm your friend. Friends share things. They talk and tease and sometimes they do more intimate things but not always. Sometimes just being near is enough."

"Yeah? That's good to know."

Evie was pleased her words seem to set Aurora at ease even though she wasn't really sure herself what she meant. Her stomach chose that moment to growl loudly. Thankful for the diversion she gave Aurora a pleading look. "Dinner? Please?"

Aurora chuckled. "The food should be ready and serving you dinner will be my pleasure. I found a dusty bottle of wine while I was setting the table. Not sure if it is any good but we can try it."

***

Dinner consisted of fish smoked to perfection. It was warm, moist, flaky and delicious. It was accompanied by bread so hot the steam nipped Evie's fingers, creamy butter that melted into the bread, a wedge of well-aged yellow cheese in a thick red rind and a sweetish fruit pickle from a glass jar that complimented everything beautifully. For dessert, to Evie's amazed delight, Aurora produced an apple pie with orange glaze. It was so good she offered to marry Aurora if she promised to make it regularly. Aurora laughed and dished her another slice. The wine Aurora mentioned was a red of uncertain vintage, hand corked in a dark green bottle. On tasting, it had a woodsy oak flavor that reminded Evie of a well-aged port, as did the potent alcohol kick of the drink that brought an instant flush to her cheeks. Altogether very pleasing.

After the meal, with her second drink in hand Evie felt mellow. Aurora sat with her long legs stretched out under the kitchen table, a contented smile on her face. It wasn't just the wine that had them both so relaxed. Even before they took the first sip Evie noticed how much more at ease they were with each other, their interaction light with lots of banter and laughter. They talked about this and that while they ate, random topics that ranged from Evie's family to far flung places Aurora had been. It was like they had passed some kind of test and were now in a freer place where they spoke like old friends catching up rather than new acquaintances getting to know each other. It was an odd feeling that made her feel slightly giddy and mischievous. Or maybe it was the wine to blame.

Timing it just right Evie asked, "So this professional you see, how good is she?"

Aurora spluttered, coughed and had to thump herself on the chest. Evie took a sip of wine to cover her smile.

"Why?" Aurora croaked out when she could finally speak.

"I've never been with someone like that. If she's really good maybe I'll pay her a visit."

"She's expensive and you don't need to pay for it. I'm sure you can hardly go anywhere without women and men throwing themselves at your feet."

"Neither do you. I bet if you walked into a nightclub half the people there would buy you drinks and try to chat you up. I know I would. But all of that is beside the point. I want to know what she's like in case I ever want to try something a little different."

"You really want to know?"

She didn't but Evie was curious what drew Aurora to that woman in particular. "That's why I asked."

After a moment's contemplation Aurora said, "She is beautiful and very sensual. She's a shifter and I suspect she is a lot older than she looks. Like I said she's discreet and very exclusive. I needed an introduction to meet her and then she sat me down for a talk to decide if she would take me on as a client. She had questions which I answered as honestly as I could, we discussed fees and payment and that was that."

"There must be plenty of women that fit that description. Why choose her in particular?"

Aurora absently swirled the wine in her glass. "I like her. Not as a love interest but as a person. In addition to providing the kind of service you might imagine she also provides a safe place for her clients. That's part of her guarantee. With the type of enemies I have that is important. I'm not exactly at my sharpest when I'm on heat."

"So, you trust this woman?"

"I've been seeing her for some time and thus far she's not given me any reason to distrust her. Besides, her reputation would be ruined if anything happened to a client so there is that."

"Aside from her do you see anyone else regularly?"

"Do I seem like the type who would go see someone like her, or anyone else, if I had a lover? I'm monogamous, Evie. Once I'm set on someone that is it. So no, I haven't seen anyone regularly or even occasionally in a very long time."

"Why?"

"I've not been interested enough in anyone to make an effort. Which is probably just as well."

"Why just as well?" Evie tilted her head into her palm her interest thoroughly piqued.

Aurora frowned, took a small sip of wine then said, "I'm not casual dating material. I tried it when I was younger but it was a disaster. The girls were keen enough to have a quick fuck but unless I'm in heat that doesn't do it for me. I get way too intense and territorial when I'm interested in someone. Not sure if that's just my personality or if it's my beast side bleeding through, driving me to find a mate – the lines can get blurry there. Plus, I was on this path of bloody vengeance which wasn't exactly conducive to romance. How about you? Is there a special someone in your life?"

"No. If there was, I wouldn't have kissed you. It's one lover at a time for me. I do go to the clubs to dance and unwind a little but it's not like when I was younger and everything seemed so exciting and new. I used to think it was just a matter of time and I'd meet someone who'd sweep me off my feet in a wild romance that would become something lasting. I've become too jaded to hold out much hope of that happening. I've seen all the moves and I'm well aware that most of the players are more interested in Evangeline Aquilar's power and wealth than in me as a person to be flattered by their overtures. So I mostly end up leaving with my friends or go home alone. It's been like that for some time now. Oh, and according to my last girlfriend I'm 'high maintenance'. What does that even mean?"

Aurora smiled and took another sip of her wine. "I'm sure I have no idea." At Evie's arched brow she burst out laughing. "You are perfectly sweet. It's not your fault she didn't know how to handle a thoroughbred."

"Did you just call me a horse?"

That made Aurora laugh even harder. "Why sound so indignant? It's okay for you to call me a horse but I can't return the favor?"

"I said you eat like a horse not that you are one. There's a vast difference."

"What I meant was that like a thoroughbred you are highly intelligent, high spirited and so strong willed you'd fight any attempt to steer you in a direction not of your choosing. If you were a horse, with those magnificent golden wings of yours, you'd be a female Pegasus. A breathtakingly beautiful, divine creature of the skies."

"Hmm…I can't decide if I should feel flattered or concerned about the way you see me. You have to admit as analogies go that was peculiar. At least it was original, I'll give you that."

Aurora gave a sheepish grin and said, "You can blame that on the wine."

"Oh?"

"I rarely drink because my system doesn't handle alcohol well. I can neutralize toxins but struggle with alcohol, how weird is that? One glass is about my limit. More and I get into trouble."

"What sort of trouble?"

"The sort where I wake up the next day appalled at the things I got up to the previous night. Alcohol messes with my self-control and one of the first things that goes is my inhibition. That's how I ended up in that strip poker game with mermaids, tree folk and wolves about to lose my bra when that smoke alarm went off."

"I forgot about that. You told me about the strip poker game and that drink was somehow involved but you were vague on details." Evie reached over and upended the bottle into Aurora's glass, tapping the side to release every last drop. "This I want to see. You sure you only have the one bottle? This will barely bring you to two glasses. Darn, if you reminded me about this earlier I would have saved more for you."

Aurora laughed again, a deep throaty uninhibited sound that caused a warm stirring low in Evie's stomach. Aurora gave the glass of wine a hesitant look, shrugged then downed it in a long gulp. "Come on, let's go to the library. I'll get the fire going and put on music."

"You have a library? Like with lots of books?"

"The real deal. Without the library I'd have gone mad up here all by myself. The winters here can be a bitch. I swear it once poured down hard for four weeks straight. There were huge waterfalls and rock slides everywhere and lightning in the sky like the old gods were having a prolonged pissing contest."

***

The moment Evie entered the library her steps faltered and she paused with one hand braced against the wall. Soft light illuminated bookshelves that stretched from the floor to the high ceiling as far as the eye could see. Aurora wasn't exaggerating when she said she had a library, there had to be thousands of books along one wall alone. On the opposite wall there were more books but there were also cabinets that held manuscripts and rolled up parchments. Wherever there was a space there were paintings. A mix of landscapes and portraits running a gambit of styles and moods, an eclectic collection. There was so much to look at that Evie couldn't take it all in. Maybe that was why her eye was drawn to the one thing different from the rest: the large desk stacked with notebooks and maps held down by marble chess pieces. There were pens and pencil cases, bottles of ink and calligraphy brushes all neatly lined up and a chair pushed out as if whoever used the desk had briefly stepped out. Aurora's backpack lay on the floor beside it.

"Evie, do you want to join me? I got the fire going. The room doesn't really need heating but I've always found it comforting to have a fire here especially when it's so cold and miserable outside. I can make tea here as well which is very handy."

Evie made her way to the doorway through which Aurora had disappeared and found a cozy sitting room with comfy chairs, a small tea table, a cabinet with an old record player and a couch placed to face a large window. Outside the light was fading fast and she could just make out the thickly vegetated mountainside and a wild sea that coiled and writhed angrily amidst tall sheer cliffs of dark grey. She took a seat on the leather couch. The material was worn and supple, giving way under her weight so she sank down into it. It was a place to relax and enjoy the view. To lie down and possibly even sleep judging by the blankets propped up at one end to form an oversized pillow. Or stretched out on the rug in front of it. Thick and soft the color of cream the rug stopped just short of the tiled area around the pot-bellied stove with its dark chimney that disappeared into the outside wall. Grilled up behind a thick partition of clear tempered glass a cheerful fire burned, pouring flickers of golden light into the room.

Aurora was on her knees beside the couch looking through a stack of vinyl records in a leather case. She would slide out an album, peer at the title and push it back down. "What kind of music do you like? Keep in mind all I have is this old record player and a somewhat antique collection. I bought a machine to play the more modern music but there is too much magic here so the electronics in the machine died and the discs were all blank before I even got to listen to one."

"Anything really. I'm not crazy about experimental blues though."

"Duly noted."

Seeing the guitar case on the stand next to the record player Evie asked, "Do you play?"

Aurora looked at her then the guitar case and back again. "A little."

"Will you play something for me?"

"Um...I'm self-taught."

"I promise I won't laugh. Please let me hear you play? I enjoy playing the piano but if my father's pained expression is anything to go by I have more enthusiasm than talent so you could hardly do worse."

"I'll play for you if you want but please don't expect too much. Like I said I'm self-taught and I'm not used to playing for other people."

"I would have been surprised if you were." Evie made a show of getting comfortable and gave Aurora an encouraging smile.

Aurora took the case from its stand carefully laid it down and almost reverently lifted out a guitar with wood the color of polished gold.

"That looks like a classic guitar? The wood grain is lovely."

Aurora nodded, smiled down at the guitar and said, "When I heard her sweet voice and saw the wood, I had to have her."

Aurora settled herself on the couch next to Evie and strummed quietly with her head cocked pausing to adjust the pegs. It took several minutes before she nodded in satisfaction. Then she started to play and Evie caught her breath forgetting to exhale for several seconds because she was so astonished. She'd expected a simple ditty or at best a passable rendition of some popular song. Instead, Aurora plucked the strings and the music that flowed into the room was as startling and pleasing as stumbling on a lush oasis in the desert fed by a well of cool sweet water. The instrument, its tone rich and mellow like well-aged liquor, sang under her fingers like a lover strummed by expert hands. Evie saw how Aurora's fingers flew over the strings to bring the complex melody to life and recognized the hand of a budding master tempering clean precision with passion. The music called to her, stirring emotions she couldn't clearly define and she wished desperately that it would not end.

After a few minutes Aurora's eyes drifted half closed. A dreamy expression softened her features and the small smile hovering on her lips drew Evie's attention to how full and sensual they were. Heat stirred low in her belly as she remembered what it had felt like to have those amazing lips and Aurora's hot mouth on her skin while she healed Lucky's scratches. She wondered wistfully how far Aurora would have gone if she hadn't interrupted her downward exploration.

A soft thud on the back of the sofa interrupted Evie's thoughts. Turning to look she found a set of yellow eyes giving her an up close and level stare. Refusing to be intimidated by something so small, despite the very real threat of razor-sharp teeth and poisonous claws so close to her face and neck, Evie narrowed her eyes and returned Lucky's stare. She was not in the mood for a repeat of the altercation in the hallway even if it did lead to Aurora ripping her shirt open to kiss and lick her all over.

The lynxhawk gave a sneezy huff, rustled its wings then sauntered closer to Aurora. Lucky made a high-pitched trilling sound and waited expectantly for Aurora to acknowledge him. When she turned her head to look at him amber sparked in her eyes and she pinned Lucky with a look that radiated so much disapproval Evie hoped never to have it leveled at her. The lynxhawk's posture immediately slumped, it ducked its head and made a noise that sounded vaguely apologetic. Aurora continued playing, her eyes never left Lucky's and the creature remained as still as a statue, only the tips of its ears twitching. This went on for so long Evie started feeling sorry for the lynxhawk and wondered if she should say something to intervene on his behalf. Lucky made another trilling noise, this time it was clearly plaintive even to her untrained ear. Aurora made a huffing noise and lowered her shoulder as if in invitation. Like a shot Lucky leapt onto her back and proceeded to drape himself across her shoulders. Aurora acknowledged the furry presence by rubbing cheeks with the creature. She continued playing, her hands never faltering as she transitioned smoothly from one piece to the next. Soon Lucky's rotating ears and swishing tail stilled and the lynxhawk drifted into a contented doze with its nose tucked into the nape of Aurora's collar.

Lucky was drawn to Aurora's presence just like she was, Evie realized with amusement. No wonder he wasn't happy finding her still here. He probably saw her as competition for Aurora's attention. Well too bad, he would just have to get used to sharing. If she played her cards right he would see a lot more of her. Resting her head on the sofa Evie allowed herself to relax back into the music. When Aurora looked like she might stop she made encouraging noises urging her to go on. This made her smile shyly and she played on once again drifting off into that dreamy look. When the music stopped Evie found the silence almost painful she missed it so much. She remained quiet hoping Aurora would continue but she sat with her hands limp and blinked as if she was coming back to herself.

"Just one more? Please?"

Aurora shook her head, "You flatter me but the wine…I think I may have had too much to drink. I'm beginning to feel it now." She flashed Evie a grin. "I better stop while you still think I can play." She briefly caressed the golden wood then she rose and gently lay the instrument back into its velvet-lined case shutting the heavy-duty locks. Disturbed by her motion Lucky rose with a languid stretch, gave Aurora's face an affectionate head-butt then flew out of the room.

Aurora smiled fondly and watched him go. "The poor thing is exhausted. He usually has lots of little naps but today he remained vigilant the whole time. He's not used to me having company aside from my mother on occasion and it confused him. He was torn between wanting to go back to his own warm den and his family and wanting to keep an eye on you. Clambering all over you was his way of trying to figure you out. I don't think he meant to hurt you. He probably just forgot to retract his claws. I'm sorry about what happened and that's not how I wanted my first guest here to be treated. After you threw him into the wall he really did want to tear into you and I'm glad I was there to stop that. You don't have to worry – he won't do anything like that again now I've made it clear I won't tolerate such behavior towards you. Lucky is very smart and he knew exactly why I was upset with him."

"I've already put it behind me. Besides, you took care of me very nicely afterwards so I'm not going to complain about lack of hospitality." She gave Aurora a sly wink that made her smile with just a hint of a blush. "I don't want to talk about that little pet terror of yours anymore. I want to know how you learned to play like that. No way are you self-taught. You're too good."

"But I am." Aurora reached into the container next to the record player and extracted an album in a faded red cover with a single guitar featuring prominently amidst spidery script. "The music came from this album and others like it I've collected over the years. It took me a while to play decently but the winters here can get long and lonely and learning kept me busy. Besides, I like music and I find playing the guitar relaxing."

"You entirely taught yourself from listening to old albums? No one helped you?" Evie struggled to keep the disbelief from her voice.

Aurora's brow furrowed as she thought about Evie's question. "I did study this man who used to play on a street corner in Porta Belua. People would applaud when he was finished and throw money in his hat. I figured he must be good for people to do that. I listened and watched to see how he placed his hands. I also have sheet music and books on how to play but I prefer to learn by listening. It's stirring to hear the passion the musicians pour into their music and it makes me want to play like that so I can feel it too. When I finally get it right it's a magic of sorts." Aurora looked flustered and a bit sheepish when she stopped talking. "I got carried away. I didn't mean to say all that."

"Aurora, you have a gift and how you play is unbelievable. You gave me shivers you played so well." To emphasize her words Evie rubbed her arms.

Aurora smiled but shook her head, "I don't really. I have good hearing and memory so I listen carefully then I copy. Anyone could do that if they practiced enough and I've had plenty of long empty days to fill. There's no great skill in that. It's just persistence and I like to work at things until I get it right."

Evie wanted to argue with her, wanted to point out there was more than repetition in how she played but she bit down on her words. What would be the point? Aurora really believed what she said and Evie guessed if she tried to convince Aurora how good she really was it would make her uncomfortable and possibly make her withdraw behind those heavy shutters. She did not want that. She didn't want to do anything that would spoil the relaxed mood. It was enough for now that she got to hear Aurora play and what an unexpected treat it had been. The best part of it was she had played *just for her.* Evie felt a warm glow streaked with possessive satisfaction at the thought.

"How about I make us a cup of tea and put on some music?"

It wasn't really a question but Evie nodded anyway. Soon the sultry voice of a woman singing in French, accompanied by a band drifted into the room. While Aurora busied herself with the kettle and cups Evie wandered back into the library to have another look. The books ranged from new hardback books to ancient leather-bound tomes that looked too fragile to touch. Evie recognized a few titles but most she didn't and it soon became apparent that the majority of the books were in languages she couldn't read or in script so incomprehensible she couldn't even guess the origin. She saw an entire section dedicated to rune magic but did not dare step over the symbols on the floor guarding the area, as the way the script became alive with movement and seemed to ooze menace when she got too close made her break out in a cold sweat. The library was truly a treasure trove of knowledge gathered, by the look of things, over centuries. It was a personal treasure that no one aside from Aurora and her Old Blood mother had access to. It was a library scholars and collectors would literally kill to get into. It made Evie feel privileged and awed that Aurora trusted her so much she'd let her see it.

Evie spotted an open doorway between two shelves. Curious she went closer and peered inside. The room was dimly lit but she caught the glint of metal on the rows of shelves and she made out something that looked like a spear or possibly an oversized sword resting on the lowest tier. On a frame hung a suit of armor reminiscent of a drawing she'd seen of a Japanese samurai except this was so big only a giant could fit it. What was something like that doing here? Intrigued Evie contemplated going inside the room to get a better look but decided against it. Aurora had explicitly warned her not to go anywhere she hadn't taken her and even though what she saw seemed to extend from the library it could also be a forbidden area Aurora had forgotten to close.

Evie backed away and made her way to the large desk beside which Aurora had left her backpack. The contents of the desk had sparked her curiosity the moment she saw it but she had made herself look around the library first so it wouldn't look like she was dying to know what Aurora was up to. Evie studied the guides and the maps held flat by chess pieces. The maps were not of Nordarra as she'd expected. They were of places in the human world she'd only heard of; Africa, Asia, America. All places on the other side of the portal in the ocean a few miles from Porta Belua that allowed trade and flow of people between the two worlds. Spread out on the side was a large map of Canada, next to it a place called Alaska. Someone, presumably Aurora, had made lots of notes in small, neat handwriting in the margins. An unsettling thought occurred to Evie. Hoping she was wrong she asked, "Aurora, when you said you didn't know when you would be back here I assumed you were going to a remote part of Nordarra. But that's not what you meant, is it? Are you planning to go through the portal?"

Aurora came and stood next to her to see what she was looking at. "Ah, yes. I'm going to the other side to explore those far lands."

"How long will you be gone?"

"Forever, if I find a place to call home."

"But why? You have a home here."

"This isn't truly a home…it's a place where I live alone. It's safe and has everything I need to survive but I want more out of life than that."

"You can't tell me in all of Nordarra you have not found a place you'd like to make a new home. You said you've traveled far so surely there must be someplace?"

"I've looked, Evie. Home to me means a place where people eagerly await my return. It means belonging. It means being wanted and needed. I'm yet to find such a place and I don't believe I'll find it here in Nordarra."

"Why not?"

"I've not been able to put down roots because the vow I made kept me on the move searching for the trophies taken from my father but I was always looking hoping to find a potential home. I thought a few times I'd found somewhere I could belong but it always turned out the same. Sooner or later people realized I'm an Old Blood and they would start to treat me differently. That I could deal with but unfortunately because of some of the things I did when I was younger and the rumor mill that blew everything out of proportion, I also have a bloody reputation. Some people become afraid when they hear those rumors and they want me to leave while others, like clan Swift Foot, want me to stay but only because they want me to fight for them. I want to get away from all of that. I want a fresh start."

"But why go so very far away? You'll have to leave most of what you own behind. You'll have to start from nothing in a place you know no one and everything is foreign."

"That's kind of the point, Evie. Aside from how people treat me I have a much bigger problem. I constantly have hunters on my trail. Some of that is due to the enemies I made while hunting for my father's killers but mostly it's because I'm an Old Blood tigress. My body is literally worth a king's ransom. You know how crazy the trade in anything shapeshifter is. If an avian drops a feather scavengers on the ground will fight to collect it. Tourists happily fork out wads of cash to smuggle an avian feather back to their world, buying into the whole 'good luck' and 'wings of angels' crap. Then there are the herbalists who grind it down into tinctures and potions believing it will do amazing things if harnessed correctly."

Evie nodded because she did indeed know this. She'd been

approached numerous times by tourists offering her ludicrous amounts of money for one of her feathers and the sentinels frequently caught people trying to climb over the walls in the hope of finding feathers around the base of their tower. As annoying as that was she never feared someone would try to kill her for her feathers. What would be the point when there were so many avians and literally millions of feathers? Aurora's pelt, on the other hand, would definitely be one of a kind. Definitely worth killing for. Evie's chest ached like someone was squeezing her heart and she had to blink back tears.

Seemingly oblivious to Evie's distress Aurora continued. "Normal tigers are hunted for their pelts and in the belief that their bodies have healing and mystical properties. From what I've read there are places in the human world where tigers are almost extinct because of that. Shapeshifters are imbued with magic so you can imagine how much more valuable and fanatical the hunt for a tiger-shifter, dead or alive. I try to blend but I'm too big and my beast too distinctive for me to go unnoticed. People tend to remember me. It only takes one sighting and soon someone is trying to find my trail. I've stopped counting how many hunters and mercenaries I've killed over the years. It stops for a while but the price keeps going up and eventually there is always someone new who thinks they can take me down. Perhaps if there was an entire clan of Old Blood tigers in the area it wouldn't be so bad but I'm the only one of my kind in this part of the world. To the hunters that makes me the ultimate trophy."

"Aurora…that's dreadful. How long have they hunted you?"

"It started after my father was murdered. There have been peaceful periods but it never lasts. This last year was particularly bad for some reason. Or maybe I'm just feeling it more. When I was younger I enjoyed the game as I saw it as a way to hone my skills but I'm long past that." Aurora sighed like she had the weight of the world on her shoulders and said with weary resignation. "It doesn't matter how good I am because there's only one of me and they keep coming. Eventually, I'm going to make a mistake or just run out of luck and then it's game over. Unless I'm willing to live in isolation I have to move to where no one knows about me. That's why I'm going to leave Nordarra. I'm going to try to pass for human in their world. Hopefully that will give me a chance to have a peaceful life doing ordinary things with friends and if I'm very lucky…a mate. It shouldn't be too hard to make a living in the human world – I'm physically strong, I've picked up many useful skills during my travels and I'm not afraid of hard work, heights, cold, dangerous seas or predatory animals. I've also learned several of their languages. Admittedly it's mostly the written format but my ear and memory are good so it shouldn't take me long to learn to speak it properly. I have a plan…" Aurora grew animated her hands tracing the map of Canada. "I'll go to places like this where it sounds like the people are friendly and welcoming even to strangers and according to the maps there are still lots of wild isolated places for the times I need to shift or have to hide for some reason. It's a big area and there are many places someone like me can cross into Alaska or other parts of the continent unseen. Yes, I think Canada should be a good place to start. I'll try new things, explore the forests and mountains of that world and visit their great libraries. Maybe I can play my guitar on street corners to see if I'm good enough that people will throw money in a hat as they did for that man. It will be quite the adventure, don't you think?"

Evie was silent, she honestly didn't know what to say. She felt shocked, disappointed and upset. Her thoughts were a jumbled mess and she could find nothing supportive to say. Not when what she really wanted to do was ask Aurora to reconsider and stay but how could she do that? Aurora was looking at her with such expectation, her eyes shining and the flush on her cheeks making her look so young. Seeing her like that, so excited and so desperately hopeful, was as startlingly unexpected as it was heartbreakingly beautiful. Aurora had just shared with her a deeply personal dream, something she was invested in. How could Evie say anything to dampen her excitement? Swallowing the lump in her throat Evie said the most neutral thing she could think of. "It sounds like you've put a lot of thought into this."

"I've been planning it for years."

"When are you going?"

"I'm going to take you to Porta Belua personally instead of asking my friends in the village to make sure you get home safely. As soon as I've dropped you off at the harbor, I'll go book a ticket for one of the tourist ships returning for a pickup. I've heard it's hard to get a cabin this late in the season but it's worth a try. There are bound to be a few humans who died during their visit or someone who decided to stay in Nordarra."

"Why so soon?" Evie couldn't help herself, the words were out before she could think of a reason not to say them.

"It is hardly soon. I've wanted to leave for many years. Now my oath is fulfilled I'm finally free to make a fresh start. It's a new beginning! I've dreamed about this for so long and it has kept me going when I felt like I couldn't take it anymore. I'm so tired, Evie. So very weary of living like this. I need a chance at something new and good."

Feeling shaken and unsteady Evie placed her hand on Aurora's arm and gave it a little squeeze. "Your plan sounds good. I just wish we had more time. We're still getting to know each other and we are already such good friends. We have this amazing connection. Or maybe it's just me who feels this way?"

"It is not just you. I can't remember ever feeling so at ease with someone. I trust you and I don't even know why. There are people I've known most of my life who I haven't told a fraction of the things I've shared with you."

Evie couldn't stand it anymore. She needed to be closer to Aurora. She needed to touch her. She closed the small distance between them and leaned her forehead against Aurora's shoulder.

"I'm going to miss you."

Strong arms wrapped around, drawing her near so their bodies pressed together in a most intimate way. This made Evie's breath hitch. Tentatively she put her arms around Aurora not wanting to read too much into it. Sometimes a hug, however intimate, was just a hug. Aurora was very emotional right now and it was entirely possible she didn't realize what she was doing.

"I won't tell anyone the things you told me or talk about the places you showed me. You have my word."

A soft lingering press of lips against her forehead. "Thank you. Those things were only for you. I'll miss you too, Evie."

Standing so close to Aurora Evie could feel her feminine curves and the flex of her muscles in the small shifts of her body. That combined with the heat coming off her was doing unsettling things to Evie's body and she struggled to keep her breathing even. She was acutely aware of Aurora's hands circling her back and shoulders in firm motions, kneading and stroking. Aurora moved her leg, semi wrapping it around Evie and she felt a different sort of heat press against her side. Oh yeah, something was definitely happening and it wasn't just her wishful thinking. She needed to see Aurora's face, she needed to be sure. Tilting her head sideways Evie saw Aurora's eyes and her own flew wide in astonishment. Aurora's eyes were so dark they looked almost black and were filled with so much naked hunger the force of it took her breath away. Then Aurora kissed her and she could not think at all. It wasn't the tentative, gentle first kiss she had expected Aurora to initiate. It was a confident, demanding kiss that took no prisoners and had Evie holding on to Aurora's shoulders for dear life, fearing if she let go she might fall. The body encasing her had become like steel. A hand descended to caress her bottom and Evie squirmed at the unexpected boldness. Through the lust haze she registered something wasn't right. Aurora had just gone from 0 to 200 miles an hour in about five minutes flat. Breaking the kiss she leaned back against the desk trying to get a better look to confirm her dawning suspicion. Aurora's pupils were too wide, like dark deep pools, and her cheeks were flushed crimson.

"Aurora, are you all right?"

"Why? Didn't you like the kiss?" Then Aurora giggled. It was a bubbly girly giggle so unlike her normal laughter it set off all Evie's remaining warning bells.

"How about it, hmm? You did say you wanted to be kissed and dined first before I go down on my knees between yours. Now I've done both. We could have so much fun. I have lots of stamina and I can go for hours. Want me to show you?" Aurora leaned in for another kiss with a goofy grin. Evie ducked away and got a kiss on the shoulder.

"Wow, I think you're drunk. Like *really* drunk."

"Possibly. Doesn't mean I can't perform. I can make you feel good, Evie, so very good. I promise."

"Oh sweetie, you really can't handle your drink. You need to go have a nap or something."

"You're turning me down? I thought you liked me? I thought you wanted me?"

"I more than like you and I definitely want you but you're so not yourself right now. I think we need to wait until you're sober before we take this any further."

"Seriously? Hmm…you smell so good."

Aurora leaned in to nibble the side of Evie's neck. She braced one hand against a bookcase while the other caressed Evie's back and sides in long strokes. Evie temporarily lost the ability to have coherent thought, reveling in the delicious sensation of Aurora's mouth exploring her throat and neckline and almost didn't react in time to halt the wandering hand sneaking up the inside of her shirt. Her breasts were her weakness and if Aurora got her hands on them what little self-control she had left would be out the window. She'd probably let Aurora take her on the desk if she put that amazing mouth on one of her sensitive nipples. Evie took a shaky step away and the other woman immediately pursued. She placed a hand on Aurora's chest to keep a little distance between them.

"I can't believe I'm saying this…but yes. We have to wait until you're sober." Evie almost choked on the words. She was painfully aroused and she longed for Aurora to tear her clothes off and fuck her senseless but this felt wrong. This wasn't her Aurora, not the carefully controlled woman she'd come to know. Not that she believed for a minute Aurora was always so tightly held but she wanted to see those guards let down willingly, not smashed to pieces by a few sips of red swirled on the tongue. She didn't want to ruin the genuine trust Aurora had shown her by accepting what she might not have offered otherwise. Especially not after everything they'd talked about this evening. Even though Aurora obviously desired her she felt sure Aurora would resent alcohol-induced sex tomorrow. A part of her argued that Aurora knew what she was doing when she downed the second glass of wine but she hadn't been the one to pour it for herself. She probably wouldn't have had more if Evie hadn't goaded her into it. Aurora even told her she didn't normally drink because she ended up doing things she regretted afterwards. Darn it! And she had such high hopes for this evening. She'd entertained visions of them naked between the sheets all day. Now she was cast in the role of a caring friend putting her inebriated buddy to bed. She sighed heavily. Who knew Aurora could get this plastered from so little? Her little sister could probably drink three times as much and be fine.

Evie's thoughts unraveled again and she stared in fascination as Aurora planted kisses on her palm and wrist. When she suckled Evie's fingertips she felt red hot spikes shoot to her sex with the flicks of Aurora's tongue.

"Do you really want to wait?"

Aurora's voice was a low purr promising dark pleasures and Evie knew if she led Aurora to bed she'd follow willingly. Surely, she must really want it to be this eager? Maybe she had the wine to help herself relax knowing full well it would end up with them having sex. Aurora's lips were just inches away, so full and ready to be kissed again. Evie felt herself waver. She removed the arm keeping them apart and cupped Aurora's cheek. Aurora's eyes half closed and she leaned into Evie's touch stroking her face against her palm.

"Evie, you're so incredibly beautiful, so amazing. I feel like I can trust you with my secrets…and my life. Someday you will make someone weep with happiness to have you as a mate."

Evie took Aurora by the hand and let her to the cozy sitting room. She took one of the folded blankets from the couch and lay it down like a sheet on the thick rug then lay another over the top. She folded back a corner and held it open. "Lie down, Aurora."

Aurora pulled the shirt over her head treating Evie to the sight of dark-tipped breasts and toned muscles that rippled as she arched. Without pause she pushed her pants down and stepped out of them. Evie felt a wave of relief on seeing the boxer briefs. Aurora's words before had been like an unwelcome cold splash dampening the heat of her desire enough to see reason but the fire was by no means extinguished and it would take very little to stir it to an inferno that would sweep her away. She was constraining herself but no amount of good intentions would stop her if Aurora stripped totally. She was a woman, not a saint. She almost lost it when Aurora went down on her knees to crawl past her to get between the blankets. She brushed Evie's hip in passing and the slight sway of her breasts as she moved had Evie biting her lip to prevent a moan from escaping.

Staring up at Evie Aurora asked, "Are you going to sleep with me?"

Evie closed her eyes for a moment and swallowed hard. "Here." She patted the sofa. "I'll be sleeping right here."

Aurora watched her with dark eyes. "That's what you want?"

No, that's not what I want! I want to fuck you but I can't because you're drunk and you will probably hate me in the morning!

"I might join you later."

"I would like that." Before Evie could reply Aurora turned on her side and her eyes fluttered shut. Within moments her breathing was deep and even.

Darn it! Evie collapsed on the couch and stared at the beautiful woman asleep at her feet. She was so conflicted it was making her feel ill. She slid her hand into her panties. She was soaked and so aroused she ached. She was tempted to give herself relief just to take the edge off. A few strokes and she stopped. No. That wasn't what she wanted and it wouldn't be enough by far. Not tonight. Her hunger was way too deep to be satisfied by a quickie when what she really wanted was Aurora between her legs, taking her until she screamed her release. Nope. Not on the same scale at all. Feeling miserable she stalked off to the bedroom to get changed for bed and find pillows and more blankets. She hoped the couch was as comfortable as it looked.

CHAPTER 18

COMFORT

After tossing and turning for what felt like an eternity Evie finally managed to fall into a fitful doze. She woke with a start, every fiber of her being on alert. Something woke her, something bad. Squinting in the low light she saw Aurora move on the floor and knew what had alarmed her. Aurora was dreaming, she must have moaned in her sleep. Turning on her side to keep an eye on the dreaming woman Evie relaxed back onto her pillow. Then the keening started. It was the most terrible sound she'd ever heard. Somewhere between a wail of lament and a scream, it was a thing dredged from a dark pit of despair and hearing it made Evie tremble. Aurora wasn't just dreaming, she was having a horrific nightmare. She raised up on an elbow to have a better look and saw Aurora had kicked off her blanket. She was crouched on arms and knees her muscles straining like she was struggling against a great weight pressing down on her. Her body was covered in a sheen of sweat making her skin glisten in the firelight and her breathing was fast and labored like she was struggling to get enough air.

Sliding off the couch to get closer to Aurora, Evie reached out a hand to shake her awake but yanked it away from the shoulder she'd been about to touch when she saw the way Aurora's skin rippled. The air around her felt charged like moments before a lightning storm and there was a dissonant hum Evie felt rather than heard that set her teeth on edge. Something was happening. Was Aurora about to shift in her sleep while stuck in a nightmare? Wouldn't it be dangerous to touch her if that is what was happening?

"Aurora, wake up!"

Aurora didn't respond.

"Aurora! Aurora! Aurora, wake up!"

Aurora threw her head back and screamed while tears streamed down her face. Evie stared in dismay at the agony and grief etched onto the dreaming woman's face. Was she having a nightmare about what happened to her and her dad? Was she reliving her capture and his death right now? No. She had to stop this. Now. Caution be damned, she would not let her friend suffer like this. She was going to wake her whatever it took! In desperation she grabbed Aurora's shoulders intending to shake her. In the blink of an eye, Evie found herself flat on her back with Aurora on top pinning her down. The body above her was strung taught as a bow and Aurora's eyes were like nothing she'd seen before. There wasn't even a fleck of green in her eyes, only a sea of amber and worse still her pupils were vertical slits like that of a large cat. There was no recognition in those eyes, no Aurora that she could see, only something other and it was staring at her like a predator would a tiny creature trapped in its paws. Evie realized she was looking directly into the eyes of Aurora's beast. Sensing Aurora's terror it must have come to the surface to defend her and she'd just interrupted a full shift. In another moment she could have had a tigress crouching over her. Evie swallowed and lay very still. She wanted Aurora on top of her but this wasn't what she had in mind.

"Aurora, it's me. Evie." Evie said speaking quietly. "You had a nightmare. I tried to wake you up. Aurora, can you hear me?"

Aurora cocked her head as if listening. She blinked and the alien eyes were human-shaped again. Her eyes were still mostly amber but Evie could see tiny flecks of green. Aurora was fighting her way back.

"Evie?" Aurora blinked again and the amber receded a little more.

Moving slowly Evie got her fingers on Aurora's arms and stroked gently. "Yes, it's Evie. I'm with you. You had a bad dream but you're awake now. It was just a dream. You are safe. Aurora, please come back to me."

Aurora lowered her head to within inches of Evie's neck, her nostrils flared and she inhaled deeply drawing in Evie's scent.

"Evie..." Aurora's eyes flew wide and it was like someone threw a light switch and suddenly she was back entirely.

"Oh no...did I hurt you?" Aurora cupped Evie's face with one hand her eyes desperately searching for an answer. "Did I?"

"I'm fine. You didn't hurt me. I woke you from a nightmare rather abruptly and you threw me on my back. That is all. What terrible nightmares you have! Come here, let me hold you."

Evie wrapped her arms around Aurora's neck and tugged gently. After a moment's resistance she allowed herself to be drawn into an embrace. Evie threaded her fingers through Aurora's hair and drew her head onto her shoulder. She ran her other hand up and down Aurora's back in what she hoped was a soothing motion. The muscles under her fingers were rock hard with tension, Aurora's skin was clammy and cold and small tremors ran through her body. It was Aurora's low body temperature that alarmed Evie most because she usually ran hot as a furnace. Since Aurora's top blanket was a tangled mess somewhere by their feet Evie reached up to the couch and drew down her own blanket. With a bit of one-handed fumbling she managed to drape it over them making sure to cover the trembling woman all the way to her neck.

"I'm mortified. I never wanted you to see me like this."

"Like what?"

"Like this…so weak and pathetic. Shaking like a child over a bad dream. What must you think of me?"

"Don't be silly. You are one of the strongest people I know. How typical of you to have the most god-awful nightmares; you're such an over achiever. Most people have run-of-the-mill bad dreams with the occasional night-terror but oh no, that's not enough for you. Your subconscious just has to take it to the next level." Evie felt Aurora's muscles relax as some of the tension left her. She tenderly kissed her forehead and asked, "Was the nightmare about what happened to you and your dad?"

"Yes."

"Do you want to talk about it?"

"No."

"Have you talked to someone about this recurring nightmare?"

"No."

"You really should. You need to talk about what still terrorizes you after all these years."

"No."

"Why not talk to me? I'm your friend and I'm offering to listen. You need to get this out. It's been festering in you. I've heard of people being plagued by nightmares but, Aurora, your father's death was such a long time ago it shouldn't still be this bad. I will listen. I promise you I won't run away screaming."

"You can't run away – I have you pinned," Aurora said dryly.

Evie gave her a smack on the shoulder and Aurora chuckled. She moved down a little so that she could see Aurora's face better. "But seriously, why won't you tell me?"

Aurora's expression became grim. "I don't want anything from that dark place touching you. Ever. I don't want that taint anywhere near you. Trust me, Evie, there's nothing good there. You won't look at me the same. I've never seen you afraid or disgusted, not once. I couldn't stand seeing that kind of look on your face."

"You already told me what happened. What is it you're so afraid of?"

"I told you some things. Just enough so you would understand why I'm so sensitive about my father's death. What I didn't tell you was what happened afterwards. I didn't tell you the things I did."

"It's okay, you can tell me. You must have wanted to talk about it so tell me now. I'm here for you. I'm your friend and I want to know. No matter how ugly you think it is I can handle it."

"I've carried this with me so long. I don't want to anymore. I thought when I found the last piece of my father and the vow was fulfilled that the dreams would stop but they haven't." Aurora sighed heavily. "I so want this to be over. Do you really think if I talk about what happened it will help?"

"There's only one way to find out. I'm no counselor but I know it's not good to keep bad memories cooped up inside. You have to let them out and the best way to do that is to tell someone what happened. It's like opening a wound that's festered. Painful, but once it's been aired and cleaned it can start to heal."

"I hate those nightmares. If talking will help I'm willing to give it a try."

"Good. I'm here for you."

Aurora went quiet as she gathered her thoughts, their breathing and the faint popping of the fire the only sounds disturbing the silence. The quiet began to stretch into minutes but Evie waited patiently. She would wait as long as it took and holding Aurora in her arms was no hardship at all. Aurora's voice when she finally spoke was so soft Evie had to strain to hear her.

"After I escaped from the cage they had me in I lost my mind for a while."

"That's understandable, you were out of your mind with grief and shock."

"It was more than that, Evie. I mean I went mad. As in bat shit out of my mind feral. I was stuck in a pit in the ground with my father's body on top of the grate. He'd fallen like that to keep the men away from me when he realized he couldn't get me out and could not get away either. In his beast form he spoke to me. He commanded me to stay awake and told me I wasn't allowed to die. That I had to hold on a little longer, that soon I would have all I needed to escape." Aurora paused to angrily swipe tears from her eyes. "My dad told me that what came next would be hard for me to endure. I thought he meant shifting. He told me I had to push through the pain and shift all the way. That once I shifted I needed to do whatever it took to escape, no matter what. I cried when he told me that. I thought he was asking the impossible of me. Before that day I had never managed a full shift, not once. I had tried, I really had even though it felt like pushing against red hot spikes. I could sense my beast and the bulk of my magic on the other side of a barrier but I could not get past to form a proper connection to either. The most I could ever manage was to shift parts of my body but only briefly and even that wasn't quite right. When I changed a hand or something else it didn't consistently take the same form. At times it would be this freakish meld that looked like nothing I'd ever seen. My dad said it was because what I had inherited from my mother and him were fighting for dominance inside me. He always said not to lose hope, it was just a matter of time. That my body and mind just had to mature enough to handle it all. My poor dad was such a terrible liar. I pretended to believe him but I'd seen toddlers move easily between their human and beast forms and they didn't act like something was trying to tear them apart from the inside. I was already eleven. I knew something was wrong. I knew I was broken somehow, flawed. My parents were from very different bloodlines. Usually, in such a union the child takes after the mother or the father but there is always a chance the magic will mix badly and the child ends up unable to shift at all. I thought that was what happened to me. I felt like such a disappointment. I had two powerful Old Blood parents but I was like neither of them. My father tried to comfort me as best he could. He still loved me even though I was broken so I tried to tell myself it didn't matter that I couldn't run with him in tiger form."

Aurora covered her face with her hand. Her breathing was quick and Evie could feel the rapid thud, thud of Aurora's heart through her chest.

"You did shift that day, didn't you?"

"Yes. I most certainly did."

"How?"

"It was my father's last gift to me. I didn't understand until they started cutting and he was there directly above me, his blood pouring down on me like warm rain. The healing power of a tiger-shifter's blood…there is truth in that but it was so much more. I felt him pour all his magic along with his blood onto me. I felt him give his life to save mine. He didn't hold back any magic to heal himself, he gave everything he had to heal what was broken in me so that I could connect with my beast and shift. So that I could escape and live. He looked at me the whole time. He could no longer speak by then but he kept looking at me until the end. He saw it. He saw my first full shift and the last thing I remember seeing before everything became a haze was my father's smile."

Aurora was sobbing, tears streamed past her fingers to drip on Evie's shoulder. Evie gently pulled her hand away. "You don't have to be ashamed of your tears. Not with me. What happened next?"

"I was very badly injured. The men had hurt me to make me scream so my father would hear my cries and come for me. I think I was dying. So much pain everywhere. It was all so horrible and I felt so pathetically small and weak. So violated and ashamed. Then I had my first full shift and *boom* everything changed. All the pain and fear disappeared along with my frail damaged body and all I felt was rage and the need to destroy. The rage felt good. It burned everything else from my mind and gave me a singular consuming focus. That body was so much better. So primal, so powerful. Even if I'd known how to shift back on my own I don't think I would have."

"How long were you like that?"

"I don't know. Days, weeks maybe longer. My memory of what happened after I shifted for the first time is fragmented at best, a jumble of images and sensations. It was the first time I truly connected with my beast and it was at a time when I was as fucked up as any person could be. My mother knows because she found me and forced me to shift back but she never said and afterwards neither of us wanted to talk about it. My father's death was too raw between us and I think how she found me scared her. The prolonged shift and my father's blood had healed my human body but my mind…" Aurora motioned to her head, "I wasn't right for some time. They called him a monster to justify what they did to him but he was a peaceful kind man. He made friends wherever he went and avoided fights whenever he could. He was happiest when he got to roam the forests and spend time with his wife and child. But they came for him, for us. They tortured me to lure him into a trap then made me watch him die while they hacked into him. I was only a child who couldn't shift so they didn't think I was dangerous and I wasn't before that day. I was just a young girl who wanted to be like her daddy. After that day I became the monster my father never was." Aurora paused and gave Evie a worried look.

Evie stroked the side of Aurora's face and gently said, "I'm listening. Take your time, we have all night. I know it feels very uncomfortable right now but you will feel better once it is all out."

Aurora nodded and said, "I killed several of them when I shifted and clawed my way out of that hole trying to escape. I was in such a frenzy I didn't even register I'd done it until I thought about it later. I ran at first but I had to go back for my dad. As messed up as I was I knew my father was dead but they were doing terrible things to him, to his body. What if some part of my father was still trapped inside, aware and suffering? I had to save him from that. When I got back there were only four men left. The others had already packed up and fled, taking with them my father's pelt and what had already been harvested. I'd never taken a beast form before then and never stalked a prey for the sole purpose of killing. That night I hunted those men as easily as if I'd done it hundreds of times. My father had taught me how to hunt from the moment I could walk and I had a powerful body with enhanced senses. Between that and my rage…so much rage… those men never stood a chance. When I was done with them I carried my father's remains away and used my claws to dig a grave for him under a giant tree. I was delirious with grief and more than a little mad at that point. I'd just killed my first people and buried a hunk of flesh and bones that was unrecognizable as the man who raised me. I was lying on my father's grave when I made the vow to retrieve what had been stolen from him. I did it while I was covered in blood; my own, my father's and those of the men I just killed. That was how the hunt started. The other murderers had gone by air and by boat and had done their best to disappear. I did whatever it took to track them down and when I found them, I showed no mercy. If they begged for their lives or tried to come up with excuses for what they had done it only made me angrier and instead of granting a quick death I took my time. It was like a different kind of madness and it lasted for years. I tried to wash away the grief and shame of what happened with their blood. I wanted to make them suffer like my father did as he lay there paralyzed, feeling every cut they made but unable to stop them. I wanted them to suffer like I did as I lay in that cage drenched in his blood. It ran into my wounds, my eyes and down my throat. I felt his blood heal my broken body even as my mind was shattering. I lost everything that was good in my life that day. I wanted to forget what happened, *I wanted it to be over*. But every time I killed another it all came back to me again. The darkness of those days fresh in my mind like putrid blood in the mouth, poisoning me over and over."

Aurora stopped talking and stared at the ceiling with a stark expression on her face. A muscle jumped in her clenched jaw and her eyes had an unsettling amber glow. Evie didn't say anything to fill the silence as she didn't feel it was the type of silence that waited for a response. Aurora wasn't done speaking, that much was clear. She just needed a moment to figure out how to continue.

"I tried to stop. When I realized what it was doing to me I tried to stop but I couldn't. The vow I made drove me to keep looking for the pieces of my father that were carried away and this repeatedly brought me into contact with the sort of things I was trying to forget. Perhaps if it wasn't for that I could have moved on and made a peaceful life for myself. I'd like to think so but…I'm not sure. For years I had nightmares almost every time I slept so I slept very little and that didn't help my mental state. At that point in my life, the hunt had become my sole reason for living. When I was at my worst if I heard a rumor about a cutter's nest I went after it and if I found one, I decimated the entire operation. Killing the cutters and saving the shifters they held captive felt like the only way I could justify being alive when by rights I should have died with my father. It didn't help that my beast relished the hunt. It's an aggressive predator and killing is what it does best but I can't blame how far I went on being a beast-shifter. I'm still the one in control. Well…mostly anyway." Aurora sighed and said, "It took me a long time to find even a small measure of peace and to feel like I was allowed to pursue the kind of life I may have had if my father hadn't been murdered. I'm so weary of blood and death. All I want is to spend my days doing ordinary things with friends and maybe if I'm very lucky with a mate by my side. I honestly don't care what I must do to make a living or where I have to live as long as I can have that. Even if it means I have to leave everything and everyone I know behind I'll do it if that's my only chance to start over with a clean slate."

***

Aurora lay very still and kept her eyes on Evie's shoulder. She'd not been able to look at Evie when she told of the people she killed and as memories of how, at times, she'd given into bloodlust and let her beast have free reign shamed her. Now she was afraid to look at Evie, afraid of what she might see on her face. She hadn't meant to share so much but once the awful truths started pouring out it was like she couldn't stop. Aurora felt raw and utterly exposed. If Evie now feared her or she found a look of revulsion on Evie's face it would be a blow from which she might never recover. She waited for her to say something. When the seconds dragged on and still no response the need to know overrode her fear and she hesitantly looked at Evie. Evie's face was streaked with silent tears and her eyes were filled with so much sorrow and compassion it shook Aurora.

Evie took a gasping breath and said, "I don't know what to say. I don't know how you survived everything that happened and manage to still have such a kind heart. What I do know is your dad must have loved you more than life itself and you must never forget that. He wanted his little girl to grow up and have a full happy life. Don't go through the rest of your life carrying the burden of guilt for what happened. Not only was his death not your fault, your father would never have wanted you to punish yourself over and over with these horrible nightmares. As for the people you killed it almost sounded like you were asking me for absolution but you don't need it. Not from me or anyone." Evie took one of Aurora's hands in hers and kissed it. "Yes you have blood on your claws but truly how could there be any other way? You stopped evil people from hurting others. Not just the ones they would have captured but also the families and friends who would have suffered for the loss of their loved ones. Imagine those poor people searching fruitlessly day after day, year after year. Not knowing what happened, suspecting cutters were involved but never knowing for sure. Or even worse...seeing what had been done to a child, a parent, a sibling or a lover. That, Aurora, would be the kind of thing that would make someone have nightmares for the rest of their life. By doing what you did, by putting your life at risk for strangers, you saved all those people from the fate you and your father suffered. And most importantly as far as I'm concerned…are you listening, Aurora?"

"Yes, I'm listening."

"Good. Most importantly because of you, I'm entirely whole. That cutter didn't get to lay a blade on me and my soul is unscarred. You saved me. Because of you, I get to go home and aside from a few bad memories of *that place* I will go on with my life as if I'd never been stuffed into a cage. You made that possible. Remember that."

Aurora had been staring into Evie's eyes, drinking her in and watching her expressions closely as she talked. She heard only truth and sincerity in her words. She saw no revulsion, no judgement, no fear and felt no subtle drawing away in the way Evie held her. She felt a massive weight lift off her and let out a deep shuddering breath she hadn't realized she'd been holding. "Thank you, Evie," she said simply. "Thank you. I can't tell you how much this means to me. You listening, what you said. All of it." Aurora wanted to say so much more, wanted desperately to convey to Evie her intense gratitude but she felt raw from her sharing and Evie's words were still settling like a healing balm. Her emotions were a jumbled turbulent mess and she needed time to calm down before she could speak more.

"Aurora, it's been my honor to be here for you. Thank you for sharing with me, for trusting me like this. Everything that is said between us will stay with me. I swear it to you."

Feeling overwhelmed emotionally Aurora closed her eyes and allowed herself to relax into Evie's embrace. It felt so good in her arms, so soft and comforting. Safe. Evie seemed to understand Aurora needed a little time to gather herself. She didn't speak, instead she let her hands do the talking, trailing fingers over Aurora's back and through her hair in a gentle caress. Eventually, Aurora opened her eyes, cleared her throat and said, "If you ever need my help, no matter with what, all you have to do is ask and I'll be there for you. What you have done for me tonight…" Aurora trailed off not knowing how to finish.

"I know you would but there's nothing owed between us, there is only that which is freely given. We are friends."

Aurora felt a smile lift her lips and said, "Yes that we are. Friends."

Evie smiled back at her and gave her a tender kiss on the cheek. "You had me worried there for a bit. Are you feeling better now? You look better."

"Yes, I'm fine now." Aurora raised herself up on an elbow and noticed Evie's shirt was darkly stained and wet from their combined tears so it clung to her. "We made your shirt wet," Aurora said smiling ruefully and rubbed at the tears that had gathered in the hollow of Evie's throat. The motion made the blanket slide from her shoulder baring her chest. Aurora looked down at herself and saw her bare breasts pressed against Evie's damp shirt. She froze. "I'm not wearing a shirt…and no pants. Why am I almost naked? Oh no...*the wine.*"

Evie couldn't help it, she giggled. "Did you only just realize that?"

Aurora scowled and tried to tuck the blanket between them but Evie would have none of it. She pushed the blanket away and tightened her arms around Aurora keeping her close. She enjoyed having her hands all over Aurora's bare back way too much and the sight of Aurora's breasts pressed against her chest had her just about giddy.

"Relax. We've been like this for ages so it would be silly to get all shy on me now. Besides, you're covered with the blanket and I'm still wearing all my clothes."

Aurora's cheeks were scarlet. "It was the wine but I only had two glasses. Wow, it must have been a lot stronger than I thought."

"That wine was more like brandy," Evie agreed. "It smacked you silly. You are an adorable drunk. Very amorous."

"Well from what I was told it was aged in an oak barrel for many years so I suppose that would account for the potency. I remember now…I came on to you and not subtly either."

"No, subtle you were not," Evie agreed.

"And you turned me down."

"I didn't want to. Trust me I *really* wanted to take you up on your offer but you were so not acting like yourself. I was afraid if we had sex you'd hate me once you sobered up."

"I wouldn't have hated you."

"But you wouldn't have been happy about it either?"

"No. That kind of losing control reminds me too much of what it's like when I go into heat. I don't like it."

"So, I did the right thing? That's a massive relief. Tucking you into bed and curling up on the couch was one of the hardest things I've ever had to do. You had me on fire. If you tell me it would have been perfectly fine to get into bed with you, I'll be hitting myself for missing out on hot, drunken sex. I'm not an angel you know."

"Evie, you're as close to an angel as I've ever known."

That took the air from under Evie's wings for several seconds. Finally, she said, "I hate to knock myself off that pedestal you've put me on but you should know my thoughts about you right now are anything but angelic."

"Are you having wicked thoughts?"

"*Very* wicked thoughts. I've been having them all day."

"Only all day? I've been having them since we met."

Evie leaned away just far enough to see Aurora's face better. "Really?"

"Oh yes."

"And what were you going to do about that?"

"I wasn't going to do anything."

"Why the heck not? I threw out so many hints just about the only thing I didn't do was throw myself at you naked. Did you think all the touching was just me being tactile? I'm not like that with everyone! I only touch people I like and every day it has gotten harder to keep my hands off you. Didn't you notice that? And I kissed you!"

"You just about drove me crazy with the touching and the kisses."

"Then why do nothing? I don't understand."

Aurora traced Evie's bottom lip with her thumb and asked, "You don't know? Really? Don't you know by now how much I care for you? To have only one night with you and then leave…how could I endure that?"

"I'd think it would be the exact opposite. If you like me that much how could you not have at least one night with me?"

"But Evie, there can be no future for us. I'm leaving and even if I wasn't how would a female beast-shifter like me fit into the life of the future ruler of an avian House?"

"Why think about that right now? Why worry about the future? What comes next is not something either of us can be sure of. Tomorrow is unwritten. The only time we have for sure is right now and here we are in bed wanting each other. Needing each other. Perhaps everything has led up to this. To give us this night, this brief moment in time. I really think we should make the best of it. Don't you?"

Aurora had absolutely no idea how to respond to that. Her arguments, such as they were, held no ground in the face of such illogical reasoning that at the same time made perfect sense. Besides, the way Evie's hands stroked all over her hips and sides stopping just short of the underside of her breasts was incredibly distracting and her brain was having a very hard time retaining the driver's seat.

"Well?" Evie demanded when she took too long to answer.

"I'm trying to think," Aurora groaned "but it is very hard with you touching me like this." Even as she spoke Aurora could feel her resistance evaporate faster than a shallow puddle under the desert sun. She was crazy about Evie and incredibly attracted to her. After everything they'd shared, one night with Evie could be enough to shatter the fragile protection left around her heart. Aurora knew this but she could no more refuse Evie than a freezing man could refuse the warmth of a fire.

She was drawn. Captivated.

She was so going to get burned.

Right now she didn't care. One night, just one night. How bad could it be? A voice tried to warn her she was fooling herself but here right now she had this incredible woman offering herself. She desperately wanted her. For one night she would have Evie no matter the price. She yearned to make this incredible woman hers, body and soul but if she could only have her body for one night she would take it. She would take *her*. Oh yes. If they were only going to have one night then she was going to make love to Evie with nothing held back. Fears of the future be damned; she probably didn't have much of one anyway. She could be killed tomorrow. That thought made Aurora feel almost cheerful. If that was the case what a wonderful last night this would be. She felt her heart rate ramp up until it thudded in her chest like a runaway horse.

"Yes, Evie. Yes. I want to make love to you." At her words, Aurora felt Evie sag against her in relief.

"Kiss me. Kiss me again like you did before. That was wonderful."

"I'm not drunk this time. It will be better."

"Promises pro—"

She didn't let Evie finish. They had both done more than enough talking, it was time for action. She sealed Evie's mouth, stroked her bottom lip with her tongue exploring the velvet softness. Evie opened wider taking her inside, sucking gently. At the explosion of heat the feel of Evie's tongue caressing her own Aurora moaned. She gripped Evie tighter, shifting to push her thigh between Evie's legs. Evie instantly tightened around the offered leg and rotated her hips in a grinding motion. Aurora could feel the moist heat of Evie's arousal on her thigh. That and the way Evie had gone straight for her breasts, teasing her rock-hard nipples between her fingertips, drove her wild. Wanting to return the favor Aurora palmed Evie's breasts through the shirt. They were bigger than her own and the moment she rubbed her thumbs over the taut nipples through the damp material Evie bucked and her kisses became somewhat frantic. Right then Aurora knew she was going to take her time feasting on Evie's sensitive nipples if she liked having them touched that much. But first, the blasted shirt had to come off. She had no trouble removing the shirt as Evie eagerly helped. She moaned when Aurora got her hands on her luscious breasts and she urged Aurora to lie on her back. She didn't care how Evie wanted her as long as she could continue to caress her bare breasts – she was fascinated by the weight and feel of them and the little sounds that touching them elicited from Evie. Evie sat up to shimmy out of her shorts and Aurora groaned at the loss of contact. The shorts got tangled around one of her ankles. Evie muttered something and sent them flying with a kick. An instant later a fully naked woman straddled her. She reached for Evie but had her hands pushed under the couch.

"Hold on to that for now," Evie commanded. "I'll make it worth your while. I promise."

"But I need to touch you."

"Soon. Please, I'm starving for a proper taste of you. If you touch me, I'm going to climax too quickly and fantasies of having you like this have had me aching for hours."

Aurora wanted to protest but Evie gave her such a searing kiss that by the time she was able to replenish the air in her lungs she was happy to let Evie do whatever she wanted. She loved the weight of Evie's silken breasts against her own and the sensation of her lover's taut nipples stroking her over-sensitive skin was driving Aurora insane with need. Evie nudged Aurora's hips to make her lift, peeled off her briefs and flung them away with a flick of her wrist. When she resettled herself between Aurora's legs she ground their mounds together. They both gasped at the contact and Aurora had her hands on Evie's ass in an instant, pushing them more firmly together.

"Wait, wait…" Evie begged and stopped moving. "I'll come if you do that."

"You started it," Aurora pointed out and nipped the side of her neck. She loved the feel of the rounded cheeks in her palms and the exquisite sensation of Evie's sex rubbing against her own and didn't want to stop. "Hmm…you feel amazing. I want my hands and mouth all over you."

Evie's chuckle was deep and throaty. "Patience, my sweet. You can do all you want soon, just let me have my way with you a little longer. Please?"

It was the please that got her. Aurora allowed Evie to move her hands back to grip the couch albeit reluctantly. Evie reclaimed her mouth in a feverish kiss and her hands continued their exploration of Aurora's body: caressing, teasing, claiming. She usually hated relinquishing control in bed but with Evie she found she didn't mind at all. In fact, she absolutely loved it. Before Aurora could recover from Evie's conquest of her mouth she went after her breasts with lips and tongue, like they were a delicacy she'd been dying to try, while her fingers played on the inside of Aurora's thighs. She stroked the curls and trailed the tips of her fingers through the heated flesh in a slow tease, over and over. Evie's light barely-there touch was exquisite torture. By the time she let go of Aurora's breasts and started working her way downwards with kisses and swirls of her tongue she had Aurora quivering, her breathing was ragged and her grip on the couch was so hard the wood creaked.

"Evie…you're killing me."

Aurora felt Evie's smile against her stomach and her fingers, on their glide-through, dipped deeper eliciting a moan from Aurora.

"I want you to remember this first time with me. No need to rush when we have all night. I promise I will take care of you as many times as you need me to."

Aurora groaned hoping she would survive Evie's ministrations without breaking the frame on the couch.

"Put a pillow behind your head."

"Hmm?"

"There's a pillow on the couch just behind you. Put it behind your head. I want you to watch what I do next."

Wordlessly, Aurora reached behind her, felt for and found the pillow. She put it behind her head as instructed. She locked eyes with Evie who gave her a slow, wicked smile. She nudged Aurora's thighs further apart and still looking at her Evie licked the length of her sex, lingering to twirl her tongue around Aurora's clit. Her eyes fluttered shut and she moaned.

"Look at me. I want you to watch me make love to you. I want your eyes to be open when I take you over the edge. I want to see your incredible eyes when you come for me. I've dreamed of it."

"I need to touch you, Evie. I need the connection."

"Then touch me."

Aurora carefully gripped Evie's shoulders mindful of her own strength. She didn't want to hurt the beautiful woman intent on giving her pleasure or leave bruises on her creamy skin.

Evie put her head back down. Her eyes remained locked with Aurora's while she claimed her pussy the way she had claimed every other part of her. Aurora found it hard to keep her eyes open and even harder to look Evie in the eye while she performed such an intimate act on her. It felt like she was allowing Evie to stare into her soul but at the same time she got to see into Evie's as well and she liked what she saw. True to her word Evie took Aurora over the edge in more ways than one.

She had two blindingly intense climaxes that hit in rapid succession and left her boneless and dazed for several minutes.

As soon as she recovered enough to move, Aurora flipped Evie onto her back and pinned her down. She squirmed against Aurora's hold but became still when she saw the excited gleam in her eyes.

"It's my turn to have my way with you. I'm going to make you come until you beg me to stop."

"I have a hearty appetite so that's hardly a worthy threat. But you can try and I'll thoroughly enjoy myself while you exhaust yourself."

Aurora's smile was delighted and more than a little predatory, as if she'd been given a challenge she absolutely relished. "You are about to find out I wasn't lying when I said I have *lots* of stamina. Let me know what you like and I'll do it for you. All. Night. Long. That's what I've dreamed of doing to you. I've fantasized of satisfying you so thoroughly you pass out in my arms in absolute bliss."

Evie heard the truth of the statement in Aurora's voice and shivered a little, a mix of excitement and nervous anticipation at the intensity of her gaze. Then Aurora's mouth claimed hers and the way she moved and touched let Evie know she was about to be fucked senseless. She sighed happily, wrapped her arms and legs around the powerful body of her lover and gave herself over to be ravaged.

A long while later Evie did have to beg her to stop. Utterly exhausted and thoroughly sated she collapsed into the warmth and security of her lover's tender embrace. She was vaguely aware of Aurora tucking a blanket over her back, a few murmured words and a gentle kiss then nothing more.

CHAPTER 19

WHAT THE HEART WANTS

When Aurora woke in the early morning hours she found Evie sprawled half on top of her. Evie's head was on her shoulder, she had thrown a leg over and her right hand gently cupped Aurora's breast. Evie's breathing was deep and even and she looked so incredibly beautiful with her long braid trailing down her back, drawing the eye to her perfectly round butt cheeks while emphasizing her narrow hips and creamy skin. It still amazed Aurora that Evie was lighter colored than her even though she spent so much time in the sun. It was like her skin had set a limit on how much sun it would absorb and simply reflected the rest back.

Aurora thought of everything that had happened the previous night, of her nightmare and how talking to Evie about it had felt like a purge. She felt different somehow…lighter…hopeful. Yes, that is what it was. She felt truly hopeful that her life was about to take a better turn for the first time in years and it was all thanks to Evie.

As if hearing her thoughts Evie stirred, muttered something incoherent and her eyes fluttered open. She gave Aurora a dreamy half asleep smile and nuzzled the side of her neck. Aurora reveled in the sensation of Evie's mouth against her neck and the feel of Evie's naked body in her arms after what to her had been a spectacular night of lovemaking. If she could wake up like this every morning, she would be the happiest woman in the world. Evie's hand tightened on Aurora's breast and it made her breath hitch. She turned her head slightly and saw Evie was now fully awake and watching her.

"Good morning." Aurora leaned in and gave her a tentative kiss not certain if that was the appropriate thing to do. She really wanted to kiss her but did Evie want to be kissed? Was this about to turn into one of those awkward after-sex affairs in which they would hurriedly dress in uncomfortable silence? She needn't have worried as Evie put a hand behind her head and deepened the kiss. Aurora responded with enthusiasm.

"That's better," Evie said when they came up for air. "That's how I like to be kissed. You pecked me like we were cousins meeting at the dock."

"I didn't want to be forward and assume too much. We've never had a morning after before."

Evie snorted. "After everything you did to me last night a kiss is hardly forward. Sometimes you have such strange notions about things." She moved her hand from Aurora's breast to stroke between her legs making Aurora gasp. Instantly her body responded, coating Evie's fingers with her arousal. "Hmm, yes you feel as good as I remembered," Evie murmured. "I wanted to make sure I didn't dream that part."

Swallowing hard Aurora said, "And I'm so happy I didn't dream you. I'm so pleased I said yes. You are incredible."

"It was that good?" Evie asked as a slow self-satisfied smile stretched her lips.

"Amazing."

Evie's smile widened, "I feel the same…just so you know. As a way of saying good morning properly would you be interested in a replay of one or two favorites before we get up? It's not light outside yet I'm sure we have time."

"Asks the woman with her hand between my legs…"

"I'm just taking the initiative."

"I like your initiative. The best good morning wake-up ever."

"Is that a yes?"

"Absolutely. I will make up for that peck and use my mouth in a way that will much better show my appreciation for the amazing night we shared."

"I love the sound of that. And afterwards?"

"A quick soak in the bathing chambers and then a hearty breakfast to prepare us for the trip to the village."

"What are you making?"

"What would you like?"

"Pancakes?"

"I'll make you the best pancakes you have ever eaten. Satisfaction guaranteed."

Evie smiled happily. "For that you'll get extra honey."

Aurora laughed and said, "I've never been so happy that I know my way around a kitchen."

"And the bedroom. Don't forget the bedroom. You're *very* good at that."

They had taken the edge off the feverish hunger that drove them into a near frenzy earlier in the night so now they were able to go a little slower. Delighting in their mutual desire and enjoyment of each other their coupling gained a playful tone and there was even a little talking and teasing between the urgent moments when bodies tensed and arched like overstrung bows before the release.

Lying on the rug in front of the big window Aurora marked the passing of time by how the greys of predawn were replaced by muted colors that became brighter, as if someone was turning a dial to sharpen the focus. Too soon they lay in a pool of light that made the sweat on their bodies glisten so it looked like they were covered in a golden sheen.

It was as Aurora tasted the salty drops on her lover's back that she admitted to herself that she was in love with Evie. She did not want it to be so but she knew it was true. Evie felt like home to her. Being with her made her feel happy, safe and content. If Evie had turned over at that moment and asked her to stay in Nordarra to be with her she would have gladly agreed even though she knew that would be as good as signing her own death warrant. If not tomorrow then surely someday soon. But Evie didn't turn and ask her to stay. She sighed and pointed out that even though she would like nothing better than for them to remain where they were it was probably time for them to get ready to leave. So Aurora stuffed the thought down as far as it would go and tried to convince herself that what she felt was only infatuation and the afterglow of great sex. It was a poor lie as she knew in her heart she had never felt about anyone the way she did about Evie even before they'd had sex and the thought of losing her hurt like a physical blow.

***

"Aurora, I've been waiting for you. Come join me?"

There was a small splash as of a body being lowered into the water and a contented sigh. Aurora paused at the bathroom doorway with the blankets they had slept on bundled in her arms. Peering in she saw Evie submerged up to her neck in the bathing pool. As Evie pushed off from the side to drift slowly to the other side her long hair, loosened from its braid, drifted around her like a golden fan. Steam rising from the water combined with the low lights that illuminated the room and added a dreamlike almost mystical quality, so it felt to Aurora like she had stumbled upon a secret pool in the forest in time to spy a nymph having an early morning swim.

"Are you coming?" Evie's voice brought Aurora out of her reverie.

"If I join you it's unlikely we'll leave today. I'll want to play in the water and make love to you again."

Evie gave a warm chuckle. "Then maybe not. As much as I'd like to stay longer and have sex till we pass out I need to get back to my flock. I'm worried about my dad's health and what Marcus might be up to in my absence. You said the boat is due tomorrow? If I miss the boat, I'll have to fly back over the open ocean to get back home or cross over the high mountain ranges. I'd prefer not to put that much strain on my wing. It's still healing."

Aurora tried not to feel disappointed. This was what she'd expected but there was a part of her that had hoped Evie would say something different. It was foolish of her to think Evie would consider delaying her return to her flock just because they'd had an amazing night together. That kind of thing only happened in romantic fairy tales, not in real life. It was a wake up call for Aurora who'd been thinking about delaying her departure from Nordarra to spend more time with Evie. Whatever fantastical notions she might have had of a future in which the two of them become a mated pair evaporated. She had momentarily forgotten Evie wasn't free to come and go as she pleased, that she literally had a tower of responsibility. For someone like Evie, her family and flock would always come first. She understood and respected this. That didn't mean she was willing to give up her own dreams and risk her life to wait at the back of a queue for the crumbs of Evie's time and affection. She'd had a lifetime of that from her mother and she would not settle for it with a lover. She should concentrate on enjoying Evie's company while she could and try hard to keep things light so as not to put a damper on the amazing time they'd had together. There was another splash of water and it reminded her Evie was probably waiting for her to say something.

"The shortest route to Porta Belua from the village is over the ocean. Until your wing is fully healed I don't think you should attempt to fly home as that area is prone to ferocious storms that appear with little warning. We need to get to the village today to make sure we don't miss the boat in case it comes early. I have a few things to take care of and as soon as I'm done I'll start breakfast. Come to the kitchen when you're ready."

"I won't be long. I'm almost finished then it's your turn."

"Soak in the pool while you can. There'll be no bath or hot water tonight. I only have the essentials in my room in the village: a washbasin and a pitcher of water, soap, a washcloth, and towels. I'm used to it and find it adequate but you might find it a let-down after this."

"You've convinced me to stay in a little longer. I love this pool and I'm going to miss this majestic bathroom of yours."

"I thought you might feel that way," Aurora said with a smile and headed to her bedroom.

Aurora found the feather while she was changing the sheets on her bed. It was one of Evie's prime feathers. Holding it between the tips of her fingers she twirled it, admiring the glossy sheen, the delicate construct and the golden color. She brought the feather close to her face and inhaled slowly. The scent was fainter than directly from the warmth of her skin but still distinctly Evie. She intended to put the feather on top of Evie's pack. A prime feather was a precious thing after all and by rights should be returned to its owner but Aurora found she couldn't let go. She wanted it. She wanted the feather as a memento of their night together and of the amazing woman it belonged to. Something of Evie to carry with her wherever she went. She ran to the study and found a slim dark case that, on closing, sealed shut. She slipped the feather inside the protective shell, hoping as she did so that it would preserve Evie's scent for a while. Then she carefully stowed the case into a hidden compartment in her guitar case. She felt a twinge of guilt at what she'd done. She should have asked Evie if it was okay for her to keep the feather but it would be like asking for a lock of hair or something equally intimate as if they were sweethearts and what if Evie said no? She didn't want to give it back. She would quietly keep the feather and avoid an awkward conversation. It was just one feather and Evie had so many. Surely, she wouldn't even be aware she'd lost one.

***

After her own bath Aurora returned to the bedroom to find Evie dressed in new flight gear. It consisted of tight-fitting pants, a padded vest with little pockets and a stylish matching jacket Evie currently wore open that artfully hid the slits designed for wings. The hood that went with the set dangled from Evie's fingers.

"I didn't know you had a second set of flight gear. Did you buy it from the trader? That set is exquisite, it fits you perfectly and the color will complement your wings beautifully. You look like a queen about to take a leisurely flight to survey your domain. I bet the trader charged you a fortune for that outfit."

Evie turned to her with a frown. "I didn't buy these. I found the clothing in the bathroom next to my own set of flight gear and assumed it was a gift from you. Are you saying these are not from you?"

Aurora leaned in to sniff the clothing. "Ah. They're from my mother."

"Your mother?" Evie's eyes went wide. "Your mother gave me these?"

"Yes, I can smell where she handled them. She probably left a note somewhere and I've missed it."

"Your mother was here?" Evie's voice was high and her eyes as big as saucers.

"Yes, I caught her scent earlier. Ah, I found the note! She put it on my bed stand on top of a giftwrapped package for me. She always wraps the things she gives me no matter what it is. I think she just wants an excuse to use some of the pretty paper she has stored away."

Aurora unfolded the note, it read:

I came to see you but you were preoccupied. Could not stay. A new book for you, hope you like it. A little something for the girl as well as it is not fitting for your companion to return to her tower dressed in rags. You have never brought anyone here before. It must be serious? She is pretty for an avian. If she betrays you, I will tear off her wings.

"What does the note say?"

"Not much, just that she dropped by."

"When do you think she was here?"

"Around midnight."

"Not while we were...you know?"

"Having sex? By the way she phrased things that would be a yes."

Evie's hand flew to her mouth, "Nooo. I was so loud!"

Aurora smirked at her. "Who's shy now?"

"That was definitely not how I wanted to make a first impression on your mother."

"Don't worry, she only dropped in briefly according to her note."

"If it's not too personal can I read what she said?"

"Sure." Aurora handed Evie the note.

Evie's brows knotted as she read. "Why would she leave me clothing? We haven't met and how did she even know to bring it?"

"You are here with me and we were having sex so she thinks we're a couple. That's her way of saying hello. Sweet of her really. As for where she got the clothing? She has an area here that's just hers. She stays there when she's visiting me or passing through the area. My mother likes to collect pretty and interesting things. That flight gear must have caught her eye and has probably been semi-forgotten in one of the storerooms. It's amazing she had something in your exact size but she's always been into collecting the oddest things. Or maybe it's just odd to me because I don't understand what she would need it for."

"Oh. Do I have to be worried about the wing tearing remark? Was that a joke?"

"It is not a joke but you'll never meet her so there is no need to worry about that."

"Wow. She sounds intense."

"You have no idea. Compared to her I'm a fluffy kitten."

"Did she come to say goodbye?"

"She doesn't know I'm leaving, so no. My guess is your presence triggered an alarm and she came to see what was going on. Bet she got a lot more than she bargained for."

"Wait, back up a moment. Did you just say she doesn't know you are going to leave Nordarra?"

"I didn't tell her I was planning to go. I saw no reason to."

"You didn't feel the need to tell your own mother you are leaving Nordarra even though you may never return?" Evie sounded shocked.

"I haven't seen her face to face in almost a year. We're not close. If she'd bothered to wait until morning to see me I would have told her. I will not wait around until she deigns to grace me with her presence."

"So, you're just going to leave without saying goodbye?"

"Why not? She does it all the time."

"But you may never see her again."

"Your point?"

Evie stared at Aurora in disbelief. "You two really don't have a good relationship."

"Having a good relationship with someone requires that person to be around for more than five minutes at a time. It's not like I can go visit her or just drop in to say hello."

"Did you ever try it? Just for laughs to see what would happen? Maybe she would be really pleased to see you?"

"I did. It almost got me killed. Like I said, her people just barely tolerate my existence. My close relatives don't acknowledge me. Turning up unannounced at one of their hallowed gatherings looking for my mother threw them into a rage."

"Wow."

"It's not personal. Most of the Old Bloods are like that. They can't stand their lineage being diluted or in my case polluted with the blood of their enemies. My mother warned me about it but I was young and foolish. I didn't believe they would really be that vicious."

"They attacked you?" At Aurora's nod Evie grabbed onto her arm as if she had to steady herself. "What did your mother do? Did she just let this happen?"

Aurora paused, a smile easing the tension from her face. "You know now that I think about it she was magnificent. There were so many of them but she flew at them like a blood-crazed feral. They were scrambling to get away from her. I'd never seen my mother so enraged. That was until she got me back here to give me a dressing down that I would never forget." Aurora's face broke into a grin. "Well, I think that's what she tried to do but she got all emotional and teary telling me never to do anything that stupid ever again. Then she made me go to bed to heal my wounds and tried to cook for me, which I can tell you was almost punishment in itself. There was a good reason my father never let her near the stove."

"If it wasn't for the part where you got attacked that could have been a sweet mother-daughter story. It sounds like she's very protective over you."

"Yeah, I suppose she is."

"You should really tell her you're going. At least write her a goodbye note. If you disappear without a trace she will worry you've died, or worse, that you got captured by cutters again. Surely you don't want that?"

Aurora recoiled in horror. "No, of course not. That's awful. I would never do such a cruel thing to my mother and it didn't even occur to me she might think that."

Seeing the look on Evie's face she threw up her hands in a defensive gesture. "All right. I get it now. I wasn't deliberately trying to be an insensitive asshole. I'll leave her a note telling her I'm going."

"As you should. Do you mind if I leave her one as well to thank her for the clothing?"

"Sure. If you want to."

"What do I call her?

"Address her as Lady Adelind."

***

It was around nine in the morning by Evie's calculation when they emerged onto a narrow path high above the sea. She took deep breaths of the salty air and if she could have kissed the sun she would have, she was that happy to see it. Taking a quick look around nothing seemed familiar to her but this wasn't surprising as landmarks from above always looked different from ground level. She was confident however that with a little time to orientate herself and maybe a short flight she would have a pretty good idea where they were. Although where they were was a considerable distance from Aurora's lair, that much she knew for sure. Aurora had once again used underground tunnels and passages to get them from her home to where they were. How Aurora knew which unremarkable rock wall hid the entrance to a passage or how to make it appear baffled Evie but she didn't ask then and she didn't intend to now. As far as she was concerned it was enough to know the tunnels and magical passages existed and that Aurora could lead her safely through them because she had absolutely no desire to travel in this manner by herself. The tunnels were way too dark and enclosed for her liking and the feel of the magic Aurora used to activate the passages made her skin crawl. It got a hundred times worse when they took shortcuts through connections that Aurora told her only existed temporarily. It had been bad enough the first time Aurora had led her through one and she had been blessedly unaware of how dangerous it was. This time around it had felt to Evie like they were performing a death-defying feat the two times she'd seen that swirling red orb counting down in the dark. It had felt like they had stepped into the lair of a one-eyed subterranean monster ready to swallow them whole if they lingered just a second too long. She had clung to Aurora's hand with both of hers, not trusting her sweaty fingers not to betray her at a critical moment and cast her adrift in the dark abyss.

"You okay, Evie?"

"I am now that we are out of that accursed place. Please tell me we are done with underground things? I don't think I can take much more."

Aurora sat down on a rock with a good view of the bay below and patted the space beside her. When Evie sat down she said, "You will be glad to hear it's all open skies from here on. We'll follow this trail to the bay below where I'll use the canoe I keep hidden in a cave to cross to the other side. After that we only have about two hours of easy walk and we'll be at the village."

"That's a relief," Evie said and gratefully took the cup of steaming tea Aurora offered her. "Hmm, this is good. Extra honey just the way I like it. It's perfect, just what I needed right now."

Aurora smiled and poured herself a cup from the small flask as well.

"It would have been even better with biscuits but I didn't have the time to bake any. I do however have these." Popping the lid on the familiar dented tin Aurora revealed two thick sandwiches.

"When did you have the time to make those?" Evie asked in amazement.

"While you were having a leisurely soak of course. Want one?"

"I'm still full from the small mountain of pancakes you fed me. How can you possibly be hungry again so soon? You ate enough for several grown men."

"It's my beast," Aurora said as she took one of the sandwiches. "I need to let it out regularly for a hunt and feed or no matter how much I eat I stay hungry and I burn through calories like my body is a raging furnace. Don't ask me how it works. All I know is that after a good hunt I don't really need to eat for days but if I put it off too long I must eat constantly or I start wasting away and become extremely bad tempered. My dad had this joke he used to say that tigers are like pregnant women – we eat for two. Although in my case I probably eat like I'm carrying triplets." Aurora gave Evie a wide grin clearly delighted at her own joke and took a large bite of her sandwich.

"Aurora…I'm so sorry. This is my fault. You were so mindful of my food preferences you only caught what I could eat. To make things worse I made you babysit me at night because I'm afraid of the dark and you didn't get to hunt and see to your own needs. I feel so selfish. Why didn't you say something? Why didn't you tell me you needed to shift and hunt?"

Aurora finished her mouthful and patted Evie's leg with a smile. "Nothing to feel bad about. I thought of it as practice. In the human world I won't be able to hunt whenever I want so I will need to compensate and make sure I eat heaps. As long as I don't get so hungry that it undermines my ability to control my beast all will be well."

Evie drew in a sharp breath. "Has that ever happened to you?"

"Not since I was a kid and didn't know to read the danger signs. I'm a grown woman and I've learned how to look after myself properly a long time ago. Try your sandwich and tell me what you think."

Evie picked up her sandwich. It was so thick she had to hold it with both hands.

"There is no way I can eat this entire sandwich. I'll be surprised if I can manage half. Why don't you have it instead? You need the extra food and I really don't."

"At least taste it. I made it especially for you."

Evie meant to say again that she really wasn't hungry in the least but there was something in the expectant way Aurora watched her that made her swallow her words and she took as large a bite of the sandwich as she could manage. Made from the leftover baked bread from the previous evening it was stuffed with smoked fish, crunchy green salad that had a spicy bite and just a hint of sweet relish. It was delicious. Her mouth too full to speak, Evie made appreciative noises. Aurora smiled happily and wolfed down the rest of her sandwich. Evie managed one more small bite then held the rest of her sandwich out to Aurora.

"Please finish it for me?"

"You don't want to keep it for later?"

"I'd rather you fill up your tummy. Besides knowing you I'm sure there'll be another meal soon. Eat, please? It will make me feel better about keeping you from hunting."

Aurora nodded and took the sandwich from her. This she also devoured in quick bites. When she was finished she licked her fingers and the palms of her hands in long strokes that reminded Evie of a cat cleaning its paws. She drank her tea and pretended not to notice Aurora's slip. She'd come to realize that Aurora worked very hard not to act like a beast-shifter and any slip was an embarrassment to her. Now that she knew Aurora had been planning to leave Nordarra Evie understood that she had an underlying motive – she'd been practicing to pass as human. Evie didn't have the heart to tell Aurora that despite her best efforts she still had numerous little tells that gave her away. There was the way she sniffed the air and the effortless feline grace in her movements that no normal human her size could hope to emulate. Then there were her eyes. No one who looked her in the eye and caught even a glimpse of Aurora's beast could be fooled into believing she was just a harmless human woman.

"Finished, Evie?"

She wordlessly handed her cup back to Aurora who stowed it then offered Evie a hand to get up. She didn't need the help but she understood that, like the sandwich, to outright refuse would hurt Aurora's feelings. Besides, she liked how gallant Aurora was with her and the way she paid attention to the little details, like that Evie liked extra honey in her tea. It made her feel special.

"What did you write my mother? That was a lot of writing for a thank you note. Were you telling her how amazing I am in bed? As true as that is it would be a really weird thing to tell my mother." Aurora easily dodged Evie's swipe, laughing as she did so.

"No, I did not. Wise-ass."

"Are you going to tell me what you said?"

"Why should I? It was a private message."

"I respect that but I hope for your sake you were very courteous and addressed her formally."

"Why?"

"My mother is very serious about things like protocol and manners and she doesn't easily forgive an insult. Just so you know not so long ago her people considered avians food; a tasty snack on the go."

"You're kidding, right? You just made that up because I won't share."

"Are you sure about that?" Aurora wiggled her eyebrows at Evie and bounced away with a merry whistle, the heavy bag slung across her shoulders not slowing her down in the least.

"You can be incorrigible, you know that?"

"That's not what you called me last night," Aurora said and flashed Evie a wicked grin.

Evie huffed out a loud breath but she couldn't help smiling. Seeing Aurora so exuberant and playful and knowing it was the aftereffect of their lovemaking made her feel all kinds of wonderful. She felt pretty good herself because of it. More than good, she felt amazing if a little tired and tender in unusual places. She felt the chemistry between them and suspected there would be serious heat between the sheets if they ever got that far but she'd been taken off guard by the lightning storm that ignited as soon as they got their hands on each other. To her delight it turned out that Aurora tasted as good as her lips everywhere and that body of hers was sculpted to perfection. Having Aurora under her and the freedom to touch her body all over and in any way she wanted had just about made her come long before Aurora had flipped her on her back and claimed every part of her in return. Just thinking of how it had been made her heart beat a little faster and set off hot flares all over. Aurora had been so generous and attentive to her needs, treating her body like it was her temple of worship but at the same time her arms and legs had encased Evie in such a way it was clear she would claim her due and not stop until she thoroughly had her way with Evie. She thought she had a healthy appetite but Aurora had been insatiable. She had explored her body with vigor and driven Evie to more climaxes in one night than she could remember having with another lover. As amazing as all that had been it was how they were with each other afterwards that had been messing with her head. She'd had plenty of good sex and even the occasional sleep-over but this had felt different. Utterly sated and exhausted she'd drifted to sleep on top of Aurora. She remembered making a feeble attempt to roll off her worrying her weight would become uncomfortable but Aurora had wrapped her arms around and said, "Please stay. I love feeling you like this." That low sultry voice and the tender kiss had undone her. She'd tucked her head under Aurora's chin, more than happy to stay exactly where she was. The last thing she'd been aware of before sleep claimed her was the strong steady sound of Aurora's heartbeat under her ear and it had made her smile thinking of the first time she fell asleep in her arms in that cave. Then the sound had represented the presence of a caring person when she needed it most and she'd felt gratitude but little else. Last night however, hearing it again after everything they'd shared, Aurora's heartbeat had been the most beautiful and comforting sound in the world.

Thinking about it made Evie feel unsettled. Things between them were still so new but some part of her already knew she would crave that sound when she went to bed on her own and she would miss the woman who provoked such unusual and powerful emotions in her. The thought of Aurora leaving Nordarra and the inevitability of another woman ending up in Aurora's bed being held like she was the most precious being in the world made Evie want to scream and hit something. It wasn't fair. She wanted an opportunity to date Aurora to see how far they could go. She was the future ruler of House Aquilar and Aurora was a beast-shifter and those were major obstacles they'd have to overcome but they had on their side a connection the likes of which Evie had never experienced and chemistry that was off the charts.

In her previous relationships Evie had always felt something was missing right from the start but ignored the signs until the inevitable rot of dissatisfaction set in and she had to end it. Over the years she'd come to the sad conclusion that she either expected too much from her partner or maybe the person she was looking for simply didn't exist. Meeting

Aurora had literally turned her world upside down. In her, Evie had found someone who exceeded her wildest dreams and she was smitten with her. Not only that, they complemented each other, slotting together like they'd known each other for years not just days. It was uncanny. What were the odds she would meet someone as amazing as Aurora again and be able to make a similar connection? With her abysmal track record she'd probably sabotage all future relationships by comparing her partner to Aurora and find her lacking in some way. Typical. She'd finally found someone she thought could be 'the one' just as that person was getting ready to leave Nordarra.

Was she really going to let this amazing woman walk out of her life? The bigger question was, did she have any say in the matter? The reality she faced was that Aurora was determined to leave. If she asked Aurora to stay, would she? Did she want to be the sort of woman who made another give up her dream and risk being resented for it? Or worse, get Aurora killed because she kept her in a place where she was hunted like a rare animal, when she wasn't even sure things between them would last? They'd only known each other for a few days after all. That was hardly enough time to warrant making decisions that would have life-altering effect.

Distracted and not paying as close attention as she should have to the uneven rocky path Evie slipped and fell. Before she hit the ground Aurora was by her side steadying her. She glanced up at Aurora intending to thank her and make a witty remark about her own clumsiness but the way Aurora looked at her stole her breath away. It was the same as when she'd made love to Evie and made her feel like she was the center of the universe. So much heat, intensity, and tenderness condensed into a single look. No one had ever looked at her quite like that and Evie felt her heart flutter in joy and nervous excitement. Then Aurora let her go and Evie could breathe again but her heart was still pounding like she'd been sent tumbling through the sky by a powerful wind blast. She was in so much trouble. She had to figure this out fast.

CHAPTER 20

OLD FRIENDS

Aurora was pleased to find the canoe where she'd left it and still in good condition. While she carried it to the water's edge her eyes roamed constantly over the water and the surrounding rocks. Nothing but birds, crabs and the expected assortment of sea creatures to be seen. Everything seemed peaceful but she wasn't fooled. The water was too still and the restless stirring of her beasts warned her there was more here than the naked eye could see.

"Evie, can you do something for me please?"

"Sure, what is it?"

"Will you shift and fly my belongings to the other side? It's only a short distance and it shouldn't be too strenuous on your wing. I have precious things in my pack that I don't want to lose and my beautiful guitar would be ruined if it got submerged in seawater."

Puzzled by Aurora's request Evie stared out over the still bay. The air was breathless, nothing stirred the water and she didn't see a discernable current. In fact, from where they stood the surface looked as flat and still as a sheet of polished glass.

"You want me to fly your belongings to the other side because you're afraid you're going to capsize?"

"It is possible."

"Uh-hum, cut the bullshit, Aurora. I really don't appreciate whatever it is you're doing right now. It's too calm and there's no way you'll capsize. Be honest with me and tell me what's really going on."

"There is a real possibility the boat might capsize but not due to my incompetence."

"But why would—"

"Mermaids. This bay is home to mermaids."

"Oh." As understanding dawned Evie scanned the water more carefully. "You see them?"

"No. But that doesn't mean they aren't here. I've known these girls a long time and we are generally on good terms but they are tempestuous. No, that's putting it too mildly. They're moody as fuck. They will be ecstatically happy to see me one day and the next day, for no apparent reason, they will be in full bitch mode. When they've been fighting with each other it's even worse. There really is no telling what kind of reception I will get."

"If you are that concerned we should go around."

"That would be a waste of time. I'll be fine. At worst I'll have to swim for the shore. Please, take my things to the other side and wait for me there. Preferably on a high ledge where you can't get yanked into the water."

Evie took hold of Aurora's face and gave her a deadly serious look. "You'd better be all right. Just so we are clear on this I'm not afraid of a bunch of scaly-tailed bitches. If one tries to drag me in, she will get wing smacked so hard she'll have a concussion that will last a week and if they put their slimy claws on you, I'll find a way to make their time on land a misery. I swear if they hurt you I'll find large rocks and drop them on the mers from so high they will never see it coming."

Aurora's eyebrows shot up and her eyes sparkled with amused curiosity. "Evie, do I sense a little hostility?"

"I had a few run-ins with mer girls at the club. They may deny it but they have terrible wing envy. I'm going to shift now – the quicker we get away from here the better."

***

"Come play with us Aurora, come play..." The voices of the mermaid sisters merged in a singsong refrain coming from all around the canoe. "Forget about the little avian; come swim with us."

"Not today, girls."

A head popped up next to the boat and demanded, "Why not? Are we no longer good enough for you? Come on, Aurora, you used to be so much fun. It's been too long, come play. A clawed hand appeared from under the water to grab the side of the canoe, rocking it. Aurora snapped out the paddle and smacked the water beside the submerged mermaid. The hand withdrew to the sound of hissing from the bobbing heads.

"Not. Today. No means no. I have somewhere to be."

"You are no fun, Aurora, no fun at all."

"We should make her join us," a voice said somewhere behind Aurora. Immediately the other mermaids took up the chant, "Yes, a swim, a swim. Let's make her join us."

The water swirled like it was birthing a whirlpool and Mistress Leni rose from the depths in slow motion. Aurora knew the dramatic entrance was to assure she was the center of attention. In her youth Leni was a legendary mermaid beauty and she was as vain as she was smart and vicious. Her daughters and granddaughters respected and feared her in equal measure. She looked out for them but she was the queen of her domain and expected to be treated as such.

On seeing her Aurora made a seated bow. "Mistress Leni, it is always an honor to gaze upon your breathtaking beauty. How magnificent your bay and how fertile the reefs of your domain."

Leni gave a regal nod and said, "Indeed, it requires hard work to keep it so, not just frivolous play." She gave the nearest mermaid a scathing look causing her to sink below the water and disappear. "Are my offspring bothering you? They should know better." The five remaining mermaids became so quiet not even a ripple disturbed the waters around them.

"No, we were merely having a discussion. It's such a hot day they were suggesting I come for a swim but I have urgent business elsewhere so it is not convenient timing."

"Is it bad timing? Or because you have an *avian* waiting for you?" The way Leni spat out the word like it tasted bad in her mouth left no doubt how she felt about avians in general.

"I do have an avian waiting for me." Aurora met Leni's gaze levelly and waited for what she knew would come next. The mermaid didn't dare tell her outright she shouldn't be with an avian but she couldn't let it go either. There was a long running animosity between avians and mers, probably to do with them being creatures of air and water respectively who rarely mixed. When they did find themselves in close proximity it wasn't long before sparks flew as evidenced by the way Evie reacted just thinking about past altercations she'd had with mers in a nightclub.

"That is strange company to keep," Leni tried again when Aurora didn't rise to the bait. "Some may disapprove. What would Lady Adelind say? Surely *her peopl*e would never associate with something so far beneath them."

Aurora almost smiled. If they were playing cards Leni had just made a desperate play, throwing in what she hoped was a trump card. Hearing she was traveling with an avian must have really rattled Leni. It probably didn't help that Evie stood waiting high on the rocks where everyone could see her.

"Mistress, my mother does not tell me how to live my life. As for my mother's people, as you know more than most about my parentage you must be aware they wouldn't piss on me if I was on fire because I'm of mixed blood. Why would I care what they think about avians or any of the other races? I won't allow their prejudices or that of anyone else to keep me from seeking the company of someone I find pleasing irrespective of what or who they are. In fact, I've been told repeatedly I should avoid the company of mers but I've ignored those warnings and I'm glad I did or I would have missed out on so much. It was your daughters who taught me to read the currents and they showed me how to ride the waves so it feels more like flying than swimming. They showed me the beauty of the coral gardens and because I was with them I got to hear the song of the giants rise from the deep. Hearing your daughters answer the call of the great ones and join them in song was one of the most magnificent things I've ever witnessed. So as far as I'm concerned it has served me well that I don't pay attention to what others think of the company I keep."

Leni studied Aurora quietly for several seconds her expression unreadable. "You swim perilous waters with the agility of a sea lion, Aurora."

"Thank you. I've had lots of practice and good teachers."

"If any of my daughters had your smooth tongue and such sharp teeth our domain would be twice the size it is. Your mother's people were arrogant fools to discard you and treat you the way they have. They think they are better than everyone else but what good all their power and magic when they are quietly disappearing into the fade. Their so-called pure blood is becoming so thick with inbreeding that soon they will have no children at all. We mers know the importance of fresh seed; we harvest it at every opportunity and look how fertile we are. So what if not every one of our offspring can swim the deeps, even land walkers are kin and they too serve a purpose. Your mother the great Lady Adelind was wise, she understood this even if her people did not. She did well to lure such a powerful, fertile male to her bed and produce you. Surely if he hadn't died they would have had many more children."

"That's not why she chose my father."

Leni made a dismissive hand gesture. "Yes yes, I know it wasn't. I saw how in love they were. My point is that her people are stuck in the past. If they keep holding fast to their old ways, one way or another it will be the death of them. Our world is changing and if they don't change with it they will become like the Ancients who built all those abandoned ruins – just a myth. You at least will not go down with them. You have forged your own path and that pleases me. May you have lots of offspring, Aurora, and may every single one of them be more prolific and formidable than your mother's kin. That, my dear, would be the best revenge of all and I would love to see that. Ah! Now that gives me an idea! When you are ready to breed let me know. I will set my girls to find you specimens. Strong shifters with good lineage because nothing but the best will do. I will look them over myself to make sure they are suitable. That will be my gift to you."

Mortified and a little worried, Aurora struggled to keep her face straight. She knew Leni meant well but this conversation had just veered off into the deep end and she didn't like the determined gleam in the mermaid's eyes. If she didn't leave soon Leni might magically produce a man or several and expect her to 'get to it' while she hovered to make sure the males were performing adequately.

"It's a generous offer but that really won't be necessary."

She heard a snicker and caught the amused expressions of Lyla and Tamar. They were facing Aurora, their backs turned so that their mother couldn't see their faces. Aurora narrowed her eyes at them which only made them grin harder flashing shark-like teeth. The girls were aware she wasn't in the least interested in their mother's offer. That conversation was years in the past and yet it seemed they had never told Leni of her preference. Odd. Either that or Leni knew and was choosing to ignore it.

"You already have someone in mind, Aurora?"

"No. I don't intend to breed."

"Really? Are you sure? The process of breeding can be very enjoyable. A well-endowed male who knows what he is doing is a day well spent."

Aurora watched, as emboldened by her sister whispering something in her ear, Lyla made her fingers into a V and used her tongue and mouth to make an exaggerated display of what she thought Aurora would like to do instead and whom with. To her annoyance, Aurora felt her cheeks heat. Mermaids could be insufferable.

"I'm very sure. I really need to go now."

"Oh…that's disappointing. If you change your mind my offer

stands."

"Yes, Aurora, we can help – all you have to do is ask. Oh yes, yes please *dooo*. We'll be happy to lend you a hand, several if you need it." Mers all around her giggled like teenaged girls delighted with a new game.

Aurora didn't look to see who said what, she put oars to water and got the boat moving at a good speed. The quicker she got away from the mers the better. She knew them well enough to know once they got going with sex jokes that the girls would try to outdo each other at her expense and nothing was considered too much or off limits. This was what she got for befriending sex-crazed mers. It did occur to her that physically they were no match for her. She was a powerful Old Blood who could snap them in half like dry twigs and she should really remind them of that. On the other hand, she had to catch them first and they'd just gang up on her and flail her with their sharp tongues. Aurora sighed and made a mental note to be more selective about her friends in the future. It was a good thing Evie wasn't close enough to overhear the conversation because she probably would have lashed out. Aurora shuddered imagining the verbal war that would have ensued with her stuck in the middle. She'd rather face an angry bear any day.

Evie waited for her on a high ledge on the other side of the bay. She stood with her hands on her hips, her wings arched aggressively and her eyes scanned the water behind Aurora. As soon as Aurora steered the canoe close to the beach she drifted down.

"Here." Aurora threw a rope at Evie who caught it with only a slight fumble. "Pull the canoe closer to shore?"

Evie obliged. Moments later Aurora with her pants rolled up to her knees, waded up to her, took the rope from her hands and hauled the canoe out of the water onto the beach.

"Thanks, you saved me getting wet. I always seem to drift back out at the last moment."

"What was that about? You were surrounded by mers and it looked like it was getting heated. I got worried I'd have to fish you out of the ocean."

"It wasn't that bad. They wanted me to come for a swim. I declined. Mers aren't good with no for an answer so we had a little standoff then their matriarch turned up and we had a talk."

"What about? You look flustered."

"I'd rather not go into it."

"Was it about me?"

"You came up. Well, not you specifically. It upset them that I was in the company of an avian. I've never associated with avians before and I think they're worried I'll become a 'feather lover' and pick avians over mers."

"After last night you're definitely a 'feather lover' even though I didn't have my wings on. We can always do it that way next time to make sure you've thoroughly earned the title," Evie said with a wicked smile. "So that's it?"

"Um yeah…more or less".

"How is it you know them so well?"

"I kind of grew up with the mers, with them being the closest kids and all that. I knew there was a good chance one or more of them would be in the area. They are actually a lot of fun when they're in a playful mood."

"What kind of playful mood?"

Catching the dangerous gleam in Evie's eyes Aurora quickly said, "Not *that* kind of playful. Mermaids are very serious about the whole reproduction thing. I'm not going to deliver in that department so they're not interested. That's just as well because, between you and me, they smell a little fishy even when they look fully human and they love drama. Dating a mer girl would be like dating all her sisters at the same time. It'd be torture. I shudder to think what it would be like to have a bad breakup with a mer. They're so vindictive it would be impossible to cross a stretch of ocean without worrying about being capsized or drowned."

"You seem to have put a lot of thought into that."

"Yeah, I kind of had a thing for a mer girl when I was a teen. It was more hormones than anything else. You know how they love to sunbathe naked and practice that whole seduction routine. I couldn't help wonder what it would be like to bed one of them. Thankfully, I got over that infatuation real fast."

"I'm thankful you're not a man. If you were, those girls would have ridden you like a prized breeding stallion in the hopes you'd pass on some of that potent Old Blood magic to their offspring."

"Evie!" Aurora stared at her in shock then giggled. "Actually, you're probably right. Mermaids were always flirting with my dad and just about served themselves up on a plate."

"How did your dad respond to that?"

"He was the perfect gentleman, always polite. If they were too persistent he would mention his life-mate, Lady Adelind. That made them back off quickly. They knew my mother would rip them to bloody shreds in a heartbeat if she heard they'd been sniffing around him."

"Would your mother really have done that?"

"Definitely. My mother is composed and cool as ice until she loses her temper, then it's like the eruption of a volcano. My dad was the only one who could talk her down when she got like that. He'd wrap his huge arms around her and just hold her." Aurora pulled a face and added, "That was usually the sign for me to go for a long run or take a book and go read somewhere because more often than not the two of them would disappear to the bedroom. The cabin was big but not *that* big and trust me no one wants to hear their parents going at it."

Evie couldn't help but be amused at the thought of a young Aurora fleeing to escape her parent's enthusiastic lovemaking. "Sounds like they were very passionate."

"They were. The bond between them was real and anyone who saw them together could see that."

Evie stretched her right wing gingerly. It was an unconscious motion that immediately caught Aurora's attention.

"Your wing, how does it feel?"

"It was a little stiff and sore during the flight but that's to be expected. It really has healed amazingly well and so much quicker than I'd have thought possible."

"That's good to hear. Do you think you can manage another flight to the village? I'll give you directions."

"Why? Am I slowing you down too much?"

"It is a little slower with you but that's not why I suggested you go on ahead. I thought you would prefer flying over walking, now that you can fly again. I'll write a note letting the villagers know you're a friend of mine and to let you use my room while I make my way there. At a jog it won't take me long."

"No, I'd prefer to walk with you."

"You would rather walk?" Aurora gave Evie a skeptical look. "Since when?"

"I didn't say that. I said I'd prefer to walk *with you*. As in I want to spend more time with you."

"You do?"

As an answer, Evie wrapped an arm around Aurora's middle and kissed her cheek. "Don't sound so surprised. We've come this far together and we can walk the last few miles to that village of yours together."

Aurora's smile was soft and happy. Basking in the warmth of Aurora's approval Evie had to resist the urge to preen, she was so pleased with herself. She liked that she'd surprised Aurora and fortunately the walk was easy enough that she didn't regret her decision. Compared to their slog through the waterlogged forest and climb over the mountains it felt like a leisurely stroll even though she had to raise her wings occasionally to prevent them from getting snagged. The rugged coastline was beautiful and there was so much to see. They passed a large colony of noisy seals and there were colorful seabirds of every description on the rocks and cliffs around them. It felt to Evie like they were surrounded by a riot of color and sound and she was so taken with her surroundings she was astonished when Aurora said, "We're almost there."

"Really? But it doesn't feel like we've been walking for two hours."

"We're on the outskirts. They built the village around a horseshoe harbor nestled between the sea and the forest. Once we get to the top of this rise we only need to cross a grassy stretch then we will be on the forest path to the village. We should run into people soon. It's such a beautiful day they'll probably have the herd grazing in the valley." Aurora tilted her head as if listening then beamed. "I was right. Can you hear them?"

Evie strained to hear over the pounding of the waves on the rocks and thought she could hear a distant tinkling sound. "I hear *something*. Not sure what it is though. It sounds musical?"

"Bells. You're hearing the bells on the goats. We should see them shortly."

The sheltered rocky path next to the sea they'd been following came out on a rise and a sudden blast of air caught Evie off guard so she had to spread her wings a little to regain her balance.

Aurora grinned at her. "The wind almost got you. There is always a wind that blows through here on this spot." She pointed up at the mountain that curved to their right and made a line tracing the stretch of grass-covered valley wedged between the mountain and the forest running down to the shore where a large herd of goats grazed. "Today the wind is mild but at the height of winter it can easily blow a person right off their feet and into the ocean if they're not careful. Down in that little valley where the animals are it's pretty sheltered though and the grazing is excellent."

Evie surveyed the grazing animals. "So close to the forest and mountains aren't they at risk of predators? I don't see anyone with the goats, won't they wander off or run away if something chases them?"

"They're not alone."

As if in response to Aurora's words several loud barks rang out. Honing in on the sound Evie spotted a massive white dog among the flock looking in their direction.

"Wow, is that a dog or a shifter? That thing is huge."

Next to her Aurora laughed. "Thor is a big boy but entirely dog. He's not the only one either, there should be more but they'll be laying low among the flock or be under cover on the perimeter."

"The goats have guard dogs? Seriously?"

"They do because the goats are very valuable to the village. Those dogs were brought up with the goats to help them imprint and they were taught to protect the herd from predators and thieves."

"So, the dogs and the goats are out here by themselves?"

"There will either be someone with the animals keeping an eye out or villagers nearby working in the forest. Trust me, our presence will not go unnoticed. They take the protection of their people and the village seriously; no stranger gets to enter unchallenged. Ingvild is walled in, gated and most of the homes built with stone."

"Why build the homes from stone when they're right next to a forest?"

"Tradition. One of the founding families of Ingvild were master stonemasons where they came from."

They were halfway across the valley ankle deep in lush green grass when a horn sounded from the edge of the forest. It gave a long note followed by two shorter ones, there was a short pause then a medium length note followed by three quick notes in rapid succession.

"Aurora…did we just get announced?"

"Dramatic isn't it? Now the whole village knows we're approaching."

"Just from those few notes?"

"Yes. It's mostly used as an early warning system and to communicate messages over distance when they can't see each other. It can get quite complex but that message roughly says: one friend and one avian on foot. Since I'm one of the few people to approach the village from this angle it's a pretty good guess they'll know it's me."

"And they called you friend?"

"I'd certainly hope so! I've been coming here as long as I can remember. My dad made friends here and would bring me to play with the other children. Shifters tend to stick to their own kind but my dad went out of his way to befriend all kinds of beings, probably because he was the only one of his kind in this part of the world. The humans I suspect he befriended more for my benefit. My parents were shapeshifters but I couldn't shift so other beast-shifter children and even the mer girls to a lesser extent made fun of me. Here it wasn't like that. The human children couldn't shift so they didn't expect me to be able to, in fact, they were impressed by how much stronger and faster I was than them. It was a nice change and helped make me feel a bit better about myself. Over the years I've made good friends here and I'm very fond of these people."

They'd been on the forest path for about fifteen minutes when there was the sound of running footsteps coming towards them. Aurora quickly moved into a little clearing, removed her packs and motioned for Evie to get off the path. Evie wondered what was happening. She worried they were about to have an unpleasant run-in of some sort but Aurora wore a huge excited grin. She planted herself in the middle of the path and waited with her legs spread wide. Curious, Evie put down her pack, her eyes darting between Aurora and the approaching footsteps. Moments later two identical sandy-haired little boys came sprinting towards them. As soon as they saw Aurora they roared and flew at her. Aurora leapt at them and scooped one up in each arm. She planted a quick kiss on their cheeks and then swung in a circle so fast the three of them were a blur of arms and legs. The boys squealed their delight and Aurora roared with laughter. When she finally put them down the boys staggered away drunkenly. One fell on his butt and sat there laughing while his brother tried valiantly to find his balance. Aurora sat down next to the seated boy and was promptly pounced on as the boys tried to wrestle her flat. She retaliated by tickling them which caused more squealing and laughter. Soon the three of them were rolling on the forest floor scattering leaves and debris as they play wrestled.

Aurora went on all fours and the boys hauled themselves up on her back excitedly. Evie watched in amusement as Aurora imitated a wild four-legged creature and the boys did their best to stay on her back while she leapt and made quick directional changes as she charged around the clearing. Inevitably one or both got flung off despite clinging like limpets but fell in a roll, tucking their arms and legs so they sprung to their feet ready for another round. Aurora would pass close to the downed passenger and pause just long enough for an arm and leg to be thrown over before she continued. The boys laughed and made whooping noises encouraging each other to hold on and Aurora to keep going.

Movement at the corner of her eye drew her attention and Evie saw a statuesque blond woman carrying an equally blond toddler approaching. She wore a long colorful embroidered skirt, a starched white blouse with fine needlework and her hair was tied in a heavy braid interwoven with pink and red ribbons that fell all the way down her back. She was beautiful and Evie might have found her attractive if it wasn't for the way her eyes locked on Aurora. There was something too proprietary in that look and Evie had to resist the urge to rustle her wings in agitation.

"Ah, so this is where you two ran off to so suddenly."

Aurora and the boys had been playing hard and the boys were making so much noise Aurora must not have heard the woman approach because at the sound of her voice she stopped so suddenly both boys flew off her back in a jumble of arms and legs. She gave them a glance to make sure they were all right, stood up and dusted herself down.

"Hello, Astrid."

"Aurora. I see you and the boys are still playing that game. They are getting too big for it, don't you think?"

Aurora shrugged and smiled sheepishly. "It's fun. If they want to play I'm not going to say no."

"Lots of fun!" One of the boys echoed grinning widely. "No one does it like Aurora, Mum, she's the best!"

Astrid pointed a finger at the boy and said sternly, "Look at your shirt, young man. It's dirty and I can see rips. That goes for both of you. Do you think it's my idea of fun trying to get the stains out and spend my days repairing clothing? I can see we need to have another long talk about this as clearly I wasn't heard the first dozen times."

One of the boys gave Aurora a beseeching look but she held up her hands, "Oh no, I'm already in enough trouble with your mother. Don't drag me into this."

"We wanted to be the first to say hello to Aurora," his brother piped up. "We didn't plan to get dirty. Things just kind of happened."

"Indeed, as it tends to when Aurora is around," Astrid said but there was no sting in her words and she was smiling. She clutched her toddler in a one armed hold to remove a leaf from Aurora's hair. "Look at you all scruffy from rolling around in the forest like a big kid. You are as wild as ever."

One of the boys at that exact moment decided to point at Evie and shout out, "Look, Mum, the lady has wings! An avian! She's an avian!"

All eyes turned to Evie. Inwardly Evie sighed, not sure if she was relieved or annoyed at the timing. She was fairly certain Astrid hadn't noticed her up to that point and she was curious to see what the woman would do next. She gave a small wave. "Hello. I'm Evangeline but my friends call me Evie."

"Please to meet you, Evangeline. I'm Astrid and these two rascals from left to right are my twins Sven and Erik. They are six and will probably make me go grey before they are ten." The boys gave identical grins and waved at Evie.

"What about me?" The little girl in her arms piped up. Her eyes were huge and a bit teary.

"My sweet little poppet, of course, I haven't forgotten you." Astrid kissed her daughter on the forehead and made soothing noises.

While their mother was preoccupied with their sister Eric tugged at Aurora's hand, beckoning her to bend down so he could whisper in her ear. When she lifted her head both boys looked at her expectantly.

"Yes, I did bring you something," Aurora said.

"Brought what?" Astrid's head snapped up and she narrowed her eyes at her sons. "Aurora, did my boys just ask you if you brought them a gift?"

"But, Mum, she always brings something when she's been away a while," Sven protested.

"That may be so but it is rude to ask."

"It's fine, Astrid, you know I don't mind. Besides, I've been excited to give it to them. I put it on top of my pack especially." Aurora hurried over to her pack and after a moment produced a carved wooden box. She rattled the box and it made a clinking sound.

"Marbles!" Eric shouted excitedly.

"Did you bring us more marbles?" Sven asked.

"I thought of the two of you when I saw these marbles which I'm reasonably sure you don't already have. I remembered there was a terrible incident with a hole in a pocket and favorites being lost. Would you like these? They're very colorful and pretty."

"Yes please." The boys chorused followed by, "Thank you, Aurora!" as she put the gift into their eager hands.

The boys gave their mother pleading looks and Astrid said, "Yes, go find your friends and play with your new marbles. But be sure to do the chores you haven't finished today tomorrow or there will be no marbles at all until I say so."

The boys agreed enthusiastically and were off at a run back the way they came. The little girl had been watching the commotion with interest and when her brothers ran off she made as if to get down and follow them. Her mother clasped her tighter and said, "Not you, missy. You stay with me."

"I have something for you as well, Tove." From behind her back Aurora produced a stuffed tiger. "A kitty for you to sleep with."

Tove grabbed the stuffed toy and rubbed it against her face. "Pretty kitty, ohhhh, so soft!"

"Say thanks to Aurora for your toy."

Tove shyly looked up at Aurora and was about to say something when her eyes went wide. She stared at the tiger in her hands then at Aurora then back again. Her brow furrowed, she pointed at Aurora and said loudly, "Kitty! Mummy, I want *that* kitty!"

Astrid gave Aurora a meaningful look. "This is what you get for letting her play with your mane. I told you she wouldn't forget seeing you like that."

"Wanna touch kitty." The little girl pushed her toy tiger into her mother's hand and reached for Aurora. When Aurora didn't immediately move closer her lips quivered and she added in a tearful voice, "*Please*?"

Aurora looked at Astrid for permission. "Only if your mum says it's okay."

"Please do otherwise my child will cry herself to sleep over it."

Aurora bent down so she was face to face with the girl in her mother's arms. "Tove, watch."

"Kitty coming?" Tove asked hopefully.

"Yes. Just for you, little one."

Aurora arched her neck rotating it slowly and as she did her shoulders broadened, her neck thickened and the planes of her face shifted gaining feline features. All the while her hair grew and changed, becoming a thick furry mane of mostly black interspersed with silvery grey and russet oranges.

The little girl clapped her hands and a gurgled laugh bubbled out. "Kitty!" She threw herself at Aurora extending so far she almost slipped out of her mother's hold. Aurora held open her arms and a smiling Astrid passed over her child. As soon as she was against Aurora Tove sunk both arms into Aurora's mane up to her elbows. Boldly the little girl explored: stroking fur, gathering hands full to sniff and burying her face in the glossy mane while making happy noises. Aurora smiled and patiently held the wiggling child secure in her arms. Tove's attention shifted to Aurora's face and she traced the altered contours with wide-eyed fascination. It wasn't long before she tried to pry open Aurora's lips.

"Teeth?" Tove enquired. "Can I see fangs?"

"*No*, leave Aurora's mouth alone," Astrid told her daughter. "When she's like this her teeth are very sharp."

Aurora's shoulders shook with laughter as the girl kept trying to pry her mouth open despite her mother's protests. Finally, Aurora took the little hands in one of her own.

"Your mummy is right about my teeth; they are too sharp for you to touch. I told you last time that teeth and hands don't go together, remember?"

The girl ducked her head shyly and nodded. "I remember. Never play with teeth!"

"Good girl…I can't let you play with my teeth but if you want, I can give you a big slobbery lick," Aurora said and made a slurping noise.

The girl squealed in equal parts protest and giggly delight. "Kitty, no licking! Yuck!" She clasped Aurora's face in her hands with the little fingers splayed wide and proceeded to rub her face against Aurora's cheeks and neck in imitation of scent marking. Aurora laughed and cradled the child even closer while a deep, resonating sound rumbled out of her chest.

"Kitty is purring!" Tove exclaimed.

"Sort of…it's called chuffing; this is how big cats purr. Do you like it better than licking?"

"Yes, much better than licking! More purring, *more*." Tove scooted downwards to lay her head against Aurora's chest, an expression of utter bliss on her face. "Kitty is purring," Tove said with approval as she listened. Her eyes half closed she snuggled, making herself comfortable in Aurora's arms.

Cradling Tove gently Aurora rocked her while making happy tiger noises. Slowly the little girl's eyes drifted closed altogether and it wasn't long before it was obvious to the adults that she was asleep. "She's in dreamland," Aurora whispered.

"Thank you," Astrid whispered back. "You're a life saver. I've been trying to get miss grumpy to sleep for hours; she's teething." Carefully she disentangled little hands from Aurora's mane. Even in sleep the toddler had a firm grip and it took her mother a while to gently pry open the tiny fingers without waking her child.

"Maybe get her a real kitten to sleep with?" Aurora suggested with a grin.

"Somehow I don't think that kind of kitty will measure up."

"At least it will purr properly. Well, as long as she doesn't pull its fur like she pulls mine."

Astrid gave Aurora a big smile. "You indulge Tove. You know she'll pull your hair if you let her play with it and yet you let her do it every time."

"At least she's not as bad as the boys were."

"Only because she's so tiny. In another year those hands will grip much harder."

Aurora groaned in mock protest making the other woman laugh. Astrid held open her arms and Aurora leaned close to pass the sleeping toddler back to her. She tucked a strand of hair away from the rosy cheeks and gently kissed Tove's forehead. "She's so pretty; she's going to be a stunner when she grows up. Just like her mother."

Astrid blushed and she gave Aurora a tender smile. "It's so good to see you. You were away longer than usual and I worried because we heard..." She faltered but then rushed on, "We heard you had hunters after you again and that you'd been shot! I was so upset that I—"

Aurora stiffened and sounding a little strained she said, "It was just a scratch wound, they barely grazed me."

"I wish those bastards would leave you alone!" Astrid hissed angrily.

"So do I," Aurora said with a sigh, "but they won't."

Astrid bit her lip and looked down while she blinked rapidly, fighting back her tears. A few seconds passed with neither woman saying anything and Evie shifted uncomfortably as she watched them. Her movement caught Astrid's eyes and she looked startled, as if she'd forgotten Evie was there. She immediately squared her shoulders and speaking to Aurora she said, "I have to get back to the village."

"You go ahead and we'll follow as soon as I've fixed this," Aurora said indicating her face.

"All right, I'll go refresh the bedding and towels in your room. I'll speak to Mother. I'm sure she'll be happy to arrange a room for your avian companion with one of the families rather than in the guest quarters. There is no one in it right now so she wouldn't have to share but a friend of yours deserves better."

"Thanks, but that won't be necessary – Evie can stay with me."

"But…there's only one bed in your room and that sofa is not big enough to sleep on," Astrid protested.

Evie stepped away from their gear to stand next to Aurora and unfurled a wing so it hugged her back. Even as she was doing it Evie chided herself for making such a possessive display but Astrid was standing way too close to Aurora for her liking. "You really don't have to find me another room, Astrid. We'll manage."

This gave Astrid pause. She frowned and looked at Evie with more interest then shifted her focus to search Aurora's eyes. Whatever she saw there made her face darken and just for a moment before she schooled her expression, she looked sad.

"Oh, I see. It is about time." Astrid tried for a cheerful smiled but it didn't reach her eyes. "Excuse me, ladies, I have to go put my little darling to bed now. Don't be a stranger, Aurora. Finn has the chess board set up and he's eager for a rematch." With a swish of her skirt Astrid turned and walked away, her child clutched tightly to her chest.

***

Aurora watched Astrid's retreating back with a mixture of sadness and relief. Tilting her head to the sky she rotated her face into the dappled sun flickering through the leafy canopy. A breeze tumbled through the woods stirring small branches and dry leaves. Aside from that, the forest seemed deceptively quiet. Aurora closed her eyes, listened with her other senses and the quiet layer drew away. She could hear the heart of the forest: birds chattering, the sound of small scurrying creatures, the snorting of a sow and her piglets grazing and a deer clambering up a steep incline nearby. Beyond the sprawling forest the sounds of the village rose like a distant hum. Inhaling deeply she picked up chimney smoke, the salty tang of the ocean and the musty earth smells of things underfoot. Imposed over everything was the awareness of the breeze caressing her face and ruffling her fur with the familiarity of an old lover. It felt like the forest was breathing on her, whispering to her of secret things and she felt her tiger stir in yearning to rediscover favorite places. She loved the forests of Nordarra and would miss it almost as much as the people in the village but she would just have to bear the loss – it was time to move on to new and better things. Aurora sighed and restored her features so she again looked entirely human. When she opened her eyes Evie was right in front of her, staring up at her with a concerned look on her face.

"Aurora, what's wrong?" Gentle fingers reached out to wipe her damp cheeks. "Why were you crying?"

"Was I? Oh...it's nothing." Embarrassed Aurora quickly dried her face with her sleeve.

Evie's brow creased into a frown. "How can you crying be nothing? Was it about her, that woman? The way she looked at you made me think there was something between you?"

"I'm sad because it just hit me that I won't be here for the twins' next birthday party and I might never feel Tove's little hands on my face again. I'm going to miss them."

"And you'll miss Astrid?"

Aurora groaned, "Why do you have to be so persistent right now?"

Evie gently cupped Aurora's face in her hands. "Because it looks like your heart is breaking and I can't stand seeing you like this. Please talk to me, tell me what's going on in that head of yours."

"I'm not grieving for her. I mourn for what she represents. Astrid is a shattered dream of the life I once thought I could have. So, to answer your question: Yes, there was something between us. Once."

"What happened?"

"We spent time together and became very close. I thought what we had was special and that we could make a life together. I thought she felt the same and assumed we had an understanding. I was wrong. I had to go away for a few months and when I came back to claim her as my mate she was engaged."

"Oh no."

Aurora shrugged, "It was for the best. Her husband is well respected and a master carpenter who provides well for them. Finn treats her kindly and he's a great father. Astrid loves her family and most of her relatives live in this close-knit community. This is the life she wanted - she's surrounded by family, friends and the safe familiarity of her world."

"Do you regret…I mean do you still have feelings for her?"

"Now? No, not like that. I'll always care about her and do whatever I can to help but only because she's my friend. Anything else is in the past. I felt sorry for myself for a long time but she was right."

"About what?"

"That I do not fit with her people. No matter how much I want to belong here, I never will."

That made Evie gasp in horror. "Astrid said *that* to you?"

"Yes, but she wasn't trying to be cruel. This is her world after all and she just saw the truth more clearly. Everyone in Ingvild is human and even though they are friendly to shapeshifters they don't want shifters living among them. Also, this is a patriarchal society and even though the women aren't subservient the community as a whole does have belief in the order of things and everyone's place in it. It's part of their traditions, integrated into their culture and it defines how they see themselves. I've been coming here since I was a child so they treat me like part honored guest and old friend. As such I'm not expected to adhere to the things they believe and within reason I can do just about whatever I want. My differences are tolerated good-naturedly, like one would accept the eccentricities of a revered distant cousin, but their acceptance of my otherness is conditional. They can only allow me this freedom as long as I remain on the outside and my visits are just temporary stopovers on the way somewhere else. A female beast-shifter like me claiming one of their prized daughters as a life-mate and then expecting to live among them like we're a normal married couple would be too much."

"Was she your first?"

Aurora hesitated before saying, "She was the first person I pursued and my first love. So yes, but that was a long time ago. We were both so young we didn't really know what was happening between us. We didn't really know who we were or what we really wanted. She loved me but everything about us scared her and worst of all there were times I could tell she was afraid of me. I would never have hurt her in a million years but all it took was seeing a glimpse of my beast when I got upset and she couldn't get away quick enough." Aurora sighed wearily. "Astrid made the right decision. I wasn't a suitable mate for her."

"Do you think she could have been the right one for you? That maybe she's the one who got away?"

"No, I don't. Someone who's afraid of me can never be right for me. How could I bear to look into the eyes of the person I love and see fear? I'd rather be alone."

While she listened Evie had unfurled her wings and wrapped them around Aurora like a second pair of arms. Her left hand rested on Aurora's hip, the right hand on her chest over her heart. When Aurora fell silent Evie slid her hands sideways and up to caress her breasts. Almost instantly nipples crested into hard peaks. She gripped the sensitive nipples between thumb and forefinger and squeezed hard making Aurora buck.

She grabbed Evie's hands and gasped, "Evie! What are you doing?"

"I am not afraid of you."

"Yes, I can tell. If anything, I'm the one who's a little afraid of you, especially right now, but that doesn't explain why you did that."

"Well, your breasts are lovely so I wanted to touch them anyway but right now my intent is to distract you. I don't want you to think about sad things anymore. I also won't have you thinking about another woman when I'm right in front of you."

"But I wasn't thinking of another woman," Aurora protested.

"Now you're not." Evie smiled wickedly and nipped the side of Aurora's neck while her hands fondled her breasts.

Aurora moaned and when she spoke her voice was low and husky. "Evie, you're playing a dangerous game."

"Am I?" She wrapped her arms around Aurora's neck and whispered in her ear, "Kiss me."

Aurora happily obeyed. If it was Evie's aim to distract her she did an excellent job; the way she kissed should be illegal it was that good. The soft warmth of her, the scent that was so distinctly Evie enveloped Aurora's senses and the world receded so there was only the woman in her arms. Aurora was foggy on the sequence of events but she found their gentle kiss had escalated to a battling of tongues and the air between them sizzled with heat as their hands roamed and their bodies angled, rubbing against each other in a way that left no doubt where they were heading. When Aurora broke the kiss she was breathless and intensely aware of her body's reaction to the incredible wonder that was Evie. She didn't want to but she had to slow things down.

"Evie, we need to stop."

"No, we don't," Evie protested as she kissed the side of Aurora's neck.

"But we do…I'm minutes away from dragging you deeper into the forest and out of your clothing," Aurora warned her.

"Is that supposed to be a threat?" Evie chuckled. "Hmm, that sounds like a fabulous idea to me."

Aurora groaned and plunged her tongue into the velvet heat of Evie's mouth. Her hands slipped under the waistband of Evie's pants onto bare skin and she caressed and massaged her way down across the rounded globes of Evie's ass towards the source of heat at the apex of her thighs. Encouraged by the approving noises Evie made she dipped her fingers lower and the moment she touched the sweet spot Evie moaned into her mouth and shivered a little. That sound was so sexy it just about undid her and Aurora realized she would do just about anything to hear Evie make it again. Evie's pleasure gave her pleasure and to be desired by this woman was a potent aphrodisiac. The sound of a voice calling up the path and another from just above answering was the only thing that stopped Aurora from following through on what could have come next. It might feel like they were isolated but they were on the pathway into the forest most frequented by the villagers and it was just a matter of time before someone came upon them. Aurora moved her hands to a safer location and Evie moaned again but this time in protest. Aurora suppressed a groan; the woman drove her wild with how open and passionate she was. The way Evie was looking at her with heavy-lidded eyes and licking her lips that were moist and swollen from their kisses made it incredibly hard to remember why she shouldn't carry her off to a more secluded spot. Trying to calm herself and ease Evie down gently she kissed her eyes, the side of her mouth and stroked fingers along the soft planes of her cheek and neck.

"You are a dangerous woman, Evie, you make me forget just about everything. Even where we are."

"Hmm, as long as you never forget about me."

"That would be impossible." She said this with such conviction that Evie laughed and pulled her head down for another kiss. This kiss was slower and softer and although the heat was still there it was more under control.

"Do you want to come with me?" The words were out before Aurora even realized she was about to speak.

"To where?"

For a moment Aurora contemplated making up something harmless but now that she'd had the thought and the words were on the tip of her tongue she had to continue. It was unlikely Evie would be interested but she wanted to put it out there…just in case. She felt excitement stir at the mere flicker of hope that Evie might say yes.

"Come with me to the human world, even if it's just for a holiday. I'll buy you return tickets so you can come back whenever you want. We can travel first class and visit interesting places. I have plenty of money so you can pick where we stay and even where we go. It's not like I have to go to Canada straight away."

Aurora felt Evie stiffen, saw the troubled shadow drift across her face and instantly the fragile flicker of hope died. It had only burned briefly but she felt bereft by how empty and cold its absence made her feel.

"Aurora, I'm sorry but—"

Aurora disentangled herself from Evie and stepped out of reach. She had to – she felt exposed, like her skin had been peeled back and she couldn't tolerate being touched. Bitter thoughts rose to the surface. She should have expected this…of course someone like Evie would think she was good enough to fuck but not worthy of more. She'd just offered her an all-expenses-paid holiday and even that couldn't entice Evie to go away with her. So much for Evie saying she wanted to spend more time with her. Aurora tried to quash the dark thoughts; they were born from an old hurt and she knew she was overreacting. But at the same time she couldn't help but feel there was a kernel of truth in there and that made her feel humiliated.

"No, it's fine. I know you have plans, commitments, things to do. I shouldn't have asked. Just got a bit carried away in the moment. I keep forgetting we're going our separate ways after tomorrow."

"Aurora—"

"It's fine Evie, forget I brought it up. Let's go to the village before they send out a search party for us. If we're lucky I can rustle us a little something to eat in the meeting hall. It's a long time until dinner and I'm starving."

CHAPTER 21

HEROIC MONSTER

They had just entered the meeting hall when a solidly built woman in her sixties came out of the kitchen drying her hands on her apron. The moment she saw Aurora her face broke into a huge smile and she threw her arms wide. "Aurora, you're back! I've been worried sick about you. Come over here and give an old woman a hug right this minute."

Aurora dropped her things and was across the room in three long strides. She gathered the older woman in a hug, lifted her off the ground and kissed her cheek. "Aida, it's so good to see you."

Smiling, Aida gave Aurora a playful smack and huffed, "That's no reason to squeeze all the air from my lungs. You're as bad as my boys!"

Aurora grinned and twirled Aida once before gently lowering the flustered woman. "And I'm as ravenous as they are for a taste of your cooking. I know it's between meals but I'm starving. Do you maybe have a little something for me and my friend? Just something to tide us over until dinner."

"For you I'll *always* have something, you know that. But first, introduce me to your friend."

"Aida, this is Evangeline Aquilar. Evie, this wonderful woman and mistress of all things food related is Aida Olsen."

"Pleased to meet you, Mistress Olsen."

"Call me Aida, we don't stand on formalities here."

"Thank you, Aida. Please, call me Evie."

"Welcome here with us, Evie. Any friend of Aurora may have a seat at my table." Introductions out of the way Aida draped a meaty arm around Aurora's waist and pulled her along. "Come into the kitchen with me, girly. Tell me what mischief you've been up to while I make you a plate."

That left Evie standing alone in the hall feeling a little lost. She decided to have a look around while she waited. The meeting hall, like most of the buildings she'd seen in the village of Ingvild, was made from blocks of hewn stone fitted so snugly she couldn't see any gaps. Clearly the work of skilled stonemasons. The slanted high roof was held up by a latticework of thick wooden beams slotted into each other and the floor was covered in squares of springy material that looked like it could be lifted up and replaced easily. When Aurora said they were going to the meeting hall she had assumed from the look of the building it would be the equivalent of an oversized hunting lodge with stuffed animal heads and weapons lining the walls but there was nothing like that here. The walls were covered in large colorful tapestries depicting village life, sunsets over the ocean and all manner of other scenes. She was no expert as such things went but it was breath-taking work and must have been the combined labor of love of many women working many years to get it done stitch by intricate stitch. It gave the place a lively and welcoming feel. It was the kind of place she could imagine families and friends gathering to talk and play or to share meals at the long wooden tables.

Evie paused in front of an oil painting that covered a massive section of one wall. It showed a large wooden ship sailing towards the portal in the middle of the ocean that was the only access between Nordarra and the human world on the other side. The deck of the ship was tightly packed with families, livestock and the kinds of things a group of people would need to make a new beginning in a wild land. It was a very dramatic scene. The ship looked like it had been in a battle. It listed badly to one side, the sails were patched and there were scorch marks on the sides. The people looked equally worn and battered and some were clearly injured but they were embracing each other, their expressions a mix of joy, relief, and hope. A large bearded man at the helm poised with an arm outstretched pointing at the portal, which for some reason was depicted as a huge golden gate. It gave the scene a deliverance feel, as if the people on the boat believed they were about to enter a holy land or a place of salvation. Curious, Evie got closer to study the busy scene inside the gate. It showed a mountainous landscape crawling with fierce animals and shapeshifters represented as beings that were half man and half beast. A huge dragon loomed in the sky. Evie wondered if this painting depicted the villagers' journey to Nordarra and if they had known what kind of creatures awaited them here before they decided to make the perilous voyage. If so, things must have been terrible where they came from for them to pack up their families and brave the dangers of Nordarra anyway.

Out of the corner of her eye Evie saw movement. Turning she saw Aurora come out of the kitchen carrying a tray with two large bowls and a pile of buttered bread. She hurried to take a seat at one of the long tables and Aurora angled towards her. Sitting down on the opposite side of her Aurora carefully lifted a bowl and put it in front of Evie.

"Oooo, hot, hot." She blew on her fingers and slid the second bowl in front of herself. "I hope you like chowder. Aida makes the most delicious seafood chowder. We were lucky she had a pot on the stove." Without waiting for Evie to reply Aurora dug in and finished her bowl of chowder and most of the bread in record time.

Aida came out of the kitchen carrying a platter piled high with an assortment of cut meats. "More, my girl?"

"Please, Aida. You know I go crazy over your chowder. I've craved it. I swear I dream about it some nights it's so good."

"Flatterer," Aida said fondly. She removed Aurora's empty bowl and slid the meat platter in its place in a practised motion. She cast an eye at Evie's mostly full bowl, gathered the tray and said, "I'll go refill this for you, Aurora. It does an old woman good to see her food appreciated."

"Thanks, you're the best. If there is fruit could we have some?"

"What kind of fruit?"

Aurora glanced at Evie.

"Anything really and thank you, the food is amazing."

"You're welcome. I will go see what I can find."

Aida came back a little while later with the tray again heavily laden with food. On it, another large bowl of chowder, more slices of buttered bread, an orange, three of the biggest guavas Evie had ever seen each the size of a man's hand and twin pitchers of chilled ginger ale.

Evie slid aside her empty bowl and shook her head at Aurora's offer to share the bread with her. She was eager for the fruit. Reverently Evie placed one of the guavas in her plate. It had a thin green skin and when she sliced it the inside was red velvet and tasted like the sweet captured remnants of summer.

Aurora was finishing her plate of meat with sips of the drink when a gangly old man with a wild grey beard and even wilder eyebrows wandered in and sat down next to her. "Ha, I knew I'd find you here. How is it you can get that woman to feed you outside of mealtime when the likes of me can't even get a morsel of dried bread out of her?"

Aurora shrugged. "Don't drag me into your mess, Hagen. It's not my problem if you still haven't patched things up with Aida."

Hagen grumbled and gave the kitchen door a disgruntled look. "Aurora, are you going to stay a while this time?"

"No, we're leaving on the first boat to Porta Belua. There should be one tomorrow."

"Hmm, shame that."

"What's happened? Something from the forest causing trouble?"

"Yeah. Got me a critter by the quarry that's proving troublesome."

"Troublesome for you? That sounds serious."

Hagen stroked his beard and nodded. "I could do with your help. Whatever is out there the dogs don't like it and the other animals are staying clear of the area. Doesn't have a good feel. I sent in the dogs to flush out what is there so I could have a look and it cost me two good hunting dogs. Dreadful loss. Baldur made it back in a terrible state. I patched him up after I pulled this out of his leg." He put a bony spike on the table. It was a mottled grey color, two feet long, thick and one end was honed to a needle's edge.

"Ah…yeah that's trouble right there."

"You recognize this? What kind of critter is it?"

"That's from a blue razorback and where there's one there is probably a mate as well because they mate for life. You do not want these things nesting in your backyard. They're like giant lizards with spikes, they are carnivorous, not fussy about what they eat and they breed quickly. To top things off they are *very* aggressive. They will think nothing of attacking and eating a grown man never mind a child playing in the wrong place."

"I've heard of those but I never expected to see one around these parts."

"I've only ever seen them up north beyond the great mountains so I wouldn't have expected them around here either. They prefer dry, hot climates and they don't like to travel far. Maybe something chased them out of their territory and they just kept going until they ended up here or, which seems more likely, someone captured one or more for the exotics trade and it escaped in transit."

Hagen paused in stroking his beard and said, "All possible. Suppose we will never know how it got here. Not important now. I'll go gather a few of the young hotheads that have been pestering me about wanting to have a go at whatever is out there."

"They'll just slow us down."

"True but it will do them good to see how this is done. I can't keep hunting forever and you're not always around to help. They need to learn because soon they will be the ones who have to protect the village."

"If they're coming along get them to bring the big spears and a medkit in case we have to stitch someone."

"Spears in that thick growth?"

"Blue razorbacks are covered in those spikes so the spears will give us a reach advantage. I'll flush them out to a place where those spears are usable. You need to prep the youngsters so they stand their ground when those things come flying at them screeching like banshees."

"How you gonna get those creatures out into the open when the dogs couldn't?"

Aurora grinned. "I've got my ways. You just make sure you take care of your end."

Hagen clapped Aurora on the shoulder. "Ha, I knew you'd be up for it. Those critters are gonna wish they took the hint and moved on. I'll go get those young ones roused and ready. Do you think you could get Aida to give me a little something before I go? Maybe a bowl of that chowder? It smells mighty good. She'll do it if you ask cos she's got a soft spot for you. Actually, she doesn't even have to know. How about you slide that extra bowl over to me…quiet like."

"Not extra and not happening, you old schemer. I'm happy to hunt for you but I will not stick my head in that bees' nest. I have to look out for my stomach and her food is mighty good, I could eat an entire pot of this chowder all by myself." To emphasize her point Aurora took a heaped spoon of chowder and ate it with slow relish. Hagen left grumbling about disrespectful children and difficult women which Aurora gleefully ignored, fully focused on enjoying the last of her meal.

"Are you seriously going to hunt that razorback or whatever it is called?"

"Looks that way, Evie."

"Can't their hunters do that?"

"They only have two hunters at the moment and the other guy went to one of the islands with his wife to visit their daughter who's expecting her first child. No telling when he'll be back. This can't wait. Besides, I don't mind helping out." Aurora mopped out her bowl with the last piece of bread. Before popping it into her mouth she paused to say, "Also I have to pay for my meals and room. They won't take my money for that so it's important to me that I'm useful to these people. They work hard to make a living and I don't want to feel like I'm a burden.

I'm glad Hagen spoke to me, it's good timing. I need to shift and I need a challenging hunt because my beast is clawing at me to be let out and fed after being denied for days." When she finished eating Aurora pushed her bowl away and stood up. "I'd better go get ready."

"How are you going to get ready?"

"I can't go like this," Aurora said pointing at herself. "I have to put on something more suitable so it's easier to shift."

"You're going to take on your beast form?"

"This is a good opportunity for me to let my beast out for a hunt before we head to Porta Belua so yes, that's the plan." Aurora took her bowl, Evie's empty dish, and their cutlery back to the kitchen. When she came out of the kitchen she headed straight for the exit. In passing, she said to Evie who was halfway through her orange, "My room is above the big warehouse. You should be able to find it easily but if not ask one of the villagers to show you the way. I don't know how long this will take so you're welcome to have a sleep or whatever. I left a couple of good books so there's that as well."

"Wait and I'll come with you? I'm almost done."

"I'm in a hurry and there is no need for you to come with me." Aurora picked up the rucksack and guitar case she'd put down by the door and left the hall.

Frowning, Evie replayed the conversation in her head; she had the distinct feeling Aurora had just given her the cold shoulder. What was that about? She finished her orange and decided to save the last two guavas for later and put them in her satchel. Trying not to look like she was hurrying she made her way over to the structure she recognized as the warehouse. She got to the top of the stairs she assumed led to Aurora's room just as the door opened. Aurora stood in the doorway with a cloak over her arm dressed only in body-hugging black boxers and a strapless bra made from the same stretchy material, which clung to her breasts.

Evie's eyes flew wide and she had to clear her throat before she could speak. "Aurora, are you going out like that? I approve of the look but I think you're going to scandalize the villagers if you step out in your underwear."

Aurora laughed and said, "I'll put the cloak on before I go outside."

"You're not putting on anything else?"

"Nope. Did you think my clothing magically disappears and reappears when I shift? Unfortunately, that's not an ability I've mastered. That's the reason I usually wear such loose clothing. It's not a fashion statement, it's practicality because I don't want to rip my clothing every time I shift. Trust me that gets old real fast. What I have on is good for shifting. If I only half shift this stretchy material will cover the important bits and if I need to become a beast I can easily slip out of what I've got on. The cloak will cover my nakedness in between shifts so as not to shock the villagers. Although I think the guys wouldn't mind seeing my bare ass but I'd probably never hear the end of it. I'm still getting sly comments from the time a couple of them saw me swimming naked."

"Aurora!" Evie could not contain her shock. This was a side of Aurora she'd not seen before and had not expected.

"Oh relax, I would never go with one of them and all the guys here know that. They don't even try to flirt with me anymore. They just like to give me a little grief now and then but it's good natured, they have a healthy respect for women in general and my fists in particular. Besides, I want to have a bit of fun. I've always been so careful trying to act as human as possible with them but I'm leaving so why not let my claws out a little?"

Evie didn't know what to say to that. She had the feeling an Aurora wanting to strut her beast side could be wilder than she or the villagers knew how to handle. She opted for a safer comment, "Where are your shoes? Are you going barefoot?"

"Yes, I have thick soles on my feet and since I'm planning to shift it's more convenient to go without." Aurora pointed a thumb over her shoulder. "The room is there. Make yourself comfortable."

Evie reached for Aurora wanting to brush her cheek with a good luck kiss but she sidestepped and made her way downstairs while pulling the cloak on, not looking back once. Blinking in confusion Evie stared at Aurora's disappearing back; this was so not like the woman she'd come to know. She didn't want to trail after her like a lost puppy but she needed to know what was going on with her. Or maybe this was just how Aurora became when she was preparing for a hunt? No, that didn't feel right. It must have something to do with her declining Aurora's offer to go away with her.

Opening the door Evie gave the room and its contents a cursory look. It had a big window, a large single bed, a small wardrobe, a fireplace, a full bookcase, one chair, a trunk, a small sofa, a rug and a mirrored stand with a white enamel washbasin on top and a set of doors down below.

Evie dropped her things and left one of her guavas on the table next to Aurora's black knife as a late night snack then made her way back down. She was not the type to wait for answers to come to her and she had no intention of lying down to have a snooze like a granny while Aurora fought a dangerous lizard. There might not be time for them to talk right now but at least Evie could go see her off.

***

Outside a small group was waiting for Aurora. Evie recognized Hagen the hunter. Beside him stood three tall sturdy young guys sporting various incarnations of attempted beard growth. Beside them, a stocky blond girl of about sixteen in leather pants and a worn padded leather jacket, her entire outfit covered in soot stains and singe marks. This was such a contrast to the colorful skirts and feminine dresses she'd seen the village women wear and it made Evie look twice. If the clothing hadn't drawn her attention, the way the girl stood with her arms folded and a dark scowl on her face would have. Catching snippets of conversation she soon realized why the girl looked so annoyed.

"You should go home, Irena – this isn't woman's work."

"Neither is working in the forge but I help my dad all the time."

"But Irena, you could get hurt."

"Hagen told me I could come along," Irena replied and set her mouth in a stubborn line. "Besides, one of you could get hurt just as easily."

"We know you are capable but you're still a girl and this is a dangerous hunt. If something happened to you your dad will beat us to death with his bare hands."

Aurora who had quietly drifted over interjected, "I'm a girl too – doesn't anyone worry something will happen to me?"

"But, Aurora, you're a shapeshifter."

"So? That makes me harder to kill not immortal. If Irena wants to come let her, she knows the risks. Besides, don't you guys want the kind of woman who can defend your home from attack and protect your children from wild animals while out in the forest? I think Irena getting experience with handling weapons is a brilliant idea. Everyone should know enough to protect their loved ones."

This quieted the guys and the girl relaxed a little, her arms unfolding to rest on her hips.

"Let's go. Keep up with me or I'll leave the lot of you behind and claim the entire kill for myself."

As Aurora led them to the gate taking her customary long strides the cloak flared to reveal her shapely bare legs. There was a wolf whistle from one of the young guys that earned him a cuff around the head from Hagen the hunter.

"Keep a civilized tongue in your head. Don't act like you've never seen a woman's legs boy."

"Not like that I haven't," the young man muttered to muted laughter of the rest and even the girl grinned.

Aurora turned to walk backwards and said in a serious voice, "I hope everyone has a strong stomach because I'm going to shift at some point either partly or all the way and you may see me doing that. All of you have seen me in tiger form at one time or another but I won't necessarily look as you remember and when my beast is riled up with battle lust, I may seem a little scary. Just keep in mind whatever you see it's still me in that body. If anyone stabs me or panic throws a spear at me there will be a reckoning. Remember the kitty is on your side. Unless you throw a spear at her…then not so much." The planes of Aurora's face moved becoming more feline. She made a snapping motion, flashing fangs and a mouth of inhumanly large teeth followed by a meaningful look at each of the young hunters. The group went very quiet and instinctively moved closer to each other. Aurora grinned at their response and gave Hagen a conspiratorial wink. He snorted and tried to hide his amusement by enthusiastically finger-combing his beard.

"Hagen, do you want to say anything before we head out? I want as little conversation as possible once we go through the gate."

"I've already said most of what I wanted to say to them before you came. Remember while we are out there keeping each other safe should be everyone's top priority. We aren't hunting rabbits; those things have killed seasoned hunting dogs with more experience than all of you youngsters combined. We're going out to hunt those razorback lizard things because Aurora tells me if we leave them they will breed quickly and be a right menace, attacking anyone or anything that gets near. Our little ones play in the forest and the women forage and gather wood. We're going out there to keep our family and neighbors safe. This isn't for sport and I don't want no glory hounds. We aim to kill quick and clean. Follow my lead, stick to the plan and everything's gonna run smooth. Any problems, that's why we got Aurora along. She knows those things and I've hunted with her many times before, there's no one better. I trust her with my life and yours. Listen carefully to any advice she gives and if she decides to go furry to deal with those critters don't get in her way."

There were murmurs from the group that Evie took to be questions but it was no longer possible for her to make out what was being said as they were moving quickly and too far away. Evie was tempted to take to the skies and follow the hunting party to act as their scout. From above she could provide the hunters with useful advice on terrain and the creatures they were hunting. She stayed grounded because she didn't think Aurora would be pleased with that. She hadn't asked her along in any capacity, in fact, it seemed like she wanted to be away from Evie so it wouldn't be a good idea to hover in the skies above her like an uninvited guest. Besides, she might prove to be a distraction to the inexperienced hunters and if the creature they were hunting was as dangerous as Aurora said it would be bad.

"You want to come have a cup of tea with me, dearie?"

Evie turned to find Aida standing in the doorway of the meeting hall.

"They'll be away for hours as these things tend to go."

"Thank you, that would be lovely."

"Good. That gives me an excuse to put my feet up while I brew us a pot. I have almond biscuits in the oven almost ready to come out so we can have those with the tea."

"You've been so generous already. You really don't have to go out of your way for me."

"Think nothing of it. Besides, any friend of Aurora's she thinks good enough to bring here starts out in my good books. I don't offer my almond biscuits to just anyone I'll let you know," Aida said with a smile.

Evie followed Aida through the big hall into a large kitchen. Aida moved with the ease of long familiarity, opening cupboards and reaching for cups and teapot without really looking, expecting what she placed to be precisely where she left it. Clearly, Aida was a woman firmly in control of her domain.

"Aida, how is it that people have shared meals here when they have their own homes? Is it a kind of tradition?"

"It is practicality not tradition although it might become that if we keep it up long enough. We have lunch in our own homes but there is breakfast, mostly hot porridge, set out early for those who want it. We have a shared dinner in the hall on account of the ethian generator that powers the stoves and cooling units in this kitchen. Everyone stores their precious foods here in their own compartments and we have a connection from the generator to the workshops as well. There are heating units under the floor of the hall that we turn on at the height of winter so we have a warm cozy place to gather. Everything is strictly regulated to make sure we don't damage the crystals. We've only had it a few years but we'd be lost without our precious ethian generator. Besides gathering for meals is a good way for extended family and neighbors to catch up. Several of the girls will come help with the preparations for the evening meal in an hour or so but for now we have peace and quiet. As much as I love having them around you wouldn't believe how noisy a few women can be. This lot chatter non-stop like a flock of birds!"

This made Evie smile. "I do actually. I have a large extended family and when all the women are together it's hard to get a word in with everyone trying to talk at the same time."

"Ah, that's nice, dear. It's good to have a large family. Do you plan to have many children?"

"I've not really given it much thought but no, probably not. I suspect my sister might. She's only seventeen but I think one day she's going to be the kind of woman who'll want lots of children of her own to boss around and look after. She tries to hide it but she has a maternal streak; she even fusses over me sometimes and I helped raise her."

"Your mother is not around?"

"She died giving birth to my sister."

"Oh…that is sad."

"Yes. I still miss her and I really wish my sister could have known our mother."

"What's your sister's name?"

"Oriana."

"That's a lovely name."

Their conversation drifted into how Evie and Aurora knew each other to which Evie gave an abbreviated version of events. She could tell Aida was curious and bursting to ask more questions but she deftly steered the conversation away from herself and the nature of her relationship with Aurora towards Aida's role in the community and questions about her family. As soon as she brought up Aida's sons she could tell she'd hit the sweet spot. The woman beamed, rested her thick muscular arms on the counter and settled in for a good talk. Soon Evie learned more about Aida's sons than she was comfortable knowing. Including the various attributes of the four wives and why they were a good match for her darling boys or, in the case of one daughter-in-law who dragged her son off to the city, not so much. The topic that was most pertinent to her however was that of her fifth and youngest son who she despaired would turn into a bachelor until it became known he was smitten with a young woman who lived on one of the small islands. This had Aida very excited and Evie got to hear a detailed account of the courtship to date. There had been lengthy letters exchanged via boat, he'd made several trips to her distant island home and slaved over handmade gifts to impress not only the pretty girl but also her parents. He was on a mission to prove he would be a good provider for their beloved only daughter. This conversation got them through their first pot of tea. As soon as Evie drained her cup Aida prepared them a fresh pot and slid a plate of warm almond biscuits fresh out of the oven between them. Evie read this as a sign of approval and decided she could finally lead the conversation in the direction of the person she really wanted to know more about. If anyone had insight on what Aurora had been like as a child it would be this woman who'd lived here her whole life and who the normally reserved Aurora was comfortable enough with to hug and ask for food.

"Aida, how long have you known Aurora?"

"She has been coming here a long time. She used to come with her father. He was a huge man even by our standards, too large to come into the meeting hall unless he bent over. He was a mountain man and lived somewhere far into those ranges. He would come to trade and chat from time to time and he always brought his little girl with him. When they came they usually stayed for a few days. She used to ride on his shoulders when she was little but as soon as she was able she carried her own pack and ran beside him. She was quick as a shot and she could outrun all the boys and even the young men when one could be goaded into competing with her. Whip-smart too, show her something once and she got it. Oh, and what a pretty child she was with those beautiful eyes and long dark hair. We knew she would turn heads when she grew up even with that wildness in her. We hoped one of the boys would catch her eye. Not many women willing to come out so far into the wild country and make it home, you know."

"Did you meet her mother?"

"Never saw his wife. He said the trip was too far for her to make but I have never known me a woman who wouldn't travel for company in such lonely country. Would have thought there wasn't really a woman out there except he was always buying pretty things and treats like a man would get for his sweetheart. And when he mentioned his wife he would smile and get this look in his eyes like he couldn't wait to see her. Made me wish my husband would go on a long trip so he could come back and look at me that way," Aida said with a chuckle.

"When did things change? I know her father was murdered. Did she come here after it happened?"

"She did but not for a while. We figured something must have happened when he didn't turn up to collect the shipment he'd already paid for. He'd been excited about it and swore he'd be waiting at the dock to pick it up as soon as the ship came in. So, when months passed and he didn't come for his packages, well, it's dangerous out there. People die all the time. In my lifetime I've seen several parties equipped with everything a group of people could need to survive in the wilds pass through here never to be heard of again. No trace of them. Poof, just gone."

"When did you see Aurora again? When did she return?"

"Our hunters saw her first. One day she came to the edge of their camp to talk to Hagen. He was a good friend of her father's and they usually stayed at his place when they came here. Aurora told Hagen they'd been ambushed by cutters and that her father had been murdered while helping her escape. She said she'd been on the trail of her father's killers ever since. Fancy that, a young girl hunting grown men. She asked him to ask the boatmen and traders if they'd seen a large group of men come out of the wilds after a hunting trip and if they'd heard rumors about anyone selling tiger parts."

"Was that all? Did Hagen say anything else?"

"He said there was something off about Aurora. She had a look about her that made him uneasy. It would have been the trauma and grief of her father's death that did that. They were so close and always together. She's never wanted to talk about what happened but I know it must have been bad. We heard about the things those cutters do. It's too horrible to think about. Whatever happened changed her and not in a good way. Hagen tried to get Aurora to come back with them. He even offered her a place with his family but she wouldn't hear of it. She wouldn't even share a meal at the fire with them she was so skittish. But she took the winter coat he offered and supplies the men could spare. Said she'd repay them for it when she came to get her father's packages and if she didn't come for it in two seasons she was probably dead and they could have that instead."

"When did you see her again?"

"Two winters later. That was when the Great Illness struck us down and almost wiped us from the face of this world."

"This sickness, was it a disease? The flu?"

"No, not the flu although it started with coughing. It was the men who came here from somewhere deep in the wilds who gave it to us. They said they'd been exploring a potential ethian mine site but we found out later they'd been digging in one of the old ruins looking for treasure. They must have picked up a sickness or brought a bad artifact with them into the village. We should have known their story was fishy because they were in an almighty hurry to keep going. It was autumn and the seas were already churned over by the storms but they were desperate to leave, flashing money for someone to take them to Porta Belua. None of us are stupid or desperate enough to try to take a boat through that gap of ragged rocks when the storms hit. It's difficult enough for an experienced crew to get through safely in good weather never mind bad. When no one would take them they paid a small fortune for one of the boats and set off as quickly as they could load themselves and their cargo. We started getting sick a day after they left. I've not before or since experienced anything like it. Like I said it started with coughing, then there was a rash all over that burned all the way into the bones and such sickness of the bowels. It was hard to breathe, to move. It was like a giant weight pressing down, we became weak and helpless like babes. We could not go out to hunt or gather food, no strength to push out our boats to fish. Wild animals broke into the big pen and carried away most of the stock. Everything that could go wrong went wrong. We rationed our remaining stores and prayed. It was a toss-up what would get us first, the illness or starvation. By the time Aurora came, there had been several deaths. The worst of the sickness had passed but it was the height of winter, our rations were almost gone and those of us who remained hardly had flesh on our bones from the wasting. It was a desperate time."

"What did Aurora do?"

"She hunted and fished. She cooked food our stomachs could tolerate and made healing teas that cooled the fevers and stopped the pain. She tended our fires, washed our soiled bedding and heated buckets of water so we had warm water to wash the filth from our bodies. I can't really describe what it was like to get clean and have a full belly again after all we'd endured. To have her do for us what we could not do for ourselves or each other. She was only a young girl then, barely in her teens, but she watched over us until spring and by that time we were more or less on our feet again. She left as soon as the first trading ship docked. It was like someone had stoked a fire that had almost burned out in the darkest coldest of nights and kept it going till the sun came again and we could walk out into the light." Aida went quiet, sniffing she wiped her face with the apron. "I sound so melodramatic that it won't surprise me if you think I'm just an exaggerating, weepy old woman but I'm telling you that girl saved us. Since then, well, she's welcome among us any time. See that big window up there above the warehouse? Glass is expensive and getting it here safely isn't easy but it was agreed if we were going to build a room for her up there it had to have a big window, the kind that opens from the inside. After what happened to her and her father we figured she would want to see the sky and know she can get out so the room didn't feel like a trap. It was the least we could do. Have you seen the room? It's not big but cozy. It has a solid bed with a good mattress, a pretty bedspread, a few essentials and a bookcase on account of how much she loves to read. We don't let anyone stay up there but her and no one is allowed to touch her things."

"How long does she usually stay?"

"Depends. She is usually just passing through or come to trade so not long, a few days maybe a week. If she's come to help with a project she will stay longer or if the winter's been particularly long and she's feeling lonely maybe a month. Longest she ever stayed at one time was half a year when she was eighteen. She said she came to help with preparations for winter but I think she was trying to get a taste of what it would be like to live with us. She didn't take to it which is a shame because she is mighty useful to have around. That girl is a hard worker and she is strong as an ox, must be the shifter in her."

"That time when she lived here for a while was that when she and Astrid became good friends? Or were they already friends before that?"

Aida's eyebrows shot up. "How did you know?"

"Oh, it was just something Aurora mentioned," Evie said hoping Aida wouldn't press for details. She'd taken a wild guess not thinking she was really on to something. She probably shouldn't be asking about it at all but she was curious and, if she had to be honest, jealous. Which was ridiculous seeing as whatever happened between Aurora and Astrid must have been a long time ago.

"Before then they were friendly enough but not close. That was the time Astrid decided she'd take Aurora under her wing to tame some of that wildness. She thought she'd do that by teaching her needlecraft and more womanly skills and ways of behaving. Astrid is such a sensible level headed girl most of the time but that notion of hers was plain foolish. She might have been older but Aurora had been taking care of herself out in the wilderness for years and even before that she was out and about with her father all the time. That girl had a strong notion of who she was and no amount of talking was going to turn her into someone different. Besides, she's a shapeshifter and everyone knows shifters aren't like regular folk. Pardon me for saying that."

Evie waived her on. "No offense taken. Please continue."

"But tried Astrid did, not that it did any good. Aurora stayed Aurora and if anything it was Astrid who changed for a little while. It wasn't like she was slacking in her chores or talking back to her elders but it was like some of Aurora's wildness got into her. She got all restless and fidgety, wanting to be with Aurora rather than do things with the other girls. I even once saw her sitting on the roof of the warehouse with Aurora. She was in her best dress and the two of them were laughing so hard I feared they would fall off. How Astrid got up that high is beyond me. I couldn't believe it was the same girl who wouldn't even climb trees with the other children when she was little out of fear she might dirty or tear her clothing." Aida shook her head a small indulgent smile on her lips. "The experience did them both good though and they've been great friends ever since. She's the one who made that lovely quilt and curtains for Aurora's room. She's such a dab hand with a needle, that girl can make just about anything. She does her family proud with her skills."

"Astrid's husband doesn't mind her making such time consuming things for someone else?"

"Of course not, why would he? They've all known each other since they were children and get on well. Finn is always going on about the interesting gifts Aurora brings for the children or how he's looking forward to talking to her about things he's read in the books she's lent him. He was the one who suggested that they should ask Aurora to be little Tove's godmother." Aida's hand flew up to cover her mouth. "That's supposed to be a secret. They still have to ask her but I know Aurora will agree. She adores that little girl, anyone can see it and who knows maybe that would make Aurora come to stay more often on account of Tove being her goddaughter."

"That's so not going to happen."

The words were out of her mouth before Evie even realized she was going to say something. Why, oh why did she have to say that out loud? Evie picked up a biscuit and stuffed it almost whole into her mouth hoping desperately that Aida hadn't heard her. But no such luck as the woman's easy warm smile was gone replaced by a flinty look squarely focused on her. That look Evie imagined would be the same one Aida would use if she caught someone stealing from her pantry or deliberately breaking one of her precious plates and it made her feel about ten years old.

"What exactly did you mean by that?"

Aida's tone was so arctic Evie wouldn't have been surprised to find the tea in her cup had frozen solid. Inwardly she groaned and cursed her own big mouth or whatever fates had conspired to let her slip something that wasn't hers to share. She contemplated for a moment making up an elaborate story to cover her mistake or flat out making a run for it but neither were mature options. Besides, given the way Aida glared at her she wouldn't put it past the older woman to tackle her like she was a naughty child if she tried to get away and sit on her until she told the truth.

"Do you think little Tove isn't good enough to be Aurora's goddaughter because she's not a shifter? Is that it?"

"No! Aida, it's nothing like that. Aurora adores little Tove, I've seen it for myself. I wasn't supposed to say anything because Aurora was going to tell everyone herself that she's leaving Nordarra. Possibly for good."

Aida looked like someone slapped her. "You are sure of this?" The older woman spoke softly her eyes searching Evie's as if she hoped to catch her in a lie.

"Yes, I'm sorry. As soon as we get to Porta Belua she's planning to book a ticket and leave."

"That's…unexpected news."

Aida looked a little lost staring at the table with unseeing eyes and she was blinking in a way that made Evie suspect she was holding back tears.

"Are you going with my sweet girl? Are you going together?"

Startled by the question Evie quickly said, "No. She's going by herself. If it's any consolation she's sad about leaving; she had tears in her eyes when she talked about how much she would miss the children."

"Then why is she leaving?"

"That is something you have to ask Aurora yourself. I've already said too much. She's so not going to be happy with me about this, you know how private she is."

"But—"

At that moment the kitchen door opened and several women, Astrid among them, came into the kitchen amidst cheerful chatter and the swish of colorful skirts.

"Your dinner helpers are here, Aida. I'll get out of your way now. Thank you for the tea and biscuits and the talk." With that Evie did the only sensible thing she could, she fled out of the kitchen before she got cornered by a group of steely-eyed women wanting to know why she had their beloved matriarch on the verge of tears.

***

Once outside Evie walked quickly trying to get distance between herself and the drama that was probably unfolding in the kitchen. What she needed was a quiet place away from the curious eyes that seemed to track her every move to process what Aida told her and to think what to do next. Soon she found herself at the back of two buildings in what looked to be a herb garden. There was a small wooden bench but she was too restless to sit. She had to get to Aurora before any of the villagers did so she could warn her they knew she was leaving and apologize to her for letting it slip. It didn't matter that she thought Aurora needed to tell these people, some of whom seemed to genuinely care for her, about her plans. It wasn't up to her to share that information and it was something she was told in confidence. Aurora would probably understand if she explained what happened. She had to make sure Aurora didn't get the impression she shared her secrets or gossiped about her. She did ask about her but it was Aida who did the sharing and she didn't tell Evie anything that everyone in the village, aside from her, didn't already know.

Evie stared in the direction the hunting party went. She would follow their path and once she found them she would look for a place to land and take Aurora aside to talk to her. Yes, that's what she would do. Her wing was still recovering and tender but as long as she was careful she could manage another short flight. She was probably overreacting but she didn't want to take any chances. Aurora had opened up to her about things she never shared with anyone so she didn't want her to worry that she'd made a mistake entrusting so much of herself to Evie.

Evie paused in her pacing when she became aware of footsteps between the buildings heading toward her location. Moments later Astrid appeared. At first, she thought the other woman must be on a mission to harvest herbs for the evening meal but the thunderous look on her face and the way she honed in on Evie quickly dispelled that notion.

"There you are. I was looking for you."

"And now you've found me." Evie couldn't keep the sarcasm out of her voice. She couldn't imagine any pleasant reason for Astrid to be seeking her out with such an expression on her face.

"Aida told us what you said. Is this your doing? Did you put this crazy idea of leaving Nordarra into Aurora's head?"

"What? No!" Evie rustled her wings in agitation at the nerve of the woman. "How is it my fault she's leaving? From what she told me she's been thinking about this a long time, much longer than she's known me. So no, I have nothing to do with it. If you want to look for someone to blame you should look at yourself."

"Me?" Astrid looked incredulous. "How can I possibly have anything to do with this?"

"You told her she didn't fit in this village. You made her feel like she didn't belong."

"I didn't say that. That is outrageous. I would never say such a horrible thing to Aurora."

"Are you sure? Aurora certainly seemed to think so."

"When did she say I said this?"

"Before you were married. When you two were…involved."

Astrid blanched and lowered her voice. "Aurora told you about that? She told me it would stay between us."

"I sort of guessed and dragged it out of her. But she gave no details aside from that you were her first love. Apparently, you told her it couldn't work because she didn't fit here."

"Oh…" Astrid paled. Reaching for the bench she lowered herself shakily. "Oh no."

"You did say that, didn't you?"

"Yes, I did. Sort of. But I didn't mean it like that. It wasn't that *she* didn't belong here, *we* didn't fit here as a couple. I didn't think it could work. It all happened so fast it was so unexpected and she was like a flame, I felt like I was on fire like she was going to burn me up. I'd never experienced anything like it. I couldn't eat. I couldn't sleep. I was obsessed with her. She turned my world upside down." Astrid took a shaky breath her hands fluttering against her flushed cheeks. "I had plans, different kind of plans that involved having children and staying near my family. That was how I always saw my life. Then Aurora happened and my future looked nothing like I imagined. I panicked. She was intense, so consuming and I was only nineteen…" Astrid's voice trailed off. "I've known Finn all my life, we grew up together and he's still my brother's best friend. He's kind and relaxed, undemanding and considerate. He wanted me and I wanted the life he could give me. I knew we would be good together. Before Aurora I thought I was in love with him. With her everything was so different it was like going down the rapids with no oar and she wasn't like she is now, all calm and reasonable. She was so wild and fierce and she could be scary when she got upset. I'm not a brave person and that was my first serious relationship. I was too inexperienced to handle the intensity that came with being with someone like her."

"So, you told her she didn't fit here and she believed you."

"But that was all so long ago. Surely, she can't still believe that? Things here have changed so much. We all changed because of her and all the travelers and traders that come through. The girls now have so much more freedom and Aurora, she is so much a part of us. She's like family. We expect her like we expect the change in seasons. We're not sure exactly when she will be back but she always turns up. She looks out for us. She got us those giant dogs to guard the flock and she interceded when we had a misunderstanding with the mermaids. When she's around she makes the scary things go away and we all sleep better knowing she's out there keeping watch over us. We trust her. We rely on her. She is our Aurora."

"I doubt she realizes she's that important to the villagers. She told no one of her plans that have been years in the making because she probably didn't think it would matter to anyone but her. She didn't expect anyone to really miss her."

Evie had been thinking about it since they arrived, trying to understand why Aurora believed she didn't belong here when these people were clearly very fond of her. Now suddenly it was like a light went on in her head and all the pieces fell into place. She talked quickly as it came to her.

"Since she was little Aurora was told she's not welcome among either her mother or father's people because she is of mixed blood and other shifter children made fun of her because she couldn't shift until she was older. As a child this human village was the only place she felt accepted. After her father was murdered she was all on her own, a visitor wherever she went. Then your people built that room especially for her as thanks for helping them in their darkest hour and told her she was welcome anytime. For a lonely person who experienced so much rejection that would have meant so much. She told me she was looking for a place to belong after her father died. That she lived here for months on end tells me she was trying to earn a place among your people. Then you two happened and the stakes got even higher. I know you were barely an adult but what you did and said devastated Aurora. She was in love with you. She thought you had chosen her as your mate. But while she was away you got engaged to a man and when she asked why you told her it was because she didn't fit into your world. I think she interpreted that to mean that she didn't belong in your life because she's a woman and that she also didn't belong in this human village because she's a shapeshifter. A double rejection delivered by someone she trusted. What a terrible blow that must have been for her."

Astrid looked like she was going to be sick. "Great vengeful dragons…what have I done? I need to talk to her. I need to make this right!"

"Right for whom? You or her? What can you possibly say to change things now? No. Leave her alone. Someone somewhere can make it right for her but it won't be you. That ship has sailed. She's leaving, don't go raking things up and confusing her. You contributed but you're not the main reason she's leaving. She's tired of being hunted like a rare animal so she wants a chance at a life where people don't know her. I don't know if she'll find what she's looking for on the other side but how can we take that dream away from her if we don't have something better to offer her in its place? How can we ask her to stay if staying could get her killed?"

"Ah…I see it now. You're in love with Aurora."

Taken aback by the blunt statement Evie struggled to find a suitable reply. "I…um…we are good friends. I care about her."

"If you've been in her bed, I'd say you're more than just good friends," Astrid said tartly.

"We're still getting to know each other. It's all very new," Evie said, reluctant to share her feelings about Aurora with Astrid.

Astrid nodded knowingly. "Take this from someone who has known her a long time: You will never meet anyone else like her. If you like who she is and how you are together then don't let her go."

"Like you did?"

Astrid shook her head. "This is not about me. I love my husband and my life. I'm content. I wouldn't exchange it but I'm so glad I had that with her, so glad she was my first. I still remember how it was with her. I never felt so alive."

"She's older now and more experienced. Trust me she is *way* better than you remember."

"I meant to be loved by her, to be the focus of all that energy and intensity. Not the fucking if you insist on being crude about it...which, by the way, was *amazing*."

Astrid got up, smoothed her clothing and flicked specks of dust from her sleeve. "I have things to do. I can't say I've enjoyed meeting you but I can see why Aurora likes you." She gave Evie a regal nod and strode off her back straight, head held high and the beautifully embroidered skirt flaring around her legs.

"And I can see why she likes you," Evie grudgingly muttered.

***

Flying low over the forest in the direction Aurora and the hunters had gone, Evie soon spotted the returning group. Circling she found a suitable spot near them to land. The girl, Irena, and the four young men sat side by side passing around a water bottle and they all watched her walk towards them. As a whole, the group that set out on the hunt eager and fresh now looked battered and tired. They had not, by the look of things, come away unscathed from their encounter with the razorback as evidenced by the girl's bandaged hand and the shredded blood splattered shirt on one of the young men. Their injuries had to be minor though because they seemed relaxed and incredibly pleased with themselves. The reason for their triumphant looks lay at their feet on a makeshift frame fashioned from spears and rope. The massive creature looked like the result of an animal orgy where a giant eight-foot lizard mated with a porcupine and possibly also with a crocodile if the teeth were anything to go by.

Evie pointed at the razorback. "That thing is hideous."

One of the guys grinned. "It sure is and it wasn't easy to kill."

"It's so big and those spikes look vicious."

"Yup and this was the smaller of the two. It is unbelievable how fast this thing moved – it rushed us quick as a horse sprinting. Good thing Aurora was there to yank it back by the tail."

"There was another?"

"Yes, Aurora drew it away from us. It must have been a huge fight. We didn't see it but the ground shook, trees fell down and the noise of them going at each other was terrible."

"We wanted to go watch but Hagen wouldn't let us," his neighbor said sullenly.

She had expected Aurora to be at the rear but scanning the path and the surrounding forest Evie saw she was nowhere in sight. Alarmed she turned on the girl and demanded, "Irena, where is Aurora?" On realizing Aurora was missing Evie had instinctively unfurled her wings in preparation for flight. This must have distracted the girl because, to Evie's annoyance, instead of answering the question Irena sat staring at her wings with her mouth gaped open.

"Wow, your wings…they're so beautiful! I've never seen an avian up close and I didn't realize your wings were so huge. Can I touch them?" Not waiting for permission, the girl jumped up and reached with a dirty hand to stroke her wing.

Evie slapped Irena's hand away. "No, you may not." She snapped her fingers in front of the girl's stunned face. "Focus. Where is Aurora? Why is she not with the group?"

"Aurora will go to the village when she's ready." It was Hagen the hunter. He'd come up to them so quietly Evie hadn't even noticed him until he spoke. "Rest time is over," Hagen said to the group. "Irena, I'll talk to Aurora's friend. You go help the boys carry that thing home."

The girl who'd been staring at Evie with wide eyes quickly took up her place at the rear and slipped one of the rope slings attached to the frame over her shoulders. At the count of three the group heaved as one to get the heavy burden off the ground and they moved towards the village at a slow shuffle.

Hagen turned back to face Evie. "Things got a bit lively and Aurora went full furry to keep the critters off the youngsters. She's changing back."

"Is she all right?"

The hunter gestured for her to wait. Once the group was out of earshot he said, "Aurora had a tussle with the big one further up from where we were. I went to go have a look once things quieted down. She'd taken it down with only a few scratches but it got her beast mightily riled up. I've seen this before. The girl just needs some time by herself to calm down and she will be right as rain. Aurora didn't want the others to see her like that so we agreed I'd lead them home and she'll come to the village when she's ready. She carries such a fierce creature inside it can't be easy on her keeping a lid on it. Once it's out it must be mighty trying to put it back and walk among us mere humans."

"Is there anything I can do for her? To help I mean."

"You could go get her some clothes. Those lizards tore right through where she left her things and I'd be surprised if there are more than a few shreds left to cover herself with. I didn't want to say it in front of the others in case the young men got it into their head to try for a peek but Aurora is partial to a swim after a hunt. There are several good swim spots around the rocks. A person who can fly should be able to spot Aurora if she's gone that way."

Evie grabbed the man's gnarled, work-roughened hands and squeezed. "Thank you."

"You're welcome young lady. I can see you're very worried about our Aurora. She could do with someone looking out for her and she needs a bit of caring for. Seeing how you're also a shifter I reckon you'd be able to see to her better than we can."

Evie took to the skies again and found the spot where Aurora must have fought with the blue razorback with ease as it looked like a tornado had set down in that area. Trees lay broken, jagged shards of wood littered the area and the earth looked like it had been churned over by giant claws. Wanting to have a better look she landed carefully amid the debris. As soon as she put her feet down she wished she'd stayed in the air. There was blood splattered in thick drops clinging from branches and in shallow dark pools on the forest floor drawing flies. Her stomach roiled at the sight and she wanted to leave the area immediately but she was determined to make sure Aurora didn't lie somewhere nearby injured or dying from a wound she'd hidden from Hagen.

It took Evie a little while to figure out which way to go. Taking a good look around she decided to follow what seemed to be the path of destruction. When she found the dead razorback her mouth dropped open and she stared in incomprehension. Was there really a gigantic sixteen-foot lizard impaled on a tree by its own spikes? How was that even possible? The thing looked like it weighed several tons. It would take many men to lift and yet somehow it was several feet off the ground stuck upright to the trunk of a forest giant. What kind of being possessed the strength and will to do such a thing? Aurora did this? How? Going closer she noticed the blue razorback was missing its tail and had been ripped open from throat to belly despite the underside being armored like a crocodile's hide. Something about the chest and stomach areas looked wrong. Holding her breath against the reek of blood and spilled guts she picked up a long branch and pulled back the torn hide to have a look inside. The chest cavity had been broken open like one would crack a crab's shell and she saw marks that were made by either giant claws or teeth as something tore into the razorback's insides. Whatever it was had fed on the great lizard devouring all the vital organs and huge chunks of flesh leaving a hollowed-out husk behind.

Evie dropped the stick and took a step back, her mind reeling and struggling to understand what she was seeing. Was this Aurora's beast at work? Or did something else come upon the carcass and have an opportunistic feed? If so what if it was still around? Evie looked around herself nervously. The forest was way too quiet and she didn't hear a single bird. This was not a good place to be. Scavengers would be drawn to the smell of blood and could be watching her from the shadows. Evie launched herself into the air. Her wing complained at the hard lift but she ignored the discomfort, relieved to be high above the forest canopy out of reach of whatever monsters lurked beneath.

Needing a few minutes to settle her thoughts Evie soared above the forest. She felt awed and more than a little shaken by what she had seen. She found it difficult to reconcile the gentle Aurora she knew with the violent force that tore into the giant lizard and killed it in such a spectacular manner. The scale of the destruction and the force with which the razorback had been slammed into the tree spoke of an enraged creature set on utterly decimating its enemy. Was this what happened when Aurora allowed her beast out? Was this what Hagen meant when he said she carried such a fierce creature inside that she needed time to calm down after she let it out? Evie took a deep breath and slowly let it out. She needed to get a grip on herself. She could not allow Aurora to see her unsettled about what she'd seen in the forest. Aurora was sensitive about what she could become when she took on her beast form and had expressed on more than one occasion her concern that Evie would be repelled or scared seeing her like that. If she caught even a hint of distress on Evie she would read it as fear of her and possibly even as a delayed rejection because of everything she'd told her the previous night. That would wound her and she would shut herself away from

Evie as surely as the sun sets in the evening. Not going to happen. She would not allow it. She would find Aurora and even if she was still a beast with blood on her muzzle she would look her in the eye without flinching. Bolstered by her determination she headed towards the village to go get Aurora a change of clothing.

***

A massive tiger the size of a draft horse hauled itself out of the water. Its eyes focused on Evie as it came towards her with unnerving feline grace, its powerful muscles rippling under sleek wet fur.

"Aurora, please tell me that's you...because if it's not I'm going to need a change of pants."

The tiger made a noise that sounded like the human equivalent of a snort. "Were you expecting another tigress?" The tiger, wet from its swim sidled up to her and vigorously shook itself, bathing Evie in a shower of salty drops.

"Eeew." Evie used her wing to shield herself from the spray. "You smell like wet cat. I thought cats don't like water."

"Tigers enjoy swimming and I like to be clean."

Evie opened her mouth to say something about cats licking themselves clean but the gleam in the tigress's eyes made her hesitate. This was Aurora but with entirely too many teeth.

"Time to change. Don't look, Evie."

"Why? I've seen you naked. More than seen you…"

"It's not about that. Seeing me change back could be upsetting."

"I'm not a delicate hothouse flower," Evie huffed. "I've seen other shapeshifters change form and I was fine. I was really hoping to see your warrior form at least once. I've now seen you in full fur why not show me the rest? Please, Aurora?"

The tigress studied her with head slightly cocked. It was such a familiar gesture Evie felt herself relax. "I'll show you my mixed form but if you scream I will be deeply offended. If you faint I'll just let you fall. Understood?"

Evie popped her hands on her hips and said, "Stop procrastinating, Aurora. If you're going to show me do it."

Evie watched as the massive beast reared up on its hind legs. There was a shimmer around it and the air felt charged, similar to the feeling in the air just before a lightning storm hit. The creature's body grew while its skin rippled. Within a few heartbeats Aurora was towering a gigantic ten feet tall and so broad across that Evie doubted she could touch her from shoulder to shoulder with her arms spread. Standing in front of her was a creature that could inspire nightmares and epic songs, a peculiar blend of human and feline predator that Evie's brain found hard to process. She was fascinated despite the alarm that made her heart hammer rapidly in her chest. She noted the most prominent features: the thick muscular limbs, the clawed feet and hands, the fur covered body topped with a head that had both human and feline features. The huge head with pointy tiger's ears tilted and amber eyes with flecks of green gave her a cautious look.

Evie inclined her head and did a dramatic clap. "Yes, tiger-girl, that's quite something. But see, no fainting or screaming over here."

The beast made an amused huffing noise. It bent down until they were almost eye to eye and smiled, showing teeth and a set of fangs that would have made a sabertooth weep with envy if one was around to see it. Evie felt her breathing become uneven and she swallowed hard.

"You've made your point, Aurora. You can be scary when you want to be." She was going for nonchalant but her voice sounded shaky even to her.

The beast immediately stepped back, a shudder ran through its body and Aurora shifted so fast one moment Evie was looking at a gigantic beast the next a woman who appeared entirely human. The sudden change was so startling that for a moment she had the two images superimposed over each other in her mind's eye. She'd always thought of Aurora as a tall, strong woman. After seeing what she could become she seemed small, almost frail and very vulnerable in her nakedness.

Evie raked her eyes over Aurora's body and greedily drank her in. She loved the way Aurora's hair floated like it was charged with ethereal current. The sight of Aurora's chocolate tipped nipples and the dark tuft of hair that covered her sex made her feel giddy. Evie realized she was breathing hard and incredibly aroused. Some part of her knew the intensity of her reaction and the timing of it was partly a delayed stress reaction. Her body looking for a way to purge all the adrenaline it had pumped into her muscles priming her for a rapid flight at seeing Aurora's beast form. All of that energy now channeled into her physical attraction to Aurora in a fierce surge of lust.

"You're so gorgeous. Your body looks like it was sculpted by the gods. Seeing you like this is making me think wicked thoughts about what we could do to each other on a leafy bed in the forest." Evie saw

Aurora's breasts contract to hard points and the way her stomach muscles clenched before she quickly put on her bra and yanked on the long t-shirt to cover herself.

"Evie, you can't look at me like that right now."

"Why not?"

Aurora scowled and slipped on the blue briefs Evie had chosen for her followed by her jeans. Evie felt stung by Aurora's response. She'd been missing her touch like an ache and she'd been hopeful once they were alone they would continue where they'd left off that morning. Unfortunately, it was clear Aurora had no such intentions even though her body said she was aroused by Evie's suggestion. Evie suppressed a sigh along with her raging libido and changed tack.

"Is it hard to come back from your beast form?"

"Yes. Sometimes I don't want to come back at all."

"Oh. That's not what I meant but okay. Why not?"

"Life seems simpler. The things that pain me drift away until there is only the purity of the hunt and the thrill of battle. Pitting my wits against that of another until only one of us remains. Life or death. Nothing else matters."

"Not even love?"

Aurora gave Evie an inscrutable look and sat down to put on her shoes. "Thanks for bringing my clothing. I dreaded having to sneak back to the village in what little was left of my other outfit. I was contemplating staying furry until I reached the room."

"I also brought you one of the guavas I saved from my meal. It's not much but I figured you'd be starving."

"Thanks, but I'm not hungry."

Evie stared at her incredulously. "Aurora, you are *always* hungry."

"I just ate."

"What did you eat? Don't tell me it was you who chewed on that thing back there? It had most of its insides missing."

"I would have preferred you didn't see that. Yes, it was me. My beast was hungry and that creature was fresh kill I took down myself. I didn't eat it in front of you. I remember how you feel about that kind of thing."

"I was joking. I didn't think you'd eat raw meat straight from a carcass."

"You forgot what I told you. I must see to the needs of my beast or I risk running into trouble. It was angry and hungry but now it's calm and well fed. This means I can have an entire evening surrounded by lots of people and as long as nothing alarming happens it will slumber."

Evie mentally slapped herself. She had just done the very thing she promised herself she wouldn't do and made an issue of something that was a sensitive topic for Aurora. Backtracking she said, "I didn't mean to make it sound like I was judging you. I'm glad you got to have a filling meal for a change. It must be awful to be hungry all the time. By the way, your tiger is much bigger than I expected and your mixed form is humongous. I'm seriously impressed. No wonder the wolf-shifters were quivering in their boots and treated you so carefully. You could have them for lunch!"

Aurora nodded thoughtfully and said, "According to my father his people are the largest and most powerful feline shifters in all of Nordarra. Where they roam the creatures they hunt are much larger than them but they thrive on the challenge and even the dragons treat them with respect."

"No way…are you serious? I thought nothing could take on a dragon and win."

"Well, according to my dad his clan and the dragons had a bloody feud but after a while it became clear they were too equally matched for either side to rise as the clear victor so they agreed to call a truce. Dragons dominate the skies and can destroy almost anything but eventually they must land and a tiger with a grudge will stalk an enemy relentlessly until it corners its prey. In a surprise attack, almost nothing can survive a fully grown tiger's strike at the neck or spine and on the ground, a tiger-shifter has the advantage over a dragon because of its agility. The tigers used to go after the dragons' wings to ground them but that didn't assure a win because even with its wings torn a dragon is still a ferocious opponent. A dragon is well armored and once it goes into a battle rage it won't stop until either it or the enemy is dead. My father said there were many accounts of tigers and dragons found dead, either near each other or still locked in battle, even in death. The losses were terrible on both sides and even though the dragons killed a lot more tigers there are fewer of them and they don't produce many children so they felt it equally. So the dragons and tigers called a truce, agreed they were equals and have avoided each other ever since."

"Wow…that's the first I've heard about a war between the tigers and dragons."

"Unless a dragon or a tiger from my father's clan told you it's unlikely you would have."

"I suppose that means avians owe your father's clan a big thanks for cutting down the dragon population."

"Why is that a good thing?"

"They used to hunt my people for sport. So I've been told."

"So you've been told?"

"You know how it is with the old stories…facts get mixed up so it's hard to know what's true. Besides, we haven't had a dragon go on a rampage or destroy a tower in my lifetime. I only know for a fact they used to do that kind of thing because my grandmother was one of the few survivors after an enraged dragon destroyed their tower. She was a child when it happened but she said it was something she would never forget. The dragon attacked at night. By morning all that was left of two hundred avians and their magnificent tower was a handful of survivors, rubble, feathers, and blood. That's what our dawn songs are about: surviving dragons that come in the night. You know the one you heard me sing in the mine that drew you to find me and save me and the wolves from that terrible place? That song is about surviving the night and the monsters that come in the dark to greet the new day. The monsters we refer to are the dragons but because we believe to use their name in song might draw one we never refer to them directly."

Aurora stared at Evie for several seconds then she threw her head back and laughed. She laughed so hard she had tears running down her face.

"What's so funny? Aurora?"

Aurora wiped tears from her eyes. After taking a few deep breaths to steady herself she said, "It's just so ironic that you singing a song about surviving monsters that come in the dark got you rescued by the likes of me."

"I still don't get why that's funny. You are not a dragon or a monster."

"Some people will disagree with you. I've been called a monster more times than I care to remember."

"That's stupid. Just because you can shift into a large beast and prefer to move around at night doesn't make you a monster. It makes you a nocturnal predator." At Aurora's raised eyebrow Evie replayed what she'd just said and felt her cheeks heat. "Granted that doesn't sound much better but you know what I mean."

Grinning Aurora said, "That doesn't sound good at all but I get you're trying to say you don't see me as a monster and I'm grateful for that."

There was the sound of their names being called and they both turned to look. Around the bay on an outcropping of rocks two women stood waving. Aurora lifted a hand and waved back. In response one of the women made a beckoning motion and pointed to the village.

"Evie, I think that's our sign to head back."

"Before we go there is something I have to tell you. I messed up. I accidentally told Aida that you're leaving. She was talking about how they were going to ask you to become Tove's godmother and how that would make you come visit more often and I said it wasn't going to happen. She cornered me and I had to explain why I said that. I'm so sorry, it just slipped out."

"I see."

"Are you upset?"

"No. I did have to tell them and you just moved things along quicker than I would have liked."

"When were you going to tell them?"

"Just before we left tomorrow. I thought it would be easier that way."

"Aurora! Seriously? Easier for whom? Your friends would have felt hurt if you didn't give them an opportunity to say goodbye properly."

"You think so?"

"I know so."

"Oh. I didn't want to hurt anyone. It seems you did a good thing by letting it slip I'm leaving Nordarra. What did Aida say when you told her?"

"She didn't say much but she seemed upset and sad."

"She was?"

"I think she sees you as a daughter or at least as one of her brood."

"Aida told me as much but I wasn't sure if she just said that to be nice. People do that sometimes. If Aida is upset with me, I'm going to get a fierce telling off. Or tears. I can't decide which is more terrifying." Aurora took a deep breath and rolled her shoulders a few times like she was preparing to grapple with a fierce opponent. "Race you back to the village?"

"You could never beat me," Evie scoffed. "Wings remember?"

Aurora gave her a sideways glance. "Wanna bet?"

Before Evie could reply Aurora took off in a blur of motion. In the few seconds it took her to realize the race was on Aurora had already covered a good distance bounding over the rocks in huge leaps. Evie launched herself into the air and pursued Aurora flying low and fast. She caught up to her on the last few meters and they entered the village together in a rush of speed and the whoosh of wings that had villagers scattering. Aurora laughed and turned her face upward to flash Evie a smile full of mischievous delight. That look made laughter bubble up in Evie's chest and it spurred her on to continue their game.

***

"You're such a cheat!" Evie shouted at Aurora as she swooped past close enough to ruffle her hair.

Aurora enjoyed their impromptu game and still high on adrenaline and the thrill of having Evie chase her, she laughed and said, "I was just evening the odds, you have wings remember. Don't be a sore loser."

"I did not lose! We got here at the same time."

Evie circled back for landing and swooped past Aurora again to give her a playful blast of air from her wings. She flew so near Aurora got the smell of feathers mixed with the scent of Evie's body that was now as familiar to her as Evie's face. It was the most glorious and magnificent smell and so shortly after a shift it stirred her at a primal level. Like an addict craving a bigger hit she covered her mouth so no one would see and flicked an inhumanly long tongue to catch the air particles. She knew she was playing with fire drawing on her other beast as it was more aggressive than her tiger and harder to deny once called upon but it had senses her tiger did not. She was instantly rewarded with the taste of Evie's excitement at the game and a tantalizing hint of her arousal which registered sweet and hot like spice in her mouth. Too quickly the taste dissolved like a snowflake on her tongue. She rumbled her frustration and watched Evie with hooded eyes. She shouldn't have resisted Evie's offer of sex. She should have buried her face in the source of that taste and drunk her full. Mesmerized she watched Evie land. Taking in the magnificence of her wings Aurora marveled at the colors reflecting off Evie's feathers in the late afternoon sun so it looked like she was decked with jewels that glittered in shades of gold and crimson. So beautiful. Evie was a shimmering, winged goddess worthy of adoration and pursuit. As the thought echoed through her mind Aurora felt a surge of possessive longing so raw and fierce in its intensity it shook her.

Landing complete Evie smiled as she walked towards Aurora. It was a broad joyous smile that shone with warmth and affection and Aurora found she was smiling too. There were villagers all around them but

Aurora's awareness of them faded to inconsequential. All that mattered to her at that moment was the woman of her dreams striding towards her with wings still slightly raised like open arms. Caught up in the moment Aurora took a step forward, her own arms reaching for Evie. She knew exactly what she would do next. She would scoop Evie up and kiss her passionately. Then she would stomp the ground until the earth shook and roar her intent to claim the beautiful woman as a mate so anyone bold and foolish enough to fight her for the right could come forward. She would kill all the challengers and lay their corpses at the feet of her queen as proof of her devotion. As the night descended over the crimson sky she would carry Evie away to her lair. There she would make love to her all night long while she told her over and over how much she loved her.

She was only a few feet from Evie when Aurora came to her senses. She stopped in her tracks like she'd been gut-punched and dropped her arms acutely aware of the rapid pounding of her own heart. She felt her beast raging at her, urging her to take Evie, compelling her to claim what she wanted most. But it had no power over her now that she realized what was going on and she shoved it back hard. Aurora was furious with herself for letting it get this far and felt the acid churn of fear in her gut at what had almost happened. It was her own out-of-control emotions and her intense desire for Evie that had brought this on. She should never have acted on impulse, drawing on that beast and allowing it close to the surface when she was in such an unsettled state. She hadn't done anything so profoundly stupid in a long time.

Aurora looked at the ground by her feet because no matter how expressionless her face Evie seemed to know exactly what was going on with her just by looking into her eyes and she didn't want Evie to see her turmoil. She drew on her years of experience to force her beast into a slumber. When it was done she let out a long breath, dizzy with relief. She'd been moments away from outing herself as more than a tiger-shifter and she would have terrified her friends by acting like a lust-crazed beast. She also would have horrified and embarrassed Evie with such a barbaric display. No woman wanted to be subjected to a public declaration of love and a desire to become a mated pair when in private they had only expressed words of affection. Evie was her friend first and her lover only temporarily. For Evie, it was just 'an affectionate sharing between friends', as she put it, and even though she'd made it clear she enjoyed their coupling and wanted to do it again, to her it was just sex.

Nothing more. She'd been lonely a long time and Evie happened to come along when she was vulnerable and touched her in ways she no longer dared hope was possible. It wasn't Evie's fault she had fallen head over heels in love with her. To think for a moment it had seemed perfectly logical to present Evie, who recoiled at the thought of Aurora eating the bloody meat of her kill, with the eviscerated bodies of slain rivals as proof she was a worthy mate. No matter what happened she would never let that beast near the surface again while Evie or any woman she was seriously interested in was around because its idea of courtship would get her labeled as psychotic.

"Aurora, what's wrong?" Evie spoke softly as if she was afraid if she raised her voice above a whisper she might spook Aurora.

Looking up Aurora saw Evie was right in front of her. The happy smile she bore moments ago had been replaced by a frown and she looked at Aurora with troubled uncertain eyes.

"Did the chasing game get your beast riled up?"

Aurora wanted to soothe the frown and the worried lines from Evie's face with her fingers but she knew that under no circumstances could she allow herself to touch her. Evie's touch affected her even more powerfully than her scent. The two together was a potent mix that hit her with such force she was left dazed and defenseless, bound to give in to her more primal desires.

"Something like that," she said telling a half-truth. "I really enjoyed our game. I'm sorry it ended with me getting weird. I hope I didn't frighten you."

Evie's frown deepened. She opened her mouth to speak but was interrupted by a commotion as the curious crowd they had drawn during their race parted for the broad shape of Aida baring down on them like a ship heading for the dock.

"Aurora…there you are. We must have a talk, young lady. Right now."

Aida's voice was loud and held an angry edge but her face was flushed and her eyes looked bruised like she'd been crying. Despite knowing the conversation with Aida would be uncomfortable she was thankful for the interruption. Surely it couldn't be worse than a determined Evie wanting to know what had just happened? She gave Evie an apologetic half smile and let Aida put an arm through hers to lead her away.

"What's this I hear about you going away, my girl? Tell me it's not true?"

Aurora groaned inwardly. From the frying pan into the fire.

CHAPTER 22

LOVERS

After their return to the village, Evie didn't see Aurora again until dinner. One of the village women collected her and directed her to a seat in the meeting hall. She was surprised and disappointed she wasn't seated beside Aurora but at least they were at the same table. The evening meal had become an impromptu feast and aside from the food that appeared from the kitchen women emerged from their homes laden with special treats and baked goods. It didn't take a genius to figure out word of Aurora leaving Nordarra had circulated and that this was the villagers' way of showing their fondness for a woman who took her food very seriously. It didn't escape her attention that Aurora dutifully added something to her plate from every dish and repeatedly declared how delicious everything was loud enough for everyone to hear. This brought smiles and nods of approval from the villagers.

After dinner the men and children built a bonfire above the high tide mark on the beach and soon people sprawled around it on blankets and chairs. An elderly man, with so much facial hair that Evie could hardly see his mouth move when he spoke, guided her to a high bench saying it was her special seat. Personally, she would have preferred a chair but she realized he thought he was being kind by offering her a seat that would accommodate her wings so she thanked him with a bright smile. As far as Evie was concerned the only good thing about the hard wooden bench was its location. She'd been placed directly opposite from where Aurora was holding court on the other side of the fire. She wasn't alone for a minute. People drifted in to talk to her all the time. As soon as one person got up another took the seat beside her. From her perch Evie saw the way Aurora interacted with the villagers and how at ease she seemed with them, laughing and smiling as with old friends. What caught her attention in particular, probably because she was looking for it, was the way Astrid kept an eye on Aurora. She pretended to be playing with her children and listening to the people around her but her attention was never away from Aurora for long. Evie knew she was way too fixated on another woman watching Aurora but she couldn't help it. She had a feeling Astrid was waiting for an opportunity to catch Aurora by herself and even though she had no right to act like a protective girlfriend she felt like one.

Evie watched out of the corner of her eye as Astrid said something to the big man next to her who nodded then gathered their kids and ushered them away, presumably to bed. As soon as Astrid approached Aurora sat up straighter. Astrid said something to her and after a moment's hesitation Aurora got up and followed Astrid to a spot a little further away from the fire. They sat down across from each other, their faces in profile, their knees not quite touching. Over the sound of people laughing and talking and the loud crackling of the fire Evie couldn't hear their conversation. Not for the first time she wished she had the hearing of a wolf, although maybe in this case it was better that she couldn't hear. Just seeing the two of them so close together made her nervous. She considered looking elsewhere but only briefly; she had to know what was going on.

Astrid was talking, her hand motions becoming increasingly agitated until Aurora stilled them in her own. She touched Astrid's face once then started to speak. Evie could see that the woman was hanging onto every word Aurora said. Her entire body arched towards her and tension tightened her frame. She started to cry. Evie held her breath as she half expected Aurora to take Astrid into her arms to comfort her but to her relief she just kept talking. Even though she couldn't hear it Evie could imagine the soothing tone of Aurora's voice and the way it deepened and resonated when she was serious. She said something that made Astrid bark a laugh and she wiped away her tears. She replied with something that had Aurora grinning and then, in a move that had Evie gritting her teeth, she put her arms around Aurora's neck and drew her down so they were cheek to cheek to whisper in her ear. When she pulled away they both looked solemn. It was hard for Evie to be sure with the flickering firelight but she thought Aurora's cheeks looked rosier than before. Astrid stood up and smiled down at the seated woman for a long moment, her expression tender and affectionate. Then she gave Aurora a nod and made her way around the outside edge of the fire disappearing in the same direction her family had gone.

Aurora watched her leave then her eyes sought Evie. Their eyes caught and held across the fire. Aurora only looked away when someone put a hand on her shoulder to get her attention. Evie realized she'd been holding her breath. The weight of Aurora's gaze had been so intense and so heavily laden with unspoken things she had felt it as keenly as a touch. She exhaled slowly and felt the shakiness in her hands. She stared down at them in astonishment. How could someone affect her so much with just a look?

Another hour passed with people coming to talk to and presumably say goodbye to Aurora. A fiddler started to play. Soon he was joined by a flute player, two guitarists and a man with a pair of hand drums. Their music was cheerful and a little rowdy. Couples and older kids who had not yet been rounded up by their parents were dancing around the bonfire amidst laughter and friendly jeering. Normally Evie would have joined in as she loved to dance but instead she politely refused several offers. She wasn't in the mood to dance, not with any of the people who asked her anyway. She was waiting. She wasn't sure for what but she knew for whom. She busied herself talking to those around her but afterwards she could not clearly remember who she had said what to. She was in a haze, her focus on the woman on the other side of the fire, everyone else merging into the nondescript blur of faces. She was thankful she grew up in a tower with people around all the time. All those conversations about nothing had honed her ability to ask questions and smile attentively to keep the other person talking while she said very little.

The moment Evie saw Aurora excuse herself from talking to an elderly man to make her way around the fire towards Evie her attention snapped back to focus. She folded her wings more tightly and scooted a little on the bench creating space for Aurora to sit next to her. They were finally going to talk. About time.

"It's been a long day, Evie. You're welcome to go to the room if you want to sleep."

Evie didn't know what she expected Aurora to say, but that definitely wasn't it. Before she could stop herself she snapped, "What am I? A feeble old woman who needs a nap?"

Aurora stared clearly taken aback by her response. "I just thought you might be tired."

"Are you going to the room now?"

"No. I'm going to stay here and talk to people for a while longer. It will probably get very late."

Evie had a suspicion Aurora wasn't planning on coming to bed at all. Not while she was in it waiting for her. The thought stung. She thought about confronting Aurora about that but things had been strained between them since she so gracelessly turned down her invitation to go away with her. Afterwards Aurora pretended it was a spur-of-the-moment thought and that she didn't take her refusal to heart but Evie knew that wasn't true. When Aurora had asked her she had looked so vulnerable and cautiously hopeful like she expected a refusal but gathered her courage to ask anyway. When Evie turned her down Aurora's shutters had come down hard. From kissing Evie passionately and being moments away from taking her on the spot, Aurora had withdrawn. She was still friendly but it hadn't escaped Evie's notice that whenever she reached for her Aurora moved ever so slightly, avoiding the contact. It was so subtly done the first time she'd thought she imagined it, by the third she recognized it for what it was. It left her feeling hurt and unsure of how to approach Aurora. She'd grown so used to the physical and emotional closeness they shared. She loved knowing she'd been allowed close in ways others had not and it had made her happy to see the way Aurora responded to her touch, leaning into her as though she unconsciously sought more of a connection. That closeness was gone. Now even though Aurora sat close enough to be heard over the sound of the music she was ever so slightly out of reach in every way that mattered.

Evie felt her temper flare. She hated that Aurora would withdraw so much so quickly just because she wouldn't go away with her. She was being utterly unreasonable. She wanted to grab her and shatter the barrier between them so that she could feel again the intense heat of the woman who had made love to her with such fervor. Just the briefest memory of their night together made her breasts feel heavy and swollen with need. Astrid was right, Evie thought resentfully. Aurora was like a fierce flame. She set her lover on fire and everything seemed brighter and more vibrant when she was around. When she withdrew it left a terrible chill so that it felt like the world had become a darker place. Well, she'd had enough of this nonsense. Aurora still wanted her, of that she was sure. She'd caught Aurora staring numerous times, her looks so smoldering Evie was surprised her clothes hadn't melted off her body. She would play dirty if that was what it took to get past her defenses. If Aurora was so afraid to touch her then she had to find a reason that they had to touch. That gave Evie an idea.

"Dance with me?" Aurora looked so startled Evie felt she should repeat the question in case she hadn't heard her properly. "Aurora, will you dance with me?"

"I can't."

"So not with me…" Evie's heart dropped. "Someone else perhaps? Maybe that pretty girl who talked to you for ages?"

"No!" Aurora looked shocked. "No, Evie," she said more quietly. "If I was going to dance with anyone it would be with you but…" Aurora opened her hands in a helpless gesture, "I don't know how. Not like what they are doing, not with a partner. I never learned. It looks easy but I'm sure I'll step on your toes or trip you up."

"You're in luck. I'm an excellent dancer and I know how to lead. I will teach you. Trust me, you'll be in good hands."

When Aurora hesitated Evie said, "We can practice on the beach. Come on, it'll be fun." Evie playfully bumped shoulders with Aurora. "Just look how much everyone is enjoying themselves. I promise I won't complain if you step on my toes. Besides dancing is a great skill to have and it will help you mingle. It would be a shame to turn down my offer. What do you say?"

Smiling Aurora said, "You're very persuasive. How can I possibly refuse when you put it like that? It does look like fun and I've always wanted to learn."

"Good."

Standing, Evie arched her back and her wings to get rid of the kink she'd gotten from sitting so long. "Oof, that hard bench did a number on my butt." She rubbed her behind absently. "The dancing will do me good, loosen up the muscles."

Next to her Aurora rose in a fluid motion and gave Evie a lingering appreciative look. "Evie, you'll give someone a heart attack stretching like that."

"Really? Who?"

"Me for starters. Although I'm sure I'm not the only one."

"Ha, I'm not interested in anyone else looking. Come on, let's go find a less crowded spot in case you're as terrible a dancer as you claim."

"I didn't say I am terrible, I said I don't know how to dance. I'm a fast learner so if you're as good as you say I'm sure I'll get it quickly."

"As I said, you're in good hands."

Evie entwined her arm with Aurora's who, to her relief, didn't stiffen or pull away but tucked her closer, offering herself as a support on the uneven sandy surface. Evie wasn't at risk of stumbling but she leaned into Aurora a little so she would know the gesture was appreciated. Aurora led them to a spot on the edge of the firelight. Close enough for them to still hear the music but far enough away that the sound of the beating surf was louder, adding its own refrain to the music. Overhead the moon was clear and bright, the air warm with only the slightest sea breeze stirring Aurora's hair so it seemed to float a little.

"Will over here work?"

"This is perfect." Evie hesitated not wanting to spoil the mood but she had to ask the question that had been on her mind. "Are you angry with me?"

"I'm not angry with you, why would you think so?"

"This is the first time since we got here that you've let me touch you. You've kept me at a distance. What am I to make of it?"

"Oh." Aurora's shoulders sagged a little and her expression became guarded.

"Talk to me? Please tell me what's going on. I'm still your friend remember? Just because we slept together that shouldn't change. I don't like how you pulled away from me so suddenly after everything we've shared."

"Evie, I…I'm not used to being so open and the things I told you have left me feeling raw and exposed. Then there's what happened between us… I don't do casual sex and it's been a long time since I've been romantically involved so that was big for me. I should have stepped back a little to gather myself but instead I rushed in and asked you to go away with me despite knowing you're eager to get back to your life. When you said no it was like a bucket of cold water to the face but that was a good thing. It made me realize I was getting way too attached to you and that I had to put a little distance between us because after tomorrow I'll probably never see you again."

"So, you were just trying to protect yourself?"

"And you..."

"No, don't do that. I'm a big girl, don't presume to know what I want or need. I make my own decisions."

"Evie, what *do* you want?"

"Right now? Right now, I want to dance with you. I want you to hold me while we move together to the music. Is that too much to ask?"

"No. I can do that. Once you show me how. You might not be so keen after I've stepped on your feet a few times. You're so dainty and your bones so light I'm worried I'll crush your toes with my big feet."

Evie laughed and squeezed Aurora's arm. "You should know by now that I'm not nearly as fragile as I look." She drew Aurora into her arms and positioned her hands where she wanted them. "Put your hands on me like so. Move closer. Feel me move. Yes…like that. No, don't look at your feet, just follow my lead. Feel where I'm going."

They danced slowly and hesitantly at first as Evie guided Aurora through a series of basic steps. She did catch on quickly and despite a few missteps Evie's toes remained intact.

"You were right this is so much fun! I should have tried it years ago." Aurora's smile was wide, her cheeks flushed with the joy of her success.

"Why didn't you?"

"I didn't have someone as amazing as you to teach me."

"I told you I was good," Evie said with a grin.

Aurora threw her head back and laughed. "Ever modest. Never change, Evie."

"I have to tell you the moves I'm showing you are best suited for dancing with a winged partner. But the principles are sound and with a little adjustment you can make it work with just about anyone."

They kept dancing, their bodies becoming more in sync with every step until they glided effortlessly together. Evie marveled at how naturally Aurora took into account the width of her wings on the turn and the way she held her like they'd danced many times before. Aurora's hand on Evie's back moved into the warm fold of her wings. She caressed the sensitive joint between back and wing, an area Evie found so erogenous it made her shiver, and she had to suppress a moan. If Aurora had fondled her breasts she could hardly have been more intimate. Did she realize this? The thought made Evie's nipples harden in arousal and she instinctively opened her wings a little to invite a deeper caress.

"Hmm…" Aurora's eyes closed and she inhaled deeply. "I love the scent that comes off you when you open your wings."

"Oh…what do I smell like?"

Aurora's eyes opened and she smiled shyly. "You'll probably think it sounds silly but the scent of your wings makes me think of the sweet, fresh fragrance of a meadow after the rain. Combine that with the warm tones of your body and the exquisite aroma when you're aroused…" Aurora inhaled and let out a shuddering breath. "Evie, your scent is a heady mix and it drives me wild."

"Wow…you smell pretty good yourself."

"I do?"

"Yes, you smell like…" Evie leaned close enough to inhale the warmth from Aurora's neck, "caramel, spice and something else. Hmm, so delicious, what is that?" Evie pressed even closer and again filled her lungs with Aurora's scent. When she exhaled her breath caressed Aurora's cheek. Aurora trembled and tightened her arms around Evie. Emboldened by how she was affecting her Evie whispered in her ear, "You smell like sex in the moonlight. Like a soft blanket before the fire with naked bodies on it."

Aurora turned a fraction so their eyes locked. Her gaze was so intensely heated Evie could feel her heart beat faster from the dark promise it held. Her breathing hitched and she felt like she wasn't getting enough air. Evie licked her lips and Aurora's gaze dropped to her mouth. That was all the invitation she needed. She unfurled her wings to create a cocoon of privacy for them then she pressed the entire length of her body against Aurora's and claimed her mouth with all the pent-up frustration and longing she'd been carrying all day.

***

Aurora didn't know quite how it happened. One moment they were just dancing having fun, the next they were all over each other kissing like their lives depended on it. She felt Evie shiver as she continued to stroke the sensitive connection between her back and wings. She felt Evie's ragged breaths in her hair and smelled Evie's desire, the hot fragrant need that was just for her, and it made her want to drag Evie to a sheltered place and rip her clothes off. It wasn't a tame spike of desire she could brush away, it was a surge of lust and want so intense she hurt from it. She wanted, no *needed* Evie naked under her. She wanted to kiss her until she was breathless. Wanted to fuck her senseless until she lay spent and utterly satisfied in her arms. She tried to be gentle but she was barely in control, kissing hard, her hands roaming under Evie's shirt, desperate to again feel the soft weight of naked breasts in her palms. She tried to slow down but Evie really wasn't helping. She was grinding her hip into Aurora's crotch, kissing with such fervor they both struggled to catch their breath and Aurora felt fingers tugging at the zipper of her jeans.

"Evie, wait..." She fumbled trying to contain the quick fingers. "Evie, if we don't stop we're going to end up naked on the spot."

"We're not stopping," Evie just about growled. "I'm not letting you an inch away from me. But..." she glanced over her spread wings that mostly hid them from the view of those still by the fire, "you're right not here. Hold on to me I saw an ideal spot earlier today."

"We're flying?" Aurora struggled to think past the lust haze. "Now? Why? Where to?"

"Yes, I'm flying us. I saw a lovely sheltered area up on the cliffs. I just need you to give me a little boost to get off the ground with our combined weight."

"Why not go to my room? We do have a bed so why not use it? No one goes into the warehouse at night so you can be as loud as you want – no one will hear."

"Aurora, I don't want to make love in a room where almost everything in it was made for you by a woman who is still carrying a torch for you. You might not get it but those things amount to the human equivalent of Astrid putting her scent all over your room. Sweetie, she put fresh flowers on your table, she made your bed and laid out towels with your name embroidered on it. That beautiful bedspread alone must have taken her months with all that fine detailed work."

"Oh." Aurora looked startled. "I honestly never thought about it like that. It's just something she's always done. It's like a hostess thing? A friendship thing? I help where I can and bring her family gifts, she keeps my room fresh and makes colorful pretty things to brighten it. Isn't that what friends do?" Aurora frowned, distress straining her voice. "Since the day she got engaged, we've never...you know. I couldn't. I'm all or nothing that's just how it is. Finn adores her. He's such a gentle, kind man and I really like him. He reminds me a little of my father and I would never do anything to—"

Evie sighed and pressed shaky fingers to Aurora's lips. "Hush...I'm sorry I shouldn't have brought it up. Maybe you're right and I am overreacting but I can't do it in there. I don't want you to be reminded of her in any way while we fuck and I want you so badly. I need you so please don't make me beg. This could be our last night and so much time has already gone. Let me spend what is left of it in your arms. You holding me like this, it's the most right I've felt since we got here."

Gently Aurora lifted Evie's chin so she could see her eyes. In the flickering reflection from the fire and the soft glow of the moon they shimmered, overfull with emotions and what Aurora feared were banked tears. She felt a sharp twist in her chest. She'd been selfish. She'd only thought of herself in keeping Evie away, afraid of what it would cost her to part from the beautiful woman if they made love again. She'd hurt her. Made her feel like she wasn't wanted, not desired. She would make love to Evie and show her how precious she was to her. That much she could do.

"Evie, you are so lovely. So wonderful. You make me weak with wanting you. I've had to hold myself back all day. Let's not waste another moment, take me wherever you want."

***

In the bright moonlight it didn't take Evie long to find the place she'd noticed during her flight that day. It was an opening high on a sheer cliff, wide enough for her to land in but sheltered from the elements. Inside she'd seen a thick covering of moss, the kind she knew to be soft and springy to the touch. It was an ideal place to bed down for the night when caught out away from the nest. As soon as she saw it she'd had a vivid fantasy of taking Aurora there and making love to her to the sound of the surf beating against the rocks far below. At the time it hadn't seemed like something likely to happen, not with the way Aurora was keeping her distance but she'd still marked the place in her mind.

She intended to slow things down once they landed because she wanted to savor every touch and kiss. She quickly realized Aurora had different plans. She barely got them down safely before Aurora lowered to her knees, snapped the tie that held up Evie's pants and peeled away her undies to caress her buttocks. A quick kiss on her bare stomach and the gentle hands shifted to take a firm grip, spreading and tilting her in one motion so her core was pressed against a hot mouth and she was being explored like she was a ripe fruit that Aurora was desperate to taste. She tried to speak but no coherent words came out and all she could do was grip Aurora's shoulders and hold on while her mouth, hot and demanding, plundered her. Her legs shook under the strain of standing amidst such an onslaught and she spread her wings, desperate for balance. A strong arm shifted to wrap around her hips anchoring her while she fell apart. Evie fisted her hands into Aurora's hair, arching so that she could have all the access she wanted. Confident her lover could and would support her weight Evie closed her eyes, drinking in the sensations, trying to memorize everything. The feel of the cool sea breeze on her bare skin and wings, the strength and warmth of Aurora's body bracing her, the intense heat of the tongue alternating between plunging her opening and lashing her clit with insistent strokes driving her higher and higher.

She was molten heat. She was on fire.

She would implode if she didn't climax soon.

Evie was dimly aware she was moaning and making frantic noises as she neared the crest. "Don't stop. Please don't stop. More. Yes, yes, yessss."

She cried out, bucking with the intensity of her release. Her legs gave way and she would have collapsed but Aurora had her. She lowered her gently taking extra care that Evie's wings didn't dig into the mossy earth beneath them. Evie briefly felt the cool air against her core left exposed by the absence of Aurora's mouth but then a warm hand slid between her thighs. Fingers caught the last tremors of her orgasm and explored her slick folds stroking the sensitive flesh with clear intent. Evie felt her body respond, eager even though she was still struggling to catch her breath from the last orgasm.

"You're going to kill me," Evie groaned as Aurora pushed her shirt and bra away to claim a nipple. "I'm still weak from the last one. You're supposed to let me recover so I can have my way with you."

"We've already established you won't die from multiple orgasms," Aurora murmured as she kissed her way up Evie's neck. "Whether you'll have the strength to walk tomorrow is another matter. I intend to use every minute until dawn to make love to you."

Evie gasped when Aurora playfully nipped her earlobe. "For someone who said she didn't want to do this again you're very enthusiastic."

"I never said I didn't want to make love to you. It has driven me near mad wanting to have you again; to kiss you, feel you, taste you. I've longed to have you touch me and hold me. I said I didn't think it was a good idea because I'm getting too attached to you. Two very different things. Now you are in my arms I'm going to show you how much I've wanted this."

"Just as well I can fly," Evie murmured. That was the last coherent thing she was able to say for a long while.

***

When Evie woke up, she found herself cradled in Aurora's arms. The light had changed and the moon was a sliver of silver amidst a smattering of stars in the clear sky.

"Aurora, why did you let me sleep? I thought you were going to make love to me until dawn."

"You passed out in my arms. You must have needed the rest."

Evie rolled over and slapped Aurora on the ass.

"A slap on the butt? Seriously? What for?"

"I can't believe you let me fall asleep like that. I wanted to take my time with you and now look, dawn is not far off and I haven't even had a proper taste."

"Really? By my count you had plenty," Aurora said with a chuckle. "By the way, there are better ways of showing your appreciation for my efforts than smacking me. Or is this your way of saying you're into kinky sex play?" Aurora made wide eyes at Evie, the corners of her mouth twitching with amusement.

Evie huffed. "This is frustration. You have this infuriating effect on me sometimes. It's the way you think, it messes with my head. Now if we miss our boat it will be your fault."

"How do you figure that?"

"Because I'm not letting you go until you've had an earth-shattering orgasm."

"I don't think that will be hard to pull off," Aurora said softly.

Slipping her hand between Aurora's legs Evie found her thighs slick with arousal, her clit so hard it felt like a tiny pebble. The muscles in her legs and torso twitched at Evie's touch.

"Oh wow…how could you stand being like this? You should've let me take care of you ages ago."

She had wanted to tease Aurora long and slow until she begged for release but Aurora had been like this for too long, pushing her own needs aside while pleasuring Evie over and over. To play with her would be cruel. What Aurora needed right now was to climax hard and have relief. She pushed Aurora's legs apart and settled herself between them. The heat that came off Aurora was intense, her smell rich and earthy, the taste of her like that of a delicious exotic fruit Evie could never get enough of. She used her lips and tongue to caress the slick folds and twirled the tip of her tongue around Aurora's clit. When she heard her moan she inserted first one finger then another, working in and out slowly. Taking her cue from the urgent way Aurora pressed into her hand and mouth she picked up the pace and thrust harder. She tried to make it last for Aurora but her need was too great and sensing she was about to peak Evie took her clit into her mouth and sucked hard. Immediately Aurora arched her back, her fingers dug into the moss while her muscles bunched and she threw her head back and a groan, low and guttural, wrenched from her body while she shook and came in waves that rippled through her body. Inside her, Evie felt the silken muscles grip her fingers hard over and over. The powerful surge of her release coated Evie's hand and it filled her with a fierce joy knowing she'd been both the source of Aurora's arousal and the instrument of her release.

When Aurora finally collapsed she draped an arm over her eyes covering her face. Evie withdrew carefully, kissed the inside of her thighs and her stomach then crawled up her length. She gathered the other woman close so that Aurora's head rested between her breasts. It didn't feel like enough so she tucked a leg over pulling her even tighter. She'd shifted her wings away to allow her lover to touch her skin on skin everywhere but now she regretted not having a wing to drape over Aurora because she had an intense desire to shield her. In the moment before she came their eyes had locked across the length of her naked body and what Evie had seen had shaken her. She had looked so vulnerable, bared by the intensity of her need and there had been a longing and a deep hunger burning in those eyes that spoke of something way beyond physical desire. Now in the aftermath of her orgasm Aurora's eyes were closed and her breathing rapid.

"Are you all right, sweetheart?"

Aurora wrapped an arm around Evie and kissed her neck. "Yes. You've undone me."

Evie couldn't help it, she giggled.

"What? What's so funny?" She tried to pull away but Evie tightened her arms and legs until Aurora got the message that she didn't intend to let her go.

"I had multiple orgasms and made so much noise I probably terrified the wildlife. You had one that lasted so long that I honestly worried it would kill you and when I ask how you are, you go all solemn and poetic on me. What an odd pair we are."

"Hmm." Aurora laid her head back down on Evie's chest, her breathing deep and even now. Relaxed. Gently, Evie stroked the side of her face, her hair and the expanse of bare back she could reach.

"I might have bitten you."

"Did you?" Evie tried to take stock. She didn't remember being bitten but she had been so aroused that just about anything Aurora did would have felt good and her limbs were still suffused with languid heat, dulling any potential aches. "Where?"

"I did bite you. Several times. Not hard but your skin is so creamy and delicate you'll probably bruise. I'm sorry about that. I wasn't deliberately putting my mark on you. I tried not to but I was so turned on I couldn't help myself. It's your scent. It excites my beast and drives me wild. I made a point not to break your skin or bite you where it can easily be seen. If you're careful with what you wear for a few days no one will know."

"Why do you think I'd care about something like that?"

"I didn't want to cause you problems when you get home. No need to explain what no one knows about."

"I suppose I should thank you for being considerate but frankly, I don't care if people know. Who I sleep with is my business."

"I'm glad you feel that way but there's no need to borrow trouble and you'll have enough to explain as it is. When it becomes known you traveled with me some people in your flock will be unhappy about that. You don't need visible love bites to complicate matters. You're the future ruler of House Aquilar and you'll need your allies and friends firmly around you, not whispers and rumors following you around."

Evie wanted to deny it but she knew, just like Aurora did, that for her as an avian to openly have a beast-shifter as a lover would have repercussions. Not just for herself but potentially for her entire House because of her status. It was one thing to discreetly take a walk on the wild side; people would pretend not to notice. Openly flaunting the bite marks of a beast-shifter was a different matter. It would send a public message about a very private relationship. Still, it irked her that Aurora felt she had to apologize for something she did in passion when she had once again given Evie one of the most memorable and fulfilling sexual experiences of her life.

"You still haven't told me where you bit me."

"On your butt, the inside of your thighs. Around that area. Only below the waistline."

"Hmm…I remember you did this thing where you sucked and bit down grazing me with your teeth. I enjoyed that."

"You seemed to and it made you climax hard."

Giggling Evie said, "I did indeed. You have my permission to do that any time you want, bite marks be damned. It is not like I intend to show my bare ass to anyone."

"I'm pleased to hear that."

"About the bites or me not showing my privates to anyone?"

"Both."

Aurora lifted herself up on an elbow and retrieved pieces of their clothing that lay within reach and draped it over them. She lay back down with her head on Evie's chest and sighed contentedly when Evie once again wrapped her arms around her and entwined their legs. Evie took the opportunity to play with Aurora's hair, loving the feel of silken strands pouring through her fingers.

"Is this all right? I'm not annoying you?"

"Love it." Aurora's voice was muffled and sleepy.

Smiling, Evie kept playing with Aurora's hair and before long she heard her breathing slow as she drifted off to sleep. Wide awake she watched the starry canopy slowly recede giving way to the early light of day while surf pounded rhythmically on the rocks below providing a comforting background drone. It felt good to trade places and be the one to keep watch while Aurora rested oblivious to the world. She enjoyed the way Aurora remained nestled against her and the way the warmth of their bodies mingled. She felt so content and safe with her and so vibrantly alive. She wished they could stay like this forever. She wished she could run away from all her responsibilities and go away with Aurora like she'd asked. What adventures they would have, what an amazing life together.

Evie's hand stilled. Wow, did she really just do that? Did she see herself and Aurora together not just for a few days or weeks but a lifetime? She'd never done that before with anyone, not even as a passing thought. The idea of being bound to someone and being with that person day in and out had always made her feel restless, constrained and slightly panicky. With Aurora she felt none of that. She wanted to be around her all the time and just the sound of Aurora's voice made her feel happy. The mind-boggling sex must have gone to her head. That's what brought this on. The woman was tireless and she knew how to strum Evie's body just so, hitting all the cords just right. Darn it. On top of that Aurora was so darkly facetted and intriguing, she had a body that would make angels weep in envy, she was smart, witty, talented and there was this undeniable connection between them. No wonder she was so intensely drawn to her. Who wouldn't want a chance at a life together with a woman like this? But Aurora was leaving

Nordarra and now they had even less time together than before. She could almost hear the clock ticking but if she allowed herself to focus on that she would be miserable and waste what little time they had left. Evie told herself not to mope or dwell on regrets. What was the point? There were no guarantees in life, all they had was now. She just had to make the most of every second she had with Aurora.

***

"We smell like sex."

"Hardly surprising all things considered. You do know how to get a girl going, Aurora."

"That I don't mind but I also have bits of moss wedged into places it really shouldn't go. We should have a swim. It'll be refreshing so early in the morning."

"By refreshing you mean we'll freeze our asses off."

"Not quite as bad as that but we will need to warm up after," Aurora admitted. "The water is deep down here but around the corner is a lovely stretch of beach we'll have all to ourselves until the tide turns. I'll race you there."

"There's no way you can descend this steep cliff; you'll fall and hurt yourself."

"I'm an excellent climber so I'd manage easily but I wasn't planning to climb down."

"No. You're not jumping from here, it's too high. You'll break something!"

"Wanna bet?"

"No, I don't."

"Don't worry, Evie, I do this kind of thing all the time. It gets the blood pumping. Bring our clothing to the beach?"

Before Evie could respond Aurora strode to the edge, turned to give her a mischievous wink and dove over the side in a flash of bare limbs. Evie rushed to the edge and with her heart in her throat watched her lover hurtle towards the ocean far below. She barely made a splash when she entered the water and after several long seconds her head popped up. She waved when she spotted Evie and gave a thumbs up.

"You're crazy!"

Aurora laughed and shouted, "Race you!" She started swimming towards the beach in long sure strokes that cleaved her through the water.

Evie measured the distance to shore and realized she had to hurry if she didn't want Aurora to beat her. She quickly gathered their clothing and bound everything together in a tight roll. She tried to find her panties but they were nowhere to be seen. She searched for fruitless minutes and finally concluded her panties probably went over the side. She was taking too long so she would just have to go without. Even if her panties were wedged into a hidden corner they were not in a wearable state anyway. Evie rushed her wings into form – it stung but only took minutes. Aurora had told her she would get faster the more she practiced but she was astounded how much she'd already improved. Helping her to shift properly was by far the greatest gift any lover had ever given her. Eager to show Aurora how quick she had shifted she took to the sky. The air as she flew to the sandy strip was frigid on her bare skin and Evie shuddered thinking what the water would be like. She landed and found a little alcove above the waterline to store their clothing just as Aurora waded up to her knees in the surf.

"Come on," Aurora said holding out her hands. "The water is lovely."

"You lie. Your nipples look hard enough to cut glass."

Aurora laughed and beckoned again, "Come."

Evie shifted her wings away then cautiously approached the water. She squealed when a wave crashed over her feet sprinkling her with icy drops. "The water is freezing!"

"Run in, that's the best way. Run and jump. If you're going to do something like this don't hesitate, don't think about it, embrace the experience." Aurora held her arms wide, "Come on, Evie. I'm waiting for you."

Screaming, Evie ran into the receding surf and when she came abreast with Aurora, she ran beside her. Together they stormed the water like it was a fortress to be conquered. Timing the waves Evie jumped. The water was so cold when she came up she was temporarily stunned. Instantly Aurora was beside Evie, her arms around her steading her, her strong legs defying the surge of the current to keep them more or less in one place.

"Lovely isn't it?"

"No, but you are." Evie wrapped her arms around Aurora's neck and kissed her soundly. Then she threw her head back and shouted, "This is amazing! I'm freezing my boobs off but I feel fantastic!"

"I told you," Aurora beamed.

"I've never done anything like this."

"Like what? Swim naked with your lover?" Aurora asked and gave Evie a gentle nip on the shoulder followed by a trail of warm open mouth kisses to the side of her neck.

"Definitely not that. Nothing like this, not with anyone. If you told me last week I'd be flying naked and early morning skinny dipping with a gorgeous woman who made love to me until I passed out I'd have written it off as wishful thinking. Thank you for this."

"Don't thank me yet. We still have to get out and get warmed up."

"Hmm…I can think of a fantastic way to warm up together."

Aurora laughed, her voice a clear happy bell. "I'm beginning to think you want to miss that boat."

"When is the next one?"

"Not for another week."

"That's too long. I'm needed back home and I *have* to get back. I'll have to fly to Porta Belua if we miss the boat."

"I know."

"I wish I could stay longer. I really do."

"Me too. You've made me happy."

"Just happy? Not ecstatically happy? My poor ego. We had nights of blistering hot sex and that's all I get?"

Aurora was still smiling but her eyes had gone darker, the playful light dimming to something wistful and sad. "You have made me very happy. The happiest I've been in a very long time. Is that better?"

"Yes."

But it wasn't better. Evie felt unsettled. The relaxed, playful mood was crumbling and she could see Aurora retreating behind her walls. She shoved hard, dunking Aurora's head under the water. She came up sputtering an instant later, a look of outrage on her face. Turning she searched and honed in on Evie who was a few feet away and rapidly backing up.

"Catch me if you can!"

The toothy grin Aurora flashed her made Evie squeal in giddy expectation and she swam in earnest. She expected Aurora to grab her when she caught up but she didn't. It became a game in which they chased each other through the waves, their naked bodies bumping and gliding like they were seals at play. Every time Aurora's body slid against hers in a flash of contact Evie felt a jolt of heat despite the cold. She could tell from the looks Aurora gave her that she felt it too. She reached for her wanting to wrap her arms and legs around Aurora's muscular body but she dodged her. Keeping a small distance between them she turned away from Evie and led the way back to the beach. As soon as Evie caught up with her in the alcove she grabbed Aurora's hand.

"Don't do that. Don't pull away from me again. Not after everything that's happened between us. We still have a little time so let's enjoy being together. Don't let this get weird now."

For a long moment Aurora stared at Evie's hand holding hers before she gently pulled free. She picked up the singlet she'd worn under her long-sleeved shirt and started to vigorously towel herself with it. "Evie, I'm not made of stone. I won't be able to walk away if we keep doing this. I already have such strong feelings for you. I don't regret making love but if we keep doing it I won't be able to let you go even if you don't want me. I don't mean I'll stalk you or anything creepy like that. I'm trying to say it takes me a long time to move on when I've become romantically attached to someone. I tried to think of what was happening between us as just physical intimacy between friends but it doesn't work like that for me. I can't do casual. I told you. I wish I was different. I wish I didn't feel things like this so intensely but I do. Evie, you take my breath away and despite only knowing you for such a short time I want to claim you as my mate. You're everything I've dreamed of in a woman and it's driving me crazy knowing you are not meant for me." She snapped the shirt over her head and shook her head like she was trying to rid herself of something. "I never meant to tell you any of this. It's my problem not yours that I feel like this. I'll meet you in the village. Don't be long because the boat won't wait for us."

"Where are you going?"

"I need a little space to clear my head and time to settle my beast. I'm too wound up and my control hasn't been this shoddy in years. If a stranger gets too close to either of us while I'm like this I might lash out. It's dangerous for me to get like this because I could accidently hurt or kill someone."

Without waiting for a reply Aurora gathered her shoes in one hand and took off at a sprint. A stunned Evie watched her go. As Aurora disappeared from view Evie became acutely aware that she was naked and shivering on a deserted beach.

***

When Evie made it back to the village she went to Aurora's room to find her bag and a change of clothing. She saw that Aurora's things were still in the same place and it didn't look like she'd been in. She had a quick wash over the hand basin to get the sea salt off her skin. Her hair had already semi-dried so she just gave it a quick brush before braiding it. After that she didn't know what to do with herself as her thoughts were in turmoil and she wasn't up to casual conversation with strangers. She sat down on the chair beside the bookcase. It faced the large window and Evie could see the village in the foreground framed by the forest on one side and the sea on the other. It was a spectacular view but Evie was too restless to find it soothing. There was something about the room that bothered her. It didn't take her long to figure out what was wrong. If she closed the curtains the room with its fireplace, bed and few pieces of furniture would feel tiny. For someone with wings or a woman of Aurora's size it would be challenging to entertain a guest in such a small space. The villagers might have thought they were being generous when they built this room for a teenaged Aurora but for a grown woman it was little more than a large closet with a pretty view. Aside from becoming claustrophobic, it must get lonely up here. She could imagine Aurora alone in this room reading or sitting quietly in the dark watching the lights in the homes of the villagers burning brightly. Which one of those homes belonged to Astrid and her family? Could Aurora see it from here? Did she watch Astrid's husband and wonder what it was like to go home to the sound of children's laughter and a lover's warm embrace? Evie shook herself to dislodge those unsettling thoughts. It made her sad and on top of how she already felt that wasn't helpful. She'd rather hold on to her anger. She had a few things to say to Aurora when the blasted woman finally showed up. She would stay here a while longer and wait for her. If Aurora didn't turn up she'd go look for her. No doubt she'd gravitate to somewhere there was food because she couldn't go long without eating something.

Thinking about food Evie noticed her giant guava still sitting on the table where she left it the previous day, right next to Aurora's black knife still in its sheath. Evie realized she was hungry and used the knife to cut the fruit into bite-sized portions. The knife that had looked so small in Aurora's hands was a perfect fit in hers. It was surprisingly light and incredibly sharp, the merest pressure against the skin of the fruit slicing deep. It was not just a tool. In the right hands it would be a lethal weapon but she would have expected Aurora to carry something a lot bigger. Her eyes fell on the sheath. It was a handmade thing of worn, hard leather that looked like it had been newly repaired but the central part looked original. Evie picked it up for closer study and saw the inscription burned into the back, faded but still there.

For Aurora. Love Dad.

Evie carefully cleaned the knife and returned it to its sheath before putting it back where she found it. It felt wrong for her to have used it so casually. No wonder the knife was so small, it was a gift to a child. Aurora had carried it with her all these years and never replaced it with another better suited to her size. It made her sad to think Aurora's dad had not been around to give his daughter another knife and all the other things she must have missed out on over the years.

Feeling restless and upset Evie stood up. She had to distract herself from those depressing thoughts. She had to do something. Thinking of the trip that lay ahead she decided to shift her wings away. They would just be in the way on a small vessel and make it impossible to go below deck. The thought came to her so easily she was shocked and amused. Previously if she had to take a trip by boat she would have been resigned to staying on deck no matter the conditions. It would never have occurred to her to shift her wings for the duration of the trip so she could be more comfortable, because among avians being seen wingless was as shameful as going naked in public. How stupid. There was no shame in going wingless, that belief was encouraged to hide how terrible avians were at shifting. Admittedly, before Aurora's intervention it was so difficult for her to shift it wouldn't have occurred to her to question convention and shift her wings away for the sake of convenience. She was not that avian anymore. She could quick-shift now and she intended to fully explore the freedom and power that came with this amazing gift. Not that she planned to broadcast she could quick-shift. She was not ready to deal with the jealousy and demands to be taught something she might not be able to pass on. Besides, it might come in handy that she could do something people didn't suspect her capable of.

***

Once Evie recovered from, what for her was the third shift in one day, she went on the hunt for Aurora. As she suspected she found her in the meeting hall with an empty plate in front of her talking to Hagen. She gave the hunter a friendly smile as she made her way towards them. Stopping next to Aurora she put a firm hand on her arm and said, "I'm sorry to interrupt but I need to borrow Aurora. It's an urgent matter that needs her attention before we leave."

Aurora gave her a wary look and for a moment it looked like she might not get up so Evie, still smiling sweetly, pressed her nails into the underside of her arm. Aurora's eyebrows shot skyward, she opened her mouth to say something but closed it again and with a nod to Hagen followed. Evie led them to Aurora's room. Once inside she pushed the door shut and with a sharp click turned the lock.

"Evie I—"

Evie slapped her. The sound cracked through the room and Aurora rocked back on her heels, her eyes wide with shock.

"That was for leaving me naked and wingless on that beach. How could you do that? You could at least have waited until I was dressed and safely in the air. That would have been the equivalent of walking your date to the door and I deserved that much at least." She leaned close, her body inches from Aurora. "It was beyond rude and callous running off like that. You made me furious. I've come to expect better from you."

Aurora stood blinking with her hand against her cheek. "Didn't you hear anything I said to you?"

"I heard everything you said but since you didn't wait to hear what I had to say we had to come to this."

"You cornering and slapping me?"

"I didn't corner you. We are having a quiet conversation."

"Evie, I'm so out of my depth right now I have no idea what to say to that."

"You can start with an apology for running off."

"Um…okay. I am sorry I left you like that. I should have waited. I wanted to but I just couldn't. You were naked. It's hard enough to resist you with your clothes on."

"Am I hard to resist right now?"

"Evie, don't do this. Please..."

"Well, am I? If I slide my hand inside your panties right now will you be wet for me?"

"For the love of…are you trying to drive me crazy! What are you doing?"

Evie leaned her forehead against Aurora's shoulder. "We had such an amazing night and this morning we were playing in the surf and I was so happy, so turned on. I thought…" Evie faltered struggling to explain why she felt so hurt. She swallowed around the lump in her throat then tried again. "I thought we would make love again or at least say goodbye properly but you suddenly withdrew and ran off. If I'm so irresistible how could you do that? How could you leave me behind like that?"

"Evie, I'm sorry. I tried to explain."

"Yes, I know. I heard you. I even think I understand but it really didn't feel good. I thought we were friends. We've shared so much I thought we could talk about anything and I don't want to get on that boat with things so weird between us."

"We will probably never see each other again after we dock."

"I don't care. We're not leaving things like this."

Aurora wrapped her arms around Evie drawing her closer, closing the small distance between them. "I don't want to leave things badly either, not when we've had such an amazing time together." Aurora sighed and said, "It feels like I've known you so much longer than just a few days."

"I know what you mean, I feel the same." Evie heaved a sigh and said, "I can't believe you're going away. I expect you to keep in contact with me. That's what friends do. Please don't disappear or I'll be worried sick wondering what happened to you."

"I'll try to keep contact but I don't know what will happen in the human world."

They stood in silence for a while, their arms wrapped around each other. Evie felt the heat from Aurora's body seep into hers and it chased away some of the cold that set in when she watched her run away on the beach. "I'm sorry I slapped you. I didn't plan that. I was just going to talk to you but I was so upset. You looked so relaxed talking to Hagen like it didn't bother you to desert me on that beach. I snapped. I'm sorry. I'm not normally like this, I seem to have these emotional outbursts around you."

"It's okay. I was shocked more than hurt."

"Can I kiss you?" Evie asked, her voice barely above a whisper. "I'd really like to kiss you."

"Only if you are willing to miss the boat and stay at least until the next one. Then you can do anything you want with me."

Evie did not reply for several heartbeats, her fingers anxiously tugging on the belt loops of Aurora's pants. "I can't. I have responsibilities, things at home that can't wait. You know that."

"Then my answer has to be no. If you kiss me now I won't let you leave this room. I won't let you get on that boat today. You drive me wild, Evie. I want you and not just your body. If you offer me your mouth I'll want more and I'll want you to stay with me."

A hard knock on the door startled them apart. Hagen's voice from the other side boomed, "The boat is in and the boys are in a hurry to keep going because it's only a quick stop. If you want to be on it before it casts off you'd better hustle."

Aurora looked at Evie waiting for her to say something. When she didn't Aurora opened the door and stepped out. "Thanks Hagen, we're coming. Give them a shout and don't let them leave without us."

CHAPTER 23

PORTA BELUA

Aurora stopped so suddenly Evie almost walked into her.

"What is it?"

She was looking at a huge man slumped against the overturned hull of a dinghy in the shade of an old tree. He was taking small sips from a flask, pausing between like he was testing to see if he could keep it down.

"You know him?"

"Yes, he's a friend of a friend. Nice guy, well, to his friends anyway. Plays a mean viola. I'm going to say a quick hello."

"Mind if I come along?"

Aurora looked momentarily surprised. "Sure, I'll introduce you."

As soon as they approached the man stood up straighter and Evie tried not to stare. He was at least seven feet tall with limbs the size of medium tree trunks and a neck thicker than her waist. Beside him she felt dwarfed, like a small child standing next to an oversized statue of a primordial man. He wore a woolly hat and most of his face was covered in a wild beard. She was used to all manner of unusual beings but the sheer size of the man gave Evie pause. Aurora had no such reservations and she smiled broadly as she clasped the giant's forearm in greeting.

"Hello, Drunn."

"Aurora..." a deep voice rumbled out of his chest. He reached out a massive hand resting it on Aurora's shoulder for a moment.

"Good to see you, Aurora, good to see you."

Noticing his glance at Evie Aurora said, "Drunn, this is Evangeline Aquilar, an avian friend of mine. Evie, this is Drunn Hammerfist." She waited for Evie and Drunn to exchange greetings then asked, "What are you doing here? I thought you don't like boats?"

"I don't. If I never again have to set foot on one of those blasted floating tubs I'd be a happy man. If anyone but Selene asked me to get on one of those death traps I'd tell them to get stuffed."

"You are doing a job for her? Out here?"

"A pickup. She's had trouble with her deliveries disappearing on route. Wanted me to make sure the next lot arrived safely."

"What's she doing now?"

"Getting ready to open a store."

"Selene a storekeeper? I don't see it. She'll be bored out of her mind in no time."

Nodding his agreement Drunn said, "I don't see it either but you know Selene, once she gets an idea in her head it gets stuck in there and no one's going to tell her she can't do it."

"I didn't say she couldn't do it, I'm just surprised. Doesn't seem like her kind of thing. If you told me she was leading a convoy into the wilds or setting off to explore a ruin, *that* I could see."

"She says she's got plans and owning a store is the start. She also just bought this huge rundown place in Old Town. It's a mess right now but it has lots of potential. Well, according to Selene," Drunn said with a shrug. "Aurora, I'm glad we ran into each other. I was going to leave you a message in the village but this is better. There is something you need to know." He paused and shifted his weight uncomfortably, his gaze flicking from Aurora to Evie and back again.

"Is it Selene's business or mine?"

"Yours."

"Then you can speak in front of Evie. I trust her."

The big head dipped in acknowledgement. "Selene said if I saw you to warn you someone is offering serious money for your head, no matter if you are in human form or beast, as long as there is proof it's you. This new contract on you is worth almost triple the last one. Whoever it is wants you dead real bad."

Aurora's eyebrows shot up, "Really? That much? Sounds personal. The cutters and trophy hunters usually want me in fur or alive."

"Yeah, it's a fortune. That kind of money will draw out all sorts. Even the ones who should know better."

"What else do you know? Any idea who's behind it?"

"That's all Selene told me. She heard about it when I was leaving."

"This happened in the last couple of days?"

Drunn nodded, his eyes flicked towards Evie and away. He cleared his throat and said, "Selene said you should be watchful of the skies because that much money is likely to draw out sky-hunters."

"I see." Aurora's face settled into an unreadable mask and she didn't react to Evie's sharp intake of breath.

"Perhaps you should think of postponing your trip to Porta Belua. Someone will recognize you. Wait them out, let the hunters come to you."

"Not this time, Drunn. I have plans, places to be."

"Hmm, you got to do what you got to do. Selene said to remind you whenever you are in Porta Belua you are welcome to stay with her. Night or day, just turn up. It shouldn't be hard to find her new place; it has a giant tree in the back."

"That's very generous of her but I won't take that kind of trouble to her door."

"Hmpf, don't worry about that, Aurora. You know what Selene's like. She's probably dying for an excuse to test one of those nasty toys of hers on a live body. Anyone who follows you to her door is asking for a world of hurt."

A smile ghosted across Aurora's lips. "She's still collecting those things?"

"She makes them now and she's tinkering with human weapons as well."

Aurora chuckled. "I pity the fool who believes that cherub face. That woman has a dark streak in her."

Drunn made an amused huffing sound, "Don't I know it. Small but deadly. For such a little thing she scares me shitless."

A call from on deck had Aurora hoisting her pack. "Time for us to go. Thanks for the warning, Drunn. All the best with the job."

"You take care, Aurora."

"I always do."

"Miss," Drunn gave Evie a cursory nod.

"Aurora, what—"

"It's nothing Evie, don't worry about it."

"How is that nothing? I was right there – I heard what he said about people wanting to kill you!" Alarm made Evie's voice shrill causing heads to turn.

"Hush. Wait until we're on the water. Too many ears."

***

It felt to Evie that the simple task of getting on board and stowing their gear below deck took forever. Once they were underway Aurora made a tour of the entire vessel, talking to the captain and various crewmen, who greeted her by name. Aurora moved with loose-limbed grace despite the rolling deck and she looked relaxed as if she didn't have a care in the world. Her eyes told a different story. Evie saw the restless flicker of her eyes as she scanned the ocean, the sky, and the coastline and the way she tracked the movement of the crew. By the time Aurora joined her at the stern, it felt like hours had passed even though it had probably only been about twenty minutes. She'd been replaying the conversation between Aurora and Drunn and her agitation levels were at an all-time high. Combined with her lingering sexual frustration and how upset and confused she felt after her confrontation with Aurora in the village she was ready to explode.

Aurora slid into the space beside her, close enough that their shoulders and thighs touched. "We can talk now. What did you want to say?"

"How can you be so calm?"

"I've had so many bounties on my head it's hard to get worked up about it. Don't worry, I'll be fine."

"But it sounds like this bounty is huge. Your friend specially sent a warning and the giant was so worried he tried to convince you not to go to Porta Belua."

"The size of the bounty won't mean anything once I'm out of Nordarra. I'm leaving, remember? I'm going to get a ticket, lay low until it's time to leave, slip quietly through the portal and disappear into the human world. They can't catch what they can't find."

"Oh. I forgot about that."

"You forgot I was leaving? Seriously?"

Evie frowned and stammered, "Yes. No. Of course, I remembered it's just...I didn't think about that." Evie threw up her hands in exasperation. "Please be careful. Promise me you will be careful? Promise me they won't get you. I'll be devastated if anything happens to you."

"Worried about me?" Aurora was smiling like it was all so very amusing.

Evie scowled at her. "Of course I am. How can you even ask such a thing?"

Worried and fuming with frustration Evie had to resist the urge to yank Aurora close and kiss her senseless until she promised to be safe. Something must have shown on her face because Aurora's smile grew wider. Leaning in she clasped the back of Evie's head and rubbed her face against Evie's cheek and neck.

"Thank you for caring. I'll be all right. Don't think about that anymore."

"Aurora?"

"Hmm?"

"Are you scent marking me?"

Aurora straightened and looked away, a hint of red on her cheeks. "No. Of course not."

"Are you sure?"

Chancing a glance at Evie Aurora saw the amused twitch at the corner of her mouth and let out a breath. "I wasn't deliberately trying to claim you. It was an instinctual response and I did it without thinking. My mind understands you're not my mate and that touching you when we are parting soon is not a good idea but my body and the other parts of me haven't gotten the message."

"Yeah, I know what you mean."

Standing side by side neither of them said anything for a while after that. Around them the deck was busy but the men only spoke to each other as they worked and avoided the area where the two of them stood. Under their feet the wooden sailboat creaked as it cleaved its way through the water, cleverly weaving around the many rocky outcroppings and small islands that jutted out of the ocean. Overhead seabirds screeched as they drifted on the breeze. After a time Aurora decided they should sit down so she made them a nest of sorts in a shady gap between tall crates by fashioning a thick length of canvas she appropriated into a makeshift seat. They lounged on it with their legs stretched out towards the water, the canvas underneath them pleasantly warm from baking in the early morning sun while the fresh sea breeze ruffled their hair. Sitting so close to Aurora Evie found it natural to rest her head against her shoulder.

"I'm going to miss you. If it wasn't for my father being sick and things in the flock being so unsettled I'd take you up on that offer of a holiday together. I love spending time with you."

In response, Aurora picked Evie up and set her down between her long legs so she came to rest with her back against Aurora's chest. "Is this okay?" Aurora asked against Evie's cheek.

Evie shut her eyes for a moment to enjoy the delicious shiver that ran through her at being held so intimately. "Yes. This feels wonderful."

"I know it's not a good idea for us to sit this close but right now I really don't care. As long as you're happy to be with me like this I'd like to enjoy the last few hours we have together."

"I'm glad you feel that way," Evie said and gave a happy sigh as she snuggled into her.

"Hmm, this is very nice but..." Aurora grabbed Evie's hips and stilled them, "don't wriggle against me like that. You don't want to play games with me right now, trust me on that. You will get a lot more than you bargained for."

Aurora's voice was so serious Evie knew she meant business. "Sorry. I didn't even realize I was doing that."

That made Aurora chuckle. "Yeah right. But to be fair it was asking for trouble putting you between my legs. It might be better if you sit next to me again."

"No." Evie wrapped Aurora's arms around her waist and kept them in place. "I like sitting like this. I'm not moving. I'll be good."

"Hmm..." Aurora made a low rumbling sound that vibrated against Evie's back giving her goosebumps. "If you're not good I'll take it as an invitation to ravish you on the spot."

She lowered her head to graze the side of Evie's neck with her teeth while simultaneously cupping Evie's breast and squeezing her nipple. Instantly Evie felt a fierce, hot surge between her legs that had her clenching her thighs and digging fingers into Aurora's arms. Aurora's nostrils flared and her hand went to undo the button on Evie's pants. Evie intercepted quickly.

"Whoa, slow down tiger! We're on the deck of a boat surrounded by sailors. I don't mind doing it outdoors but not with an audience."

Aurora groaned loudly. "Sorry, I got carried away. I'll be good too."

Evie giggled and fanned her flushed cheeks. "We are a dangerous combination."

"That we are," Aurora agreed.

Aurora rested her hands on the canvas and Evie tried to sit still even though she was on fire and acutely aware of every inch of Aurora's body against her. She needed a distraction, they both did.

"Aurora, can I ask you something?"

"Sure."

"Selene, the woman you and Drunn were talking about, how do you know her? What does she do?"

"Selene? She is in the rare goods trade. The sort of things that are old or powerful. Preferably both. She got her start by excavating in the old ruins. Most of the places that are known have long been picked clean but there are a couple that even the most experienced treasure hunters avoid because they are infamous deathtraps. That's where Selene went. What she found gave her the startup money for other ventures. She doesn't deal in body parts or exotic beings but in the circles she moves in she hears about those who do. She knew what I was after and she gave me several good leads over the years."

"Why did she do that? Wouldn't that be risky in her line of business?"

"A few years back she got into a bit of trouble and I helped her out. We became friends after that."

"So, she does it out of friendship?"

"Yes, and she has a fierce hatred of those who make a profit off the suffering of humans and shapeshifters. Selene had to fend for herself from when she was very young. She told me of some of the things she saw on the streets and the close calls she had with the bastards who grab children for use in the flesh market."

"Have you known her for a while?"

"Several years. Not that I see her that often."

"Is she an older woman?"

"Not sure how old she is. If I had to guess I'd say she's in her mid-twenties. I wouldn't call that older."

Evie turned so she could see Aurora's face better. "What does Selene look like?"

"Red hair and she's on the tiny side. She is slender and very agile with quick hands and feet."

"Is she pretty?"

Aurora's eyebrows shot up. "Why am I getting the feeling you really want to ask me something else?"

"Drunn made it sound like Selene is very eager for you to stay with her. That made me wonder how intimately she knows you. Have you slept with her?"

"Why? Because she's a woman and I sometimes stay with her? No, there has never been anything between us. I'm not even sure which way she swings. I've seen her flirt with both men and woman but with Selene it can be hard to tell if she's serious or just being playful. It never occurred to me to ask."

"Why not?"

"She's been a good friend and someone I'd trust to watch my back in a fight. For me that's a rare and precious commodity. There is no chemistry between us so I honestly don't care what she does in her bedroom and she's not felt the need to tell me."

"Does she know you like women?"

"She knows."

"You told her?"

"I didn't have to tell her. We know some of the same people so...Selene knows. She also has a habit of trying to introduce me to and I quote, 'nice women'. She denies she's trying to set me up but it's all too coincidental. I have to give her credit though, she seems to know a lot of hot, adventurous women keen for a walk on the wild side."

"Does she really?" Evie struggled to keep her voice neutral. She hadn't even met the woman and she already knew she disliked Selene.

"No." Aurora grinned. "I made that up. A bit of wishful thinking on my part. Evie, I wish you could see your face because that shade of red is lovely on you."

Evie let out a sharp laugh. "I can't believe you did that. You had me thinking very unkind thoughts about your friend. Dropping her off a cliff came to mind."

"I couldn't resist joking with you. You're so cute when you get all fired up."

"But you will meet beautiful women where you are going."

"I certainly hope so but I'd be surprised if any of them can compete with you."

Evie didn't know what to say to that so she took a page from Aurora's book and said nothing at all. The thought of Aurora leaving was like a sore spot she was desperately trying to avoid and she didn't want to think about what would happen when they reached Porta Belua. She resettled herself so that she rested comfortably against Aurora and did her best to stay in the moment. Evie inhaled the salty fresh air, drawing it deeply into her lungs and marveled at the scenery. It really was a lovely day to be at sea. She rarely traveled by boat and it was such a treat to watch the world go by snug in their private little corner. She knew there were other people near but the way Aurora arranged their cozy nest made it feel like it was just the two of them and she was pleased she got to have Aurora all to herself again. The strain that set in between them after the beach and their talk in the village wasn't entirely gone. There remained too much unresolved between them, but things were definitely better. That Aurora allowed her this physically close again and had been so open about her desire for Evie spoke volumes.

As they passed a large rock Evie saw two mermaids sunning themselves and she turned to ask Aurora if she knew them. The words stilled on her lips when she saw Aurora's eyes were shut. She watched her closely for about a minute expecting her eyes to fly open at any moment but she didn't stir, her breathing deep and even, her limbs relaxed. A combination of lack of sleep and the lulling motion of the boat must have gotten the better of her. Careful not to disturb her Evie lay her head down so she could hear Aurora's heartbeat. Aurora needed her rest. She needed to be fresh and alert for any trouble that might await her in Porta Belua. Despite her own tiredness Evie knew she would remain awake. She wanted to savor every minute even if it was bittersweet. In addition, she felt intensely protective of the sleeping woman. Aurora would probably wake up the moment someone approached them but it made her feel good keeping watch while she slept.

Studying her sleeping lover it occurred to Evie that even though they were such opposites: a nocturnal beast-shifter and a sun-loving avian respectively, in her opinion their trust in each other had allowed them to use their differences to their advantage instead of it being a hindrance. They were more complete somehow when they were together. Evie wasn't afraid of the dark when Aurora was near, knowing the other woman wouldn't let anything harm her. Aurora, in turn, had allowed herself to cat-nap by day in places she would normally have found too exposed because Evie's scent reassured her she was keeping watch. Evie imagined what a spectacular sight it would be to have Aurora snoozing in tiger form in the private garden-terrace outside her office. She was nervous going to the night market, even with sentinels watching her back, but with Aurora by her side keeping other beast-shifters at a respectful distance, she'd be able to relax and she knew they would have fun exploring the numerous stalls together.

Evie smiled wistfully. It was a silly fantasy but there was a feeling of such rightness to it that her heart ached wondering if Aurora would want to share such a dream, or a version of it, with her. If only Aurora wasn't leaving she would wake her right now and ask her to be her girlfriend. No, not her girlfriend. To someone like Aurora that would sound too casual, as if Evie was just trying her out to see if she fitted. She would offer to become her mate. The thought terrified and excited her in equal measures. That was a short step away from becoming Aurora's life-mate which in beast-shifter terms was like getting married. This was insane, what was she thinking? It was way too quick! Except now that the idea was in her head she couldn't let go and the more she thought about it the less terrified and more excited she became.

Evie considered the potential negative reaction of her flock and other avians to her being in a serious relationship with a tigress and found she no longer cared. The only opinions that mattered to her were those of her father and sister and she was convinced they too would become enamored with Aurora once they got to know her. Evie sighed when she realized she'd once again allowed herself to drift into wishful thinking. Unless Aurora had a drastic change of plans before they reached Porta Belua, they would say goodbye on this deck and probably never see each other again. She really needed to follow her own advice and stay in the moment, no matter how difficult it was proving to be.

***

Aurora slept for hours, seemingly dead to the world. Even when Evie had to move as she was getting cramps from being in one position too long Aurora remained motionless aside from a small flutter under her eyelids. What finally woke her was when a deckhand came too close to their little nest. Evie saw Aurora's nostrils flare and felt her muscles tense an instant before her eyes flew open. Her head swiveled to pin the intruder with unblinking amber eyes, the pupils narrow slits like those of a large jungle cat. Evie had seen Aurora and this man talk on board with the familiarity of old acquaintances but at that moment there was no recognition in her eyes, there was only the calculation of a predator honed in on its prey. Evie knew instinctively Aurora would attack without hesitation if the man made a sudden movement towards them. He seemed to recognize the danger as well because he froze in place and paled under his tan.

Moving slowly Evie raised a hand to Aurora's cheek. Keeping her voice low and soothing she said, "Aurora, you're safe. We're on the boat to Porta Belua. You fell asleep. Everything is all right, there's no danger here. You know this man and he's a friend."

A shudder went through Aurora. She closed her eyes briefly. When she reopened them her eyes were human and forest green with only a few amber specks. "Jornan, what can I do for you?"

Jornan cleared his throat and said, "We are past the spire rocks approaching the harbor. You usually go below deck before we get this far."

"Thank you, it was good of you to come tell me. Like Evie said I fell asleep." Aurora gave a lopsided smile. "Sorry about the death stare, Jornan, I'm cranky when I wake up suddenly from a deep sleep."

Jornan gave a dismissive wave. "Think nothing of it. My Lillie is foul as a winter's storm if I talk to her before she's awake properly in the morning."

Despite the man's assurance, Evie sensed Aurora's discomfort at her slip and possibly at the way Jornan found them all wrapped up in each other. Meaning to draw the man's attention away from Aurora she moved to get up but Aurora clamped her thighs around Evie's hips letting her know she wanted her to stay. Evie relaxed against her, smiled up at the man studying them curiously and said, "Jornan…that name is so familiar. Are you perhaps Aida's fourth son, the one with his second child on the way?"

Jornan's face broke into a broad smile. "That I am. You met my mother?"

"Yes, we had tea together and she let me try her almond biscuits hot out of the oven. They were divine."

"That they are, Miss. My mother doesn't let just anyone try those so you must have made a mighty good impression." There was a call from the deck behind him and Jornan gave them a quick nod before he hurried away.

As soon as they were alone Aurora scrubbed at her face. "I can't believe I fell asleep and slept so deeply. I've never fallen asleep on deck like this before."

"You slept for ages."

"It feels like it. No wonder my butt has gone to sleep." Aurora wriggled her hips and grimaced. "Yup, pins and needles, here it comes."

"You want me to massage it better?" Evie asked sweetly. "I have good hands." She wiggled her fingers for Aurora to see. "You'll be *amazed* at what I can do with these."

That made Aurora grin. "You're so wicked, Evie."

They both got to their feet a little stiffly. Aurora rubbed the back of her neck, stretched her arms above her head and there was the sound of something popping in her back.

"Ah, that feels better. Did you fall asleep as well?"

"No, I stayed awake to enjoy the scenery and watch you drool in your sleep."

Aurora's eyes flew wide and she wiped at her mouth.

"I'm just kidding."

Aurora stared at Evie, an uncertain expression on her face. "Do I snore?"

"No, you don't."

"That's a relief. I always wondered about that. I haven't heard myself snore but I've had no one to ask so I couldn't know for sure."

"No, you're fine. We're going below deck now?"

"I need to since I want to remain out of sight as long as possible but you can stay here if you want."

"I'll come along and keep you company."

Aurora led them below deck past stacked bags and wooden boxes to the corner where she'd stowed her things.

"You weren't worried one of the crew would riffle through your things?"

"Who would be stupid enough to steal from a beast-shifter or mess with my things? I'd pick up the scent and on board like this there would be no escape."

"I didn't think about that. That's handy."

Aurora opened the large backpack, pulled out a selection of clothing and changed quickly. When she was done she wore dark blue jeans of the sort sold in bulk at the market, a black shirt, a brown leather jacket that came past her hips and a pair of black low-heeled boots. She brushed her hair which had grown several inches already after her shift the previous day and put on a grey cap with a wide rim that hid a good portion of her face.

"Evie, what do you think?" Aurora slouched a little, stuck her hands in her pockets and did a loose-limbed walk that was nothing like her normal purposeful stride or the way she sometimes prowled. The changes were subtle but remarkable. The walk along with the clothing made Aurora look like a woman heading off to meet with friends. A very human woman. Add the backpack and guitar and to the casual observer she may pass as a tourist.

"That so doesn't look like you. Good, but not you."

"That's the point," Aurora said, smiling. "I want to look different. It's inevitable that someone who knows me will recognize me and there is only so much I can do about my height but hopefully this will let me blend a little. Look, I even got these." She slid on a pair of sunglasses to complete the look. "This will hide my eyes. I have contacts too but I'm saving them as a last resort. They are irritating."

"Hmm, you look so sexy right now but those sunglasses can wait. I love your eyes so don't hide them yet." Evie took off the sunglasses and slid them back into their case. Then she adjusted Aurora's jacket, smoothing non-existent creases and removed her hat so she could push her fingers through Aurora's silky hair. "I wish I had make-up on me to accentuate your cheeks and those amazing lips."

"I have some."

"Nooo? Really? The woman who cuts her own hair with a knife uses makeup?"

"You're never going to let that go, are you?"

"Nope."

"It's only lipstick and tinted moisturizer." Aurora bit her lip. "I'm not sure how to use the other stuff."

Evie rubbed her thumb over Aurora's lower lip. "You don't need those other things because you're already stunning."

Aurora caught Evie's thumb between her lips and sucked the tip. Evie licked her lips mesmerized by the way Aurora was staring at her. That dark, hungry look was back. She felt her heart rate pick up in response and parts of her tightened and readied with enthusiasm for hot sex she knew wasn't going to happen. Frustration gnawed at her and she pulled her hand away. It would be better if she went above deck and stayed away from Aurora. This was just torture. She took a step backwards but Aurora grabbed her hips and drew her flush so their bodies crushed together and slid a leg between Evie's thighs, anchoring her there. Instinctively Evie clenched her thighs and ground against the offered leg.

Breathlessly she gasped, "Aurora, what are you doing?"

Aurora ran the tips of her fingers along Evie's jaw and the curve of her ear. "I can smell your desire and it's been driving me crazy. I can't take it anymore." She tightened her grip on Evie's ass, sliding her up and down against the taut muscles of her leg. "Do you think you could come like this?"

Evie had her arms around Aurora's neck and the exquisite friction against her crotch had her panting a little. "I'm so turned on right now I could go off just about any way but what about the things you said before?"

"Don't you want to?"

"Of course I want to."

"Then come for me, sweetheart. Please come for me."

"Aurora…hmm this feels so good."

"Hush darling, be as quiet as you can. There are people just above us."

Evie rode Aurora's leg, loving the feel of muscles flexing under her, loving the way Aurora held her and pushed her to the edge and in no time at all she bit onto Aurora's shoulder to muffle her scream as she came. Everything happened so hard and fast she felt a little dizzy. Aurora kissed the side of her neck, slid her off gently then lowered herself between Evie's legs and begun to undo her pants.

"Aurora, wait!" Evie wrapped her fingers in Aurora's hair and tugged urgently trying to pull her back up. "Someone could come down."

"I. Don't. Care." It sounded more like a growl than words. "I can smell you and I have to taste you *right now*."

"Aurora—" That was all she got out before Aurora's mouth was on her and she had to stuff her own arm into her mouth to muffle her moans. This was not a gentle exploration meant to build her up slowly. It was an urgent lashing of tongue, a bold claiming of lips and the graze of teeth. It was so aggressive. So intense. Almost too much. She tried to draw away a little but Aurora wouldn't let her. Arms like steel held her fast until she came so hard she saw stars. Panting, her eyes half closed, arms braced on the bulkhead to remain standing Evie felt Aurora spread her folds with her hands. She gave Evie a kiss on the inside of each thigh then she gently licked her clean with long deliberate strokes of her tongue. No one had ever done that. It was a little shocking and so erotic that she climaxed again. By the time Evie could think, see and breathe properly Aurora had pulled her pants back up and was tiding her shirt for her.

"Aurora…what was that?"

Aurora ran her hands up and down Evie's hips in a caress, her eyes so dark they looked almost black. "Think of it as a parting gift."

Evie put her hand against Aurora's chest and shoved her hard up against the bulkhead. "Did you really think this would only go one way?"

Aurora glanced over Evie's shoulder towards the door. "We are out of time. We're in the harbor nearing the dock."

"I. Don't. Care. Undo your pants for me. I want in."

"Evie—"

"No, don't Evie me. You just fucked me senseless, I'm not letting you go until I've been inside you and felt you go for me. *Now,* Aurora!"

Aurora's eyebrows shot up at the aggressive command but she didn't resist when Evie popped the button on her jeans and shoved her hand inside her briefs to cup her.

"Oh sweetie...you're soaked."

"Hmm..." Aurora's eyes fluttered shut. She gripped Evie's shoulders as clever fingers entered her and began to work their magic. She came quickly and quietly with her head bowed on Evie's shoulder, her entire body shuddering with her release. Evie waited until the last wave passed then eased out of her gently and just as Aurora had done for her, Evie tidied her clothing. Her mind was awhirl with the suddenness and aggressiveness of their coupling. It almost felt like they'd had rough make-up sex but they were parting not staying together so what did that make this? A goodbye fuck? But she didn't want this to be the last time. It couldn't be the last time...they hadn't even done it in a bed yet! Preoccupied with her thoughts it took Evie a moment to register the dampness on her shoulder.

"Aurora, are you crying?"

"No."

She lifted Aurora's face from her shoulder. "Yes, you are. Please tell me what's wrong?"

Aurora rubbed angrily at her face. "It's nothing. Please tell me I didn't hurt you before? I didn't mean to be so rough."

"You didn't hurt me. I'm fine. Are you though?"

"I'm fine," Aurora said but she wouldn't meet Evie's eyes, instead gathering her up for a tight hug. "Thank you for this."

"I think I'm the one who should say thanks but what changed your mind? When I tried to kiss you at the village you wouldn't even allow that. Why this? Why now?"

"Why? Because I lost my mind and couldn't keep my hands off you. I tried but when you touch me and look at me the way you do and I smell your desire it drives me crazy. It feels a lot like when I'm on heat but I burn only for you."

"Are you saying you were overwhelmed by lust for me? That you lost control? Not that I'm complaining but it just seems out of character for you."

Aurora snorted. "Evie, you really don't know me as well as you think you do."

"What does that mean?"

"It doesn't matter."

"Tell me, Aurora, you know I don't like unanswered questions. It will drive me mad trying to figure out what you meant."

"It means when I lose control I lose it on a grand scale and no, it wasn't just lust for you. You were hungry and I was driven to take care of your need. I couldn't stand you walking away from me like that."

"Aurora…you're a complex woman."

"Or maybe I'm just very horny for you."

This made Evie burst out in laughter. "I can live with that."

Aurora was smiling now too. "We're docking so let's leave before someone comes down here for cargo and finds the place smelling like sex. I don't think I can handle Jornan giving me knowing looks. He's always been a terrible tease and he would think it's funny to make a sly comment. That would be a bad move. If he as much as looks at you funny I'll throw him overboard. Unless you still want to shift your wings? You probably don't want to turn up at your tower wingless. I'll go stand at the top of the stairs and make sure no one comes down until you're done shifting."

Evie felt her face go hot with potential embarrassment and she quickly grabbed her bag. "I'm fine like this. I'd rather just get out of here and as for my wings…I'd rather get home quietly without drawing attention. People will notice an avian disembarking from a ship but without my wings I'm just another traveler. That suits me fine. I don't want to risk you being seen by the wrong kind of people because I flashed my wings."

"Any shifter with half a nose will still know you're an avian. The scent is not so strong without your wings but it is still there."

"Perhaps. But at least I'm not hoisting a flag announcing what I am. Besides, to pick up my scent someone would have to get close enough to me to do that in the first place and I bet sorting out who smells of what gets harder in a moving crowd and this time of day that's exactly what I'll be heading into on the way home."

Halfway up the stairs Evie grabbed the back of Aurora's shirt and pulled her to a stop. "Wait…we didn't say goodbye. I want at least another kiss."

"We can say goodbye in a little while. I'm escorting you home."

"But you said as soon as we docked we would go our separate ways?"

"I said that before we were lovers. Now there is no way I'd let you walk through the city by yourself. I need to make sure you get home safely. If I don't the worry will eat me alive and I'll have to come find you to make sure no one grabbed you on the way."

"That seems rather unlikely?"

Aurora shrugged. "I'm walking you home. I'm dropping you off at your front door, or gate. Whatever. You don't really have a say in this. Besides, this is the least I can do for my date, don't you think? I remember someone saying something like that this morning just after she slapped me for my poor manners." Aurora turned to give Evie a mischievous grin. "I try to learn from my mistakes. I offered to give you time to shift your wings and I made sure you were fully dressed this time. I've definitely improved my game."

Evie put a shaky hand to Aurora's cheek. There was no mark where she struck her but she felt guilt and regret twist sharply in her chest. "I'm so very sorry about that. I swear I'll never do it again."

Aurora took Evie's palm and kissed it. "I already accepted your apology so don't dwell on that. Come on, let's get you home."

"I'm quite capable of walking a few streets on my own, you really don't have to accompany me," Evie protested. "I was upset and unreasonable when I threw that old-fashioned notion at you."

"I *will* walk you home, Evie. I've brought you this far and I want to make sure you get home safely. Even if I didn't care about you so much I would still do it because I gave you my word to deliver you back to your people unharmed. There are too many unanswered questions about the people involved in that operation at the mine. I don't like that. Too many unknowns and it might mean you have enemies closer than you realize. Watch the people around you carefully and please don't go on solo flights without sentinels to guard you. I won't be around to look for you if you don't come home when you're supposed to."

"That feels like a lifetime ago, so unreal. Surreal even. I wish I could forget it ever happened. I definitely want to forget the things I saw in that horrible place."

"Forgetting would be nice but you don't have the luxury of becoming complacent. You can't afford to think there is no danger just because you are home. It's the enemy you don't suspect that is the most dangerous. Promise me you will be extra careful?"

"I promise. You will be careful too?"

"Always."

***

Aurora had already paid for their trip with the cargo vessel and she didn't seem to feel the need to say goodbye to anyone so aside from a nod here and there they left mostly unacknowledged. They wove their way around cargo being uploaded and offloaded on the dock and the humans and shifters, shouting and scurrying as they went about their tasks. This was not the dock that catered to the tourists arriving and departing through the portal in the ocean; it had a shabbier well used and slightly chaotic feel to it. It was the type of place where rotten planks were replaced because it would not do to have cargo fall into the sea, not because anyone cared how it looked. The area smelled of fish, salt, grease, freshly hewn timber, the sweat of working men and women and the excrement of livestock waiting in a pen. Into this mix drifted the smells produced by the many food vendors. They catered to the dock workers, merchants and the travelers who weren't lucky enough to secure a berth on a boat where meals were included in the fare and had to stock up on food that wouldn't spoil on the voyage to whatever island or remote inlet they were heading.

Amidst the bustle of locals the stray group of tourists looked conspicuous in the way they clustered together and gawked at everything. Aurora led them on a route to pass behind the tourists and they saw the middle-aged woman with a wide-brimmed hat and striped blue and white dress break from the group. She approached a horned man in deep conversation with a scantily clad mermaid beside one of the food stalls. Ignoring their curious looks she stood a little in front of him, held a camera at arm's length and posed smiling broadly. She checked something on the display then stood next to the horned man. She said something to him, put her arm around his waist and made ready to take another photo. The mermaid's expression instantly became thunderous. She slapped the camera out of the woman's hands, grabbed her hair and dragged her literally kicking and screaming to the water's edge and threw her in. Satisfied, the mer sauntered back to the horned man who held out his arm to her with a broad smile. The two of them disappeared into an alley, utterly ignoring the commotion that broke out as the woman's friends tried to fish her out. The locals watched the whole thing go down with varying degrees of interest but aside from an elderly man who offered them a length of rope to throw to the woman, who was treading water doggy style, no one rushed to help.

"That woman got off lightly," Evie commented quietly to Aurora.

"Yup. Never try to muscle in on a mermaid getting ready to drag her man off for a little action. She was lucky the mer had other plans and didn't take her for an extended tour of the ocean floor."

"I think the poor woman was just trying to take a photo with them."

"Without asking…and she touched the man. Bad move. I've seen the booklet that comes with the disclaimer they make tourists sign before they are allowed to come here. It's a mini guide packed with things not to do if they want to survive the experience. Not touching any kind of shifter without permission is on the first page just before and I quote: 'Don't try to pull a feather from an avian's wing'."

Evie pulled a face. "I had a tourist try to do that once. Unbelievable. The idiot actually thought I wouldn't feel it."

"What did you do?"

"Let's just say he got a lot more than he bargained for."

Aurora shot her a grin and chuckled. "I'll bet."

***

Once they were a little way from the dock Evie took the lead guiding them down familiar paths to her home. She found she was walking slower than she normally would and instead of taking the shortest path she took the scenic route. If Aurora noticed she didn't comment. Her eyes busy and calculating, she stayed close and Evie saw her nostrils twitch as she processed a myriad of smells. Evie knew not to talk to Aurora when she got that watchful look. She tried to see their surroundings through her eyes, observing the narrow busy streets and the noisy bustling crowd that even she found overwhelming at times. How hard must this be for Aurora with her enhanced hearing and keen sense of smell? How was she tolerating so many strangers streaming past in such close proximity? Evie absently put a hand on Aurora's arm to soothe her and was rewarded with a smile that made her heart skip a beat. It never ceased to amaze her how breathtakingly beautiful Aurora was when she smiled. Evie slowed her pace a little more. There really was no need to hurry.

When Evie spotted one of her favorite eateries she came to a stop. "Have you had pastries from that place over there?" She pointed down an alley where a chalkboard on the pavement advertised a variety of specials for the day.

"Can't say I have. Are they good?"

"The best. Everything is freshly made and so few people know how amazing their food is. Let me buy us something to eat? I'd love for you to try a few pasties."

"That's probably not a good idea. That will take time and we should keep moving."

"It's in a quiet alley and you'll see if anyone comes from either side."

Aurora's eyes flicked up and down the alley. She started to shake her head.

"Please? I'd like to feed you at least once for all the times you cooked for me and it won't take long. You missed lunch so that tummy of yours must be demanding something to eat by now."

"I am hungry and those pasties smell good even from here. I still don't think this is a good idea but all right, let's have one last meal together."

Evie gave a happy little clap and said, "Great! This is going to be lovely. I'll get us a pitcher of their fresh fruit juice to have with our meal."

"I'll follow behind to make sure we don't have hunters on our trail."

"Sure. What kind of filling would you like? Something sweet or savory?"

"Both? You know their specialties so you pick. I'll enjoy anything you get me."

Evie nodded and hurried to place their order. She was going to go crazy and take as many as they had ready. There was no one seated at any of the tables and when she got to the counter she didn't see anyone there either. Evie stared sullenly at the glass partition that kept her from her prize. Hot pasties of every description lined one side, the delicious sweet offerings in the chilled cabinet beside it. She peered around anxiously but she was still the only person in the entire place. She would have thought the place was deserted if it wasn't for the pasties and the music coming from the kitchen. Unbelievable. The one time she was in a hurry there was no one to serve her. If someone didn't turn up soon she was going to hop over the counter, help herself and leave the money.

"Hello? Anyone there?"

"Yes, beautiful angel...I'm right here."

Turning her head to the side she saw a handsome dark haired man coming towards her. He had an apron on, was carrying an assortment of vegetables in a crate and sported a rakish, confident smile.

"You work here?"

He put the crate of vegetables down on one of the tables, removed his apron and sauntered over. Coming to stand right next to her he popped an elbow on the counter and his smile brightened a few more degrees.

"I do, just started this week. Good timing otherwise I would not have had the good fortune to meet you. What can I do for you? Just name it, anything at all. Avians aren't usually my type, I prefer wolf bitches, but for a pretty little thing like you I'd make an exception.

Evie rolled her eyes at what had to be one of the worst pickup lines she'd heard in ages. Before she could give him the verbal response he deserved a voice from behind her said, "You will step away from her. That is *all* you will do."

Evie had become used to the stealthy, quick way Aurora moved so she wasn't surprised to see her appear almost out of thin air but it startled the guy. He straightened and stared warily at Aurora but didn't move away.

"I'm entitled to talk to a pretty girl if I want. Why should I—"

He didn't get to finish his sentence. In a blur of motion Aurora was right in front of him. She towered over him and was making a deep rumbling sound laced with so much menace it gave Evie chills. That was not the truly alarming part. The air around Aurora shimmered and felt charged like the moment just before a lightning strike, a warning Aurora was moments away from a full shift. Looking at her from the side Evie could see Aurora's jaw thickening, sharp ridges rose under the skin of her face like something was about to burst to the surface and her hands had become huge paw like things with gleaming claws that looked like they could rend armor. To top it off aggression, raw and primal, emanated from her like a living thing coiled to strike. Even standing next to her Evie found it hard to look at Aurora because some primitive part of the brain warned that to meet her eyes in challenge would be a very bad idea.

The man froze and stared at Aurora, doing an excellent impression of a rabbit caught in headlights. He sucked in a breath and his nostrils flared. "You must be Au-ro-ra, the Old Blood tigress. I heard about you but never thought I'd—"

A louder rumble from Aurora and her lips peeled back to reveal teeth that looked powerful and viciously sharp. The man looked down abruptly and he slowly moved away from them, his body slumped in the imitation of wolfish submission. If he had a tail Evie felt sure he would have tucked it.

"I meant no offense, Old Blood. I did not realize the female is mated. I made a mistake."

Aurora's voice came out low and guttural. "LEAVE."

He nodded once and with his eyes averted scurried into the kitchen. Aurora tracked him with amber eyes. As soon as he disappeared from view she put pressure on the small of Evie's back and guided her out of the little eatery. On the way to the dumpster behind which Aurora had hidden her things Evie felt the paw become a hand again. Aurora quickly gathered up everything and angled to get past Evie to continue on their way, never once looking directly at her. Evie blocked her way and with gentle pressure on her face made Aurora look at her.

"Wait, you have something on your lip."

"What?"

She stroked her thumb along Aurora's jaw, "An impressive set of fangs. I think you made that young guy pee himself a little."

"Good! He's a wolf so he would have detected my scent on you. He should know better than to be sniffing around you like that!"

Evie arched an eyebrow. "Your scent, hmm? I don't think he was actually sniffing me though."

"He was a stranger, he stood too close. Near enough to touch or attack."

"What would you have done if he touched me?"

Aurora snarled baring her teeth. "He would have lost that hand and anything else I saw fit to take!"

Evie tried to soothe the tense muscles in Aurora's back with firm strokes of her palm. Keeping her voice low she asked, "What's wrong? I've never seen you like this, not even when you were protecting me at the wolf camp. Then there's the way you shifted just now. I might be wrong but it didn't look like you had control over that. What is going on?"

Aurora half closed her eyes and taking deep breaths retracted the fangs and settled her face back to a normal shape. Her eyes when she looked at Evie were human but what stared out of them was something wild, barely tethered. "I'm having self-control issues today."

"Yes, I noticed. Why?"

"I tried to tell you when we were at the beach. In short, it's about you but it's not your fault. Even before we had sex you put all my protective instincts in overdrive. He's a male shifter, a wolf, an unknown. Danger. He got too close to you and I wanted to kill him. It wasn't personal. I'm sure he is probably a nice enough guy just trying to chat up a pretty girl but it wasn't the human side of me thinking. It was an instinctive response."

"Protecting your territory?"

Aurora nodded, a blush coloring her cheeks. "It's the sex. Right now you smell like my mate. My beast is aggressively territorial; add that to how I feel about you and it becomes a volatile combination. This is embarrassing, I didn't want you to see me like this." Aurora rolled her shoulders and glared at the eatery's door. "I'd go apologise to the little shit but in my current mood it's likely I'll rip out his throat instead."

"I'd rather you didn't do that," Evie commented dryly.

Aurora grinned. "I'd rather not do that either. It just occurred to me that there is at least one good thing about us parting ways now. You won't have to deal with this beastly side of me. I was as bad as a mer going all possessive on you like that. We had amazing moments and incredible sex, that's probably as good as it gets. We say goodbye on a high. Good memories. Let's get you home so you can get back to your life. I promise not to snarl at anyone else unless you want me to."

***

As they came into view of Evie's home she said, "We're here, well almost. That's my tower at the end of the street and there's the gate to the Aquilar compound."

Aurora gave a low whistle, "That's an impressive tower and solid looking walls. Not a small compound either. House Aquilar must be doing very well to have a place like this in the city. I'm happy for you, Evie."

"I suppose. I rarely see it from street level and to me, it's just home. Come inside with me. Come meet my family. My father will want to thank you and I'd love for you to meet my sister. Oriana is witty, kind and very feisty. I think you'll like her."

Aurora shook her head. "Thanks, but I can't. Not right now. In that tower I'll be in close confines with a crowd of strangers who will most likely swarm all over you. I'm not calm enough to handle that rationally. It's bad enough you got to see my little outburst; I'd hate it if I embarrassed you in front of your people. Besides, I have a lot of things to take care of before I go through the portal. I don't even have a ticket yet. I'll stay here until you're safely inside. Give me a goodbye wave from one of the balconies."

"Aurora, wait! I've been thinking about it a lot and I don't think you should go."

Aurora frowned. Her expression lost its warmth and her eyes became wary. "You want to talk me out of going *now*? Here on a street corner?"

"If not now, when?" Feeling the urgency of the moment Evie rushed on. "I've kept my thoughts to myself but I can't stay silent any longer. I don't think you realize that you will always have to hide what you are in the human world. The humans outside of Nordarra think shapeshifters are monsters. I know there are those who accept us, some even adore or worship us but they are in the minority. If you think having hunters on your trail here is bad can you imagine how much worse it will be if you are discovered in their world? The way I understand it the trade in rare animals, dead or alive, is the third biggest illegal market in their world. That's the reason the hunt for our pelts and the theft of young continue despite the risk of punishment by death because humans are willing to pay the most exorbitant prices. No contraband is supposed to pass through the portal but it's such a lucrative business all kinds of things still get smuggled out. You must know all this. If you go to the human world you will always have to be vigilant not to let anyone find out what you are. You won't be able to shift where anyone can see you; if you slip up and act like you did with that guy at the eatery it will be over. You won't be able to talk about the life you lived before without the risk of outing yourself. Aurora, you will have to pretend an entire part of you doesn't exist. Will you be able to live like that? Will you lie to your lover? Will you lie to your friends? You might think you're just not telling them things but inside you'll know you're lying. You will try to protect your secret and eventually your lover will feel you are hiding something. Your lie of omission will create distance isolating you from everyone around you. I honestly think in the human world you'll be lonelier than you were in that sanctuary of yours. You should stay. You already have a life here with people who care about you. Friends who will stand with you. You should not allow anyone or anything to drive you away. Nordarra is your home...you belong *here.* I'm sure we can find out who put that price on your head and make it go away. There must be a way to make it so no one will think about hunting you for your pelt ever again."

Evie reached for Aurora's hand but she jerked away. She seemed unsteady on her feet and her face was deathly pale like she'd just received bad news.

"Don't run away. You're not alone I—"

She didn't get to finish her sentence. Aurora abruptly swung away and with a few strides of her long legs she was across the road rapidly weaving through the crowd. Within moments the throng of people swallowed her.

Evie fought the urge to chase after her. She'd already done that once today, twice was more than her pride could handle. Besides what good would it do? Evie stood with a hand on her heart feeling a heartbeat that was heavy and painful in her chest as she recalled the emotions on Aurora's face while she spoke. The shock and confusion she could handle but that look of despair would haunt her. Aurora had looked at her as if she'd just given her a mortal wound. Should she have said nothing? Should she have let her go with the hope of a wonderful new life waiting for her? Maybe she was wrong and it would all work out for Aurora but she'd heard enough of the world on the other side of the portal to know it could be a harsh place, even more so than their own. But she didn't have to say it quite like that. She'd felt a trapped desperation build in her since they got on the boat and she knew their time together was almost over. She had tried her best to ignore it but when she saw Aurora ready to walk away something inside her broke. The words she'd been holding inside spilled out raw, harsh even. She had convinced herself she should tell Aurora what was so glaringly obvious to her, that she was telling her for her own good. As soon as she felt the hollow sadness at seeing Aurora leave without a backwards glance Evie knew her motives for wanting her to stay were not as altruistic as she led herself to believe. She wanted Aurora to stay *for her,* to be *with her*. She wanted her to stay because she would miss her terribly and the thought of never being in Aurora's arms again made her want to cry.

CHAPTER 24

SEPARATION

Aurora felt like she was in a daze and kept moving by instinct. The noise of the crowd had receded to an indistinct buzzing noise and all she heard was Evie's words replaying in her head like a stuck record. How could Evie do this to her? She'd shared her most private hopes and dreams with her and just as she got ready to start her new life Evie poured doubt over everything leaving her feeling distressed and battling waves of hopelessness. She had only one plan for when she finally fulfilled her vow. *Only one*. Leaving her old life behind to start over was going to be her reward for all the years she'd lived a half-life, searching and waiting for her vow to be fulfilled. She felt as petulant as a child who'd been waiting all summer for an ice-cream to have it slapped out of her hands into the mud before she even got a taste.

Aurora rolled her shoulders and shook her head to dislodge the melancholy that wanted to take root. She was being melodramatic. Nothing was lost and no one could take her dream away unless she allowed it. It's not as if she didn't know there were risks so nothing had changed. It was almost funny that Evie worried that she would have to hide what she was. She'd had years of practice doing precisely that. She discovered the true nature of her beast the first time she had shifted and aside from her mother she'd never been able to tell a single soul. Granted, pretending she was a tiger-shifter was easy compared to pretending she was just human but she would manage. She had to.

Aurora sighed wearily. No, Evie hadn't given her a good enough reasons to stay and her own feelings for the beautiful woman were an added motivation to leave sooner rather than later. She was in love with Evie. There was no point trying to deny it and fighting how she felt was useless. She wanted Evie as a life-mate and, if she'd been given the chance, would have made Evie the center of her world. If Evie had even once indicated that she was interested in having more than a fling Aurora would have stayed in Nordarra despite the risks, but…she never did. She should have asked Evie how she felt about her but she had been too afraid she'd push her into admitting out loud that she didn't see Aurora as a suitable partner. She'd put everything on the line once before and hearing those words from the woman she'd loved had been so devastating it had taken her years to recover. Being older had not made her heart more shatterproof and she hadn't been brave enough to ask the question. Instead she had tried to read the signs but all knew for sure was that Evie cared about her and enjoyed their lovemaking. What she wasn't clear on was how meaningful any of that actually was. What did Evie call sex again? 'An affectionate sharing between friends'. Those words have been stuck in her mind like a thorn. She hadn't understood what Evie meant when she said it and now she was doubly confused. It sounded so casual, so dismissive. Did it mean Evie saw her as just a friend she had sex with? If that was the case how would she cope if she stayed to be with Evie and it turned out all she was interested in was sex now and then when she had a free evening? Or worse, what if Evie only wanted the friendship part now that she was back among her own people and picked an avian lover over her? Aurora fought to shut down the image of Evie on a bed surrounded by numerous naked winged lovers, her head thrown back as she cried out in rapture. The thought of someone else making love to Evie was maddening and she wanted to tear those phantom lovers to shreds so badly she could taste the hot metallic tang of their blood.

Aurora's skin burned as if something on the inside was trying to claw its way out and she knew that was a warning to get her raging emotions under control or she would shift. Desperate to get out of the jostling flow of people Aurora stepped into an empty looking store. She feigned interest in a display of bags while she took deep calming breaths. The owner of the store must have bought into her portrayal as a tourist because he bounded towards her holding out an expensive looking leather bag with gilded dragons stitched into the motif and launched into an enthusiastic sales pitch. He wasn't blocking the doorway but she would have to step around him to leave and in her current state of mind Aurora didn't like that at all. She watched the man out of the corner of her eye hoping he would go away if she ignored him. When she realized he had no intention of leaving her alone she faced him directly. Instantly the smile slid off his face and he swallowed hard, his adam's apple bobbing nervously.

"You are in my way." Aurora thought she had spoken quietly and politely, simply stating a fact, but the man clutched the bag to his chest like a shield and stumbled out of her way as if she had threatened to disembowel him.

"My humblest apologies, beast-lord." The man made a deep bow and remained that way until Aurora left the store.

Cursing under her breath Aurora slid on her sunglasses. If she had any hope of passing as a human she had to remember to keep her eyes covered, especially when she was upset. She would have to be more vigilant; Evie was right about that part. Remembering the salesman Aurora did a double take. Did he call her a beast-lord? How odd. The human had a heavy accent that made her think he'd not been in Nordarra long so perhaps the way he acknowledged she was a beast-shifter was a cultural thing? Or did seeing a reflection of her beast in her eyes scare the poor man senseless? If he was that skittish she wondered how he would cope if he ran into a pack of rowdy young wolves, come into town to blow off steam. If he bowed and acted submissively like that they would find it amusing and probably leave him alone but if he ran…

Aurora pushed the man out of her mind. She had enough problems of her own. What she needed to do was get off the streets. Not that she had been wandering aimlessly. Even though she'd not been thinking clearly she'd instinctively angled towards one of her safe places. Normally she wouldn't have felt any qualms about being by herself for an evening but after spending almost every moment with Evie for so long she couldn't stomach the thought of being alone with only her own miserable thoughts for company. She wanted to see a friendly face. She wanted pleasant conversation over a hearty meal with someone she trusted to watch her back. She would go find Selene's new place and see if she was home. A small voice chided that she would put Selene in danger going there but she quashed the warning. She would be extra careful to make sure she wasn't being followed and Selene had been such a steadfast friend that she deserved a face-to-face goodbye. It both amused and annoyed her to realize this was Evie's influence coming through loud and clear. Before Evie's little lecture in the village it wouldn't have occurred to her that Selene might feel hurt if she left without saying goodbye.

***

Old Town was on the outskirts of the sprawling city on a sloping mountainside overlooking the sea near where the original harbor used to be. Aurora had been to Old Town only briefly years ago but she found its winding cobblestone streets and stately old homes virtually unchanged. Compared to the part of the city she'd just come from this area had a quieter more sedate feel to it as if the inhabitants were happy to go about life in a slower undisturbed pace. Even the storefronts with their high arches and old-fashioned gilded writing advertising their services looked like the remnant of a different era and Aurora found she liked it. On one of the side streets there was a group of young children playing a ball game that involved a lot of running and shouting and Aurora saw a grandfatherly old man had dragged a chair onto the sidewalk so he could watch while smoking his pipe. The children looked like they were having so much fun she would have liked to watch them play for a little while but kept moving so as not to draw attention to herself.

She kept angling upward. Drunn had said there was a giant tree in the back of Selene's new place and Aurora had a rough recollection of where she'd seen an exceptionally large tree. She smelled the tree long before she saw it. After the smells of the busy city the earthy forest scent of it wafted to her on the salty evening breeze like the perfume of an old friend and she was drawn to it. When she found it in the enclosed courtyard she stared up at it in wonder, amazed that such a magnificent old tree had survived the expansion all around it. The huge old multi-story house next to the tree was covered in ivy and had an abandoned feel about it but she heard the rhythmical thump of music from somewhere inside and found Selene's green Jeep in the back so she knew she was in the right place. She tried knocking at a door in the front first. When there was no response she circled round to the back where she found a door with a rusty knocker. The door, like the rest of the property, had been subjected to years of neglect and though not rotten yet, cracks in the protective coating had allowed water to seep in so the door was swollen in places. She knocked the weighted ring against the metal plate. The sound it made was surprisingly loud and she cringed at making so much noise. The music turned off and a few minutes later there was the sound of a key being turned in the lock. She heard Selene cursing on the other side as she wrestled with the unyielding door. It opened inch by slow inch until there was a gap wide enough for Aurora to see a petite woman with a mop of fiery red hair peer up at her. As soon as Selene recognized her she flashed a brilliant smile.

"Aurora! What a lovely surprise!"

"Need help with the door?"

"If you don't mind."

Aurora put a little weight behind her push and the door slid open easily.

"Show-off," Selene said cheerfully. "I usually use one of the other entrances because this door is way too much of a workout for me."

Aurora opened her mouth to reply but she found herself staring in fascination at the peculiar sight in front of her. Selene had a harassed look about her of someone who'd been interrupted while doing important work. Her short hair, the shade of a well-stoked fire, stuck up in all directions like a series of exclamation marks and her face was covered in inky smudges. She wore a frayed green turtleneck jersey, faded jeans and a full-length leather apron that was stained with various dyes, chemical burns, and grease. What was most striking however was the shotgun the size of a small cannon strapped to her with a padded sling. Selene's right hand rested loosely on the barrel, her fingers within easy reach of the trigger. Instinctively Aurora moved to the side so Selene would have to turn to get a clear shot at her but to her relief her friend didn't make a threatening move. Aurora cleared her throat and said, "I knocked on the other side but you didn't hear me."

Selene shrugged. "It's a big old place with lots of weird noises. I thought I heard knocking but there is something on the roof that makes a tapping noise at the slightest breeze so I assumed it was that blasted thing again."

"It didn't help that you had your music playing so loudly," Aurora couldn't help point out.

"I like my music loud. It helps me concentrate when I'm working and I need it to drown out all the creaks and groans this old place makes. I swear if I didn't know the walls and foundations were sound I'd think it was going to crash down on me at any moment. But never mind all that. It is good to see you, Aurora!"

"Are you sure?" Aurora pointed at the weapon. "I've had warmer welcomes."

Selene looked at the huge gun strapped to her side as if surprised to see it. "This is not meant for you. Obviously. I was working on it when you knocked."

Selene moved the weapon so the barrel pointed at the floor then she straightened and in a formal tone said, "Come in, my friend. Be welcome in my new home. My food is your food. My sanctuary, your sanctuary."

Aurora made a small bow of acceptance then said, "You may not want to offer me sanctuary, Selene. I tried to be careful about not being followed here but there are so many eyes in this city there is bound to be unpleasant company on my heels. I don't want to cause you trouble."

Selene's eyes narrowed and a shadow of something hard and dangerous flitted across her face then she smiled and the cheerful young woman was back. "You know me, Aurora, if trouble doesn't find me, I find it. If anyone comes here hunting for you it will be an excellent opportunity for me to test my new toys. I've just finished altering this girl on my arm and I'd love an opportunity to try her out on something more lively than stuffed dummies. Come in and close that cumbersome door behind you."

Without waiting for a reply Selene disappeared inside. Aurora closed the door, turned the oversized key in the lock and followed her friend into a wide hallway.

"Selene, that weapon is almost as tall as you and it looks heavy. How do you fire that thing without getting knocked on your ass or getting your arm ripped out of its socket?"

"Trade secrets, my friend, trade secrets. All I'm willing to say is it is amazing what adding the right kind of rune magic can do for a weapon." Selene gave a wide impish grin and winked. "Truth be told I'd only fire this weapon as a last resort because even with the improvements I've made she still kicks like a mule. She's not meant for me; I'm sprucing her up as a special thank you gift for Drunn. I've been sending him all over the place by boat and you know how much he hates those things. I worry about him running errands for me. He relies too much on his huge size and strength to keep him safe. He doesn't consider quick enemies could easily surround him and if they keep out of reach of those massive paws of his he could be in serious trouble. The way I see it with this big girl by his side he'll have an edge. Drunn can't shoot for shit but with this he only has to aim in the general direction and he will hit the target. I also strengthened the barrel and added a custom grip so he can swing her like a cudgel. Versatility is important in a weapon, don't you agree? I've been working hard to surprise him with it when he gets back."

"If you meet him at the door with it as you did me, I'm sure he will be *very* surprised."

"Yeah, ha-ha very funny. Here on the right is the kitchen. Put your things down and take a seat at the table. I'll put on a pot of tea. So just to warn you that aside from my work area, the bedroom and bathroom, this is the only other place that is currently clean enough to inhabit. If you decide to go for an exploratory wander be warned you are likely to end up covered in spider webs. The previous owner really let this place go. Aurora, what are you doing here? I'm happy to see you but there is a huge price on your head. This is not a good time for you to be in Porta Belua."

"I know. Drunn told me when I ran into him."

"If you know about the bounty does it mean you've come to root out the source to shut this thing down? If that's the case you will need someone to watch your back. I nominate myself. If you give me a few hours I can call in a few favors and get backup. Give me a day and with enough coin I can hire a company of elite mercs so we can blow this thing out of the water with style. If it's going to go down in Porta Belua we might as well use it as a stage and make a statement that reminds everyone, loud and clear, that you are not to be messed with. I know a guy who runs a clean operation and once he's committed he and his mercs stay bought. He's not cheap but the good ones aren't. How are you for money? If you are short I can loan you. I'd give it to you but this place is draining me dry. I swear builders and plumbers are worse than loan sharks. There is *no way* replacing rusty pipes and rotten planks can cost as much as they are trying to charge me! Do you perhaps know a good plumber who's not a rip-off artist? Would you like cake? I have a big chocolate cake begging to be eaten freshly baked this morning. Silly question, of course you'd like some. Here let me cut you a big piece. It's a gift from the grandmother of the young guy who's trying to convince me to hire him. Well, it's more like an attempted bribe than a gift. I told him he wasn't what I was looking for but he's been turning up anyway offering to help. I have to admit I admire how tenaciously persistent he's been and using his grandmother's baking to soften me up is a stroke of genius."

"Selene, slow down. You're going a mile a minute. Do I get to reply to any of that?"

"Oh, sorry. I'm a bit hyped, I've been living off pots of coffee trying to get through the hundred and ten things I've got going. I know I should squeeze in a few hours' sleep sometime soon but there is so much to do!"

"Sit down, Selene. Eat some of that cake and give me a chance to talk. I have something to tell you."

"That doesn't sound good."

"It's not good or bad. Not really. Sit down because you're fluttering about like a hummingbird and you're making me dizzy."

Selene gave Aurora a speculative look and sat down at the table. She lay the gun down so the barrel faced the kitchen door and helped herself to a big slice of cake. "What's going on?"

"I'm leaving Nordarra."

"As in *leaving,* leaving?"

"Yes."

"When?"

"As soon as I can arrange passage."

"Why? Is it because of the bounty on your pelt? That's never fazed you before. I know it's a fortune but we can figure out how to shut this down."

"I always planned to leave Nordarra once I fulfilled my vow and in this past week, I finally did it. It's time for a fresh start. Now I can finally go see what it's like on the other side. This latest bounty has reinforced it's a good time to leave. It's getting harder, Selene. They are using high powered sniper rifles now. I'm good but it's difficult to defend myself against an enemy that hides under cover and shoots from a mile away."

"You got shot?"

"Yeah."

Selene inhaled sharply. "When?"

"A few months ago."

"Where?"

Aurora tapped her chest. "The bullet just missed my heart and clipped a lung. I thought I was going to suffocate in my own blood. I've had close calls before but as I lay there I honestly thought that was it. That the hunters had finally got me."

"But you made it…"

"Yeah. I managed a shift and regenerated enough to get myself up and moving before they could get to me but it was a harsh wake-up call. It used to be about skill, preparation and remaining vigilant so I had an edge. Now every time I leave the forest it feels like I'm rolling the dice. It is just a matter of time before my luck runs out."

Selene, her hands clenched into fists, stared up at the ceiling for a long minute. When she looked back at Aurora her eyes were shiny dark pools of anger.

"Did you kill the bastard who shot you?"

Aurora nodded. "It was a four-man team. Once I was well enough I tracked them down and we played a little game of cat and mouse. I won."

Selene bared her teeth in a feral grin. "Excellent! That's what I want to hear. How about I make us dinner? I bet you're hungry after your trip."

"I could eat a little something."

Selene laughed and gave Aurora's hand an affectionate squeeze. "That, my friend, is a massive understatement."

They ended up making dinner together. Or rather Selene washed and chopped while Aurora did the actual cooking. Selene's initial plan was to throw something in a wok and use her little one ring camp cooker since she hadn't gotten around to cleaning the ancient wood stove. There was some good-natured arguing and Aurora got the stove cleaned out, stoked and working in record time. Soon it was radiating heat into the chilly high-ceilinged kitchen like a mini-furnace. Selene extracted pots and pans from the boxes marked 'kitchen' that stood in the corner of the room while Aurora scrutinized the meager ingredients in the cupboard and cooler. After some deliberation, they agreed Aurora would make a goat curry with rice and naan bread. While Aurora cooked Selene disappeared for a time. She came back freshly washed, smartly dressed for an evening in the city and shivering. She headed straight for the stove to warm herself. Standing beside Aurora she barely came up to her chest.

"What's wrong with you? What's with the shivering?"

"There is no hot water and the bathroom is like a slippery freezer with those awful tiles underfoot. Well, there is hot water but only a trickle. The plumber said something about lack of pressure and rusted valves so until that's fixed I have to endure brisk cold showers. That's what you're getting too unless you want to boil water on the stove for a wash."

"A cold shower doesn't bother me, Selene. As long as I can get clean I'm happy. I have to ask, what's with you buying this place? It's big and in a great area but it needs a ton of work."

"It does," Selene agreed. "But it has great potential, the location is perfect for what I have in mind *and* I got it at a fraction of its actual worth. Now I just have to ride out the bumpy stretch and fix things one item at a time. When I'm done with this place it will be amazing. Don't worry, I have a plan. Several actually."

Aurora nodded thoughtfully as she carried the food to the table. "That tree in the courtyard is massive."

"That it is. That tree is also the reason this side of the house is so cold.

It is always in the shade. I dread to think what it is going to be like in winter."

"You won't cut the tree down, will you? It's very old."

"I wouldn't dare. Protecting the tree was the main condition of sale. That was the reason I could afford this place at all. I'd tell you how it all went down but it's a long story with lots of boring details and not important right now. What is important is the bounty on your head and getting you safely out of Porta Belua. I've been trying to find out who's behind it since I heard about it. I have a few good leads but it's been hard going to get the information because everyone knows we are friends. I'll head out after dinner to follow up. Until we know exactly who we are dealing with I suggest you stay out of sight. I'll make all the travel arrangements for you. Anything else you need just tell me and I will take care of it."

"But, Selene, you told me how busy you are."

"There's nothing that can't wait until you are safely away. This is more important."

"But—"

"No buts. Let me do this for you. Please, Aurora. We've never talked about it but I haven't forgotten that I owe you my life. This is hardly repayment but it is something I can do for you. Let me help you. Please."

Aurora gave a slow nod. "Thank you, I'd appreciate your help. You have to let me work around the place while you're out. I can't do nothing while I wait. I need to stay busy or all the things I've got on my mind are going to drive me crazy. My knowledge of plumbing is very basic but I can have a look at the shower. I'm better at building and making things. Point me toward what you need fixed most urgently, give me some tools and supplies, and I'll see what I can do."

Selene beamed. "You have a deal. I feel like I'm taking advantage of you but for hot showers I'll do pretty much anything at this point."

Aurora returned Selene's smile and for the first time since she dropped off Evie felt a little better. It was good to feel useful and have a friend who was concerned about her. She dished herself a hearty plate and started to eat. Across the table Selene dished herself a sizable portion as well and dug in enthusiastically.

"Yum, this curry is so tasty! I'd forgotten how well you can cook. Now I find out you can build and fix things as well. You've got the goods, girl. It's a mystery that some woman hasn't snaffled you up yet. You're a keeper." Selene paused with the fork halfway to her mouth to squint at Aurora. "What's with the look you just gave me?"

"What look?"

"The one that said I'm trying to sell you rotten fish."

"Those things aren't enough to make someone want to be with me."

"Not by themselves perhaps but you've got the whole package going. You just need to put yourself out there. Get to know new people, mingle with the ladies. How else are you going to meet that special someone?"

"I did meet someone special." The words were out before she could stop them and Aurora instantly regretted it.

"You did? What is her name?"

"Evie."

"That is wonderful, Aurora! I'm so happy you finally found a mate."

Aurora shook her head and kept her eyes on her plate. She resumed eating even though the food had become thick and tasteless in her mouth.

"Oh. It didn't work out. I'm so sorry."

"Yeah. Me too."

When they were done eating Selene did the washing up and Aurora went for a quick shower. When she got back to the kitchen Selene was pouring hot milk into two large mugs.

"I made hot chocolate. Something to warm you up from the inside after the cold shower."

"I actually found it refreshing but I'll never say no to hot chocolate," Aurora said and took an appreciative sip. "Selene, I have a favor to ask. Three actually. I'd do it myself but as you pointed out its better for me to remain out of sight."

"What do you need?"

"A voucher for the Royal Hotel's luxury couples' package."

"For you?"

Aurora snorted, "I wish. It's for Oswald of clan Swift Foot. He did me a favor."

"Sure, that's easy enough."

"Yeah, I thought I would start with the easy one first. You're not going to like my next request."

Aurora put a black ledger onto the table. "I took this off a cutter. It was his personal log and he kept meticulous notes. In addition to noting the type of shifters captured, what he harvested and how long each person lasted, he also wrote down their names and clan affiliations. She slid the ledger across the table to Selene. "Can you see to it that the relatives of the people in this book are notified they are dead? It will give them no peace of mind but at least they can stop searching."

Selene glared at the ledger as if it was a venomous snake. "Where did you get that?"

"In the ethian mine near the Black Paw trading post. There was a hidden section set up with cages and a harvesting room. It's a human operated mine but I picked up the scent of avians."

"This is going to cause a shit storm of epic proportions, Aurora. Heads will roll over this. Literally."

"I know. It might be better if you keep what I said about the avians to yourself. I don't know who they were and I'd hate for an innocent flock to be accused."

Selene opened the book with the tips of her fingers as if she was loathed to touch it. She leafed through it expressionless, turning the pages faster and faster. She paused at a page as something caught her attention. Her jaw clenched and she slammed the book shut.

"Someone you know?"

Selene nodded wordlessly.

"I'm sorry."

"Yeah. Me too. I only met him a few times but he seemed like a likeable guy. What a horrible way to die. Where you able to rescue anyone?"

"Two wolves and Evie. The wolves were in bad shape especially the female but I did briefly see them in the forest so hopefully they both survived and made it home.

"Evie as in *your* Evie?"

"She's not mine but yes, the same Evie. Her full name is Evangeline Aquilar."

"Wait I know that name…do you mean Lord Augustus Aquilar, the head of House Aquilar's oldest daughter?"

When Aurora nodded Selene gave a low whistle. "From what I've heard he adores his daughters and Evangeline is his right hand. When he finds out another avian House grabbed her and stuffed her in a cutter's cage he will go feral on whoever is responsible. Was she badly hurt?"

"Fortunately she'd not been there long enough for anything bad to happen but she did get shot in the wing while we were leaving. To make things worse she broke that wing in a bad landing. She couldn't fly while the wing healed so I offered to get her back to Porta Belua. We spent the last week together and I dropped her off at her home before coming here."

"She's one lucky lady."

"This brings me to the other favor, Selene. I'm very fond of Evie. She said something I didn't like as we were saying goodbye and I stormed off. I don't want that to be how she remembers me. I'd like to send her a gift so she knows I'm not angry with her."

"You want me to deliver the gift for you?"

"I want you to get it made for me first. What I want is very specific."

"What do you have in mind?"

As Aurora explained Selene's eyes grew wide. "That will cost a fortune. If you want to have it done right with those kinds of materials, I'll have to employ a master jeweler of exceptional skill. I can think of only a handful of people that good and only one I trust to be totally discreet. You have to understand with such a tight time frame there will be no room for negotiation on the cost."

"I don't care about the cost. Offer whatever you have to get it done."

"Aurora, are you sure? Is that girl worth something like this?"

"To me she is."

"Wow, you don't mess around. Okay, if this is what you want I'll make sure you get it. You've given me plenty to do tonight so I'd better get moving."

"Thanks, I really appreciate you doing this for me."

Selene gave a dismissive wave. "I told you I'll help you with anything you need. Oh, I almost forgot to tell you, I put fresh sheets on my bed. You're welcome to use it. It's unlikely I'll make it back till morning so you will have it all to yourself. Tomorrow I'll hunt down the box that has the extra bedding in it and you can help me assemble the spare bed for you."

Aurora thought of Evie's reaction if she found out she'd slept in Selene's bed, albeit innocently, and she could hear the agitated rustling of her wings as clearly as if Evie stood right behind her. It made her smile.

"That is generous of you but I'll be all right. It's such a lovely night I prefer to sleep in the tree."

"Are you sure? My bed is comfortable and big enough even for you."

"Once I get underway I'll be cooped up on a ship for weeks so I'd like to sleep outside while I can. It will also give me an advantage if an enemy comes here looking for me."

Selene's lips twitched in an amused smile. "In other words, you're planning to lie in wait for potential prey."

Aurora saluted Selene with her mug. "You know me well."

Selene squeezed her arm and said, "I wish you good hunting my friend. Please try not to scare my neighbors while you're at it. I'm still trying to make a good first impression."

"Don't worry, unless I want to be seen your neighbors won't know I'm out there."

***

Evie shut the door to her suite with a relieved sigh. She was finally alone. Since arriving home she'd had to deal with endless questions and people trying to monopolize her time. She only shared the bare bones of what happened to her, making it sound like she got blown off course and injured during a severe storm so she'd had to make her way back on foot and by boat. She had intended to tell her flock everything that happened but when she heard that her uncle Marcus was entertaining Raven of House Ravir as his personal guest it had sounded multiple alarms and she had decided full disclosure could wait. She didn't trust Lord Raven's daughter and every time they met her dislike for the avian woman grew more intense. Which was a shame because when they were children she had liked Raven and thought they would become friends. Unfortunately, over the years Raven had become more like her father and she now had the same hard eyes and a way of watching that reminded Evie of a vulture waiting to swoop down at the first sign of weakness. Her father's lingering illness was drawing predators and as his successor she had to appear strong. Anything she said to members of her flock would reach Marcus's ears and he would tell Raven. For the time being, she didn't want either of them to know she'd been caught and stuffed in a cage or that she had needed the help of a beast-shifter to escape. It had only been a few months since she turned down House Ravir's offer of an alliance and publicly humiliated her uncle for trying to strong-arm her into a marriage with Lord Nero's son and she had no doubt they were looking for ammunition to use against her. Evie was pleased that on arrival at the gates she'd had the foresight to insist the sentinels escort her straight to her suite so she could quickly wash, shift her wings and change into attire fitting to her status before the rest of the flock saw her. She could imagine the derisive comments her uncle would have made and Raven's superior smirk had they seen Evie wingless and rumpled from traveling.

It was only when she was alone with her father and Oriana that she revealed how she'd been captured and talked about the things she saw in the cutter's lab. Her father had been so furious he immediately wanted to gather a squadron of warriors armed with explosives to fly to the ethian mine so that they could level the buildings to the ground. Her father tried to hide the extent of his illness but Evie had felt him tremble from the effort of standing to give her a welcoming hug and she worried his pride would compel Lord Augustus to accompany the squadron. She had argued for caution. She'd described the heavy weaponry at the mine and told him of her suspicions that an avian House was involved. He had reluctantly agreed with her they had to find out who their adversaries were so they could plan accordingly before making a move.

Once her father calmed down enough to stop rustling his wings she told them about Aurora. She told them about their first encounter in the mine and the agreement they made to work together to get away from that place. She explained that she got shot in the wing as they were escaping and broke it on landing and how, instead of abandoning her, Aurora had taken care of her and promised to get her safely home. It was at this point that her father mentioned that he had heard stories about Aurora the tigress but he wouldn't say what, urging Evie to continue her story. Her sister gasped when she told them about going into the village of wolves hostile to avians and she had to reassure Oriana she'd never been in any real danger because she'd been under Aurora's protection. She told them that Aurora commanded so much respect among clan Swift Foot that most of the wolves had given her a wide berth and that she had almost killed the woman who scared and insulted Evie. She described their stay with the friendly humans of Ingvild. She made it clear that Aurora had become a dear and trusted friend in the short time they were together. What she carefully omitted was how close they'd become, to where Aurora shared Old Blood secrets with her and they'd become lovers. Some things she knew she could never share with anyone because of her promises to Aurora. As for the intimacies they'd shared she felt too protective of those precious memories to share them with anyone. Not even with the two people who meant the most to her in the entire world. Her father, always a perceptive man, had watched her with sharp knowing eyes and she got the feeling he knew she was keeping secrets. She also knew he respected her too much to pry into his daughter's private affairs, trusting that she would not withhold anything that could put their House at risk.

In her suite, Evie opened the door to her balcony and stared out over the familiar sight of the city. Her eyes drifted towards the night market where ethian lamps were being lit. It was open day and night but only truly came alive after sunset. Unlike many other businesses in the city the night market was run almost exclusively by shifters and was as much an entertainment and neutral gathering hub for shapeshifters in Porta Belua as it was a place to buy and sell. The gathering clouds promised rain later but it was such a warm evening she knew the market would be bustling with all kinds of shifters and gawking tourists hoping to see the nocturnal beings that rarely ventured out before dark. She wondered if Aurora would be there. It was unlikely as she was trying to keep a low profile but if she needed to get supplies for her trip that would be the best place to go. Evie considered flying to the market in the hope of finding Aurora but quickly dismissed the thought. The night market was a sprawling labyrinth with lots of hidden corners; she could walk right past Aurora and never see her. Besides, she was physically exhausted and emotionally drained after all the ups and downs of the day. She desperately wanted a hot bath and then she needed to go to sleep. Tomorrow she would have a ton of work because of her absence and she would have to be up at the break of day to join her flock in singing the dawn song.

Glancing at her bed it occurred to Evie that it would be the first night in a week she would sleep without Aurora beside her. She knew that the bed was going to feel cold and empty without her. Where was Aurora sleeping tonight? Was she alone or perhaps with that Selene woman who was so eager for Aurora to stay with her? Aurora said there was no chemistry between them but for a smart woman she could be oblivious about some things. Just because she wasn't attracted to Selene didn't mean the other woman was equally unaffected. Evie slammed the drawer shut that held her sleepwear and marched off to the bathroom. Enough already. That kind of thinking would drive her crazy.

Evie had just finished toweling off and slipped on a top when she heard Oriana's voice at the bathroom door.

"Evie, you in there?"

Before Evie could ask Oriana to wait she pushed the door open and came inside.

"There you are! Evie, I..." Oriana paused mid-sentence and her eyebrows shot up. "Wow. How did you get those bruises on your butt?"

Oriana tilted her head sideways to get a better look. "Are those bite marks? Evie did you know you have bite marks on your butt and between your—"

Mortified Evie quickly yanked on her pants. "I know."

"Who did that to you? I mean..." Oriana paused to stare at her face. "Wow, I don't think I've ever seen you blush that hard. Not even that time when I caught you and your girlfriend about to—"

"Never mind that, Oriana," Evie quickly interrupted. "How many times do I have to tell you to wait for an answer after you've knocked? You can't just walk in!"

"But if I waited I would have missed out on seeing your love-bite riddled ass. So the woman you mentioned, I assume this means you two became more than just good friends?"

"Yes."

"A beast-shifter...oooh la-la, I didn't know you liked your girls that wild. She didn't hurt you, did she? She must have gotten rough to leave bruises."

"No, Aurora didn't get rough with me. Not that it's any of your business but she's an incredibly gentle and passionate lover. She just got excited."

"And bit you all over your ass?"

"It wasn't really bites even though she used her teeth a little. She also used her tongue to..." Evie stopped suddenly and held her hand up in a warding gesture. "Oh no, this is *not* happening. I'm not sharing sex details with my little sister. It's just something she does when she's excited and she was *very* excited. It didn't hurt at all; in fact, it was very erotic the way she did it." Evie could feel the heat on her cheeks spread down her neck.

"Oooo, *very* excited. You don't say. By the look of you, she wasn't the only one."

Evie giggled and threw a wet towel at her sister. "You're too young for this kind of conversation."

"Oh please, I'm seventeen and we've always talked openly about stuff. We're best buddies remember? Or has that changed?"

"No, of course not. Actually, I do need to talk about Aurora and I trust you not to blab to anyone."

"Never. What's said between us stays between us. That's our thing. My ears are your vault. Tell me more about this girl. Is she pretty?"

"Aurora is a woman not a girl and she's stunning. Taller than me and very strong. Don't you dare tell anyone but she carried me down a mountain in the dark while it was raining. That was just after we escaped and I broke my wing. There were people with dogs searching for us and I kept falling on the slippery rocks. I would never have gotten away on my own. She was amazing, Oriana, so sure-footed and graceful even with me on her back and she was tireless. That woman has so much stamina she can literally go for hours." As she said this Evie thought of the way Aurora smiled when she promised to pleasure Evie until she begged her to stop. She bit her lip and wished Aurora would magically materialize in her bed. What she wouldn't give to find her naked between the sheets waiting for her.

"Evie, you really have it bad for this woman."

"I do. I think she might have been *the one*. I know we weren't together that long but we spent almost every moment in each other's company. I've never connected with anyone like I did with her and she made me feel so safe. I knew she wouldn't let anybody or anything hurt me while she was around. The way she kissed and made love to me made me feel like I was the most precious person in the world. I've never felt so adored and desired." Evie sighed heavily her expression becoming troubled. "I'm rambling and not making sense."

"You're making perfect sense. You're in love with her."

"I am."

"What did she say when you told her?" Oriana asked.

"When I told her what?"

"That you're in love with her."

"I...I never told her."

"Why not?"

"She was leaving and I…it all seemed so quick."

"But you told her how much she means to you, right? I'm still new at the whole dating and love thing but I kind of assumed that's how this works."

"She knows I care about her but now that I think about it I never actually said…" Evie trailed off as she frantically searched her memories. Evie grabbed her sister's shoulder to steady herself as the realization hit. "Oh no. I never told Aurora how much she means to me. I didn't tell her how amazing she made me feel. She asked me to go away with her and I said I couldn't. When she told me she wanted me as her mate I was so stunned I said nothing. I wouldn't even agree to stay an extra week with her. Oriana, this is bad! I know how Aurora thinks. She would have brooded over this and concluded I wasn't interested in a serious relationship with her. After everything we shared that would have hurt her so badly. But I am. I want her! Oh…was *that* why she cried after we made love on the boat? Did she think it was just sex to me…that she was only a fling?" Evie groaned. "Yes, of course, she would think that because that's what she's learned to expect and I never told her I loved her. How did I fuck up so badly? I feel like I'm going to be sick."

***

To Aurora's delight she found that the height of the giant tree combined with the position of Selene's property meant she could literally see for miles in every direction while she herself was hidden from view by the dense foliage. She had taken her tiger form to stay dry in fur as it rained intermittently and it also allowed her to take full advantage of her tiger's superb hearing and night vision. Occasionally, just to make sure she didn't miss anything she would snake out a long tongue to test the air gathering scents that were too delicate for her tiger to detect. Aurora felt at home in the ancient tree with its familiar forest smell. The branch on which she lay was thick and sturdy so once she felt she was reasonably familiar with the sounds and smells of the neighborhood she put her head on her paws and relaxed into a light doze. Just before sunrise she moved to a different part of the tree from where she could see the top half of Evie's tower. It was too far away to identify Evie among her people but she could see the gathered flock on the balconies raise their wings as the sun rose. For a moment as the wind blew from the direction of the tower she thought she heard snippets of a dawn song but it was likely only her imagination. She watched as the avians of House Aquilar launched into the air until the sky around the tower was filled with winged figures circling higher and higher. Even from so far away it was a magnificent sight and she wished she knew which one was Evie.

It was with a mixture of regret and relief that she made herself look away when she heard Selene return. She watched Selene get out of the Jeep and pretend to stretch a stiff back so she could look up at the tree. Aurora lay flat and motionless, the predator in her delighted in knowing she blended so well into the background it would be near impossible for Selene to spot her. She was tempted to jump down beside her friend as a joke but she didn't. It was not a good idea to give Selene a fright. She had lightning quick reflexes and her years of surviving as an orphan on the streets of Porta Belua taught her to lash out first and ask questions later. She once had to dodge a hot pan filled with scrambled eggs because she came up behind Selene too quietly. Whatever weapons Selene had concealed under that jacket of hers would do a lot worse than a pan.

Aurora moved to where she would be visible and once Selene saw her she stretched her long body to give her friend a moment to get used to the sight of her before she jumped down. She padded over to Selene who had gone very still. She watched Aurora warily and took care not to make direct eye contact while she embraced her beast so completely. Aurora remembered wistfully how boldly Evie studied her the first time she saw her in tiger form. If Evie was here she would have strode up to meet her and had her hands buried in her fur by now. She never realized how much she enjoyed being touched until Evie had touched her all the time. Why had none of her friends ever felt so free with her? Was it her fault for being physically aloof or was it that Evie played by her own rules and totally ignored all Aurora's boundaries? Not that she wanted just anyone to touch her the way Evie did but Selene was such a good friend she should not be this cautious to avoid acting in a way that could be perceived as a challenge for dominance. Acting on impulse Aurora lowered her head and rubbed her cheek affectionately against Selene's shoulder. Selene made a startled noise and became rigid. Aurora remained motionless, waiting for her friend to make the next move. After a few seconds she relaxed and cautiously rested her hand on Aurora's massive head. Aurora chuffed to show her approval.

"We are friends, Selene. No matter what form I'm in you do not have to be afraid of me. I hope you know this?"

Selene gently worked her fingers into Aurora's fur. "I know. I was just being respectful and cautious. When you're in beast form you are magnificently terrifying."

Aurora turned so she could see Selene's expression and this time her friend did not look away. What she saw was genuine affection and sincerity but no fear. "For the record, I feel the same way when I see you carrying a weapon that could blow a fist-sized hole in my chest. Respectful and cautious." This made Selene grin like a kid who'd just been given a box of candy. Aurora huffed in amusement and headed toward the house. "I hope you brought lots of food because fixing that shower of yours has given me a monstrous appetite."

Behind her Selene laughed delightedly and went to the Jeep to grab a crate of groceries. Inside Aurora quickly shifted back to human. Once dressed she joined Selene in the kitchen.

"Did you really get the hot water going?"

"I did. The pressure is more like light rain than a downpour but the water will run as hot as you want it."

"That's amazing! You've made my day."

Aurora grinned happily and set about brewing a pot of tea.

Selene got a cake tin from the cupboard and popped it open to offer Aurora the biscuits inside. "I have good news for you."

"Yeah?"

"I got the jeweler to accept your commission. I thought he was going to faint from excitement when he saw the materials he got to work with and he was already furiously busy when I left. I'm not sure he will get it done before you leave though. I got your ticket and paperwork sorted. You're leaving tomorrow."

"So soon?"

"Everything fell into place. You did say you wanted to leave as quickly as possible?"

"I did."

"In other news – that ethian mine shut down."

"It has?"

"For now. Apparently, someone threw a freezer full of shapeshifter body parts along with the cutter responsible off the mountain to go splat where everyone could see it. Was that your handiwork?" When Aurora nodded Selene grunted in a manner that said that's what she suspected. "The miners had a look-see up top and found a lab with cages and all the guards dead, their necks snapped like dried twigs. It made a powerful impression. The miners are third to fifth generation Nordarrans, many have a shapeshifter somewhere in the family tree and most have shifter friends so they were furious to discover a cutter's nest right under their noses. What you did to the cutter and the guards they took as a warning from an angry shifter that bad things would happen to anyone who continued to work at the mine. The remaining guards tried to prevent the workers from leaving and things got ugly. By the time all was said and done the miners raided everything they could from the site and made a run for Porta Belua. They've been arriving for the last two days telling everyone they knew nothing about the existence of a cutter's lab, pointing fingers firmly at the owners."

"Who are the owners?"

"Good question. I had to grease a few palms to get all the juicy info.

On the surface everything looks legit. According to official records the mine changed hands two years ago and was bought by a company registered here in Porta Belua. All good so far. However, when I tried to find out who actually owns the company it quickly became clear someone put a lot of effort into obscuring the trail."

"Why such secrecy for a legitimate operation?" Aurora asked.

"Precisely. My contact told me the majority shareholder is a human named Carlos. He is a native of Nordarra who left to go make his fortune in the human world. According to my contact he only returned recently but he's had agents quietly at work for him for a few years now buying into all kinds of investments in preparation for his homecoming. Now here comes the intriguing part: House Ravir's people have been acting as his agents. They negotiated the sale of the mine and wait for it…House Ravir owns a third of the shares in the company that bought the mine."

"Our mystery human and House Ravir are business partners? The plot thickens."

"If you think that's interesting wait until you hear the rest. Word is House Ravir leveraged themselves hard to buy into the mine because they assumed they would recoup their costs quickly. What the avians didn't realize because none of them could go down those narrow passages to have a look was that all the big crystals were harvested just before the mine was sold. That left the little ones that would take years to grow to profitable size. In the meantime, the ethian veins had to be nurtured and the mine maintained and protected if they didn't want to lose their claim."

Aurora mused on this. Now she understood why the crystals in the mine were so small. She'd only found the large crystals because she crawled into a spider's nest in desperate hope of finding something decent. It was ironic that the cutters that owned the mine never knew what great riches lay within their reach. The miners, very sensibly, would have avoided the nests of the venomous creatures. Why risk their lives for set wages? It was only her promise to Yutu that had driven her to venture where no one else would go. She might be able to neutralize toxins but spider bites still hurt like crazy and having them crawl all over her had been nasty.

"So, you're saying House Ravir was in debt and losing money?"

"They were hemorrhaging thousands of credits a month. House Ravir, unlike House Aquilar, is not known for being business savvy and they were struggling financially even before the mine deal. They raked up debt everywhere and my contact said he heard a reliable rumor that House Ravir was perilously close to losing their tower because they couldn't repay their loans. The only thing that kept the creditors at bay was the logistics of trying to wrestle the tower away from such a militant flock. Then about a year ago their fortunes miraculously started improving."

"I can guess why."

"Yeah. It's an ugly business but extremely profitable for those with the stomach for such things. House Ravir has a long history of getting their hands bloody for profit. I heard they have ties with Black Paw and, for the right price, will act as scouts for hunters. There hasn't been a rumor of them working with cutters but desperate people will do desperate things."

"Evie told me House Ravir pushed hard to create an alliance with House Aquilar. She said her father didn't trust them and she couldn't stand to be in the same room as Lord Nero or his psychotic children so she deliberately derailed the negotiations despite her uncle Marcus advocating for the alliance. I'm so glad she did. Once word gets out anyone associated with House Ravir will be ruined."

"Unfortunately, once the business at the mine and the content of the ledger become widely known it is going to taint every avian flock to some extent. It's a real shame. The avians were just beginning to shake their reputation as sky-hunters for the slavers and cutters. Now, because of one greedy House, they're all going to be dragged back into the mud."

Aurora frowned. "I hope this won't affect Evie's House too badly."

"I wouldn't worry about it. Augustus Aquilar has worked hard for many years to distance his House publicly from any flock that still carried a whiff of involvement with those kinds of practices. House Aquilar should be fine. It will help their cause that Evangeline Aquilar was seen with you in the city and that according to rumors in the night market you almost bit a wolf who tried to get cozy with her. There is even a rumor you marked her as your mate?"

"Ah…so much for sneaking undetected into the city."

"Care to tell me what happened?"

"Evie and I had been intimate shortly before we had a run in with a male wolf. He propositioned Evie. It made me so furious I started shifting without even being aware of it. If he hadn't backed off I would have killed him."

"I see." Selene picked up her cup and took a sip of her tea. "How did

Evie react to this?"

"She wasn't upset or afraid if that's what you're asking. She helped me calm down. Evie is very good at that."

Selene took another sip of her tea her expression thoughtful. "Most avians would be too afraid to go near an upset beast-shifter and when you get angry it's no joke. Your Evie sounds like a remarkable woman. Are you sure you two can't work things out?"

"Don't poke at this, Selene. It is what it is."

Selene put her cup down and patted Aurora's clenched fist where it lay on the kitchen table. "I'm sorry. It is just that I've never seen you like this about anyone but you're right, it's none of my business. I'll leave it alone."

"That would be for the best." Aurora sighed and gave Selene a rueful smile. "Did you manage to find out who put the big bounty on me?"

"Not yet, but it wouldn't surprise me if it's connected to what happened at the mine. The timing is just too coincidental."

"Well, it hardly matters now. I'll be leaving tomorrow."

CHAPTER 25

DANGEROUS VISITORS

In her sitting room Evie lowered herself wearily into a chair. It was after midnight and aside from stretching her wings for a short flight during the dawn song that morning she'd been stuck inside all day. She wanted to go look for Aurora but she'd been unable to leave. She'd had a quick tour of the mira gardens to check on progress. After that she'd had a marathon of meetings and endlessly dealing with people who should be able to take care of the House business assigned to them without needing so much input from her. It was good to have her opinion valued but on more than one occasion she'd had to bite her tongue to not give a sharp reply. Her people had fluttered around her like nervous children in need of reassurance. She had never experienced anything like it and on a day she so badly wanted to be elsewhere it had been particularly trying.

Evie knew it was her father's illness that had the flock so unsettled. Lord Augustus had always been such a powerful presence, a figure to look up to. At the same time, he was an approachable leader who knew his people well. Under his leadership the flock had prospered and through his shrewd but fair dealings with other shapeshifters and humans, built a reputation for House Aquilar that gave its members respectability and a measure of protection that didn't rely on squadrons of armed warriors circling their tower. By shapeshifter standards her father was still a man in his prime and it had been shocking for Evie to see her father go backwards so quickly over the course of one year. The progressive illness had eaten away at the once vigorous man reducing him to a husk of what he used to be. His plumage was dull with bare patches and the fire in his eyes that had always shone so brightly had become dimmed by pain and frustration at the weakness of his body. The physicians had tried everything but since none of them could diagnose the cause of his illness all they could offer were remedies to alleviate his symptoms. As her father weakened he had handed more responsibilities over to her, to where she had to juggle more than either of them expected her to have to take up so soon. Despite how difficult it had been she thought she had done a reasonable job. Not as good as her father but she genuinely cared for her people and did her best. In her unexplained week-long absence the flock seemed to have developed a new found appreciation for her and it had taken her by surprise how many people had come to tell her they were happy she got home safely and seemed genuine about it.

Evie knew she was generally well liked and respected but she suspected in this instance it had more to do with the flock's concern with Marcus's behavior in her absence. Evie had had many complaints about the way he strutted around like he was Lord of the Tower. Mostly it was his arrogant and disruptive behavior that had ruffled feathers but there were two incidents she could not overlook. The first incident was financial and the other involved a serious breach of security. That morning the head accountant, a steely-eyed woman named Reva, told her she'd received a request for repayment on a substantial loan underwritten by House Aquilar on behalf of Marcus that she swore had never been authorized. This followed on the heels of Evie blocking his access to credit tokens only the previous month after she found out he'd been pressuring one of the junior accountants into letting him have those without going through the proper channels. When she had an audit done on what the tokens had been used for it turned out House Aquilar had been footing the bill for his extravagant parties and debt raked up at several gambling halls. She had made it clear to him then that House Aquilar was not his personal bank and that she would take serious action if he tried to pull another stunt like that again.

The accountant had just gone when she'd been told that Marcus had taken Raven on a tour of the tower and tried to bully the sentinels into letting them into restricted areas that contained the armory and the research laboratories. Fortunately, the sentinels had stood fast and refused, citing breach of House protocol. Evie had been speechless with fury when she heard what he'd done. In her eyes, he had gone from being a puffed-up peacock with delusions of grandeur and an occasional menace to a danger to the security of House Aquilar. Only a few members of House Aquilar were granted access to those areas and yet her idiot uncle thought it would be a good idea to take the heir of a rival avian House for a guided tour. As far as she was concerned it was the last straw. She would not tolerate such behavior from other members of her flock and he'd been allowed to get away with too much for too long. Marcus had to go.

She had already spoken with the head of security to make sure his eviction would be handled quietly and efficiently. She would not allow the man to upset the flock or her father with a dying swan act. She would have had him thrown out after dinner but her father had already been asleep when she had gone to his suite and she owed him an explanation before she kicked out his half-brother. Once she spoke with her father in the morning Marcus would be removed from his luxury suite and not be allowed back into the tower. As much as she was tempted to strip him of all support, she wouldn't touch the monthly allowance her father gave him because it wouldn't do for the Lord of the Tower's half-brother to live in squalor. He would, however, be cut off from all other House resources. If he curbed his extravagant spending he could live in comfort. If not, well, he was an adult. It was time he acted like one and faced the consequences of his actions.

Evie rotated her neck to get rid of the stiffness brought on by the stresses of the day. Tomorrow as soon as she dealt with Marcus, she would go look for Aurora. No matter what. She knew from experience it was a slow process organizing passage to leave Nordarra but she still felt the clock ticking and it was not a good feeling. She couldn't afford to let another day slip away without actively trying to find her. She would start with that friend of hers, Selene. The one who had a place in Old Town. She probably knew where Aurora was or could get a message to her that Evie wanted to see her. Even with how busy she'd been her thoughts had never been far from Aurora and she'd felt her absence like a constant ache. After her mini-breakdown in her bathroom the previous evening she'd felt utterly miserable. She'd spent hours replaying their time together and she had been appalled that she'd missed so many of Aurora's subtle and not so subtle signals that she was interested in a serious relationship with her. She had been so blinded by Aurora's plans to go away and the worries of what was happening back home that she had suppressed her desire to tell Aurora she loved her and wanted them to be together. She would not make that mistake again. When she saw Aurora she would tell her how much she meant to her and that she wanted to become her mate.

As soon as she'd made the decision to fight for Aurora Evie had felt the rightness of it. She knew there would be some in the shapeshifter community who would be outraged by their joining but she didn't care.

As long as Aurora still wanted her she knew they would make it work. The way she saw the future she was bound to a lifetime of service for the good of her House. Despite being groomed for the responsibility, giving up so much of her freedom had never sat easily with her but she'd thought she had a lot more time to play before her wings were clipped. If she was to become ruler of House Aquilar years ahead of schedule she wanted at least one thing just for herself that made her truly happy. She wanted Aurora. Her flock would accept it or they could go pluck their own feathers for all she cared. She hoped she'd be able to convince Aurora to stay. She spent every free moment working on her arguments. She even worked out a plan to keep the hunters off Aurora's trail permanently. If Aurora wouldn't listen to reason she planned to seduce her. She would do whatever it took. Not that it would be a hardship to drag Aurora off to bed to convince her they belonged together. Fantasies about the many ways she could show Aurora just how well they fit together had pleasantly distracted her during several of the more tedious meetings she'd had to endure.

Evie got out of the chair and went inside to get ready for bed, locking the balcony door behind her. She was almost at her bedroom door when she heard a knock. Evie frowned; who would bother her so late? She had given strict instructions that unless there was an emergency she didn't want to see anyone until morning. The knock repeated and to her surprise, Evie realized the sound was not coming from the door to her suite but the balcony. That must mean it was Oriana because the guards would allow no one else near her balcony this time of night. Evie came to an abrupt halt when she saw the balcony door she just locked was wide open. Made from reinforced glass and spell crafted to withstand severe weather and physical attacks, it was also meant to have a tamper proof lock. In addition to her door being open several of the lights that had previously illuminated her sitting room were out so the room had more shadows than she liked.

"Hello? Who's there?"

There was movement on the darkened balcony and she saw the figure of a woman dressed in a long flowing robe. She had her hood drawn so her face was cast in shadows.

"A friendly visitor. If you will treat me as such."

"Who are you?"

"You should invite me in."

"Since you've already opened the door you hardly need my

permission to enter. However, if you wish to be treated like a friendly visitor you will tell me your name and give me the opportunity to decide if you are welcome here."

"You know my daughter Aurora."

"Lady Adelind?"

"You may call me that."

Cautiously Evie approached the doorway. "How do I know you are really Lady Adelind? I don't know what Aurora's mother looks like."

The woman studied her for a moment then produced a folded piece of paper and opened it for Evie to see. Evie recognized the paper and her own handwriting. It was the note she had written to Aurora's mother.

"If that is not enough proof I can mention that I saw you in a library. Although at the time you were preoccupied with my daughter and unlikely to have noticed my brief presence."

Evie felt her face go red hot with embarrassment. She desperately wanted to look anywhere but at the woman who had seen her having sex with her daughter but she stiffened her back and said, "Lady Adelind, I welcome you as a guest to my home. Please come in."

Lady Adelind inclined her head, accepting the invitation and came inside. As she came into the light Evie saw her more clearly and felt her mouth go dry. She had the face of a statue, perfectly sculpted and equally chilly. Her grey eyes shone with razor-sharp intelligence and the haughty confidence one saw in those accustomed to wielding great power. Movement on Lady Adelind's robe caught her eye. At first, she wasn't sure what she was seeing then she realized that the midnight-blue robe shimmered with silver runes woven into elaborate patterns that seemed to be moving. Curious, she focused, trying to see one of the patterns more clearly but the runes immediately changed shape and she felt a sharp stab behind her eyeballs. She quickly looked away. When Aurora said her mother knew advanced rune magic she wasn't kidding. What the heck was she dealing with? More importantly, what the heck was Lady Adelind doing here in the middle of the night? Trying not to show how unnerved she was Evie schooled her expression and drew on her polite hostess persona. She offered Lady Adelind the first choice of chairs and took a seat across from her.

"Would you like refreshments? I can call for tea to be brought up if you desire?"

"No. I do not wish my presence here to be known. We have important matters to discuss, Evangeline Aquilar."

"We do?"

"Yes. I want to know how you came to be in the sanctuary and who you told of its existence."

"I told no one. Aurora made me give an oath that I would never speak of it. As for why I was there, why not ask your daughter? She was the one who took me there."

"I am asking *you*."

Evie could not think of a good reason not to answer Aurora's mother and plenty of reasons why withholding the information could be a bad idea so she gave a brief summary of how they met and their journey together.

When Evie was done Lady Adelind sat quietly as if reviewing what Evie had told her. She nodded and said, "What you told me explains the foundation of your relationship. Aurora is cautious when it comes to intimate relationships and I know for a fact she has never taken anyone else home. Therefore, you must be dear to her and someone that she trusts. Aurora is a good judge of character but I had to meet you for myself to make an assessment. Call it parental concern if you like. Now on to the other matter I've come to discuss with you. The note. In it you said things I found curious."

"Curious how?"

"You implied my behavior has alienated my daughter. You urged me to speak with her and make things right before she left Nordarra. What behavior are you referring to?"

"Are you sure this is a conversation you want to have with me? Wouldn't it be better to speak to Aurora directly?"

"It pains me to admit there are things amiss in our relationship. I have no idea how to broach the subject with Aurora and even if I could find the right words to ask her why she acts towards me the way she does it is likely she wouldn't tell me. You, on the other hand, seem to be privy to information I am not. I demand you tell me."

Evie felt herself stiffen at the woman's impertinent demand. Lady Adelind was clearly a woman accustomed to getting her way but if she thought she could bark orders and have Evangeline Aquilar blindly obey she would be sorely disappointed. Her magic robe wasn't *that* impressive. Evie locked eyes with Lady Adelind and said, "I won't share what Aurora told me in confidence just because you demand it."

Surprise and a hint of approval showed on Lady Adelind's face. She gave Evie a long thoughtful look. "It was my understanding from your note that you hoped to see a greater closeness between me and my daughter. Correct?" At Evie's nod she continued. "Have you considered that what you know may be the key to us reconnecting?" She waited a moment for that to sink in. "Tell me what you know, Evangeline. Please." It sounded like the proud woman almost choked on the please. Evie felt herself soften.

"Lady Adelind, what I have to say will not be easy to hear. Aurora never spoke badly of you but the picture she painted of your relationship wasn't pretty."

"My daughter is often a mystery to me. She doesn't scream or shout, she holds things inside. She is my only child. I wish to understand her. I want to hear everything."

"Aurora told me how she was captured and how her father died. She told me of the things that happened and the vow she made. She said you became cold towards her after her father died. That you could not stand to touch her and were rarely around. She thinks you blame her for his death as she blames herself."

"I see. Aurora has it wrong. The truth is so much worse."

"I don't understand?"

Lady Adelind sighed like she carried the weight of the world on her shoulders and said, "To understand what I mean I have to tell you a story. It's both a love story and a tragedy. Of lovers who were never meant to be together but defied the odds and did the worst thing possible; they had a child. Aurora's father came from a lineage that has been tied to the magic of this land for centuries. His people strive to keep their line pure so as not to dilute the power that was gifted to them. This is something Valen's people and mine have in common. To stay pure his clan stay secluded in one of the ancient forests. It is a vast place inhabited by great beasts the likes of which I've not seen elsewhere and the winters there are the most terrible I've ever experienced. It is truly a place only the strongest survive."

"Is that where you met Aurora's father?"

"Yes. I was passing through the area. I'd been warned about the unpredictable weather but I was only meant to be there briefly, a few days at most. I thought I could handle whatever weather came my way but I got caught in a snowstorm of epic proportions. Total white out so that I couldn't tell up from down. The rivers froze solid, ice weighed me down so it was difficult to move and every breath felt like swallowing razor blades. Lost and half frozen I stumbled into what I thought was a cave looking for shelter only to find it was someone's home."

"Aurora's father?"

Lady Adelind nodded. "Valen was in beast form but I recognized what he was and asked for shelter and hospitality in the tongue of his people. His people and mine have clashed in the past. It does not translate well but we are the equivalent of honored enemies. We have been at peace a long time but we do the best we can to avoid one another. It's a courtesy and a precaution. I expected his response to be as cold as the frozen lands he called home but he was nothing like I expected. He laughed and told me my pronunciation was terrible but I was welcome all the same. He offered me a place by his fire, a seat at his table and safety in exchange for stories from the world outside his people's territories. It was a relentless, bitter storm that lasted weeks. He changed to man so he could tend the fire I needed for warmth and so we could talk more easily. His tiger was huge and magnificent but as a man, he took my breath away. He was so big and powerful but so gentle. He moved carefully so he wouldn't frighten me with his size. He was so easy to talk to and had such an inquisitive mind, we spoke for hours and it felt like mere minutes. He wooed me and before long we became lovers. More than lovers. I knew I had found the one person who made me feel complete. Valen wanted me to stay and become his life-mate but that was impossible for so many reasons." Lady Adelind paused and stared off into the distance retrieving old memories. "Valen told me he would follow me anywhere. He said he would abandon the great forest and frozen shadow lands of his clan to be with me. I didn't believe he would really give up that much for me. I told him if he was willing to do that I'd find a way for us to be together. But he did it. He threw a pack on his back and followed me halfway across the continent. Then he built us a home and grew my favorite flowers outside our bedroom window so I'd smell the sweet scent drifting in on the evening breeze. Those years with him, those precious days and nights were the happiest of my life. I've never known a love like that and no matter how long I live it is unlikely anyone will love me half as well as Valen loved me."

"So, Aurora really was a product of your love?"

"Yes. He wanted us to have a child so badly. He begged me. I knew it was a bad idea. Our bloodlines are ancient and carry too many things that could mix badly. There was a lot that could go wrong. Even if we produced a normal child our offspring would not be welcomed by his people or mine. Our child would be an outcast destined for a lonely life.

He said he would make it his mission to make connections among the tribes of younger shapeshifters and humans so that our child could mingle with their children and make friends among all of them. For every concern I had he would come up with a counter argument. He wore me down. I took so much from him that I could not deny him a child."

Lady Adelind went quiet again but Evie sensed the story was far from over. There was something about the way the woman held herself that reminded her of Aurora when she was contemplating what to say next, if anything at all. Evie didn't try to fill the silence waiting instead for Lady Adelind to decide how much she would share.

"As soon as Aurora was born and Valen handed her to me to suckle I knew I had made a terrible mistake. She was mostly in human form but her little hands on my chest kept changing: hand, paw, claw and then a hideous mix. I was terrified. I knew that meant our child was a chimera. Normally a child of mixed lineage takes after either parent when it comes to shifting with the human form as the base. This is how it should be and even that can be too much for some to handle if the heritage is a rich and powerful one. You would not have experienced this yourself but beast-shifter children are taught to have disciplined minds and to create harmony between their human and beast selves. This is so they can harness the strengths that come with the ability to shapeshift without being swept away by the more primal impulses that come with it. Chimeras can access everything that comes with their mixed lineage. Not only can they make a full shift to another form they can also draw parts of it like just claws or fangs or whatever they have learned to do. Some powerful shifters of the Old Blood can still become a creature that is half man half beast but what makes chimeras unique is that they can draw from several forms at once to become something entirely different. However, in doing so they open themselves to a raging torrent, with all they carry within fighting for dominance with the carrier's consciousness. That is a terrible onslaught that few minds can survive intact. Thankfully a chimera is rarely conceived and even less likely to make it to term. If one survives in most instances it becomes a ferocious, crazed monster in a nightmarish body that is in a perpetual state of hunger and bloodlust. For this reason, if Aurora had been born among my people, they would have killed her instantly."

Shocked, Evie struggled not to let her dismay show. "Would you really have killed your child? Your own baby?"

"I saw a grown chimera once. It was a hideous, rampaging, crazed thing that had to be put down and it was not easily done. So yes, I would have smothered my own child rather than risk having to hunt her later."

"But you didn't."

"I could not." Lady Adelind took a deep shuddering breath. "Valen was beside me the whole time and all he saw was his beautiful daughter, the result of our love. He thought it was cute she could shift like that. He didn't understand what it meant. His happiness was my weakness, I could not take that joy away from him. I could not kill her and I could not tell him that she was an abomination. I was desperate."

"What did you do?"

"I did the only thing that made sense at the time. I suppressed her ability to shift, locking her in human form to at least give her a chance to develop normally. All she could do was alter small parts of herself like fingers or eyes but she could not hold it for long. Valen was so distressed about that. He longed for his daughter to run with him in beast form and he hoped it would be just a matter of time until she managed it. He was convinced her part shifting was proof she would. Knowing she couldn't and that I was the cause was a terrible burden but I consoled myself it was either that or kill our daughter. I told myself over and over I'd done the right thing. I was even proud of the complexity of the spell I wove. Aurora could feel her beasts calling to her so she kept trying to break down the barrier she felt but did not understand to connect with them. She fought so valiantly but she never stood a chance. She was only a child and I had set my considerable magic against her." The padded chair on which Lady Adelind sat groaned and Evie saw the metal of the armrest squeeze through her fingers like putty. "So good was my binding that when those men took turns to rape my little girl, she could not break free. When they broke her bones and burned her, she was helpless to defend herself. They tortured her and she could do nothing but suffer and bleed because of me. Valen died trying to save our daughter because I withheld from her the power that was hers by birth out of fear of what she might become. I was so arrogant, so superior in my conviction that I'd done the right thing. I was the worst kind of fool. For years I've wondered if Valen suspected what I had done. If that was why he chose to bleed all over Aurora knowing the power of his blood, so old and powerful made even more potent at the time of his death, would set her free from my binding so that she could save herself."

"They raped Aurora?" Evie's voice was barely a whisper.

"She didn't tell you? No, of course, she wouldn't have. What was I thinking? Yes, they raped her. I don't know if it was just to draw out her father or because she was such a beautiful child. Whatever the reason it scarred her. I think next to her father's death, being violated like that was what damaged her the most."

"That's horrific. No wonder she went out of her mind for a while."

Lady Adelind nodded. "Indeed. When I found her and saw the state she was in I feared the worst. For some time after I worried she was not entirely sane. She endured so much and she had to learn to cope with such a complex heritage. It is a testament to her immense strength of will that despite all of that she managed to become the woman she is today. I am so proud of her."

Evie felt sick after hearing Lady Adelind's account of what happened to Aurora. What Aurora shared about what happened to her and her father had been awful to hear but that had not been the worst of it. It had either been too hard for her to speak about or she had tried to spare Evie the full horror of what had been done to her. Evie tasted bile in her mouth and wondered if she would have to excuse herself to go throw up. Before she could make up her mind Lady Adelind continued speaking.

"Now you know the truth you must see I never blamed my daughter for her father's death and not for a moment have I stopped loving her. Aurora means more to me than you can possibly comprehend. It is simply that I hate myself. Every time I look in her eyes and see the scars on her soul I know that was my doing. It is unbearable."

"So, what? You wouldn't touch Aurora because her pain made you uncomfortable? You were all she had left and she needed you to be there for her. She desperately needed her mother. Instead, you left her all alone in that so-called sanctuary to fend for herself. That, lady, is called abandonment." Evie knew her anger bled into her voice but she didn't care.

Lady Adelind gave a dismissive flick of her fingers. "Aurora was always an independent child and much closer to her father than me. They spent so much time together and I was the mother who visited but never stayed. He was warm, patient and easy to be with. Affectionate. I'm not. He found ways to make us work as a family. He made everything all right somehow. After he died she became so wild and obsessed with vengeance that it was difficult to find her, getting near her in any meaningful way was near impossible. Without Valen I didn't know how to bridge the divide. I never abandoned her. I saw her whenever I could. I taught her whatever she would accept from me. I taught her how to shift and how to contain the beasts so they did not control her. I showed her the secret places of the ancient ones and how to use that knowledge to keep hidden. I made sure she had a safe place to return to and that she had access to plenty of food, resources and knowledge. I shielded her from my people. I kept her safe to the best of my ability."

"You kept her safe to the best of your ability? Really? If that's true then your ability is severely lacking." Evie's voice dripped with sarcasm.

"What is that supposed to mean?" Lady Adelind's expression hardened and there was a dangerous gleam in her eyes.

"Do you know why she's leaving Nordarra?"

"She's after adventure and discovery – Aurora has always been curious about the world beyond the portal."

"No! It's because she's tired of being hunted like her father. How can you not know this?"

"What are you talking about?" Lady Adelind demanded. Shock and disbelief warred on her face. "Who dares to hunt my daughter?"

"The cutters and exotic animal hunters. They are after her because she is an Old Blood tigress."

"How long has this been going on?"

"Years. From the sound of things since her father's death."

"That's not possible. She would have told me. *Someone* would have told me! I knew Aurora had the occasional pursuer but I assumed it was because of her hunt for her father's killers."

"At one time that was probably the main reason but not anymore. Dead or alive she is worth a fortune on the black market. She has killed so many hunters but the price keeps going up so the cycle continues. I tried to persuade her to find a way to make that stop but it has been going on for such a long time I don't think she can see it ever ending. It's too much. Constantly being on guard for traps and hunters has worn her down. She can never relax. She wants to settle down with a mate and have a normal life but she doesn't think that's possible in Nordarra. She thinks she must leave or eventually what happened to her father will happen to her. Can you imagine what that must be like for her? To live in fear she will one day find herself back in a cage at the mercy of cutters? Or even worse, to have someone she loves tortured and killed because of her? She barely survived what happened the first time and she's still plagued by horrific nightmares."

"You've painted a grim picture, Evangeline."

Lost in thought Lady Adelind sat expressionless and motionless as a statue and Evie knew instinctively not to speak to her. If Aurora's mother breathed or blinked Evie couldn't see it. The only thing that moved was the hem of her robe where the evening breeze stirred it but only slightly as if it too was afraid to disturb the woman. When Lady Adelind finally spoke her voice was low and thoughtful. "You have given me much to think about. You were bold to speak to me the way you have little avian but that is the way when love stirs the heart – it makes one reckless. However, since you did it on behalf of my daughter, I will overlook it."

"I was reckless? How so?"

"I can tell you have no idea who or what I am. Normally I wouldn't tolerate being lectured by the likes of you. Clearly Aurora kept her word and said nothing. Either that or you're not just reckless but stupid as well and my daughter would never fall for such a woman."

Evie bristled at the arrogance of the woman but she decided to bite her tongue. She had a personal question she wanted to ask Lady Adelind and she wouldn't get an answer if she antagonized her more. "Lady Adelind, Aurora said you are a direct descendant of the Old Bloods as well but wouldn't tell me what kind of shapeshifter you are. Would you mind telling me?"

Lady Adelind regarded her impassively, the blue light of the moon making her look even colder. "What else did Aurora tell you about me?"

"Aside from what I already shared? Very little. Odd snippets of conversation. Like when I asked her if you were joking about tearing off my wings if I betrayed her, she said you were serious and when I wrote you that note she said hopefully I'd been polite because your people used to eat avians. I honestly don't know if she was just messing with me. Sometimes Aurora's sense of humor can be a little odd."

Lady Adelind smiled showing a mouth full of teeth that gleamed unnaturally and looked too pointy to be entirely human. "My daughter does have a peculiar sense of humor and in her roundabout way she did tell you what I am. Think about the old stories. Do you recall which Old Bloods used to hunt avians for food and sport? Who filled your little hearts with such terror you sang with joy to see the dawn? Think about it. Tell me when it comes to you."

Evie inhaled sharply and her eyes grew wide. "Nooo, you're not a…you can't be a…"

"I can't be what? Say it if you dare." Lady Adelind tilted her head, one flawless eyebrow raised in challenge.

"A dragon. Are you a dragon?"

Lady Adelind blinked and suddenly Evie found herself pinned by cold reptilian eyes. "Well done, little avian. You would do well to keep this and everything else I told you to yourself. I like you, Evangeline, but my daughter's secrets are not to be shared. If you break her trust or breathe a single word of what I've told you to anyone you will witness first-hand the wrath of a dragon. I will annihilate your entire flock so that when I'm finished only blood, ash and feathers will remain. I'll make you watch the destruction of everything you hold dear and when I'm done, I'll eat your treacherous heart. This I swear to you on my scales."

Lady Adelind flashed Evie a terrifying smile full of sharp teeth and menace. Then she walked out on to the balcony and disappeared over the side. An instant later a massive dark scaled dragon whooshed up into the sky. The power of the creature's wings caused so much backdraft it made the curtains flap and staggered Evie back several feet. Evie raced to the balcony craning her neck to find where the dragon had gone. There was no trace of Lady Adelind anywhere, even though the evening was bright and clear enough for her to see for miles.

***

Evie rarely felt the need to fortify herself with a drink but after Lady Adelind's dramatic departure she went over to her drinks cabinet and poured herself a brandy. After a sip of the smooth liquor she was pleased to note her hands shook only a little. Not bad considering she'd just had a dragon threaten to kill her entire flock and rip out her heart. She had a lot to think about and no one she could talk to about any of it. She'd been shocked to hear Lady Adelind call Aurora a chimera. Evie recalled reading about chimeras when her tutor delved into ancient Nordarran lore. Most of the creatures described in those old texts were so outrageously powerful or strange that she had always assumed the writers embellished or made up the mythical beings. She still struggled to accept that Aurora was a chimera but why would her mother lie? That would explain why Aurora said she didn't intend to have children and on more than one occasion had alluded to being called a monster. If those old books were to be believed chimeras could morph into such powerful monstrosities even the mighty dragons feared them.

Aurora is a chimera. Evie poked at the revelation a little more to see if it changed how she felt about her. It didn't. So, the woman she wanted as her mate had an actual dragon for a mother and hid how powerful and dangerous she truly was. That was hardly surprising all things considered. What really upset her and brought her to the verge of tears was Lady Adelind's description of the torture Aurora had suffered at the hands of her father's killers. She'd never been the kind to fantasize about killing but if she had it in her power to turn back time she would personally lead an aerial assault against those evil people and command her warriors to show no mercy. At least they were all dead. No…not all of them. Aurora said that their leader escaped to the human world and she lost his trail. After so many years he would not be easy to locate but she would hire agents to continue the search and if he was found she would have that despicable man killed and his heart brought back as a gift for Aurora. Evie grimaced at her bloodthirsty thoughts and downed the rest of her drink. Less than an hour in the company of a dragon and she was already thinking like one.

Evie was still standing with the glass in hand contemplating if it was wise to have another brandy when she heard a noise at her door. Glancing at her clock she saw it was almost two in the morning. Odd. Even Oriana wouldn't come to her this late, not unless there was an emergency, and then she would be shouting and pounding on the door. Evie registered with alarm that the sound she was hearing was someone unlocking her door. She looked around frantically and just had enough time to grab a corkscrew from the cabinet when the door swung open. As if in slow motion she saw a tall avian male with a hawkish nose enter her sitting room. She really should have backed into the shadows but she was so outraged at seeing Marcus sneak into her suite in the middle of the night that she blurted out, "What are you doing here?"

Her uncle paused and looked startled to see her standing in her sitting room when he probably expected her to be sound asleep. He got shoved out of the way and behind him Raven Ravir appeared holding a needle-gun. As soon as Evie saw it something clicked in her mind and she was on the move towards the closest exit, her balcony. She veered towards her room when she saw her escape blocked by an avian in sky-hunter garb landing on her balcony. She heard the whoosh behind her and deflected the first dart with a blast of air from her wing so it fell harmlessly to the floor. There was cursing behind her as Raven reloaded.

Evie made it to her room and rushed to slam the reinforced door shut so she could engage the locks but a foot got shoved into the gap at the last moment. Terrified, Evie cried out and slashed blindly with the corkscrew. Marcus wailed in pain and to her relief he withdrew his foot. Just as she was about to slide the lock in place the door got rammed and she flew backwards with the force of the impact. Staggering and struggling to regain her balance she saw the avian male from the balcony come at her with outstretched arms so she whipped out a wing aiming for his head. Convinced she was fighting for her life she held nothing back and connected to his temple with a satisfying thump that vibrated through her wing. Dazed, he slumped to the floor. She picked up a heavy glass figurine of a dragon and threw it at Marcus but he ducked and she heard it smash to pieces in the room behind him. Raven darted through the doorway and Evie saw her level the weapon and pull the trigger. She tried to get out of the way but there was nowhere to go and she felt the sharp sting as the dart hit her chest. She yanked it out immediately but she knew she was in serious trouble. If the needle was filled with something similar to what she was shot with at the mine she had seconds before her muscles turned to jelly. She tried to fall back to the bathroom but her desperation wasn't enough to overcome the drug and she stumbled on numb legs. There was another sharp sting as a dart grazed her shoulder in passing. The world tilted and the floor came flying up at her. Evie tried to move but her body felt like it was weighted down with boulders. She tried to scream but all that came out was a low moan. Her face pressed into the thick carpet, she struggled to breathe and her uncle's voice sounded like a distant echo over the drumming of her own heart. She closed her eyes when she saw a woman's boots and braced for a kick in the head or a crushing blow to her ribs but to her surprise, Raven only gave her a sharp poke in the side. She didn't react. If they thought she was unconscious she might be able to use that to her advantage. If she was going to survive whatever this was, she couldn't afford to panic. Evie fought against the haze trying to claim her mind and honed in on the angry voices above her. It sounded like her uncle and Raven were having an argument.

"Quietly in and out. That is what you said, Raven. Your man knocked over a table and there is glass and blood everywhere!"

"Blame it on your own incompetence, Marcus. You said she would be asleep. The mess we made is minimal and most of it is you dripping blood on the floor. Wrap that wound, you fool! Don't just stand there and look at yourself like you expect someone else to do it. I'm not sticking around for the clean-up, that's your responsibility. You'd better do a good job if you don't want someone to become suspicious."

"I can't believe the little cunt cut me. Take her away. Get rid of the bitch. Make sure it looks like she had an accident. She recently had an injury to her right wing so it shouldn't be hard to make it look like it gave in while she was having one of her solo flights."

"I know why we are here. Remember, you owe us. Oriana's hand in marriage to my brother, an alliance between our Houses and a half share in the profits from the mira products."

"Aquimar wasn't part of the deal! I will never be able to sell something like that to the flock!"

"It is part of the deal now and you will make it happen. Did you think you could just keep asking for help and the price would remain the same? It doesn't work like that. Don't try to wiggle your way out of this. You know if you cross my father he will do a lot worse than pluck your feathers."

"All right I'll do it. No need to threaten me, Raven. As soon as I'm Lord of the Tower I will deliver on my part."

"You keep saying that. Lord Nero is out of patience and he wants what you promised him. Up the dose. Finish it."

"It will look suspicious if Augustus dies now."

"Nonsense. It's perfect timing. Lord Augustus is a sick man, the grief and strain of his beloved daughter's second disappearance is exactly the kind of thing that would finish him off. As soon as he is dead her corpse will be found in a ravine. For this to work the timing must be right, no more than a day or two delay or it will look suspicious."

"That wasn't the plan! She was supposed to die immediately and then I kill him."

"Marcus, you talk big but you're weak on delivery. You've been poisoning Lord Augustus for a year and he's still not dead. I'm keeping Evie alive until he is. How's that for motivation?"

"But—"

"Stop whining, you pathetic worm! We've done everything but hand House Aquilar to you on a plate. Grow a pair and do your part. Kill Lord Augustus. No more excuses."

Evie felt as she was rolled into a net but what was happening to her seemed inconsequential now that she knew her uncle was going to murder her father and she was helpless to prevent it. Evie's last despairing thought before darkness claimed her was that she was going to die and Aurora would never know she loved her.

CHAPTER 26

FINDING EVIE

Aurora stared at the pendant in the box. "This is beautiful, Selene. So elegant. I like how all the elements were incorporated. This is even better than I imagined. Your jeweler friend truly is a master."

"Not to mention a miracle worker getting it done so quickly. I expect the bonus you offered on top of the asking price was a great motivator."

Aurora held the pendant up by the chain so she could see it from all sides and Selene whistled appreciatively. "Wow…that's exquisite."

"Do you think Evie will like it?"

"If she doesn't the woman is blind or has no taste. That is a work of art. If someone had that made especially for me I'd count myself incredibly lucky."

Aurora smiled and admired how the play of light brought out various colors in the design. "I really want her to like it. I hope she'll wear it and think of me." Feeling embarrassed she'd spoken so openly Aurora carefully put the pendant back into the box. She added the note she had written, engaged the lock adding a little magic so only Evie could open it and then she carefully wrapped the box in the pretty paper Selene had the foresight to get for her. Her hands felt big and clumsy wrestling the slippery silk ribbon into a tidy bow and trying to do it on the dashboard of Selene's vehicle didn't help but Aurora was pleased with the end result. When she looked up she caught Selene studying her thoughtfully.

"You are in love with her."

Aurora saw no point in trying to deny it. She gave a helpless shrug and carefully placed the package in the vehicle's glove compartment.

Selene sighed and said, "If I'd known that I wouldn't have pushed so hard to get you a ticket out of here. If the boat wasn't leaving shortly I'd make you go see her. Even if you two couldn't get past whatever is keeping you apart at least you would have been able to take the necklace to her yourself. A gift like this…you deserve to see the expression on Evie's face when she sees it for the first time."

"I would have liked that but at least I got to see what the necklace looks like. You'll make sure she gets it?"

"Of course. You have my word I will put it in her hands."

"Thanks, Selene. Do I get a hug goodbye?"

"You just try and leave this vehicle without giving me a hug!" Selene leaned into Aurora's chest and said, "I'm going to miss you."

"I will miss you too. Thank you for being such a good friend."

Selene made a noise against Aurora's shoulder that sounded suspiciously like a sob and hugged her harder. After a few seconds Selene pulled away and said, "I'm going to show you how good a friend I am by kicking you out of my vehicle and driving like a pack of feral wolves are chasing me to get this gift to your Evie. The Aquilar Tower is only a short distance from here so I can probably get there before your boat leaves."

"You don't have to do that."

"Aurora, would you say you and Evie had something special?"

"I thought so."

"Do you think she cares about you?"

Aurora thought about how Evie had used her hands and words to soothe her after her nightmares and how upset and worried she'd been when she heard there was a price on Aurora's head. She remembered the affection in Evie's eyes when she looked at her and wished she had tried to see her again. If she turned up at her tower surely Evie wouldn't have turned her away? Perhaps they could have had another night together. What she wouldn't give to get drunk just one more time on Evie's intoxicating scent. For a moment Aurora thought she smelled the familiar blend of feathers and sensuous woman that was so distinctly Evie and she had to suppress a shudder at the intensity of her longing.

"Yes. Evie cares about me. I know that much for sure."

"That is good to hear. Aurora you said you stormed off because you two had a disagreement. You said the gift was your way of letting her know you're not upset with her?"

"Yeah?"

"It sounds to me like you are trying to make things right with her before you go?"

"Yes. And your point is?"

"My point is that she probably also feels bad about the way you two parted ways. What if Evie also wants to set things right between you two but she can't because she doesn't know where to find you?"

Aurora frowned and her expression became troubled. "That was the second time in one day I felt overwhelmed and ran off on her instead of staying to talk things through. Evie is big on talking and listening and getting things resolved. You're right, she will be unhappy about the way we left things. At the very least she'll want to tell me off for running away again. Okay, Selene. Go give her the necklace and tell her where I am. Hurry. The boat is leaving soon and I intend to be on it."

***

From the deck of the Mary-Jane Aurora watched as the anchor was lifted and the fishermen used oars to push the little vessel away from the wooden jetty. She scanned the air and road for what felt like the hundredth time but still no sign of Evie or Selene. She fought the waves of disappointment and told herself it was for the best. She missed Evie so much all it would take right now was the merest suggestion Evie wanted her and she would postpone her trip. Which would be a silly thing to do so late in the game. She was already on the boat and Selene had gone to a lot of trouble getting everything organized for her. The crew of this vessel was giving up an entire morning's fishing so she didn't have to take the ferry taking tourists through the portal to the ship waiting on the other side. Despite the late booking Selene had even secured a single cabin with a balcony for her on that vessel. Something for which Aurora was incredibly thankful as she would need frequent respite from the other passengers to keep her beasts calm.

Aurora heard the engine start and the distance between the dock and boat slowly grew as the captain eased them away. She swept the skyline one last time hoping to see golden wings but aside from a few seabirds drifting high above the skies remained conspicuously empty. With a heavy heart she put her hand into her jacket and touched the case that held Evie's feather.

"I would have liked to see you one more time but I suppose this is it. Goodbye, Evie."

Another quick glance towards Aquilar Tower then Aurora pushed off from the railing and made herself move to the side of the boat that obscured her view of the city so she couldn't keep looking for someone who wasn't coming. Aurora had just made herself comfortable against the wheelhouse wall when she heard the urgent honking of a vehicle.

Peering around the corner she saw Selene's Jeep speeding toward the dock. Inside the wheelhouse the captain throttled down to an idle, stuck his head out of a little side window and said, "What has gotten into that girl? She's driving like a mad woman and making enough noise to wake the dead."

The Jeep came to a screeching halt and Selene flew out of the vehicle. The moment her feet touched the ground she was running. "Wait! Stop! Aurora! Aurora, where are you?"

Aurora quickly stepped into view and waved at Selene.

"What is it?"

"Aurora you have to get off! I need to talk to you."

"Too late. We're leaving."

"It is about Evie. She's in trouble."

"What kind of trouble?"

"Her sister will be here in a moment and she will explain everything. Joel, come back. Aurora needs to talk to someone."

"We're gonna run late, Selene," the captain protested. "We're already cutting it close."

"You can make up the lost time. Drinks on me for the crew and a six-course dinner for you and the missus at the Royal. That's a fancy place; you know she's been dying to go there for your anniversary. What will she say when she hears she missed out because you turned me down, Joel?"

"You drive a hard bargain. Fifteen minutes on the clock and not a second more or your friend won't make her connection."

Aurora saw movement in the sky and watched as an avian girl dove to land beside Selene. She was tall, willowy and fine boned with long hair the color of sun-kissed wheat done up in an intricate braid similar to the kind Evie favored. Her features were sharper and her curves less full but her resemblance to Evie was unmistakable. Aurora took a running leap to clear the boat's railing and the watery expanse to the dock that had grown to several meters. Behind her there were shouts and curses from on deck. She ignored it. Her focus entirely on the girl who looked so much like a younger unfinished version of Evie.

"Are you Evie's sister Oriana?"

The girl stared up at Aurora in wide-eyed wonder. She blinked and said, "I am. You must be Aurora. Evie tried to describe you to me. I thought she was exaggerating but wow…I totally get it now. I'm so glad we got to you in time."

Exaggerate about what? Aurora wanted to ask but dismissed it as unimportant. "I still have no idea what's going on. How is Evie in trouble?"

"My sister is missing."

"Are you sure about that? Perhaps she went for a solo flight to stretch her wings?"

Oriana adamantly shook her head. "She's been way too busy for that kind of thing and the sentinels would have noticed her taking off. I know something bad has happened to her. Evie told me to come get her just before daybreak so we could stand side by side during the dawn song but she wasn't in her room or anywhere else in the tower. That's not like my sister. If she makes plans with someone she doesn't change her mind and take off without saying anything. I think someone kidnapped her."

"Why?"

"When I went into her room there were little things out of place but it wasn't until I saw her bowl of fruit was untouched that I knew something was seriously wrong. Evie devours fruit like other people breathe air. She can't get enough. If she didn't touch her fruit that must mean she wasn't there to eat it. No one saw her leave so she must have been taken. I've got the sentinels and everyone else looking for Evie but I have a feeling they won't find her. I told my dad she's missing and he got very upset but he's so sick this morning I don't see him being much help. My uncle said I'm overreacting and stirring the flock into a frenzy for nothing."

"You are right to be concerned. You did well to get your flock looking for Evie."

"Will you help me find her? She said you saved her life and protected her. She trusts you. The way she talked about you made it sound like you could do just about anything. Evie said you're a beast-shifter. Some kind of cat? That must mean you're good at sniffing things out and tracking. I need you to come to her room and use that nose of yours to figure out what happened."

Selene stiffened and gave Oriana a sharp look. "You mind your manners when you speak to Aurora. I don't know how you talk to people in that tower of yours but you would do well to remember that you're not in it now. Didn't anyone tell you to be respectful when you address a beast-shifter, especially when you don't know what you're dealing with? Calling Aurora a cat would be like me calling you a fat pigeon and telling her to come sniff like she's a dog...are you out of your bloody mind? You pull that crap with the wrong person and you'll get your wings torn off."

Oriana stared at Selene with teenaged indignation. "No one would call me a pigeon, that's just stupid. I'm nothing like a pigeon and I'm definitely not fat." Oriana gave Aurora a speculative look. "I apologize. I didn't mean to be disrespectful, it's just that right now I couldn't care less what you are. I'm frantic with worry about my sister and the last time Evie disappeared it was because she'd been captured and shot. All I'm interested in is if you think you can find my sister and bring her home. Can you do that?"

"I will find Evie even if I have to tear this city apart. If she was taken out of her home against her will or harmed in any way whoever is responsible will die by my claws."

"That's the best thing I've heard all morning. Finally, someone willing to do something not just flap their wings and talk, talk, talk like that's going to get her back. I can see why Evie is crazy about you – you're a woman who gets things done. I like that."

"I'm glad I meet with your approval," Aurora said dryly.

"It's a relief for both of us. It would have been really awkward if I didn't like my sister's girlfriend."

"She told you I'm her girlfriend?"

"No, but you are clearly her something. Her very serious something. I've never seen my sister in such a state over losing someone and you put love bites on her butt and she let you. Plus, you hear she's in trouble and you jump off a boat to find out what's wrong. If that doesn't mean you two have something special I don't know what does."

Aurora cocked her head and gave Evie's sister a thoughtful look. "Oriana, how old are you?"

"I'm seventeen," Oriana said hands on hips, her wings arching just a little. She tried to meet Aurora's intense stare and lasted all of three seconds before she got flustered and looked away. Aurora smiled.

"What's so funny?"

"You remind me so much of your sister. She does the same thing with her wings when she tries to boss me around."

"Does it work?"

"Sometimes."

Aurora turned to address Selene. "Can you get them to unload my gear and take it back to your place? Looks like I'm not leaving today."

***

In Evie's bedroom, at the place she had fallen and other avians had stood around her, Aurora knelt and inhaled deeply, committing all the scents to memory. Even if these avians hid in a crowd she would be able to identify them as surely as if she had a photo. Aurora clenched her fists and fought to contain her anger. Evie was supposed to be safe in her den among her own people and yet avians had come into her most private space and taken her away. Evie must have been so afraid especially at the last when she lay helpless at her attackers' feet but how valiantly she fought before they took her down. When she found who did this to Evie she would make them pay.

Aurora strode to the sitting room where she had made Oriana wait. Some of her anger must have shown because the young avian took one look at her face and took a step backwards.

"Is she dead?" Oriana whispered.

"No, Evie was alive when she was taken. Her attackers came in the early morning hours. They probably expected to find her helpless in bed but she was awake and put up a fight. Two came through the main door, a male and female and another male through the balcony. Once they subdued her the female and the male from the balcony flew away with her. The other male went back into the tower but not unscathed. Evie cut him with something. He tried to clean up the drops but there is no hiding the smell of blood."

"Can you tell where they took her?"

"If they left on foot I could track them but they flew away hours ago and since I'm not familiar with the scent of those two I can't guess where they might have taken her."

"Then what do we do? Now I only have confirmation my sister was kidnapped but I'm no closer to finding her."

"Not true. We are going to ask the traitor who let the attackers into Evie's suite. Or rather I will ask the questions and if you have the stomach for it you can watch."

"What do you need me to do? How can I help?"

"Get your people to stay out of my way. I'm scared for Evie and furious she was taken from the place she was supposed to be safe. As far as I'm concerned anyone in this tower who is not you or your father is a potential enemy. I will tear to shreds anyone who tries to stop me from getting the answers I need to rescue Evie."

"What? No! You can't do that. I didn't bring you here to hurt my flock."

"I told you before you brought me here I would kill whoever is responsible for Evie being taken from her home."

"Yes, but I thought it would be people out there. Not *my* people."

"Oriana, there is something rotten in House Aquilar. Someone with a key unlocked her door and let her attackers in. Evie would have screamed while she fought but no one came to her aid or saw two avians fly away with her. That means the sentinels on guard were either incredibly lax in their duties or they were in on Evie's kidnapping. I don't have the time to figure out which it is and frankly, I don't care. They let her be taken and in my eyes that makes them guilty by default."

"But—"

"Oriana, we are wasting time talking. Evie could be in a cutter's cage as we speak. Moving through the tower will be quicker if I don't have to clear a path to my target but I will do whatever it takes to get my claws into the person who betrayed Evie." Aurora held her hand out to Oriana palm up. "Oriana Aquilar, will you help me save your sister or must I do this on my own?"

Oriana had been nervously watching Aurora, her wings drawn tightly around herself in a protective gesture. Now a change came over the young woman. Her feathers puffed up and she arched her wings aggressively. She took a step forward and clasped Aurora's hand squeezing hard.

"Find the traitor and save my sister. I'll fly by your side and clear the way."

On hearing Oriana's answer Aurora bared her teeth and said, "Let's hunt."

Honed in on the traitor's scent Aurora wove her way through the tower at a fast walk while Oriana hovered near. She wanted to run but they were already drawing attention and she heard the word 'beast' rustle in the air. The word was like a spark in a dry forest, not quite a flame but it would take very little for the mild alarm she sensed in the avians to ignite into full-blown panic. Four armored sentinels appeared and headed straight for Aurora with steely looks. Oriana immediately flew to intercept and spoke to them in an urgent whisper accompanied by sharp hand gestures. While Aurora waited she kept her eyes averted and tried to look as harmless as possible. Standing still when everything in her strained to be moving was difficult but she had to give Oriana a chance to avert confrontation. Aurora heard murmurs of protest but

Oriana proved to be as formidable as her older sister because despite their misgivings the sentinels motioned for them to continue. Inwardly Aurora sighed with relief. A fight now would have been a waste of valuable time and despite the impression she gave Oriana to get her to cooperate she wanted to avoid bloodshed. This was Evie's flock. These avians were Evie's family and friends, her entire world revolved around them. She had to keep her claws sheathed because she was so angry if she fought now she could lose control of her beast and if that happened there would be carnage in Evie's home. She was here to save Evie, not destroy her world in the process. With that in mind, Aurora continued her hunt for the traitor. She stopped when the scent trail went beyond a locked door. Aurora pressed the tips of her fingers against the grain and said, "He lives here."

"But…these are my uncle's rooms."

"Your father's half-brother Marcus? The one with a Ravir woman for a mother?"

"Yes."

"Evie doesn't like him."

"Neither do I. Very few people do because he's an obnoxious pain in the butt but I find it hard to believe he's involved in Evie's kidnapping."

"Let's find out."

The door was locked but a swift kick sent the heavy door flying off its hinges. A quick look inside confirmed what her ears already told her; Marcus wasn't there.

"Are you sure?" Oriana's voice was uncertain and the way she huddled under her wings made her look very young. She wanted her to be wrong Aurora realized. Even though she didn't like Marcus Oriana also didn't want a family member to be capable of such a terrible betrayal.

"I'm sure. Do you remember I told you Evie made one of her attackers bleed?"

"Yes?"

Aurora followed her nose and found stuffed in the clothing hamper a torn, bloodstained shirt. She held the shirt out to Oriana who took it reluctantly. "The blood is only a few hours old. See how it hasn't gone black yet." Aurora was heading back towards the broken door to continue her search for Marcus when she caught the hint of a familiar smell. She stopped so abruptly Oriana almost ran into her. Aurora inhaled deeply rotating her head to pinpoint the smell.

"What is it?" Oriana whispered. She was watching Aurora closely, the bloodied shirt dangling from her fingers.

"I smell poison."

"Here?"

Aurora nodded and pointed at a wall panel. "The poison is there. Oriana, can you think of a reason why your uncle would keep poison in his room?"

"I can't think of a reason for anyone to keep poison in their room. What kind of poison?"

"I'm familiar with this smell. It is faint but it is the toxin excreted by a little yellow frog that lives in some forests. They are abundant where I live and the lynxhawks eat them as a delicacy but most animals are warned away by that scent. They know that even a touch can cause a severe reaction and make them sick for days."

Oriana paled. "What kind of reaction?"

"It would depend on the creature and how much toxin we're talking about but in humans and avians I'd expect seizures and muscle weakness. There would be other symptoms too but those would be the worst."

"My dad has been sick. What you describe sounds like what's been happening to him for the last year. He just comes right then he has another attack that leaves him weaker than before."

"If Marcus has been poisoning your dad with that toxin for a year it's a miracle he's still alive."

"He's been taking large dosages of our most potent mira potion every day."

Aurora nodded. "That explains why he's still alive. This toxin isn't lethal in small dosages but there is a cumulative effect, without the mira potions speeding up his healing he would have gone into a coma and died after the third or fourth application."

"When my father hears—"

Before Oriana could finish Aurora grabbed her by the shoulders and moved her away from the open balcony. "Oriana, we are about to have company."

As if on cue armored sentinels burst into the room with the loud stomping of feet and rustling of wings. The ones that entered through the door angled to train long metal spears on Aurora while the two who flew through the balcony drew wicked looking swords. Aurora stood still with her hands by her sides and tried once again to look as harmless as possible. Kicking the door in probably wasn't her best move. If there had been any doubt she was a beast-shifter, breaking a reinforced security door with a single kick would have dispelled that. Avians rarely let beast-shifters into their towers and here she was destroying things and alone with the youngest of Lord Aquilar's daughters just hours after her sister disappeared. No wonder the avians were in a flutter. Aurora watched as a sentinel rushed to draw Oriana away from her side and had to resist the urge to snarl and shield the girl with her body. Evie's sister wasn't in danger. If she acted rashly now the situation would quickly escalate into violence. To her surprise, Oriana flicked her wing at the woman's face when she tried to grab her so she had to jump to avoid being struck.

"What is the meaning of this?" Oriana raised herself up to her full height and arched her wings aggressively. "Who authorized this?"

"I did."

There was the sound of a cane tapping on the floor and an avian male with dull, patchy plumage appeared in the doorway. He was immaculately dressed and wore a red and gold sash around his hips that bore the crest of House Aquilar and the hand on the cane bore an elaborate signet ring. His clothing was of the highest quality but hung loosely on his tall frame. There were beads of perspiration on his forehead and despite the liberal application of cologne to Aurora the stench of sickness was unmistakable.

"Daddy!" Oriana rushed to her father and wrapped her arms around him. A little tension went out of Lord Aquilar's shoulders and he stroked Oriana's head in a gesture that spoke of affection and relief.

That was all the confirmation Aurora needed. She made a small bow in his direction and said, "Greetings, Lord Augustus Aquilar. I had hoped to meet you someday but not under these circumstances."

"You have me at a disadvantage. Who are you and what are you doing in my tower?"

"Dad, this is Aurora, Evie's beast-shifter friend, the one she told us about. She was on a boat leaving Nordarra but when she heard Evie was missing she came to help find her."

Lord Augustus gave Aurora a questioning look. "You are the one who rescued my daughter and brought her home?"

Aurora inclined her head slightly. "I am."

Lord Augustus nodded thoughtfully and told the guards to put their weapons away. "You match the description of the Old Blood tigress I've heard about and Evie spoke highly of you but you still need to explain yourself. Why did you break into Marcus's suite?"

"He was in on Evie's kidnapping, Dad. She was taken from her bedroom last night. Aurora followed his scent all the way here and look at this..." Oriana held up the blood-stained shirt. "Evie fought him and cut him. That's not all. Aurora said she can smell poison behind that wooden panel. She said she recognizes it because it smells like a poisonous frog that excretes that scent as a warning to be left alone. Did I get that right, Aurora?"

Aurora nodded. "You got the gist of it."

"Aurora told me what that poison does and it sounds like what happens when you have an attack."

Lord Augustus swayed like he'd been struck. He stared from the bloody shirt in Oriana's hands to Aurora.

"This is true?"

"Yes. The man you call brother is a snake."

"The poison...show me."

Aurora went to the wooden panel and slid it back to reveal row upon row of different colognes, oils, and lotions. She pushed them all aside and carefully removed from the back a small green glass bottle. She held it up for everyone to see. "This is it. It was opened recently. The odor still lingers on the rim."

The sentinel who had not sheathed his sword when Lord Aquilar told them to put their weapons away but merely lowered it to his side, stabbed it in Aurora's direction and shouted, "What a load of dragon dung! That is just cologne. You are nothing but a filthy beast come to mire the good name of Lord Marcus. He is worth ten times the likes of you!"

"You dare call me a filthy beast and a liar?" Aurora bared her teeth in a vicious smile. "Such an insult can't go unpunished." In a smooth motion she removed the glass stopper and splashed some of the liquid into the man's face. The entire room went so quiet one could hear a needle drop, all eyes fixed on the sentinel. For a moment nothing happened. Then his eyes rolled back in his head, he collapsed and started seizing, the back of his heels drumming on the wooden floor in a staccato beat.

Lord Aquilar stared at the man for several seconds and when he looked up his face was suffused with rage. "Get him. Bring Marcus to me. NOW. If he tries to fly away break his wings!"

Two sentinels promptly disappeared to fulfill his command. The woman who had tried to drag Oriana to safety was staring at the convulsing man in horror. "I'll get a healer, my Lord."

"You will do no such thing." Lord Augustus rustled his wings and wearily lowered himself into one of the seats.

"But…why not?"

"He made it clear where his loyalty lies when he called my bastard half-brother Lord. That is a title only used for the current Lord of the Tower. I'm not dead yet and even if I was my daughters are next in line. I smell treachery. Might as well begin the purge. You can, however, take him away. I have experienced what is happening to him many times and I have no desire to sit here and watch it. Everyone except Aurora wait outside. You too, Oriana."

Oriana opened her mouth as if to object, cast an eye at the seizing man being carried away and scurried out of the room with the rest of the sentinels in tow.

Once everyone was gone Lord Augustus lowered his voice to a whisper and said, "There is very little time to speak freely. Getting Evie back is more important than whether I live or die but I need to know if there is hope for me. You seem to know this poison. Tell me, Aurora, is it enough that the poisoner has been stopped or is it too late? Am I a dead man walking?"

"Lord Augustus, if you were a human your organs would have been irreversibly damaged by now and stopped working. Fortunately, you're a shapeshifter. Given enough time your body will purge the poison and you will recover fully. Keep taking the mira potions. It has kept you alive thus far and it will continue to aid you."

Lord Augustus bowed his head and let out a shuddering breath. "Thank you. I feel like a man who's just had his death sentence repealed. Now tell me honestly, can you find Evie?"

"Will you allow me to question your brother as I see fit? No interference."

"Snake of a half-brother. Yes. You may do whatever you see fit but don't kill him. Whatever his involvement in this he's still family."

***

Evie's uncle was escorted in by two stone-faced sentinels. Marcus looked like he was at least twenty years younger than Lord Augustus. His beautiful silver-grey plumage shone with health and vitality, he had a fine-boned almost delicate look about him that some avians had and it was only his beak-like nose that tipped him towards handsome rather than pretty. He was dressed in what looked like an imitation of courtly attire of some bygone era. Whereas Lord Augustus dressed elegantly but simply and only wore a single sash and the ring of office to denote his position Marcus was decked out like a peacock in full preen. His clothing tailored to perfection, he was swathed in layers of rich fabric embroidered with the red and gold motif of House Aquilar. Even his bootstraps were embossed with the Aquilar crest. Marcus strutted into the room with an air of righteous indignation, his feathers puffed up to show his displeasure. Comparing the two men Aurora noted that despite his prolonged illness Lord Augustus radiated confidence and authority whereas Marcus swaggered like he had something to prove. If Lord Augustus was a sixteen-pointer stag well established in his domain, Marcus was a new horn trying to muscle into his territory by making a flashy display.

Putting all the pieces together Aurora concluded that Marcus was, despite his delusions of grandeur, smart enough to realize he was no match for the old bull in an open challenge. Even if by some miracle he managed to overthrow Lord Augustus he would still have to deal with the daughters and an angry flock. Staging his brother's murder would raise suspicion. On the other hand, if Augustus wasted away slowly from a mystery disease a cunning person could use that as an opportunity to establish himself more firmly. This raised the question: How devious was Marcus? Evie had dismissed him as a puffed-up peacock and an occasional trouble maker but he had been poisoning her father for a year without anyone suspecting a thing. He also presented an offer of alliance from House Ravir when House Aquilar desperately needed more wings in the skies to patrol their trade routes. Coincidence or something far more sinister? Perhaps Marcus was a more cunning predator than Evie realized. His mistake was to think he could manipulate his niece. Aurora knew first-hand how strong-willed and determined Evie was. She wouldn't meekly do as she was told and despite being an avian she could act as territorial as any beast-shifter. Evie might look sweet and gentle but her claws, when she chose to unsheathe them, were lethal. From what Evie told her Marcus found this out the hard way when he'd tried to undermine her authority during the negotiations and tried to strong-arm Evie into marrying Titus Ravir. Her response had shut the door on the deal and left Marcus publicly humiliated. For someone who seemed to put a lot of stock into how he appeared to others that must have been a brutal blow. Yet another reason for him to want to get rid of Evie. It wouldn't surprise her if he had a plan in the works for Oriana too. Aurora fought the urge to snap Marcus's neck. The man truly was a snake. Lord Augustus had welcomed him into the tower and allowed him to use the Aquilar name even though he was an illegitimate child but instead of showing gratitude he had tried to get rid of his own family. Bitterness rose to fuel her anger. What she wouldn't have given to be offered such a gift. If her father's clan or her mother's people had offered her even a fraction of the welcome Marcus had been given by the Aquilars she would have given her life to protect them.

Marcus came to a standstill in front of Lord Augustus and said, "There you are, Augustus. What is the meaning of this? Why did you have me dragged away from my meal? I was just about to have a slice of warm honey cake. The cream would have gone runny by now."

Lord Augustus's grip on his cane became white-knuckled. "Your niece is missing and you whine about missing your dessert?"

Aurora's anger towards the man who helped kidnap Evie flared into rage and she pounced. She saw the shock and disbelief in Marcus's eyes as he lay sprawled on his back with her weight pinning him down. She bared her fangs and roared into his terrified face. "WHERE IS EVIE?"

"I don't know what you are talking about!" Marcus screamed. "Guards, get her off me! Oh god, someone get this beast off me!"

"Sentinels stay where you are. No one moves unless I say so." Lord Augustus's voice rang out loud and clear.

"Augustus, what are you doing? Brother, why have you let this animal loose on me?"

"I have reason to believe you have been up to no good. I'd advise you to answer the young woman. She looks very angry to me."

Angry didn't even come close to describing the inferno of rage clawing at Aurora's insides. She wanted to tear out Marcus's throat but instead, she tore open his shirt to reveal the bandage on his chest. She ripped it off and the cut that ran from below his collar bone to his navel started bleeding again.

"Evie cut you good but this is nothing compared to what I will do to you if you don't tell me where she is." Aurora lifted a hand for Marcus to see and elongated her nails several inches, the tips honed to a razor's edge. She stroked his cheek lightly and blood ran in streaks.

"No, not the face! Oh god, not the face!"

"I want you to know that Lord Augustus asked me not to kill you so I won't. I will do something worse. I'm going to bite and tear pieces off your body bit by bit. I'll start with your hands then move to your feet. The wings will have to go, as will your nose and ears. But don't worry I'll leave your eyes so you can see the pity and revulsion on people's faces when they see the stump of a man you've become. Everything will grow back eventually. That's assuming you have someone to feed you and keep you alive that long. Now that you know what I plan, how many body parts you lose is up to you. Tell me what I want to know and I'll stop. Lie to me and I will take an extra-large bite." Aurora lifted Marcus' left hand to her mouth and bit off all but the thumb with a sharp snap. She spat the bloody fingers into his face.

"You took all my fingers!"

Marcus was screaming hysterically so Aurora slapped him. The force of the impact left him momentarily dazed and silent.

"You lied to me. I know you were in her suite when she was taken – your stink and blood were all over the place. You are the one who let in the avians who took her. Are you going to call me a liar and deny it?"

"You're right, I was there. I let them in. Please don't bite me again!

"Let who in?"

"Raven Ravir and her man."

"Why? What kind of deal did you strike with them? Tell me everything."

When Marcus hesitated Aurora lifted his other hand to her mouth and peeled back her lips to show him her teeth. Wanting to hurry the interrogation along she let her tiger come close to the surface so he could feel its presence and see it looking out of her eyes. Staring up at her Marcus pissed himself and squealed like a dying rabbit.

"No, no, no please don't! I beg you! It was just business! They take Evie off my hands and when I'm Lord of the Tower I will give them the alliance they want and Oriana's hand in marriage. It benefits both houses and I need money. I have debts, large ones. I borrowed from people that take the saying 'paying in a pound of flesh' literally. This House is so wealthy and the Aquilar personal fortune is huge but Evie wouldn't let me have a measly cent; she kept blocking me at every turn. It's not right! I should be the next Lord of the Tower when Augustus dies, not her! I got a tiny inheritance and have to live off the scraps my brother gives me. It's not fair!"

Aurora tossed Marcus into the air and spun him around so she stood behind him. She grabbed hold of his wings, lifted them away from his back and struck at the connecting joints. Her claws cleaved through bone and flesh as easily as a hot knife through butter and wings fluttered to the ground. Marcus clutched at his back and fell to the ground screaming. One of the sentinels ran out of the room and there was the sound of vomiting.

"Why did you take his wings?" Lord Augustus asked from his seat. "Was he lying?"

"No, he was telling the truth."

"Then why?"

"He admitted to betraying Evie. He doesn't deserve to fly." Aurora poked Marcus with her boot. "Where did they take her?"

"You took my wings. You goddamn bitch you took my wings." Marcus was blubbering like a small child. "Do you really think I care what you do to me next?"

Aurora lifted his chin with a claw so he could see her face. "You have plenty more to lose. You can still walk and piss like a man. If you don't tell me what I want to know by the time I'm done you will beg for death. Answer my question. Where is Evie?"

Marcus stared at her through a haze of pain and hatred. He sucked in his cheeks and Aurora was ready to avoid a glob of spittle when he spat, "Dead! She's dead! That was my price. I wanted her dead. Right now she is worm food or better yet, getting sliced up and bottled. One day some wealthy prick is going to rub his dick with 'Cream of Evie' to get a hard-on. Fat rendered from a female avian is supposed to cure impotence, did you know that?" Marcus was laughing hysterically. "Oh, the irony. I hope that happens, it's what that bitch deserves."

Aurora stumbled away from Marcus. The world was spinning and it felt like she couldn't get enough air. She heard the tap of the cane as Lord Augustus got up from his seat and walked over to the man he once called brother. She watched through a haze as he raised his cane and struck the fallen man so hard Aurora heard Marcus's skull crack. Lord Augustus grabbed Marcus by the bloody stump of his wings, dragged him to the balcony and with the strength of a man possessed threw him off the building. Aurora shifted her hands and face back to human shape and went to stand beside him. Together they stared at the mangled remains of Marcus where he lay shattered in a pool of crimson on the marble paving far below. An avian rushed to land by the fallen man while others hovered in the air staring at the balcony where Lord Augustus and Aurora stood side by side.

"It was too quick a death," Lord Augustus said as if speaking to himself. "I should have kept him alive and made him suffer for the rest of his life." Lord Augustus slumped against the wall, his head bowed over his cane. "My daughter is dead. My Evie, my beautiful golden angel is dead."

"No."

"No?" Lord Augustus's head snapped up.

"No. I refuse to believe that. She was alive when they took her away. I smelled the sedative they used to knock her out. Why bother to sedate her? Why not kill her right there and then if that was their intent all along? There is no difference between carrying a dead person or an unconscious one. Marcus might have made an agreement with Raven to kill Evie but until I see a body I'm going to believe she's still alive. What he said before he died was the desperate last strike of a man who knew he was doomed. He knew he could not escape me and when I was done with him, he would still be faced with your wrath. Life as he knew it was over."

"Yes. I see what you mean." Lord Augustus raised himself up to his full height and said, "I will ready warriors, fly to Ravir Tower and demand my daughter's release."

"What if they won't give her back or deny they have her?"

"Then I will declare war on House Ravir. I will decimate them!"

"Could you win in an armed battle with House Ravir? They are a very militant flock. I've seen their tower. It's heavily fortified and always swarming with sentinels."

"Are you suggesting House Aquilar is weak?"

"I'm saying you need to think of this as a hostage situation. We don't know where they are keeping Evie or what they will do when you confront them with an armed force. Best case scenario they demand a ransom. Worst case they kill her. Our priority is to find Evie and rescue her. Open dialogue with House Ravir and let them know that you know they have her. From what I've heard you are a savvy negotiator and a brilliant businessman so now would be a good time to pull out all the stops. Give them incentives to keep her alive and buy me time so I can find out where they have her hidden."

"What are you going to do?"

"There is someone I can ask for help to locate Evie. As long as Evie breathes this person will be able to pinpoint her exact location."

Lord Augustus gave Aurora a hard stare. "Why didn't you do that right from the start?"

"I'm not on the best footing with this person and honestly, it didn't even occur to me until now to ask her for help. She's a very powerful Old Blood and she doesn't like to get involved in the affairs of the lesser races so this is a long shot. However, we have a history and mutual obligation. I think she'll help me if I ask."

"How can I assist you? What do you need? The considerable resources of House Aquilar are at your disposal. Just ask and it will be done."

"Have the roof cleared and draw all your people inside. If you value the lives of your people do not come out until I say so. If she thinks this is a trap or that I've been taken captive by avians it's going to turn into an epically bad day for House Aquilar. Once the roof has been cleared I will send out a call and see if she'll come to speak to me."

"And if the Old Blood doesn't heed your call?"

"Then I'm going to tear Ravir Tower apart floor by floor looking for Evie."

***

Lord Augustus had the rooftop cleared in record time and the avians were inside their tower with all the shutters closed. Before the tower went into lockdown he sent avians speeding off in various directions on what Aurora assumed were important errands. Aurora found a sheltered spot and used a borrowed charcoal pencil to draw the summoning spell that would call her mother. She had a good memory but she still had to think carefully about the alignment of the overlapping circles and had to redraw one of the runes. Her mother would no doubt scold her when she saw the sloppy work. In the middle had to go the offering to identify the person seeking an audience. That is where she would place her hair. Her mother had said she should use more hair if the call was urgent. How much exactly did this situation call for? Aurora sighed in frustration; what a terrible time to rely on a spell she'd never tried before. It was a miracle she remembered it at all since she'd been adamant she would never call on her mother for help.

After a short contemplation she decided she would rather create a bonfire than a measly smoke signal. Time to go all out. Aurora pushed her fingers through her short hair, gathered it in a bunch and cut so close to the root she felt the cold metal of the blade glide against her scalp. She lay the hair carefully in the designated space and repeated the process until she couldn't find anything long enough to cut. She checked all the runes and interlocking patterns one more time to make sure there weren't any glaring mistakes then activated the spell using her magic. The runes glowed a dull yellowish green but the hair did not ignite like her mother said it would. Disappointed and wondering what she'd done wrong Aurora was about to remove her hair and start again when her hair turned into a seething mass of green flame. Good. Now she would wait to see if her mother turned up. She would wait an hour, no more.

Twenty minutes later Aurora heard a thud behind her. Turning she saw her mother stride towards her with billowing robes. She was scowling and she somehow managed to look worried and annoyed at the same time.

"Aurora, what is going on? What is the emergency? Why have you called me here of all places? If these avians have harmed you I will reduce this tower to rubble." Adelind paused in her tirade to look at the summoning spell and its contents with disgust. "I said use a few hairs if you need me not shave off all your hair. I thought you must be dying. I stormed out of an important meeting I—"

"I need your help mother. Evie has been kidnapped."

"Evie?"

"Evangeline Aquilar, the girl who was with me at the sanctuary."

"Ah, your avian lover."

"Yes, my avian lover. Mother, you were in her rooms last night. What were you doing there?"

"I did not take the girl. I had questions in regards to the note she left me. We spoke and then I left. It was an informative conversation and I was impressed with Evangeline. She has courage for one of her kind and she cares about you a great deal."

Aurora sagged with relief.

"Did you think I harmed her?"

"No. But it was baffling to find your scent in her sitting room and it's been bothering me. I had to know why you were there for my own peace of mind. I called because I need your help to find Evie. I could do it but it would take a lot longer than if you looked for her and the people who took her have had her for hours already. I don't even want to think about what they may be doing to her. The thought of someone hurting or violating her is terrifying. I have to save her!"

Aurora had grabbed hold of her mother's arm while she spoke. Adelind looked at the hand on her arm then studied Aurora's frantic face. "This girl must be very important to you. It's been so long since you've asked me for anything and you've never called me like this."

"Please, Mother. If you want me to beg I will. Is that what you want? Do you want me to go on my knees?"

"No!" Adelind glared at her daughter. "No, don't you dare. I'm not trying to make you beg, I am just trying to understand your behavior. This is so out of character for you. Tell me, does Evangeline feel about you the way you do about her?"

"I don't think so but that doesn't matter. I would tear this world apart for her. Please, will you help me?"

"Of course, I will help you. I will find your girl and accompany you on this quest to rescue her. Do you have something of hers I can use?"

Aurora reached into her jacket and removed a slim flat case. She carefully unsealed it and showed her Evie's feather nestled within. Adelind removed the feather and twirled it slowly between her fingers.

"Ah, this will do nicely. A primary feather is a precious thing. Did Evangeline gift this to you as a token of her affection?"

"She didn't really give it to me," Aurora admitted. "She left it in my bed."

Adelind's mouth twitched in a smile. "I think that counts as 'giving it to you'. The way you two went at it no wonder the girl left feathers behind."

Aurora's stared at her mother in stunned silence. She cleared her throat and asked, "Mother, did you just make a sex joke at my expense?"

Adelind gave a dismissive wave. "Aurora, we are both adults. I walked in and straight back out when I saw what was happening. You two were in the library for goodness sake and you have *never* brought anyone home before so there was no way I could have known. Next time I'll listen before I enter although I'd like to point out, that's what the bedroom is for."

Aurora was staring at her mother as if she had never seen her before. She absently ran her hand over her shorn head and said, "Mother, I really don't want to have this kind of conversation with you. Especially right now. But for what it is worth I had no idea you have such a wicked sense of humor."

"There are a lot of things you don't know about me, like there are a lot of things I don't know about you. We should really try to remedy that, this distance between us…it pains me. Once you've gotten Evangeline home we should have dinner and talk. Is that a deal?"

"Is what a deal?"

"I'll find your Evie and you'll repay me with a meal. You haven't cooked for me in years. I always loved your baking. Can you make those little tarts with the cherry filling, the ones your dad used to make? I've craved those."

"Um…sure. If that's what you want. We can have dinner and I'll even bake the tarts, just like Dad used to make."

"And talk," Lady Adelind added urgently. "We really need to talk. There are things I have to tell you." Her right hand darted from the robe and she tentatively touched Aurora's cheek. Aurora barely had time to register the slight tremor in her mother's fingers before she snatched her hand back.

"Sure…" Aurora drawled out the word and wondered if she looked as startled and confused as she felt. She couldn't remember the last time her mother had touched her. "I don't know what to make of your sudden desire to spend time with me but we can talk about that. Later. Right now, I need you to concentrate on finding Evie."

CHAPTER 27

IN A BAD PLACE

When Evie woke she felt confused and disorientated. She couldn't understand why she was lying on her sore wing and wrapped in a net. When her sluggish mind finally recalled the kidnapping she felt vaguely surprised that she was still alive. After the initial relief came panic and she had to fight her instinctive response to struggle against the bindings. Evie's thoughts went to her father and she wondered if he was still alive. She was determined to believe that he was. Her father was ill, not stupid. Her disappearance would make him very suspicious especially when he heard she planned to have Marcus expelled. She had to believe he would figure out in time that his half-brother was a traitorous snake. The alternative was unthinkable. Evie told herself not to dwell on what was happening at home. She had to save herself before she could help anyone else. She had to focus on escaping.

The pep talk helped to make the panic recede and Evie felt her mind clear. The first thing she did was to take stock of what condition she was in. She was nauseous, her head felt like it had been stuffed with cotton and her mouth tasted like bile. She was hot and her sweat drenched clothing stuck uncomfortably to her skin as though she'd been left to bake in the midday sun but it was probably just her body trying to flush out the sedative she'd been injected with. She felt bruised and battered as if she'd been roughly treated but nothing seemed broken and since she was still fully dressed and wrapped in a net at least no one had taken liberties with her body while she was unconscious. In comparison to not being dead or having parts of her body missing she knew it shouldn't be important but Evie almost cried with relief.

Peering through her lashes Evie saw it was day and she was in a stone structure with a sturdy door, reinforced walls and lashed down roofing. It was the type of design she'd seen in buildings meant to withstand extreme weather. The floor against her cheek had a metallic feel. She turned her head a fraction and her heart almost stopped when she saw the thick metal bars inches away. Evie's queasy stomach flooded with acid when she realized she was once again in a cage. She made herself lie motionless while she fought to bring her uneven breathing under control. Straining to listen over the pounding of her own heart Evie heard nothing aside from wind howling over the roof so she took a chance and slowly lifted her head to get a better look at her surroundings. She was in a small storeroom. The door on the far side was closed and presumably locked and she was in a cage but the cage door was slightly open. Whoever dumped her here probably thought it was overkill to lock the door of the cage when the captive was unconscious and wrapped up tighter than a turkey about to be stuffed in the oven. Either that or it was an oversight. Whatever the reason if she wanted to escape she had to get out before someone locked her cage or she'd be at the mercy of whoever held the keys to that door. To get out of the cage she first had to get out of the net. She knew how to do that. She would shift her wings away and that would give her a lot more room to move. Once free she would find a way out of the storeroom and fly away. Evie suspected it wasn't going to be that easy but it gave her hope and that was something she desperately needed.

About fifteen minutes later Evie staggered out of the cage. Her limbs were shaking, she was panting and sweat-slicked. Aside from the time her wing was broken and Aurora forced her to shift this was the worst shift she endured. The sedative Raven put in those darts did not play nice with shifter physiology and a week ago it was unlikely she would have been able to overcome the side effects of the drug to shift at all. Evie wiped the sweat from her brow and felt ridiculously smug that she'd not only managed to shift but she'd done it in such a short time despite being drugged. With her wings gone and her everything lubricated with a copious amount of sweat she had practically slipped out of the net.

Evie made her way to the storeroom door and found it was locked. No real surprise there. She went over to one of the tiny windows and cautiously peeked out. What she saw made her heart drop. She was not on the ground like she suspected but on the roof of a building. On the roof of an avian tower to be exact. Outside she saw a winged sentinel dressed in House Ravir's flight armor perched on the edge of the roof, his gaze cast outward as he scanned the skies and surrounding mountains. Evie swore silently. She recognized the area and the sentinel confirmed she must be at Tower Ravir. The place was fortified to the teeth and according to reports there were always dozens of sentinels on patrol. She was an excellent flyer but she didn't like her odds of evading that many pursuers out in the open. Evie stared at the sky and what she saw made her smile as another plan started to take shape. Thick grey clouds clustered above, the heralds of an impending storm. It wasn't raining yet but it would soon pour down and that would drastically reduce visibility. She would fly into the heavy cloud cover, a dangerous thing to do during a storm but it would give her a fighting chance. But first things first, bar the door so no one could get in. Hopefully, that would make her captors think she'd fortified herself inside when in fact she planned to squeeze through one of the tiny windows. A child would have difficulty getting through but she was fined boned, slender and highly motivated. She would get through even if she had to scrape her boobs raw.

***

Some time later Evie found herself hiding in a gap between the roofing and what might be an old chimney flue. She had congratulated herself on spotting the small opening but now she was trapped. The roof had become a hive of activity as sentinels landed to get out of the sky before the storm hit and Raven had turned up with company. The wind was picking up making it harder to hear but Evie caught snippets of conversation when the wind blew her way. From it she deduced the man with Raven was eager to see the captive Evangeline Aquilar. Evie didn't know why the man was interested in her. She knew for a fact she had never seen him before because he was not someone she would forget. He was bald with bronze skin, built like someone who worked out so he could break things with his bare hands and he had a sneer on his face that looked like it lived there permanently. He was smoking a black cigar that gave off a sweet cloying stench. This told Evie he had to be human because it was rare for a shapeshifter to smoke and no beast-shifter with a half-decent nose would be able to tolerate that sickly smell. He was the type who at first glance looked like a common thug but the cut of his clothing spoke of wealth and he had two huge bodyguards shadowing him. The guard on the left sported a bulge under his jacket so Evie assumed he was a human carrying a firearm. Firearms were on the list of items not allowed through the portal but that didn't mean there were none around, just that the few who possessed such weapons had to pay a fortune to own one. The guard with the greasy hair tied into a ponytail radiated a different sort of danger. He tracked the movements of the sentinels with an unsettling gleam in his eyes and the way his lips curled in a half snarl gave him away as a wolf-shifter. The presence of a wolf in their tower caused an agitated stirring among the sentinels and they watched him with equal interest, their wings arched in readiness to spring into motion at a moment's notice.

Evie drew her eyes away from the silent battle to focus on what was happening between Raven and the angry man. She couldn't make out everything that was being said but she gathered he wasn't happy about the barred door and Raven was on the receiving end. He was ranting at her, standing so close that spittle flew into her face. Raven's feathers were puffed up with fury but instead of lashing out as she so clearly wanted to she stood in stone-faced silence. Evie found this astounding. Raven was infamous for her vicious temper and acid tongue and Evie couldn't believe she was allowing a human to speak to her like that. The only time she'd ever seen Raven silently endure verbal abuse was when it came out of the mouth of her father, Lord Nero Ravir. By all accounts, Lord Nero ruled his House with an iron fist and she wouldn't be surprised if Raven was afraid of him. What Evie was afraid of was that Raven's people would break down the door and find out she was missing and start looking for her. From her teenaged encounters with Raven she knew to be wary of her but her trepidation about being at Raven's mercy had nothing on the primal dread caused by the sight of cigar-man. It wasn't just that he was a large aggressive male, he radiated so much menace it triggered every one of Evie's flight instincts. She knew without understanding why that she should do everything in her power to stay away from him.

The breeze blew her way again and Evie heard Raven say, "She can't go anywhere, she's trapped. Marcus may try to weasel out. Alive she is leverage. If the plan goes to crap she can still be used for ransom. House Aquilar is one of the wealthiest flocks in Nordarra and Lord Augustus will pay handsomely to get her back."

"I don't care. Bring her to me. She is mine now."

There was a flash of thunder and the dark clouds tore open. From her little hidey-hole, Evie watched in disbelief as the sentinels, instead of seeking cover inside, squatted all along the edge of the roof and arched their wings into canopies to shield themselves from the deluge while they guarded their flock. She didn't expect such dedication. The sentinels from her own House were not this vigilant. Belatedly Evie realized this was probably why she was in this mess. She eyed the sentinels sourly; they had just derailed her plan to escape during the storm. At least the downpour had chased away Raven's odious companions. Unperturbed by the rain Raven watched the human and his bodyguards run to get off the roof. Even through the rain Evie could see hostility radiate off the woman. Raven's dark eyes bore daggers into the man's back. There was so much loathing on her face Evie knew if she was capable of such magic Raven would have called down lightning to strike him and his companions dead.

She was still standing in the same spot when a sentinel approached her and said something to her. In response Raven turned to look towards Evie's hiding place. Crap. One of the eagle-eyed sentinels must have spotted her. As if to confirm her fear several avians moved into view blocking her only exit. She'd been caught. She had nowhere to go and even if she had her wings she could not slip past that many avians to attempt escape. Evie closed her eyes for a moment to gather her courage, took a deep breath then scrambled out of her hiding place to stand in the open under an overhang. She was wingless and filthy but she held her head high and glared defiantly at the other avians. She was Evangeline Aquilar, daughter of Lord Augustus Aquilar and she would not shame her flock by being dragged out of her hiding place like a drowned rat.

When Raven saw that Evie couldn't fly away she made a hand signal and the sentinels immediately returned to their previous positions. She joined Evie under the overhang, looked her up and down slowly and said, "So this is how you got out. No wings. I didn't think you'd wake for several hours never mind shift and manage an escape. I'd applaud your effort but since you're still a captive there really isn't any point."

"Hello, Raven. I'd say it's good to see you again but it really isn't."

A ghost of a smile flickered on Raven's lips. "Hello, Evie. You're as fiery as I remembered. Good to see that hasn't changed."

"Unfortunately, you have. I would never have imagined the girl I used to play with when we were kids would one day kidnap me out of my room and stuff me in a cage."

Raven shrugged. "We're no longer children. In the game of life we do whatever we must to win. There are no rules to protect the weak from the strong, only the cunning and ruthless survive. I tried to tell you that."

Evie studied the woman in front of her. Raven had dark hair, dark wings and eyes as inscrutable as the night. Hard lines were edged in around her mouth and eyes making her look years older than she was. It felt like a hundred years since they had laughed as they rode the breeze, testing their new wings. What happened to that girl she knew? Why did she become a woman with eyes full of bitterness and rage? They hadn't been friends exactly but she'd liked Raven and during the annual gatherings they had always teamed up when it was time for the games where the boys were pitted against the girls. The boys were bigger and faster but between the two of them they often came up with a plan that gave the girls enough of an edge to win. That was before the games became too serious to be fun and Raven turned into a certifiable bitch. Mentally Evie shook herself. What was the point of musing about the past? It wouldn't change what Raven had become or help her get free and she needed to focus on the now to try to gather as much information as possible while Raven was still talkative.

"So…I assume I'm here because my uncle struck a deal with your father?"

"Yes. That and you wouldn't become Titus's wife. My father took that rather personally."

"Can you blame me? I know he's your brother but he's so not my type."

"Titus isn't anyone's type. No one sane anyway."

Surprised at the venom in Raven's voice Evie decided to push for more and asked, "Who's the human with the stinky cigars?"

"You don't know him?"

Evie shook her head.

Raven's mouth turned down like she tasted something bad. "That's Carlos. He is a wealthy business associate."

"I overheard some of what was said. Why does he want me?"

"I'm not sure why that bastard wants to get his paws on you, aside from the obvious. He wasn't even supposed to be here today but when my father told him we have you he got very excited. He called you 'Aurora's mate'."

Evie blinked in surprise. "Why would he call me that?"

"You haven't become the mate of a female beast-shifter?"

"No. But I do know Aurora. What I don't understand is how he knows I know her or why he would call me her mate. I only met her about a week ago."

"It's unfortunate Carlos thinks you're important to her because he was foaming at the mouth like a rabid dog when he said Aurora's name.

Their bad blood is about to spill all over you. I've argued to keep you alive to give us options if Marcus tries to renege on the deal but Carlos wants you and what Carlos wants my Lord Father gives. That's what happens when one person owns the debt of an entire House. My father calls him our golden goose but he's the one who holds the noose around our necks." Raven turned her head and spat.

"I take it you're not a fan of Mister Golden Goose?"

"He 'entertained' himself at the expense of one of my friends and the arrogant fucker struts around our tower with a semi-feral wolf in tow. That, Evie, isn't even the half of it. While you were my responsibility I had some say about what happened to you but once you're in his hands there is nothing I can do for you. For what it's worth I'm sorry I didn't give you an overdose when I had the chance."

"How about instead of being sorry you didn't kill me you apologize for kidnapping me in the first place."

Raven shook her head. "I was following orders. I do as I'm told like everyone else. That's how it works. I'd have nothing to do with this mad scheme if it was up to me. We are going to be hit with a shit-storm if the other flocks find out we supported the poisoner who knocked off Lord Augustus and we abducted and killed House Aquilar's golden princess. Your father is highly respected and you've always been popular, Evie. No one likes my family. The other flocks fear us but we can't force them to do business with us or entice their young to join our House just because we have a formidable air-force. A show of force or the murder of the heads of a rival House might have been how success was measured in my grandfather's days but that is not what appeals to the younger generations. The world has changed, we have to as well if we want our House to prosper. I can see it clear as day but my opinion doesn't matter."

"Of course your opinion matters. Raven, why are you acting like you're a powerless puppet? You are Raven Ravir, heir to House Ravir. When you speak your people obey. You just made a hand motion and all the sentinels did as they were told. Whatever you may think, these people look to you for leadership. I bet if you let me fly away they wouldn't question you."

Raven was quiet for a moment when she spoke her voice was laced with bitterness. "You really have no clue. Yes, the sentinels would obey whatever order I give but I don't dare defy my father's wishes. In your world, you are the beloved oldest child and your father a benevolent ruler who adores his daughters. Not everyone can live in a fairytale. In my world, my father has already chosen his preferred heir and it is most definitely not me. I'm only insurance in case his perverted shit of a son dies or he needs to breed me for offspring to maintain his bloodline. He'd try for more sons himself but he's been firing blanks for years and thus far Titus hasn't been able to sire a single child despite fucking anything he can shove his dick into. That is my reality. As long as I toe the line and continue to prove my usefulness Lord Nero lets me be. However, if I give him even the slightest excuse he'll have me strung up by my wings and whipped to within an inch of my life, just like anyone else. I've learned that lesson the hard way."

"Raven…I had no idea. That's dreadful."

"Very few people do. Certainly no one outside of House Ravir."

"I must really be doomed if you're telling me this."

"Pretty much. I hoped if I kept you alive long enough something would happen to allow you to go home again but now it would take a miracle to save you. As soon as it stops raining Carlos or one of his men will come for you."

"Why did you try to save me, Raven? I thought you don't like me."

"I liked you plenty when we were kids. You were one of the few people who were genuinely kind to me. You and your mother when she was still alive."

"Then why did you start treating me so badly? You were horrible. Always saying nasty things and trying to hurt me. You plucked out my feathers and pushed me into a river. I almost drowned!"

Raven shrugged and looked a little sheepish. "I was a messed up angry teenager and you had the life I wanted. I was a vindictive bitch. I still am."

Realizing that was likely to be the closest thing to an apology she'd ever get from Raven Evie decided to play a hunch and asked her next question. "Does your flock own shares in the ethian mine near the Black Paw trading post?"

Raven gave her a suspicious look. "Why do you ask and why in that tone?"

"Why do you hesitate to answer? There is great prestige in owning an ethian mine."

"There is…but you know I can't talk about House business."

"You already have and as you pointed out I'm a condemned woman. What's the harm in telling me?"

Raven nodded and said, "We do own shares in the ethian mine but Lord Nero decreed it had to remain a secret. He wanted to buy it outright but the best we could manage was a third of the shares, the controlling two-thirds belong to a human. It rankles his pride that House Ravir could not even buy equal shares. He thinks if the other flocks find out it'll look like we are subservient to a human."

"I see. I had a stopover at that mine about a week ago after I got blown off course in a storm. Did you hear about that?"

"Titus was there checking that everything was running smoothly but he didn't mention seeing you. Not that we talk unless we have to. He doesn't tell me anything about his business and that place has been his responsibility from the start. The only time I hear anything is when he gloats about how much money the mine is making for the flock. What's the big deal about you being there anyway?"

Evie studied Raven thoughtfully. "You don't know, do you? Either that or you're a very good liar."

"Don't know what?"

"About the cutter's den operating inside the mine. Cages, a processing laboratory and until last week captives as well."

Raven did a slow blink and said, "No. That can't be. You must be mistaken."

"It's the truth. I got stuffed into a cutter's cage just for landing there. I was just resting my wings but I assume someone thought I saw more than I did. Or perhaps since the agreement with Marcus was to get rid of me Titus thought that was a golden opportunity to make me disappear. It would have worked. I was so far off course no one would have thought to look for me in that area. The only reason I escaped is because Aurora, the beast-shifter you asked about, discovered the cages and freed me and the captive wolves."

Raven was staring at her in stone-faced silence, a muscle twitching in her cheek.

"You *really* didn't know?"

Raven shook her head and said, "Un-fucking-believable. Now so many things make sense. I knew something fishy was going on when I heard Titus was flying boxes of chemicals and laboratory equipment to the mine but I assumed they were powdering crystal shards to turn into drugs. It's nasty stuff but the high is unbelievable and worth a fortune on the black market. But a cutter's lab? That's madness! If the other shifters find out about this our flock is going to be in a world of trouble."

"That business will taint every flock, not just yours. It is going to turn the other shapeshifters against all of us again. It's only been in the last few years that we've been able to visit the night markets without being harassed or attacked."

Raven's mouth set in a bitter slash. "Do you think I don't know? Operating a cutter's den is suicide."

"You said House Ravir owns a third of the shares so who owns the rest?"

"Carlos owns the majority shares. He's our wealthy business partner, remember? His men run the mine. Ah…now I understand why he got so feral about that Aurora woman. He must have found out she was the one who let you and the others escape. If she hasn't spread the word by now the wolves will howl it to the moon. That operation is blown."

"What can you tell me about Carlos?"

"Trying to get to know your enemy? It won't be much use to you but I'll tell you everything I know. Carlos grew up in Nordarra and from what I've picked up my father used to do business with him even then and they were drinking buddies. I think Carlos used to go by a different name and there was something about him having to leave in a hurry because he ran afoul of a crazed beast-shifter. Apparently, it all worked out because he hooked up with 'the right people', whatever that means, and made a fortune in America."

"Do you think Lord Nero knows what they've been doing at the mine?"

"Of course, my father's spies are everywhere. There is no way my brother would do something like this without clearing it with him first. He may be the chosen heir but that doesn't mean he's immune from punishment."

"This is messed up, Raven. Really messed up."

"Welcome to my world."

"No thanks. I'd rather be out of your world and back in my own. Preferably soon."

Raven snorted and said, "I can still go find the needle gun and give you an overdose? That would get you out of here fast."

Evie gave Raven a dirty look letting her know exactly what she thought of that suggestion.

"I'm trying to be nice. It's a serious offer and you should take it. It will be a quick, painless death."

"That is a definite NO. You need more practice at being nice. Offering to kill me really doesn't fill my heart with warm feelings towards you."

Raven shrugged. "You made your choice. Remember I offered to give you an out. I've done some bad things but I make my kills quick and clean. That bastard gets off on making people scream and from what I've heard with women he takes twice as long and lets his men join in. I don't need to tell you what that means."

Evie wrapped her arms protectively around herself but it did little to ward off the deathly chill of Raven's words. She felt her hands trembling and hoped Raven wouldn't see through the thin veneer of her bravado. Swallowing hard she said, "As long as it's raining I still have time. Something good can still happen to turn things around. This can't be how my life ends – I have so many things I still want to do."

Raven shifted making herself a little more comfortable under the overhang. "What sort of things?"

"You really want to know?"

"Sure. Let me live vicariously through you for a few minutes. Like you pointed out it's pissing down. We have a little time."

"First, I'll make Marcus pay for what he's done."

"That goes without saying. What else?"

Evie stared into the rain that was coming down so hard she could barely make out the edge of the roof and had a feeling of déjà vu. The last time it rained this hard she was on Aurora's back while she ran down a mountain to get them to safety. What she wouldn't give to feel Aurora's warm strong body carrying her away right now. Evie closed her eyes for a moment then said, "There's a woman…I didn't tell her I loved her when I had the chance. I should have told her I want her in my life permanently but I didn't and she went away. If I die without seeing her again that will be my biggest regret. What makes this doubly tragic is if I had told her she probably would have been with me last night and you wouldn't have been able to abduct me even if you had a squadron of warriors with you."

"You reckon your avian girlfriend is that tough?" Raven asked with a smirk.

"She's not an avian."

"Beast-shifter?"

Evie nodded. "A tigress. She's so sleek and powerful that just watching her walk into a room is an experience."

Raven whistled and said, "A tigress? That's an audacious catch even for you. You don't do anything by half. Now I want you to live just so I can witness the drama when you try to introduce something as predatory as that into your flock. Talk about letting the cat loose in a tower full of birds. So, what's your tigress like?"

Evie tried for a smile and said, "I'd invite you for dinner so you could meet her yourself."

"As your guest or as her meal?" Raven asked with a grin.

"That's funny. I'd laugh if I wasn't so stressed. Who knew you had a sense of humor? It's a shame you were such a bitch because I think we could have been friends."

"I'm still a bitch."

"True. You're also deranged with the offering to kill me every few minutes but if you let me go I'll overlook it. It's not too late to turn things around, Raven, all you have to do is give the word and I'll be gone. If you let me go I vow that only Marcus will be held accountable. It can all stop now – there is no need for more bad things to happen."

"Good try, Evie, but this is out of my hands."

"Please let me go? I beg you."

Raven folded her arms across her chest and looked away from Evie. "I can't."

They stood in uncomfortable silence after that. Evie expected Raven to leave but she remained where she was, her face an inscrutable mask. Evie figured she was either guarding her or standing vigil like for someone condemned to death. Neither thought comforted her but she was thankful Raven was delaying her handover to Carlos.

Raven obviously didn't want to talk to her anymore so Evie decided instead of trying to draw the other woman into conversation she would use the precious time to shift her wings. It was something one only did in private but she wasn't likely to get privacy any time soon. She needed the options her wings would give her; a chance to fly away or fight if she had to. Shifting was easier this time, which let her know the lingering effects of the sedative was wearing off, but it still took her five agonizing minutes to shift. When her wings whooshed into existence Raven gave a startled grunt. She recovered quickly and at her barked command sentinels surrounded them. Point made. Even with wings Evie wasn't getting away.

"You're full of surprises. How did you shift so fast?"

"It wasn't that fast. I've been working at it since we started talking," Evie lied.

"That's still very quick and it's the second time you've shifted today.

How did you manage it?"

"Let me go and I'll let you in on the secret."

Raven gave her a sour look. "I'd forgotten what a pain in the ass you can be."

Evie ignored the comment and flexed her wings. Her golden color and wingspan always drew admiring gazes and now was no different; she could feel the weight of multiple eyes as the sentinels looked at her with more interest. She knew her wings were beautiful but she wasn't trying to impress the other avians. She wanted them to see her wings and think, *"She's an avian. She's one of us."* She wanted that image firmly planted in their minds when the human and his bodyguards tried to drag her away. There was more than one way of fighting and she was going to play the distressed pretty avian female to the hilt. It might not make the least difference but she was out of options. Next to her Raven shifted uncomfortably. Glancing at her she saw that Raven was looking at her with narrowed eyes.

"Evie, what are you doing?"

"What does it look like? I'm stretching my wings. Don't you stretch your wings after you've shifted?"

Raven gave a non-committal grunt. With nothing else to do Evie studied the sentinels more closely. Between the rain and the hoods they wore drawn low over their faces it was difficult to see them properly but Evie recognized one of the women as someone she danced with at a club and two of the males looked familiar to her. She was still wondering if she could use any of this to her advantage when the rain that had been pouring down stopped as suddenly as it started. Evie looked up at the skies that were still dark grey with clouds and hoped it was just a brief pause. Raven swore and when Evie followed her gaze she saw Carlos and his men coming through the door. He paused to take in the scene on the roof then bore down on them to stop a few feet away. His eyes went from Raven to Evie and his lips peeled back in an ugly smile. He looked Evie up and down letting his eyes drift across her wings and linger on her breasts.

"Evangeline Aquilar, I heard you were a lovely thing but the rumors didn't do you justice. Good. It's so much fun to play with pretty things and avian girls are a special treat."

Behind him, the human snickered and the wolf leered at Evie with undisguised lust. Evie shuddered and drew her wings tightly around herself. Next to her Raven's mouth drew into a thin hard line.

Carlos leaned in and said, "I couldn't have asked for better bait. I'm going to take lots of photos and spread it everywhere to make sure Aurora sees how much fun we are having with you. If she's got as much of a soft spot for her little avian as I've heard it will flush out the elusive tigress and when she turns up to rescue you…BOOM, she's dead."

Evie reacted without thinking, she lashed at him with her wing and only missed the strike to his temple because the wolf-shifter yanked his boss out of reach.

Carlos angrily shook off the wolf's hold. He stabbed an accusing finger at Raven. "Why haven't you tied her up? I want that bitch's wings bound."

Raven unhinged her jaws and said through tight lips, "No. If you want to bind her wings do it yourself. I will not lay a finger on her to help you and neither will any of my people."

"Lord Nero commanded you to obey me," Carlos snarled.

"No, he did not. My Lord father instructed me to let you take her, nothing more. There she is. Take her if you can."

Evie grabbed Raven's arm as she started walking away. Pitching her voice so everyone could hear she said, "Raven, please don't hand me over to this cutter. I beg you. Lord Augustus will pay handsomely to have me returned unharmed and our Houses can put this disagreement behind us. There will be war with my flock and no peace with any of the other flocks if you hand over the heir of House Aquilar to be tortured by humans and wolves."

Raven shook off Evie's arm and went to stand some distance away with her back turned so she couldn't see what was happening behind her. Her wings were arched aggressively and the sentinels beside her shifted uneasily, their eyes darting between Raven, Evie, and Carlos.

Realizing she was on her own Evie bolted to the side of the building and tried to take flight. The wolf jumped on her from behind and brought her down hard. She tried to scramble away from him but he grabbed her by the wings and started dragging her to the waiting Carlos. Evie screamed in pain and terror. She tried to dig in with her legs and clawed at the grooves in the rock trying to get away but she was no match for the wolf's strength. She got yanked to her feet by her wings and she saw several of her golden feathers strewn along the path she'd been dragged. She struck at Carlos when he came into view but for a human he was surprisingly quick and avoided her blow. There was a thud and Evie doubled over in pain. Winded and in shock Evie realized

Carlos just punched her in the gut. No one had ever hit her with such clear intent to inflict pain and her mind struggled to cope with the horror. Before she could recover she got yanked upright by the wolf. He held her from behind and Carlos pressed his face into hers. His eyes were filled with so much fury she knew he was beyond reason. Perhaps it was his anger that made him forget he still had an avian audience or perhaps he was so used to doing whatever he wanted he thought no one would dare to object when he grabbed hold of Evie shirt and tore it open. He had long unkempt nails and the vicious force with which he tore Evie's shirt meant he also left a bloody trail down her chest and across one breast. Evie screamed and tried to cover herself but Carlos was all over her. She tried desperately to dislodge his hands from painfully squeezing her breasts but the wolf pinned both arms along with her wings. Evie threw her weight back against the wolf and kicked out with all her strength. She felt vicious satisfaction when her kick landed solidly and she heard the agonized grunt of a man who'd been hit where it hurt most. Her victory was short lived as an instant later a blow struck the back of her head. She went limp as stars flickered in the dark before her eyes and she was dimly aware she could taste blood from where she bit her own tongue.

From somewhere to her side Evie heard Raven roar, "ENOUGH! Get that feral mutt off her!"

There was a flurry of wings and angry shouts but Evie couldn't follow what was going on over the din in her head. She got shoved to the side and with no time to brace herself she hit the roof hard. Her stomach heaved and in a daze she pushed herself up into a sitting position expecting to throw up but nothing happened. As soon as she had her wits about her Evie tied her torn shirt as best she could. It hurt to turn her head but she forced herself to look around. It took her a moment to comprehend what she was seeing. Carlos lay on his side clutching his crotch, the human guard kneeled with his hands tied behind his back and the wolf lay on the ground with unseeing eyes, a thin trail of blood seeping out from under him. Standing over the wolf with a bloody spear in his hands was one of the males she had thought looked familiar. She recognized him now from a brief meeting when her cousin Innes had shyly introduced the new man in her life to the flock.

"Hello, Lorenzo."

Lorenzo nodded but kept his eyes averted. "Hello, Evie."

Evie heard raised voices and saw Raven was having a heated

discussion with half a dozen sentinels. Evie unsteadily got back to her feet. She tentatively flexed her bruised wings and almost wept in relief to find they were still in working order. Good, that meant she could fly and that was exactly what she would do while everyone was distracted. She walked to the edge of the roof intending to launch herself over the side but a firm hand grabbed her wrist. Panicked she tried to shake off the hand but it was no use, Lorenzo held fast. Feeling oddly betrayed she stared up at him. Lorenzo looked uncomfortable and very grim.

"You can't leave, Evie. Not unless Raven says so. Please don't struggle I don't want to hurt you."

Raven broke from the gathering, she skirted around the downed Carlos and grabbed hold of Evie's other arm.

"Come, Evie. *Move*. Quickly now!"

Before Evie could open her mouth to ask what was happening she was force-marched off the roof by Raven and Lorenzo. When she tried to dig in her heels Raven yanked her hard. "I'm trying to help you!" Raven ground out through gritted teeth. Seeing no better option Evie followed.

As they passed through the guard room Lorenzo scooped up a discarded flight jacket and wordlessly stuffed it into Evie's arms. She shot him a grateful look and wrestled her wings and arms into it on the move. She felt less exposed with her torn shirt covered but she still had to resist the urge to draw her wings around herself protectively. So many curious eyes tracked her movement and none of it felt friendly. Wordlessly they hurried down several flights of stairs. Raven stopped in front of a locked door, fished a key out of her pocket to unlock it and pushed Evie inside. It only took Evie a moment to notice the barred windows and that access to the balcony was blocked by a metal gate bolted into the floor and ceiling.

Furious she turned on Raven. "How is stuffing me into another cage helping me?" Evie hissed.

"This is for your own protection. I'm the only one who has a key to this room. It's true you can't leave but no one can get to you either. Trust me right now that's a good thing. It will buy time while I figure out what to do next. If you believe in any deity now would be a good time to pray for help."

With those parting words, Raven shut the door in Evie's face and there was the sound of a key turning in the lock. Evie stared at the metal door and told herself firmly she wasn't allowed to cry. She rested both palms on the door and listened with her ear pressed to the door but the metal was either too thick or the room had been made soundproof because she heard nothing aside from her own pounding heart and rapid breathing. Turning away from the door Evie surveyed her new prison. It was empty, not even a chair to sit on or a rug to cover the bare floor. On the upside, she didn't see manacles on the wall or torture equipment either. Evie strode to the other side of the room to inspect the gate that blocked access to the balcony. It was odd that a prison would have a balcony but it was probably already there when the room got repurposed to serve as a holding cell. Rather than remove the balcony it was easier to add the gate. Experimentally Evie pulled on the lever in the wall. She didn't really think anything would happen but to her surprise, it retracted the balcony screen. If her circumstances weren't so dire she would have marveled at the sight that greeted her. Ravir Tower was on a high mountain that could only be reached by flight and Evie saw stretched out before her majestic snowcapped mountain ranges, rain swollen clouds and far below a valley with a river writhing through it like a thick green snake. A blast of cold wet air ruffled her feathers; it was raining again. Evie gripped the thick metal bars that kept her from flying away and stared longingly at the dark skies beyond. As she watched lightning fork in the distance she automatically counted down the seconds until she heard the accompanying boom. If only she could get out she'd happily throw herself into that storm. No matter how dangerous it was to fly in such bad weather she'd give half her feathers to be out there rather than remain a captive of House Ravir.

CHAPTER 28

RECKONING

Despair washed over Evie and she closed her eyes against the sting of tears. As soon as she did the scene on the roof replayed in her head and she started to shiver as the shock of what almost happened hit her. She opened her eyes and stared up at the stormy sky willing herself not to think of the fate that awaited her if she got handed to Carlos. Evie was so lost in her dark thoughts it took her a moment to register the low whisper of her name. At first, she thought she imagined it but then she heard it again. Scanning the balcony she saw the top of a head and a pair of familiar green eyes staring at her. Evie's jaw dropped and she stared in disbelief. Aurora? Here? How was that possible? Aurora looked between the room and Evie, her eyebrows raised in question.

"It's just me," Evie mouthed at her.

Aurora nodded her understanding and pulled herself up onto the balcony. She put a finger to her mouth cautioning Evie to be quiet and made her way to the barred doorway. She took a quick peek into the room behind Evie then took hold of two bars bending them out of the way like they were made from rubber. Aurora squeezed through the gap and Evie immediately touched her to make sure she was real.

"Aurora, I can't believe you climbed all the way up here. It's so high, what if you fell?"

Aurora gave her a mischievous grin and said, "I told you I can climb really well. Getting up here wasn't difficult, the challenge was getting to you without being seen." Aurora turned her attention back to the bolted gate and as thunder rumbled in the wake of another lightning strike she ripped out the metal bars so a person with large wings could get through.

Evie stared at the effortless display of power. She knew Aurora was strong but this was on an entirely different scale. It reminded her of the way Lady Adelind destroyed the armrest of the chair she'd been sitting on. She had squeezed the metal frame in a fit of anger so it pooled through her fingers like putty. Aurora must really have dragon blood in her veins, Evie thought. Wow…and they had made love.

Evie waited impatiently for her to finish. As soon as Aurora turned to face her Evie threw herself into her arms. The moment she felt the familiar comfort of Aurora's embrace the fear that had gripped her like a vice released and she blurted out, "You came for me. I didn't think anyone knew where I was but somehow you found me. I'm so happy to see you."

Aurora scooped her up so Evie ended up with her legs wrapped around her waist. Aurora kissed the side of her neck and murmured into Evie's hair, "I was so worried about you. I thought I was going to lose my mind when Oriana told me you were missing. I was so angry with Marcus for what he did. Your father was furious."

"My father is alive? Marcus planned to kill him."

"I know. Don't worry he is very much alive and he will get better now he's not being poisoned."

Evie whimpered with relief. "When I get home I'm going to have Marcus's wings clipped for the suffering he caused."

"That may be a bit redundant…your uncle is dead."

"You killed him?"

"No, your dad did that. I just ripped off his wings and bit off a few fingers to make him talk."

Evie's eyebrows flew up and she said, "Sounds like you and my father had a very interesting bonding session."

"Something like that. You are precious to him and he wants you home safe. We have that in common."

"I'm precious to you?"

"The most precious thing in the world."

Evie tilted her head and claimed Aurora's mouth in a hungry kiss. The kiss only lasted a few seconds but it was intense with Evie trying to convey so many complex emotions at once.

"You really are happy to see me," Aurora said a little breathlessly when she pulled away. "I'd like nothing better than to have you kiss me like that all day but not here. We are still in enemy territory and your kisses are very distracting."

"I know but I had to kiss you. I was so afraid I'd lost you and would never get to do that again. When I thought I was about to die all I could think of was you."

Aurora's arms tightened around Evie. "If you say things like that to me I won't be able to let you go."

"That's good. I don't want you to ever let me go. We have a lot to talk about but you are right this is not the right place or time. Let's get out of here."

As Aurora set her down she said, "I got your clothing wet and dirty. Sorry about that."

"I was already like that and even if I had been in pristine clothing I wouldn't have cared because that greeting was totally worth it." Something that had been nagging at her since Aurora's arrival finally registered and she exclaimed, "What have you done to your lovely hair?"

Aurora grinned and stroked what little remained of her hair. "I know it looks bad but I was in a hurry and no scissors."

"Typical. I leave you alone for two days and you go back to hacking your hair off with a knife." Evie glided her palms over Aurora's head tugging at the uneven tufts of hair. "You made such a mess."

"It was for a good cause; I was trying to find you."

"How did cutting your hair help you find me?" Evie asked incredulously. This I've got to hear."

Aurora's grin froze and her body became rigid with tension. "Evie...I smell blood on your wings and chest. You've been injured."

"It's nothing. I lost a few feathers and it's just a scratch in the front."

Unconvinced Aurora opened the loaned jacket and reached for the knot Evie tied to keep her shirt closed after Carlos tore it open. Evie blocked her.

"Please let me see. I need to know how bad it is."

Evie relented and moved her hands out of the way. Aurora gasped when she saw the ripening bruises and the ripped bra. She gently traced the red finger marks imprinted on Evie's creamy skin and stared at the swollen breast with the bloody cut. Looking down at herself Evie had to admit it looked bad. Feeling ashamed despite knowing she had done her best to prevent the man from touching her Evie retied the knot with shaky fingers. She didn't realize she was crying until Aurora cupped her face and tried to wipe the tears away with her thumbs.

"Evie, who did this to you?" Aurora's voice was low and dangerous. Where her hand rested on Aurora's arm Evie could feel the spike of power nip at her fingers as Aurora's beast surged close to the surface.

"It's nothing. It looks worse than it is. I wasn't raped. I'm all right.

Really I am."

"How can this be nothing? Someone tore your clothing and hurt you." She pressed her face against Evie's chest and inhaled deeply. Evie felt Aurora's arm ripple and had to yank her hand away as it suddenly felt like she was touching red-hot steel. When Evie saw her face she almost took a step back. Aurora's inhuman eyes were amber slits with only the barest traces of green and filled with so much anger it terrified her even though she knew none of it was directed at her.

"The man who put his hands on you…tell me everything you can about him. Tell me what happened. It is important that you leave nothing out."

Evie tried not to show how alarmed she was at the way Aurora's features were becoming more beastly by the second. She already had fangs, her shorn hair was growing into a thick mane and Evie knew from the way the air around Aurora shimmered that she was moments away from making a full shift. She worried what she was about to tell Aurora would only make her angrier and push her closer to losing control but she couldn't withhold information from her. Especially not when Aurora looked at her like *that*. Evie told her everything that happened. She described the man with the stinky cigar and told all she had learned about him from Raven. When she was done Aurora covered her face with her hands and said nothing for several long seconds. When she finally spoke her voice sounded odd and Evie had to strain to understand her.

"It's been so long. I thought I was mistaken. How could it be the same man? He escaped. Gone without a trace. Why would he be here now after all this time? But it is the same scent. Impossible to forget. In my nightmares I still smell the stink of him all over me like the spray of a rutting animal. I hear his voice jeering the others on. The smell of my burning flesh and the reek of those fucking cigars are seared into my mind. He took my father from me and destroyed my world. As if that wasn't enough just as I'm finally ready to put it all behind me he comes back and puts his stink on my beautiful winged angel. He hurt my sweet Evie." Aurora's breathing became uneven and her hands turned into massive paws with gleaming claws that resembled curved daggers. "How dare he touch my Evie. *Die*. He must *die*. I'm going to rip his fucking heart out!"

Aurora dropped her hands and this time Evie did take a jerky step away, she couldn't help it. Aurora's amber eyes glowed with rage akin to madness and hatred contorted her face so that Evie hardly recognized the woman she thought she knew. Aurora blinked and the last of her human features disappeared. The beast before Evie had a tiger's facial structure and black horns the texture of polished stone grew out from beside her temples curving past her ears and over her scalp. Her bare feet had grown to balance her bigger bulk and sprouted nails like that of a giant cat. Aurora tore off her clothing just as massive arms and legs burst the seams. Evie stared in shock at the scales that covered Aurora's body like living armor. As Evie watched it spread up around her neck and over her face like dark ink and disappeared into her hairline. A long thick tail covered in barb-like protrusions appeared; it uncoiled like a living thing and whipped the air behind Aurora's back.

The chimera opened its massive maw and in a voice that rumbled like thunder declared, "Blood debt is owed. Today I will kill my father's murderer. For allying with the cutter and aiding the traitor who tried to kill you and your father I declare war on House Ravir. They put the one I love in the hands of my greatest enemy and for this I will show them no mercy. I will bathe in the blood of Ravir's slain and piss on what's left of their corpses. When I'm done this great tower will be reduced to a burial mound."

The beast picked up one of the bars it had torn off the window and threw it like a spear at the door. It went right through the solid metal and there was the sound of a muffled scream from the other side. Lightning quick the beast charged the door taking a section of the rock wall with it as it burst into the hallway beyond. Its roar was so deafening Evie had to clamp hands over her ears. There was a moment of utter silence as if the world was holding its breath then there was a scream, high pitched and panicky, lasting only a moment before it got cut short. There was running, shouting and the whoosh of wings as terrified avians tried to get away from the crazed beast in their tower. The building shook with impact so that the chandelier above Evie's head swung like an earthquake had hit the building. Rooted to the spot Evie stared at the hole in the wall through which she could hear the sound of destruction as a monstrous creature rapidly moved through the tower in pursuit of its prey. Above the sound of things breaking Evie could hear the terrified screams as death tore through Ravir Tower in the form of a chimera berserk with rage.

Movement on the balcony caught her eye and Evie swung around to see Raven hovering in the air. She was staring at the destroyed metal grate and the bars that lay strewn like broken toothpicks beside it. Her eyes flicked to Evie then lingered on the gaping hole in the wall where there used to be a door. She landed on the balcony and carefully climbed through the opening. There was another impact and again the entire building shook. It was too much for the chandelier; it broke free from its mooring and shattered into a thousand pieces when it hit the floor. Raven flew over the debris and peered into the tower. There was another thunderous roar and she hastily retreated back into the room.

With wild eyes Raven asked, "Evie, what the fuck is that?"

"That is the woman I told you about. She came for me."

Raven stared at her incredulously. "You said your girlfriend is a tigress. Whatever is loose in there is not a tigress!"

"If you dare to get close enough you will see she is." Among other things...Evie added quietly to herself. "Aurora is an Old Blood. That is her mixed warrior form. I did tell you she is powerful."

Raven stared at her in horror. "An Old Blood? Your tigress girlfriend is an *Old Blood* with a warrior form?" At Evie's nod Raven visibly shuddered and whispered, "Deities protect us. An Old Blood is on a killing spree in my home."

The howls of someone in mortal pain poured into the room and Evie flinched. Raven paled another shade and narrowed her eyes at Evie. She took a determined step toward Evie and said, "She came for you. You must stop her."

Evie picked up one of the broken bars with a sharp end and pointed it at Raven. "Back off. I won't be taken captive again. I will skewer you if you try to put hands on me."

Raven stopped and held up her hands. "Evie, my people are dying. She is slaughtering them. Can't you hear the screams? I beg you, make her stop."

"I don't know if I can. I've never seen her this angry."

"Because we kidnapped you?"

"She was angry about that but it was finding out Carlos is here that pushed her over the edge."

"Carlos? What did he do to her?"

"He's the cutter who murdered her father in front of her. She's hunted him since she was eleven years old and Aurora is the angry beast-shifter who made him flee to America. She was only going to rescue me but when she found his scent on me and saw the way he tore my clothing she went berserk."

Raven punched the wall with a white-knuckled fist. "That right there is the reason why it is suicide to do business with cutters! There is always a relative or friend out for revenge. It never ends."

"Where is Carlos now? Still up top? She is hunting him and anyone who gets in her way is collateral damage."

"She'll leave once she's got him?" Raven asked hopefully.

"I...don't know. Like I said I've never seen her this angry."

"What would happen if you called to her from outside the tower? Would that make her leave? You said she came here for you."

Not liking the calculating look in Raven's eyes and the way her body tensed for motion Evie backed up towards the balcony, all the while keeping the spike trained on Raven. "Don't even think of using me as bait to lure her out. If you'd let me go when I begged you to free me your people wouldn't be dying right now."

Evie stopped when she felt a hand press into the small of her back. A chill ran down her spine and she turned expecting to find a sentinel behind her. What she found instead was possibly more alarming. The robed figure of Lady Adelind stood behind her. She had her hood drawn and the only part of her that was visible was a portion of her face. Cool grey eyes with a hint of amber met hers and Lady Adelind said, "Is the black feathered female troublesome, Evangeline? I've been waiting for you – is she responsible for your delay?"

Evie was so startled to see Aurora's mother, the dragon lady, that it took her a moment to gather her wits. The first thing she did was make as respectful a bow as she could manage under the circumstances. "Lady Adelind. It's...a surprise to see you here."

Lady Adelind inclined her head acknowledging the greeting. "Indeed. I'm rather surprised myself. When I started the day I didn't expect to accompany Aurora on a rescue mission for her avian lover and yet here I am. So, why haven't you left yet? Aurora opened your cage and there is no reason for you to linger here. If the avian is preventing your departure kill her." When Evie didn't make a move Lady Adelind sighed and reached for the spike in her hand. "I'll do it for you. You're clearly too squeamish to kill one of your own kind."

The robe fell away from her arm and Evie saw that instead of skin Lady Adelind had thick scales and her fingers were tipped with long nails that looked like talons. Evie dropped the metal bar like it was on fire. "Thank you for the gracious offer but that won't be necessary.

Raven was just leaving."

Raven was staring at Lady Adelind's hand. Fear warred with disbelief in her dark eyes. "Evie, is that a dra—"

Evie cut Raven off before she could finish. "You should go, Raven. NOW. While you still can."

Evie had to give Raven credit, she had superb survival instincts. She might not have understood exactly what was going on but she got the warning and didn't hesitate to act. She twirled on her heel and flew into the tower, gambling she could evade the raging beast rather than try to squeeze past the amber-eyed Lady Adelind. Smart woman.

"Why did you let her live?" Lady Adelind asked curiously. "I know who she is. Raven Ravir is no friend of yours."

"No, but she's not my enemy either. At least I don't think so." Seeing Lady Adelind's skeptical look Evie reluctantly added, "She saved me from being raped."

"I overheard your conversation. By taking you captive in the first place she put you in such a vulnerable position. You do not owe her mercy."

"You heard what I said to her? Then you heard that..." Evie faltered not wanting to tell Lady Adelind her husband's murderer was in the tower in case she lost her cool composure and went berserk as Aurora did. The last thing she wanted was to be in the room with an angry dragon.

"Did I hear that the man who tortured my daughter and murdered Valen is the one who rough handled you? Yes, I heard. I will help Aurora exact vengeance but first I must escort you to safety. That was Aurora's purpose in coming here but the scent of her enemy has driven her mad with rage. My daughter rarely asks me for anything and that she summoned me to locate you tells me you are very important to her. It would not do to have you recaptured or killed after all the trouble she went through to rescue you, Evangeline."

"Aurora said she was going to destroy the tower and everyone in it because they were working with Carlos. Will she really do that?"

"Aurora doesn't make idle threats and as enraged as she is right now I have no doubt she will decimate this place."

"Then we have to stop her! You could do it. You could stop her."

"Perhaps but why would I? House Ravir made an alliance with my enemy and harmed my daughter's lover. Those are unforgivable transgressions. Blood is owed."

"But there are several hundred avians in this tower. They're not all guilty."

"It doesn't matter. The leaders of this House set this in motion. They drew Aurora here by taking you captive. If House Ravir had acted honorably and treated you as a valued hostage, assuring your wellbeing while negotiating with House Aquilar Aurora would have rescued you and left the matter to be resolved between your Houses. Instead, she finds you reeking of fear and blood with her enemy's scent all over you. Unforgivable. She will turn this place into rubble. If the avians want to live they should abandon their tower."

"But there will be a nursery with wingless little ones somewhere in this tower. What if they can't get out in time? When Aurora comes back to her senses it will devastate her if she hurt the children. She'll never forgive herself."

Lady Adelind frowned and said, "Unfortunately you are right. She won't harm children even in the state she's in but falling debris will be as fatal as a strike from her claws. This is a conundrum. Calming her enough to listen to reason will be difficult."

"There must be a way. What if we—"

Lady Adelind held up her hand motioning for Evie to be quiet and tilted her head from side to side listening. She closed her eyes for a moment and sighed. When she reopened them her eyes shone with amber fire. "I can no longer escort you to safety and as for protecting the avian children…forget about it. Go home. Perhaps between the two of us we could have calmed Aurora but the situation has escalated significantly. I have to go and you should leave *immediately*."

"What can be worse than Aurora raging out of control destroying the place?"

"Evangeline, they are just avians. If it wasn't for Aurora's interest in you and the valid point you made about the guilt she'd load on herself if she killed the little ones their death would mean nothing to me. I'm older than I look and it is not polite to mention such things but I remember when we thought of your kind as little more than a tasty snack."

Evie swallowed hard and asked timidly, "If you don't mind me asking, Lady Adelind, what did you hear that has you so concerned?"

"More of my kind are heading this way."

"More dragons?" Evie's voice was so high it was barely a squeak.

"Aurora roared like a dragon. We can hear each other over long distances and unfortunately, she was heard. There are several males on the way, drawn to the sound of a young dragoness in distress. They are coming to investigate what has enraged a female so much that she would attack an avian compound by day. Females are precious. There are fewer of us than males which makes the competition to mate fierce. Those males are not only coming to protect a female they also want to make a good impression on her. If they think it will please the female to see this place destroyed they will compete to kill the most avians and pile the bodies to present to her as trophies or, if she was so inclined, as food."

"Eeew…that's revolting."

Lady Adelind nodded her agreement. "We work hard to act civilized and that kind of behavior is frowned on but there is nothing like the draw of sex combined with the smell of blood and the exhilaration of battle to bring our dragon's most primal urges to the fore."

"I don't understand. If female dragons are so precious why have they treated Aurora so poorly? The way she told it your people would have killed her if it wasn't for your intervention."

"That's because they think Aurora takes after my beloved Valen. They've only ever seen her as a tiger and they don't know she can take the form of a dragon as well."

"Why didn't you tell them? Wouldn't that have made them treat her better?"

"Once they thought she was a tigress we had to stick to that lie. That part of her was all Aurora could allow anyone to see."

"But why?"

"Isn't it obvious? Only a chimera can take more than one beast form. Remember I told you my people kill our chimera babies? Chimeras of dragon blood are the nightmare creatures my people fear as your kind fear us. They already hated Aurora because our feud with her father's clan cost us so many lives. That we had to agree to a truce was a bitter blow to our collective ego and the older dragons still remember that bloody struggle like it was yesterday. They didn't dare touch Aurora because of my position and the certainty of my wrath. Those males are coming here expecting to see a dragoness who they hope to woo to become a mate. It is possible she will be in full dragon form by the time they get here but it is more likely they will see a monstrosity that is part dragon combined with whatever Aurora is drawing on to help her in battle. I'm not sure what will happen if they see her like that but my kind tends to lash out when we are upset. I will try to reason with them but it is likely I'll have to physically intervene to prevent them from attacking her. One thing is sure, they'll have to kill me first to lay a single claw on my daughter."

Without thinking, Evie stepped forward and put her hand on Lady Adelind's arm. "That sounds dangerous. Will you be all right? Is there anything I can do to help?"

Lady Adelind tilted her head and looked at Evie as if she was studying a curious specimen. "How could you possibly help me?"

"I don't know. That was probably a silly thing to say but I don't want you to get killed." Realizing she still had her hand on Lady Adelind's arm Evie quickly removed it.

"What an extraordinary soul you are. No wonder my daughter is so infatuated with you. There is no need to fear for me; I know how to deal with my kind. It is *you* who must take care to stay alive. Aurora will be inconsolable if anything happened to you. When you fly home make sure to stay out of the cloud cover because you do not want to meet what's coming. You need to go *now,* Evangeline. Forget about the children of this flock, they are not your responsibility and it's up to the guardians of this House to look after their young. Soon the skies above this tower will be filled with angry dragons and this will not be a safe place for anyone. Least of all avians."

***

Once Lady Adelind left Evie had a moment of indecision. She wanted to go home to her family and flock but she couldn't abandon Aurora. Indirectly she'd brought her here. She came to rescue her and now Aurora was lost in her old nightmare, tearing the place apart in search of the one responsible for her pain. Killing Carlos would vent a lot of her fury. Once that was done Evie felt she had a chance of convincing Aurora to come away with her.

The other reason she couldn't leave was the people in the tower. They were already dealing with a worst-case scenario – a furious Old Blood among them. They didn't know their tower was about to become the focal point of angry dragons as well. Even if the dragons didn't target the avians directly any confrontation between the giants of the sky would have them stuck in the crossfire. Since dragons have no regard for avian life it was a massacre waiting to happen. Evie's heart clenched with fear. They weren't members of her flock, not her responsibility and she'd been treated so badly she shouldn't care what happened to any of them. But she did. She had to warn them. She had to find Raven and tell her to evacuate. She was the only one in authority who might listen to her.

Evie balled her fists, took a fortifying breath and stepped through the broken doorway. It was eerily quiet. After the initial roars and commotion Aurora had gone quiet but there had been intermittent screams so she knew Aurora was still in the tower. She was no longer raging out of control; she was stalking her prey. A chilling thought. Masonry crunched under her foot and for a moment she stood transfixed, her eye on the shattered door and the avian that lay impaled beneath it. Raven must have left someone to guard her door. She could only see the man's leg so she couldn't tell if it was Lorenzo. She looked away quickly hoping it wasn't.

Despite there being plenty of windows it was murky inside. The storm was upon them and it had gotten so dark it was like twilight. She saw lights here and there but they were lonely things, probably part of an emergency system designed to turn on when the ethian generator was down. Something Aurora had done must have taken out the power. There was an acrid stench in the air that burned her lungs when she inhaled too deeply and she caught an alarming whiff of smoke. Evie hoped there wasn't a fire somewhere. The inside of this tower was like a hollow tube, not wide enough to really fly but it allowed enough room for avians to drift down or rise slowly between floors. Flames would spread like wildfire in a place like this

Evie heard people calling to each other on the floors above and below interspersed with confused shouts and terrified wails. She went down on her hands and knees to stay out of sight and peered over the edge trying to catch a glimpse of Aurora or Raven.

"Hiding from your murderous girlfriend?"

Evie almost jumped out of her skin and swore when she saw Raven land behind her. Lorenzo was beside her and a handful of sentinels landed around them in a tight cluster.

"I was looking for you."

"Me? Why?" Curious Raven stepped away from the group to stand in front of Evie. "What are you still doing here, Evie? I expected you to be long gone."

Evie took Raven by the arm and turned her so they had a little privacy. Speaking urgently she said, "You have to evacuate the tower. Quickly. Get everyone as far away from here as you can."

"So that your tigress can rampage in the tower unopposed? What kind of fool do you take me for?" Raven snarled and ripped her arm away.

Evie thrust a hand at the giant beast-shaped hole in the stone wall where there used to be a door and hissed, "She burst through that wall without breaking stride. Have you seen her yet? Have you seen how quickly she moves? Have you seen how big and powerful she is? Have you seen the size of her claws and fangs? She is an Old Blood, Raven. An *Old Blood*. Your people are in a close quarter's battle with a predator who outclasses them in every way. Your sentinels may be well trained but we both know our people need open skies and room to move to take down a beast-shifter. Don't pretend you think fighting an Old Blood hand-to-claw inside your tower will end well."

"If you hung around just to tell me that you've wasted your breath and my time. I already know we are up against a formidable opponent. But this is our tower and we won't give it up without a fight!"

Evie heaved an exasperated sigh and said, "Aurora doesn't want to claim your bloody tower! She has no use for it. I already told you she is after Carlos. Getting in her way will only get your people killed." Raven made as if to turn away from her and Evie grabbed her sleeve. "I was looking for you to warn you about something else. There are several dragons on the way and I have it on good authority they are going to be furious when they get here. Anyone in the air will be in danger. Your tower may not survive."

While they spoke Lorenzo had moved up beside Raven in a guard position. His posture defensive, a hand on his sword, his eyes restlessly scanning the shadows. His eyes now flew to Evie and he gave her an incredulous look. "Dragons? I haven't seen one in years. Why would we suddenly have dragons on the way? Why at the same time as there is an Old Blood loose in the tower? That doesn't make any sense. I like you, Evie, but now you're blowing smoke. I don't know what you are trying to do but that story is so outrageous no one is going to believe it. Raven, please…we must keep moving. We have our orders."

Raven didn't move or speak. She stared at Evie with a look in her eyes that said she'd been thinking about Lady Adelind and Evie had just confirmed what she suspected. She'd seen a dragon. She knew she couldn't discount Evie's warning because she'd seen her talk to a dragon. Raven was in shock struggling to process what this meant.

Evie softened her voice and used the same words Raven had spoken to her as she dragged her off the roof. "Raven, I'm trying to help you."

Raven's head whipped up and she silenced Lorenzo with a sharp motion of her hand when he tried to speak. "Did that woman, Lady Adelind, tell you dragons are coming here?

"Yes."

"Why? How do you know her? What was she doing here?"

Evie shook her head. "You don't get to ask me those questions. I've gone out of my way to tell you this. I could have left without saying anything."

"If what you are saying is true, we are doomed. We can't even contain the tigress. A squadron of our best warriors was sent to stop the beast. They wore full battle armor and they were armed to the teeth and yet no one came back. *Not one.* Now we have dragons as well…deities help us! This is a dark day for House Ravir."

"It doesn't have to be like that. Evacuate the tower. You must have protocols for a breach. You must have designated places your people can retreat to when the tower is no longer safe."

"We can't abandon our tower," Raven balked. "We have to fight. We must—"

"How will you fight dragons? Even if you manage to injure one what about the rest? It's suicide, Raven. This…" Evie waved at the walls, "is just stone and metal. You can rebuild the tower if it falls."

"Maybe your flock could afford to rebuild, mine can't," Raven said bitterly. "My father will never give the order to abandon Ravir Tower. It was built by his great-great-grandfather. He will sacrifice as many people as it takes to protect our family's legacy."

"Raven, that's madness! The tower is important, I agree, but in the end it is just a place. The people are the true strength and the heart of the House. They cannot be replaced. It's the Lord's duty to protect the flock above all else."

"My father doesn't think like that. To him the tower is the symbol of the Lord's power and a display of a flock's might. It's the glue that binds. Without a tower he will no longer be Lord of the Tower. It is the obligation of the Lord of the House to provide a home for his people and a tower to keep them safe. If this tower falls it means he has failed in his duty to the flock and the people are released of their obligations. They could leave and join other flocks without needing his permission. It will be the end of House Ravir. He would do *anything* to prevent that. In his mind people are dispensable, this tower is not."

Evie stared at Raven in shocked silence.

Raven gave a weary shrug. "I'm simply telling you how it is."

Rallying, Evie shook her head and said, "No. You are telling me what your father would do. Just because he is willing to sacrifice his people it doesn't mean you have to allow that to happen. This flock is as much yours as it is his. These are your people and they are your responsibility. You've known them your whole life. They look up to you for leadership and protection. If it comes down to it what will *you* choose? The tower or the people?"

Raven spoke but her words got drowned out by a deafening roar within the tower. There was an answering bellow from outside moments before something large impacted the top of the building with such force the entire building shuddered. Evie watched in horror as large chunks of stone wall cascaded past the windows. A steel ballista with the giant bolt still mounted hit one of the balconies, tearing right through it. Evie ran to a window and hesitantly peered out. She glimpsed a dragon's tail curled around the top of the building before she had to duck to avoid being hit by falling rubble. That was a massive dragon. Was that Lady Adelind? Or someone else? Did it really matter? Whoever it was just destroyed the top floors and took out the primary defensive weaponry simply by landing on the roof.

A horn sounded outside. Evie assumed the alert was for the dragon on the roof but one of Raven's people shouted and pointed to the east at a dozen sentinels heading towards the tower. Peering through the rain haze Evie saw a red dragon swoop out of the cloud cover directly above them. It extended its talons and tore through the sentinels' tight formation sending them tumbling to the ground in a flutter of torn wings and severed limbs. An avian who escaped the initial onslaught made a desperate attempt to get away from the pursuing dragon only to have massive jaws chomp down on her. One moment there were wings sticking out the sides of its mouth and then they were gone as the dragon swallowed its prey whole. The red dragon rose back into the cloud cover disappeared from view but there was no mistaking its direction – it was heading straight for the tower.

Evie turned to face Lorenzo. "Still think I'm blowing smoke? Your flock now face two dragons and there are more on the way."

Evie and Raven locked eyes. Raven's face was an unreadable mask and Evie couldn't tell what the woman was thinking. Raven shifted her attention to Lorenzo and the sentinels clustered around her. They were all standing tall but their eyes as they stared at Raven were dull and resigned as if they expected the worst and were steeling themselves for an impossible battle.

"What do we do, Raven?" Lorenzo asked. "What is your command?"

"We evacuate. Vena and Asheron, go ring the bells. Seema and Belek, I want you two to activate the additional escape protocols. We must get our people to safety. Hurry!" There were surprised looks but the sentinels immediately burst into flight.

Lorenzo looked at Raven with a mix of admiration and worry. "He will disinherit you for this."

Raven rustled her wings defiantly and said, "There will be nothing to inherit if the tower is rubble and we are all dead."

"I'll help get the children out," Evie offered. "Where is the nursery? Do you have a safe place nearby we can take them?"

"Yes, my father had an armored vault built into the mountain behind us. Officially it's used to store precious things but it also functions as a fallback shelter. He was supposed to be the only one with access but I know how to get in. We will gather the children and anyone unable to fly we find along the way and take them there. Everyone, let's move!"

CHAPTER 29

FIRE AND BLOOD

They were running toward the vault. The adults herded the children under the shelter of their spread wings, shielding them from the icy torrential downpour and the view of the dragons. Evie was carrying a wingless child and had another by the hand. An old man with crooked wings and a bent back hobbled to the side and scooped up a little girl who had fallen.

"Raven, how much further?" Evie shouted.

"We are almost there. It's just around that outcropping."

A furious roar from behind them sent shivers down Evie's spine and by reflex she glanced back to see what was happening. Ravir Tower, the pride of House Ravir was on fire. Smoke seeped from the spider web of cracks circling the walls and billowed from open doorways. The rain pouring in through the destroyed roof was keeping the fire at bay in the top floors but on the lower levels the windows were tinted red with the blaze of the raging inferno. A few avians who hadn't abandoned the tower when the evacuation bells rang were making their escape, diving to stay as close to the ground as possible to avoid the dragons circling above. Evie noticed a group heading in the same direction they were going. In the heavy rain visibility was poor but she recognized Lord Nero and his son Titus in the front. His personal guards surrounded him and one of the sentinels carried a man. An entire section of the tower wall burst outwards and a huge creature that looked vaguely like a tiger surged into the air in pursuit of its prey. Dark wings appeared where there had been none a moment before and with claws extended and snapping jaw it tore through the back of Lord Nero's guard. Armored sentinels tumbled to the ground like broken dolls and the beast dove after them. Evie hastily looked away.

"Raven! Look! Your father and Carlos are heading this way. Aurora has Carlos's scent and she's coming after them."

Raven glanced back over her shoulder and swore. She grabbed hold of Lorenzo's arm and shouted, "Get to the vault. Make sure they don't close it before we are inside."

"But, Raven, it's my duty to protect you."

"GO. That is an order! If my father gets in before us he will lock the fucking door to save himself and we'll be left outside at the mercy of the dragons and that blood-crazed tigress. You keep that door open no matter what."

Lorenzo paled visibly, he looked at the approaching avians flying low and then at the terrified children and adults running for the vault. The beast roared again and this time the sound was a lot louder. It was on its way. From within the cloud cover a dragon bellowed as if in answer. Lorenzo visibly shuddered and balled his fists. "Raven, I will keep the door open for you. I swear this on my life." Then he flew off flying so low his wings almost clipped the ground.

When they rounded the outcropping Evie saw a door shaped hole in the side of the mountain. Lorenzo was inside seemingly in a heated argument with two sentinels wearing the colors of Lord Nero's personal guard. As soon as he saw Lord Nero and his party swoop towards the opening he positioned himself in front of a large wheel and drew his sword. He spread his legs wide and even from where she was Evie could see the determined set of his jaw. True to Raven's prediction as soon as he was inside Lord Nero made a gesture towards the wheel and two sentinels peeled from his side.

"Does that wheel close the door?" Evie asked Raven.

"Yes! It's only the first of several doors but once that one is sealed from the inside we are not getting in."

Lorenzo shouted at the men, pointed his sword at Raven's group and then settled himself in a fighting stance. The men paused, looked at Raven and the approaching children then turned to look at Lord Nero. Lord Nero barked another order and the men instantly drew their own swords and attacked. Lorenzo moved in a flurry of motion and the two men stumbled back. One clutched his arm and the other dragged a wing. Two others took their place. Lorenzo flicked blood from his sword and watched the circling men with a grim determination.

"Wow, he's fast," Evie gasped between breaths. Running over mushy earth, bent forward with her wings extended while carrying one wiggly child and dragging another by the hand was exhausting.

"Lorenzo is one of the best fighters in the flock! Even two at a time he will keep them at bay. A few more minutes is all we need. We're going to make it!"

A loud boom ran out and crimson blossomed on Lorenzo's chest. He staggered backwards and clutched at the hole in his chest with an expression of confusion that quickly turned into dawning horror.

"Nooooo!" Raven screamed.

The sword clattered out of his hands and Lorenzo turned his head to stare out the door towards Raven. "I'm sorry," he mouthed as he toppled sideways. The sentinels parted and Carlos walked up to the fallen man. He took aim and shot Lorenzo point blank between the eyes.

"You bastard!"

Carlos's head swiveled and he locked eyes with Raven. He grinned and lifted the gun as if to take aim at her but lowered it when Lord Nero came to stand beside him.

"Lord Nero, please don't close the door!" Raven begged. "The children can't fly and they need shelter. Please help us!"

Lord Nero watched his daughter with cold dead eyes. His gaze swept past the children and their frantic minders as if they weren't there to focus on something behind them.

"Father, please! Wait, I'm almost there! Don't let me die out here."

Raven took to the air heading for the door with a child in her arms. Beside Lord Nero Carlos was also staring at something in the distance. His eyes widened and terror contorted his face. He spoke urgently to Lord Nero who nodded. He made a circling motion and the door lowered; sealing shut with a loud hiss just as Raven landed. She hit the door with her fists, screaming for someone to let her in but no one did.

Evie stopped running and got jostled by the children streaming past her towards the locked door. They were so set on the task they'd been given to keep moving towards the vault that they continued on even though they were now heading to a dead end. The child in her arms wriggled to be let down so she let him go and he stumbled after the rest. The children surged up against the door like a living wave then stopped and looked up at Raven expectantly. She was oblivious. Still pounding on the door her pleading had turned into a bitter tirade laced with curses. The adults gathered around the children and spread their wings over their charges while they spoke in urgent whispers.

A chill ran down Evie's spine and she spun around to look behind her. A massive tiger shaped beast was approaching. It was sheathed in jet black scales, a ridge of spikes ran from the back of the neck to the hindquarters and the long tail was covered in barbs that looked like it could flail a man to death with a single strike. The wings were gone and huge paws and legs propelled it forward at breath-taking speed. The beast's powerful body radiated agile power and death. Evie caught a glimpse of the beast's eyes and she shuddered. Volcanic rage and bloodlust burned like demonic fire in the depths.

That is what death looks like when it comes for you, Evie thought. There was no escaping that creature. Nothing short of death would stop it and it was coming straight for them. Or rather it was heading straight towards the vault to get Carlos and they just happened to be in the way. But what about the children? Surely Aurora wouldn't hurt the children? That's when it dawned on Evie that the beast probably couldn't see them. The adults had formed a tight formation overlapping their wings to create a canopy for the children to shelter under and in the process hidden them from view. The beast would only see the adults and it would show them no mercy. Aurora had declared war on House Ravir and to her those people would be little more than a temporary obstacle barring her way. She would tear into the adults and the children would die with them.

Evie wanted to shout at them to get away from the door but it was already too late. The beast would be on them in moments. Even if they heard her and responded immediately they couldn't get out of the way in time. They were as good as dead unless someone could convince Aurora to let them go. Of the avians present the only one who stood a chance of reasoning with her was Evie. She'd have to step into Aurora's path and try to get through to her. Evie trembled. That wasn't the kind woman she'd fallen in love with and definitely not the gentle woman who made her feel so safe. That was a furious beast set on destruction.

Her mind flashed to Aurora killing the giant armored lizards that threatened Ingvild village. That was the first time she got to see more than a glimpse of the predatory beast that Aurora hid so well. She had stared in awe and horror at the broken remains of the monstrosity Aurora had killed and fed on and finally understood why Aurora had been afraid Evie would recoil if she saw that side of her. Later that day she'd seen Aurora's tiger form as well as a gigantic warrior form that was a blend of human and tiger. She had been awed but not afraid and she had congratulated herself on how fearless she'd been in her response. What she hadn't known was that Aurora had been very careful to show her the tame version. That beast was a kitten on a leash compared to what was heading her way now. This was Aurora at her most primal and ferocious.

Evie reminded herself that as scary as it was to see Aurora like this it was also this beastly side of her that gave Aurora the power and drive to protect those she cared about. This was that side of her temporarily out of control. Evie had a choice. She could fear the beast she saw or trust the woman inside wouldn't hurt her, no matter what. She'd seen Aurora claw her way back to control repeatedly at the sound of her voice and scent. She had to believe this time would be no different. Evie grabbed hold of the memory of Aurora cradling her protectively and stepped into the beast's path. She opened her wings and moved them ever so slightly trying to waft her scent in Aurora's direction. She took a deep breath, imagined she was about to sing a dawn song while a gale blew into her face and projected her voice with all the power she could muster. She sang Aurora's name in a refrain hoping desperately she'd be heard. Evie saw the beast's ears unpin to rotate forward and saw the nostrils flare. Encouraged Evie kept singing Aurora's name and moved her wings a little faster. The beast jumped, clearing the last fifty feet in a single leap to land right in front of Evie in a spray of pebbles. Evie froze and tried not to panic at suddenly finding herself face to face with a predator that was so large she could walk underneath it without ducking her head.

"Aurora, I think you just made me pee myself a little," Evie spoke without thinking. Stress had loosed her tongue to say the first thing that came to her.

The beast huffed at her and Evie struggled not to gag at the reek of flesh on its breath and the sight of the blood-drenched claws and muzzle. Its eyes fixed on Evie, the beast prowled back and forth in front of her growling in agitation while the tail flicked restlessly. Staring into the beast's eyes Evie saw sparks of green flare in the amber, saw the way Aurora was fighting for control.

"Aurora, it's Evie. You know it's me, right? Please say something, the growling is unnerving."

The growling stopped and the beast stood still. It cocked its head in the same way Aurora did when she was carefully listening and Evie felt the tight band around her chest ease a little.

"Aurora?"

The beast crouched to bring its massive head level with Evie and took a deep breath. When it exhaled on her Evie smelled incense, scorched spice, and something that burnt her throat with a metallic aftertaste.

"Evie…what are you doing here? You should be home."

Evie almost sagged with relief to hear Aurora's voice come out of the beast's mouth. "I helped get the children out of the tower. I knew you wouldn't want them to get hurt."

"Children?" The beast asked and its brow furrowed into a frown. "No children. Only adults. Warriors. *Prey.*"

"No Aurora, not just warriors. Not just prey. Wingless little ones as well. Families. Look behind me. The adults are sheltering children under their wings."

The beast stared over Evie's wings and shock registered on its face. "Children?"

"Yes, children. You will let them pass?

"I don't kill children."

"And the adults with them? Will you let them go? The children need the adults to look after them."

The beast rumbled its discontent and started prowling back and forth again, its eyes on the avians huddled by the door. Evie prayed no one would get it in their head to make a bid for escape at that very moment. Aurora's mind was too intertwined with her beasts right now, any sudden movement and she would pounce.

"Aurora, those people didn't know Lord Nero and his son were running a cutter's den and they had nothing to do with my kidnapping. They aren't guilty. Please let them go."

The beast paused beside Evie. "Tell the children and their protectors to go. My fight is not with them."

Evie turned and raised her voice to be heard above the rain. "Get away from the door. She is after the cutter in the vault with Lord Nero. Not you. Don't run and don't try to fly away. Move slowly. Go now."

There were uncertain whispers and Evie saw the fearful looks cast at Aurora. Gathering her courage she reached out slowly and put her hand on the beast's leg. The scale covered flesh felt alien to her touch and magic nipped at her hand so her palm and fingers tingled from it. She saw wide eyes and the whispers intensified but the fact that the beast didn't devour her on the spot seemed to be enough to bolster their collective confidence. As soon as one person started moving the rest followed. The beast watched them with unwavering focus, motionless aside from the flicking tail. That is until Raven passed. She was trailing in the back sheltering the children in the rear. The beast waited until all the children were out of sight behind a bend in the path then moved quick as lightning. It hooked Raven and slammed her onto her back, a massive paw covering her entire chest.

"This one is guilty. I know her scent. She took you from your room. She must die."

"I'm not the one you want! I was just following orders," Raven choked out clawing at the paw on her chest. "Help me, Evie! Please tell her I'm speaking the truth."

"Aurora, she didn't have a choice. She had to obey her Lord's orders."

"She is guilty," the beast insisted. "You were hurt. You could have died. Blood is owed. *She must die.*"

Evie went on her knees beside the downed woman. She leaned over Raven and angled into Aurora's view so she was locked onto her instead of Raven. When Evie looked into Aurora's eyes she saw the tiny green sparks were drowning in a sea of amber; soon they would be all gone. Aurora had marked Raven as prey and the fury she dammed to listen to Evie was flooding back. Aurora didn't care why Raven kidnapped Evie, only that she did. If she wanted to save Raven's life she had to act fast.

"Aurora, give her life to me. I'm the one who was taken, it is my blood that was spilled. Let me decide when and how she dies. Give her to me. Please?"

"That is your wish?"

"It is."

"Then so it will be."

The beast unsheathed its claws, wrapped them around Raven's chest and lifted her so they were eye to eye. "Raven Ravir, your life now belongs to Evangeline Aquilar. A blood debt owed. Do you understand?"

Raven looked like a terrified doll in the beast's paw. Her eyes on the beast's mouth her wings flapped with the trapped desperation of an animal convinced it was about to die. "Yes! I understand! Please don't eat me!"

The beast gave a disgusted grunt and flung Raven in the direction of the fleeing avians. Evie held her breath as Raven tumbled helplessly through the air, certain she would smack into the rock wall, but Raven got her wings into play just in time. Raven's chest heaved with her frantic breaths and she hovered unsteadily. She touched her side, stared at the blood on her palm then met Evie's gaze with inscrutable dark eyes.

The beast roared and they both turned to watch Aurora charge the sealed door. The metal buckled at the first blow. It wouldn't last long, that much was obvious, and once Aurora got into the vault neither would the people inside. Evie glanced at Raven to see her reaction to her father and brother's imminent death. Raven's teeth were bared in a vicious smile. Raven spat. It was a slow deliberate motion filled with a lifetime of loathing and a manic glee that Evie found deeply disturbing. Then Raven flew away without looking back once.

***

Debris flew into the air as Aurora tore at the rock surrounding the locked door forcing Evie to retreat to a safer distance. Noticing a small overhang she huddled under it. It provided some shelter from the rain and she could still see what Aurora was doing without getting hit. A dragon's leg appeared in her field of vision. Evie blinked hoping it was just an illusion brought on by stress and fatigue but the leg didn't disappear. Instead, it shimmered and a moment later morphed into Lady Adelind. Evie felt momentary relief it wasn't one of the other dragons but her heart did an unsteady thump at the unnatural way Lady Adelind's head swiveled to hone in on her. They stared at each other through the rain curtain. Not knowing what else to do Evie made space for Aurora's mother to stand beside her under the overhang. Lady Adelind hesitated for a moment then walked over and joined her.

"Miserable weather," Lady Adelind commented as she shook the rain from her robe.

"Terrible weather for flying," Evie agreed even as a part of her screamed at the absurdity of talking about the weather when so much else was happening.

"She has him cornered in there?"

"Yes, the cutter fled inside with Lord Nero and his personal guard."

"Good. It will be over soon."

Noting a bloody tear in the sleeve of Lady Adelind's robe Evie asked tentatively. "Lady Adelind did you come to an understanding with the other dragons? They won't attack Aurora?"

"For now." She said this with such icy finality Evie knew it was a warning not to push for more information.

Evie turned her attention back to the vault where the sound of tearing metal let her know that Aurora had dug her way in. There was a staccato of shots, a brief silence, then the screaming started. It was the desperate sound of people dying and Evie tried to tune out everything but the rain drumming on the rocks. She refused to feel sorry for Lord Nero and his psychotic son. They put people in cages, profiting off their suffering and death. In doing so they had drenched the name of House Ravir in blood and the kind of filth that would taint every member of their flock for years to come. As for Carlos...she still felt the effect of the cutter's brutal hands on her and she was pleased that when Aurora was done with him he would be unable to hurt anyone ever again. She did feel regret for the sentinels dying to protect their Lord but she reminded herself that those warriors would have killed her without hesitation at Lord Nero's command.

The beast tore through the avians quickly and their voices fell still. Not everyone was granted swift execution. A singular male voice cried out, swearing defiantly. The cursing turned to begging, then screaming. It was a horrible sound filled with mortal pain and terror accompanied by the furious snarls of a beast. Long after Carlos stopped screaming the beast raged on. To her it sounded like a series of ferocious roars, no more intelligible than any other animal noise. But the longer it went on it seemed to her there was a rhythmic cadence to the roars, like someone shouting the same thing over and over. It suddenly occurred to Evie that Aurora could be speaking in tiger or even dragon tongue. If so…what was she saying? She turned to ask Lady Adelind but the question died on her lips. The woman's face was edged with sorrow and her very human grey eyes were overflowing with soundless tears. Evie quickly looked away. She didn't have to be a genius to know the proud woman would resent a virtual stranger witnessing her tears.

Finally, after what felt to Evie like an eternity, the beast fell silent. She heard a woman's sobs. It was a lost heartbroken sound and she automatically took a step forward to go comfort Aurora but Lady Adelind put a hand on Evie's shoulder and shook her head.

"She will not want you to see her like that."

"I've seen her cry before."

"That's not what I'm referring to."

It took Evie a moment to understand. "She wouldn't want me to see what she did?"

"No."

"Then I will wait for her to come out."

"Evangeline, when Aurora comes out of there she's not going to be in a good state of mind. She just killed the man responsible for Valen's murder. She will need time by herself to process and grieve. Then there is everything that happened here today. She has a lot to work through.

She will want to go to the forest. She will want to go to her father's grave. I will go with her. We need to do this together."

"I want to be there for her too." Evie gave Lady Adelind a cautious look trying to read her reaction. "I understand the two of you need family time. What just happened is so big. It's good that you were here to help her and to watch over her. It's what she needed. I don't want to get in the way it's just...I really want to be there for her. She needs to know I'm there for her."

Lady Adelind gave a thoughtful nod. "There is also the matter of my people. Once we've been to Valen's grave I need to present her officially. Not just as my daughter the tigress but as a chimera. She will have to demonstrate that she can control her beasts or they won't leave her alone."

"I can't imagine Aurora being pleased with that."

"She will hate it," Lady Adelind said flatly, "but it must be done. I'll fight beside her if it comes to that but even together we can't defeat them all in battle. We must come to an accord with the Dragon Council."

Evie was quiet for a few seconds then she asked, "Lady Adelind, what is it you are trying to tell me?"

"Aurora will be away for a while."

"How long? A week, a month…months?"

"It will take as long as it takes."

Evie looked away so Aurora's mother wouldn't see her expression and slowly counted to ten. It had been a nerve-wracking day and her temper was frayed. She couldn't afford to snap at the dragon lady because she was frustrated with her answer. When she felt calmer she said, "I have to speak to Aurora before she goes. She needs to know I'll be waiting for her."

"You've known her for less than a month. Will you really wait for her?"

"I will. I love her. We are going to be life-mates."

Lady Adelind arched a brow at Evie's bold statement. "Is Aurora aware of this?"

"I haven't told her in so many words but I will."

Lady Adelind's stare intensified becoming a searing weighty thing that pressed in on her so it was hard to breathe. It felt like the woman was trying to pry her open to peer into her soul. A voice in the back of her head screamed at Evie to lower her gaze to relieve the strain but she gritted her teeth and held on.

"Aurora killed many avians and destroyed their tower. You are an avian. This doesn't bother you?"

Evie contemplated for a moment then she said, "Most of the people fled when the evacuation bells rang and we saved the children. As for the destruction of the tower…if House Ravir grabbed my little sister Oriana and did to her what almost happened to me today, I would have done everything in my power to level their tower to the ground. No one hurts the people I love and gets away with it. Aurora is doubly fierce when it comes to protecting the people she cares about. Today was the equivalent of a perfect storm for her. She saved me from House Ravir's cutter's cage and brought me safely home. That should have been the end of it but they abducted her lover and handed me over to the man who murdered her father and almost tortured her to death. If that's not asking for trouble I don't know what is. So, my answer to your question is this: I do not hold anything that happened here today against her."

A smile flickered across Lady Adelind's lips. She gave a small nod and said, "If this is truly how you feel Evangeline then perhaps there can be a future for the two of you."

***

When Aurora finally came out of the vault she was human, naked and covered in gore from head to toe. Evie had schooled herself to expect some blood but it still came as a shock to see Aurora in such a state. Silently she thanked Lady Adelind for keeping her out of the vault. She was still struggling to comprehend the scale of destruction Aurora was capable of when she unleashed her beasts so she probably wasn't ready for the carnage inside.

Keeping to the shadows Aurora stepped into the heavy downpour. She tilted her face into the rain letting the water cascade down her body. The way the crimson washed out of her hair made it look to Evie like Aurora was crying bloody tears. Aurora opened her eyes and stared directly at Evie. Her eyes were dark pits of pain sprinkled with the last smoldering vestiges of her anger. But mostly she looked resigned as if steeling herself for a mortal blow.

It dawned on Evie that Aurora chose to stand where she did deliberately. She knew Evie was outside watching the doorway. She wanted Evie to look her full and see the aftermath of her battle. She had stripped herself of all her defenses – no longer an armored beast but a naked, vulnerable woman. She was waiting for Evie to make the next move. To judge her. From the look on her face Evie could tell Aurora feared she'd be called a monster and be pushed away yet again like she had so many times in her life but still she stood, waiting. It was the bravest thing Evie had ever seen. She took a fortifying breath and stepped into the rain. The water was icy cold and made her shiver. Aurora stood motionless but the closer Evie came the more palpable the tension in Aurora's body and her expression alternated between hope and fear. Evie's heart hammered in her chest; they were on the razor's edge. One wrong word from her and Aurora would disappear from her life as surely as if she had died today. She would brood and draw her anguish and the shame of her rejection around her like a shield and she wouldn't let Evie close again. Evie walked right up to her, standing so close she could feel the heat radiate off Aurora's naked body like a stoked fire. Slowly she unfurled her wings to create a canopy to shield them from the rain somewhat and give them a little privacy. Aurora trembled when Evie's wings brushed her bare skin. She gently cupped Aurora's face and said, "It is over now. You got him."

Aurora's composure broke and she started to cry. "Thank you for getting the children out of the tower. Thank you for stopping me. I didn't see them. I couldn't have lived with myself if I—"

"Hush, I know. You didn't. Everything's going to be all right." Evie put her arms around Aurora and drew her into an embrace. Aurora bowed down resting her forehead on Evie's shoulder. "You're trembling. We should get you out of the rain. It's freezing and you're naked."

"The rain is good…it's cleaning me. But even if I stand under it for hours it won't be enough to wash this day away."

Evie didn't know what to say to that so she tried to give comfort with her body instead, soothing with her hands and sheltering Aurora with her wings.

Aurora stirred restlessly and said, "I have to leave."

"I know. Take me with you?"

"No. It's not safe for you around me right now."

"Aurora, I'm not afraid of you. I trust you with my life and I know you would never hurt me."

"I can't tell you how happy that makes me. That's not the problem, they are…" Aurora pointed up at the sky and Evie saw dark shapes circling in the clouds above. The tip of a dragon's wing broke through the cloud cover like the fin of a monstrous shark breaching the water. Was that odd rumble thunder or the voice of an angry dragon? Evie shuddered and drew her wings more tightly around them.

"My mother said she told you what I really am?"

"Yes, she did."

"That is such a relief. It's been such a burden not being able to tell anyone. The dragons didn't know, not until today. We hid it from them all these years. Now I must deal with the fallout of outing myself as a chimera to those arrogant fuckers. I can hear how upset they are. Go home, Evie. Your father and Oriana will be worried sick about you."

Aurora tried to pull away but Evie kept her close. Staring into her eyes she said, "I love you. I wanted to wait for a romantic moment to tell you but this can't wait. I love you and I want us to be together. I want to be your mate."

"You do?" Aurora's eyes flew wide in surprised wonder.

"Yes, I do."

Aurora pointed at the burning tower. "But how can you want to be with me after seeing me do that?"

"So you lost your temper and destroyed Ravir Tower. You had good reasons for your anger. If I was in your shoes and could turn into a powerful beast I probably would have done the same. I don't care that you are a chimera and I know you don't care that I'm an avian. I know we have some things to work out but we can talk about that later. All that is important right now is that I tell you that I love you and that I want us to have a life together. Do you love me? I think you do but I need to hear you say it."

Aurora gently touched Evie's cheek and said, "Evie, I love you more than life itself."

Joy flooded Evie like a warm tidal wave. "Those are the most beautiful words I've ever heard. You have just made me a *very* happy woman. Now that's settled, promise me you'll come back to me as soon as you can."

"I don't know what's going to happen with the dragons. It might not be safe for you to have me around. I don't want to put you in danger."

"Aurora, I don't want to hear excuses. I want you to give me your word that you will come back. You always keep your word. If you promise I know you will return. Please promise me."

"I promise I will come back as soon as I can."

Evie smiled. "I'll be waiting for you."

Aurora removed Evie's hands from around her neck and held them gently in her own. "I had something made for you. A gift. Selene will bring it to you. If you change your mind leave a note with her then I'll know to stay away."

"I'm not going to change my mind."

"Evie, listen to me, please. It's not just about you and me, you have an entire flock to consider. You may not have a choice."

"But—"

Aurora squeezed Evie's hands and said, "It will break my heart to lose you. I'd rather read the words than have you tell me to my face you no longer want to be with me."

"Sweetheart, even after our first night apart I was going to find you and beg you not to leave. I cried myself to sleep thinking I'd lost you."

"I need you to be sure. Promise me you will use the time we are apart wisely and think this through carefully. In a few weeks you may not feel like you do right now. I will not resent you if you decide being with me is not what you really want."

With a resigned sigh Evie said, "All right. I won't change my mind but I will do as you ask and think about our future very carefully. I promise."

CHAPTER 30

THE GIFT

"Hello. Are you Selene? Aurora's friend?"

The petite redhead locked her Jeep and gave Evie an appraising look.

"Yeah. Who wants to know?"

"I am Evangeline Aquilar but please call me Evie."

"Oriana looks a lot like you so yeah, I guess you could be Evie. What can I do for you?"

Evie frowned and said, "Aurora said she left something for me in your safekeeping?"

"Yes, she did."

Evie's frown deepened. "Why haven't you brought it to me? Aurora said you would. It's been a week."

Selene impatiently tapped the car keys against the side of her leg. "I've been away. You are looking at a woman who hasn't slept in her own bed, or any bed for that matter, in days."

"You just got back?"

"Yup. Come inside. I was going to find you tomorrow but since you're here now it will save me the trip."

Evie followed Selene into the ramshackle old house.

"Have you been waiting long?"

"No, only about ten minutes."

"Lucky you. I should have gone grocery shopping on the way home but I wasn't in the mood. Wanna cup of tea? I'm pretty sure there is half a cake wrapped up in the cooler. It will be a tad dry by now but a good dunking will sort that. I'm happy to share if you want some."

"Um, thanks but no. The gift? I'm eager to see it."

"Sure. Come this way. What happened to Aurora after she rescued you and wrecked Ravir's tower? I know she took off and I'm pretty sure she hasn't been back. Have you heard from her?"

"No, nothing. You haven't heard anything either?"

Selene shook her head and sighed. "Rumors…but nothing I'd put any trust in. Since you were there, is it true there were dragons? I heard one attacked the tower. Did you see any of that?"

Evie had been asked that question repeatedly so she gave her prepared answer. "There was a torrential storm so it was hard to see what was going on most of the time but I did see dragons around the tower."

"Do you know what they were doing there?"

"I didn't fly up to one to ask."

Selene flashed her a toothy grin. "Fair enough." She let Evie into the house and led her down a long hallway to a closed door. "This is the guest bedroom. I put Aurora's things and your gift in there."

Evie followed Selene into the room. She came to a standstill when she saw Aurora's backpack and guitar case propped against a double bed. Evie sat down on the bed and lifted the guitar up beside her. After a moment's hesitation she popped open the case and gently ran her fingers over the honeycomb woodgrain.

"Selene, have you heard her play?"

"No. I didn't even know Aurora played until I saw the guitar. Is she any good?"

"She plays beautifully. To hear her is to want to weep with joy."

Selene didn't reply. When Evie looked up she saw the other woman was studying her thoughtfully.

"You love her?"

"I do," Evie said simply, allowing the truth of the statement into her eyes and the wistfulness of her smile.

Selene nodded and looked away. "That's good because Aurora is head over heels for you. She's never in all the years I've known her been interested in anyone so for her this is serious. She's not one of those people who flitters from one lover to another."

"I know."

Selene locked eyes with Evie and said, "I did some asking around about you. You've had heaps of girlfriends and they don't last, a few weeks or months at most. You get bored and move on."

"It's true I've had a few girlfriends but I didn't end things just because I was bored."

"I don't care why your relationships didn't last. What I'm saying is I see a troubling trend and I don't want Aurora to be just another short-term conquest for you. She's a lifetime commitment kind of person, you realize this right? She is one of the most loyal people I've ever met. She doesn't let people in easily but once she's decided you're her person she will defend you tooth and claw and stand by your side no matter what. That kind of person doesn't come around every day. If you treat her like you did the others it will break her heart. Evie, if you toy with my friend's affection or deliberately hurt her you and I are going to have the worst kind of trouble."

Evie sighed and carefully closed the guitar case. "I don't have to explain myself to you but since you're Aurora's friend and I hope we can be friends as well I will share something very personal with you. I told my father, Lord Augustus, that I intend to become Aurora's mate. So you see, I'm more serious about her than you can possibly understand. I know without a doubt I've found the person I've been looking for my whole life and there is no way I'm letting her go. She's mine and I'm definitely hers. I want a life with her. I'd go to her right now if I could but where she's gone, I can't follow. I have to wait for her to come to me like she promised. This has been the longest week of my life. I don't know how I'm going to cope if she stays away for months."

Selene quietly mulled over Evie's words. She nodded as if to herself and her face broke into a smile wide enough to show dimples. She held out a brown box for Evie to take. "Aurora's gift is inside. I'll give you privacy to open it."

"Thank you. I'd appreciate that."

Selene gave a one-handed wave over her shoulder and left the room. The door closed behind her with a soft click.

Evie's attention shifted to the cardboard box on her lap. She lifted the lid and found a gift wrapped in pretty paper and tied with a silk bow. Evie carefully removed the paper, taking care not to tear it. Out came a small round box carved from a crystalline blue stone that shone like polished glass. The sides were covered in intricate engravings that looked like overlapping wings in flight. She slid her finger along the seam trying to find a way to open the box and felt a sharp prick like a bee sting. She drew her thumb away to inspect it and saw the imprint of a rune hover on her skin for a moment before disappearing. There was a hiss and the lid slid open to reveal a silk lined case with a necklace nestled within. She extracted the tiny card with her name on it. It was made from embossed paper and when she opened the card she saw precise, neat handwriting with Aurora's name signed in a flourish at the bottom.

Dearest Evie

The time we spent together was precious to me and so are you. Thank you for everything.

I'm sorry about the way we parted. I didn't mean to storm off like that.

About the necklace – I found one of your primary feathers and kept it without asking if I could. I'd like you to have this gift in return as I have no intention of giving up the only memento I have of our time together. I hope that you will wear the necklace occasionally and remember me kindly.

Please accept this gift with my sincerest best wishes for you.

May you always fly freely wherever and whenever you wish.

May you always have a light to guide your way, night or day.

May you always have someone watch over you.

May you no longer fear the dark now you know not only monsters favor it.

Love Aurora

Evie put the card down on the bed and carefully extracted the necklace. Suspended from the silver chain hung a dark oval disk that showed a female avian soaring over a lake under a full moon. The miniature carving of the avian was exquisitely done in a pearl-like substance that appeared white at first but changed color depending on the angle of light. It was as she was admiring the play of light that she noticed there was something inside the moon. It was too small to see clearly at first but when she focused her vision she saw a tiger under a tree. The rendering was so well done she could see patterns in the fur and the green crystals used for eyes. Tracking the tiger's gaze she saw it was watching the girl. It was a masterful work created by someone with great skill and so personalized that Evie knew Aurora must have had it commissioned at great expense. It was beautiful and a thoughtful keepsake to remind Evie of the evenings the two of them spent under the full moon and the tree probably represented the one in Aurora's garden. Evie smiled remembering how she woke from falling asleep under it to find Aurora had covered her with a blanket and even slipped one under her head.

Evie became aware of a tingling in her hands. At first, the feeling was faint but it became stronger the longer she held the necklace. It wasn't unpleasant but the sensation was traveling up her arms which was disconcerting. If she didn't know the gift was from Aurora Evie would have worried there was something harmful embedded in the necklace and dropped it. She checked the disk for magic runes but there were none that she could see. It was smooth like polished stone, had a metallic sheen and was surprisingly light for how thick it was. Something tugged at her memory. There was something about the color of the disc and the tingling in her hands that seemed familiar.

When the answer came to her Evie gasped. The oval disk wasn't some rare stone or metal, this was a dragon's scale. Altered in shape but definitely a dragon's scale. If she had never seen a dragon up close it would never have occurred to her because it wasn't like dragons left their scales around for people to examine. Extremely rare and reputed to be imbued with the most potent magic dragon scales were highly coveted even by other shapeshifters. A single scale sold on the black market was worth a pile of ethian crystals.

Evie felt her hands shake as she realized that Aurora had had one of her own scales shaped into a piece of jewelry for her. With unsteady fingers she took up Aurora's note and reread it. This time she saw the play of words and could hear the things Aurora didn't explicitly say but were there between the lines. The dark scale that was the backdrop for the entire piece was meant to represent night, the time her nocturnal lover felt most at ease. The full moon was meant to chase away the dark and light Evie's way so she wouldn't be afraid. Hidden inside the moon the tigress watching over her, keeping her safe. So many layers of symbolism only the two of them would understand but it was the dragon scale that was Aurora's true message. She didn't just leave Evie a piece of sentimental jewelry in exchange for a feather, she'd given Evie a piece of her secret self. It was a secret hidden in plain sight. Like the woman who gave it this gift was so much more than it appeared to be. If Evie wore this around her neck all a casual observer would see was a beautiful necklace that depicted an avian flying at night as the tigress hid in the moon. But the true secret wasn't the watchful tigress, it was the dragon scale masquerading as merely a backdrop. Aurora must have wanted to tell Evie she was a chimera but she couldn't so she'd hinted at her secret this way. It was so subtly done that if she didn't already know she would have missed the message entirely. It was so like Aurora to give a gift of great significance and mindboggling value and try to pass it off as an equal exchange for a feather.

Evie clutched the necklace to her heart and whispered. "Sweetheart, where are you? I miss you so much. I'm waiting for you. Please come to me." Evie pressed her lips to Aurora's dragon scale and burst into tears because for a moment the way it hummed against her lips it had felt like a kiss.

CHAPTER 31

REUNION

It was sunset when Aurora arrived at Selene's door. She knocked loud enough to be heard above the music and a minute later she helped Selene wrestle open her heavy door. Before she could say hello Selene grabbed her around the middle and surprised her with a fierce hug.

"Aurora, you're alive! Where have you been all this time? I was worried! No one knew what happened to you. Are you all right? Wow, you made a powerful statement bashing up House Ravir. You destroyed their freaking tower! Great work. No one is going to mess with you in a hurry. What's with the dragons turning up at the same time? You wouldn't believe the crazy rumors flying around. Everyone has a theory on why they were there. People have been pestering me for information because they know we're friends. I keep telling them I wasn't there and I haven't seen you so how am I supposed to know? Great news…that big bounty on your head? Gone! That's what happens when you kill the person responsible. I've been dying to tell you I found out Carlos has been paying frontmen for years to put bounties on your pelt. Apparently, he wanted to come back to Nordarra but he was shit scared of you. Rightly so. He barely got back and you shredded his ass. Wish I was there to see that. Bet he pissed himself when he saw you coming. And you saved Evie! Knew you would. I forget my manners, come in my friend. We can talk inside while I make you a cup of tea. So much to tell you. Did you travel far? You look a bit worn out."

Aurora smiled at Selene's exuberant welcome and the overload of information that gushed out of her non-stop. It was a sign her friend was either very happy to see her or was on a sleepless coffee binge trying to finish a project. Knowing Selene it was probably both. After her initial blast of energetic chatter she would settle down to more sedate conversation.

"Hello, Selene, it's good to see you too. I'm okay. I traveled several days almost non-stop to get back to Porta Belua. I couldn't come earlier.

Had things to take care of I'd rather not discuss."

Selene gave her a curious look but nodded her understanding. "As delighted as I am to see you, I suspect you didn't travel for days on end just to see me?"

"Evie…we have unfinished business."

Again Selene nodded her understanding. "I thought so. Do you want to stay here while you two sort things out?"

"If that's all right?"

"Of course, you know you are always welcome."

"While I'm here I'll sort out that door for you and see what else I can do. Repairs for food and board."

Selene beamed and clapped Aurora on the arm. "It's a shame we're not into each other because I'd love to have you around more. You're so useful! Plumber, carpenter, cook and the list goes on. You're like several tradesmen all for the price of a bed and meals. An absolute bargain!"

Aurora burst out laughing. "It's probably just as well we're only friends. With our size difference could you imagine the looks we'd get if we were dating? I'm well over six foot and you're um…"

"Tiny?"

"Petite."

"Whatever. Oh, by the way, I put your things in your room."

"I have a room? Since when?"

"Since you left all your stuff with me and I needed to prepare a guest room anyway. Just so you know, if anything has been disturbed it wasn't me."

That stopped Aurora in her tracks and she gave Selene a questioning look.

"Your Evie. She came over a few days after you left. She wanted her gift. She tagged along when I went to go get it from your room. I thought she might want to open your gift in private so I left her to it. I got busy and forgot she was here. When I realized how much time had passed I assumed she'd gone but to my surprise, I found Evie was still here. She'd unrolled your sleeping bag on top of the bed, crawled inside and was fast asleep."

"She was?"

"Yup. She got rid of her wings and made herself right at home. That surprised the heck out of me I can tell you. I've never seen a grown avian without wings. She looked so peaceful I didn't have the heart to wake her."

"How long was she asleep?"

"Hours. The woman must have been exhausted. I had to wake her eventually because the sentinels on my roof were becoming agitated. I didn't want them to break down my doors to 'rescue' their sleeping princess."

"Have you seen Evie since? Did she leave me a note?"

"She came around again last week asking if I'd heard from you but she didn't leave a message. Were you expecting one?"

Staring out the window toward the Aquilar tower Aurora didn't reply.

"Aurora?"

Aurora mentally shook herself and said, "I need to see her. It's almost dark and probably rude to turn up so late but she is so close. If I wait until tomorrow to go see Evie it's going to drive me crazy. Can I use your shower?"

"Want to be fresh and sweet smelling for your reunion with the pretty avian? Oooo...are you blushing? That's so cute. You know your way around, help yourself. Are you hungry? Want me to make you something before you go?"

"I'm in a hurry. I'm just going to shower and go."

"Hot chocolate. That's what I'll make. Won't take you more than a minute to down a big mug."

"Sounds good. Thanks, Selene."

***

Evie heard her sister's familiar knock on the door a moment before she pushed it open to shout, "Evie, are you here?"

Evie sighed. She wasn't in the mood for company but she didn't have the heart to send Oriana away.

"I'm on the couch in the sitting room. Come in."

"Why are there no lights on? Evie...where are your wings?"

From her seat on the couch where Evie sat with her legs drawn up to her chest she turned to give her sister a dark look. "Where do you think they are?"

"Oh wow...someone is testy." Oriana plonked down next to Evie and took a moment to arrange her wings comfortably. "And very broody."

"I'm not broody. I never brood."

"You could have fooled me. You're sitting alone in the dark staring out at the city with a melancholic look on your face. That's the very definition of brooding. I don't think I've ever seen you sitting in the dark. Like ever. Not on purpose anyway and when are you ever without your wings? Just wow again to that one."

"It's not that dark, Oriana, it's barely dusk. As for my wings? I didn't feel like having them on. It's not like I'm planning to fly anywhere tonight and it's so much more comfortable sleeping without them. I love that I can lie on my back and fall asleep looking up at the moon."

Oriana stared at Evie. "Who are you and what have you done with my sister?"

"I'm fine," Evie grumbled. "I'm just thinking out loud."

Oriana's forehead creased into a frown. "You've changed. The old Evie would never have shifted her wings just to sleep more comfortably. I'm seriously worried. What is going on with you?"

"I'm…not quite myself. I feel different after everything that happened and things that didn't bother me before annoy the heck out of me now."

"Like?"

"Like the jokes they made at dinner about beast-shifters. Those fur and flea jokes are disgusting, juvenile and plain ignorant. Beast-shifters are super clean and their fur doesn't stink! We have plenty of cats in the tower being fussed over and sleeping in people's beds and I've never heard anyone complain that their fur stinks."

"Ah…now I understand what's going on. This is about your tigress. Do you miss, Aurora?"

Evie's face crumbled and she wiped a tear from her cheek. "Would you miss your wings if you lost them tomorrow and could never fly again?"

"Of course, that would be terrible. Without them I wouldn't be me anymore. I'd be incomplete."

"That's how I feel about Aurora. Like something essential is missing and now I have this constant ache inside. I've never felt like this before and it scares me. It's been nine weeks and I haven't heard a thing. What if Aurora never comes back? Will I be like this forever?"

"Wow, that's intense. I was going to go to a party and tell you afterwards that I saw Aurora but now I'm glad I came straight home."

Evie shot upright and grabbed her sister's arm. "You saw Aurora? Where, when?"

"About half an hour ago near the night market."

"You're sure it was her?"

Oriana scoffed. "Evie, I've met Aurora. She is very memorable and I'd have to be senile to mistake someone else for her. I also talked to her, so yeah, it was definitely Aurora."

"You talked to her?" Evie stared at Oriana as if she had just told her she saw a wolf sprout wings.

"Geez, you're slow tonight. Yes, I talked to her and boy, she looked hot. Dangerous but hot. Not that I'm into girls but if I was, I'd love to have a go with someone like her. I was with Fredric and Isa and I thought they were going to wet themselves when she came up to say hello. They thought we were too high up and the sides of the building too smooth for any beast-shifter to climb up to mess with us but she was up there in no time at all. Plus, she looked so hot. Did I mention that part? Fredric denied it but he had the hugest boner and Isa drooled so hard I worried she was going to rip off her own clothing and throw herself on Aurora. It was embarrassing. Good thing I stayed cool and collected."

"Oriana, what the heck are you talking about? Where did you see her? What did she say?"

"A group of us met up to listen to the band playing in the square while we had pizza and drinks."

"You know you shouldn't drink and fly. It's not safe," Evie said on reflex with no actual heat.

"Whatever, *Mother,* we were just having cider and we were eating. Now do you want to hear the rest of the story or not?"

"Yes, yes, go on."

"Sooo, we were sitting on the roof *eating pizza,* people watching and listening to music when Aurora strolled past below. I called out to her and boom, just like that, she climbed the building. That was awesome by the way – your girlfriend really knows how to make an entrance and she wasn't even breathing hard."

"What did she say?"

"Not much, just that it was good to see me again and she asked if you were home. I asked Aurora when she'd gotten back and she said she'd just arrived. Then I introduced her to Fredric and Isa. They offered her some of our pizza and cider but she didn't want any and after that she left. Awesome exit too. She walked to the side of the building and jumped. We rushed to have a look and I thought for sure she was going to be a pancake down below but she was nowhere to be seen."

"So, you're telling me Aurora is back and in the city?"

"Yeah, the evidence seems to point that way."

"If she was coming to see me straight away she would have been here by now. I bet she was heading to Selene's place to see if I left her a note. Yes, that's where she would have gone. So that's where I'm going."

Evie got up, yanked her shirt over her head, clenched her fists and concentrated with all her might. Instantly her wings popped into existence with a whoosh of air that knocked a bowl of fruit from the side table sending peaches and strawberries tumbling to the carpet.

Oriana jumped several feet into the air and perched on the back of the couch like a startled cat. "Evie, how did you do that? That's impossible!"

"Of course it isn't because you just saw me do it. We just need to be taught how to quick-shift and I was taught by the best."

Oriana cocked her head to the side, confusion and doubt all over her face. "Grandma taught you how to quick-shift your wings?"

"Not a chance, grandma's technique is horrible! Aurora taught me. She's amazing." Evie walked to the balcony and prepared to launch herself into flight.

"Evie, wait!"

Annoyed at the interruption but caught by the urgent tone in her sister's voice Evie paused. "What is it?"

"You should really put on a shirt first. Unless it's your plan to flash everyone with eyes your boobs?"

Evie felt herself go crimson. She stepped back from the balcony and hastily folded her arms over her chest to cover herself. "A shirt would be good." Looking down at herself Evie added, "And probably pants that are not pajama bottoms, and a pair of shoes. Thank you, Oriana, that was a close one."

***

Evie was about to knock when Selene opened the door. Selene was carrying a large mug of hot chocolate in one hand and Evie saw a flash of something metallic in the other before it disappeared under Selene's jacket.

"Hello, Selene."

"Evie…"

"Is she here?"

Selene leaned against the doorframe, took a leisurely drink from her mug then said, "Yup, she turned up a short while ago."

Evie waited for Selene to say something more or to invite her in but Selene just watched her with wry amusement.

"Is she all right?"

"Yeah, she seems fine."

Selene took a sip and then another and in the awkward silence that set in Evie could hear distant laughter and the sound of birds settling down for the night in the huge old tree. She strained to hear movement in the house but there was nothing and she couldn't see anyone in the hallway behind Selene. Evie fiddled with her necklace and her fingers automatically traced the now familiar shapes of the avian and her watchful guardian, her mind seeking comfort in Aurora's message. When she'd heard Aurora was back she was so excited she'd rushed to be with her. Now she was beginning to feel unsure of herself. Perhaps this was a mistake? Should she have waited for Aurora to come to her? Was Selene blocking her because Aurora didn't want to see her?

Selene raised her cup to have another sip but when she heard water run into the drain she straightened and motioned Evie inside. "*Finally*, it took her long enough. I was stalling to make sure Aurora was in the shower before I invited you in."

"Um…why?"

"If I let you in earlier you'd have caught her before her shower. You'd be at the kitchen table right now with her offering you a cup of tea and fretting that she didn't have time to have a shower after traveling for days to see you. Now you can wait in her room and skip straight to the fun part," Selene said and gave Evie a mischievous wink.

For a moment Evie was speechless as her mind rallied to adjust to the unexpected direction of the conversation. "I haven't seen her in over two months. Do you think she'll mind if I wait in her bedroom?"

"Are you here to tell Aurora it's over between you two?"

"What? No! Definitely not."

"Then yeah…the way I read the signs she will be *very* happy to see you. By the way, I'm heading out for the evening and I don't expect to be back till morning. You two will have the place all to yourselves for the night."

"Selene…thanks."

Selene saluted Evie with her mug and grinned. "I'm just giving you two privacy. Make the best of it." Not waiting for Evie to reply Selene disappeared down the hallway whistling a cheerful tune.

***

Aurora lingered in the shower, her arms braced on the sides, her head bowed. She had meant to take a very quick shower but the hot water was so soothing on her aching muscles. She always prided herself on her stamina and could outrun just about anything but she wasn't flying fit. A few weeks of flying didn't undo a lifetime of pretending she didn't have wings and it certainly didn't prepare her to battle gale force winds for close to a day to get over the mountain ranges. She was sore and tired. She'd been tempted to curl up for a snooze in the forest just outside of Porta Belua but she had pushed herself to continue because Evie was waiting for her. At least she hoped so. It had been months and so much could have happened to change Evie's mind about them. Fear was the other reason she lingered in the shower. The hope she'd held so close to her heart felt like a flimsy dream now that she was about to see Evie again and all the doubts she'd been able to suppress while she faced the dragons and fought to make her way back to Evie bloomed in her chest so that it was hard to breathe. The last time she hurried back to be with a woman who said she'd wait for her Aurora had returned to find her lover had chosen another in her absence. It had been a crushing blow and it was hard not to fear similar disappointment. At least there was no note from Evie calling things off between them and Selene said Evie came looking for her. Surely those were encouraging signs? Aurora rolled her shoulders and pushed away from the wall. Only one way to find out. Time to get out of the shower and go see Evie.

As soon as Aurora entered the hallway she smelled Evie. She froze and tested the air, half-convinced she imagined it but there was no mistaking that tantalizing scent. Instantly she was in pursuit of the source, her body moving as if it had a will of its own and in a few strides she was in her bedroom. Standing by the bed Evie turned and their eyes locked.

"Evie, you're here!" The words came out in a rush. Aurora's heart was beating so loudly she was sure Evie would hear it. "I was on my way to see you."

Evie's eyes darkened and her lips curved up in a smile. "Were you coming like that? Because if you were...I *love* the outfit."

Momentarily confused Aurora looked at herself and saw she was only wearing a towel and a very tiny one at that. It barely covered her butt. She blushed and tried to pull it down a little but that bared more of her breasts. Evie's smile widened.

"No, of course not. My clothing is on the chair."

"Hmm, I'm glad I got here before you had time to put it on."

Flustered and struggling to find a suitable comeback Aurora's eyes caught the nervous way Evie fingered the necklace around her neck. It was the necklace she'd given her. Evie was stroking it compulsively like she was trying to draw courage from it. Looking closer Aurora saw the tight way Evie held her wings and behind the laughter in her eyes there was vulnerability. Despite her brazen words Evie was nervous too. If Evie could be bold so could she. Aurora moved closer so there was less than an arm's length between them.

"You're wearing my necklace."

"I never take it off."

"Do you like it?"

"I love it. It's so beautiful and a piece of you I can carry with me always."

Aurora smiled and gently put her hands on Evie's waist. "You are in my bedroom and you're wearing my necklace. Does that mean what I hope it does?"

Instead of answering the question Evie slid her arms around Aurora's neck and kissed her. Evie's lips were warm velvet gliding against her own, soft but insistent. She probed with her tongue and Aurora opened for her. Aurora groaned as the taste of strawberries and peaches flooded her mouth and she wondered if Evie's arousal would taste as sweet. She desperately wanted to find out. Evie's kisses were hungry and she pressed her body hard up against Aurora so she felt every contour of her body. She slid her hand under the back of Evie's shirt so she could feel the warmth of her bare skin then down a little so she could feel the perfect rounds of Evie's ass move under her palm as she strained to get closer. Their kisses were them speaking without words as their bodies sought and gave reassurance to questions their fearful minds were yet to express. They rocked together and as Evie's hands caressed her shoulders and back with aching tenderness Aurora felt tension seep out of her body and something inside her uncoiled. She let out a shuddering breath and Evie drew back to search her eyes. Whatever she saw there made her smile and she made a happy humming sound.

"Does that answer your question, my love?"

Her mind a haze of want and contentment at having Evie back in her arms, Aurora stared at her in confusion. When it dawned on her what she meant Aurora was shocked at how utterly Evie had derailed her thoughts. She closed her eyes for a moment to gather her courage then asked the question she was afraid to ask but had to for her own sanity.

"Evie, I don't want to assume the kisses and you being here with me means more to you than it actually does. I need you to say it. I need you to tell me so I know for sure."

"I rushed over as soon as I heard you were back. I'm in your arms. This is me showing you I am yours. It means I want to be your mate."

Aurora swallowed hard. "My mate…are you sure?" She gently cupped Evie's cheek and moaned when Evie turned her face to kiss her palm.

"I've missed your hands. So strong but gentle all over me. Your fingers are so long and elegant. How I've missed your fingers inside me. Hmm, you taste *so good*."

Evie followed that comment up by swirling her tongue around Aurora's thumb and sucking the tip. Aurora's stomach muscles clenched and it took all her self-control to pull her hand away so Evie would look at her. Apparently they were both easy to distract. She had done a lot of thinking during their separation and there were things that had to be said.

"Evie, please don't offer to be my mate unless you are sure. You know what I am. My beasts are very territorial and so am I when it comes to what belongs to me. Telling me you want to be my mate is not the same as just being my girlfriend. You understand that, right? There is no rush. If you want to date for a while to get to know me better I'll give you all the time and space you need. I don't want you to feel pressured into a serious relationship just to keep me around. We can take it as slow or fast as you want. All I ask is that you be very clear with me where we stand so there's no misunderstanding."

"Is going slow what you want?" Evie countered, her voice sharp and laced with hurt. "Is this your way of telling me you need more time together to be sure about us?"

"No, I already know all the things that really matter about you. I want you to be mine. I was trying to be considerate."

"Aurora, it's sweet you are trying to be considerate but truthfully I was already yours after the first time we made love. I just wasn't ready to admit it to myself. I don't want a casual girlfriend who I only get to spend time with if we both happen to have a free evening and I want to be in your bed every night not just occasionally. We are way past that. Are you worried you'll scare me off if you act too territorial?" At Aurora's hesitant nod Evie smiled. "Do you really think you are the only one with a possessive streak? No more drunken strip poker games for you unless it's with me and I have to be honest, the thought of you swimming naked with those mermaid bitches makes me want to hit something." Evie rustled her wings in mock aggression and it made

Aurora laugh. "Now we've got that out of the way, please tell me you're not still thinking of leaving Nordarra?"

"No, Evie. You are here, how can I leave? I love you."

Evie let out a happy sigh. "That's such a relief. I love you too, Aurora. I love you with all my heart. I've missed you so much. Every day you've been away has felt like an eternity."

Aurora tightened her hold possessively and Evie reciprocated by draping her wings over her shoulders. Aurora shivered at the feel of warm silky feathers against her bare skin. She buried her nose in the warmth of Evie's wing and inhaled greedily, loving how Evie's sweet scent enveloped her. Heat pooled between her thighs making her slick with need.

"You smell so good. It makes me want to..." Aurora faltered feeling overwhelmed by the intensity of her feelings for Evie.

Evie caressed Aurora's face, her eyes soft and happy. "Go on. Tell me."

"You smell like safety and home. So comforting, but at the same time your scent is a powerful aphrodisiac that drives me a little crazy and after being away from you for so long I want to rip your clothes off and claim every inch of you. I've craved your scent, your touch, the nearness of you. You're intoxicating. I've not even had a taste of you and I'm already feeling a little drunk."

Evie gave a throaty laugh and palmed one of Aurora's rock-hard nipples straining against the flimsy towel. "You know how to make a woman feel desired. It makes me so happy to hear you say those things." Evie rested her cheek against Aurora's chest and said, "I've missed the sound of your heartbeat and your arms around me. I feel so safe and loved when you hold me. I know nothing can harm me while you're near. At night alone in my cold bed I tried to drive away my fears by remembering what this felt like but hugging a pillow is a very poor substitute for you."

Evie felt Aurora's body tense and when she looked up at her she saw that the dreamy expression from a moment ago had been replaced by predatory alertness. "Why were you afraid, sweetheart? Did someone threaten you? Tell me who it was. It won't happen again." Aurora tilted her head inquiringly. "Or is it political? Are the other flocks giving House Aquilar trouble because of what happened with House Ravir?"

Because she was looking for it Evie saw the amber flames ignite in the green of Aurora's eyes and it made her think of coals in the forest.

Carefully tended it would provide gentle heat and protection but stoked too high it would turn into a raging forest fire bent on destruction. It was the difference between cuddling up with the protective tigress or provoking the dragon's rage. Such a fine line. Aurora was watching her expectantly and Evie realized that because Aurora loved and trusted her she had the power to push her either way. It was a power she didn't expect and didn't particularly want but if she became Aurora's mate it would be hers all the same. The thought made Evie's mouth go dry and she made a mental note to always pay careful attention when she spoke to Aurora. She didn't want to accidentally unleash her on harmless foe.

"It's all right, no one threatened me and the other flocks aren't giving us trouble. When they heard what despicable things House Ravir had been up to and saw what happened to them, as a result, the other flocks couldn't sever ties with Ravir quick enough. When I said I was afraid I meant of losing you. I was afraid *for you*. I had a taste of what life with you would be like and I longed for that so badly it hurt. The business with the dragons...are you okay? What happened?"

Aurora relaxed and pulled a face like she tasted something bad. "The dragons are a colossal pain in the ass. It was better when my so-called relatives ignored me and pretended I don't exist. Their sudden interest in me is unsettling. My life isn't in danger so let's leave that conversation for another day. Thinking about them puts me in a foul mood and I won't let anything spoil our reunion. I forgot to ask, how's your father?"

"He's feeling so much better. Every day he's a little stronger and it's wonderful to see. He told me what happened and how you saved his life. All that time we never caught on that Marcus was poisoning him. You were in the tower less than an hour and put it all together."

"Only because I have a superb sense of smell and I was in the right place at the right time. Marcus's time was up. That's all."

"Yes but—"

"Evie, please don't make my role bigger than it was. I was only there for you. It was a happy coincidence I got to help your father."

Sensing Aurora's discomfort Evie relented. She wouldn't gain anything by pushing Aurora to accept thanks she didn't want. She would find other ways to show her gratitude. Ways both of them would find thoroughly enjoyable and provide mutual satisfaction. The thought excited Evie. There was something she'd been aching to do since Aurora walked into the room steamy from her shower, her gorgeous body covered only in a barely-there towel. Using her nose to nuzzle the towel out of the way she licked the drops of water that trickled from Aurora's wet hair to cling to the damp hollow between her breasts. Loving the taste and feel of Aurora fresh from her shower she took her time, licking along the watery trail, tracking it backwards across Aurora's collarbone to the vulnerable plane of her throat. Aurora moaned and arched her neck to give Evie more access so she pressed warm open mouth kisses on the heated skin. She slipped a hand under the towel and caressed the inside of Aurora's thighs. She ran her fingers slowly up and down brushing against the damp curls at the apex. She did that a few times and Aurora's breathing became ragged and her skin broke out in goosebumps. Evie meant to take it slow but she couldn't resist the need to dip her fingers into the welcoming heat. Aurora hissed in a breath and swayed unsteadily so Evie maneuvered them to the bed. She pushed at Aurora's shoulders letting her know she wanted her to sit down then she straddled her. Aurora watched her wrestle with the knot that held the towel in place and smiled when Evie muttered her frustration at not being able to undo it. She placed a hand over Evie's trembling hands, squeezed gently and loosened the tight knot for her. She withdrew her hand leaving Evie to finish what she'd started. Evie licked her lips and slowly parted the towel to bare Aurora. Her breath caught in her throat. Even though she had held fast to her memories of Aurora's sculpted body nothing could compare with the reality. Reverently she cradled Aurora's breasts in her palms and ran her tongue over the dark nipples. She reveled in Aurora's sharp intake of breath as she sucked first one then the other into her mouth. She wanted to linger there but she had so much more to explore. Promising herself she would return to give Aurora's breasts all the attention they deserved, Evie let her hands glide down to remap the hard ridges of Aurora's abs, the narrow waist that flared into broad shoulders then down over her hips and between her powerful thighs to the slick folds that quivered at her touch. She dipped deeper and felt the walls of Aurora's pussy throb around her fingers. She was right on the edge. Evie held still while she considered what to do. Back off and tease Aurora nice and slow or give her the relief she needed? One look into her lover's eyes and she had her answer. She gently but firmly pushed her down on her back then kissed her way down Aurora's body until she was between her legs. She unfurled her wings slowly and glided the inside of her wings over Aurora's naked body. Aurora moaned and arched into her.

"Evie..." Aurora's voice was husky and thick with desire. "Evie, your feathers are like warm silk. Your scent…your scent is all over me." When she lifted her head to stare at Evie her eyes looked glazed. "Are you trying to drive me insane? Do you have any idea what you're doing to me?"

"You like when I touch you like that?"

"I *love* it."

Evie hummed with delight and took Aurora in her mouth. She wasn't gentle. She sucked hard while flicking her tongue across the sensitive bud. Aurora cried out her name and her body bowed with the intensity of her release. Her walls clamped down on Evie's fingers and feeling Aurora come for her was such a turn on Evie almost climaxed as well. She left her fingers inside Aurora long after the last contractions finished, reluctant to give up the intimate contact.

"Was that good, my love?"

"Hmm…you've undone me. My muscles feel like jelly. I'll need a few minutes to recover."

Feeling immensely pleased with herself Evie crawled up Aurora's body and lay her head on her chest. She listened as Aurora's breathing and heart rate slowed down and felt deep contentment settle over her. So right…this felt so right. She wanted this always. She wanted this woman, her mate, her love with her always. She resettled a wing over her naked lover covering her and heard Aurora's happy sigh. She only lifted her head from Aurora's chest when she felt her move. Aurora raised up on her elbows and Evie felt a rush of nervous anticipation when she saw the predatory gleam in her eyes. Evie licked her lips and saw Aurora's eyes fasten on her mouth before raking over her clothed body as if she wore nothing at all.

"I've got my strength back. We are way overdue getting you undressed." Aurora tucked at Evie's shirt. "I want you naked. I need to touch you, feel you. I'm starving for a taste of you."

Aurora's hands brushed against her breasts through the shirt and Evie ached to have Aurora's hands and mouth on them without the cloth barrier. She tried to help but in their urgency they were getting in each other's way and her wings made it harder to get her clothes off. Frustrated she shifted them away.

Aurora gave a grunt of surprise and paused in the process of unhooking Evie's bra to stare at her. Her face broke into a brilliant smile and she said, "So quick. Sweetheart, you've been practising."

Basking in her lover's approval Evie laughed and did a happy wiggle as Aurora peeled her out of the rest of her clothing in record time. "Every day at least twice a day. As you can see, I've become very good at it."

"You're amazing. Congratulations, you can now shift as quickly as a dragon."

"Truly?"

"Yes. I'm so proud of you."

Aurora lifted Evie onto her lap so she straddled her again and they both gasped as their naked bodies came into full contact.

"Oh…oh, how I've missed this." Evie lay her head on Aurora's chest. Warm hands cupped her ass and Aurora tucked her tighter so her wet sex was splayed open against Aurora's stomach. She could smell her own arousal and felt it coat her lover's skin. For a moment Evie was tempted to feel embarrassed but then Aurora inhaled audibly and she made a sound that was somewhere between a happy moan and a possessive growl. The sound vibrated through Evie's body causing shivers down her spine and her clit throbbed painfully.

"And I've missed this. I've missed you. I love you." Aurora's voice was low and husky.

Her own breathing ragged, Evie whispered in her ear, "I'm yours. Your mate. Take me. Claim me. *Please.*"

Aurora captured Evie's face between her palms and tilted her head up for a kiss. Just before her mouth descended Evie saw Aurora's eyes. They were so dark they were almost black and feverish with desire. Evie felt her own excitement go through the roof. She remembered that look. Knew it meant Aurora was going to fuck her senseless. She'd given up count how many nights she'd awoken in a lust sweat after dreaming about that look. Finally, she'd get all that went with it for real and experience a climax not brought on by her own desperate hands. Climaxes… she corrected with a groan as Aurora claimed a nipple exactly the way she liked. That was the other thing she remembered with delight: Aurora's insatiable appetite for her.

Soon Evie's breasts felt like ripe fruit ready to burst from all the attention lavished on them and she was an aching, quivering mess. Aurora's hands and mouth were all over her driving her into a frenzy but never lingered where she needed them most. She couldn't take it anymore. Frantic with need Evie tried to push Aurora's hand between her legs. She got a nip on the shoulder and found herself on her back, her legs spread wide with Aurora's fingers buried inside her while her hot mouth feasted on Evie's sex. She tried to hold on to enjoy the sensation of Aurora thrusting in and out of her and the feel of her tongue doing wondrous things but Evie had been driven right to the edge. That on top of two months of lustful wanting and worrying meant her body had a will of its own. It wanted release and it wanted it *now*. Her climax hit hard and fast. She fisted her hands in the sheets and rode out the waves of pleasure cascading outwards from her core until finally she lay limp, her body flushed with languid heat. Aurora carefully removed her fingers and kissed her thighs.

"Was that good, sweetheart?"

"Spectacular," was the only word Evie could muster.

Aurora gave a toothy grin and while she kept eye contact she lowered her head to suckle Evie's clit. Evie watched her through heavy eyes and didn't protest that she was too spent from her earth-shattering orgasm to have another so quickly. She knew her body would rally for Aurora and it did. With enthusiasm. Later Aurora's body did the same for her. Multiple times. They were both gloriously exhausted and well sated by the time they passed out in each other's arms.

***

When Aurora woke Evie was sprawled on top of her. Their limbs entwined so for a moment it was hard for her sleep befuddled brain to figure out where she ended and Evie began. Evie's hair had come undone and it covered them like a golden fan. Aurora breathed in, finding pleasure and comfort in the way their scents mingled. They were silky feathers and warm fur, sun-drenched skies and moonlit earth. Evie's lighter sweeter fragrance infused with her earthier tones and overlaying their unique scent was the smell of sex. Aurora felt herself grinning from ear to ear and stretched languidly. Disturbed by her lover's movement Evie lifted her head and stared at Aurora with sleepy eyes. When she saw the way Aurora was smiling she raised a questioning eyebrow.

"I'm happy," Aurora said as explanation. "You've made me ecstatically happy."

Evie smiled and lay her head back on Aurora's shoulder. "I love you."

"Hmm…I'll never get tired of hearing that."

"That's good because I'm going to tell you a lot. With my words and my body, every day."

Aurora trailed her fingers down Evie's back in a gentle caress. "I'll be yours as long as you want me."

"I'm not going to change my mind."

Aurora kissed Evie's forehead. "It's still dark. Sleep some more. I'll wake you in time to go join your flock for the dawn song."

Evie wanted to protest and press her point but she could hardly keep her eyes open. Lulled by the steady heartbeat under her ear and the warmth of Aurora's embrace she drifted off to sleep.

***

Aurora propped herself up on an elbow to watch Evie get ready for her work day. She was sitting in bed beside Aurora naked from the waist up with the blanket pooled around her hips. She was tidying her hair. Aurora was fixated on the slight sway of the rose-tinted nipples as Evie brushed out her long hair. When Evie lifted her arms to start braiding, her body stretched in an arc. The light filtering through the curtains cascaded over her body in a golden haze further emphasizing her feminine curves and the silkiness of her skin.

Evie's eyes met Aurora's and her hands stilled in motion. She swallowed hard and said, "You can't look at me like that right now."

"Why not? You're beautiful. It's impossible for me not to admire you."

"When you look at me like that I can hardly think. I want to throw down this brush, crawl right back into your arms and forget I have a whole day of meetings scheduled."

Aurora leaned in and starting from Evie's hip she trailed her lips and the tip of her tongue all the way up to the curve of Evie's breast. She gave Evie a wicked smile and gently grazed her nipple with her teeth followed by the soothing swirl of her tongue. Evie trembled and leaned back onto her arms offering her breasts up to Aurora's hungry mouth.

"Not fair," she groaned. "You know that's my weakness."

Aurora's hand slid up the inside of Evie's thigh. She automatically spread her legs and Aurora cupped her with firm pressure. Lifting her head from Evie's breast Aurora said, "I think we have time for one more before you have to go to your boring meetings. A little something to tide you over until tonight. Unless you really need to go right now?"

Evie knew if she let Aurora make love to her again she would miss attending her flock's dawn song but she didn't care. At that moment the only thing that mattered was the way her lover's naked body pressed against her offering mind melting pleasure. "I have a little more time," she said weakly and moaned her approval when Aurora's strong body settled on hers.

***

Evie smiled when she felt the now familiar buzz of Aurora's dragon scale as she put the necklace back around her neck. She shifted her wings in preparation of the flight home and watched as Aurora slid into her jeans and put on an old t-shirt.

"What are your plans for today?"

"While you are in meetings I'll be playing handyman around here. The place needs a lot of work and I told Selene I'd help out."

"You're good with fixing things?"

"Yes, over the years I learned a lot from the villagers of Ingvild."

"Hmm, you're such a talented woman. You really can do all kinds of amazing things with those hands of yours. I can definitely attest to that."

Aurora grinned and pounced on Evie from across the room. Evie gave a startled squeal which turned into a moan when Aurora kissed her. They were both a little breathless when the kiss ended.

"I really have to go."

"I know."

"You'll spend the evening with me? I'm planning a romantic dinner."

"Of course. Where would you like to meet?"

"Meet me at Aquilar Tower."

"Are you sure you want us to meet there? There will be no going back once the word is out that we are together. You know our relationship will upset some members of your flock, I am a predatory beast-shifter after all and they're avians. Won't they be afraid to have me in the tower after what I did to House Ravir? Won't they resent you for being with me?"

Evie clasped Aurora's face in her hands and said in a serious voice, "House Ravir tried to kill my father and kidnapped me. My flock is furious with them. If you hadn't destroyed Ravir Tower my father would have had to retaliate on principle and going wing to wing with such a militant flock would have cost us dearly. My people realize this. As for individuals unhappy about our relationship…let me deal with that. I'm not Astrid or any of the other people who turned their backs on you because you didn't fit into their perfectly ordered world and you know I'm not afraid of what you are. So please stop worrying, my love, I've made up my mind about us. If this relationship ends because one of us walked away it won't be me. I want you to come to Aquilar Tower tonight because I want everyone to know you are mine. I'm sorry if that sounds overly possessive but that's just how it is. I plan on making it clear to anyone with eyes that we are mated. I hope you don't mind."

"I don't mind at all that you want to claim me as yours. As long as you understand that also means you're mine."

In reply, Evie gave Aurora a tender kiss and said, "I'm so glad to hear that. I don't even know myself anymore, I've never been so possessive in my life. I fear if I lose you, I might lose my mind."

Aurora clasped the back of Evie's neck and rubbed their cheeks together while a deep happy sound that reminded Evie of a cat purring rumbled out of her chest. "The feeling is mutual, sweetheart."

***

When the time came to get ready for her dinner date with Evie Aurora took a long shower and washed vigorously to get all the sawdust off her skin and out of her hair. She found her tube of nice smelling moisturizer and applied it liberally. She put on a black bra and matching briefs. Next the tailored black pants and a burgundy silk blouse that buttoned up the front. She put on the boots she'd polished to within an inch of their lives and brushed her hair that had regrown to hang past her shoulders after the brutal cut she'd given herself. As a finishing touch she carefully applied lipstick. Aurora stood in front of the mirror and gave herself a critical look. She thought she looked good but maybe instead of fixing Selene's door and then working on the roof she should have gotten a professional haircut. Her thick hair was shiny and lush but looked a little wild. Aurora tucked a strand of hair away from her face and sighed. It was too late for that; she was as ready as she was going to be. She put on her jacket, slipped on the exquisite diamond cufflinks that were a parting gift from her mother and went looking for Selene. When Selene had heard she was going to dinner with Evie and meeting her at the Aquilar Tower she had immediately insisted on driving Aurora there. She'd gratefully accepted. The weather didn't know what it wanted to do and with her luck she'd get soaked on the way.

When she walked into the kitchen Selene put down her cup and let out a long wolf whistle. "*Very* nice."

"You think so? Is this okay for a romantic dinner somewhere nice?"

Aurora fidgeted nervously with her cufflinks and wondered if the jacket put too much emphasis on her broad shoulders but it also hugged her curves and went well with the rest of her outfit so hopefully that would balance things out. When Evie told her to dress smartly for their date she should have asked her where they were going. What if she wasn't dressed appropriately?

"Don't look so nervous. Aurora, you're a stunning woman and in that outfit you're going to turn heads. You've got that tall, dark and smoldering look going. Add that to the way you move and it screams danger and sex. If I took you dancing, I'd have to pry the girls off you with a crowbar. Evie is going to get all hot and bothered when she sees you. I hope you two are planning a private dinner because I saw that steamy kiss on the porch and the way Evie looked at you as she flew off. I'll be surprised if you two make it to dessert with all your clothes on."

Aurora grinned even as she felt her cheeks heat. "I'll take that to mean I look all right. Thanks for the confidence booster, Selene."

***

Aurora was approaching one of the sentinels on guard at the gate of the Aquilar complex when Oriana drifted down from above and promptly gave her a full-bodied hug.

"Aurora, you're here! I've been watching for you. Good to see you! Wow, you look *amazing*. I'm your personal escort courtesy of Evie."

Feeling startled by the enthusiastic welcome Aurora awkwardly patted Oriana's shoulder. "Hello, Oriana, it's good to see you too."

"Evie will meet you in the main hall. I'll take you there."

Aurora followed and soon found herself in what looked like a grand ballroom complete with a high ceiling and a spiraling staircase. The room was packed with avians talking in groups while sipping from delicate long-necked glasses or lounging on comfortable couches as they watched the couples on the dancefloor sway gracefully to the lively tunes of a string quartet.

"Is this a party, Oriana?" Aurora asked softly.

"Sort of. It's a formal dinner preceded by a little dancing and fancy booze to help people unwind and afterwards there will be more entertainment. It's supposed to be a fun get-together for our people and we usually have representatives from other flocks and some of our trading partners attend as well. We used to have these frequently before my father became sick. He loves to entertain and see people have a good time. Evie would have preferred not to be here tonight but she has to make a showing or it will look bad."

"Oh, I see," Aurora said trying to hide her disappointment. When Evie said she was planning a romantic dinner she'd expected a private setting for their first date as a couple, not a formal dinner with Evie's flock. Now instead of stealing kisses, she'd have to make polite conversation with strangers and instead of a relaxing meal, she'd have to put up with dozens of avians scrutinizing her every move. If this was how Evie wanted to let everyone know they are together she should have warned her. She didn't like being the center of attention and being in a confined space with a crowd of potential enemies agitated her beasts. Aurora took a fortifying breath and willed them to be calm. This was Evie's world and if she wanted to share her life, she would have to learn how to endure these kinds of events. Mentally Aurora shook herself. She would do *better* than endure, she would be on her best behavior and make Evie proud to be her mate.

Aurora got jarred out of her thoughts when she noticed Lord Augustus heading straight for her. He looked so much better than the last time she saw him. His cane was gone, his plumage was less dull, there was vigorous new growth in all the balding spots and his eyes sparkled with life. Clearly, Augustus was a man on the mend and he knew it. A hush fell over the room when he came to a standstill in front of Aurora. She bowed her head in polite acknowledgement. "Lord Augustus. It is pleasing to see you look so well."

Lord Augustus returned the bow then said in a voice that carried, "I'm looking good because of you. I owe you a great debt for saving not only my life but that of my daughter twice over. As Lord of Aquilar Tower I welcome you to our home. I'd invite you to be my honored guest but Evie already claimed that right for herself. I will not even have the pleasure of your company at dinner as she's determined to have you all to herself. Come walk with me. Let us talk a little before she comes and whisks you away."

Lord Augustus was still speaking to her but Aurora was no longer paying attention. On the other side of the room Evie was coming down the stairs in a dress that clung to her like it was molded to her body. It was a spectacular sea-green creation that emphasized Evie's sensuous curves and dipped low in the front so it drew the eye to Aurora's necklace nestled between ample breasts. Evie's golden wings shone like the sun and her long hair was styled in artful curls that tumbled across her shoulders. If Aurora believed in angels she would have thought she was looking at one. Their eyes met across the crowded room and Evie smiled. It was a radiant smile that made Aurora's heart do a happy flutter. Evie's hips gained a seductive sway that had her mesmerized and she couldn't look away even if she'd wanted to.

It took Aurora a moment to register someone was tugging at her sleeve. Glaring at the offending hand on her arm she found Oriana grinning up at her. "Breathe, Aurora. You look as if you're about to faint."

Aurora sucked in a breath of air and on the exhale she gasped, "She's so beautiful."

Beside her Lord Augustus beamed with fatherly pride. "Yes, she is. Evie takes after her mother."

Evie paused on the last step and made a small motion with her head beckoning Aurora to come to her. Aurora felt herself moving forward even as she said to no one in particular, "I have to go to her."

"No doubt about that," Augustus said with an amused sparkle in his eyes. "Evie is putting on quite the show for you. Linger at your peril."

Aurora was almost at Evie's side when a handsome male with silver grey wings stepped in front of her. He smiled roguishly and oblivious to Aurora's scowl he did a graceful bow that ended with him holding his hand out to Evie. "Beautiful lady, may I have this dance?"

Aurora suppressed the urge to bare her teeth and roar in the face of the male who'd cut in front of her. Opting for a more civilized approach she clamped a hand on his shoulder and moved him out of her way. "She's already taken…this dance is mine."

The avian looked equal parts startled and annoyed. He turned to confront Aurora but whatever he meant to say died on his lips the moment his eyes met hers.

A smiling and amused looking Evie descended the last step to take Aurora's offered hand and she held on to it as they walked to the dancefloor.

As she drew Evie into her arms Aurora whispered into her ear, "You'd better lead. This is only my second time dancing and *everyone* is watching."

Evie kissed her cheek and said, "You'll be fine. We'll take it nice and slow. Ignore the people, relax and imagine it's just you and me dancing on the beach."

"Oh really? I remember us getting hot and heavy while dancing on the beach. I don't think your father would approve of me ravishing his daughter on the dancefloor with the entire flock watching."

Evie gave a low, hungry moan and tightened her hold on Aurora. "Hmm, I remember. We'll dance for a while then leave. My father and Oriana can entertain without me tonight. I made plans for us and I'm dying to get you alone."

"Do your plans involve feeding me as well? Aurora asked teasingly. "You did promise me dinner."

Evie laughed. "Of course, I ordered lots of delicious food. You won't go hungry when you're with me and for my own selfish reasons I want to make sure you have *lots* of energy."

They slowly increased speed as Aurora reacquainted herself with the steps Evie had taught her. Evie's face shone with happiness and she didn't seem to care that her partner was the least experienced dancer on the floor and the only person without wings in the ballroom. It made Aurora's heart swell and she fervently hoped that she would have many opportunities to hone her dance skills with Evie and maybe someday she'd get to show off her gleaming dragon wings among the feathered hoard without causing pandemonium.

With Evie guiding their movements so they glided effortlessly between the other couples Aurora relaxed and began to genuinely enjoy herself, despite all the eyes on them, and was a little disappointed when the music stopped. An announcement was made for everyone to move to the dining hall but instead of following the crowd Evie flashed her an excited grin and led the way to an exit on the other side of the room.

Aurora eagerly followed. She didn't know where they were going and it didn't matter in the least. She had found her mate and she would follow Evie anywhere.

Walking hand-in-hand through her tower with Aurora Evie felt like she was gliding on air and her heart was so filled with happiness that she felt like she might burst with joy. She brushed Aurora's back with her wing in an open display of affection and felt the gentle buzz of Aurora's dragon scale flare into a pulse that sent a tiny shockwave through her body. Curious as to the cause Evie stared up at her mate and for a brief moment she saw in Aurora's eyes the amber shapes of a tiger and a dragon watching her. Aurora beamed at her and the ghostly figures vanished but the protective warmth emanating from the necklace remained.

THE END

ABOUT THE AUTHOR

Emily Noon always liked reading fantasies with a dark twist and if there was a romance between strong main characters to sweeten the deal, even better. After years of working in libraries while in secret creating magical worlds and lightly torturing her characters before giving them a happy ending, she decided to let them loose on the unsuspecting world. Aurora's Angel is her debut novel but won't be her last. It can't be because now she's let this lot out the other people running around in her head are demanding to have their stories told as well.

If you'd like to connect with Emily or find out what she's working on next you can find her at:

www.emilynoonbooks.com
Facebook: @authoremilynoon
Twitter: Emily Noon@EmilyNoonAuthor

A note from Emily

Thank you for reading my debut novel.
Please leave a review online if you enjoyed Aurora and Evie's story.
I'd really appreciate that.

Made in the USA
Monee, IL
01 October 2022